THE FATHER'S TALE

MICHAEL D. O'BRIEN

THE
FATHER'S
TALE

A Novel

IGNATIUS PRESS   SAN FRANCISCO

Front cover image: *Boy and Sailboat* Anonymous

Cover design by Roxanne Mei Lum

© 2011 by Ignatius Press, San Francisco
Paperback edition published in 2019
All rights reserved
ISBN 978-1-62164-365-4
Library of Congress Control Number 2011926371
Printed in the United States of America ♾

With love and gratitude to my sister in Beijing (who must remain unnamed, a flower of Christ in China) and to her spiritual children. And to the unknown martyrs of Russia and China, whose sacrifices will be revealed at the time of harvest.

Let no one deceive himself. If anyone among you thinks that he is wise in this age, let him become a fool that he may become wise. For the wisdom of the world is folly with God.
—I Corinthians 3:18–19

CONTENTS

PROLOGUE

In late February of a year not long past, Dr. Irina Filippovna, a physician, was crossing the interminable expanse of the taiga on the Trans-Siberian Railroad and happened to be an unwilling witness to a singularly odd event. Though the coach in which she rode was third class, the seat hard, and her fellow passengers in foul or despairing moods due to the recent disruption of rail service by ecology protestors, she had planned to sleep away much of the journey between Novosibirsk and Irkutsk. She had delivered a lecture on immunology at a medical institute in the former city and had hoped to disembark in the latter without undue trouble, and from there to make her way by bus and horse-drawn sleigh to her home village, where she maintained a small but necessary practice.

A handsome woman in her early forties, she was a widow with two sons to support. It was her custom to work with quiet determination to keep her life as simple as possible in order to bring what remained of her family through these times–the sociopolitical situation that now seemed more confused in some ways than it had been under the Communist regime. She had no love for anything that remained of the state's apparent omnipotence and its omnivorousness. Neither did she waste energy trying to understand the universe in other terms, for what might or might not lie beyond it could never be proved by science. She was in her own estimation a mother and a scientist. She often reminded herself that she had a good deal to be grateful for, especially her husband, whom she had loved as no other in her life, and her sons, who were

9

now, if it might be expressed in this way, her very life. She was a person with a complicated but by no means unique personal history. An intellectual, though an impoverished one, she was neither political nor naïve. She entertained no sentimental illusions about her native land, yet in her soul she loved it fiercely, even as she doubted the existence of the soul.

It was her habit from time to time to adjust what she called her "Russian mask", the impenetrable neutral expression that projected an attitude of indifference and resignation, for it had a tendency to slip from her face at inopportune moments, usually those moments that she later dismissed as lapses "for humanitarian reasons". She was not indifferent and she was not resigned, but she had throughout her lifetime learned that it was best to hide the more personal elements of her character—and certainly before strangers. She was, she told herself, immune.

Thus, when from the corner of her eye she observed an unhappy man on the seat across the aisle, she noted the fact but attributed no significance to his presence. He appeared at first glance to be little different from several others in the coach, hunched as he was inside a dirty greatcoat, gaunt, haggard around the eyes, scowling, unshaven. He was about her age, perhaps a bit older. From time to time he lifted his left hand, favoring it as if it were sprained or burned, and pressed it to the frosted glass of the window beside him. Yes, a burn, she decided, assessing his wincing, the livid red disk on his palm, and the weeping blisters. She considered offering him an antibiotic salve from the medical bag at her feet but thought the better of it. His hair, dyed a glaringly artificial yellow, stood up in spikes, like that of a decadent American rock star. Not a few young Russians in the big cities affected the same appearance, but in a middle-aged man it was repulsive. She decided not to make contact. He might be drunk or a criminal, or both, but clearly he was a disturbed person, and the hundreds of versts yet to cross could all too easily degenerate into tribulation. The country was full of irrational, dispossessed people like him. Though she felt a momentary impulse to help, she warned herself against involvement and firmly put the poor fool from her thoughts.

Hoping to nap a little before the next jarring rumble across the next nameless frozen waterway that drained the limitless void, she closed her eyes. She had just succeeded in dozing off when his voice brought her fully awake again. He was now declaiming in a strange accent, quoting poetry. A closer inspection of the pathetically intense monologist revealed that his features did not precisely fit any templates of the numerous racial groups in the country. What was he? Where was he from? Well, no matter; it was not her concern.

Feeling more irritated than disgusted, she noted that he was reciting to a very pretty girl seated opposite him and that she was crying. The foreigner, succumbing to infatuation or desire or simple madness, was trying to console her with verse. Then he reached into his pocket and, to the astonishment of all the surrounding passengers, suddenly burst into flames. Yes, fire and smoke. An enterprising old man threw a cup of water onto the fellow's pants, and the fire went out. Now the fool was convulsing in agony. Collapsed onto his seat, he was grimacing in extreme pain.

Dr. Filippovna sighed, shook her head, and reached into her medical bag.

PART ONE

1. *The End of His Life*

On the first Sunday of Advent in the previous year, a man named Alexander Graham said a prayer that was to have unforeseen consequences.

He lived on Oak Avenue in Halcyon, a town of twelve hundred souls situated in the forested hill country north of Lake Ontario. Because his home was only a few blocks from his parish church, he went out that evening into a snowstorm and trudged up the street with the intention of making a brief visit to the Blessed Sacrament. Although he was not an exceptionally pious person, he had of late been haunted by a sense that his life was over, or soon would be, and he wished to speak to God about it.

The church windows were dark, but he found the side door unlocked. Inside the vestibule he stamped his feet on the slush mat to rid his boots of snow and blindly located the door into the nave. The interior was warm, lit only by the flicker of amber vigil lights ranked in front of statues and by the ruby tabernacle lamp hanging over the high altar. They cast a subdued glow, enough for him to see his way down the aisle to his customary pew. This was on the left side, halfway to the front, beside a pillar. The soft mutter of candles, the scent of beeswax and incense hanging in the air, the faint echoes in the dome, the audible hush—these were, for him, the atmosphere of an entire world. He had been baptized in this church and had never worshipped in another. Its every detail was so deeply embedded in him that he could not have imagined life without it.

A quiet and dignified man, in his late forties, he was accustomed to living his life without attracting undue notice. In fact, he preferred it this way. If there had been any other parishioners present in the church, they would have felt little inclination to wonder why he was there, still less to approach him. He sensed that his relationship with God was much the same as his relationship with his fellow human beings.

He knelt, made the sign of the cross, and began to recite the prayers that were habitual to him. He said them mentally, carefully, trying as best he could to mean each word. It was a rare thing for him to experience any feeling connected to prayer, and indeed, if he had wanted to recall such scattered incidents, he would have had to reach back many years in search of the most recent memory. It did not matter to him. Emotions, he was certain, were unreliable and irrelevant to the labor of religious faith.

Nevertheless, on this particular evening, an errant mood took hold of him. Perhaps because he was tired and feeling the weight of his solitude, his attention drifted and the formal prayers fell silent. At any other time, he would have reengaged his will and resumed praying, but for some reason he could not. He bowed his head and rested his forehead in one hand, remaining motionless for several minutes without a single thought or image occupying his mind. Eventually he stirred and sighed.

"I think", he whispered to the Presence in the tabernacle, "my life is over."

He did not expect a response, and he heard none. He was not pessimistic by nature, nor was he prone to depression, and so this vague sense of termination, or completion, was not the result of morbidity. He had no desire to die, though it must be said that he was not excessively attached to life. Since the death of his wife some years before, and the departure of his two sons to college, he had become less and less connected to other human beings. He had been a virtuous husband and a conscientious and affectionate father, though a somewhat distracted one. And now the life of his small family had reached that phase when its form begins to be absorbed into the larger community.

He missed his deceased wife very badly at times, but there was no bringing her back. He missed his sons, but they were launched into the world, busily making their own lives. They would revisit Halcyon from time to time, but the law of return, he knew, was not eternal. He supposed that, for his sons, home now represented a fixed node in a wheeling universe, an anchor, or a kind of icon they occasionally touched and perhaps even reverenced, as one respects a tradition that had once been useful but has lost its mystique. They loved him, yes, but their temperaments were those of a different generation—active, enthusiastic, plunged into the stimuli of life in a way that he had never been. Thus, he was alone. That he had loved, and loved with a measure of sacrifice, he did not question. He had given them what he had to give. But he now felt some regret that he had not known them as well as he might have. Nor had they understood him, for he was a relatively silent man, bookish and dutiful.

He wondered if the old time bomb in his chest was nearing its long-expected detonation. For more than thirty years he had lived under its threat, and to tell the truth, he had long ago ceased to be worried about it. Was this sense of impending finality a hint from God? *Get ready, Alex, tidy your books, make the last notations in your records, for the account is about to be closed.*

Looking up at the tabernacle, he said, "Do whatever you want with me."

On the following evening, Halcyon prepared for a winter's sleep beneath a sky turbulent with spiraling stars and jets of green aurora borealis. The hundred gabled rooftops of the old town core were merry with icicles refracting the Christmas lights that had appeared on homes and shops during the past week, competing with the luminous sky. The air was completely still, and the smoke from chimneys rose straight up into darkness. When occasionally a car passed slowly along icy Main Street, its tires would whine, mingling with the laughter of boys making their way home from the town rink with hockey sticks and skates dangling from their shoulders. Few other people were out on the sidewalks, it being after eight o'clock and the region groaning under an early cold snap.

Braving the arctic air with a determination—and pleasure—that was uncharacteristic of the populace as a whole, Alex came out onto the steps of the old brownstone that was his residence and place of business, locking the door behind him. Though it was his habit to keep the lights of his bookshop burning and the door open to nocturnal browsers until ten o'clock each night—Sundays excepted, when it was closed all day—he had been possessed by a desire for an early walk beneath the stars. He now stood for a few moments, buttoning the toggles of his dark blue naval parka, tightening his scarf, pulling fur-lined gloves onto his fingers. Hatless (he disliked hats), though protected by a shock of once-blond hair threaded with strands of gray, he felt the first sting of the subzero temperature on his ears, a sensation that invigorated rather than dissuaded him.

As he surveyed his neighborhood, he thought, as he had done countless times before, that there was no place on earth as lovely as Halcyon. This peculiar loyalty was due in part to the fact that he had rarely traveled beyond the town and the back roads of the surrounding hill country, which offered circuitous rambles that always returned him to the exact center of the world. Indeed, he had never traveled farther than Toronto, a two-hour drive to the south. He had visited there only once in his life and had not been afflicted with a desire to repeat the experience. He had been born in Halcyon, as had four generations of his forefathers, and he considered himself fortunate because of it. If his life had failed to be entirely placid, he was thankful that his troubled years, now fading, were more than outweighed by the years during which he had known much happiness.

Alex inhaled sharply, avoiding the lure of certain memories, and turned his attention to the scene before him, a sight that always reassured him that although life was imperfect, its cardinal rule was the preponderance of order. His shop was situated on a quiet avenue a minute's walk from Main, close to the highest point of town, from where one could view most of the roofs and all of the encircling hills. On distant hilltops a few sparks from solitary farms could be seen. Their snow-covered fields shimmered under a rising moon, bordered by black stands of conifers and the paler lacework of deciduous woods. The town itself sat on a bluff in the valley of the Clementine River, at the big bend where a dam had been built in the early 1800s. The heavy stonework had not crumbled and the sluice gates remained in operation, but the gutted ruin of the gristmill that it had once serviced—Halcyon Grain and Feed—and around which the town had grown stood as a silent reminder that times had changed.

He blew a few puffs of frost and felt a moment's surprise when sparkles of color materialized in the microscopic crystals of his breath. He smiled and thought to himself, *There's always something new. I've lived for more than four decades, and never before have I noticed this.*

He stepped down onto the sidewalk and blew more puffs, this time directly toward the brighter lights of Main. Again and again the sparkles appeared, shimmering, falling in slow motion until they dissipated.

He was so intrigued by the phenomenon that he failed to hear approaching footsteps.

"You all right, Alex?"

Looking up, he saw Maria Sabbatino standing three paces away, frowning.

"I'm fine, Maria. I was watching lights in the frost."

"Oh", she said, her large black eyes peering at him from under a fringe of silver hair, chopped down to bangs. Her eyebrows, thick like a man's, were joined in consternation, her expression suspicious above two round olive cheeks inflamed with plum red—the identical twin sister of a portrait in the book on Pompeii.

"Alex, you have supper tonight? You eating?"

"I had supper tonight, Maria. I'm eating."

"Maybe you drink too much today, no?"

"No drink today, Maria."

"Please, Alex, don't drinka too much, you go for the walk and you fall down nobody see you and you freeza ta death. That's okay for you, maybe you go to heaven, but thinka da boys, thinka da peoples who cry over you coffin, eh?"

Alex smiled, then chuckled.

"How come you laugh? It'sa no joke you fall down freeza ta death!"

Hoping that it did not sound patronizing, he chuckled again—not because of her dialect, and certainly not because she was something of a figure of fun in town, but because of the absurdity of her notion that people would cry over his coffin.

Who would cry over my coffin? he wondered. *Only those who drinka too much from the keg of emotional indulgence. Those who are addicted to the pleasures of Grand Mourning—the funerary bargain hunters!*

He did not intend these thoughts unkindly, and they contained not a trace of self-pity. It was merely his habit mentally to correct the false assumptions that people were forever uttering in his presence, and, of course, the assumptions that appeared from time to time within his own mind.

20

"Maria, look at this." He pointed to the lights of Main and blew a cloud of frost. "Have you ever noticed those sparkles before?"

She shrugged. "I never see it before. So what, Alex? So, you got sparkles. Can you cook sparkles?"

She threw her right hand up in a gesture that might have been intelligible to her countrymen and that perhaps expressed a willingness to probe deeper into mysteries as long as she retained her rights of cynical caution and severe maternal disapproval. Alex knew the gesture well, though he had not succeeded in translating it perfectly during the months Maria had worked for him during Carol's final illness. He had supposed it was part of a deaf-and-dumb alphabet, a kind of visual code that was useful in discussions about fate, death, wages, pasta recipes, and the subterfuges of teenage boys. It was so flexible that it could mean, alternatively: It's a mere nothing; it doesn't matter! It breaks your heart, so what can you say! Ha, I've seen it all before! You can't fool me! Life is a bad business! You think I'm stupid; don't waste my time! et cetera. To the unfamiliar eye the gesture could seem dismissive, but it was intended, he supposed, as a mode of intimate communication. It could be read properly only if one had learned the lexicon of facial expressions and tones of voice that accompanied the precise, swift lash of the upthrust arm, palm open, resignation and protest linked in uneasy union, the distinctive product of millennia of Roman life (the empire, not the city, for he knew that Maria was from the impoverished south, the dry-hot hills of Calabria).

Alex, Anglo-Saxon Celt that he was, had not yet decoded the lexicon. It was, perhaps, unnecessary to learn it, for in the alternative language of shared suffering, which almost always has a limited vocabulary, they understood one another quite well. He was grateful that Maria was his neighbor and fellow parishioner—and rescuer, for once, several years ago, she had saved his life. She had stepped in when everything fell apart, had become the cook, the household organizer, the chief scold, the petty tyrant of the kitchen, and in unguarded moments, a mourner. He had surprised her as she was weeping in the pantry one day. "*Povera, povera* Carolina!" she had sobbed. "Poor boys, no mama, no mama!" Gut-wrenching, cathartic. Cathartic most of all for the three stoic males who had until that moment held their pain within, resigned to their fate. Maria's wildly extravagant sobbing had driven Alex and his two sons to the privacy of their bedrooms, where each, in the company of his own memories, gave in at last to grief.

"Christmas shopping?" he asked, pointing at the large paper bag in her left hand (the right was always kept free for gestures).

"*Sì*, I finda something fora Paolo. Nice scarfs and a mitt. He no need, but he come home sometime for visit. Then he need!"

Paolo, her son, more idolized and more anguished over than a dissolute fifteenth-century Florentine prince, was a computer analyst in a place that Maria referred to, in tones of disdain, as "Valle Silicone", California.

"And for Bruno, I getta dis."

For the first time Maria smiled, and though it would have seemed a grudging smile to all who did not know her, Alex knew that it was a veritable outburst, containing fountains of affection and tolerance. On the scale of her emotional life there were no blocked-out zones, but histrionics were reserved for the funerals and weddings of those who were only loosely connected to her. Her deepest emotions were almost entirely interior.

She showed him a plastic bag full of leather and wires.

"Electrica worka glove!" she said triumphantly. "Batteries included. Forty-nina ninety-five! When he worka night shift on da track, he no freeza da hands." Speaking with animation, she tore open the plastic wrapper and was preparing to demonstrate how the battery pack could be affixed to a coat sleeve by Velcro straps.

He stopped her—no, no, no—laughing. "It's too cold, Maria. Show me another time."

"*Ecco!* Okay, okay, maybe another time. You come our place after Midnight Mass, have a *cicchetto da vino*, and Bruno show you da glove."

As she rewrapped her gift, he looked down fondly at her head, capped with a bowl of imitation leopard fur, and felt an irrational desire to lurch forward and hug her clumsily, to kiss the top of her head—a filial impulse that would have distressed and confused her. He did not give in to it.

The repacking completed, she looked up, squinted, and said in a threatening voice, "You hear from those boys this Christmas?"

"Not yet. I expect they'll send cards."

"Children! We breaka da body for them, breaka da soul, cry da guts out, give everything, and wadda we get?"

"Grandchildren?" Alex suggested.

"I tell you what we get, we get they breaka da heart!" She thumped her chest with her gesturing hand.

Alex nodded sagely, murmuring, blowing smaller puffs, without sparkles.

"Alex," she said, changing tone, peering at him shrewdly, "Carolina, she's a gone, how many, five years now?" With a philosophical air, she made a small sign of the cross on her chest.

He nodded again, uncomfortable.

"It'sa time you find a gooda woman, marry ina church before God, she look after you. You need *somebody* look after you. Looka dose ears! You don't find somebody pretty soon, Alex, you gonna stand ina street every night blow sparkles and dey take you away in ambulance to hospital for da *matto-pazzo* peoples!" Circular motion at her temple, made with the revolving fur mitt of the right hand.

"*Matto-pazzo*? Ah, you mean crazy."

She nodded somberly. "*Sì*, crazy. I know you *not* crazy, Alex, but tonight I see you stand out ina cold, stare at nothing, blow cloud of the mouth and see sparkle. Maybe somebody don't know you, he think—*matto-pazzo!*"

"That's if I don't fall down and *freeza* to death."

She slapped his wrist with the right-hand mitt. "No joke about it! Think about what I say."

"All right, Maria, I'll think about it."

She went away up the street, a hunched sixty-year-old, not quite five feet tall, with sun in her blood, bundled against the numbing dark of the unnatural New World, worrying about anything and everything. He was touched by her concern but knew he would not consider for a minute her suggestion, the panacea offered by maternal hearts whenever they encountered the tragedy, the scandal, the gash in the cosmos created by an unattached male. No one could ever replace Carol. That part of his life was over.

Turning away from the glow of Main, he walked up Oak in the direction of the crest, where the spires of three churches formed the crown of Halcyon. The tallest of the three was Saint Mary of the Angels, a neogothic dream of pale rose stone and masterful stained glass that drew upward everything in its vicinity. Saint Paul's Anglican, modern, steel and glass, was on the opposite side of the street. The monolithic Findley Memorial United, red granite capped by a crenellated war tower, was half a block farther along, beyond which the avenue began to descend again in a long arc that girded the bluffs and eventually led to the river.

As he approached the grounds of Saint Mary's, Alex paused momentarily at the walkway leading to the front doors. Recalling his prayer of the day before—*Do whatever you want with me*—he wondered at himself. Surely that was precisely what God always did with his creatures. Why, then, had he felt the need to state the obvious? What had he meant by it? What had he been asking—if indeed he had been asking anything? Well, it did not matter, because the odd mood that had precipitated the prayer was now gone.

The muffled strains of a choir practicing Christmas carols hung in the air. It grew suddenly louder when the front door of Saint Mary's opened and two figures stepped outside, a teenage boy and a small girl. They skipped down the steps and turned onto the sidewalk ahead of him, where they broke into a run. He noted their poor clothing and their anxious faces as they passed. They disappeared hand in hand around a corner onto a cross street, heading toward Lowertown and the river. He did not recall having seen them before and supposed they belonged to one of the new families that had moved into the rent-subsidized housing the county administration had built last year at the foot of the bluffs.

Blowing more puffs, he moved on.

Although most of Alex's life was preoccupied with scholarly pursuits, with polite literary exchanges with customers, with keeping accurate financial records in his shop, and with the deflection of irrational assumptions, he did occasionally indulge in musings that verged on the poetic, or at least the dipping of a toe into erratic streams of consciousness. These lapses never overwhelmed him or possessed him but were rather carefully chosen moments of intuition. They were not productive in the sense of genuine creativity, for he was not a poet or painter or musician, but they were useful in that they provided him with a kind of relaxation of the mind. Other men took to drink or verse, or worse, but Alex would lock the door of his shop and set forth to wander at random in the dark hills that were as familiar to him as his labyrinthine bookshelves and the hyperion heights of the town. These small exercises in imprecision, in imitation of abandonment, kept him supple.

Maria Sabbatino was wrong in assuming that he, like many a widower, had taken to drink. In fact, he never felt the desire to drink, and when he shared his single New Year's Eve toast with Father Toby upstairs in the parlor above the shop, it was always poured from the same bottle of amontillado, recognizable by its label: a red crusader's cross emblazoned on a gold shield surmounted by a tiny three-dimensional chalice embedded in the black Spanish glass. The level of liquor in the bottle was a little lower each year, a detail that Father Toby commented on with dry amusement. And that was that. See you next year, same time, same place, same bottle. Five years ago, three weeks after Carol's funeral, Maria had surprised him one morning as he upended a bottle of Seagram's whiskey that had belonged to his father, glugging down a throatful, hoping it would ease the killer bite of anguish. It didn't. Its only effect had been to convince Maria that he had a drinking problem, an assumption from which she would never thereafter be dislodged.

Oak crested and began to descend. If he followed it another eight blocks, he would come to the edge of town at the bridge over the Clementine, which would take him into the north hills, his favorite walk, two hours more or less, depending on the weather. But for some inexplicable reason, he felt a desire to take his least favorite route, which was straight down the bluff to the gristmill dam, across the dam's walkway (treacherous but exhilarating), and up into the escarpment through Dogpatch Run. The Run or Dogpatch, as it was known locally, was officially named Wolfe's Ravine Road, but its more unflattering title derived from the cluster of decrepit buildings, many of them clapboard houses and sheds built in the 1800s, clinging to the sides of the gravel road that climbed the ravine. Mill workers and river men had once lived there, but its golden era was long over. Many of the buildings were now empty, and those that were not soon would be, for the relief housing across the waters in Halcyon was irresistible.

The Run's attraction was that it took him to the top of the escarpment at a point where he could see beyond the bend of the river and watch it wind away through the hills to the south, in the direction of Lake Ontario. Moreover, from that height, and that height alone, one could look down upon the whole of Halcyon, which at night became an encrustment of fiery jewels, resting on the shadowed collar of a beautiful recumbent woman, sleeping in her gown, its white satin folds modest and elegant but stirring. In summer the gown was green. As a young man he had often gone there in order to feel the sharp sweetness of longing for the mysterious feminine principle, an ache that would have translated itself into the customary social skills, the elaborate plots and schedules of courtship, if he had not been so abysmally shy, if he had not been an only child, if he had not been the heir to a family tradition of eccentricity, if he had not been the magistrate's son. As if that were not enough, he had spent two years of his early adolescence in bed, recovering from the ravages of rheumatic fever. In those days the disease damaged the heart, they said, and the only cure was total inactivity. During convalescence, he had plunged deeper into the world of books, and remained there. Thus, what might have been a transient state—a young man's diffident temperament—became his permanent form.

Later, Carol came into his life like a miracle, changing him at the core, kindling a fire on the hearthstone, though the architecture of his personality had already set. He was essentially an introvert, a structure erected with skill and patience by master craftsmen, with solid wood doors that locked and windows that could be shuttered instantly, permitting no passersby a view into the interior. Yet the heart continued to beat, the coal glowed. If there was now no longer any fuel to throw onto it, Alex was not greatly dispirited by this, for he was content with his life. His one wrestling match with despair was over, the memory of it fading, leaving only residual marks. It was necessary to guard against any recurrence, however, any vulnerability to the killer bite. For even the most cursory glance at the human condition provided ample evidence that no ordinary murderer was at large. A serial killer was on the loose, and the heart was his preferred target. The heart was the most exposed organ of all.

Even so, Alex was not so enclosed within himself that he presumed upon any kind of absolute security. He knew that a guarded existence, even the apparent serenity of a bibliophile's life, was no sure defense. *You must remain flexible*, he told himself, *to a degree—as much as you can.* He knew that if he did not, he could easily atrophy in middle age, shrink, shrivel, and calcify into a gnome in a Dickensian shop. Become the old curiosity itself. If, instead, he walked abroad upon his own familiar high moors, he would see vast landscapes and keep muscle and heart and mind alive to the possibilities in an infinitely large and surprising universe.

Turning off Oak, he went down the steep incline of Tamarack (avenues were deciduous, streets coniferous), going slowly, digging in his heels with each step to avoid a fall. Arriving without mishap at the riverside road, he turned left and walked a half block upriver toward the dam. There, at the valley's narrowest point, the river was only thirty or forty feet wide, its waters accelerating for the rush through the gorge and over the lip of the dam, thundering onto the rocks below. Nearing the steps to the catwalk, he heard high-pitched shouts but paid them no heed, assuming that children were making noise at the skating rink down the road. The roar of water pouring over the dam's spillway muffled all other sounds. As he mounted the steps of the catwalk, he glanced down to his left, the high side of the dam, expecting to see only the semicircle of ale-brown water in front of the sluice.

Two children were in the water, their mouths opening and closing in inaudible screams. They were clinging to the edge of the ice on the town side. One of them had the other under an arm, and both were pawing frantically at the ice shelf, trying to grab hold, but chunks kept breaking off, and in the second or two of stunned horror during which Alex stared at the scene, they slipped closer to the sluice gate, pulled by the current.

If it had been summer, they would have gone over. But the current was weaker at this time of year, the water level low, though he estimated that at their position it would be over their heads. He leaped from the catwalk, dropping four feet, landing in snow, and struggled with all his might toward them. He could hear them now, a high-pitched wail from one mouth and cries from the other.

"Hang on, hang on!" Alex called.

He burst over the snow hump at the edge of the river and sprawled facedown across the ice. It made crackling-splintering noises beneath him as he struggled out of his duffel parka. They were at least ten feet away, and their faces turned to him: a young girl screaming in gulps, an older boy gasping, "Help! Help!"

"I'm coming! I'm coming!" Alex shouted. "Hang on!"

Their eyes were wild with terror, spray frozen on their faces and clothing. Alex slid his body toward the edge, trying to get close enough to fling the parka to them, hoping to use it as a rope to pull them to safety. Moving forward slowly—a few inches, six inches, a foot—he prayed for time. He flung the parka, but it thudded on the ice just short of the boy's frantically grasping right hand. A chunk of ice broke away under him, but as he scrambled for a grip on the shelf he did not let go of the girl.

With his elbows and knees, Alex pushed himself forward, then threw the parka again. This time the boy's hand grappled it. Alex pulled hard, but the weight of the children was too great. He needed to get closer. He thrust forward once more, expecting to slide, but instead the ice buckled under him and he plunged beneath the surface.

The shock of the cold water stunned him, and in the sudden darkness he felt for a moment that he was losing consciousness. Kicking hard, he resurfaced, pushed away the chunks of ice floe, and lashed his way slowly toward the children. The tug of the current increased as he approached them, and his legs were dragged downward. His boots hit the rocky bottom of the riverbed. The water level was just above the sternum of his chest. Three feet away the children's eyes were rolling, and the boy's arm was sliding off the shelf again, a body length from where the river plunged over the dam.

Alex forced his dead legs to move, one step, another. Another. The water level was now at his neck.

The boy let go of the ice just as Alex half-swam, half-leaped between him and the dam. Grabbing the children's arms, he swiveled around toward the shore, dragging them after him. Straining his toes downward, he searched with his feet, hoping to touch a stone, a submerged log, anything that would give him purchase. Without warning, one leg refused to go down full length; it no longer had any feeling, and he did not know if it had cramped or had hit something on the bottom. He pushed with his hips, and his body was propelled forward. The dead weight of the children followed with agonizing slowness.

Close to the shore he stood upright and found that the water was just above his knees. The ice shelf shattered before him with every step. Shaking uncontrollably, numb in all his extremities, he pulled the girl into his arms and staggered toward solid ground. He dragged her onto the shore and laid her down on the snow, then turned back for the boy, who was gasping loudly, trying to rise on all fours. Alex grabbed him around the chest and pulled him up, and together they staggered out of the water. As he fell to the ground, Alex saw people running toward him; he heard car horns beeping, doors slamming, shouts, cries; and in the few seconds before he closed his eyes, he saw galaxies slowly revolving in the open places that are high above the enclosures of the heart.

In his sleep he dreamed of light, and the light became a presence. And the presence became a voice.

You must go back, whispered the voice. *You have work to do.*

He opened his eyes and saw a white room and white lights, and Father Toby with a purple stole around his neck, and a doctor standing beside him with a stethoscope on his neck.

"Alex!" Father Toby's mouth opening and closing until the sound merged with his lips. "Alex, can you hear me?"

"He's back, Father", the doctor said. "It was a close call, but he's going to make it."

Later, he awoke and saw Father Toby in a chair beside the bed, reading a magazine, his legs stretched out, crossed at the ankles. Down the hall beyond the open doorway, a red exit light shone and people dressed in green uniforms passed briskly back and forth.

Alex's body was connected by wires to machines that beeped regularly. His lungs ached and bubbled, his face hurt, his hands throbbed, screaming in pain. When he lifted them, he saw that the fingers were bandaged.

"Oh!" he croaked.

Father Toby looked up, and seeing that Alex was awake, he pulled his chair close to the bed.

"Hi, buddy", he said in a low voice. "How are you feeling?"

"Sore", he croaked. "Hurts to breathe."

"Breathing's gonna hurt for a while. Do you know where you are?"

"*Matto-pazzo.*"

"*Matto-pazzo?*"

"*Matto-pazzo* hospital."

"That's right, you're in the hospital. Do you remember what happened?"

"Swimming."

"Yes, you went for a little swim."

Sharp pains stabbed at the corners of his mouth, in his lips, everywhere.

"Look, you'd better not talk. Just rest. You have pneumonia, but you're pulling through just fine."

A nurse came in, and Father Toby stood.

"He's coming out of it", the priest said to her. "A little confused, but I think our Alex is still with us."

"Hot!" Alex said.

"You've got a fever, but the chills can return at any time", said Father Toby. "We have to keep you bundled."

"Freeza to death. Batteries included."

Both the nurse and the priest looked down at him with worried expressions.

He slept.

Later, he woke up and saw daylight pouring in through the window, and a vase of flowers, red, white, violet, yellow, the blossoms opening as he watched, their colors changing steadily, the tendrils of perfume uncurling and flowing through the room.

He slept again.

When he awoke, there was a poinsettia bursting into flames on a window shelf, and beyond it, stars. Christmas music down the hall. And church bells.

A young nurse came into the room and changed a bag of liquid that dripped into a tube taped to his forearm. Then she helped him to sit up in bed. She fed him a bowl of thin, salty soup, spoonful by spoonful. Her arm around his shoulders felt wonderful. Worth dying for, worth almost-dying for.

"You're so warm", he croaked. "You're so beautiful!" Then he jerked back in dismay over this uninhibited blurting. She gave him a little ironic smile and made him take another spoonful.

When Father Toby came by later, she said, "Keep an eye on this one, will you, Father? What a tiger."

"A rogue indeed he is", said the priest.

When she left the room, Father Toby sat down on the end of the bed.

"Tiger?" he said with an arched eyebrow. "Good to see you back in the land of the living, Alex. Feeling better? Any chills?"

Alex shook his head.

"Fever?"

"No, but my hands hurt. My feet hurt. My face too."

"You had us worried there for a while. But you'll be going home soon, I think."

"What day is it?"

"December fourteenth."

"That can't be."

"Yes, it can. You've been out of it for a while."

When Alex had absorbed this, he asked, "How are the children?"

"The two kids? They stayed in the children's ward for a couple of days, then went home."

"How did it happen? How did they fall into the water?"

"A neighbor was supposed to pick them up after choir practice at Saint Mary's. But the streets were icy and she didn't have tires good enough to get up to the crest. They'd agreed to meet down on the river road by the dam. When they got there, the boy figured out that the woman was delayed. They didn't want to stand there and freeze, so they decided to take a shortcut across the river and meet her on the other side."

"Didn't they know how dangerous that was? Why did they cross so close to the spillway?"

"It wasn't the boy's fault. He wanted to cross farther from the dam, but the girl ran ahead of him. He shouted at her to stop, but it was too late. She fell through, and he went in after her." Father Toby shuddered. "Thank God you came along."

"I'm glad they're safe. Why haven't they sent me home?"

"First you were in shock and had hypothermia, and then you had some kind of cardiac arrest. No permanent damage, they think, but then pneumonia set in, and they're still a bit worried about your heart, considering your history. Something to do with that time you left school—grade ten, wasn't it? You were in bed quite a while."

"Two years."

"Doc Hendricks told me your circulation isn't what it should be. They want to keep an eye on you. He'll tell you more, no doubt."

"That's good", said Alex drowsily.

"I have to get back to the parish now for confessions, but I'll pop in later. Would you like me to bring you some books?"

"No thank you." He felt hot again, his thoughts blurring.

When he opened his eyes again it was daylight, and Father Toby was reading in the chair.

"Who's taking care of the store?" Alex asked.

Father Toby looked up, closed the book, and smiled.

"Nobody, as far as I know. Maria Sabbatino came by, lamented audibly over you, and asked for your keys. I gave them to her. I thought you wouldn't mind, her being your housekeeper a few years back. She said she wanted to go in and tidy up before you got home, put some food in the fridge, decorate for Christmas."

Alex groaned. "That wasn't necessary. I never decorate anyway. Not since the boys left. Not since...well, Carol always did that."

The old ache started up with a vengeance. Father Toby saw it, recognized it, and dragged his chair closer to the bed.

"Hey, buddy," he said with a big smile, "did you know you're quite a hero?"

Alex stared at him blankly.

"Yup. Whole town's in love with you."

"Oh."

"It was on the front page of the *Halcyon Leader*, hit the Toronto papers too, and got sixty seconds on the CBC *National*—the Christmas angle, community feeling, heroism isn't dead after all. That sort of thing."

"What nonsense!"

"Hey, Alex, your big swim brightened up a lot of hearts. Faith in humanity, et cetera."

"It could have happened to anyone."

"Maybe so. Fact is, it happened to you."

"That boy saved his little sister. I just happened to be there."

"And just happened to save the both of them."

Alex burst into a fit of coughing. When it was over, he said, "Look, let's not make too much of this. I'd rather people forget about it."

"That family's not going to forget about it."

"I wish they would. I wish everybody would."

"They won't, you know."

"I expect they will."

"What's more, you're just the sort of hero people love—a humble hero."

"It's not humility. I just want to get back to my life and not have to deal with people's assumptions."

Father Toby cocked a curious eye at him.

"What assumptions?"

Alex shrugged. "False images."

"And what might those be?"

"I don't know. People start expecting things from you; people want to know you."

"What's wrong with people wanting to know you?"

Alex's chest began to heave with the bubbling in his lungs. He leaned over a stainless steel bowl until it was finished, then lay back exhausted.

"Take it easy, guy. No more talking. You need rest."

Alex nodded and closed his eyes.

When he opened them again, he saw Father Toby coming into the room wearing an overcoat, brushing snowflakes from his shoulders.

"Morning, hero."

"Don't call me that."

"Why not? It's true."

"It's not true."

"What's the matter? Can't take a little praise?"

Father Toby furrowed his brow and gave Alex his most analytical look.

"Why are you looking at me that way, Father?"

"What way, Alex?"

"That way?"

"What way?"

"That way."

So ensued an old game they had played off and on since boyhood. Its rules had changed over the years, and its meaning would have been unreadable to all but the two participants. Both understood what it was about. By descending into irrational and childish behavior, they established equilibrium between themselves. It was a war of wills that for all its intensity was entirely friendly. It had early on developed into an exercise for strengthening the character of two rather reflective temperaments, much as ordinary boys will push, shove, and explode into wrestling matches without a hint of animosity, then jump up and go off arm in arm to face the world.

"What way, *Worm*?" This was Toby's old nickname for Alex and his bookworm ways.

"That way, *Toffee*." Alex's old name for Toby, who had once been addicted to Mackintosh's Toffee. Toby's family name was McIntosh.

"What way?"

"That way."

As the exchange ran through its predictable course, Alex was pursuing a different line of thought. It struck him that Father Toby was his only close friend, in fact his only friend, and that he had been a presence in his life for a long time. Although he valued the relationship, he realized that he was not dependent on it, and if it were to fade out of his life, as did so many other things, so many other people, he would not miss it overmuch. By contrast, Father Toby had several close friends, for his good-hearted, outgoing nature drew others to him. He sustained them and was loyal to them. The short, fat, shy Toby who had been Alex's boon companion in their childhood was no longer the boy he once had been. His outcast status had gradually dissolved during the years Alex was abed. A genius for hockey and the resulting disappearance of fat, the kicking in of the pituitary gland at the age of fifteen and a truly amazing growth spurt, the delirious happiness he had felt at his own metamorphosis had altered him forever. The suffering of his early years had been converted into a kind of wry wisdom. The flaccid piety of his childhood had become, at some point along the way, something robust and deep, leading him eventually to ordination.

As they played the old word game, Alex began to read things between the lines of the script. He saw that in recent years he had not been half the friend to Father Toby that the priest had been to him. He saw also that he might have misunderstood their relationship. He had always assumed that Father Toby genuinely liked him, perhaps admired the scholarly direction that his life had taken. He had supposed it was a case of a late-blooming extrovert being drawn to the quiet waters of a perennial introvert—a comfortable complementarity. Now he wondered if Father Toby, yeoman Catholic that he was, charitable man that he was, felt sorry for him, considered him to be a lonely soul in need of a friend.

If that were so, then a very large assumption in Alex's life needed to dissolve.

He stopped the game in midsentence.

"Father, tell me the truth."

"What truth?"

"Why were you looking at me that way?"

"What way?"

"I'm really asking you."

Father Toby laughed, looked at the floor.

"Alex—"

"I can take it. Come on, tell me."

"You're a sick man. Relax."

"You looked at me in that certain way, the one you use when you're about to tell me something about myself I don't want to hear. The spiritual direction look."

Father Toby waved it away. "You're imagining things."

They regarded each other with amiable, masked expressions.

"Sounds to me like you're evading", said Alex.

"What's there to evade? Look, you're feeling low right now, Alex, and you've been through a lot during the past few years. Don't read too much into things."

The next day he opened his eyes to find Maria standing at the foot of the bed, her eyes wet, gazing at him as if he were a wax bambino in a crèche. She was telling him something about keys, but he couldn't concentrate. Then, very proudly and with a proprietary air, she explained that Bruno had rescued his duffel parka from the river. Parishioners had taken up a collection to have it dry-cleaned.

"Here it is", she said, opening the bedside locker. "Like anew, like a coat shoulda be, clean for first time ina *five* years!"

He closed his eyes and drifted away.

Dr. Hendricks came by the bedside later in the morning and gave Alex the details about his physical condition, told him he had passed the most recent series of tests with good marks—the graphs of the electrocardiograms and monitor indicated no damage to his heart. However, because of the pneumonia, he wanted to keep Alex under observation a few more days.

"Father Toby says I had a cardiac arrest", Alex prompted.

Hendricks, a minimalist and a reassurer, frowned slightly. "I would say there were irregularities in your heartbeat."

"Did I die?"

"Technically speaking, yes. There was no pulse for thirty seconds, and you turned a lovely shade of blue. We got you started up again fairly quickly. Aside from high blood pressure, which is pneumonia related, you're doing well. For the time being, it's steady as she goes. Just avoid jumping into frozen rivers for a while, and you should be fine."

Unwired at last, relieved of the sound of incessant beeping, Alex got out of bed and shuffled around the room, investigating the forest of potted plants and floral arrangements. Feeling dizzy and very weak in his legs, he was nevertheless glad to see that the flowers had returned to normal behavior; they no longer unfurled their petals in time-lapse photography, and their currents of perfume had become invisible. The gift cards contained some names that he recognized, but many of the cards were from strangers. There was a packet of envelopes on the bedside table, and the one on top was from his eldest son. He sat on the edge of the bed and opened it.

Dear Dad,

I'm so proud of you. It's all over the news here in Toronto. Even one of the lawyers at Osgoode Hall asked me if we're related. I wanted to jump on the first train to Halcyon the minute I heard, but with bar exams only weeks away, I'm afraid if I come up for air I won't make it. I've been phoning Dr. Hendricks each day, and he says you're going to be fine. I feel awful that I can't be there for you right now, but I hope to get home for two days at Christmas. I want to hear all about it from the horse's mouth, though the CBC beat you to it. Ha ha!

I've got some news of my own to tell you.

Does Andrew know what happened? I tried to call him, but there's been no answer so far.

Get well soon,
Jacob

The young nurse came into the room late in the afternoon and told him he had visitors. She went out into the ward hallway and returned a moment later with two children. A girl seven or eight years of age came in first, followed by a boy of about fifteen. The nurse patted their shoulders fondly, then said, "I'll leave you three with each other", and went out, closing the door.

Alex's visitors stood at the foot of the bed, at first barely able to look him in the eye. They seemed uncomfortable, uncertain about what to say. The rims of their ears were flaming red with purple scabs. The girl's head was down, but her eyes looked up at Alex with a mixture of shyness and familiarity. She had a sweet, guileless face with blue eyes; her blond hair was carefully braided. The boy stared at the floor; then his eyes flashed up quickly and just as quickly looked away.

A lean, guarded face. Brown eyes under an unruly thatch of black hair. He whisked a blue tuque off his head and snatched a knitted wool cap from his sister's.

"Hello", Alex offered.

"Hello", they replied in solemn unison.

The boy nudged the girl forward. She handed Alex an envelope and stepped back a pace.

"We want to thank you for saving us", the boy mumbled awkwardly. "For pulling us out of the river."

The girl's face lit up. "We almost *drownded*!" she exclaimed.

"Drowned", her brother corrected.

"We'd be dead! And our mum'd be brokin-har...brokin-hart..."

"Brokenhearted", said the boy.

Alex smiled at them. He said to the boy, "It looked to me as though you did most of it. You kept your sister from drowning. How long were you in the water?"

"I don't know", he shrugged. "A few minutes, maybe."

"What are your names?"

"I'm Jamie; this is Hannah."

"Well, I'm glad to meet you. Do you know my name?"

Jamie nodded. Hannah came to the edge of the bed and said fervently, "You're Mr. Graham! You *saved* us!"

The boy rolled his tuque nervously.

"Uh, well, it was nice to meet you", he said. "We just wanted to stop by and say thanks. The nurse said we could only stay a minute. We gotta catch the last school bus."

"All right, Jamie and Hannah. Thank you for coming. I'm very glad you're okay now."

"My mum says thanks too", Hannah put in. "She wrote you a letter."

He watched them go down the hallway, puzzling over their demeanor. He supposed that the children of the poor lacked confidence.

41

He was exhausted by the visit, which had been somewhat strained. He had never been good at talking with children, a corollary of his lack of communication skills with human beings in general. He put the envelope they had given him onto the bedside table, closed his eyes, and slept.

At suppertime he ate a full meal without assistance from the nurse. After a cup of hot tea and an agonized clearing of his lungs, he opened the envelope. The letter was handwritten on lined paper, dated three days after the accident.

Dear Mr. Graham,

I am at a loss for words to express my thanks for your courageous act. You risked your life to save Jamie and Hannah. I will be forever grateful. I cannot repay you (I know you're the kind of man who wouldn't want payment anyway), but please know there is one family in this world who won't ever forget what you've done.

I know you are a busy man and have your own life, which must be very full, but if you can find a little time, we would be so happy if you would visit our place and have a meal with us. We live up on Concession 4 above Wolfe's Ravine.

I phoned the hospital, and they say you are still very ill, but going to recover. I thank God for this. All of us here (eight of us) pray for you every day.

Yours sincerely,
Mrs. Theresa Colley

P.S. I would have come into town to thank you in person, Mr. Graham, but unfortunately we do not have a car at present.

He put the letter back into its envelope and placed it on the table. A wave of sadness washed over him as he pondered their life, so much of which was revealed in a few short sentences.

The letter had not said "my husband and I wish to thank you", but simply "I". Where was the husband, if there was

42

one? She had signed it "Mrs.", so there must be one. The girl was innocent; the boy had seen some painful things. There had been a hint of wariness, even cynicism. Perhaps his mother was a woman who had trouble with men, and the boy had sustained some damage because of it. The girl no doubt would pattern herself on the mother and sustain her own damage, though that would come later.

The mention of payment. Why had it arisen? Perhaps because she was struggling to get by, had her pride, and needed to pay her way through life, avoiding the obligations and humiliation that she would incur by accepting charity. On the other hand, she had invited him to a meal in her home; if it was a genuine offer, she considered the hospitality of her family something worthy of respect.

She had apologized for not thanking him in person, explaining that she had no car. It was unusual for country people to be without a car. Was it in the service station for repairs? Had it been repossessed? Had her husband driven off with it and not returned?

Alex sat up abruptly in bed and gave himself a mental rebuke. This was judgment, he told himself. Prejudice. He reminded himself that many women were in difficult straits through no fault of their own. Why had he presumed the worst? Of course, the latest statistics on failed marriages were bad—60 percent and climbing. However, she might be a widow struggling heroically to raise her children on limited resources.

As Father Toby had rightly said, he was low, he was in that state which made him prone to imagining things. The mind, the mind! Ever ready to project its assumptions on others, on the community, on the whole world. Human relationships were so complicated and always veering in the direction of the irrational. Better to get back to his shop and his books as soon as possible.

2. *Back to Normal*

Dr. Hendricks sent him home on the twentieth of December, pumped full of antibiotics and stern admonishments to rest, releasing him only on condition that he keep the shop closed until after New Year's. When the taxi pulled up to the curb, Alex glanced with fondness at the sign in his front window: Kingfisher Books. The silver-blue feathers flashed in the afternoon sun, the jeweled eye winked at him, the crest tilted in regal acknowledgment of his return.

He tried to pay the driver, a man named Jedediah Smythe, who had been his grade-school classmate years ago but whose life had seldom connected with his own since then. Jed refused his money, saying, "This one's on me, Mr. Graham."

"You're not serious."

"Uh-huh, I'm serious."

"But why?"

"Do I need a reason?"

"That's very generous of you, but I can't let you do it."

"The next time you save somebody's life, you get another free ride."

"I didn't do anything that others wouldn't have done."

"Yeah, right." Jed tipped his cap. "Well, Merry Christmas, Mr. Graham, and take it easy, eh."

He rolled up the window and spun his tires on the slick avenue until the cab slid forward. Alex watched it disappear over the hump at the height of Oak.

Oh dear, it was already starting. The public persona. The hero. And why did Jed always call him "Mr. Graham"?

Shaking his head, he went up the steps, noting that someone had scraped them clean of snow. Unlocking the shop door, he went inside, inhaling with pleasure the smell of aging books and ancient varnish. Looking around at the dark wainscoting and paneled ceiling, greeting silently the rows of crowded bookshelves, he nearly trod on a drift of envelopes scattered beneath the mail slot. It cost him some effort to bend down and gather them up. Fortunately, his desk was near the door, and he went to it on wobbly legs, sat down, and without removing his parka and boots began sorting the mail. A few bills, some business letters, and several dozen Christmas cards (rarely in the past had he received more than ten). He did not open any, reading only the return addresses, most of which were from names he did not recognize. There was nothing from England.

There was one from Jacob. Smiling, Alex slit the envelope with his letter opener and removed a card that at first glance seemed to be a photograph of a construction site. Upon closer inspection he saw that it was an abstract artwork made of aluminum, titled *Angel*.

Hey, Dad,

My informants tell me they're letting you out on good behavior within a couple of days. That's wonderful news. I'm sure you're going to be busy over the holidays now that you're the town hero. I had hoped to get home for a day or so during vacation, but something great has happened.

I wanted to tell you in person, but it's not working out as I'd planned. I've met someone very special. Her family is fairly well off, and they've invited me to go with them to Whistler over Christmas. It's one of those once-in-a-lifetime deals, a complete vacation package at the best ski resort in British Columbia, in the whole world, actually. They're paying my way.

Don't worry—it's a family outing, and we'll be constantly chaperoned. We'll be back the end of the first week in January. Any chance you can come to Toronto to meet her? Give me a call before you come.

Lots of love. Merry Christmas!

Jacob

What is her name, Jacob? Who is she? What is she like?

After hanging his parka on the coat stand and removing his boots and setting them neatly on the entrance mat, he checked the grandfather clock, which had stopped during his stay in the hospital. He reset the hands to the correct minute and hour, wound the spring, and went upstairs to his living quarters. There he found that the parlor had been festooned with what he guessed were Italian decorations, colored streamers crisscrossing the room, chocolate saints dangling on threads from the chandelier, and dishes of odd-looking candy on every table. The kitchen was as shiny clean as a hospital ward, the linoleum scrubbed and waxed for the first time in years, the refrigerator full of plastic containers with little notes taped to them.

His bedroom was not significantly altered, though the stacks of books piled along the walls had been made less tipsy, and it looked as if someone had dusted. On his bedside table he discovered a vase of red carnations beside Carol's photograph. The carved wooden crucifix over the bed had been cleaned, the corpus wiped free of dust and oiled. The threadbare carpet had been vacuumed, the pictures on the wall straightened. His four-poster bed had been changed too and was no longer a tumble of sweaty pillows, musky blankets, and sheets gone gray but a work of pristine purity: crisp white linen that looked as if it had been boiled and starched, turned down like a fold in a page and covered with a blue blanket elaborately trimmed with maroon crocheting.

The mark of Maria was everywhere.

He felt grateful for her many kindnesses and thought he should call her on the phone, but he was suddenly so weary that he lay down on the bed and fell asleep.

On Christmas Eve his lungs had improved enough that he decided to brave the night air and go to Midnight Mass. He dressed himself in a suit and tie, shined his shoes, and from deep in the recesses of his bedroom closet brought forth one of his most valued possessions, the overcoat that had belonged to his grandfather. It was of a length and cut that had gone out of style generations ago, and the silk lining was somewhat thin, but the herringbone tweed of its outer layer seemed almost as good as the day it was made. It weighed twice as much as any modern coat, sitting on his shoulders just right, bestowing a sense not only of warmth but also of tradition, dignity, substance. To this he added another treasured possession, a Scottish wool scarf, the clan Graham tartan, forest green with black crosses.

For most of the year Saint Mary's was only three-quarters full on Sundays, but tonight there was standing room only, as was usual at Christmas. The pipe organ in the choir loft was played with more-than-usual gusto by the elderly Miss Dufort, with her younger sister, the junior Miss Dufort, turning pages. The pastor, Monsignor Penney, and Father Toby concelebrated. The sanctuary was crowded with altar boys, one of whom was Jamie Colley. The homily, a meditation on the incarnational aspect of the Catholic faith, was delivered by Father Toby, but Alex found it hard to concentrate, though he was sure the points were as excellent as the heartfelt delivery. He tried to pray throughout Mass but was exhausted and distracted by the inrush of sensory stimuli. The post-Communion hymn was provided by the children of the parish, who gathered around the Nativity scene and sang a faltering "Carol of the Bells", shaking handbells of many kinds. Hannah Colley was among them. Alex resisted the urge to scan the pews in search of a husbandless woman surrounded by several children.

After the closing prayers, the recessional hymn—"This Day So Rich in Joys"—began with a grand swell from the organ. The faithful stumbled their way through banal lyrics that had been grafted onto the Bach composition. Mercifully, the words were drowned out by the volume of the hundred-year-old, German pipes. When the hymn was over, the crowd erupted into exuberant conversation in the pews, many streaming toward the exits, children running up and down the aisles. Only a handful of people knelt praying before the crèche beneath the altar.

Alex genuflected in the aisle and tried to go upstream against the traffic, hoping to remain unseen as he made his way toward a side door. His attempt at invisibility failed, however, because for every few feet of progress he made, someone would reach out and shake his hand, thump him on the back, say things that could not be heard above the din. At one point Bruno and Maria Sabbatino blocked his passage and hugged him. Alex thanked Maria for all she had done for him. Her eyes watered, and she lashed her gesturing arm dismissively. Bruno insisted that Alex come over for a sip of wine and a view of the "electrica worka" gloves, but Alex declined.

Arriving at the emergency exit to the left of the sanctuary, he pushed the door bar and was out, free! The air was much colder than it had been earlier in the evening, and he began to cough. Muffling his face with his scarf, he hastened down the back alley, cut left onto a cross street, and was home within minutes.

By now it was almost two o'clock in the morning, and the lateness of the hour combined with his illness drove him slowly up the staircase in the direction of bed. He was in no mood to celebrate. The thought of a sip of wine or a bite from a mincemeat pie, or even of listening to a single Christmas record, evoked in him a feeling of existential woe, of yawning absence. In such situations a precipitate departure into the realm of sleep was the best thing to do.

He thought of Andrew suddenly, feeling a moment of unease, for the boy had never before failed to make contact at Christmas. He wondered if his son had sent a card or a letter, and he told himself that surely he must have. Perhaps it had been waylaid by the British postal service, had missed the mail jet, and was now crossing the Atlantic by sailing ship, or as a note in a bottle. Andrew had always been somewhat absentminded about time, schedules, and deadlines. He was very bright, more gifted intellectually than Jacob, but easily swayed by impulse; he was inconsistent and lacking in the juridical qualities of weight and systematic balance in which Jacob excelled. Andrew might call tomorrow. On the other hand, he might simply forget to do so.

At first Alex hesitated, counting the time zones. Then, realizing that it was already seven in the morning in England, he picked up the receiver of the bedside phone. He put it down on the cradle. He might wake the boy. However, if he went to bed now and phoned later in the day, Andrew would probably be out celebrating with friends. He picked up the receiver again and, consulting his address book, dialed the number of Tyburne College.

It took a minute for the overseas lines to connect and for the double buzz of the English phone ring to begin. When the call was answered, Alex listened to a recorded message:

"You have reached Tyburne College, Oxford. Our office is closed until December twenty-seventh. If you wish to transfer your call to the office of a professor or the room of a student, please press the extension number now. If you wish to leave a recorded message, please do so after the sound of the tone.

The staff and students of Tyburne wish you a happy Christmas and a prosperous new year."

Alex did not know Andrew's extension, so after the beep, he said, "Good evening. This is Alex Graham calling from Canada. I'm trying to reach my son Andrew, a student at Tyburne. Could you please ask him to ring me up at home? Happy Christmas to all of you. And to all a good night."

He hung up smiling to himself, pleased that he had been able to use the British expression "ring me up", which he recalled from World War II RAF movies. "Happy Christmas" was their version of "Merry Christmas", and a better version, it seemed to him, for making merry was different from making happiness. Deciding that he was incapable of both, he went to bed, taking with him the *Christmas Books* of Charles Dickens, the Oxford Illustrated edition, and a dreadfully dense tome that he had recently acquired for the shop, a study of nineteenth-century Russian revolutionary movements, written sixty years before the Bolshevik Revolution by an expatriate Decembrist living in Paris. It was so delightfully soporific that, if Dickens failed, the Russians would surely put him to sleep. And in this, as in so many other matters, Alex was right.

He awoke feeling ill again and stayed in bed throughout the twenty-fifth and twenty-sixth, alternately reading and sleeping, rising only to force a bit of food and drink down his throat. There were knocks on the shop door downstairs, but he did not answer them. There were no phone calls. He took a hot shower at one point, and afterward, while he was shaving, he noticed in the half-steamed mirror that he was thinner than usual. He weighed himself and was surprised to find that he had lost nearly twelve pounds, an amount he could scarcely afford to lose. He had kept himself in good shape, at least on the level of frame and muscle, with only a trace of middle age spread beginning to show at the waist, but it now looked as if these reserves had melted away. At twenty paces he might have passed for a young athlete, though up close the markings and scorings of time became obvious. He went to the kitchen, where he warmed up one of Maria's casseroles and forced himself to eat a portion of it.

On the morning of the twenty-seventh, he placed another call to Oxford. This time it was answered by a live human being. He had half-expected one of those cold English tones, perfectly correct and utterly chilling (another prejudice!), the kind he had frequently encountered when ordering rare and out-of-print volumes from dealers in London. He was pleasantly surprised by a friendly male voice.

"Oh yes, Mr. Graham. We checked the machine on Christmas Day, sir, and found your memo. Thanks so much for the jolly message. We put a note under the door of Andrew's room. Did he ring you back?"

"Not yet. Have you spoken with him?"

"No, but that's not unusual at this time of year. We keep a fairly close watch on the students during term—we're more like a community here than an institution, not a typical Oxford college, as I'm sure you realize."

"I do. Andrew's very happy there."

"I expect he is, sir. However, there are upwards of sixty young men in the house, so we aren't always able to put a precise finger on their comings and goings. Some of them have classes in other colleges. Some are in tutorials, and a few have teaching positions elsewhere. And at this time of year, they do tend to scatter. Only a handful have stayed on over the holidays."

"Andrew wasn't one of them?"

"It appears not. I expect he has gone off with a chum. Many of our lads invite foreign students home for Christmas."

"But you aren't certain?"

"I'm sorry, I'm not. But I will keep trying."

"Thank you so much, Mr. . . ."

"Groves. John Groves, sir. I'm the secretary of the college."

"I very much appreciate your help, Mr. Groves. You see, I haven't heard from Andrew for some time, and I'm beginning to get a little concerned. It's quite unlike him."

"He hasn't written to you?"

"Not since autumn."

"Did he e-mail?"

"I'm afraid I don't have it. I'm not online, as they say."

Groves chuckled.

"Forgive me, Mr. Graham, but I should tell you that this often happens. The young people from abroad get quite swept up in our way of life—the history and culture, you know. And of course, the lure of London. They sometimes forget to call home, as it were. They eventually settle down."

"I see. Well, that's most reassuring."

"Students are due to return on January thirteenth. If your son hasn't contacted you before then, I should think he will when he sees the note. I'll also remind him personally."

Alex hung up feeling a little foolish. He should have known there was a simple explanation. When he had told Groves that Andrew's failure to contact home was quite unlike the boy, he had not been entirely accurate. Andrew had been known to miss a birthday more than once, even his own, and his tardiness was proverbial. Jacob liked to quip that Andrew suffered from "chrono-dementia", a condition that rendered his younger brother incapable of knowing the time of day at any given moment. It was a family joke, but there was some truth to it. It was certainly not a medical condition—more a characteristic of temperament—for Andrew was easily drawn aside into the thousand and one fascinating tributaries of life without regard for his central purpose. He had obtained his bachelor's degree in history at the University of Toronto by spurts of sheer brilliance but in a mode that would have been alien to the more methodical Jacob.

Andrew had written three times since August and had phoned once in late October. He had sounded enthusiastic about his new life, chatting about many extracurricular interests—a debate he was involved in at a place called the Oxford Union—and exciting friendships, everything except the content of his master's program. He was registered at Magdalen College, but his home was Tyburne. Tyburne was not, strictly speaking, a college of the university. There were thirty-eight colleges officially under the umbrella of Oxford University, but the city was also home to several permanent private institutions. Tyburne was one of the latter, a smaller institute that offered courses in the field of history and culture, though it was primarily a residence for Roman Catholics studying at the established colleges. It boasted a seminar room, an admirable library, and a chapel. It was something of an anomaly, for none of its buildings was more than ten years old, it was modern and comfortable, and it was "papist" territory in a university whose successive boards of governors had not, since the Reformation, permitted the establishment of a single accredited Catholic college.

Alex had sacrificed a great deal to send Andrew to Oxford. A partial scholarship had helped, as had the boy's earnings from his summer employment, but these had by no means supplied the bulk of the cost. Alex had cashed in the last of his inheritance (his father's old savings bonds) and emptied his own account, risking the future of the Kingfisher in the process. Nevertheless, the risk was worth it. Andrew might be erratic, but he was gifted and deserved a chance. Alex's pleasure that a son of his was surpassing him was due, in part, to the fact that after high school he had not gone to university, for his marks were mediocre, his health poor, and his interest in leaving Halcyon practically nil, though he had known moments when the lure of other places had captivated his imagination.

Late in the afternoon, feeling directionless, he decided to reacquaint himself with the rooms below. He draped a scarf about his neck, wrapped himself in his frayed plaid dressing gown, and taking one step at a time, holding onto the banister all the way, descended to the lower hallway. He paused at the bottom, catching his breath, then turned right into the largest of the four ground-floor rooms. His lungs seemed somewhat better, but the lethargy and dizziness were still returning at awkward moments. He dropped into one of the two easy chairs that he kept by the fireplace for customers and laid his head back, resting. He loved this room, for it had been the family parlor when he was a boy. Radiant with memories, it was the core of the only house in which he had ever lived. He closed his eyes and drifted back to the beginnings.

Crawling on hands and knees, little Alex pushed painted lead soldiers around the battlefield between Daddy's office and the dining room. Jumping ahead a few years, he saw himself stretched out on the hearth rug, reading his way through Narnia books, the heat from elm coals baking one side of his face.

"That's enough for one night, Alexander. Did you do your homework?"

"No, Mama."

The river of time flowed on, and he found himself smiling at Carol, and she at him, over a game of Scrabble on the card table, gazing at each other as they sought to win with longer and cleverer words while his father grumbled over the *Globe and Mail* in the corner armchair, and the grandfather clock chimed nine bells. And Alex spelled out "I love you" with the little block letters. Then she spelled out "I love you too." And Alex, after a search through the heap of letters, replied, "We will dance like the three deer." And she blushed.

The following year, while Mother and Father discussed something urgent behind the closed door of the office across the hall, Alex and Carol sat facing each other in the armchairs flanking the fireplace and listened to the flames and the wind in the chimney. Unable to restrain himself any longer, Alex flung himself down on one knee like a knight, took both of Carol's hands in his, and asked her to marry him. And she wrote in the palm of his hand with her fingertip, "Yes." But she wrote more legibly with a glance as swift and shy as the aerial calligraphy of bees fulfilling oriental circuits, or the dance of autumn deer. And then they looked together without speaking into the wells of their eyes, where small fires flickered.

Still later, Alex and his fiancée stood on either side of Mother, greeting the veterans, lawyers, judges, and priests who had come to pay their respects in a room still dominated by the presence of the judge. The coffin was laid out beneath the parlor windows, draped with the old national flag, medals, and a cross, the air drugged by the syrupy scents of gladiolas, roses, chrysanthemums, and evergreen wreaths.

"He was a great man, Martha, a great man."

Leaving his mother for a moment, Alex went to his father's office and found the violin sitting on top of the safe. Returning to the parlor, he laid it on the coffin, making his mother burst into sobs.

Other memories followed: Carol all in white, Mother in pink, the women kissing each other, beaming with happiness, wine glasses clinking all around, Father Toby grinning, calling for silence.

"Here's to a marriage made in heaven!" he declared. "And let's hope we see a hockey team of little Alexanders skating around here before too long!"

Roaring laughter erupted from the guests crowding into the room to raise their glasses. Carol was blushing again,

Alex smiling as he stared at the floor, hating all the scrutiny, longing for the train ride to Quebec City, where they could finally be alone together, could take the silent walks they both so loved, soaking up the ancient streets, the saints, the great river, the continuity of history as fluid as water.

On their return from their honeymoon, Mother brought them into this room and held their hands tightly, her eyes brimming, saying, "Now I won't have any arguments about it. It's my gift to you both to help you get started in life. The legal work is already completed. I'll be very happy in Toronto—these new condominiums are the most practical inventions, and I've always thought this house was too big for a small family like ours. I know that if your father were here today, he would approve. The house is yours to do with whatever you like."

"But Mother," Carol cried, "won't you be lonely?"

"I'll miss you both very much, but the city's only a couple of hours away, and the train is very efficient. We'll see each other often. And I'll tell you a little secret: I never was all that comfortable in Halcyon. I'm a simpler person than Angus was. I wasn't born here, and, well, a judge's wife..."

She did not finish the explanation, and no one ever thought to ask what she had been about to say.

"There's a small legacy from Angus for you," she added, "not quite enough to live on, but two young people in love don't need much, do they?"

And they didn't, really. Mother moved to her condominium, and Carol and Alex moved into the master bedroom of "Halcyon Home", as they liked to call it in the early years. They dreamed and planned and prayed and in the end settled upon the idea of a bookstore. And that was the beginning of their great adventure.

"But what will we call it?" Carol asked, six months later, four months pregnant, as they unpacked boxes of books or hammered shelves together.

"You mean if it's a boy?" asked Alex.

"I mean the bookshop."

"Haven't given it much thought. How about the Three Dancing Deer Bookshop?"

"Ummm", she frowned, furrowing her brow so beautifully that he could not resist the impulse to kiss her.

"Stop that, now, Mister. We need to do some serious thinking here if we want to open in two weeks."

"We'll never open. You're too distracting."

She made a ridiculous face that was a proven method for killing passion. They fell onto the couch laughing.

"Well, what about it?" he asked.

"What about what?"

"The three deer."

"Nope", she said, shaking her head. "Too intimate. That's for you and me and nobody else."

"What'll we call it, then?"

"How about Halcyon Bookshop?"

"Unimaginative."

"True. Any suggestions?"

They held hands and pondered it for a few minutes.

"The Kingfisher!" Alex exclaimed, sitting upright. "Halcyon is the old name for the Greek myth of the kingfisher."

"Now that sounds like a winner", Carol said, nodding. "Yup, I think that's it."

They shook hands on it, then kissed and got back to work.

Jacob was born, and before long he was toddling across the parlor, knocking over stacks of books, climbing shelves, bothering the book browsers with a hundred unanswerable questions.

"Carol, he's driving me crazy, and driving off customers too. Can you come get him?"

"Time for your nap, Jakey-boy", she said with a grin, scooping him up. "Sorry, Mr. Findley. I hope he wasn't bothering you."

"Not at all, not at all", said the octogenarian Mr. Findley, the wealthiest man in town, all jowls and mutton-chop whiskers. "He's a bright lad and will go far in this world. However, it seems he has made a little rip in this first edition of Goldsmith. You might want to consider a modest discount, as I am quite interested in purchasing it."

In the blink of an eye Andrew was there too, chewing the spines of dictionaries, playing with stationery, scattering correspondence across the floor.

And so it went. Before he knew it the boys were going off to school at Saint Mary's, Mother went into a nursing home, Carol's large clan of people stampeded in like buffalo one summer and departed, sales rose and fell. Mother died. Then came Carol's first bout with cancer, followed by remission. And relief. Sadness too, because the doctor said she would never be able to have more children. The legacy was used up, and the income from the sale of books was never quite enough. They sold the violin, which turned out to be valuable, made in the same town and era as Stradivarius', though of lesser quality. The piano was also sold, along with Father's law books and a few other things. So the family and the bookshop survived.

Opening his eyes, Alex looked about the parlor, which was now the main room of the Kingfisher. The walls were lined with oak shelves that ceased ascending only when they met the ornate cornices of the twelve-foot-high ceiling; they were fully loaded and spilling over into piles wherever space had been found. Freestanding shelves divided the room into nooks and alcoves, so that the whole resembled an overcrowded library, containing approximately twenty-four thousand volumes. Sixteen thousand other titles were lodged in the three smaller ground-floor rooms. One contained classical and modern literature, another art and history books, and the third was the Russian collection. This was the smallest room and, in terms of numbers, the least significant. It contained no more than two thousand titles, yet it was the product of thirty years of research and a considerable investment of money and effort. In fact, it was Alex's chief love.

Much of this collection was composed of standard works: Tolstoy, Dostoyevsky, and Chekhov, in various twentieth-century translations, as well as writers such as Pasternak and Sholokov who had been published under the Soviets. Solzhenitsyn had a section of his own, as did the dissident poets, some of whose works had been obtained through intermediaries in Germany and Switzerland. Many of the books were ordinary nonfiction covering a wide variety of subjects, written in English, French, German, and Russian, some prerevolutionary, some Soviet era, some post-Soviet— but all dealing with one or another aspect of the Rus and regions that had fallen into the embrace of the czarist and Soviet empires. There was little Marxist material, and Alex had flagged the few books of that genre with red self-stick notes on which he had written: "Propaganda—historical interest only".

The distinctive characteristic of his collection was its unusually high number of older Russian works. It was well known to scholars of Slavic studies throughout North America and had not gone unnoticed in Europe as well, for Alex had spared no expense in obtaining rare books in the Russian language. Fully a quarter of the volumes had been published before the Revolution, including some coveted prizes such as first editions of Turgenev's *Fathers and Sons*, Pushkin's *Eugene Onegin*, Lermontov's *A Hero of Our Times*, and, most extraordinary of all, a copy of *Dead Souls* signed by Gogol.

Alex had taught himself the Cyrillic alphabet at the age of fourteen, when he was recovering from rheumatic fever. Lying horizontal with nothing to do while his heart ticked and tocked through interminable days and weeks, he had read the hundreds of *National Geographic*s stacked beside his bed, and somewhere in the second month of convalescence had come upon an article about Siberia. So alien was that land, yet so strangely familiar, that his heart had hammered dangerously as his fascination grew. There was a lovely apple-cheeked girl in one of the pictures, her dancing eyes framed by an oval of red fur—he fell in love on the spot. There was a boy his own age galloping a hairy pony across an ice-covered lake—instantly they became friends. He knew them, though he could not explain why this was so.

That evening, when his father peeked in to chat for a few minutes, Alex asked him to buy a Russian-English dictionary.

"Russian?" his father said. "Worried about a Communist invasion, are we?"

"No, Father", he replied, holding up the magazine to illustrate. "It's...it's...it's..."

It was fire and ice. It was life radiating heat in what appeared to be a temperature zone of absolute zero. Frosty clouds boiled from all lips as if breath were the materialization of soul-speech.

"It's like Greek", he said, pointing to a sign in a photograph of an Arctic railway station.

Because Alex had only recently taught himself the Greek alphabet and was presently working his way through *The Iliad* in the original language, and because—well, because of the heart problem—his father cautioned against taking on too much at once.

"A prodigious aptitude for languages is in the Graham blood, Alexander; I'll not deny it. But you should concentrate on one at a time."

"I can do both. The letters are really close. Besides—"

"No, Alexander."

"Please, Father."

"I said no."

Alex puzzled over the bitter compression of his father's mouth and the anguish in his eyes. Then he understood. His father thought it would be pointless, a waste of time and money, because Alex might not live long enough to derive any benefit from it.

"Is a straight line the fastest way to get from one place to another?" the boy asked.

"Yes", said the judge with a frown.

"But Einstein says space is curved. Maybe that means we can arrive at the destination by cutting across the arc of the curve."

"I don't quite follow you, Alexander."

"Or maybe it's like one eye and two eyes."

"I think you'd better explain."

The boy put the palm of his hand over one eye. "See, Father?"

"Er...what, precisely, do you want me to see?"

"One eye sees the same thing as two eyes."

"Yes..."

Alex sat bolt upright and all in a rush babbled with intense conviction: "One eye sees flat and two eyes see deep, but deep is invisible, and you discover the deep is there only when it's not there, so maybe deep is a kind of curve in space, or a curve in the mind, but I wouldn't want to say it's a curve in time, because that's impossible because of the physics of light-speed and our biology, but with two alphabets—"

"Calm down, Alexander, calm down", Angus said, forcing the boy's shoulders back onto the pillow. "Now just rest. You're all flushed, and your pulse is racing."

Alex could feel the artery in his neck fluttering and his thoughts sloshing this way and that, mixing everything in the swamp of the imagination. He heard galloping hooves in his ears. Then he felt his mother's hand on his forehead, stroking, stroking. It was impossible to keep his eyes open, which made everything no-deep, or maybe it was all-deep, and he dropped mercifully into sleep.

The next day, he sat up in bed and asked for the Meccano construction set. He made a spaceship with it and slept again.

The following afternoon, Toby came to visit (Mother said he was allowed only one hour, because Toby was...well, he was clumsy and he broke things, though always by accident). When Mother went downstairs to make hot chocolate for the boys, Alex told him he had overheard the doctor say he might not make it.

"Might not make it?" Toby said with a whine in his voice. "What's that supposed to mean?"

Alex shrugged. He asked Toby to bring him the model sailing schooner that sat on top of the bookcase. When his friend had done so, Alex held it in his hands for a few moments, then pushed it onto Toby's lap.

"I want you to have it."

"I don't want it", Toby mumbled, his lower lip quivering in a face as round as a pumpkin. The stubby fingers, nails bitten down to the quick, caressed the boat lovingly.

"It's yours now."

"I don't want it", he squealed again, and his face went all blubbery.

"You *have* to take it. I'm going to *die!*"

At which point both boys heard a gasp and looked up. Mother was standing at the door, her face contorting with pain. She turned and walked hurriedly down the hallway.

Toby took the boat home. And that night Alex's father brought him a Russian-English dictionary.

"Father, do you think you could ask Layo to visit me?" Alex asked with a calculating look.

"Who on earth is Layo?" his father said with a worried look.

Two years earlier, Alex, age twelve, had been sitting by the Clementine where it flowed through the forest a mile north of town. His seat was a particular flat rock where he was accustomed to go from time to time to ponder things. He had always been alone there, and always happy, as the waters flowed past in tangential waves. Startled from his reverie by a soft whizzing sound, he noticed an old man standing a few paces downstream, whipping a fishing pole from which a line hurtled across one of the deep pools of the river. For a time they remained without speaking, conscious of each other. Alex returned to staring at the current, wishing the man would go away. The old man glanced at him occasionally, and perhaps he too was hoping for solitude.

When a carp came thrashing out of the river on the end of the line, and the old man knelt to extract the hook, Alex could not stop himself from approaching. The fish was fat and metallic, gasping its final protest, flapping its body in a symmetry of optical illusions, silver scales shimmering into black, then to white, then to silver again, the fluid work of art slowly changing into the dignity of still forms.

The old man looked up.

"Water", he said.

Alex regarded him curiously.

"You look a long time at water, little boy", the man said with a thick foreign accent.

Alex could think of no reply.

"You waiting for a golden fish to speak to you?"

"Fish do not speak", Alex said, eyeing the other suspiciously.

"Fish speak. In my land they speak very much—perhaps too much."

"What do you mean?"

"What do I mean? What do I mean?" the old man sighed in a patient tone. "That is not possible to tell you, little boy."

"I am not a little boy."

"If you insist. You are not a little boy."

"But what do you mean?"

"Why should I tell you?"

"Because I like to know things."

"Ask the fish, then."

"The fish don't speak."

"No? Ah, well, that is because in this land the fish are not magic. Nothing is magic here."

Alex continued to watch as the fish's head was sliced off with a serrated knife.

"In my land is a boy like you", said the old man as he cut away the fins and the tail.

"Who is he?"

"My grandson."

"Oh." The circular shape, circular sound, a miniature affirmation of the expanding cosmos.

"He is far away—far, far away."

"Where?"

"The land of the archangel."

"Where is that?"

"East. North."

"Will he come to see you here?"

"Never again will I see him."

"Oh..." The shape of the cosmos bending, the ovoid collapsing into a flat line, the circular sound compressed into a dying note of music.

"Time", sighed the old man. "Oy, time, time."

"*Kronos*", said the boy.

"*Kronos*? Is not English?"

"It's Greek."

"Ah, like Russian."

And so it was that the old man entered Alex's life. He was the new janitor of the school. He lived in a single room at the back of Saint Mary's. He tended the boiler, shoveled snow from the walkways, and read quietly to himself in his free time. That was about all there was to know, it seemed. But a few interesting details were forthcoming: he attended Sunday Mass but did not receive Communion. And on the wall of his room, which Alex entered once to deliver a note from the teacher, there was an odd little painting of a woman pressing a baby to her breast, mother and child cheek to cheek.

"*Bogoroditsa*", said the old man, pointing to the woman. "God-bearer."

"And you?" asked the boy bravely.

"Leonid", said the old man, pointing to the center of his chest.

"Layo*need*", Alex repeated somberly.

"Who on earth is Layo?" his father asked again.

"Layo at the school."

"You mean the janitor? Why on earth would you want him? Oh, I see—to help you with Russian. I doubt he'd be interested, Alexander, and we don't really know much about him."

"I've talked with him. He's good. I know he's good."

So poor Leonid Vozhinsky was dragged in eventually, to sit on a chair beside the bed, dictionary in hand, staring at the little rich boy. Leonid looked like Father Christmas, though thinner and lacking a beard: his cheeks were red, his nose a button, his twinkling eyes nearly oriental. Father was in court that day, Mother nervously hovering. She put a cup of tea into the visitor's hands and went out, leaving the door ajar.

Leonid's shabby workman's clothes were obviously an embarrassment to him, for after swallowing the tea in two gulps, he twisted his cloth cap with large square hands, opened it again, and covered a hole in the knee of his pants with it.

The old Russian and the boy looked at each other for a time.

Finally, Leonid cleared his throat and murmured, "The river is frozen."

"I know", said the boy.

"You are sad not to see it?"

"Yes."

"In summer, when you are no longer sick, I will take you to the place where we met."

"Yes," Alex said with elation, "please."

"Please. In Russian this is *pazhalusta*."

"Pazhalusta!" Alexander whispered, trying the word as if it were a key turning in a lock.

Leonid smiled. "You like it?"

"Yes, I like it."

"Good. So—now we begin." He opened the dictionary, his face heavy with ancient ironies.

During the two years that followed, Leonid brought many books, precious Russian books, mostly stories for children and young adults. He read aloud from them and pointed at the pictures as if Alex were a child. Alex's parents obediently purchased records and cassette tapes to supplement these sessions. Then came Leonid's brutal demands for memorization, composition exercises, and translation of paragraphs. Success was rewarded by short stories read aloud. Eventually the man and boy began to make up stories. Leonid's Russian fairy tales. Alex's childish fantasies. Leonid was particularly demanding about accents.

"Vocabulary is a dead carp", he pronounced emphatically. "He is dumb and gray."

"Vocabulary is a *fish*?" Alex said, wrinkling his brow.

"With accent, the carp swims, he jumps, he is gold!"

"Fish have accents?"

Tapping his head: "Knowing is not seeing, Aleksandr."

Tapping his chest: "Engineering is not art."

Sticking out his tongue and waggling it: "Talking is not speaking."

"Talking is not speaking", Alex replied dubiously. "What do you mean?"

"Music in the tongue! Poetry!" ·

"But what do you *mean*?" he pleaded.

"Nothing. You are too young to understand."

"No I'm not. Tell me."

"*Nyet.*"

"*Pazhalusta!*"

This was countered by Leonid's most impressive weapon, more daunting than his temper: a stare from an impervious steel mask.

Another day, in a sweeter mood, he said, "What shall we read this morning, Sasha?"

"Why do you call me Sasha?" Alex demanded, for he knew that Sasha was the little cat in *Peter and the Wolf.*

"Sasha is diminutive of Aleksandr", Leonid explained.

"I'd rather you not call me that, please."

"I will call you Sashenka, then."

This was worse—babyish and slightly feminine. Alex shook his head.

"You could call me Alexei", he suggested.

"Alexei is not diminutive of Aleksandr."

"But it is!" Alex protested.

"*Nyet!* Different names. Sasha is from Aleksandr. *Alyosha* is from Alexei."

"Then I'll be Alyosha."

"*Nyet*, foolish boy!" said Leonid, growing hot in the face. "You understand nothing. Sasha is Sasha; Alyosha is Alyosha."

At an impasse, they tried to stare each other down.

"Can't you bend the rules?" Alex said after a while.

"*Nyet.*"

"Just a little?"

"*Nyet, nyet!*"

"If I ask the golden fish, he'll grant me a wish, and then you'll have to call me Alyosha."

"Ha! Go ask him, then."

"I will. When I'm better."

"Then get better."

Strangely, Leonid began to shake with silent laughter.

"What's the matter?" Alex asked.

"You. You're the matter."

"Oh. I'm sorry", Alex said, genuinely repentant. "I didn't mean to be rude."

"No, no, it's good to see you fight, Sashenka."

"Don't call me that!"

"Come, fight me more. Fight me hard. Like the fishy on the line."

With all the formality accessible to a young person of superior social station, Alex said, "I would prefer you to call me Alyosha or to call me nothing."

Leonid grinned. "Cannot do it."

"You can if you want to."

"No, little English boy, I cannot. Do you want me to destroy the Russian language, the Russian tradition, just to make you happy?"

"Uh...no."

"Good. Now tell me why you like this Alyosha name so much."

"I don't know."

"Is it the fairy tale? Is it because of *Alyosha the Fool and the Firebird*?"

"No."

But, in fact, it was. For Alyosha the crippled orphan grew tall, strong, and handsome after capturing the magic firebird and presenting it to the king, who adopted the boy and rewarded him with a palace and a mountain of gold. And thus he became Prince Alyosha the Wise.

"So. I will make compromise", Leonid stated. "I will call you Alik. It is also diminutive of Aleksandr."

"Ah-*leek*", Alex murmured, not enthused, but glad for a minor victory.

After Alex's vocabulary had reached a certain critical mass, they agreed to speak together only in Russian. Comprehension grew in mysterious leaps, never in a straight line, always curves, waves, tangents.

"When did you come to Canada?" Alex asked at one point.

"I forget", Leonid shrugged.

"Have you always been a janitor?"

"No."

"What did you do before you came here?"

The old man stared out the bedroom window and would not answer.

"Did you fish?"

"Yes, I fished", he said abstractly, nodding. "Always I have fished."

"Where is your family?"

The face mutated into the mask.

"Are they in Russia?"

No answer.

"Archangelsk? Is that where they live?"

"You are a very clever boy. Perhaps too clever."

"In the east and the north?"

"Do not ask", breathed the old man, as bitter as an Arctic wind.

So Alex learned there were regions you did not approach. Though other subjects were permitted:

"Did you catch carp in Russia?"

"Yes."

"Did they taste good?"

"Very good. Like chicken. Like the magic fish that grants wishes."

"Really?" said Alex, wide-eyed.

This brought on one of Leonid's very rare laughs. "Of course, really. In Russia all golden fishes grant wishes."

"That's why they taste so good?"

"*Da!* That's why they taste so good."

Such answers were possible only because water was the point at which the curves of two lives had intersected.

"You pronounce like a little Russian", Leonid said toward the end of those two years. "Not perfect, but it is…" He cast about for the right description. "It is rare; it is an astonishment."

"A prodigious aptitude for languages is in the Graham blood", Alex said in Russian.

"Oo, so clever, Alik", Leonid sang in a mocking tone. "If you do not die, you will be a big professor someday!"

But where the water was going, Alexander Graham could not yet comprehend, not with one eye, not with two eyes. Though all fables agreed that the water went to the sea, the sea remained beyond the line of sight, beyond the edge of the world.

When he was sixteen and more or less recovered, it was too late to ask the old man more daring questions—by then he had gone away to Toronto, or somewhere beyond. He left as soon as Alex was pronounced well again. It was autumn, the streets of Halcyon carpeted with gold and blood red, washed black by rain, cold seeping into the land, pushing it toward its annual sleep. Judge Graham drove Leonid to the bus stop at the café out on Highway 11. Alex went along too, hiding the ache, crushing the words inside him that would have betrayed a conspiracy of eloquence. Leonid scowled when he shook hands with the boy, scowled harder when the judge placed an envelope into his hands, his face unreadable as he crammed it into his pocket.

Climbing the steps into the bus, he turned around and said, "*Vada*, Aleksandr." Then, as if correcting himself, or permitting himself a great liberty, he whispered, "*Vada, Alyosha.*"

Water. Their first and final theme.

And was gone forever.

Alex coughed and pushed aside the memories. He took a last glance around his bookshop, got unsteadily to his feet, and went upstairs. There he put himself to bed, where he remained until the following morning. After breakfast he ventured down to the parlor and resumed the process of remembering.

He was seventeen, imprisoned in high school, hating it. During his free time he read more-advanced Russian books, listened to language tapes, acquired comprehensive dictionaries, practiced his accent, missed Layo, wondered why his friend never made contact.

Then he was eighteen, walking for hours each day, alone. Swimming in summer, alone. Alone in his bedroom, tackling the monumental novels—*War and Peace, The Brothers Karamazov, Quiet Flows the Don, Dr. Zhivago.* First the English edition, then the Russian, comparing the original text to the translation as he went along. The translation of great literature, he learned, was as much an art as a science, and few of the English translations he read possessed the art. Technically competent, the translators too often delivered the body of the work intact but lost its soul. Dead carp and live carp.

Alex now began to suspect that the real Russia—its character, its soul—was practically unknown in the West. Intrigued by this idea, then captivated by it, he soon became wholly devoted. As his infatuation flowered into a genuine passion throughout his nineteenth and twentieth years, he did not really stop to ask himself why this should be so. Only the entry of Carol into his life moderated the passion, prevented it from becoming an obsession. Throughout one winter he tried to write a Russian novel, complete with dialect. The finished product, a tragic tale about a rosy-cheeked girl and a pony-riding boy who lived by the White Sea of Arctic Russia, whose pure love was destroyed by a vicious Communist commissar, was so predictable and so dull that even its author was bored by it. It ran to 180 looseleaf, lined pages, all of which Alex burned before it was read by anyone else—not that anyone in his known world could have deciphered the penned Cyrillic script. Although his growing understanding of human psychology—derived largely from Dostoyevsky—enabled him to attempt from time to time a little self-reflection, the sense of irony this induced was wholly consistent with the Slavic soul.

"All Russophiles are romantics", he had frequently admonished himself during that period of his life. Yet he had been happy to remain a romantic, for Russia was distanced by an ocean and an iron curtain, injecting a bitter sweetness into his unrequited love. Years later, when the curtain was at last torn down, exposing the remnant soul, he was older, worried sick over his ailing wife, and in no condition to explore in person the land he had so often dreamed of. A year after her death he had toyed with the idea of travel, an impulse derived wholly from his desperation to escape the looming void of despair. Though he had gone so far as to obtain a passport, the document had not been used and no doubt would remain forever archived in a shoebox in his bedroom closet.

From where he now sat in the parlor, he could look straight across the central hallway into the Russian room, which was situated on the south side of the building. The sun shone through the front window panes, casting the pattern of its leaded glass onto the hardwood floors. A shaft of light cut across the only decoration in the room, a small painting of Vladimir Soloviev that hung on the wall above a cabinet of religious material: liturgical books, folios of icon prints, the writings of religious philosophers, and lives of Russian saints.

He gazed for some minutes at the room, cheered by the light within it and warmed by a thousand memories associated with it. This was the heart of the building, its true hearth. He wished suddenly for a cup of strong black tea, poured from a boiling samovar. He did own one; he had fired it up once or twice in the past, but it now sat in a corner of the Russian room, its silver body cracked, tarnished, radiating its mystique. How fine and consoling it would be to sip the steaming liquid and resurrect from memory those lines that had meant so much to him.

He whispered aloud a passage from Turgenev:

"In the days of doubts, in the days of oppressive reflections concerning the destiny of my native land, you alone are my strength and my staff, O great, mighty, true, and free Russian tongue! If you were not, how could one do anything else but fall into despair at the sight of all that is taking place in our homeland? It is past all belief that such a tongue is given to any but a great people!"

Yes, a great people. But a people torn by internal contradictions: look west to Europe, look east to the Orient. Look upward to God, look down to the soil. Look outward to the world of action, look inward to contemplation. Violence and mysticism, the village and the void, the icon and the sword.

It was Dostoyevsky, more than Turgenev, who became the conscience of his people—his passion the icon of Russia's passion—articulator of their anguish, their sins, their rage, their grievous lamentations and endlessly renewed hopes. Alex often asked himself if this essentially spiritual cry, echoed and reechoed throughout their literature, was the thing that drew him to the Russians. Why did their pain seem to tower above the countless sufferings of other peoples? Was it because they had grappled at close quarters with the raw elements of existence in a way no other people had? Or was it because they were more articulate about it, had spoken about life as no others did, testifying that heaven and hell were all around us, and within us? Bearing witness to stark warfare of the soul amid intoxicating, glorious *being*? Beauty and death on every tongue, from serf to prince?

Perhaps.

Of course, the struggle against death was not a Russian phenomenon. But in North America it was kept within its proper category, as an endnote to life. There, it was the central story.

In brooding moments, Alex wondered at his decades-old fascination with that country. Was there not something pathetic about a man such as himself who hardly dared venture beyond the borders of his safe and orderly environment, who could understand the East only as an armchair adventure? Though he was an unimportant man, and knew it, he did not want to dismiss out of hand any other explanations. Could it be that God had wished to preserve the genius of Russia in small islands of exile, waiting for the time when her culture was free to take root again in native soil? If so, Alex's peculiar interest had fulfilled its purpose.

Is my life over? Surely it must be over.

Possibly. But his guardianship of an alien legacy was not yet complete. Last year, he had written to a man named Serov in Saint Petersburg, a contact of a rare-book dealer in Berlin, offering to sell him the entire Russian collection of Kingfisher Books. So far he had received no response. Considering the present state of things over there, the man might not have received the letter. Hearing nothing after months of waiting, Alex had made a tortuous effort via telephone, speaking his own dialect of literary-leonidian Russian, in hope of obtaining the number of any Serov living in Saint Petersburg on Kanal Griboedova. The operator had found none. Neither was there a listing in the city for the name of Serov's company, Petrovsky Rare Books and Manuscripts. He had phoned

Berlin, but his German contact could offer no explanation other than:

"The situation is unstable at present. You might try again by post."

He had written once more but had not yet received a reply.

Usually it did not take much to excite one or another aspect of Alex's elaborate affair with Russia, but today he had had enough. Sighing, he got up from the armchair, crossed the hall, and closed the French doors of the Russian room. Then he shuffled to the stairs and went up to his apartment, followed by ticking and tocking and the familiar chimes.

3. *Do You Really See Us?*

The twenty-ninth of December dawned bright and blue, and as the sun rose, the eaves began to drip with meltwater. Alex was tempted to go walking outside in the unseasonably warm weather, but it cost him something to get out of bed, and when he tried to dress himself he gave up halfway through. He dragged himself to the bathroom to clear his lungs. The dizziness was gone, but the weight of exhaustion was still pressing down, and he went back to bed for the morning. Later in the day Father Toby phoned to check on him and begged off their annual New Year's toast, since he would be offering the vigil Mass at the parish's mission chapel in Maplewoods. Dr. Hendricks dropped in to interrogate him and give him a physical examination. His lungs were improving, the doctor said, and his body temperature was down to near normal, but his blood pressure was still higher than it should be. "Back to bed", the doctor commanded.

Andrew did not phone that day, no doubt because he had not yet returned to Oxford.

The thirtieth was similarly uneventful. Hendricks dropped by again on the morning of New Year's Eve, took some readings, and said that Alex's temperature had now leveled out at normal and that his blood pressure was dropping nicely. Still, he warned, don't push your luck. No going outside, no opening the shop for customers. Alex had permission to get dressed and to putter about the house if he so wished, but he needed another week or two without demands of any sort.

"Can you survive the income loss?" the doctor asked.

"Uh, well, not really."

"That's too bad", Hendricks shot back. "But I guarantee that if you throw yourself into work too soon, you'll have a relapse."

"I'm not worried about that."

"Oh, aren't you", Hendricks replied. "Listen, Alex, pneumonia was the biggest killer on the planet before the advent of antibiotics, and it's still one of the biggest. Relapses are common for at least a year after you've had it. So don't take chances."

"Okay", he said halfheartedly, toying with the idea of opening the shop two days hence, gambling on the possibility that Hendricks wouldn't hear about it.

Hendricks, who had pulled him out of the birth canal, knew him well. Reading Alex's mind, he wagged a finger.

"Don't try it. If you want to die with balanced books, that's your choice, but don't say I didn't warn you."

"The logic of that is obscure", Alex said, smiling.

"My point, precisely."

In the early evening, he dressed in his brown suit, with a white shirt and a knitted green tie. Inspecting himself in the bureau mirror, he saw a trimmer Alex than he remembered, a man who appeared to be ten years younger than his age. The recent loss of weight, combined with hair that was only beginning to show its actual age, added to the illusion of general well-being. He could sustain that charade as long as no one peered too closely, or asked him to speak, or expected anything of him that required physical strength.

He wondered if he should ignore Dr. Hendricks' orders and attend the Mass at Saint Mary's. Hendricks lived on the other side of town and worshipped sensibly on Sunday mornings at Findley Memorial United. Alex had very much missed receiving the sacraments, and he told himself that he was now recovered sufficiently to risk the weather. About nine thirty

77

he bundled up in his duffel parka, scarves, an old wool hat of Jacob's, mitts, and fleece-lined boots and went out onto the avenue. The five-minute walk demanded some effort, and despite the scarf across his face, he felt his upper chest beginning to rasp by the time he arrived at the front door of Saint Mary's.

The church was not nearly as full as it had been on Christmas Eve. Most of the regulars were there, though not many visitors. When he caught himself glancing around in search of the Colley family, he stopped it at once and forced his attention onto the prayer book before him, reading and rereading the lines of its inscription: "Gilbert Alphonsus Graham, in memory of First Holy Communion, Feast of Corpus Christi, 1863, Saint Mary of the Angels, Halcyon, York County, Upper Canada."

The next morning, Alex woke with a wracking cough. *A minor relapse*, he told himself, and did not get up until noon. Father Toby phoned to wish him a happy new year, mentioning in the course of the conversation that he was leaving for a few days to see his family in Toronto. His parents were living there, retired to a suburb of the city. Alex never quite understood why the McIntoshes had left Halcyon; they were second-generation Halcyonites, after all, and they had a son who was a priest in the town, a fact of which they were enormously proud. He supposed they had been drawn by the lure of the malls, better medical care, and efficient apartments. Perhaps they had merely grown tired of a lifetime at the lowest social level, had been called river rats and bottom feeders too many times for erasure from their memories. The city drew a lot of people away, some to escape the stifling unwritten rules of the town, some to better jobs, some to a more stimulating pace of life. The young almost never returned to live in Halcyon.

Andrew did not phone that day.

The cough steadily improved throughout the week, and on Monday Alex opened the Kingfisher for business. Neighbors, seeing the OPEN sign in the window, popped in to say hello and to congratulate him on rescuing the two children. Late in the afternoon a few regular customers came by on their way home from work, bought more than was usual for them, and asked about his health. There were more congratulations, and Alex resigned himself to his new image, which he hoped would fade quickly. He made a profit of $184 that day, and was grateful for it, because there was a stack of bills to be paid, the shop's checking account was close to overdraft, and his personal account was not in any better condition. His only other resource was a small savings account that he had left untouched for years, about $300 that he had been hoarding for who knows what—a cheap coffin, perhaps.

The next day was busy, as word got around that the shop was open. In the morning the principal of Saint Mary's school phoned in an order for more than a hundred books, explaining, with a certain overeagerness, that it was time to enrich the blood of the school library. She sent a check at the lunch hour, couriered by hand—in fact, by the hand of Jamie Colley. The boy was as taciturn as before, stopping only long enough to purchase a book on chess strategy for himself, leaving immediately upon completion of the transaction. By suppertime, the Kingfisher was bustling with browsers and buyers. When Alex locked up that night and sat down at his desk to add up the sales, he found that he had made an unprecedented total of over $1,600. People were being generous, he realized. They had deduced that his weeks of convalescence had not been kind to his business. It was a revelation to him that they would do such a thing. He understood well enough the first flush of civic approval, for the rescue had been front-page news in a small town's life, a ripple in a pond. But he was perplexed by the evidence that people were capable of doing more, of putting their money, literally, where their mouth was. He was humbled and gratified by it but felt certain that this too would fade.

By Wednesday, the fourteenth of January, Andrew still had not phoned. On Thursday morning Alex placed a call to Tyburne College and asked for John Groves. When Groves came on the line, he told Alex that all the students had returned except Andrew.

"The young men were required to be in the house last night at the latest. He knows the rules, Mr. Graham, but he may have been delayed through no fault of his own. I expect he'll arrive today or call to let us know what happened. Classes begin tomorrow, and I'm sure he wouldn't want to be late for that."

"So you still don't know where he went?"

"I've asked around. He chums with two or three men on his floor, but they have no idea where he went for the holidays. It's quite possible that he teamed up with someone at Magdalen. As you know, he takes classes there."

"When he does come in, please ask him to ring me immediately. It doesn't matter what hour." Alex hesitated, then said, "I'm beginning to worry a little."

"I can understand that, sir. I would too, if I were in your place. However, I shouldn't worry overmuch. There's a simple explanation, I'm sure."

"Yes, there must be."

At eight thirty the next morning, the bedside phone rang. He picked it up and mumbled, "Hello."

"Good afternoon, Mr. Graham; this is John Groves. I suppose I should say good morning? I hope I haven't disturbed you too early."

"Have you heard from Andrew? Has he returned?"

"Actually, no. We're beginning to feel a little concerned ourselves."

"Has anything happened?"

"Not that we're aware of. But I did want to get back to you to let you know the situation. Andrew has still not contacted us to tell us where he is or to explain the cause of the delay."

Alex felt his worry tighten into a coil of anxiety.

"But where could he have gone?"

"We still don't know. One of the fellows mentioned that Andrew might have made friends somewhere in Oxford town, people not associated with either Tyburne or Magdalen. He emphasized that it was just a guess."

"I see."

"May I ask, sir, if your son has done anything like this in the past, disappearing without leaving a message?"

"No. He tends to be forgetful, but this is beyond the usual."

"It does seem that. However, there's not much more we can do until he chooses to show himself."

"Have you checked his room?"

"The bursar and I went in with the passkey and had a look around, but we found nothing out of the ordinary. It would appear he hasn't been there since the end of term."

"Were his suitcases there?"

"Yes, two of them."

"He also had a large kit bag. It's blue with stripes down the sides."

"There was no bag of that description."

"Was there a note?"

"We thought of that also, and checked carefully. There was no note. I must say the room was tidy, as tidy as one can expect from a young person these days. It all looked quite normal."

"I wonder if the police should be notified."

"The police? If you wish, I will call them. They might turn up something."

"I would appreciate it very much. I'm sorry for the trouble."

"Not at all, Mr. Graham. Not at all."

After Sunday morning Mass, Alex took Father Toby aside on the front steps of the church. When he recounted what had happened, the priest furrowed his brow and said reassuring things but obviously didn't know what to make of it. His vestments billowing in the wind, he stamped his feet to keep them from freezing.

"I'll pray for Andrew, Alex. But you can't help the situation by worrying. You're thousands of miles away, and there's nothing you can do at the moment." Father Toby whacked him on the back. "Hey, don't you remember that kid who was always riding all over town on his bike, getting into a thousand scrapes, always late for supper?"

"I remember. He hasn't changed."

"Remember the time he biked north to the Stone Giant? Remember when we found him two days later?"

"Yes. Huddled under the rock, watching the river go by."

"Right. And remember how he looked that day?"

Alex sighed. "Exhausted and hungry, scratched from the bushes. Burns on his fingers from trying to light a campfire between the giant's feet."

"Don't you remember how happy he looked? Remember what he said when you asked him why he'd done it?"

"He said he had to see the stone man and ask him a question."

"Did he ever tell you if he got an answer?"

"I don't think so. Anyway, I never would have done something like that at his age. Ten years old!"

"Andrew's a dreamer. He just went a bit farther than you ever did."

"He was always so irresponsible. If only I had spent more time with him, taught him something."

"You taught him a lot."

Alex threw up his hands. "What did I teach him? What did I ever teach either of my boys?"

82

Father Toby gave him a long look.

"You taught them every moment of their lives until they left home. You gave them a father who had faith. You gave them a father who loved their mother. You gave them their love of learning."

Alex, his eyes blinking rapidly, leaned forward and clenched his fist with vehement intensity. The last people leaving the church looked at him curiously as they passed.

"I gave them so little—so little."

"You gave them more than most children get from their fathers."

"I poured everything into that bookshop. It ate up all my time and energy, not to mention every spare dollar. And what for? I'll tell you what for: so I could have a cozy slot in life, so I could curl up in a corner and read my book and not let the world get at me. Worse than that, I made my family pay for it."

"No, no, no—" Father Toby shook his head.

"And I did it because I wasn't good for anything else, that's why."

"Stop it", Father Toby said irritably. "It's obvious to me you're worried, you're feeling helpless, and it's starting to tie you in knots."

The two men eyed each other uneasily.

"Now relax, just relax", Father Toby said firmly. "He's a college student two days late for classes after the Christmas holidays. He's going to walk into that place today or tomorrow, and everyone's going to be very embarrassed for overreacting."

Alex nodded, rubbing his face.

"Then you're going to give him a lecture he'll never forget."

"Yes, that too."

"And after that he'll get his degree, come home, get married, set himself up in the suburbs, and become a really pathetic conformist, right?"

"You're probably right. Most people end up that way."

"It's the way of all flesh, buddy."

"I have to get home", Alex mumbled distractedly, turning away.

Father Toby watched him go off down the street, noting especially the hunched shoulders and the omission of a good-bye, which in his long experience of Alex Graham was unprecedented.

Alex spent the rest of the morning and early afternoon beside the downstairs telephone, trying to concentrate on a book and failing miserably. At one point he climbed the stairs and wandered from bedroom to bedroom, sensing distinct silences, sensing absences. Jacob's room was dominated by electronic equipment, musical and computer related, and shelves of neatly arranged, categorized books that informed. Model airplanes dangled on strings from the ceiling, and a complex Meccano invention (a mysterious machine of some sort) sat in a favored place on a wall bracket. A crucifix hung above the head of the bed, which was neatly covered with a quilt Carol had made for Jacob the year she was dying. On the wall facing the foot of the bed hung a framed print of a medieval knight on horseback charging into battle with raised sword. Alex had seen it many times before, but now it made him pause for some reflection about his older son.

He pushed open the door of Andrew's room and entered. For some minutes he remained motionless, gazing about him, straining for new understanding of the familiar objects within: a battered, half-deflated soccer ball sitting on the dresser beside a sports trophy; a glass jar on the window sill containing dry weed stalks with unusual seed pods; a three-foot-long papier-mâché whale suspended by twine from the ceiling, which Andrew had made in high school art class, complete with a little manikin Jonah popping out of its mouth; shelves packed with literature, histories, sketching manuals, and comic books randomly mixed with Christian religious material; the walls decorated with charcoal drawings of faces, mostly beautiful girls and elderly people, each of the images striving for portrayal of character; the bed rather loosely made, covered with the quilt Carol had made for Andrew the year she died. Here too there was a crucifix above the head of the bed. Below it, a framed poem in unsteady preadolescent calligraphy:

> My bed is like a little boat;
> Nurse helps me in when I embark;
> She girds me in my sailor's coat
> And starts me in the dark.
>
> At night I go on board and say
> Good night to all my friends on shore;
> I shut my eyes and sail away
> And see and hear no more.
>
> And sometimes things to bed I take,
> As prudent sailors have to do:
> Perhaps a slice of wedding cake,
> Perhaps a toy or two.
>
> All night across the dark we steer:
> But when the day returns at last,
> Safe in my room, beside the pier,
> I find my vessel fast.
>
> —R. L. Stevenson
>   (penned by the hand of
>   Sir Andrew Angus Lancelot Graham)

Alex had never noticed the "Lancelot" before. It was his son's invention, an idealization, a self-expansion. He recalled reciting the poem to Jacob and Andrew when they were little, a son tucked under each arm, page after page of *A Child's Garden of Verses*, the boys ever eager to turn the pages before the poem was done, racing ahead, wanting more and more and more. They knew all the verses by heart from these bedtime readings and corrected him whenever he got a word wrong. They loved habit, thrived on traditions. Those had been good times, happy times. Now all these years later he felt anew its momentary joy, its innocence and union. Where had it gone?

Around three o'clock the ship's bell rang, and he went downstairs to find Father Toby at the front door, stamping his feet and beating the cold from his ribs with his arms. His car was idling at the curb.

"Hi, just wanted to see if Andrew checked in."

"Nothing yet."

"Hey, how about we go for a drive? It'll get your mind off things."

"I'd better not, in case there's a call."

"The phone'll be here when you get back. Turn on the answering machine."

"I don't have an answering machine."

Father Toby shook his head. "No computer either. No e-mail, no Web browsing. How on earth do you keep this business running?"

"The way people have been doing it for hundreds of years."

"A big black ledger and a quill?" Father Toby laughed. "Well, it won't ruin your business if you get some fresh air. Let's go."

"Thanks. Maybe another time."

"Get your coat. This is your pastor talking."

"You're the *assistant* pastor."

"Whatever. Come on, it'll do you good. That way you won't tear the kid's head off when he phones."

Alex considered it for a minute. "All right", he said, and went to find his coat and boots.

They drove up to the crest of Oak and turned onto Tamarack, the nose of Father Toby's Japanese compact tilting down the steep incline. At the bottom they turned left onto Riverside Road, and half a block farther on they cruised slowly past the dam. Alex stared at it and turned in his seat to catch a glimpse of the water on the high side. When they had passed it, he looked forward again and stared straight ahead through the windshield.

"Hero", Father Toby said in a barely audible voice. Before Alex could say anything, Father Toby began to whistle an irritating little tune that seemed to have no melody whatsoever.

Alex ignored him.

They crossed the bridge over the Clementine and drove up into the hills on the other side of the river. It was the sort of day that depressed most people, heavy with midwinter murk underneath a dirty blanket of cloud rolling northward, threatening a deluge of snow. The higher wooded hills were bending before the wind, a million finger bones clawing the ceiling of their prison.

The weather matched Alex's mood exactly, but it did not seem to affect Father Toby in the least. He whistled his nonsensical tune all the way up to the T junction at Concession Road 4. The road ran along the top of the escarpment, northwest to southeast, and Alex knew it well, for it was part of his favorite walk. Father Toby turned right.

"Where are we going?" Alex asked.

"Nowhere. Just riding around. How do you like the scenery?"

"Truly bleak."

"Mmmm."

"Mmmm?"

"Mmmm-mmm."

"Oh, I see. Mmmm-mmm."

It was an improvement over the whistling.

When they passed the cutoff leading to Dogpatch, Alex turned in his seat to catch a last glimpse of Halcyon. The late afternoon was darker now, and when the car passed a gap in the maple stands, he saw that the village had taken on its finest form, the jewel on the collar of a beautiful woman. Then stretches of pine forest began, cutting off the view.

"You should get out more", Father Toby said, as if to the air. "You're becoming a full-blown recluse."

"I'm happy enough."

"Are you? Don't you ever get lonely?"

"I have my memories."

"After Carol died did you ever have a good cry, scream, kick a door in?"

"I've cried, Toby. You want me to do it in public?"

"You're burying yourself, Alex. You're slowly killing yourself in that bookshop of yours."

"I'm not killing myself. I prefer a quiet life."

"Alone. Always alone."

"I like silence."

"Yeah, but what do you mean by silence?"

"Silence is silence."

"I disagree", Father Toby said, his face going into spiritual direction mode. "I think there's a good kind of silence and a bad kind of silence."

"And you think my kind's bad. You don't like how I am, so it must, therefore, be bad."

"I didn't say I don't like how you are."

"Seems to me you did."

"If we talked more often, maybe you wouldn't jump to such conclusions."

"Talk", Alex grimaced.

"People who are all locked up inside never ask what other people really mean. They never take the trouble to find out."

"Words", Alex muttered with an edge of contempt. He resisted the impulse to blurt out that words did not bring the dead back to life.

"You've built your life on books and you despise words?"

"I don't despise words; I just don't trust them in people's mouths."

Father Toby laughed and said no more. About a half mile farther along, he decelerated and pulled over to the shoulder by a mailbox. The snow-blocked lane curved up the hillside to a small house nestled among a copse of birches. There were no tire tracks, only a single footpath through the snow. The name on the mailbox was Roger Colley.

"Hmmm, this is where the Colleys live", Father Toby said, as if recalling a vague memory. "Want to stop in for a minute?"

"No. I should be getting back."

"Okay, if you insist. But now that we're here, I really should go in for a moment. I won't be long." Without waiting for Alex's reply, he got out of the car. He didn't close the door.

"Why don't you come with me? You promised you'd visit them sometime."

"I promised no such thing."

"Oh? I thought you did. They think you did too."

"Well, I didn't", Alex said firmly. "I'll just wait here and enjoy the silence, if you don't mind."

Father Toby shrugged and began whistling. He shut the door with a bang.

At that point both men noticed a small figure running down the hill toward them, slipping and sliding on the path. It was a child. The child fell, picked itself up, then kept running.

It was Hannah Colley.

Arriving at the car, she hugged Father Toby, then pressed her face to the window of the driver's side. When she saw Alex she began jumping up and down.

"You came! You came! I knew you'd come!"

Leaning down, Father Toby peered over her shoulder and smiled at Alex.

Alex got out of the car.

"Mr. Graham, Mr. Graham!" she sang.

"Hello, Hannah."

"You came to visit us!" she said with pure delight.

"That's right", Father Toby answered. "Mr. Graham came to visit you, Hannah. You lead the way."

The girl skipped ahead of them, arriving at the house well in advance.

On the way up, Alex glanced at his watch more than once. "Please make it quick", he muttered.

"Relax, buddy, relax. We won't stay long."

It was a small clapboard bungalow with whitewashed siding, light blue shutters, and red window boxes. The front door was royal blue. Wood smoke came from the chimney and blew earthward in the wind, filling the air with the aroma of burning birch. There was a sagging barn out back, its tin roof flapping and twanging, and from a shed came the sound of a crowing rooster. Beyond that, there was a log cabin with smoke rising from its chimney.

A large tawny dog of uncertain ancestry was lying on the porch of the house, blocking the doorway. It raised rheumy eyes at the visitors, then rolled over onto its side and went back to sleep.

"You have to step over Clovis", the girl explained.

Father Toby extended his arm to knock on the door just as it opened.

Of the many assumptions Alex Graham had been guilty of during his life, the picture he had formed of Theresa Colley was one of the most inaccurate. He had been sure that the woman who wrote to thank him for saving her children was a member of the victim class. He had envisaged a troubled marriage, now over by one means or another, leaving a great deal of bitterness in its wake. On the few occasions when he had thought about her, he felt certain she would be overweight and tense, prematurely gray (or at least covering it with hair dye), a smoker, and if not a drinker, at least an addict of soap operas. There would be a hard edge to her.

He had not meant the prejudgment unkindly, for the description fit several women who lived in the region. Although he did not know any of them personally, from time to time he saw them shopping or going to church or dropping their children off at school. He thought they were probably courageous women on the whole, carrying burdens that would have crushed many a man. He certainly would not have thought ill of Theresa Colley if she had fit the pattern. But she did not.

The woman who stepped out onto the porch was not like any he had met before.

"Father," she said, reaching over the dog, "let me give you a hand. Watch your step—the porch is icy. Please don't mind Clovis; he's a little slow."

"Aren't we all, Theresa."

In a flash Alex took in several details. Her voice was gentle but also clear and steady. She was of medium height and build, with a fine face and blue-gray eyes that had a lot going on behind them. Her dark blond hair was gathered into a single braid down her back.

When the visitors were safely inside the entrance hall, she looked straight into Alex's eyes and offered her hand.

"Mr. Graham, I'm Theresa Colley. We're so glad you could come."

"I'm glad to be here", Alex mumbled, shaking her hand abstractly, inclining slightly—she was the sort of person you instinctively bowed toward—for she was both warm and dignified in a completely natural manner, without stiffness or pretense.

Her clothing was simple: a tan cardigan, white blouse, and calf-length skirt printed with small pink roses. Slippers. A tiny silver crucifix on a chain around her neck. And a plain gold wedding band on her left ring finger.

"I've just made a pot of tea", she said, turning to Father Toby. "And I think the cookie jar raiders left us something. Can you join us?"

A guileless smile that lit up everything in the vicinity.

"We'd love to", Father Toby said.

No earrings, no makeup. She didn't need any.

At that moment a large rust-colored rabbit hopped around a corner and passed them on its way to the front parlor.

The two men raised their eyebrows, Father Toby grinning, Alex a little stunned.

"She's expecting any day now", Theresa said. "The weather's been so cold, and we didn't want the babies born out in the shed." She looked fondly at the creature and added, "She's house-trained."

The rabbit crossed the carpet and plopped down beside the fireplace, where a rack of birch logs was blazing behind a wire screen.

It was not a fancy room, Alex saw. There were homey couches and chairs that looked as if they had been used by more than one generation, and by many kinds of creatures. Here and there were pieces of rustic crockery filled with dried flowers. She was artistic, he noted, or at least tasteful in her poverty. Other details swam into view: three standing shelves stuffed with children's books; a battered upright piano missing some ivory; a wicker basket full of wool skeins, knitting needles, and a half-finished, child-size sweater.

The room's earth tones were highlighted by a few bright splashes here and there: a red bird carved and painted by a childish hand sat on the coffee table, a teal blue ceramic lamp lit the corner, and a tallow-yellow candle shone in its brass holder on the windowsill. Hanging on the bricks above the mantelpiece was an oil painting of a lighthouse on a rocky coast, battered by thundering seas. Alex wondered if it was a metaphor for her life. In the far corner a pedestal table served as the household altar, with a white porcelain madonna, a Bible, and a tangle of rosaries. On the wall above the couch hung a wooden crucifix that looked very old. She had faith. But then he already knew she had faith.

Father Toby turned a circle in the room and asked, "Where are the kids?"

"The youngest is having his nap", she said. "Jamie took the rest up the hill tobogganing. I think Hannah ran to tell them you've arrived."

She invited Father Toby and Alex to sit down on the couch, and when they were comfortable she left the room.

"Well, what do you think?" Father Toby whispered to Alex.

Alex regarded him coolly. "About what?"

"Theresa."

"I think she's a pleasant person", he replied evenly. "Where is the husband?"

Father Toby looked startled. "You don't know?"

Alex shook his head.

"He died in a canoeing accident on Georgian Bay a year and a half ago. I thought you knew."

"I'm sorry. I guess I should have known, but I don't follow the news much."

"I'm surprised you didn't hear about it. Everybody in town knew the family. They moved here about four years ago. Roger Colley taught at Saint Mary's school. He once told me he liked to buy books at the Kingfisher. It had atmosphere, he said. You sure you don't remember him? Late thirtyish, going bald, suit and tie, liked to read history."

"Oh yes, I remember", Alex said vaguely. People came and went in his line of work, and about five years ago he had stopped paying close attention to them.

Theresa Colley returned bearing a loaded tray, which she set on the coffee table in front of her guests.

"There we are, gentlemen. I hope you like your tea strong. And I must apologize—we have only some homemade bread and butter and the last of the Christmas cake."

"Fabulous!" Father Toby enthused. "A real feast, Theresa."

She smiled, looking at Alex. "We would have made something more special for you, but Father didn't give us much warning. When he phoned this morning to say you were coming, the girls insisted we bake you some bread."

Alex looked at Father Toby out of the corner of his eye. The priest got terribly busy hovering over the plates, trying to choose what he would eat.

"Don't be shy", she said, filling the cups from a crackled brown teapot.

Seated in an armchair facing the couch, she sipped her tea as the men selected pieces of bread and cake. They remained in uneasy silence for a minute, wondering what to say to each other. Finally Theresa set the cup on its saucer, put it on a side table, and leaned forward, clasping her hands together.

"Mr. Graham, I . . ." She furrowed her brow. "I don't know how to tell you this. I tried to say it in my note, but the written word is always so inadequate, isn't it?"

Alex nodded. Father Toby nodded too.

"Since the night you rescued Hannah and Jamie, I've spent a lot of time composing what I would say to you in person. It was all very heartfelt and grand, the things I wanted to say. But I'm suddenly at a loss for words."

"Your note said everything, Mrs. Colley."

She smiled sadly. "Did it? I feel it didn't. There's no way I can express to you what you've done for us. If you hadn't been there, I don't think—" She paused, tears filling her eyes. "I don't think I could have survived it."

She sat back, quickly retrieved her cup, and drank from it.

Alex sat staring at her like a wooden soldier.

Father Toby cleared his throat. "Our Alex is a man of few words himself, Theresa. His silences are his greatest eloquence."

Theresa smiled and wiped her eyes.

"I think he's a very courageous fellow, Father."

"He is indeed."

Alex began to squirm. He was about to issue a denial when they were all saved by a bang on a door somewhere on the other side of the kitchen. Theresa leaped up and went to answer it. A babble of voices came from that direction, and a minute later several children burst into the room, eyes bright, cheeks flaming red. The sound of a squalling baby erupted from another direction.

Hannah made the introductions. There was a shy twelve-year-old girl named Clare (who picked up the rabbit and cradled it like an infant), and two un-shy redheaded seven-year-old twins named Gil and Robbie, who pushed in close to inspect, first the guests, then the contents of the plates. They threw themselves onto their knees beside the coffee table and plundered the feast, pausing now and then to gaze curiously at the mythological Mr. Graham, the man who had saved their brother and sister.

Theresa returned with a two-year-old in her arms.

"This is Joseph", she said to Alex. "Not in his best state, but basically human." Joseph took one look at Alex, howled and twisted away, hiding himself in his mother's shoulder.

"And you know Jamie", she added. Jamie had entered unnoticed and stood leaning against the hall doorway, watching. He nodded somberly at the guests. The span of emotion between the two rescued children was puzzling, for Hannah's adulation sharply contrasted her brother's apparent coldness. Alex wondered what was troubling the boy.

Everyone made small talk for several minutes, until the children lost interest in the guests and began to tell their mother the details of their afternoon adventure.

Alex and Father Toby were content to listen without direct involvement. From their solitude—for both men lived in relative solitude—they now began to wonder how much they had missed by escaping the tumult of life in a large family. They marveled at the vitality of feeling and form, the complexity of relationships, the responsibility of demands among a group of children who ranged in age from babyhood to midteens. They wondered, also, how Theresa managed to make it all work.

"Jamie," she said, "does Grandpa know it's teatime?"

"I told him", the boy answered. "He said he'll be in soon."

The chatter resumed, and five minutes later the back door opened, then closed with a thud. A burly man entered the living room through the kitchen-dining area and stopped short, scowling at the guests. He wore patched jeans, logger's boots, and a checked red bush jacket. His white hair was brushed back over the dome of his brow, and a grizzled beard hung halfway down his barrel chest. His face was brown, heavily lined, the eyes blue behind wire-rim spectacles. The eyes seemed intent on intimidating the guests.

Theresa went over to him and took his hand.

"Come and meet Mr. Graham", she said, gently pulling him into the room.

"Graham?" the old man said, as if he didn't like the taste of the name.

Alex rose and shook hands with him, but the piercing blue eyes looked away, suddenly reticent.

"Mr. Graham is the man who rescued Jamie and Hannah", she explained.

"Oh, *that* Graham", he said gruffly, as if it were not a matter of significance, then turned and went back to the dining room, where he sat down at the table, his back to the guests. Immediately, the three youngest children ran to him and began to crawl onto his lap and into his arms.

The old man busied himself setting up chess pieces on a board, letting the children help.

"Jamie," he grumbled, "you promised me a game."

"I'll play later, Grandpa", said the boy. "After they go."

"Boris Spassky today, Bobby Fischer tomorrow—that's what I say", the grandfather replied.

"That is my father", Theresa said with a smile, without a note of apology, though in a low voice. "His name is Edward Phillips. He has been unwell lately."

"I am not unwell", the old man roared. "And I am not deaf!" The children giggled and hugged him. He hugged them in return.

"Mr. Graham is the owner of Kingfisher Books", she called to him. "He's a friend of ours, Papa."

The old man stood, and children fell laughing from him like monkeys dropping from a tree.

"Eh? What's that? Did you say *kingfisher*?"

He came over to the couch and towered above Alex.

"Do you realize what the kingfisher is?" he growled in a low voice.

"I think I do", Alex answered uncertainly.

"Do you know that the kingfisher is a nonpasserine bird, a member of the family Alcedinidae, bright feathered, usually iridescent blue with the assistance of sunlight, crested, with a short tail and a long, stout, sharp bill?"

Alex nodded in affirmation.

"Ha! That is data! But do you really understand its presence in the world? Or is it merely decoration—the bird on the five-dollar bill?"

Alex politely refrained from replying.

"Do you know what the halcyon is?" Mr. Phillips went on. "It is not the usual definition, is it? It is not golden, prosperous, or pacific, is it?" The old man's eyes flashed about the room. "Do you see us, Graham? Do you really see us?"

"Papa...", his daughter murmured, trying to ease him away from what looked very much like an impending diatribe.

"These, Graham, are my offspring and the labor of my love, nurtured in adversity! How can I tell them that the light is dying and soon may be lost? How should I impart the knowledge of the halcyon, lest it cease to pass from generation unto generation?"

Alex grasped at a thread:

"I have always been intrigued by the Greek myth of the halcyon, sir."

"Have you? That is rare in these times. Few now realize that it is the bird above all other birds, held in ancient legend to nest at sea about the time of the winter solstice. It calms the waves for the sake of its chicks, incubating within their shells."

"Yes", said Alex. "It is the father of the fathers of all kingfishers, though it is greater than those we now call kingfisher."

The old man nodded triumphantly, then returned to the dining room table, where he sat down with a look of grave satisfaction.

Alex glanced at his watch with a stab of anxiety.

"I'm afraid we have to go. I'm waiting for a call at home."

He stood. Father Toby stood with him. Theresa and the children accompanied them to the hallway, where the younger ones helped the guests find their coats and boots.

Theresa shook her head, smiling but puzzled.

"How extraordinary", she said to Alex. "Do you know you're the first person we've met here who seems to understand him? People think he's...well, you know how people are. Did you really know what he meant?"

"Actually, yes, I did", Alex said. "It made perfect sense to me."

Father Toby looked bemused and patted Alex's shoulder in a patronizing manner, preparing to make a witty remark.

"Your father is a fine man, Mrs. Colley. Thank you for introducing us."

She looked gratified by this and reached out, shaking his hand once more.

"We hope you'll come back. It would mean so much to us. The children have made me promise to invite you to supper, so that our family can thank you properly."

"Oh no, you don't have to do that. I wouldn't want to be a bother. I'm very glad that Jamie and Hannah are safe and well, but really, you shouldn't think you owe me anything."

Her face fell, and he instantly regretted the thoughtless remark.

"It's not a question of owing or not owing", she said seriously, carefully. "It's that we would like to. I have made a promise to the children. And you must bring Father Toby as well."

"A capital idea, Theresa!" Father Toby interjected. "When can we come?"

Bypassing Alex, she said, "Would a Sunday be good?"

"Perfect", Father Toby said.

"What about four o'clock the Sunday after next?"

"We'll be here on the dot."

"Come earlier if you wish." She turned back to Alex and smiled. "There, it's done. We're not formal here, so you can wear comfortable clothing. If the weather's fine, you might want to go sledding with the children."

Father Toby began to ease Alex toward the front door, but they were stopped by a bellow from the entrance to the living room. The old man stood there raising his right arm.

"Kingfishers catch fire!" he shouted at Alex.

"As dragonflies draw flame!" Alex replied.

These utterances totally perplexed everyone else, leaving only one solution. Father Toby grasped the opportunity and bustled Alex out the front door, followed by a chorus of good-byes. Both men tripped over the dog but came to no harm.

As they drove back to town in the dark, neither of them said anything for the first few minutes. Alex seemed to huddle inside his parka, chin down.

"What on earth were you saying to the old man?" Father Toby asked.

"We were conversing on a high plane, unintelligible to mere mortals."

"I'm impressed. Thanks for humoring him."

"Humoring him? I think Mr. Phillips is a prize human being, Father."

"I'm glad you think so. Theresa and her kids think so too, but they're the only ones who do. He's mentally ill, you know."

"Then that makes two of us."

"No, seriously, he is. He used to be a high school teacher in Toronto, but he had a nervous breakdown and retired early."

"I see. Well, he struck me as an intelligent man."

"He probably is—or was. Theresa told me he's been working on a book for years—for decades, actually. Something he started as a young man and has been tinkering with ever since. He works in a cabin behind the house. It's a log shed, winterized but primitive. He spends most of the day out there carving wooden ships and toys for the kids or picking away on an old manual typewriter."

"What's the book he's writing?"

"Theresa told me once. It's about an English poet."

"Gerard Manley Hopkins?"

"Could be."

"Mr. Phillips recited a line from one of his poems."

"The kingfisher thing?"

"That's right."

"Anyway," Father Toby said, "you should see his workshop. I love going in there. It's wild."

"In what way is it wild?"

"Totally topsy-turvy. Wood shavings all over the floor. A ton of books, mostly about poetry and animals. One whole wall filled with quotations, painted on the logs. A big workbench along the opposite wall, with every kind of hand tool you can imagine. There's no electricity in there, so he heats it with a woodstove, and a couple of old ship's lanterns are the only lighting. He has a cot where he can take naps during the day. It even has a stuffed snowy owl."

"It sounds like a wonderful place."

"It is. If I were a kid, I'd spend a lot of time out back with Grandpa. The Colley kids do, especially the boys. He's eccentric, but he's great with them. He moved up here last year after Roger Colley died."

"Mrs. Colley has a lot to carry."

"She does. It hasn't been easy for her."

"They don't seem to be doing well. There's no car, and the buildings need repairs. The children's clothes seem worn out."

"Uh-huh, shabby but clean. They have self-respect."

"She must do a lot of mending."

"That, and the fact that she buys most of their clothes at the secondhand shop."

"Didn't her husband have life insurance?"

"I'm afraid not. Maybe he was an optimist, but more likely while he was alive they put every dime they had into paying off the house and land."

"How do they survive now?"

"I think they live on her father's old-age pension and whatever the school board gave him for retirement pension—not a fabulous sum. The kids sell eggs, shovel snow."

"How do they get around without a car?"

"The neighbors are helpful. People in the area think pretty highly of Theresa. They get rides to Mass and grocery shopping."

"I see."

"And of course the older boy—Jamie—he works for hire at farms up and down the road."

"Speaking of Jamie, I'm a bit puzzled by him. He's so stiff and unfriendly, you'd think I did him a disservice by rescuing him."

Father Toby glanced at Alex sideways. "Is that what you think?"

"I don't know what to think. He seems troubled."

Father Toby did not answer immediately. He turned left onto Wolfe's Ravine Road and went down it in the direction of the valley bottom. At the intersection by the dam, he turned right onto the river road and headed toward Clementine Bridge.

"The boy was with his father when he died", Father Toby said.

"He was? How did it happen?"

"It happened a year ago last summer. A group of men and their sons—most of them teachers Roger had known in Toronto—went on a canoe trip to Georgian Bay. There were five canoes all together. On the second or third day into the trip, they were paddling about two miles offshore, crossing a wide bay, looking for a site where they could camp for the night. Everybody was in high spirits, and Roger, who was an enthusiastic kind of guy, suggested they go out farther past the mouth of the bay to a rocky island just off the head of land. It was maybe three miles away. Everybody agreed that an island would be safe from bears, and more fun for the boys, so they started toward it. It was an hour before sunset, so they thought it would be easy enough to reach the island and set up camp before dark.

"A wind came up, and the paddling got harder. They were pretty tired to begin with, and this was too much for some of them. It looked as if it would take a lot of heavy paddling going against the wind. Four of the canoes decided to turn back. Roger and Jamie insisted they could make it to the island and declared they would go on alone. The others tried to argue them out of it, but Roger was not one to quit when they were so close to their goal. Both parties agreed to make fires as soon as they beached, so they wouldn't lose sight of each other.

"Roger and Jamie were still about a mile from the island when the wind started to blow hard; the waves got so high that the canoe started to roll. They steered the bow into the wind, hoping to ride it out, but the wind veered at one point, and the canoe capsized. A gust flipped it high, and when it came down, the metal gunwale hit Roger on the head. It didn't knock him out, but he was stunned, and it took him a minute to get his senses back.

"Both of them had life jackets on, and the smartest thing they could have done would've been to hang onto the canoe. It was the kind that has flotation tanks and doesn't sink, but it was swamped and filled with water. It was getting dark by then, and the waves were so high that they couldn't see the canoe anywhere. By that time the people in the other canoes had beached and were setting up camp. The storm was one of those passing summer squalls, wild but short-lived. The clouds finally swept away, and then the moon lit everything up. The wind died down.

"When the men on the shore heard faint cries for help, they jumped in their canoes, taking flashlights with them, and paddled hard in the direction of the sound. Half an hour later they found Roger and Jamie. The boy was conscious, his arms wrapped around his father. He was frightened and shivering from the cold water, but otherwise unharmed. They got him into one canoe, and Roger into another. He had a nasty cut on his forehead that was bleeding steadily. There was a big purple bruise around it, and a lot of swelling. He'd breathed some water too, because it was bubbling out of his mouth every time his chest rose and fell. They had to get his lungs clear, but while they were trying, he just sighed and—"

"He died."

"Yes, just like that, he died."

Alex looked up to find that the car was parked in front of his home, the engine idling.

He shook his head. "That's terrible. That poor family."

Father Toby exhaled loudly.

"So, you see, when Jamie and Hannah had their accident at the dam, it must have been a double nightmare for the boy. It was like it was happening all over again."

"I see."

"If he seems troubled, Alex, it's not because he's unfriendly or ungrateful. He's trying to work it out. He's still grieving over his father, and he's wondering what the hell life is all about."

"I guess if I were in his shoes I'd be wondering too: why God let it happen, and why it almost happened twice."

"Exactly."

They sat without speaking for several seconds.

"That was a setup", Alex said.

"What do you mean?" Father Toby replied.

"You arranged that."

"Arranged what?"

"You know exactly what I mean."

"Oh, you mean the visit to the Colleys?" Father Toby said innocently.

"You are utterly transparent."

Father Toby chuckled.

"It was not a good idea", Alex mumbled irritably.

"Why not?"

"Because it could build up false expectations."

"For a guy who's not interested, you sure asked a lot of questions about them. And you agreed to go back for supper, didn't you?"

"I didn't agree. I was hijacked."

"Was it that painful?"

Alex turned sideways on the seat and stared at him. "Don't ever do that to me again."

Father Toby glanced at him nervously.

"You can't fix other people", Alex went on. "You can't tinker with people's lives. We're not chess pieces. We're not puppets. We're not little cutout cardboard characters that you play with. Life doesn't work that way."

"I'm sorry. I thought—"

"You thought?" Alex interrupted. "Did you think you could fix me—poor dysfunctional Alex—and solve her situation— poor burdened Mrs. Colley—in one shot? Lonely widower, lonely widow, stick 'em together and you get a nice solution?"

Father Toby put his right hand on the wheel and stared straight ahead through the windshield.

"No, I didn't think that."

"You certainly did. It's so obvious, so utterly predictable, so—"

"Alex, why are you angry?"

"I'm not angry; I'm disgusted. I do not like being manipulated."

"It's not manipulation. I just provided an opportunity for you to meet some good people, people who, by the way, are now connected to you, whether you like it or not."

"I saved their lives. Isn't that enough?"

"They're human beings, Alex, not items in a newscast."

"I know they're human beings. But I already have a life of my own."

"Life's an adventure."

"Thanks for the cliché, but I've had my adventure, and it's over."

"I'm glad to see you've got it all figured out."

"I want things to get back to normal now, and I'd appreciate it if you don't pull this sort of trick on me again."

Father Toby gave Alex a long look.

"You know, way back long ago this morning you said something that was very insightful. For one brief moment you took a look at yourself and came up with an honest answer. Remember?"

"Remember what?" Alex snapped.

"You said you'd crawled into your books so life couldn't get at you."

"Did I? I take it back."

"You shouldn't. You shouldn't take that one back, because it's true."

Alex opened his mouth to say something, then closed it.

"But it's only part of the truth. I think you really don't know yourself."

"Oh please! Spare me the pop psychology", Alex huffed.

"You *are* a courageous man", Father Toby replied slowly. "And you're also afraid of something."

Alex's mouth tightened. He looked at Father Toby coldly and got out of the car. He slammed the door, went up the steps to the Kingfisher, and let himself in.

Without removing his coat or turning on the lights, he sat down on the bench beside the hall phone and glared unseeing at the floor. A minute later he heard the sound of Father Toby's car driving away.

He spent a miserable evening alone, pacing through the house, upstairs and downstairs, analyzing, remembering, discarding assumptions and accruing a set of new ones. Nothing was clear, nothing about his obscure temperament added up. At one point he went so far as to bang his fist into the wall, making the pictures tilt on their hooks. Because he was really quite a mild person, this outburst rather alarmed him. He threw himself down onto the sofa and sat staring at empty space.

"Why *am* I so angry?" he growled.

Because you're lonely, he thought. *Because you really would like to get to know that woman but don't want to take on her family.*

"So I'm selfish? Is that it?" he snapped in self-defense.

It's because you think it would cost too much to change.

"Well, it would!"

Maybe not as much as you think.

"I'm not going to throw my life away on a roll of the dice—on a *maybe*!"

You'd prefer to sit here and baby-sit your books for the rest of your life?

"Yes indeed! I'd like that very much."

What about the permanent ache in your heart?

"Shut up about the permanent ache in my heart! I don't give a damn about it. Anyway, this is all about sex, nothing more."

Sex? Nothing more than sex?

Alex fumed a while longer, and when the inner dialogue subsided a little, he began to reflect. He told himself that if one dug deep enough, one would find that everything was rooted in preservation of the species. He had no argument with sex itself, for he was neither a prude nor a puritan. He did not fear it, nor did he idolize it, and his memory of it was allied with the greatest joys of his life, the love he and Carol had shared.

No, his argument in these latter years was with the unfairness of life, the demonstrable and voluminous evidence that gifts of great power—such as attractiveness and strength— were handed out at random, seemingly without regard for the effect on the recipients or for the converse effects upon those who were left empty-handed. At its most primitive, the driving force of society was carnal; at its most refined, it was a question of aesthetics. Beauty was intricately connected to sex, yet it seemed to reach for what was beyond the physical. There was something missing in his critique, he knew, but he did not feel compelled to find out what it was. What purpose would that have served? He had his solitude, which was enough for him.

4. *Citizen of the Month*

Alex went to bed furious and depressed, an unusual mixture for him, and after a fitful sleep he awoke in the same condition. Outside his bedroom window the weather gave every indication of being as nasty as his temper, the wind howling and sleet slapping the window panes. A Shakespearean morning, tragic, threatening him with blasted heaths, blood-stained daggers, and drowned princes.

He got up and made coffee for himself.

When his mind was more or less functioning again, he placed a call to Tyburne. Groves told him there was nothing new to report.

"Aren't the police doing anything?" Alex said sharply.

"Mr. Graham, I think you may be overreacting a little. They are very reluctant to get up a big manhunt when your son has only been missing a few days. If it were a matter of a few months and some hint of foul play, that would be a more serious situation, but for now—"

"More serious? Don't they consider the fact that something critical could happen while they wait around?"

"They're not just sitting on their hands, sir. The police in this country have a lot of real crimes to solve, and they have no time to spare for suppositions. College students go off on larks all the time—and very irresponsible it is—but the police can't chase after every one of them."

Groves suggested that Alex send him a recent photograph of Andrew, which he offered to take to the Oxford police.

He might be able to convince them to send copies of it to other police agencies in Europe.

"France is the most likely place to look", Groves said. "It's a Mecca for the young people, both for culture and night life. Since the Chunnel opened, you would think the Strait of Dover had dried up completely. It's the parting of the Red Sea."

"What is a chunnel?" Alex asked.

"The new tunnel under the channel." Groves paused. "In the old days, when the English Channel was blocked by dirty weather, you would see headlines in the newspapers— 'Channel Closed by Fog: Continent Isolated'."

"Mr. Groves," said Alex, ignoring the attempt at humor, "would you advise the police that I'll send a photo by express mail today?"

"Fine, sir, I'll do that. And I'll contact you the moment we have any news."

Alex rummaged in the fridge and found that some of Maria's food had gone bad. He emptied the offending containers into a plastic bag and took it down to the garbage cans in the side alley. The sleet had coated everything outside with ice. Over a breakfast of dry toast, hard-boiled eggs, and more black coffee, he flipped the pages of a photo album and found a snapshot of Andrew that Jacob had taken last summer with his Leica. He looked intensely at the image— examined it more closely, in fact, than he had ever done before. He was saddened by this, for he knew that his lack of attention, or more precisely his failure to contemplate the uniqueness of his son, was a symptom of his general abstraction from the flesh-and-blood reality of life. Now that Andrew was missing, the absolute *otherness* of him hit Alex like a blow.

There was nothing in the face before him that he did not already know, but he now saw that the knowing had been gathered obliquely throughout their years of living together, an impressionistic collage of words and deeds imprinted haphazardly in the mind. Of course, if it were demanded of him, he would be able to compose a rational summation of Andrew's personality, a few perceptive and concise sentences. He would say, "Andrew Graham is healthy, intelligent, good-natured, possessed of an inquisitive and adventurous spirit, sanguine of temperament, impetuous at times, but capable of dedicated activity in fields that interest him."

Yes, this was true. But it had all the warmth of a report card or a letter of recommendation from a disinterested employer.

The photo cut its subject off at the waist. It showed a strikingly handsome young man in a pale green T-shirt standing against a hedge of purple lilacs, holding his checkered soccer ball under the crook of one arm. His other arm crossed a broad chest, his forearm brown and sinewy, his large hand firmly gripping the ball with splayed fingers. It had been taken during a break from exertion, for his face glowed with perspiration, his cheeks were ruddy, and his blond hair was pushed askew off his forehead in a fan of damp spikes. The wedge-shaped scar on his left temple was just visible (Andrew, age eleven, had once tossed a Swiss Army knife into the air while showing off to his older brother).

Alex suddenly realized how much of Carol there was in him, in his bone structure especially; his wide cheekbones and the dome of his skull were from her family, with the exception of his solid chin, which was an inheritance from Alex's father. Like all the Grahams, his nose was straight and fine, his teeth white and slightly crowded, his lips parting in a grin that had charmed everyone from his babyhood onward. His eyes, Alex realized with a start, were the same as his own—deep set, sensitive, though animated with a hint of mischief and wry humor, looking outward at the world with pleasure. The quintessence of openness. By contrast,

Alex's eyes appeared in photographs and mirrors as closed windows, eyes that looked inward for the most part. When they occasionally looked out at the world, it was with gravity and cautious approbation.

Elbow on the table, forehead in hand, Alex whispered, "Where are you, Andrew?"

He removed the photograph from the album, wrote his son's name on the back, and put it into an envelope addressed to John Groves at Tyburne College. Then he went downstairs to the shop and sat at his desk. There was a stack of bills waiting for him, neglected for over a month. He spent the better part of an hour writing out checks, and when he balanced the checkbook at the end, factoring in the money he had not yet deposited, he found that the account was practically empty. This was not unwelcome, however, for he had expected it to be overdrawn. He reminded himself to stop in at the bank when he took the mail to the post office later in the morning.

He went upstairs for more coffee, took the last pill from the bottle of antibiotics, and lay down for a catnap. The ring of the bedside phone woke him. It was Jacob. He asked after Alex's health and sounded relieved when Alex told him that he was almost back to normal. Then Jacob launched into a ten-minute description of his holiday in the Rockies, disclosing in passing the name of the young woman in his life. It was Meg, and she was the daughter of a senior partner in a Toronto law firm. She was a "keeper", he said.

"A keeper?" Alex queried.

"Like permanent", Jacob replied.

Alex was fairly certain that Jacob meant marriage, because the boy was socially conservative and a regular churchgoer. If his faith had lately seemed eclipsed by his interest in law, this was probably no more than a temporary adjustment of priorities. For Jacob, religion was a necessary component of life, essential to a reasonable and orderly existence but of no greater import than a good education, physical health, and mental hygiene. He was a responsible boy and had never given his father a moment of grief. An incarnation of his grandfather Graham, he was very much a young magistrate in the making. There was no arrogance in him, Alex was pleased to see, but neither was there an excess of imagination.

Of the two sons, Jacob was the one more like Alex, though only proximately so. His unadventurous spirit resembled that of his father, but there the similarity ended. He loved to talk, and his conversation was always about structures, systems, the significance of certain collations of data, and the codifying of objects and people. As a boy he had liked to build things in the basement: edifices of crates and cast-off lumber, engines made from nuts and bolts and old copper pipes, and structures from his grandfather's extensive collection of Meccano sets. He was inventive where Andrew was creative. He collected stamps and coins, while Andrew collected abandoned bird nests and odd-shaped stones. Jacob liked to draw buildings and machines with drafting pen and ruler; Andrew loved to draw arabesques of wind and landscape, the movement of birds, and the idiosyncrasies of people's faces, using charcoal and pastel sticks that snapped in his fingers. Jacob searched out intricate ideas and dependable principles; Andrew was lured by feeling and surprise.

Despite these differences, both boys had been gifted with kind and affectionate natures, and this combined with their physical appearance made them popular with adults and sought after by friends. If Andrew was handsome, Jacob was more so. He was brown eyed and olive skinned (Carol's contribution), shorter than his younger brother but more prone to develop muscle. On the high school playing fields, Jacob had been a studied athlete, Andrew a flamboyant one, and both were successful at it. Girls fell in love with them instantly, saved from disaster only by the Graham tradition of respect and manners—and, Alex made sure, the Catholic tradition of manly virtue.

Alex considered it a very great blessing that his sons had navigated their way safely through the pop culture of the 1980s and '90s, which he had seen spawning in the earlier decades of the "sexual revolution". Their upbringing, their peculiar ancestors, and a richly cultured home life had helped. Both were leaders, each in his own way. Jacob was the leader of many, Andrew the leader of few, though these tended to be other individualists. Throughout their years in grade school and high school, the pattern remained consistent. As the university years began, Jacob became more staid, steadfast, set upon his course, showing every sign of continuing the Graham habit of stability. If he returned to Halcyon one day and set up a law practice, he would in short order become one of its leading citizens. By contrast, Andrew drifted in and out of some undefined tangential path into a future that was unclear even to himself. Andrew could easily—to quote Maria Sabbatino—breaka your heart.

Alex snapped out of his reverie, remembering he was on the phone with Jacob. When he was finally able to interrupt the flow of talk, he told him that Andrew was missing. Jacob seemed more irritated than alarmed, though he grew increasingly silent as the details mounted.

"They're sending his photo to the police in Europe?" he said in a quiet voice. "That sounds serious."

"They might send it, or they might not. They think I'm overreacting."

"Are you okay? Are you hanging in there?"

"It's very frustrating."

"It must be. I wish I'd known earlier."

"I left several messages on your answering machine. When you didn't phone back, I assumed—"

"Sorry about that. I didn't get a single one. The tape's been garbling messages lately, and I just haven't had the time or the cash to replace the dang thing. Look, Dad, I have to meet a professor for lunch, so I'd better go. I'll be at the apartment tonight. Can you give me a call if anything happens?"

"All right. Please pray for your brother."

"I will. And don't worry too much about him. You know what he's like."

Alex paused. "What is he like, Jacob?"

There was a defensive note in the reply: "Unpredictable. He's always been that way."

Alex said nothing.

"Well, I'd better run. God bless, Dad."

"God bless you, Jacob."

After Alex hung up, he sighed, then went downstairs, gathered the mail and bank books, and tucked them into a leather valise. He put on his parka and boots and went out into the storm.

The icy sidewalks were treacherous, but he walked carefully to Main and turned onto it without a single slip. He kept his head down, but several people nodded as they passed, saying, "Well done, Mr. Graham!" or "Way to go!" The notoriety was becoming tedious.

At the post office, he threw his business mail into the lobby slot, then went inside and purchased an express envelope in which to send the photograph to Oxford, enduring yet another congratulation from the postmistress. After that, he walked two blocks to the precise center of Halcyon, the intersection of Main and Dominion, where stood the imposing granite edifice of his bank. At one time it had been a branch of the Imperial Bank of Commerce, but it was now the head office of Clementine Valley Credit Union. It was managed by Charles Findley Jr., a suave and courtly fellow who had once beaten Alex black and blue in the seventh grade. There were Catholic Findleys and Protestant Findleys, and the Catholic branch of the clan was definitely the less edifying.

The bank's architecture was early Victorian, but the interior decor was modern, with designer chairs, pile carpets, art by local painters, and a line of computers operated by charming girls. With an animated face, one of the tellers mouthed his name to catch his attention, and pointed to a framed photo on the courtesy desk. It was a color blowup of himself. Where on earth had they gotten a photo? From Father Toby, maybe? There was a vase of flowers beside it, and on the wall above it, a sign: "Citizen of the Month".

As he made the deposit, the teller gazed at him fondly and said, "You were our citizen for December, Mr. Graham. But Mr. Findley insisted you should have January too. Isn't that great?"

"Uh, yes. That's very nice. Thank you."

"Oh no, don't thank us. *We* should thank *you*."

At that moment, Charles Findley Jr. walked out of an office behind the counter and spotted Alex.

"Al!" he said and strode over, his face alight with his best golf-and-country-club expression, his right arm reaching past the teller to shake Alex's hand. "Great to have you up and running."

"Oh yes. Thank you", Alex mumbled.

"Did you see the shrine?" Charles asked with a sideways smile, pointing to the photo.

"I did. That's very kind of you."

His business completed, Alex stepped aside from the wicket and turned away. But Charles came around from behind the counter and stood in front of him. Charles began to speak, which was his penchant, and people began to listen. Out of the corner of his eye, Alex saw other customers turning their heads slightly in order not to miss any of the details. The most important man in town was speaking to the current heroic figure in town—the citizen of the month.

Alex watched Charles' mouth opening and closing, the play of charm and emphasis, hands doing this and that in the air, the body language that can be accomplished convincingly only by a successful man. For most of the thirty-five years since the beating, Alex had regarded Charles as an inscrutable life-form. And he thought that Charles probably regarded him in the same way. Charles was the son of the most important man in town, who himself had been the son of the most important man in town, who in turn—and so forth, all the way back to the early years of pioneer Canada. Even as a child, he had dominated every environment he happened to be in. Tall for his age, smart, good-looking, he had been a prime candidate for the primary position in the pecking order of Halcyon and the surrounding region, not to mention the farthest domains of the Clementine valley. Charles had never liked competitors, and Alex had been competition simply because he was the son of the second-most-important man in town.

At the time of their first altercation, Alex had weighed twenty or thirty pounds less than Charles, was two inches shorter, quiet, and apparently nonaggressive. But after his humiliating defeat, Alex had lifted barbells for six months. Then, at the end of the last day of the school year, he had waited outside the gates of Saint Mary's school yard for Charles to emerge, faced him squarely, and said, "You're a bully. You're going to stop it."

When Charles sneered in reply, Alex popped him on the mouth with his fist. Charles had staggered back, more astonished than hurt, wiped a little blood off his lips, stared at Alex, stared at his bloody fingers, shook his head, laughed, then, fighting back tears, wheeled and stomped off. The crowd of Charles' admirers had scattered, completely puzzled by the incident, for both Alex's act and Charles' reaction did not fit the laws of their world. No more words had passed between the two boys during the confrontation, but from then on Charles Findley Jr. ceased provoking Alex. In fact, they avoided each other altogether until Alex fell ill and disappeared from sight, leaving the collective memory to fade as his fellow students swept onward into the more interesting dramas of adolescence.

In the ensuing years, Charles had proved to be every inch a winner. He was now a fairly wealthy man, head of the Heritage Society, the local Chamber of Commerce, and the hospital board. In addition, he was building a multimillion-dollar golf club in the lower hills south of town, and condominiums for a winter ski resort in the higher hills two miles to the northwest. He was trim and elegant, with tailored suits, shoes from Italy, a Florida tan, and styled hair that went silver at forty with no loss of élan. He had owned at various times a Porsche, a BMW, a Ferrari, and two successive wives, neither of them locals. He was busy courting a third, rumored to be a high-power Toronto lawyer. He was admired throughout the region for giving it class, for drawing investors and employment, for restoring sections of the town to their nineteenth-century splendor, and for being a model of success in a community that had seen better days. To be fair, it should be added that he was in all his business dealings an irreproachable man. His younger brother, Elgin Findley, owner of Findley Real Estate, which monopolized land sales in the area, did not enjoy a similar reputation. The brothers (the brothers Karamazov, Alex thought of them) were close, but different in all aspects other than physical appearance and style. Elgin was a wheeler-dealer, a millionaire, also a veteran of exotic marriages. He drove Cadillacs, which he traded in annually. He bought and sold land to his advantage so often that he was widely suspected of dishonesty. Yet his skills in this business were so subtle that he could be resented only by the overly suspicious or by those who had a year or two to meditate on what they had signed away. Charles provided mortgages for Elgin's clientele. There was no conflict of interest—on any level of the meaning of that term.

Charles was still talking, exuding amicable sincerity, his left arm extended, his hand clasped firmly on Alex's bicep. Alex stared at the fingers, then at the lips, amazed that he had once bloodied them.

"I hope you'll consider it", said Charles. "It's definitely within the provisos of the heritage committee's guidelines. I foresee a day, especially after the Old Mill is restored next summer, when Halcyon will have a second renaissance. Antique and handicraft shops are going to open all along the river, concentrating by the dam. And when the resort and the golf club come online, this town is going to boom!"

"Well, that's good", Alex said, not knowing what the man was talking about.

"So, older residents may want to think about selling downtown properties at a profit and buying in low from the subdivision that Elgin's building. It's a win-win situation, Al." Charles gave him an encouraging smile and squeezed his arm. "We'll talk again. Come in and see me anytime."

"Uh, sure. Thanks, Charles."

"Not at all, Al."

Alex returned to the bookshop without mishap. The bad weather had prevented many people from venturing forth on the streets, and thus the Kingfisher did not see any customers throughout the remainder of the morning and the early afternoon. Feeling somewhat drained by his outing, he sat by the fireplace for an hour, sipping another cup of black coffee, mentally composing an apology to Father Toby, wondering if he should phone him. He decided to call the rectory after supper, then went to the poetry section and found a copy of Hopkins' collected works, an old interest renewed by the exchange he had had with Mr. Phillips the day before.

Shortly before three, Alex heard the bell of the shop's front entrance and saw a shadow enter the hallway. He inserted a forefinger into the Hopkins book to mark his place.

The shadow paused for a moment, then came into the main room followed by a man. Whoever he was, he was not a local customer, and bore even less resemblance to the out-of-town trade that occasionally visited the shop. He was about thirty years of age, hollow cheeked with a few days' growth of beard. His untidy hair under a sailor's cap was black and wet, his skin was swarthy, and his jet eyes flickered about the room as if unsure of what they wanted. His shoulders were hunched inside a navy pea jacket, hands thrust into its pockets, collar up. His green workmen's trousers were wet to the knees, and his shoes (not boots) were scuffed, down at the heel, dripping slush onto the hardwood floor.

Alex wondered if he was a vagabond or a thief.

"You are bookstore?" the man said in heavily accented English. It sounded European, though his face might also be Middle Eastern. Iranian, perhaps, or Turkish.

Alex nodded. "Yes. May I help you?"

"You help I find book?"

"Certainly. What are you interested in?"

"Book about Russia."

Alex closed the Hopkins, got up, and went past the man into the hall. He opened the french doors of the Russian room and pointed inside.

"Thank you", said the man.

"I see you are a traveler", Alex said. "How did you hear about this shop?"

"They say it at gas station on road, I have coffee at, the lady tell me come here find this place. Very interesting." He entered the Russian room and stood gazing about. His eyes lingered on the samovar. Then he turned and glanced at Alex.

"Why you have Russia book this place?"

"I am interested in Russia."

The man looked momentarily surprised, but there was an intensity lingering within the glance.

"Is little village. Is no-place. Nothing like this in Toronto."

The man scanned the shelves for a moment, then turned to Alex again.

"Do you speak my language?" he asked in Russian.

"Yes," Alex replied in kind, "though my accent is not accomplished, as you can hear."

"You speak very well, I think", the man returned. "Your accent is odd. Did you learn Russian from a language course or from our famous writers?"

Thus ended the prospect of stilted conversation with a dark ghost, and before both men there opened vistas of elaborate and rewarding communication.

"I learned mostly from a friend", Alex said. "But yes, also from Dostoyevsky and Turgenev."

"It is to be expected, for these are writers well known to the West. In Toronto I have met many people who can speak at length about their themes and styles."

Alex assessed the comment. Vagabonds and thieves usually did not discuss "themes and styles".

"May I ask, sir, why you are traveling through this remote territory? I do not wish to pry into your personal affairs, but I feel a certain sympathy for exiles from the Rus."

For the first time, the man smiled, a transient flicker across his mouth. Was it a tentative response to the humanity implicit in the inquiry, an instinctive thawing to a stranger's unsolicited warmth? Or was he merely amused by the formal character of Alex's diction?

"I have been working in the mines in the north. I am returning to the city, where my wife and daughter live."

"What brings you here?"

"I was hitchhiking. How fortunate for me that I stopped at the café to warm myself. The waitress, hearing my accent, asked me about my nationality, and when I informed her, she told me about your shop. I was curious to see it."

"Are you an immigrant?"

The man nodded. "Since two years. I will become a citizen."

"May I offer you a cup of coffee?"

The Russian's face thawed another degree.

"That is hospitable of you", he replied with a genuine, if brief, smile. "I would be grateful."

"Please examine the books. I must go to make the coffee, and then I shall return shortly. It would have been my pleasure to make you black tea in the samovar; but regrettably it is not presently in working order."

Alex went upstairs to the kitchen and set the coffee machine to work. As he rummaged in the cupboards for sugar, bread, butter, and a small bottle of vodka, he recalled that during the entire lifetime of Kingfisher Books, a period spanning more than twenty-five years, he had met only five Russians. Three had arrived without notice one day, a long time before the fall of the Soviet regime, heavyset men in shiny, ill-fitting suits and gaudy ties. They introduced themselves in correct English, explaining that they were members of the Tolstoy Society of Russia, visiting in Toronto to give talks at a conference, a joint venture of the Soviet and Canadian governments. They purchased a number of literary works, old and new, but nothing by Leo Tolstoy. One of them cornered Alex in the hallway and gave him a long explanation of the beneficial work of the Soviet Writers' Union, which out of politeness Alex made no effort to debate. However, he happened to notice, while glancing in a hall mirror that reflected a corner of the Russian room, that one of the other visitors surreptitiously pocketed a paperback copy of *The Gulag Archipelago*, which had just been published. Alex said nothing, counting the incident well worth the price of the book.

A year later a bright-eyed, prickly woman in her late sixties spent an afternoon in the Russian room and purchased a great number of titles, which she asked Alex to ship to the Toronto college where she was a professor of Slavonic studies. Born in Vladimir-Suzdal, she had come to Canada after the Second World War. During the next year or so, she sent mail orders for more books, but the exchange ended in the early eighties. Alex supposed she had died. Three years elapsed before his next Russian. She entered the shop on a Saturday morning in spring, a young woman in her midtwenties, accompanied by an elderly couple whom Alex thought must be her Canadian hosts or guardians. She spoke no English. Alex thought at first that she was an exchange student, but when he saw a delicate Byzantine cross hanging on a chain about her neck, he suspected she was a refugee of some kind. He spoke with her briefly in Russian, but she deflected his probing questions with skill, and he learned nothing about her other than that she was interested in the religious writings of Soloviev, which she said were difficult to find in the Soviet Union. She purchased *Russia and the Universal Church* and *War, Progress, and the End of History*. He never saw her again.

The man downstairs was his sixth Russian (not counting Leonid Vozhinsky, who was a category unto himself—simply Layo).

When the coffee was ready, Alex put the sugar, milk, vodka, bread, and butter onto a tray with the pot and carried it down to the shop. He set it on a side table beside the fireplace armchairs and called to the Russian.

The man came into the room warily, a book in hand, and sat where Alex indicated. Alex took the seat opposite him and poured the coffee. They ate and drank in silence, the visitor staring into the flames, visibly relaxing as the heat penetrated his damp clothes. After a time he looked up and said:

"This is unexpected. I have not experienced such..." He did not complete the comment but looked away, his eyes darker, if possible, than they had been until that moment.

"What have you selected?" Alex asked, indicating the book in the other's hand.

"It is *Grani*. Several issues bound into a single volume. If I had known, if I had known of the existence of such a journal..." He waved the book in the air. "For so many years, for so many years! How many times during those years would a single page of this have brought a ray of sun into our winter world? Yet we did not know of its existence. We thought they ruled everything, you see. There were rumors, of course. But how could we know with any certainty? Russia is a land that specializes in rumors."

"You did not know about *Grani*?"

The Russian shook his head. "We guessed that some of our true literature was getting out. How much, we did not know. We heard about Solzhenitsyn, of course, because of *Ivan Denisovich* and all the furor it had caused. But to obtain a copy was difficult, and to find his other works was impossible. Some—Isaac Babel and Anna Akhmatova, for example—they were suppressed, but even in my generation one could locate copies under the table. Other names—Mandelshtam, Grossman, Daniel—these were beyond reach, especially after the *oprichniki* began to crack down."

"To crack down on the dissidents, you mean?"

The Russian raised his eyebrows with a weary sarcasm that was not intentionally offensive.

"I do not mean the pampered writers of Peredelkino."

"Did you know any dissidents?"

"Personally? No." The Russian shook his head. "My generation knew of them, and we revered them. But where could you meet these people? They were older, they lived in distant cities, we did not have their addresses, and to inquire for them would have brought great trouble upon us. I was a boy living in a backwater during the years when the West began to hear about them. I wrote poetry, my friends wrote poetry, we all hated the poetry killers, but what could we do! Become another Sholokhov? Join the Writers' Union and be like the caged sables who published in *Moskva*?"

"I have several back issues of *Moskva*, if you would like to see them."

"You should burn them. They are worthless."

"Surely you know more about these matters than I do," Alex replied, "but I have read some excellent writing in *Moskva*. Though most of it is politically safe."

The Russian gave him a cold look. "It is not the articles in themselves but the compromised lives they represent."

"I see." Alex took a long sip of his coffee.

"Few have eyes to see. For men such as you—and please do not misunderstand me; I apprehend that you are a man of honor and culture—our sorrow can be perceived only as a distant drama. For many in the West—of course, I do not say this about you—but for many, the struggle of our true writers was crisis as art form. We provided you with theater."

"Theater?"

"Our drama excited your imaginations, did it not? You admired us—and you feared us. In the West, even when you admire passionate conviction, you find it safer to admire it from a distance. Here, everyone must become a happy consumer of entertainment."

Alex stared at him, realizing suddenly that the man before him was something more than merely educated or articulate.

His hands, swollen and cracked by Canadian mines, did not match a mind that had been sharpened in the kind of adversity Alex had never known. Many on both sides of the Atlantic were capable of holding forth intellectually, but this man was cutting through the veneer on some level of perception that was distinctly Russian.

"I do not deny it", Alex said at last. "For most of my life I have felt that the things I love are slowly being destroyed."

"Destroyed? What do you mean? There is no KGB in this land."

In answer, Alex got up and went to the Russian collection. Returning shortly, he sat down and opened a small volume.

"Solzhenitsyn", he explained. "This is his Nobel lecture. Have you read it?"

"Of course."

"Do you recall this passage? 'Woe to that nation whose literature is interrupted by the interference of force. This is not simply a violation of the "freedom of the press": it is the locking up of the national heart, the excision of the national memory. Such a nation does not remember itself, it is deprived of its spiritual unity, and although its population supposedly have a common language, fellow countrymen suddenly stop understanding each other. Mute generations live out their lives and die without telling their story either to their own or to a future generation.'"

"What is the point you wish to make?" the Russian asked.

"What was crushed by brutal force in your land is dying quietly, discreetly, suffocating from lack of oxygen in my land. Here there is no overt violence to alert us to the presence of our enemy. My people look without seeing, listen without hearing. But we are not all like that. For some of us it was not a case of watching theater, it was not crisis as entertainment. You must understand that some of us had eyes to see."

"What did you think you saw?"

"We recognized ourselves in you."

The Russian looked down at the journal in his hands. "Did you?" he said.

Alex reached for the vodka bottle and offered it. "More?"

"A little, please", the Russian said, and held out his cup.

"So, in *Grani* you have found something that is significant for you?"

"Yes. Facets, fragments. Europe is a heap of ironies, which would be difficult for you to understand. *Grani*, this literary journal of Russian exiles, specializing in samizdat, was published in Frankfurt. My grandfather was killed by the Germans during the Patriotic War. My father was wounded in battle by them, and I can still see before my eyes the scars upon his body. Yet the Germans have helped to preserve Russian literature, Mr. Kingfisher."

Alex leaned forward and offered his hand. "My name is not Kingfisher. I am Alexander Graham."

The Russian shook his hand but did not offer his own name in full, saying only, "I am Oleg."

"How did you leave Russia, Oleg?"

"I was raised in Vyborg, near the Finnish border. My wife also is from Vyborg. My family, what remains of it, lives there still."

"Your parents are alive?"

"My mother lives with my sister. My father died in Afghanistan."

"I am sorry."

"He was a soldier. But he killed no one. He worked in a medical unit."

"And you yourself, may I ask, were you a miner in Russia?"

Oleg laughed shortly. "I was a teacher. Of literature." He held up his hands, palms toward Alex. "Now I am a miner."

"How did you come to the West?"

"My wife and I walked across the border into Finland."

"You walked? You did not emigrate?"

Oleg raised his eyebrows and turned down his mouth.

"Scientists and athletes emigrate. Also, the state dumps many criminals into the West—they too are very official, very legal émigrés. People such as me do not emigrate so easily."

"Yet you are here."

"As you can see." He spread his arms wide. "Think of me as a cosmic tourist."

"A refugee?"

"Yes. We journeyed more than a hundred kilometers through forests. More than once we came close to death. But..."

Who can explain fate? his look implied.

"But you survived", Alex said.

"Yes, we survived. And so our daughter was conceived in Helsinki and born in Toronto."

He opened the bound copy of *Grani* and resumed reading quietly to himself.

The bell rang and two elderly women entered the shop, hooting and giggling about the inclement weather. It was the Dufort sisters, looking for a birthday gift for a friend. Alex suggested a few titles, and after looking at the books, they selected one. There followed a protracted discussion about Alex's health, something about mustard plasters and whiskey. He escorted them to the front door, where they insisted on kissing his cheek, defending this outrageous display of emotion on the grounds that they had not yet had a chance to congratulate him for his daring rescue of the Colley children.

"Such lovely children", the elder Miss Dufort said.

"And such a fine, brave woman, their mother", added the junior Miss Dufort.

When Alex returned to the main room, he saw that the armchair was empty. Oleg had gone back to the Russian room and was now concentrating on the collection. Alex left him to it, sat down at his desk, and opened the Hopkins. He read for a while, until he was roused from the book by the chimes of the grandfather clock striking the hour of five. Checking on Oleg, he found him bent over a book in the dissident-poetry section.

Intrigued by the oceanic spaces that existed between him and the Russian, he thought he would like to translate a Western poem for him. In an anthology of English poets, he found Dylan Thomas' "Fern Hill" and spent close to an hour translating it. He wrote on a large notepad, crossing out and rewriting, crossing out again and rewriting over and over, shifting tone and balance, substituting more-precise words, striking them off the page and restoring the more intuitive expressions. It was a frustrating process, for he saw how much was lost. The literal meaning was not difficult, but the "soul" of the work was intimately connected to the sound of the words, the music within them, and Alex now realized that this was something so delicate it did not easily survive the flight. To hurl the Welshman's word over the turbulent sea of Babel would demand the creation of an entirely new poem in the Russian language. And Alex was no poet.

Nevertheless, he completed the translation in the hope that the poem's meaning would survive—enough to offer Oleg a hint that beneath the blindness and the deafness of an affluent society, there was a flicker of soul. He also translated a few lines from "Do not go gentle into that good night", hoping to impart the sense of Thomas' intention, for this was a simpler work, less romantic.

When the clock struck six, Oleg brought an armload of books and put it on the desk in front of Alex.

"I will purchase these. I must find more. When do you close the business for the night?"

"I need not close. You may stay as long as you wish."

Oleg returned to the Russian room.

Warming more and more to the challenge of soul-translation, Alex opened the Hopkins and plunged into "That Nature Is a Heraclitean Fire". Here he found a difficulty greater than he had encountered in the Dylan Thomas, for Hopkins was the consummate master of poetry as music. Indeed, translation stumbled and collapsed at every turn, for the meaning was utterly dependent on the music, sense so married to sound that Alex began to ask himself if the act of divorcing them was a violation. But he argued that this was not so; words had power in themselves, and though the poetic genius be weakened, Oleg would learn that fire still burned in the West. Alex completed a few lines before Oleg returned to the desk with more books.

"This is enough for now", he said. "I will visit you again one day. When I am rich I will come with a truck to purchase everything!" Followed by a smile that seemed self-deprecating, grateful, and overwhelmed by the embarrassment of riches.

Oleg had selected more than two dozen books: the dissident poets, Turgenev's *Fathers and Sons* in English, *Report from Darkness* by a former prison camp inmate named Belov, Vasily Grossman's *Life and Fate* in French and English editions, and bound volumes of *Grani*. He paid for them with hundred-dollar bills, extracting two from a wallet crammed with money. When Alex gave him the change, he was not sure how he would package the books for easy carrying. He asked the Russian to wait while he went upstairs. Rummaging in the closet of Jacob's bedroom, he found an old gym bag that he carried back down to the shop. The books fitted into it, and when Oleg lifted it, the handle straps did not tear away from the fabric.

"This is good. I thank you. Now I must go."

Alex invited him to supper, adding that if he wished he was also welcome to stay overnight in one of the unused bedrooms. But the Russian declined, explaining that his wife and daughter were expecting him. The city was only a two-hour drive away, he said, and the ride might be good. Alex looked out the front display window and saw that the sky had cleared. The maintenance crews would now be sanding and salting the highway to Toronto, and Oleg stood a good chance of arriving home that night.

"At least you must permit me to make a meal for you", he said.

"If you insist", Oleg replied formally.

They went upstairs to the kitchen, where the Russian sat at the table and watched Alex beating about in the fridge and cupboards.

"There doesn't seem to be much that would make a proper meal", Alex apologized.

"No matter. Bread is enough."

Then Alex recalled that there was one of Maria's meals in the freezer. When he opened it, he saw that it was Italian meatballs in gravy. He put the dish into the oven.

"It's frozen", he explained. "It may take awhile."

"The hour is still early."

That was followed by a search for a pot in which to boil water for noodles. That done, he plugged in the electric kettle.

"Tea", Alex said.

While the tea was steeping between them in the old pot he had used since Carol's death, Alex suddenly felt the uniqueness of the moment. His mood was elevated for the first time in weeks, and he felt, moreover, an energy and enthusiasm that he had not experienced in years. He even attempted to joke with his guest.

"I expect you think all North Americans are cut from the same cloth."

Oleg shrugged a qualification but said nothing.

"I want you to know that Canadians are very different from Americans." Oleg did not look convinced. "You see, in this pot is real tea, strong tea, richly flavored tea. This is Canadian tea. Of course, we can sometimes buy tea from the United States, and on the occasions when we make the mistake of doing so we rediscover that Americans do not have real tea. They call it tea, but it is not tea. It has no taste; indeed, on the rare occasions when it is found to have a little taste, it is most unpleasant. We say this is God's punishment for the Boston Tea Party."

"Bosetone teepartee", Oleg enunciated. "What is a bosetone teepartee?"

"When the American colonists cast off British rule, the people of Boston threw a shipment of tea into the bay, in protest against the unjust tea tax."

Oleg produced a weary smile. "Only in this land do you begin a revolution with the spilling of tea! In Russia all revolutions begin with the spilling of blood."

Alex filled Oleg's cup. "Taste it. This is *real* tea."

Oleg sipped, then his face soured theatrically. "Oy! This is not tea!"

"You don't think so?"

"No, this is—I do not wish to offend you, for you have been a generous host—this is ditchwater."

Both men began to laugh for no reason at all. And it struck Alex how pleasant it was to know that Russians were capable of laughter. Humor, regardless of how silly it was, unlocked doors that rational discourse and even poetry could not open.

"May I read something to you while we wait?" Alex asked.

"Of course." Oleg added sugar to his ditchwater, sipped, and seemed satisfied.

Alex flipped through the anthology and found "Fern Hill". He read it aloud in English. At the end he looked up and asked, "Did you understand it?"

Oleg shrugged his all-purpose gesture. "A little. It is about youth and memory."

Then Alex proceeded to read aloud his translation of the poem into Russian.

Oleg listened, his face revealing nothing. When Alex had finished, Oleg tilted his head reflectively and said, "Now the meaning is clear. But it is no longer poetry."

Alex nodded, leaning forward intently. "Exactly. And this is our dilemma. Are we not at this moment breaking open the shell of language, exposing its secret core, the flow of perception from heart to heart?"

"The heart? Perhaps."

"Would you like to hear another?"

"Please."

Alex read in English the full text of "Do not go gentle into that good night".

"My vocabulary is limited", Oleg said with a note of dissatisfaction. "Yet I think it is about death?"

"That is correct."

Alex then read to him a Russian translation of the final lines.

Oleg frowned. "To rage against the dying of the light—what does this mean? Is the poet advocating a rebellion against nature?"

"He is expressing life's protest against annihilation, I think."

Oleg said nothing for a minute, staring at the cup in his hands, his eyes blinking rapidly.

"Who wrote it?" he said at last.

"A man named Dylan Thomas."

"Ah yes, the man who drank. I have read about him, but this is my first encounter with his poetry. How striking that the words of his heart do not match the image of his life. But it is always that way."

"It is often that way."

"All public images are lies, though we should look at them and study them."

"This is true, my guest. Will you forgive me if I make a confession? When you came into the shop this afternoon I thought you might be a thief."

Oleg's eyes grew ironic without any other alteration of his expression.

"And I too have a confession. When I came into your shop, I thought to myself, this Mr. Kingfisher is a dry man, a man who knows only books. He has not suffered. He will be educated and ignorant. But now I see that I was wrong. Have you suffered? I think surely you must have."

"All men suffer", Alex said.

Once again Oleg shrugged. Alex was beginning to realize that his physical lexicon was as variegated as Maria Sabbatino's.

Reaching for the Hopkins book, Alex said, "Now I will offer you a very difficult poem. It is a dangerous poem, for it is capable of throwing up barriers. At the same time, if the one who hears it has the key, this poem unlocks doors and throws a bridge across the void that separates one people from another."

Oleg eyed him cautiously.

Pausing, Alex realized that he had been overwhelming the visitor with a quantity of verbiage—intimate and intense verbiage—a violation of social restraint so unlike him that it gave him a pang of self-doubt.

Oleg gestured with his hand. "It sounds a formidable poem."

"It is."

Oleg smiled. "Then you must begin."

Alex read the entire text of "That Nature Is a Heraclitean Fire" in English. Upon completion he looked up and gazed inquiringly at Oleg.

The Russian shook his head sadly. "I hear faint music behind the walls, but the door is locked to me."

Alex then read his translation of a single stanza from the poem:

"Man, how fast his firedint, | his mark on mind, is gone!
Both are in an unfathomable, all is in an enormous dark
Drowned. O pity and indig | nation! Manshape that shone..."

With the foregoing works, Alex had not made near as much effort as he had with this short extract. He had called upon every fiber of creative intuition within himself—which was not an overwhelming amount—in order to translate the poem as a poem. And although he had been forced to abandon some of the dazzling juxtaposition of sounds, he had found Russian words that substituted for what was lost, retaining the meaning and much of the cadence.

He looked up and was surprised to see tears in Oleg's eyes.

The oven's buzzer went off, startling both of them. Alex busied himself with getting the casserole dish out to cool and the spaghetti noodles boiled. That done, he sat down at the table. He wondered if he should say his customary grace before meals. The Russian was clearly not a Communist, but it was unlikely that he was a Christian. It was possible he was a Jew, but more probably he was an atheist or an agnostic. Alex made the sign of the cross and prayed a silent grace. Oleg observed with curiosity.

As they ate, the visitor seemed to drop back into the realm of his private thoughts. At one point he surfaced and said, "Who wrote the last poem?"

Alex told him, then asked, "Did you like it?"

"One does not *like* dangerous things. One hates them or is fascinated by them."

"It seemed to me that the poem moved you."

"Yes. But not because I found a key. I have no key. It was as if the music came through the wall and the door without opening them. They dissolved before my eyes, and I thought for an instant that I was looking into the heart of my own people. I do not understand why this is so."

"Nor I. At least, I cannot claim to know why these things happen."

"The people were singing, but it was a song of grief. Something had died, but they did not know what it was."

Oleg said no more. When supper was finished he glanced at his watch and murmured that it was after eight o'clock and that he must leave. Alex insisted on calling for a taxi, explaining that the streets in Halcyon would not yet be sanded, and it was a two-mile walk back to the highway. When the lights of Jed's cab drew up to the curb outside, he helped Oleg carry the books to the vehicle. He gave Jed ten dollars and asked him to take Oleg to the café out on number 11, where there was a better chance of catching a ride with Toronto-bound truckers.

Oleg offered his hand. Alex shook it.

"Good-bye, Mr. Kingfisher. It is my wish that we will meet again one day."

"That is my wish also. And you must bring your wife and daughter. In the meantime, I shall have my samovar repaired."

"And I shall bring real tea."

Then he got into the front passenger seat, and Jed drove off with him.

5. A Really Boring Guy

Alex checked his watch and saw that it was only eight thirty. He felt heartened, as if his winter world had been struck by Oleg's winter world, and the collision had produced a burst of light. Then he remembered two dark things: he had hurt his only friend, and Andrew was missing. After donning parka, scarf, and boots, he walked to Saint Mary's and knocked on the rectory door. Father Toby opened it, grinned, and exclaimed, "Hey!"

"Father Toby, I—"

"Alex, come on in."

"Father Toby, I just came to apologize."

"Apologize for what? Okay, if you need to, apology accepted. But don't sweat the small stuff, buddy. I wasn't offended."

"You weren't?"

"Nah. I felt bad for you, that's all."

"Then you forgive me?"

"For slamming my car door too hard?"

"That, and for being angry with you when you were only trying to help."

"Okay, okay, buddy, if you need forgiving, of course I forgive you."

"I was wondering if you'd be interested in taking a walk with me."

"A walk? Where do you want to go?"

"I haven't hiked up in the hills since my big swim. Tonight is the first time I feel strong enough for it."

"I'd be glad to, but isn't it kind of slippery out there?"

"Sanding and salting is probably underway by now. Want to give it a try?"

"Let's go!"

The church walkway and public sidewalk were still icy, but a sand truck had passed minutes before, and they had no trouble as long as they stayed on the street. The weather was colder than it had been an hour before but warm enough for walking. There was no wind.

It took ten minutes to reach the Clementine Bridge, and they crossed the river in companionable silence. On the other side the road began to climb, and they slowed their pace for the steep grade.

"Any word about Andrew?" Father Toby asked.

"Nothing."

"That's a terrible worry, Alex. I'm praying steady for him. And for you too."

"Thanks."

"I hope you're not letting your imagination get the better of you."

"I'm not, or at least I'm trying not to. I have those sickening moments when I think the phone will ring and a voice thousands of miles away will tell me my son is dead. When I think about that, I feel as if I'll go crazy. But it passes, and then deep down something inside takes over and I know. He's in trouble, but he's alive. Somewhere he's alive. I just don't know where."

It took awhile for the two men to reach the top of the escarpment. At the T junction they turned left onto Concession 4 and walked northwest along the rim of the hills, saying little. Half an hour later they reached the highway and turned around for the homeward leg of the journey.

The snowfields were luminous blue beneath the moon. Sparks of satellites crossed paths with the blinking lights of jetliners passing so high that their roar could not be heard. The road was a ribbon of shadow ahead. Alex filled his lungs with the sharp oxygen, glad that they no longer contained the specter of pneumonia.

"How come you're feeling so good all of a sudden?" Father Toby asked.

"I had a visitor today who helped me see something. It lifted my spirits, and when that happened my body started feeling stronger."

He told Father Toby about Oleg and asked him if he could explain why the experience seemed to have affected his physical health so positively. Father Toby said he wasn't sure how it worked, but it was interesting because it underlined the connection between body, mind, and spirit.

"Maybe all those foreign books and foreign visitors give you a shot in the arm", he suggested.

"I don't get many foreign visitors. You could count on your fingers the number of foreigners I've met in all these years."

"Still, your life is kind of exotic by local standards. You've got a window that looks into a bigger world."

"A window? Maybe, but a window isn't a door."

They mused on that until Father Toby broke the silence: "D'you remember what I said last night about you not knowing who you are? It was a stupid thing to say."

"Not so stupid. But maybe we don't need to be in such a rush to figure ourselves out. Just to exist as a human being is phenomenal. Maybe all I need to know is what God allows me to see."

. "So, what do you see?"

"Well, I'm a small man, Father. And I'm a dull man. Actually, I'm a really boring person."

Father Toby laughed.

"You called me a hero, Toby. The fact is, I'm no hero. I'm a coward."

Father Toby snorted. "Come on, Alex."

"Oh, I don't deny that I jumped into the river. But that's not what I mean."

"What do you mean, then?"

"It's something else, something in me that wants things always to remain the same, always safe. It's a basic fear of life, I guess. I've never admitted that to anyone, and I guess I've never admitted it to myself, but it's the truth."

Father Toby whacked Alex on the back. "Tell you a little secret, Alex. The fact is, we're all cowards. That's the basic human material. And anyone who says he isn't, really is one. Are heroes fearless? Nah! Heroes are the guys who overcome their fears."

"Something I have yet to accomplish."

"Hiding inside every coward is a hero. He just doesn't know it yet."

"That's a fine view of humanity, Father. How beautiful this world would be if it were true."

"It *is* true. Take it from me", he laughed. "Call it the personal testimony of a scared and depressed kid who once was the biggest loser in the Clementine valley."

Another quarter of a mile passed before Father Toby spoke again.

"Can I tell you a story?" he said.

"What kind of story?"

"Something I made up. It's fiction."

Alex glanced at him, intrigued. Father Toby slowed his pace, hands in pockets, collar of his black coat pulled up around his Roman collar, black trousers tucked into black rubber galoshes. Black hair parted on the left side, immaculately shaven, clean-cut. Clean life. Every inch a good priest— but in no way a literary type.

Speaking in a tone that an older man might have used when telling a bedtime tale to a grandchild, he began:

"A long time ago in a country far away, there was a small town. It was moderately prosperous and smug, containing the usual number of winners and losers, saints and sinners. It was built on a hill, and the winners lived at the top of the hill, the losers at the bottom.

"On the top of the hill there lived a family who had it made. The father of the family had an important job, and everybody in town respected him. He had an only son. They lived in a big house full of books and art and interesting things like microscopes and toy railroad engines, and butterfly collections, and comic books from England and France. Beautiful flowers grew in the front yard. This son of theirs was so smart that everybody in town said he was going to grow up to be like his father, and maybe go on to be famous someday. He wore new shoes and sharp clothes. He was rich. He was the son of a winner, and he was going to be a winner too. He was a quiet kid, but everybody thought it was because he was superior and unique and didn't need friends.

"At the bottom of the hill there lived another boy. This kid was definitely inferior. He was not premium human stock. He was not smart. He lived in an old tar-paper house with an outhouse behind it. Potatoes grew in the front yard. His home contained no interesting things. It had a black-and-white television set that was never turned off. He had a sister, and she was inferior too. His mother and father were inferior. Nobody in the town ever called them that, but they knew that's what they were. The boy loved his mother and father very much, because they were good and they loved him. They worked hard to put food on the table. There was lots of food. His father worked in a gristmill loading sacks of grain. All his life he did that. His mother took in laundry and mending. It was straight out of a fairy tale. It was a tearjerker.

"The boy was fat. His hair was the color of a dead mouse. It was always cut close to his scalp because that saved money.

He wore horn-rimmed glasses. He looked like the fat kids in 'Far Side' cartoons. He wore patched clothes and shoes with soles that flapped now and then. His mother glued the shoes together whenever they fell apart. The boy went to kindergarten and learned that he was fat and inferior. He was the son of a loser, and he was going to grow up to be a loser. Each year, he got fatter and more inferior. His mother saved some money and took him to see a doctor. The doctor said he had a glandular problem. There was nothing he could do about it. He was a quiet kid, but everyone knew that it was because he was inferior and not unique and didn't have friends even though he needed them.

"The boy's parents were very religious. They sent him to Mass every day. Sometimes he'd go up to the church on the top of the hill and ask God to make him thin. God didn't answer him. He just got fatter. When he became an altar boy, he burst the seams of every black robe he tried on. The only ones that fit were too long for his short legs. Once, he tripped on the hem during Mass and fell flat on his face. People tried not to laugh, but they couldn't help themselves.

"One day when he was eleven years old, he decided he'd had enough. At school recess some bullies pushed him around, calling him names. They called him Pillsbury Doughboy and Michelin Man. Most of the bullies were superior human stock. Some girls were watching it, and worst of all, one of those girls was somebody he had a crush on, though she didn't know it. He lay in the snow of the school yard, trying to get up. He couldn't, no matter how hard he tried. No one would help him up. He began to cry. They stood around him in a circle, laughing. They called him Blubber Face. Then the bell rang, and they went inside the schoolhouse.

"That was the lowest moment in his life. The boy lay in the snow and decided that his life was not worth living. He hoped a tree would fall on him, but it didn't. He hoped he would freeze to death, but he had too much insulation for that. No earthquakes or plagues came to his rescue. He asked God to snuff him out, but God wouldn't do it.

"He lay there for half an hour. The teacher didn't notice him missing from the class. After a while he tried getting up again, but he managed only to roll over onto his side. He looked at the schoolroom windows. Then a face came to one of the windows, where the pencil sharpener was screwed to the sill. It was the rich kid who lived on the hill. The rich kid stared at him and stopped turning the crank of the pencil sharpener. He didn't laugh. He just looked very serious. Then his face disappeared from the window.

"A minute later the rich kid was kneeling down beside him. The rich kid didn't have a coat on. He didn't have boots on. He began to shiver. He asked the fat kid if he had fallen down. The fat kid didn't answer. The rich kid helped him to stand up. Then he helped him to walk into the school lobby.

"The rich kid said they should go into their classroom. The fat kid said no, he was going home and never coming back and nobody would ever see him again. He didn't say it to get pity. He said it because it was a fact. The rich kid thought about it. Then he said it would be sad if he didn't come back. He went down the hall to the coat racks and got his coat and boots. Then he asked if he could walk the fat kid home. The fat kid said, 'You'll get in trouble.' The rich kid said, 'That's okay.'

"They walked down the hill together in the middle of the school day, which was a criminal act. It meant adults would make you pay for it when they found out. But the rich kid didn't talk about that. He didn't talk about anything. When they got to the tar-paper house, they went inside, and the fat kid told his mother he had fallen down and didn't feel well.

"The mother was a very kind person. She made hot choco-late for the boys. Then she went back to her ironing. The rich kid said the fat kid was lucky because he lived beside the river. Did he catch fish in the river? Did he swim in it? Did he ever walk across the dam? The fat kid said no to every question. Then the rich kid asked him if he ever walked in the hills; did he like hiking? The fat kid said no, he didn't do any of that stuff. Getting out of bed each morning was hard enough. It nearly killed him just getting to school and back each day. He huffed and puffed all the way up and all the way down. But he didn't say any of that.

"The next day the fat kid decided he would go to school one more day. At recess the rich kid walked around the school yard with him. He didn't say a word. After school he asked the fat kid if he would like to come to his house. He said it was only a short walk from the school. The fat kid was scared of the rich kid's father, because the father was a very important man, and he sent people to jail. But he went anyway. When your life is over, what do you have to lose?

"The rich kid showed him a spaceship he was making with some pieces of metal and bolts called Meccano. The fat boy made a truck with them. The rich kid said he should take it home and keep it. They read comics together, but not the kind you bought in the drugstore. These were about a boy named Tintin and a runty person named Asterix.

"The fat kid decided he wouldn't die just yet. He and his friend lived happily ever after."

Alex and Father Toby walked on, saying nothing. They turned onto the road that led down into the valley of the Clementine.

"Whatever happened to the fat kid?" Alex asked.

"He got older."

"Did he ever get thin?"

"That's the surprising part. When he was about thirteen years old, the rich kid got really sick and had to go to the hospital. The fat kid was allowed to visit him now and then, a few minutes at a time. One day, the rich kid asked him if he'd ever thought about playing hockey. The fat kid said no. After a couple of months, the rich kid went home from hospital, but he was still sick and had to stay in bed a long time. He wasn't allowed to have visitors, except on weekends, and then only for an hour. The rich kid slept a lot.

"So one Saturday afternoon, the fat kid had nothing to do, and he wandered down the street to the local skating rink. He watched the strong boys play hockey. They ignored him. They just didn't see him. He didn't care if they saw him or not. He went back every Saturday to watch them, just so he could tell the rich kid he was thinking about hockey. One day, they were short a few players, and one of the big guys skated over and said, 'Hey, Michelin Man, want to play goalie?' The fat boy said okay and parked himself in the goalie net. His body stopped a few pucks just by being in the way. It hurt, but he felt good when the guys cheered.

"All that winter he went back every Saturday, and every so often they needed him to stand in the net and stop pucks. He kept an eye on what happened to pucks out there on the ice, and soon he got to know what they would do and where they would go. He learned to shoot out his leg or arm and stop them when they came his way. He developed a reputation. The guys stopped calling him names. They asked him to play goalie every Saturday.

"His parents gave him skates and a hockey stick for his birthday. That was in the summertime, but he didn't mind. He was the first man down at the rink in November, when they flooded it. He tried on his new skates and wobbled around the goalie net a little. By midwinter he had stopped falling down, his ankles got stronger, and from time to time he went out of the net toward the center line. He went night and day to the rink, whenever the ice was deserted, practicing his skating, his shots, his braking, and his back-skating.

During one game, he saved a play that would have lost the game for his side. The guys cheered, and somebody even whacked him on the back and said, 'Way to go!' No one ever again called him Pillsbury Doughboy or Michelin Man.

"Then a strange and terrifying thing began to happen. Just after he started high school, his body began to grow. It grew like Jack's beanstalk, and the fat began to melt off. It took two and a half years for it all to go, and when it was gone it turned out that Tarzan had been hiding inside of it all that time. He was shocked whenever he looked in the bathroom mirror. His father stopped buzzing his hair down to the scalp, and the pimples went away. Girls began to look at him. Girls actually began to say hi in the halls. It was bizarre. It was like a body transplant. It was like a brain transplant. No, it was a life transplant! A cosmic ray had zapped him and turned him into something else. It was a miracle."

"What happened next?"

"Well, the kid—we can't call him the fat kid anymore— went on to become so good at hockey that he made it to Junior A's. Then he got scouted for the NHL, but he turned it down. Crazy, eh? He'd decided he wanted to go to university, and so he did. Got a degree, became very popular. He made a few mistakes along the way. Didn't know how to handle all that success. Almost got married a few times, but either he or she would call it off each time. In the end he decided to go study theology, and after that he had the rest of his life. It was a great life."

"That's a wonderful story, Father Toby. I love a happy ending."

"Me too."

"What happened to the rich kid?"

"He got better and grew up too. He stayed at home and studied on his own, and after his parents died he used the money they left him to start a business. It turned out that his family wasn't as rich as everybody thought, so it wasn't a big business. But he liked it."

"Was he happy?"

"I think so. Did I mention that he was kind of a dull fellow? Well, you see, it didn't take much to make him happy."

"He was really a boring guy."

"Yup, that never changed."

Alex chuckled.

"Father Toby?"

"Yeah?"

"Can I tell you a story?"

"Sure, I'd love to hear a story. Is it a made-up one?"

"Totally."

They had reached the bridge now and turned left to cross it. Using the same tone Father Toby had used, Alex began his tale:

"Long ago in a country far away, there was a small town, prosperous and smug, containing the usual number of winners and losers, saints and sinners. It was built on a hill, and the winners lived at the top of the hill, the losers at the bottom. Saints and sinners were distributed equally."

"Really? Equally?"

"Don't distract me. Anyway, on the top of the hill there lived a family who seemed to have it made. The father of the family had an important job, and everybody in town respected him. He had an only son. People thought of him as the rich kid. They lived in a big house full of books and art and interesting things. This son of theirs was so smart that everyone said he was going to grow up to be like his father, a lawyer and a judge, and maybe go on to be famous someday. He was the son of a winner, and he was going to be a winner too. He was a quiet lad, but people thought it was because he was superior and unique and didn't need friends.

"This was not so. He needed friends badly, but throughout his short life he had learned that every time he made a friend, the problem of his richness and his important father got in the way and ruined things. His father was a big man, and the son felt very small under his shadow. He loved his father and mother and appreciated all the things they had done for him and all the fascinating objects they had given him. At one time he had thought of becoming a lawyer or a judge like his father, but he knew that if he did, people would always be afraid of him because of it, or admire him for it, and they would never really see him. He didn't like attracting attention to himself, because when people talked to him they were really talking to his father through him. He wasn't certain how he knew this, but he knew it was true. Besides, it interrupted his real life. He lived in the realm of inner thoughts, and these were his chief pleasure. He dreamed of far-off places. He walked alone along the hilltops.

"He wasn't afraid of other people. He just wasn't interested in impressing anyone. From time to time he felt lonely, though never for long. He had numerous books in which he found companions.

"One day, while walking through the town, he went into a grocery store to buy a bottle of apple juice, which he intended to take with him on one of his rambles. He had just entered an aisle lined with bottles when a girl who worked in the store entered the aisle at the opposite end. He knew who she was. Everyone knew who she was. Her name was Darla Conniker, and she was mentally retarded, as they used to say. She was the only mentally handicapped person in the town. She lived with her parents down on the flats. She was in her teens, had been taken out of school after failing grade five for the third time, and now worked as a part-time shelf stocker. A simple, friendly girl, she was big and clumsy. She was often laughed at. Most people were kind to her, but the younger set, the superior human stock, and the inferior as well, enjoyed calling her names just to watch her face fall.

She never retaliated, just went about her business as if she hadn't heard.

"The quiet boy saw that Darla was carrying a crate of pop bottles. She stumbled and dropped the crate. The bottles smashed, and Darla burst into wails as broken glass flew in every direction and liquid went running down the aisle. The quiet boy thought he should go to help her, but because he was the sort of person who must reflect a little before making even the simplest decision, he hesitated. Darla's wails became loud sobs, and she threw herself onto her knees and began picking up the glass with her bare hands.

"At that moment, another boy entered the aisle at Darla's end. He was the same age as the quiet boy. He got down on his knees beside her and began picking up the glass with his fingers. 'Don't cry, Darla, don't cry', he said to her. 'You didn't mean to do it. Don't cry, now; I'll help you pick it up.' But she cried even louder. He pulled a handkerchief from his pocket and wiped her face with it. Then he wrapped it around her fingers, which were bleeding. 'Don't cry, Darla. It's just a little accident; everybody has accidents. Don't cry.' Over and over he said it. The quiet boy watched them until Mr. Collins, the grocer, arrived with a mop and pail.

"Who was Darla's helper, you may ask? It was a fat boy who lived down by the river in a tar-paper house. The quiet boy knew who he was. He never thought of him as the fat boy, but that was what people called him. The manager looked angry, but in fact he was merely worried about the blood on Darla's hands. The fat boy stood up and said, 'It's my fault. I bumped into her. Don't fire her, Mr. Collins, please don't fire her.'

"Mr. Collins replied, 'I'm not going to fire her, son. And I don't think you bumped into her. Now, Darla, you go see Mrs. Collins, and she'll put a bandage on your cuts.'

"So the quiet boy went away and walked in the hills think-ing about what he had witnessed. Sometime after that, during the following winter, the quiet boy went to the window of his classroom one day to sharpen a pencil. He looked out the window, and his life was never again the same."

"That's the end of the story?" Father Toby asked, head down, smiling to himself.

"Yes. Did you like it?"

"A bit thin in the action department, but good characterization. Did everybody live happily ever after?"

"Yes, they did."

Father Toby and Alex looked up to find themselves standing in the street in front of the rectory. Father Toby checked his wristwatch. "What! It's almost midnight!"

"How could that be! Sorry for keeping you up past your bedtime. We'd better call it a day."

"Yeah, I guess we'd better. Good night, Worm."

"Good night, Toffee."

They gave each other a few back thumps and parted with promises that they would call each other in the morning.

6. *A Voice in the Night*

Alex woke up feeling happier than he had in months. He stretched in his bed, yawning, eyeing the shaft of sunlight bisecting the room. The sensation of contentment persisted for a moment or two, until it was shattered by the thought of Andrew's continued disappearance. Each day, the pattern was the same. A flash of peace, then a plunge into gloom as consciousness returned, and with it the full impact of his situation.

In order to delay the inevitable foreboding, he threw back the bedcovers, got up, and padded to the bathroom. After shaving, he dressed himself in his best business suit, a blue button-down shirt, his brightest tie, and socks that nearly matched. Brown loafers completed the camouflage.

He whistled a tune from nowhere, faking the frivolous sounds of a jolly burgher leaping into yet another productive day. Stepping into the living room, he knelt, said his morning prayers, and read a passage from the Bible; after that he ate toast, drank coffee, and placed a call to England.

Groves told him that the photograph had arrived and that he had passed it on to the Oxford police. They had not turned up anything yet. Not a single lead.

Alex went downstairs at nine o'clock to open the shop but was repelled by the prospect of sitting at his desk with nothing to think about other than the possibility that his son was lost somewhere in the world, unable to contact his family, perhaps in agony. The bookshop suddenly seemed a voluminous emptiness containing only the poisonous gas of irrational fears. Unbidden images raced through Alex's imagination:

bullet wounds, bludgeoned skulls, torture chambers, the scenes replacing one another in quick succession, inflating the atmosphere of helpless terror. He hastened into his coat and boots and left.

Hurrying down Oak, he turned left onto Main, covering three or four blocks without seeing any details of the street. Then he crossed at the intersection of Victoria and continued downhill on that street in the direction of the Clementine River. It would take him forty minutes to circle the town, and the final quarter of the route he intended to take at full speed, uphill, burning off adrenaline. At the bottom of Victoria he realized that he was approaching Collins' Supervalu grocery. Not knowing why, he went inside.

Darla Conniker spotted him, lumbered over, threw her arms around him, and cried at a high pitch, "Alex, howarya?"

"I'm well, Darla. How are you?"

"I'm good, Alex."

"I know you're *good*, Darla. But I asked how are you?"

This old joke sent her into peals of laughter. She stood off at arm's length, bent double, hooting. She wiped her eyes with the red grocer's apron.

"I'm a little bit sick in the tummy t'day, Alex."

"How come you're sick in the tummy?"

"I ate too much. I always eat too much. Mum 'n' me watched *Flintstones* last night. Mum says, 'Darla, let's have a brontoburger.' She made me a brontoburger. Hoo-boy! Too much!"

More peals of laughter. Two hundred and twenty pounds, frizzled gray hair, eyes like an angel, her only moral flaw an inordinate lifelong passion for hamburgers. Pure Darla.

Alex could not stop himself from smiling. She was infectious. Her mental age, somewhere between six and eight. Her biological age, maybe early fifties. Her soul status, well in advance of many a Halcyonite.

Her face fell. "After the brontoburger, Mum 'n' me said a rosary for Andy."

"Andrew? Why did you pray for Andrew?"

Darla leaned close and whispered, "Father Toby said I should pray for Andy. He got lost. He got in trouble. I pray for him every day."

Alex choked with emotion. "Thanks, Darla. He needs your prayers."

She patted his arms.

"Don't worry, Alex, don't worry. God love Andy very much. I seen him pick up Andy in his hands. Andy's sleeping."

"Andy's sleeping?"

"Yup, right between two trees. Big black one, kinda spooky, and the other one was on fire, real hot. So I says to Jesus, 'Look, Lord, that's my Andy-boy who got lost. You gotta look after him. You gotta bring him back to Alex. That's my little Andy-boy who I take on the pony rides.'"

The old mechanical horse, a plastic pinto, a dime a ride, had been removed from the lobby of Collins' grocery fifteen years ago, along with the gumball machine. But Darla never forgot the important things.

"You saw Andy", Alex murmured, resisting an impulse to shake his head.

She nodded vigorously up and down. "Uh-huh. I seen him—you know—at Mass. After Communion. And God said, 'Pray for Andy, and pray for Alex.'"

"Anything else?"

"Yup, I seen other pictures. Lots of trains. And a lake and fire in the water. And a purple fish."

"A purple fish?"

"Yup. There was lotsa other fish. Black fish. And orange fish. And a pinto fish."

"A pinto fish?"

"The lady of the river touched that one and made it gold."

Alex, rational Catholic that he was, and son of rational Catholics, was ever nervous about mystical phenomena. But he had learned early in life to extend a certain attention to Darla's "pictures". During the darkest moments of his near-fatal rheumatic fever, Darla, age eighteen or so, had appeared at the front door of the Graham home one afternoon, knocking insistently until Alex's mother answered.

"I gotta see Alex!" Darla had informed her.

When his mother explained that the doctor wasn't allowing visitors, Darla pleaded, "But I gotta see him!"

Mother stood firm. "I'm very sorry, but you can't."

"But I gotta, I *gotta!*"

"I said no, dear."

Frustrated, pouting, Darla thrust a bag of jelly doughnuts into Mrs. Graham's hands and said, "This is for Alex. Tell him he ain't gonna die. Jesus said he gonna grow up and be a big man."

"Oh Darla", his mother had said. "Thank you so much for the doughnuts. But Alexander is very ill."

"Yup", Darla said. "But he ain't gonna kick the bucket. Tell him he gotta walk. He gotta climb hills all the time till he get strong."

She turned on her heels and trotted off with a wave of her hand.

Alex, flat on his back, heard about what she had said when his mother related the story to Dr. Hendricks outside the bedroom door. They thought he was sleeping.

"She hears voices, does she?" Hendricks said irritably. "The poor Connikers. They've got their hands full with that girl."

"She's a sweet child, Doctor. Perhaps she has intuitions about things that most of us miss."

"She's more than retarded, Mrs. Graham. There are symptoms of schizophrenia. Did she want to visit your son?"

"Yes, she seemed quite insistent."

"It wouldn't be wise at this stage. It might build up false hopes."

Any further knowledge of his fate was veiled to Alex by a stifled sob and muffled consultation. Nevertheless, he knew Darla was God's messenger.

She was too ridiculous to become the resident fortune-teller, too much the fool to become the oracle of Halcyon. She had tempers and fits of depression, no doubt about it. But she loved Jesus and children and cats. She had conveyed more than a few uncanny messages during the ensuing years—and not only to Alex. Toby, for instance, had been informed in his thirteenth year that he would one day cease to be fat. Resigned to the inescapable fate of inferiority, he had stared at the messenger as if she were mocking him, though her own girth softened the blow. But he remembered her words. Others in town had received harsher cryptograms from on high, but these were easily blown off by those who did not want to hear.

Alex, however, had taught himself to walk again—in fact, to walk as he never had before. The summer following his release from the prison of bed, he began to do secretly what never would have been allowed if his parents had known: uphill and downhill he trudged for hours every day, week after week, month after month, year after year. As he gained strength he ventured ever farther into new territory, impelled by a preternatural sense of rightness, an irrational certainty that obedience to Darla would stand him in good stead one day.

Standing now in Collins' grocery, decades later, all he could do was to ask her to keep praying for Andrew. She promised she would. They said good-bye, and Alex went out onto Victoria Street feeling a little dazed, pondering her pictures, making no sense of them. At the base of Victoria, he turned left onto Riverside and increased his pace. Farther along he came to the iron gates of the cemetery, paused, and then went in. Passing through a forest of crosses, madonnas, and angels, he tromped through heavy snowdrifts and arrived after considerable effort at Carol's grave by the riverbank. He read the inscription on the tombstone for the thousandth time, noting also his own name and birth date beside hers. The only information missing was the date of his death.

Then he read the poem she had asked him to put on the stone, lines from her beloved Emily Dickinson:

> This quiet Dust was Gentlemen and Ladies,
>   And Lads and Girls;
> Was laughter and ability and sighing,
>   And frocks and curls.
> This passive place a Summer's nimble mansion,
>   Where Bloom and Bees
> Fulfilled their Oriental Circuit,
>   Then ceased like these.

She had insisted on the poem. Insisted most of all on the three deer inscribed in the granite above the text. As always, they danced in a circle, surmounted by a cross.

Other memories flooded in. An early conversation before their courtship had begun in earnest:

"You really should listen to this, Alexander", she said, her eyes dancing as they read their books side by side on the park bench by the dam, their knees almost touching. Golden maple leaves drifted through the sky in whimsical circuits, and bees lingered in the autumn heat.

"What did you say, Carol?" he murmured, tearing his eyes from Thucydides on the Peloponnesian War.

She stuck her face close to his, pushing her volume of poetry on top of his book. She was so clownish and so pretty that it took his breath away. He cleared his throat. "Could you repeat that, please?"

She laughed. "Read this. It's much more interesting than hopletes."

"Hoplites", he corrected.

"Read it!" she pleaded.

He read it. Dickinson again, birds and wind and feelings. It all rhymed. It rhymed too much.

"Very nice, Carol."

Grinning, she jumped to her feet, gathered an armload of leaves, and threw them at him. Sputtering, he dropped his book and stared at her. Then, on an impulse, he scooped up some leaves and hurled them back. She ran. He chased her. It ended with their first kiss. Short, pure, utterly intoxicating.

Years later, one evening as she nursed three-month-old Andrew in the rocking chair by their bed, a somber reflective look played on her features. He was stretched out beside her reading Josephus' *The Jewish War*, relaxing after a busy day in the shop. She began to croon to the baby, and it broke his concentration.

He watched them for a while, then tried to focus on the text.

"Can you read me something, Alex?"

"Okay." He scanned a few pages, then began to recite: "'Where is the mighty city? Where now is the city that was believed to have God for her Founder? She has been torn up by the roots, and the only memorial of her that is left is the camp of her destroyers that still occupies her ruins! Old men with streaming eyes sit by the ashes of the Shrine—'"

"Something gentler", she interrupted.

"Gentler?"

"Some poetry."

"Emily?"

"Yes, Emily."

He found her big volume of the collected works and opened it at random. More birds and bees and feelings. He began to recite, dryly.

"That's okay", she interrupted, nuzzling the baby's downy skull with her lips. "You don't have to read."

"Sorry. It's hard to concentrate. I'm not always sure what she's talking about."

"Poetry isn't *about* things, Alex. It's not a book of facts."

"I know—"

"It's a window—a window inside you. Or maybe a poem opens the window. Yes, it's like that. Into a bigger universe, with fresh wind and horizons that you can't see the end of." She began to croon again. He closed the Dickinson and laid it on top of Josephus.

Kissing, kissing, gently kissing the child's sleeping face.

"This is the poem", she whispered. "This is the poem."

She had loved. She had asked little of life and given everything. Longing for many children, she had taught him to long for them also, and in doing so had helped him to believe in life's victory over death. But a quirk of biology had not let her have them—the cancer after Andrew's birth, the damaged organs, the long remission, then the final blow.

Now at her grave, Alex began to talk to her, but not as if she were there beneath the blanket of snow; rather, he spoke as if he had arrived at a station where communication was likely, at the place where her body waited for the reunion of flesh and spirit. Resurrection morning. The Last Day. The day when all the ache of human weakness, all unfairness, all damage would be lifted up into the light of restoration.

Did she hear him? It seemed a nebulous zone of theology. Or had it been defined? He wasn't sure. Maybe angels carried messages to heaven, just as they seemed to carry them to earth. Regardless, he spoke to her about everything he had felt since Andrew's disappearance.

"Where is he, Carol? Are you watching what's going on? Are you allowed to see us? We had so much together, my love. They were wonderful years. Even the times when you were ill. But I always thought it would be me who would go first. Why is life so seldom the way we think it will be?

"I was twenty-one years old when we married. We had seventeen years of joy, and then four hard years, and now it's five years since you were taken."

As always, Alex righted the tumbling universe into a fixed order by the assertion of measurement: numbers, sizes, volumes, masses, enclosures of space, lapses of time.

"I'm forty-seven, Carol, and I miss you so much. I can't bring you back. But if you're somewhere near God, ask him to bring me to you soon. I'm finished. I can't hear you or see you. I can't touch you. I can't find Andrew, and I hardly know Jacob, and I think I've made a mess of life. I don't know what to do."

Then he wept the kind of silent tears that only grieving men know.

After that he retraced his steps, arrived at the Kingfisher, and opened the shop for another day's business.

Father Toby phoned at lunchtime to see if there was any word from Oxford. Alex told him that the photograph had arrived and had been given to the British police. Father Toby said he would not stop praying until Andrew was found.

There were few customers during the afternoon. Several children came in around four o'clock, looking for titles their teachers had recommended. Helping them search through the shelves filled the bleak hour before sunset, dulling the ache that was now becoming chronic. When he found the shop deserted just after four, he decided to close early and went upstairs.

Too tired to make a meal for himself, he stretched out on the bed, dozed off, and slept. He was waked by the ringing of the bedside telephone. Glancing at his wristwatch, he noted that it was just after six o'clock. He groped about and lifted the receiver.

"Hello", he mumbled.

At first the line only hummed and crackled, with faint conversations bleeding through the wires. Then came the muffled sound of people laughing, followed by low background babble.

"Who is this?" Alex asked. "Who's there?"

"Dad?" said a quiet voice.

"Jacob?"

"Dad, it's me."

Alex shot upright in bed and swung his feet to the floor.

"Andrew!"

"I . . ."

"Where are you? Are you all right?"

"Yes, I'm fine."

"Why haven't you called?"

No answer.

"Son, are you there?"

"I'm here." But only just there, for the voice was so weak that Alex strained to hear it.

"Where have you been? You've got to phone Tyburne and let them know where you are."

A long pause.

"I can't do that."

Now an ominous suspicion began to infiltrate Alex's mind. The voice was Andrew's yet unlike Andrew's, for it was subdued, guarded, giving away nothing.

"Are you in trouble?"

"No."

"But where are you?" Alex insisted. "I've been worried sick about you."

"You shouldn't be."

"Are there people with you? Can you speak freely?"

"I can speak freely."

"Then talk to me, Andrew! What's going on?"

"Dad, you wouldn't understand."

"Are you a captive?"

"No. I'm not a captive."

Lurid scenarios flashed through Alex's mind. "If someone's there pointing a gun at you, making you lie, just say something that would sound normal to them but would be absurd to you and me. Ask me to give your mother a kiss."

"It's not like that."

"Then you're really all right?"

"I've never felt this happy before..."

Alex pressed the phone receiver so tightly against his ear that it began to hurt.

"Tell me! Please tell me the truth: are you all right?"

"I'm very, very well. Dad, it would be hard for you to grasp what I've found. It's probably the most important thing happening on the planet."

"What is so important that you disappeared from school and your family without a word of explanation?"

"If you could see what I'm seeing, you wouldn't be so worried. Someday...maybe someday you can join me."

"Where? Where can I meet you?"

"For the time being, that's not possible. You see, this is the initial stage of ascending."

"Ascending?"

"Yes, I'm part of it, and very few people are this privileged. To ascend with the convergence is..."

"Convergence? What do you mean, *convergence*?"

"It would be impossible to explain it all now. Soon the whole world will know."

"Andrew! Where are you?"

"I have to go."

"Go where?"

"They don't like us to use the phone system. It's vulnerable."

"Vulnerable to what?"

"To planetary entropy."

"Planetary entropy?" Alex repeated slowly.

Silence.

"Is it because *they* don't want you talking to other people?"

"Yes. I really shouldn't, but I thought you'd be worrying."

"I *am* worried. You're not telling me anything."

"Dad, you've got to stop being afraid all the time. Just trust me. I'm involved in something much bigger than all of us, something far better than—"

"Who are *they*, Andrew?"

"I have to go now."

The line went dead.

Stunned, disbelieving, Alex stared at the receiver.

He pressed the o button. When an operator came on the line, he told her that he had just received an anonymous call and wanted to trace the number from which it had been placed. She told him to hang up, promising to call back in a few minutes.

Face in hands, rocking slightly on the edge of his bed, he waited. When the phone rang, he grabbed it off the hook. The operator told him that the anonymous call had originated in England. Did he want her to contact the British Telephone System for further information? Yes, he did.

He listened while she conversed with an overseas operator, growing more impatient when the inquiry was passed on to another department, then another. A third English operator told the Canadian operator that the call had been made at a public phone in the village of Cricklewood.

"Where is Cricklewood?" Alex interjected.

"In Berkshire", said the English voice.

"Can you please tell me, what is the closest city?"

"I believe that would be Swindon, sir."

"Is it anywhere near Oxford?"

"Yes, Oxford is also close to Cricklewood."

"How far?"

Submitting to interrogation was apparently beyond the normal requirements for personnel giving information; the English operator's voice cooled noticeably.

"I couldn't say for certain. An hour's drive, perhaps. Oxford is to the north of the village; Swindon is to the west. Is that all?"

"Sir, would you like to ring the party?" the Canadian operator asked.

"Yes, please." Alex checked his watch. It was now almost twenty minutes since Andrew's call.

The British operator made the connections, and Alex listened to a phone ringing in the night in a distant land, in a place he had never seen or heard of. A place with its own history and inhabitants. Including, possibly, *they*. After ten rings the receiver was lifted from the hook, then replaced, terminating the call.

"That number does not respond", said the English operator.

"There's nothing more we can do", said the Canadian operator. "You might try again by dialing the number yourself, sir." She gave him the Cricklewood number, which he jotted down on a pad of paper.

"Thank you, operator."

He tried dialing it again, but this time there was no answer. Frustrated, more worried than ever, he got up and paced about the room.

At least Andrew was alive, and more or less coherent.

But *ascending*? *Convergence*? *Planetary entropy*? What did that mean?

Cricklewood? What on earth was Cricklewood? It was probably one of a thousand little places in the British Isles, each with its quaint name, each containing its quorum of *they*s.

Andrew, Andrew, where are you? What has happened?

He tried calling the number three more times that evening, with no response. He spent a sleepless night, tossing and turning, and praying, but nothing would quell his agitation.

At seven in the morning he realized it was noon in England. He dialed Tyburne College and got Groves on the line. He told him that Andrew was alive and had contacted him but that the conversation had been bewildering. He mentioned the unusual words Andrew had used: *convergence, ascending,* and *planetary entropy.* Groves did not know what to make of it. He promised to contact the police and assured Alex that he would ask that an investigator drive down to Cricklewood to see what could be found, if anything.

After sunrise, Alex phoned Father Toby and related what had happened. Father Toby was perplexed, though he suggested something that had also crossed Alex's mind.

"The terms Andrew used sound a bit like esoteric religion. I wouldn't want to jump to conclusions, Alex, but he might have gotten involved with one of those English movements."

"You mean New Age psychics or something like that?"

"On the other hand, maybe he's just off on a tangent— astronomy or philosophy, or any number of quite legitimate things. I suggest you sit tight and see if the authorities find his trail."

Alex spent the rest of the day totally distracted, his mind thousands of miles away from the selling of books. More than once, customers pointed out that he had given them too much change.

He closed the shop early and went to five o'clock Mass, offering it for Andrew, begging God to bring the boy to his senses. Boy? Andrew was a man now, legally independent, fully within his rights to remain out of communication. After the closing hymn, Father Toby came down the aisle to Alex's pew and asked if he had heard anything more.

"Nothing." Alex shook his head. "Not a word."

"Want to come into the rectory for a cup of coffee?"

"No thanks", Alex said. "I'd better get back to the shop in case there's a call from England."

He was just unlocking the front door when the phone began to ring. Shedding coat, keys, and boots as he dashed down the hall, he picked up the receiver on the seventh ring.

"Hello."

"Mr. Graham?"

"Yes, yes, this is Alex Graham."

"This is Detective Helm of the Oxford police."

"Have you found Andrew?"

"I'm afraid not, sir. I did drive down to Cricklewood earlier today—it's a bit of a drive, you know. We've turned up a few facts. But they're not really conclusive."

"What did you find?"

"Well, your son was there last night. He rang you from a pub in the village. Cricklewood is a small place, rather off the beaten track. It's the crossroads of one of the back roads that cut across the Berkshires and one that comes down from Oxford. About two dozen houses, all told. It's a center for the surrounding twenty or thirty miles. There's not much in that region except sheep farms and badgers."

"Did anyone see him?"

"The proprietor of the establishment recalls a young man who came in around eleven. It was after closing time, but the locals had a darts competition going on, and the place was crowded. We're assuming the young man was your son. His description certainly matches the photo you sent. No one paid much attention to him, but he did order fish and chips for four, to take out. The woman who took his order thought he was an American. She identified the photo positively. No one came in with him. While his food was being made up, he placed a call from the pay phone."

"Did she say whether or not he had been in before?"

"I asked her that because it could indicate he was living in the region. But she didn't recall seeing him before. However, I did check elsewhere in town. While he was in the pub, it appears, the other people he was with were buying petrol at the station next door."

"Then their car can be traced."

"Unfortunately, no. The owner of the petrol station didn't note the license number, and the driver paid with cash, you see. However, I did find out that the vehicle contained four people. One, it seems, was your son, another a young man of about the same age, a young woman, and an older man at the wheel. The owner of the station was reasonably certain they were all foreigners, except for the woman. He thought the driver might be German or Scandinavian. The other young man was Indian or Pakistani. When your son returned from the pub, he said something to the others explaining the delay in getting the food, and his accent sounded North American. People usually assume that means from the United States."

"And that's all you've learned?"

"We know that the car was a late-model, dark blue Mercedes."

"Can it be traced?"

"That would be a monumental task. There must be thousands of vehicles fitting the description in the United Kingdom. And we wouldn't want to undertake that kind of search unless there was clear evidence that a crime had been committed." He paused. "Your son is twenty-three years old, I take it?"

"That's correct."

"Well, it's not as if he were a minor. He is of legal age to do as he likes, and I'm sorry to say that includes not calling home as often as he should."

"So you've ruled out any possibility of his being abducted?"

"If he had been abducted, Mr. Graham, he wouldn't have been allowed to go into the pub, and certainly not unaccompanied. And in the unlikely event that he found himself separated from his captors, he surely would have asked someone for help. As it stands, he seems to have bought them fish and chips."

"Yes, that's true."

"So, you see, from my perspective, there's really no evidence that anything criminal has occurred. Your son is alive, and appears to be in good health and in his right mind. There's nothing more we can do. I hope you understand."

"Mr. Helm, is there a possibility that he has been brainwashed?"

"Brainwashed? What, by a cult, you mean? I suppose it's a possibility. But even if that were the case, there would be nothing we could do about it. Membership in religious associations isn't illegal, and however much one may dislike their ideas, anything they do short of infringement of freedom of action is outside police jurisdiction."

"But I've heard so much about what these cults do to people's minds."

"Quite so. However, such cases are very sticky and nearly impossible to prosecute, because the victims almost always defend the very people who seduce them into the cult. We have no way of proving anything."

"Have you had any personal experience with such cases?"

"A little. The cases ended inconclusively. I should point out also that most cultic activity is in the larger cities, though it sometimes springs up in the environs of prehistoric monuments. Stonehenge, for example, or Findhorn. Berkshire is rather quiet in that regard."

"I see."

Nonplussed, Alex stared at the floor, shaking his head.

"Mr. Graham, are you still there?"

"I'm here."

"I'm sorry, sir. It must be a great worry for you, but there's really nothing more we can do."

"Nothing at all?"

"If anything untoward should happen, I expect it will get back to us. Until then, we have to consider it a dormant case."

There was no more to say, but Alex clung to him.

"Dormant?"

"On the records, but sleeping."

"What do you mean, *sleeping*?"

"Mr. Graham," Helm said in a decent but firm voice, "this is long distance at our expense. I'm afraid I have to ring off now."

Pacing back and forth throughout the house, Alex grew more frantic by the minute. In the end, he forced himself to undress and got into bed. Nothing would bring sleep, however, and even his prayers seemed to be no more than scraps of empty words, disconnected, rambling, fired in the direction of a silent heaven, unable to escape the force of gravity.

Long past midnight the bedside phone rang, startling him out of a half sleep.

"Dad, it's me."

Once again the low voice came through the wire, just above a whisper, something dark and diseased flowing into Alex's room along with it.

"Andrew! Where are you? You *must* tell me where you are!"

"I have to..."

Alex waited, but Andrew did not complete the sentence.

"Please, son, I'm dreadfully worried about you."

"We're going away."

"Where are you going?"

"To the nucleus of all spiritual energy."

Horrified, Alex now realized that whatever had captured Andrew was indeed spiritual. Moreover, it was taking his son away.

"Don't go", he pleaded. "I'm begging you, don't go!"

"I have to go." Now the tone was wooden.

"Why do you have to? Is someone making you go?"

"No. It's not like that."

Searching frantically for anything that would keep Andrew on the line, a handhold, a lifeline, a thread, Alex blurted:

"Tell me about the two trees!"

There was a pause, and then Andrew said in a puzzled tone, "Two trees?"

"Were you sleeping between two trees, a black tree and a tree on fire?"

"Oh. Yes, I see what you mean. The tree of knowledge and the tree of life. Good and evil. It's a symbol, Dad. It's what we're doing. Not the old biblical myth, but the real thing, what mankind's been waiting for all these ages. The light and the shadow are one. But...but how did you know about the trees?"

"Darla told me. She said you're in trouble."

"Darla?" he replied dreamily, as if reaching for a vague memory.

"You know who Darla is!" Alex cried into the phone. "Darla! She gave you pony rides."

"Oh yes. The pinto. I was in the pinto last night."

"You were in a Mercedes last night, Andrew. A dark blue Mercedes."

"How did you know that?" A flicker of interest, but the volume fading.

Alex was just about to tell him everything when he heard another voice, faint, as if it came from behind Andrew: "Who are you talking to?"

Silence. The hum of transatlantic wires.

"It is not permitted", the voice said, so far away that Alex barely made out the words. Deep, carefully articulated, the accent foreign, the *r* rolled.

Suddenly the line went dead.

Alex tapped the o button. Hoping to repeat the minor victory of the preceding day, he retraced his steps through the telephone systems of two countries, only to be told that the call had been placed at a pay phone in London. He jotted down the street address of the booth.

He dialed the number, and let it ring twenty times before hanging up.

At the break of dawn Alex got up and dressed. He went to the 8:00 A.M. Mass, and afterward, when Father Toby joined him on the front steps of the church, he related the details of the latest phone call.

"I'm going over there. I've got to find out what's happening to him."

"Fly to England?"

"Yes. I'll go today."

"Are you sure, Alex? Maybe you should wait. If the police—"

"The police! They can't do anything. They told me so themselves."

"Then what do you think you can accomplish, even if you do manage to find him?"

"I don't know. But I have to try. I have to talk with him face-to-face. Maybe he'll listen to me."

"All right, if you have to go, you have to go. I'd probably do the same if I were in your shoes. But it's pretty short notice. What will you do for money?"

Alex's heart sank. Money!

"You don't have any money, right?"

"I'm afraid not. I just paid all the bills, and the cash in the till wouldn't amount to more than a couple of hundred dollars."

"I can lend you some."

"No, I couldn't accept it. You're as poor as a church mouse."

"All too true."

"I'll think of something."

"The ticket will cost a fair bit. I can give you what I have, which isn't much—I've been helping my folks pay off their condo. I think I can scrape together four hundred dollars. But even if we pool our resources, it still doesn't make enough for the airfare. Don't you have a credit card?"

"I've never needed one."

"I've never needed one either."

"Well then, I have no alternative but to go talk to Charles."

Father Toby frowned. "Do you have to? What about Jacob?"

"He's up to his ears in debt."

Both men folded their arms, thinking.

"Yes, I'll go to the bank", Alex said, tightening his lips. "I'll get a loan."

He turned on his heels and went quickly down the street in the direction of Main.

As usual, when Alex entered the Clementine Valley Credit Union, he sensed that he was entering an old and honored institution, a cornerstone of the region's stability. For a man who had rarely traveled beyond the valley, it seemed to be one of the great power points on the planet. He had always done business there, his single share (mandatory for account holders) entitling him to the minor status enjoyed by all. But now, nervous and embarrassed, he had come with hat in hand to beg.

Waiting at the end of the hall that led to the executive offices, he rehearsed what he would say to Charles, choosing the wording carefully so as not to offer him anything that would feed his reputed appetite for details about his customers' private lives. Doubtless, Charles garnered far too much of that by perusing the checking accounts, where the spending habits of Halcyon were exposed to his analytical eye.

"Listen, Charles," Alex composed, fighting a temptation to bitterness, "my son has been captured by a dangerous band of fanatics and is being whisked off someplace in search of the nucleus of all spiritual energy. I must find him and rescue him if I can. I want to leave today, but my account is empty. Can you give me a bucket of money, please?"

Definitely the wrong approach.

"Charles, I've just received word from England that my son is not well, and I must fly over to be with him. Unfortunately, I'm caught a bit short at the moment. Would you consider giving me a loan?"

A much better approach.

Glancing about, Alex saw that he was still citizen of the month. He looked away. A moment later, a secretary led him into the spacious office of Charles Findley Jr., general manager. Charles rose from behind a vast teakwood desk and greeted Alex warmly with a shake of the hand.

"Al, great to see you! Sit down, sit down over here by the fireplace."

It was a real fireplace, burning real applewood logs. A real Irish setter snoozed in front of it. When they were seated across from each other in two leather armchairs, Alex began to feel uncannily as if he were a shabby foreigner.

"Can I get you some coffee?" his host offered.

"N-no thanks. I—"

"You sure? How about a hot toddy?"

Alex shook his head. Charles beamed at him, exuding a perfect blend of friendliness and good business sense.

"What can I do for you today, Al?"

"Charles, I've just received word that my son is not well, and I have to fly over to England to be with him. Unfortunately, I'm caught a bit short at the moment. Would you consider giving me a loan?"

"I'm sorry to hear it. I hope it's not serious—your son, I mean. Andrew, isn't it?"

"Uh, yes, it's Andrew."

"A fine young man. You say he's unwell?"

"I'm not sure just how unwell he is. I think I should be there with him."

"How large a loan were you interested in, Al?"

Alex shook his head and looked at his hands folded on his knees. He had forgotten to think about that.

"You're not sure?"

"Now that you mention it, I'm not."

Charles smiled. "You'll need the plane fare, won't you? And hotels and meals. How long are you intending to stay over there?"

"I don't know. It will depend on..."

On whether or not I find my missing son. On whether or not the nucleus of all spiritual energy is a fixed point on the compass and is, in fact, a findable place.

"It'll depend on his health", Alex said shortly.

"He may or may not take some time to recover?"

"Yes."

Charles crossed his legs and gazed into the fire. He reached down and scratched the ears of his dog.

"I see no problem. No problem at all. We'd be glad to give you a loan. But I guess I should ask, how is your credit rating?"

"I'm not sure what a credit rating is. I don't think I have one."

Charles smiled paternally. "Oh, I'm sure you've got one. I'll check on that and get back to you in a few days."

"A few days?" Alex said, alarmed.

"Yes, that's the ordinary procedure. It's just a formality."

"Excuse me, Charles," Alex said, leaning toward his host, "but the situation is really urgent. I need to go today, if I can get a seat on a plane."

Charles' face grew solemn. "I see. It's that serious, is it?"

"Yes. It is."

"If I recall correctly, you don't have any credit cards, at least not with us."

"None. Not with you, not with anyone."

"That makes it more difficult. However, you are a share-holder and a longtime account holder with no record of irre-sponsibility." Charles chuckled indulgently. "So I think we can waive the usual rigmarole. How about we give you a line of credit?"

"Thank you so much. I'd really appreciate it."

"Now we need to discuss how much to lend you. Plane fare will probably be around eight or nine hundred. A few months ago I took a lady friend of mine to London to see a play, so I know how pricey it can get. Then there are the taxis and hotels and meals. It can add up pretty fast. I think you're looking at a few thousand dollars, maybe more if you have to stay longer—hotels, fees to rebook your return flight, that sort of thing."

"That's a lot of money", Alex murmured.

Charles nodded sympathetically.

"I suggest we transfer three thousand in credit into your checking account, just to be on the safe side. I think we can do it this morning without any fuss and bother. Of course, we'll need some collateral."

"Collateral?"

"Yes, something that will stand as a promise of repayment, if through no fault of your own the loan defaults—no pun intended." A smile.

"Oh, I see. What do you suggest I use as collateral?"

"Your car?"

"I don't drive."

"Ah. Well, anything else of value, I suppose."

"The books."

Charles looked pained. "How much do you think they're worth?"

"The collection is worth a hundred thousand dollars at the very least."

"That's impressive." He firmed his lips, pondering. "The problem with books is, they're not really considered a liquid asset—I mean, an asset that can be readily liquidated for cash."

"Actually, Charles, I've supported my family for twenty-five years by doing just that."

"Yes, but it took twenty-five years, didn't it? That's the problem, you see. The board of directors would think it rather cavalier of me to approve a loan on that basis. The value of books tends to depreciate, especially used books. They can be redeemed for money only in dribs and drabs over long periods of time. I'm afraid I'm under certain constraints, despite our long friendship, Al."

Our long friendship?

"So, you see, we'd need something more solid as collateral."

"Solid?"

I thought you wanted liquid!

Looking mildly irritated, but controlling it, Charles said, "Solid that will liquefy at need."

Alex knew what was coming but decided to let Charles do his own dirty work.

"Al, you might want to consider your property on Oak. As a building it's not really worth much, but the land may be valuable someday. We would consider it as collateral. Real estate is in a slump right now, so its market value is low, but I think we can accept your property as a pledge of security to protect our interests."

Squirming inside, trying to keep his face blank, Alex saw everything that could go wrong. What if it took a long time to find Andrew? Suppose he couldn't make the loan payments. He might lose everything.

Charles stared at the fire again, scratching the dog's ear. It rolled over onto its back.

"I guess I have no choice", Alex said at last.

"It does seem your only option at this time."

"What if I'm delayed over there? What if I have trouble getting back in time to get the business bringing in money again?"

Charles wrinkled his brow. "If that were to happen, you could call us from overseas and apply for an extension of funds."

"I could lose my house and business, couldn't I, if I were unable to make the payments?"

"A very remote possibility. So remote as to be practically unthinkable. Rest assured that the credit union is here to serve you, not the other way around. We're not a bank. Our borrowers are our shareholders. *You* own the union. If you find yourself in a financial crunch, you just contact us, and we can transfer additional loan funds directly into your account. Of course, we have to start charging interest from the word go." He sighed. "That's the world of finance, Al. It's how the thing works. It's how it all keeps rollin' along."

"I guess it is."

Alex had a few terse thoughts on that subject but decided this was not the moment for debate.

It took an hour. When all the papers were signed, he went home to locate his checkbook and to make some phone calls. The travel agent over in Maplewoods found him a seat on a flight leaving that night from Toronto. Alex dug out his passport from the shoebox in which he kept useless official documents. Then he packed hastily, throwing a few items of clothing into an old gym bag, and some reading material into a shoulder bag.

He also decided to wear his grandfather's heavy tweed coat, which he felt might communicate an impression of stability to his unstable son. He also chose his favorite wool scarf, the blue-green Graham tartan. As a last thought he rummaged in the poetry section of the shop, where he found the hardcover volume of Hopkins' selected poems and letters and a cracked paperback edition of the complete poems. He stuffed them into the shoulder bag and ran to answer the ship's bell that Father Toby was clanging with a certain urgency.

They drove over to Maplewoods to pick up the ticket, and from there they doubled back to Highway 11 and turned south. The journey seemed longer to Alex than it really was, the two-hour drive dominated by a growing fear caused by a mixture of his desperate worry over Andrew, his apprehension at leaving beloved Halcyon, the lowering darkness of winter dusk, the uncertainties of the journey ahead, and the increasing insecurity on every level of his life. Father Toby's encouraging small talk and helpful hints for international travel could not dispel the feeling that he was about to enter into disaster.

7. The Safety of the Cage

Premonitions of disaster are not terror, and thus Alex was able to abandon himself to the experience. He had never before flown on an airplane, and he was not afraid of death. He was, however, mildly disturbed by the front-page headlines in the newspaper a stewardess had given him, dire warnings about another terrorism alert. North American intelligence agencies had uncovered plots to sabotage flights to Europe during the coming forty-eight hours. Alex supposed this was the reason why so many of the seats around him were empty.

He reminded himself that airports were well protected by security measures and that he was riding in a vehicle designed by experts and piloted by experts, with a long history of proven dependability, and that more people died crossing streets in New York City than in airplane disasters. Of course, this might be a lie propagated by airline companies. Perhaps thousands died each year, flocks of humans blasted out of the skies by the shotgun of fate, plummeting to earth, littering the landscape like dead passenger pigeons.

Waves of snow and air, wakes of roaring engines, and sea lanes of phosphorescent light ripped past the disk of window, his body pressed against the seat, strapped in, his heart hammering faster while a massive city shrank into a toy model beneath him, the frail metal tube tilting up, up, up, and he knew only one thing—he knew that eventually it must invert the trajectory and go down.

When the tube leveled off above the clouds, the roaring declined to a steady hum, and Alex's ears popped. He righted his inner gyroscope by rummaging in his bag for something to read. His hand hit one of the Hopkins books and pulled it out. His eyes alighted on "The Caged Skylark".

Man's mounting spirit in his bone-house, mean house, dwells—

And further on:

> Both sing sometimes the sweetest, sweetest spells,
> Yet both droop deadly sometimes in their cells
> Or wring their barriers in bursts of fear or rage.

"To rise, you must abandon everything," Alex said to himself, "most of all the safety of the cage. But first you must see the cage for what it is."

He sighed and put the book away. The energy required for esoteric poems was, for once, outweighing the comfort they provided. The accumulated sleeplessness of the previous two days began to take its toll. He fell into a light doze for a while, but it did not last. For much of the eight-hour flight, he was in and out of consciousness. There was some bad weather over the mid-Atlantic, and from then on he sat staring out the window at nothing until the sky turned red in the east.

When the jet's wheels hit the surface of Britain, Alex yawned and stretched and regarded what could be seen from the little window as the aircraft taxied toward Heathrow terminal. After the plane halted and the doors opened, he was the last passenger to get off.

Inside, a customs agent took one look at him, asked if he had anything to declare, and waved him through without checking his baggage. He walked out into the lobby and stopped short when he saw two hundred people staring at him. Many held signs that read "Claridges", "Windsor House", "London Hilton", and the like; there were a few bowler hats and swallowtail coats, several saris and burnouses, a single

Japanese kimono, and the usual variety of modern Western dress. Several races were represented in the welcoming party, though most appeared to be Anglo-Saxon. Disoriented, unsure of what to do next, Alex wandered through the lobby searching for an information booth. When he found one, he asked the East Indian woman at the desk how he could get to Oxford. She gave him directions, then sent him off with a wink.

The England of Alex's imagination was confirmed by the weather. When he exited Heathrow's main terminal building, he penetrated a fog that was turning into drizzle. Mercifully, only a few steps away he found the route to the trains, and assisted by courteous English people who gave him directions, he boarded one that took him to London. Arriving at Paddington Station, he purchased a ticket for the final stage of his journey.

The train for Oxford departed at ten. As it navigated through the city, Alex was amazed by the size of London. He noted also the faces of people in his carriage, most of whom probably had always lived in England, oblivious to the existence of Halcyon, the precise center of the world. Among the passengers were some whom Alex took to be hardy farmers, and others who were undoubtedly academics, and, of course, several young men out of their minds with love, scribbling in journals or on letter paper. There were more-sedate students hunched over books, as well as businessmen who looked as if they had been cloned from Charles Findley. There were rounded country women with dyed hair and plastic shopping bags resting on the scuffed toes of their running shoes, sighing with each other over the weighty matters of matchmaking and rural politics. Also present were serene old men who had seen more than one war, and tense young men who were longing for a new one. There was a bearded, disheveled eccentric muttering to himself, though he was restrained, Alex supposed, by

English social protocol. And there were children who looked as if they had just returned from Narnia.

The rolling countryside began to appear as the fog thinned. Puzzle pieces gradually coalesced, clippings of farm fields, sheep grazing on pastures, white swans drifting on a canal. A rail station crowded with Africans in native garments ripped past, followed by a ridgetop castle that glided by slowly, then more fields, more hedgerows, more villages clustering beside streams and bunched in dips of the terrain, picketed by winter trees. A Norman church, a factory, three children bending over a stone fence to see the speeding bullet, waving their red hands. Laundry flapping. Signals of the rail system. Ding-ding-ding-ding, Doppler effects and crumbling brick abutments. Bridges crossed, tunnels bored, daggers of blue horizon appearing, more water, more sheep on more fields, the grids of hedgerows and the groves of oak.

A superhighway veered close to the rail line, darted under, and continued northward on the other side. Countless matchbox cars rocketed past at speeds faster than the train's.

More farms, villages, and copses of winter trees.

More children standing on stone fences, waving—*I greet, I greet, I greet you!*

Alex wondered if they were flattening pennies on the rail. He recalled a nonsense rhyme that Andrew had loved as a child.

> Bobby on the railroad
> Picking up stones,
> Along came an engine
> And broke Bobby's bones.
> "Oh!" said Bobby. "That's not fair!"
> "Oh", said the engineer. "You shouldn't be there!"

Andrew had sung it and skipped to it for years, never failing to laugh at the punch line. Alex had puzzled over this.

Whenever he analyzed it, the ditty seemed to him a choice for justice over mercy. Considering that it was about a child who got a rough deal at the hands of an adult, a system, and a great big powerful machine, what was so funny?

Had it offered Andrew a glimpse of himself caught in a moment of folly? Perhaps when he had laughed at the stubborn little boy who ignored the lessons of reality he was really laughing at himself, for he knew deep down that he often behaved like Bobby, that he too was capable of foolish things when driven by his own tiny, dynamic will.

Jacob had always been annoyed by the song. His sympathy was entirely with the engine and its driver. Jacob knew about engineering. He did not laugh about the ditty, and never had. It now occurred to Alex, northbound on an English train, that he might have been wrong about his two boys. As a young father he had often been concerned about what kind of man Andrew would grow up to be, and never worried about Jacob. Andrew's devil-may-care approach to life was latent with danger. Jacob's seemed destined for stability. Sensible Jacob would not break his parents' hearts.

Though it seemed to Alex that Andrew was fulfilling the early premonition, he was now struck by a parallel worry, one he had not considered until this moment. Jacob too was Bobby. And the problem of the will became more difficult to the degree that the elder son was unable to feel amusement at himself, which implied that he felt no need for correction. If the pursuit of his will were to become a grave and sensible business, he risked becoming incapable of laughing at himself, and thus less able to know himself, and in the end that much more a slave to himself.

Alex wondered why he had not seen this before. Had he worried so much over the weaknesses in Andrew's character that he had not given near enough attention to Jacob's? He had failed both of his sons, it seemed.

In the early afternoon, Alex walked out of Oxford Station. He looked toward the city with a mixture of apprehension and anticipation, the former chiefly due to the fear that his journey would prove fruitless, the latter to his wonder that he was now standing in one of the great cultural centers of the world. Ancient spires and stone towers crowned the skyline. Students with long trailing scarves whisked past him. Unidentifiable birds squabbled beneath the shrubs. Black humpbacked taxis drew up to the curb, antique in design but shining new. It was like stepping back through time: turn one way, and you were in the thirteenth century; turn another, and you were in the 1940s; turn another, and it was the modern age. Yet it was a medieval city at the core.

Despite the urgency of the tasks ahead, he felt a thrill of recognition. This sensation was not so much the result of the photographs of Oxford that he had seen as it was an ethos permeating the very atmosphere and upon which the city had been built. Oxford was a community of scholars, people who were dedicated to books, studied from them and taught from them, built their lives on them. There were dozens of colleges here, most of them hundreds of years old, several of them founded more than seven centuries ago. Alex stood at the station entrance for a few minutes drinking it all in, regretting that it had taken a crisis to bring him out of his safe little world. From this perspective it was difficult not to feel that Halcyon was an isolated backwater.

He hailed one of the black taxis and asked the driver to take him to Tyburne College. When he offered a slip of paper on which the address was written, the driver waved it away.

"Don't need it, sir. I know every house in town. I'll have you there in ten minutes."

Tyburne was located in the southeast corner of Oxford, by the Cherwell, one of the city's two rivers. It was on Saint

Clement's Street, a tributary of High Street. Magdalen College was a five-minute walk north along High, just on the other side of Magdalen Bridge. The driver pointed it out as they passed. He called it "Maudlin".

The car turned off Saint Clement's and passed through an open gate into a cobblestone courtyard walled on all sides by the Tyburne compound. Alex paid his fare, got out, and stood gazing up at the main building, a three-story brick edifice of seventeenth-century design, only five years old. He climbed the steps to the front entrance and went into a brightly lit foyer, his shoes clicking on shining parquet floors. Directly in front of him, on a wall between two floor-to-ceiling windows, there hung a life-size Gothic crucifix of polychromed wood. To the right was an annex containing easy chairs, a coffee table, and a full bookshelf. To the left, a corridor led to what Alex supposed were classrooms, the chapel building, and a refectory. The smell of cooking food came from that direction, mingled with the sound of conversation echoing faintly off the walls. He went down the corridor, seeking its source. A few paces along he came to an office wicket where two men were in discussion behind the counter.

"Excuse me", Alex said.

They turned toward him with expectant faces. One was an elderly priest in a Roman collar, tall but bent, his eyes watery blue, tufts of white hair springing from the sides of his nearly bald head. The other was middle-aged, shorter, dark haired, round cheeked. He was wearing a checkered black-and-white blazer and a knitted blue tie.

When Alex introduced himself, both men leaned forward with expressions of surprise and concern. One of them was Father Turner, master of the house, and the other no less than its secretary, John Groves. As they shook hands, Alex asked if there had been any news of Andrew.

"I'm afraid not", Groves said. "Father Turner spoke with the police again this morning, and they told him there is nothing more that can be done at present."

"That's what they told me also", Alex replied, shaking his head.

"We feel quite badly about all this, Mr. Graham", the priest said. "We've been over it again and again with the students, especially those who are Andrew's friends. No one seems able to remember a single thing that could offer an explanation."

Alex began to sink into his own thoughts. The two men observed him for a moment; then Father Turner asked if he had had lunch.

"Not yet", Alex murmured. "I'm not very hungry."

"Would you care to join us at table? Won't you at least have a cup of tea?"

Alex thanked them and said he would.

They led him farther down the corridor to a refectory that was a long room with high ceilings and wall-to-wall glass on one side. Capable of seating a hundred, it was half-full with students scattered at tables in groups of threes and fours. There was a high table on a raised platform at the end of the room, and a large facsimile painting of Holbein's *Thomas More* on the wall behind it. Here Father Turner and John Groves seated themselves with Alex between them. A cheery atmosphere pervaded the room, with much animated conversation at the tables.

A waitress brought three meals on a trolley, and Alex suddenly reversed his decision about not eating. As the old woman served them, Groves thanked her in a pleasant way, while Father Turner asked about her health and jested a little to get her laughing.

The priest prayed the blessing, and they began to eat what appeared to be a typical English lunch—fish and chips, a plate of white bread, and an unappetizing pudding that Groves urged upon Alex.

Father Turner smiled sympathetically. "John, I'm sure poor Mr. Graham is suffering from culture shock. Leave him be."

The two men bantered for a few minutes, but Alex's attention wandered toward the windows, which overlooked an herb garden, pruned ornamental trees, and a branch of the Cherwell.

Where are you, Andrew? Why aren't you here?

"Have you found a place to stay?" Father Turner asked.

"Not yet. Can you recommend an inexpensive hotel?"

"Unfortunately, there is no such thing as an inexpensive hotel in Oxford. You could try one of the bed-and-breakfasts in town, but if I might suggest it, you are more than welcome to stay with us, since Andrew's room is unoccupied."

"That's very kind of you, but I don't want to inconvenience you."

Taking his cue from the priest, John Groves said, "We really don't know how long it will take you to locate your son. If you're forced to stay on, it could get horribly expensive. Do consider it, Mr. Graham. You would be our guest, and it would free you to rove around and take your proper time at it."

"That would be a great help to me. I'm afraid my budget is rather tight."

"Then it's done", Father Turner said with finality.

While Alex ate his pudding the priest turned sideways in his chair and began to write in a notebook. He tore a sheet of paper from it and gave it to Groves.

"John, this is a list of Andrew's tutors at Magdalen. Can you connect Mr. Graham with them, arrange some appointments? One of them may be able to throw light on the lad's thinking during the past few months."

"I'll get to that straightaway", Groves said.

Alex felt his tension begin to ease. Something was being done. He was not alone.

Father Turner put a hand on Alex's shoulder. "It's not much to go on, but it is a first step and may lead to unexpected answers. We'll do whatever else we can to help."

"Thank you—thank you very much."

Father Turner stood. "I have to go prepare for a class now, but I expect we'll see each other at tea. John will show you the ropes and get you settled in. Please feel free to call me if you need to discuss anything."

Alex stood, thanked him again, and watched the old man walk out of the room. Students greeted the priest as he passed their tables, and Alex saw that he was regarded by them with a mixture of great respect and affection.

"Father Turner is very kind", Alex said.

"Yes, he is", Groves said. "An altogether rare sort of man. You wouldn't think it to look at him, but he's one of the world's foremost historians of the Reformation. He has three doctorates—history, law, and philosophy. He studied under Gilson, Maritain, and a mob of other names. He's brilliant and quite uncanny at reading students' minds."

"I wonder what he thinks of Andrew."

"He did say last fall, just before end of term, that he had noticed Andrew was not attending daily Mass."

"Was he especially worried about it?"

"Yes, I think one could say that. You see, although students are often unable to attend everything at Tyburne, for various good reasons, when it becomes a pattern we begin to feel some concern."

Alex pondered that. "Did Andrew stop attending Sunday Mass?"

"No, not exactly. I mean, he stopped attending here at chapel. I believe he was going to Mass somewhere else, probably over at the Oratory church. As for our daily Mass and evening prayers, they aren't mandatory, though we do encourage the students to attend as frequently as possible. We're not a boarding house; our reason for existence here is primarily to provide a spiritual *pied è terre* in a very secular environment."

"A refuge."

"More accurately, a home away from home for young Catholics. But they are men, after all, not boys. So we presume a certain maturity and freedom of choice in the spiritual life."

"I see. And you think that Andrew was drifting away?"

"I'm not certain about that. Father Turner sensed that it might be the case. When your son started to drop out of the liturgical life of the house, Father asked him about it. Andrew told him that his academic schedule made it difficult for him to attend. He said he was going to Mass at the Oratory. We took him at his word."

"Do you think he was telling the truth?" Alex asked carefully.

Groves shifted uneasily in his chair and looked down at the table. "Yes, I think so."

"I think so too. My son is an honest person. Although he can be erratic and undisciplined, it would be totally out of character for him to lie."

Groves looked back at Alex and did not reply.

"Mr. Graham, why don't I show you Andrew's room?"

Groves insisted on carrying Alex's gym bag upstairs to the third floor, where they turned right and entered the residential wing of the college. The corridors were floored with cinnamon-colored tile, the white walls were unembellished, and at the end of the hall a marble statue of the Blessed Virgin gazed maternally at Alex and Groves. In an annex containing twelve oak doors, they stopped in front of Andrew's room— 3-12. A card in a slot beneath the number read "Andrew Graham". Penned in red ink below the name was a maple leaf. Groves unlocked the door and let him in.

"Here we are, Mr. Graham. I'll leave these duplicate keys with you. This one's the room key, this one's for Andrew's storage closet, and this one will let you in the front door. We lock up at eleven every night, but if you forget your keys and are caught out after hours, you can always ring the bell. My rooms are just beside the office, and I'll let you in."

"Thank you so much, Mr. Groves."

"Please call me John."

"And I'm Alex."

"Righto, Alex. Now you must let me know if you need anything. I'm always about the place, and as Father Turner said, we want to do whatever we can to help. The WC—that's toilets and showers—are down the hall. Make yourself at home."

When he was gone, Alex shut the door and looked about the room.

It was approximately ten feet square and contained a single bed, a recessed wardrobe-closet, built-in bureau drawers, a desk, and a freestanding bookshelf. The window overlooked the gardens and river, and beyond them lay a series of meadows. Alex started when he thought he saw an antlered stag cross a sward of grass, then disappear into a stand of trees. For a man from the New World it was a scene of great beauty, a modern Camelot. Moreover, for a man who had never been to university it was almost shrinelike. Here was a true academy where the best minds of the world sought truth.

Tearing his eyes away from the window, Alex scrutinized the contents of the room. The desk to the right of the window was cluttered, but there seemed to be a kind of order to it: piles of notes, another pile of textbooks and pamphlets, a computer and printer, stacked trays of blank paper, envelopes, pens, pushpins, and other stationery. A cork bulletin board on the wall above the desk was crowded with schedules, photographs, and notes. Alex wanted to go through it right away, but he reminded himself that the Tyburne staff had doubtless sifted it carefully, and he needed to rest.

He lay down on the bed and fell asleep. Three hours later he awoke to a rap on the door and the sound of a bell ringing softly in the distance.

"Mr. Graham? Alex? Are you awake?"

Bleary eyed, Alex opened the door to see John Groves smiling at him.

"Catching up on lost sleep, are you? Good. Do you feel ready for a spot of tea? I have a few developments for you."

Downstairs in the refectory, Groves told him that he had contacted the Oxford police and informed them that Alex was in town and staying at Tyburne. He had also arranged a meeting for him with some Magdalen professors later that evening.

"If you could go to the visitor's desk in the Gatehouse at about nine o'clock, they'll meet you there. Also, I've rounded up a few of the lads here. Andrew's chums." Groves checked his wristwatch. "We're getting together with them fifteen minutes from now. They want to meet you, and I expect you'll have a few questions to ask them as well."

"Do they know anything?"

"I think they're as perplexed as we are. However, it's possible they'll recall some detail that could provide a lead."

"I hope so. I truly hope so. You called them Andrew's chums. Are they close friends?"

"I shouldn't say close. But your son was well liked. He was one of our shiners—academically, that is. The students here are all heavily loaded with studies, so social life is not a big part of the average day."

"Was there anyone who knew his comings and goings?"

"I expect they all know each other's comings and goings to some extent. But it isn't as if their every move is watched. As I said, they're fairly busy, and so a student could go his own way without people noticing. If anyone knows Andrew well, it's a lad by the name of Perce Trainor. He'll be joining us after tea. You could ask him."

They met in a lounge beside the office on the main floor. Groves led Alex into the room and introduced him to the half dozen young men who were standing around waiting for him. He shook hands with each of them: three Englishmen, one American, one from Northern Ireland, and the youngest of them all, a man from Nigeria. Distracted, worried, Alex did not catch their names. They all sat down on chairs and sofas.

The American was outgoing and vocal, as were two of the Englishmen. These three were like Andrew in temperament, and it did not surprise Alex that they were his son's friends. The other Englishman was a withdrawn, scholarly type. The Irishman was acerbic, with a lightning wit that made the others laugh despite themselves. The Nigerian was serious, soft-spoken, and self-effacing.

John Groves told them about the current status of the search for Andrew, which was, in short, that they had very little to go on. They remained silent, studying Alex, perhaps wondering what their own parents would have felt if they had been in the same situation.

Alex asked if they had noticed anything unusual about Andrew's behavior during the previous few months. None had.

Were there any people he was seeing regularly outside the college?

"As far as we know, only his tutors at Magdalen", someone replied.

Had any unusual visitors come to Tyburne asking for Andrew?

They all shook their heads.

At an impasse, Alex could think of nothing more to ask. The uncomfortable silence was broken by a student who entered the room, books in arm, apologizing.

"Sorry'm late." His accent sounded vaguely Australian.

"Ah, Perce", Groves said. "Come and meet Andrew's father."

The newcomer thrust out his hand. He was a ruddy, sturdy fellow in blue jeans and a rugby sweatshirt emblazoned with the letters of a club in Auckland, New Zealand.

"Perce Trainor, Mr. Graham. I'm sorry about what's happened. Is there anything we can do to help?"

"I'm hoping to find information that could point to Andrew's whereabouts."

He repeated the questions he had asked the others, with the same results.

"How well did you know my son?" Alex asked.

Trainor thought before replying. "We're mates, I'd say. My room's beside Andrew's, so we got to know each other a fair bit. He's a good lot, your son, Mr. Graham, so I can't for the life of me figure out why he's disappeared."

"Did he ever discuss a girlfriend?"

"No. He didn't have a girlfriend. I guess none of us here do. Not for lack of trying." Everyone chuckled. "He was interested in a girl from Saint Hilda's College for a few weeks last October; she takes a class at Magdalen with us. But that didn't last too long; she got engaged to another fellow."

"Was he very disappointed?"

"Oh yeah, but nothing he'd kill himself over."

"Kill himself?" Alex repeated uneasily.

"Sorry, I didn't mean it like that. He was taken with her, all right, but it came and went fair quick. For a couple of weeks it was Romeo and Juliet, the Bridge of Sighs, but it was all one-sided. She wasn't interested. It was unrequited to the max."

"It was platonic", explained one of the outgoing Englishmen.

"Prototypical", said the Irishman.

"Mythopoetical", said the graver Englishman.

"Pandemic", said the American.

Suddenly they were all smiling ruefully, all except Groves, Alex, Perce, and the Nigerian.

"Straighten up, lads", Groves said. "This is not a joking matter."

"Sorry, Mr. Graham", said Perce. "They're just poking fun at themselves. You see, it was the kind of thing that hits everyone at one time or another. Powerful stuff, but it doesn't last, and you get over it. Andrew was back to his old self within a week. We laughed about it, him and me."

"You're saying it wasn't in any way an experience that depressed him."

"No, nothing like that."

Looking around the circle, Alex asked if they recalled hearing his son speak about strange philosophical or religious ideas or use unusual expressions.

None of them did.

Alex then went on to describe his last telephone conversations with Andrew. The students grew serious again when he recounted the odd phrases Andrew had used.

"Nucleus of all spiritual energy?" Perce said with a frown. "That doesn't sound like Andrew."

"Sounds kind of New Agey", the American suggested.

"And what did he mean by 'planetary entropy'?" the Irishman asked.

"Literally, it means the breakdown of the material universe, specifically the planet earth", interjected the grave Englishman.

Turning to him, Alex asked, "What do you think he meant by 'ascending with the convergence'?"

Furrowing his brow, he replied, "One could develop an exegesis, I suppose. Ascension, for example, has different meanings for various religions."

"Mr. Farnsworth is in graduate philosophy and dabbles in theology", Groves explained to Alex with a small smile. "Give us an exegesis, would you, Eric?"

"Well, it's just a guess, but I'd say that the juxtaposition of the words *ascending* and *convergence* indicates an interest in transcending the material order. That's not necessarily unorthodox, because Christianity is quite concerned with both ascension and unity..."

He went on at length, losing most of the listeners in the room, until Groves interjected:

"Do you mean that the expression Andrew used isn't necessarily a sign that he's fallen in with a bad lot?"

"It's hard to say. You see, the word *convergence* may not be what *we* mean by the term: the cosmos moving toward a restoration of the divine harmony God intended from the beginning. The widespread loss of genuine metaphysics has fostered a host of aberrations, and into the vacuum all sorts of perverse metaphysics are now pouring..."

He was about to lose them again, when Alex asked for clarification. "What would it mean, then, if he has fallen in with a bad lot?"

"Convergence in their cosmology might mean a dissolving into a single entity. In other words, he may have fallen into a nest of monists."

"What is a monist?" Groves asked.

"One who believes that all reality is a single, organic whole with no independent parts. Therefore, in their view all divisions are illusion."

"Sounds like Hinduism t'me", said Perce.

"Esoteric Hinduism and Buddhism have monistic elements", Eric replied.

"So, are you saying Andrew might have become involved with Eastern religion?" Alex asked.

"It's a possibility. But there are all kinds of monists running about these days. And not only in Asia. They do a brisk business here in England. And, I daresay, in America."

"Can you give me an example?"

"The occult movements. Also many of the mind-control cults."

"Dear God", Alex breathed.

"Monists like to try to reconcile the irreconcilable", Eric went on. "They're fond of redefining good and evil. In the worst cases, they advocate a marriage of heaven and hell."

"Excuse me", Perce interjected. "What Eric says is true, I'm sure. But there's no evidence that Andrew's got himself involved with any of these groups. No evidence at all. People use bad expressions all the time, even ordinary blokes like me. It's just part of the culture."

"Like *vibes*", the Irishman suggested.

Eric replied: "You've got a point, Perce. People use cultic phrases for all kinds of harmless things: *vibes* for feelings, 'psychic powers' for intuitions, *karma* for coincidence and fate, et cetera."

"Which leaves us where we started", John Groves said. He stood. "Alex, is there anything else you want to ask?"

Alex shook his head slowly. "No. But I would be grateful if you could let me know if anything else comes to mind, anything at all that might provide a hint of where my son has gone. No matter how small."

In subdued voices the students promised that they would and filed out of the room talking among themselves. Groves left also, leaving Alex alone with the Nigerian boy.

Boy? It was difficult not to think of him as such, for he looked no more than eighteen years old, and his luminous face was childlike to the point of sweetness. Short, slender, dressed in a white T-shirt, slacks, and sandals.

"God is watching over your son, Mr. Graham", he said. His diction was perfect, the accent cultured, educated British, containing the faintest hint of Africa. "Many are the sufferings of a father's heart. God himself is the Father of all, is he not?"

Alex nodded in agreement, then asked: "Are you a student at Tyburne?"

"I am in residence here, completing my doctoral thesis in theology."

"And you knew Andrew."

"We spoke together many times. I am very fond of your son. He is a good young man."

Thankful for a word of merit in Andrew's favor, Alex felt the cloud of foreboding lift a little.

"I'm glad you think this of him", he said.

"His aspirations are noble. He is a person of the heart, is he not?"

"Yes, but that heart of his has often got him into predicaments. It may be the cause of his present troubles."

"It may be so. Yet I wonder which is the greater danger: to be a fine intellect without a heart or to be a fine heart without an intellect."

"He is not without intellect."

"This is true. But he is at times ruled by impulse. He is young."

Alex looked at the smiling youth before him, wondering how he could make such a statement.

The Nigerian stood and said with an authority beyond his years, "I will pray for you to be at peace as you search. My sense is that this difficulty is for a purpose."

"A purpose?"

"It is within the plans of the Father's will. He will bring good from it. Trust in this."

Humbled by the maturity of this young Christian, Alex could only offer his hand in farewell.

At seven o'clock he went into the empty chapel and knelt in approximately the same spot he was accustomed to in Saint Mary of the Angels. He was momentarily distracted by the beauty of the architecture, which was based on a seventeenth-century design by Christopher Wren. The lighting was subdued, and the tabernacle was in the center of the sanctuary, with a vigil lamp flickering beside it. He wanted to pray, but the cumulative effect of exhaustion, worry, and the crowding together of too much new experience made concentration difficult.

A few minutes later, the young men whom Alex had just met entered from a side door and knelt in the front pew. Shortly after, three or four more students joined them. One of them said an introductory prayer aloud, an intercession for Andrew Graham; then they began to pray the rosary in unison. Alex found his rosary in his right-hand pocket and prayed with them.

·

8. *A Triad of Sages*

At eight thirty he went out onto Saint Clement's Street and turned north. The weather was still chilly, the winter sky starry above the obscuring city lights. Despite the lateness of the hour (or more accurately, despite its being an hour that would have been late in Halcyon), the streets were full of cars. Students, most of whom seemed blessed with vigor, good looks, and the earmarks of keen intelligence, strode briskly in several directions. Alex began to feel not only very tired, but old.

Even so, the night air revived him a little, and he quickened his pace across Magdalen Bridge, which traversed the Cherwell. Looking down to his right, he saw rowing punts tied to a splay of docks at the farthest bank. Above them towered the fifteenth-century buildings of Magdalen College.

The entrance to the college was a door in the Porter's Lodge at the extreme left of the Gatehouse, a three-story stone building extending along High Street from the bell tower. Alex explained his business to a man behind the visitor's desk.

"Oh yes, Mr. Graham, I was told to expect you. Follow me, please."

Partway along a paneled hallway, the porter rapped on an oak door, opened it, and nodded Alex inside.

Three men were seated in overstuffed chairs, conversing with each other. The air was full of smoke. Pausing their discussion, they looked up. Each of them was dressed in an appropriately tweedy fashion, one brown, two gray. One of the grays was about thirty years of age; the other two men were well into their sixties.

"Hello, I'm Alex Graham."

They stood and greeted him. Hands were shaken, a pipe unmouthed, a pair of reading glasses removed. Three pairs of eyes inspected him as the introductions were made. Their expressions were not unfriendly, but Alex saw in them a distance caused by their status, their erudition, and the fact that their lives were full to the brim with people. He understood that the meeting would be courteous but impersonal.

For no accountable reason, the image of Darla Conniker flashed across his mind. He uttered a short laugh. There were no Darlas on this campus, he thought, and laughed again. Then he told himself that laughing for no good reason was a poor way to make a first impression. What had caused it? Was it the stark contrast between the corridors of this institution and the aisles of Collins' grocery? Had it torn open an old grievance—privilege, unfairness, riches, and poverty—strewn it across the spectrum of human existence as if an ontological bomb had exploded in the remote past, leaving debris that defied explanation, refuted justice? Perhaps in the face of it, one could only cry or laugh.

The professors gazed at him curiously. Then the oldest, introducing himself as Professor Whitfield, invited him to sit down on an embroidered chair that looked as if it belonged in a museum. The chair seemed too delicate, but Alex did as he was asked.

The three Englishmen muttered to each other about tea and buns in some obscure ritualistic manner known to them all but opaque to their guest. The youngest, a don named Kebble, went to a sideboard and poured tea. When they were all settled in a semicircle, the tea ceremony moving along properly, Alex listened to more preambles, trying to fix in his mind the alien categories they presented to him: it seemed they were all doctors of their fields and all "fellows" of Magdalen, but one was a don and two were professors, and this combined with other terms such as *lecturer* and *tutor*, left him confused about the hierarchy in the room.

Whitfield leaned forward and began.

"Mr. Graham, we understand that you are looking for your son, who has disappeared. The people at Tyburne have asked us to discuss with you any thoughts we might have on his state of mind since he arrived here last autumn."

"Yes, I would be grateful for anything you could tell me. So far, I don't have much to go on, and your insights might give me a clue."

"A clue", said Hewlitt, the other professor. "That sounds rather like a mystery story. Do you suspect foul play, Mr. Graham?"

"No, actually, I don't. At least not in the sense of crime."

"Are you implying some other kind of foul play?" Kebble asked.

"Perhaps", Alex said.

They listened attentively as he described Andrew's two cryptic telephone calls.

"This occurred *after* his failure to return to Tyburne in the new year?" Whitfield asked.

"Yes. My fear is that he may be involved with some kind of esoteric religious group and has gone off with them."

Whitfield leaned back in his chair and tamped his pipe. He relit it from a large box of wooden matches emblazoned with the image of a swan. He took two or three puffs, staring at the ceiling, lost in thought. Then he turned to the others.

"Dr. Kebble taught your son philosophy. Dr. Hewlitt had him for English, and I for history. Combined, our fields cover a fair amount of a man's thinking. Let's start with you, Kebble."

The young don cleared his throat. "Yes. Well, I should begin by saying that Andrew was—forgive me, *is*—a good student. By no means the best we have this year, but brighter than average. He mastered the subject without too much difficulty. His papers were well written and often contained insights that surprised me."

"Why did they surprise you?" Alex asked.

"They revealed a mind that was truly interested. Occasionally I had to sit back and think about a point he was making, and more often than not had to agree with him. He could dazzle, but the dazzle was in fits and starts, you see. Like so many of our North American students, his education was spotty, lacking in systematic coherence. But the raw material of his mind, if you will, was highly motivated. I sensed someone who had aptitude, an *appetite* for truth. I thought he could very well achieve some distinction in the field, if he applied himself."

"Did you sense in his writing any preoccupation with religious thought?"

Kebble pondered the question. "Not really. Now and then he would compare the medieval philosophical world view to the monistic religions of the East, but there was nothing unusual in that. It wasn't unconnected to the material we were covering."

"Did he seem to favor an Eastern world view?"

"No, I wouldn't say so. My memory may be a little hazy, but my impression in retrospect is that he always took the scholarly approach."

"He was detached?"

"I would say so."

"Not overly fascinated by the subject of monism?"

"I think that is the case—he was objective."

Alex saw Kebble hesitating.

"Was there anything in his behavior that concerned you?"

"Well, I must say his academic year is now seriously in question. He has fallen a fair bit behind. And there is the question of missed appointments. I am still waiting for two papers from him that were due before the Christmas break."

"Can you tell me about his attitude?"

"Yes. That is an aspect that may be useful. When he arrived at Magdalen, he was like many of our students, terribly enthusiastic, excited to be here, asking more than his share of questions at each session, arguing ideas, offering rather a lot of qualifications to my points, et cetera—that sort of thing. It's quite normal. Usually students settle down fairly quickly, pick up our pace, learn the ropes of rational discourse, so to speak. And of course your son fell into the pattern. But in November he became silent."

"Silent?"

"Yes. It was as if he was listening, yet not listening. He stopped arguing altogether, stopped asserting. His work was still good. But his mind seemed elsewhere."

"I was told that he fell in love about that time", Alex said.

Kebble raised his eyebrows. "Did he? That would explain it, then."

Hewlitt intervened at this point. "Actually, I don't think it does. The young lady Andrew fell in love with was in my graduate seminar. I watched it happen, and then I watched it peter out. I've seen it countless times, Mr. Graham, and it was a classic case. It occurred in early October and came and went like a passing storm. He seemed quite all right after that. I doubt his disappearance is connected to it."

"Are you sure, Professor? What do you know about this young lady?"

Hewlitt looked chagrined. "She is indefatigably faithful to such things as schedules, appointments, and prayers in chapel. She is not an outstanding student, nor is she in the least drawn to the mysterious East. She is engaged to a young Anglican divine, and they seem very happy."

"I see."

Whitfield said, "Hewlitt, can you tell us about his approach to your material?"

"I would say his performance in English was very much as Kebble describes it. A bright mind, a little erratic, and of course the spotty grounding—no offense, Mr. Graham; it's the North American handicap." He said it with a smile. "He was obviously well read, better read, in fact, than other foreign students I've taught over the years. But again, and I say it with respect for the young man, there was a lack of systematic coherence in his thinking."

"That's fairly typical of this generation, wouldn't you say?" Whitfield said, pointing his pipe stem at Hewlitt. "Regardless of their origins."

"I suppose you're right", Hewlitt admitted. "Though we don't want word of that to get across the Atlantic."

The three Englishmen chuckled conspiratorially.

Hewlitt continued: "You asked about Eastern religion, Mr. Graham. And I can see why you're asking. The terminology your son used in the phone calls seems to indicate some new vocabulary in his life, one drawn from the esoteric. My field in English is the medieval period, but I also teach the Elizabethans up to the Romantics. There is very little there that would inflame a young fellow in the direction of cultic religion. Some of the Romantics dabbled in it, of course, but they remained essentially men of sensuous mood and dream—Coleridge hinting at mystery and magic, Wordsworth playing the poet-prophet. It was the spirit of the age. Their writings were undoubtedly works of genius. However, you couldn't categorize such writing as serious religious thinking."

"What about Blake?" Whitfield said.

"Yes, there is Blake." Hewlitt paused, musing. "Definitely, there is Blake." He looked down at his hands folded around his teacup, as if he were trying to recapture an elusive memory.

"Yes, that may be it", he said, looking up.

"Have you thought of something, Professor?" Alex asked.

"Possibly. In the normal course of studies, it would have meant little or nothing. But..."

"Perhaps you should trot it out, Hewlitt", Whitfield said.

"I had a disagreement with your son around mid-November. He had submitted a paper on the role of idealized communities in medieval and Elizabethan literature. He used More's *Utopia* and Bacon's *The New Atlantis*, connecting them to poetic works such as Spenser's *The Faerie Queene* and Malory's *Le Morte d'Arthur*. He handled this material quite ably. But he kept leaping all over the map, pulling in various utopian visions from Plato to Blake. I told him that we would read Blake toward spring of this year and that he was getting ahead of himself."

"How did he respond to that?"

"Suppressed displeasure, to put it mildly. He became a little heated, pushed right up to the boundary line of disrespect."

"That is quite unlike Andrew", Alex said. "I'm sorry."

"Please, do not worry, Mr. Graham. It happens. But my point is this: it was an indication that he needed to develop a certain academic discipline. That is, he needed to focus."

"I think what Hewlitt means", Whitfield said, turning to Alex, "is that unless a student learns a period in depth, and restricts himself to it, it is all too easy for him to jump to conclusions. He brings to his subject *a priori* opinions. He becomes enamored of his own pet theories and fails to learn from the scholars who have gone before him."

"I see. So you're saying my son was guilty of this?"

Hewlitt replied. "*Guilty* is too strong a word. It's not a moral failing, merely an immaturity in understanding what we're about here. We not only teach a body of information, you see; we also try to impart some methodology. Without those skills, students tend to go off on a thousand tangents."

"You say he referred to Blake", Whitfield pressed. "What did he think of him?"

"As I recall, he quoted him several times in his paper—extracts from *The Marriage of Heaven and Hell* and *All Religions Are One*. I wasn't happy about it."

"Why weren't you?" Alex asked.

"Mainly for the reason I already mentioned—he was getting ahead of himself. But also because he was quoting Blake out of context. He had no real understanding of Blake's times. I faulted him for it, and he didn't understand why. I see now that he must have been more interested in larger questions—metaphysical questions."

Whitfield turned to Alex. "Are you familiar with Blake, Mr. Graham?"

"I've read some of his poems, especially *Songs of Innocence*. As Professor Hewlitt says, he is metaphysical."

"Quite", Whitfield said abruptly. "The problem with him, however, is that he liked his spirituality hot, without any of the cool reason of organized religion, and without its moral constraints."

Hewlitt shot him a reproving glance: "You're a bit out of your field, aren't you, Whitfield? Blake's complex irony is often misinterpreted."

"I understand his irony. It's his fearful asymmetry that bothers me."

For no more than a second, the two professors locked eyes. Then they both glanced away and assumed the neutral expression that Alex, though he was unfamiliar with British university life, recognized as an attempt to maintain a veneer of academic objectivity. The veneer was thin, and for several minutes the learned men continued to exchange words as if there were no others present.

"Blake was making a valiant effort to respiritualize England", Hewlitt said in a dry tone. "He despised the 'dark Satanic mills' of the Industrial Revolution and what they were doing to mankind."

"Yes," Whitfield countered with matching dryness, "and he reacted in so totally subjective a manner that the dark Satanic mills have been succeeded by the brightly lit Satanic laboratories of our times."

Hewlitt looked irritated. "Blake longed to build the New Jerusalem 'in England's green and pleasant land'. Why would you quarrel with that?"

"My quarrel is with his arrogance, not with his desire for the heavenly city. Men cannot build the New Jerusalem."

"That remains to be seen. In the meantime, we now live in a dialectic of genuine progress. And Blake was one of its forerunners, a new mystic, unconstrained by the stultifying forces of structured religion."

"Dear me, Hewlitt, are you really saying that the world could be saved by Blakean mysticism? Surely there is nothing so much in need of rational constraint, of wise laws and prudence, as mysticism. Mysticism without reason is like a nuclear reactor without safety measures. Call it progress if you will, but it so often becomes a Chernobyl."

"Hyperbole, Whitfield, sheer hyperbole! Your Celtic origins, no doubt."

"No doubt. But I think you would agree that the high mystics of the Enlightenment have played God for several generations now, trying to build their versions of the New Jerusalem. You may have noticed that England is no longer pleasant."

"But it *is* still green!" Kebble inserted, trying to break up his sparring colleagues. No one paid him any attention.

Sensing an old dispute between the two senior professors, Alex tried to bring the discussion back on track. "When did Andrew write this paper?" he asked.

"That would have been in early November", Hewlitt said, turning to him with relief.

"And how did he behave after that?"

"In a way similar to what Kebble observed: he fell silent in class."

"What about his written work?"

"His papers remained technically competent, above average. But it seemed to me that the heart had gone out of them. I felt some regret over that, wondered if I had handled the boy properly."

The four men contemplated their empty cups. Kebble jumped up and went for the teapot.

"None of us would have done it differently, I expect", said Whitfield. "It seems to me that hindsight makes prophets of us all."

"Indeed", said Kebble. "Still, one can only wonder how deeply he *was* affected by people like Blake."

"There is no way to tell at this point", answered Whitfield. "For all we know, he won the Irish Sweepstakes and flew off to Monte Carlo. For some people that is the nucleus of all spiritual energy."

The joke fell flat.

Alex turned to Whitfield. "You taught him history?"

"Yes. I found him to be likable, intelligent—an able student. He came here with an undergraduate degree in history, so he had a background in the subject, albeit somewhat revisionist, of course. But he's bright—very bright—and it didn't take him long to see through the mess of pottage he'd been given by some of the new historians. It was a self-correcting process, and I think that says a lot in his favor. He did it very much on his own, Mr. Graham, and it demonstrates that he is genuinely interested in pursuing truth. I gave him a few helpful books."

"Dawson, no doubt", jibed Hewlitt.

"Absolutely right", Whitfield countered pleasantly. "There is no better cultural historian. Andrew took to him like a duck to water."

"Professor, would you say that Andrew's behavior in your tutorials or lectures matches the descriptions of Dr. Hewlitt and Dr. Kebble?"

"Yes, very much so. An initial burst of enthusiasm, followed in November by a rapid decline into silence. There is nothing of significance I can add to their accounts."

Kebble stood and checked his wristwatch. "Well, it's getting on. I have two children who need tucking in. Is there anything else you would care to ask, Mr. Graham?"

"I don't think so. Thank you for your time."

Hewlitt stood and shook Alex's hand.

"I too am called by the exigencies of domestic bliss. I'm sorry we couldn't tell you more. If you want to discuss this further, do let me know. I'm at your disposal."

They departed, leaving Alex alone with Whitfield. The professor relit his pipe and sat back, regarding Alex thoughtfully.

"You look quite done in, Mr. Graham."

"I haven't had much sleep during the past few days."

"Jet lag thrown into the bargain, I'd wager."

"Yes, but I'm too worried to sleep just yet. At every moment I can't help wondering where he is."

"It must be terribly frustrating. Why don't you come up to my rooms? I have a bottle of sherry hidden in the wainscoting."

"That's very kind of you. You're sure it wouldn't be a bother?"

"A bother? Not at all. It would rescue me from the task of marking six comparisons of Toynbee's and Spengler's views of history."

Alex and Whitfield walked side by side through the college cloister and out onto a second and larger green behind the old building. On the far side of it, a three-story edifice of pale stone loomed from north to south.

"That's the New Building", Whitfield said. "More than two hundred years old. The college was founded centuries earlier, in 1458. Even so, it's a relative latecomer compared with Balliol and Exeter."

"You're surrounded by a sense of history", said Alex. "In Canada we revere buildings that are barely a century old."

"Tell me, Mr. Graham, what do you mean by 'a sense of history'?"

"I'm not sure exactly. Perhaps that the past is present, that we live connected to a chain of events."

"That we are not adrift in the cosmos?" Whitfield prompted.

"Yes, something like that. It seems so much easier to feel anchored to reality in a place like this."

"Does it?" Whitfield asked doubtfully.

"You don't think so?"

"Perhaps a person from the New World is hit by our history more strongly than we are. With less to connect you to the past, you recognize what's missing. We suffer from the opposite."

"Which is?"

"Overfamiliarity. Familiarity breeds contempt, or at the very least it breeds indifference. Here the younger generation zooms in and out of these buildings as if they were erected in a month by a machine, at the command of a zoning committee, and they hardly give it a thought. I wonder how many of them realize that every stone is saturated in blood, sweat, and prayer, with grief and holiness. The stones cry out, Mr. Graham, but none can hear."

"You seem to hear."

"Do I? I wonder about that. In the country of the blind, a one-eyed man seems a visionary, I suppose. But he is also a bit of a griffin."

"I beg your pardon?"

"A mythological creature. A sort of Mr. Chips with wings."

Alex laughed. It was his first real laugh in many a day.

"Well, here we are", Whitfield said. "There's no use idling. The past is present, but the present is also present."

The professor led Alex up a stairway to the third floor and turned into an echoing hallway. Whitfield's rooms were farther down the hall, on the right. He unlocked the door and led the way into a cozy, high-ceilinged chamber that seemed to be a combination parlor-classroom. There were bookshelves, a fireplace surrounded by a sofa and armchairs, a conference desk with wooden chairs, and various paraphernalia of a historian's life: a balsa-wood model of the Parthenon on a side table, a rusted sword with ornate handle hanging above the fire, a Greek wine amphora on the mantel board, a case of ancient coins. On the coffee table sat a human skull with an iron arrowhead embedded in it.

Whitfield smiled and said, "Very useful for convincing students that history is not a chain of abstractions."

"I see. A visual aid", Alex said.

"Quite. I tell them this fellow here had a degree from Magdalen College."

"Really? Did he?"

Whitfield laughed. "Sheer hyperbole. It's Scottish. I dug it out of a field below Stirling Castle. Poor fellow was slain in 1304 by Edward Longshanks, king of England."

He crossed over to the window and drew aside the curtain.

"You must come back in daytime and see my view." He pointed out into the dark. "My rooms overlook the deer park."

"I thought I saw a deer this afternoon from my window at Tyburne."

"I'm sure you did. The grove borders both Tyburne and Magdalen. Have a seat, Mr. Graham."

Whitfield took off his jacket, loosened his tie, and turned up an electric heater in the fireplace. Opening the glass door of a wall cabinet, he removed a bottle and two sherry glasses and passed one to Alex. They settled into the armchairs to sip their drinks.

Alex felt his tension beginning to ease. Whitfield said nothing for a few minutes, apparently listening to a clock ticking on the mantelpiece.

"Do you live here?" Alex asked.

"I sleep here sometimes when scheduling is tight. My wife is away right now, doing research at Princeton. She's on sabbatical from the University Science Centre."

"Where do you usually live?"

"We have a cottage in a village north of here. A place called Wootton."

Whitfield refilled Alex's glass. The effect of strong drink was beginning to revive his optimism. He suddenly felt certain that Andrew would soon return, disillusioned with the realm of pseudofaerie; he would be older, wiser, and ready to search for the true enchantment of the world.

"Where did you study, Graham?"

"Clementine Valley Regional High School."

"I meant your university."

"I'm afraid I never went to one", said Alex in an apologetic tone.

"Are you serious?"

"Quite serious."

"Hmmm. I would have taken you for a doctor of something or other. You have the look."

"What look is that?"

"Abstracted, hooked on a thesis or two."

"Well, if the truth be known, I'm a lowly bookseller in a small town in a sparsely populated corner of a nation whose recorded history is brief."

"Still, you seem to have educated yourself, and that's an admirable thing."

"Am I educated? I rather doubt it. To quote your Professor Hewlitt, I think my 'systematic coherence' is rather rickety."

"Your son—Andrew—he's bookish like you. He looks like you too, but the similarities end there, if I guess right."

"You guess right. He is a dreamer and a searcher. He ventures far beyond where his father ever dared to tread."

"You say it with such sadness."

Alex shrugged.

"Are you angry with him?"

"There are moments when I'm in anguish over him; at times I'm overwhelmed with love for him; and then there are the moments when I'd gladly give him a thrashing for this lunacy."

Alex rubbed his forehead with his right hand.

"I know what it is to agonize over a child", Whitfield said quietly.

"You have children?"

"Three. All grown. One boy is a petroleum engineer working for the Saudi government, and the other boy is an investment broker in London. Our daughter lives in an institution for the mentally handicapped."

"Oh, I am sorry."

"Don't be sorry. She cannot walk, and she can barely speak, but she communicates with her heart. Do you know what I mean, Graham?"

"Yes, I do", Alex said. "I have a friend like that. She is pure of heart, and I love her."

Whitfield seemed moved by this. He said nothing for a few moments. Finally, raising his glass in salutation, he said in a low voice, "I like you more and more, Graham. I'm going to do what I can to help you find your son."

Whitfield walked him back to Tyburne. After three glasses of sherry, Alex was a little unsteady on his feet. The professor took his arm more than once to save him from stepping off the curb, and Alex began to feel toward him a real comradeship.

"I suggest you try to get some sleep tonight, Graham. Then tomorrow, if you like, I could show you a few of the sights of our illustrious past. What do you say?"

"I shay it's a worthy shuggestion."

"Excellent, mashter booksheller. How about I pick you up on the front steps at nine thirty sharp?"

"Agreed."

Alex slept deeply that night. At seven thirty he woke to the sound of a bell, got up, took a hot shower down the hall, shaved, and dressed casually. Feeling better than he had for weeks, he went in search of breakfast. On the ground floor, he saw students streaming into the chapel and joined them.

Mass was about to begin. Two acolytes in white albs were lighting the altar candles with tapers. One of them was a Chinese student he had not met; the other was Perce Trainor. The greatest surprise of all was the celebrant. The Nigerian processed to the sanctuary during the opening hymn, his green vestments flowing behind him, too large for his frame. The palms of his hands were pressed together on his breast, his face recollected. The dignity that Alex had noticed yesterday was evident, but its meaning was now magnified. The priest offered Mass with total absorption in what was occurring on the altar. His homily was eloquent, his intercessory prayers simple.

After the recessional hymn, Alex sat for several minutes with his eyes closed, resting in the Eucharistic peace, asking God that in the tangled weave of England he might discover a thread leading to his son.

The chapel was nearly empty when the priest left the sacristy and came down the aisle to Alex's pew. He was dressed in a black suit and Roman collar and was carrying a leather briefcase.

"I offered the Mass for our Andrew", he whispered.

"Thank you, Father. Father...?"

"Father Xavier Ukoh, Mr. Graham."

"I am grateful for your prayers."

"I will continue to pray until you find him. I feel certain that you will find him."

"Do you have a few moments to talk with me, Father?"

"Certainly." He sat down beside Alex.

"May I ask you some questions about my son?"

"Yes, of course."

"Did he confide in you?"

Father Xavier considered the question. "We discussed some things."

"In your conversations outside of confession, did he tell you anything that concerns his disappearance?"

"No. Our conversations were not intellectual, and when they touched upon spiritual matters it was always in a general way. For the most part he asked me about my family and my country. My country has suffered greatly, and he was interested in its history. And he told me about Halcyon and the places he loved in the wilderness. He hoped that I would see it someday."

"Did you sense that anything was going wrong with his thinking?"

The priest shook his head. "I saw little of him from November onward. You understand, our lives are so busy here. So busy."

"Did he tell you about a girl he was in love with?"

"Yes. It was not a great disturbance. A week, two weeks, three weeks and it was over. It was not deep, and he quickly recovered his equilibrium."

"So you think it's unconnected to his disappearance?"

"In my estimation, something else has intervened in his life, something we do not know about."

Alex stared at the floor.

"What am I to do?" he said, as if speaking to himself.

"You must trust", said the priest. "And you must not lose your peace."

When he had gone, Alex knelt down and prayed for peace, for divine guidance—and for a miracle.

Whitfield was waiting for him on the front steps, squinting at the breaking overcast, lighting his perennial pipe.

"Graham!" he hailed. "The streets are wet, but passable. Is there anything you'd especially like to see in fabled Oxford?"

"I'm not much of a tourist, Professor. What I need most is a bit of fresh air and some exercise."

"All right. Maybe later we can see the Bodleian and the other sights." Patting the seat of a bicycle leaning against a lamppost, he pointed to another one beside it. "John Groves has lent you his vintage Dutch cycle. Hop on!"

The winter sun was not strong, but it had broken through the overcast sufficiently to melt a light snowfall that had occurred during the night. It was now dispelling the mist that clung to turrets and lingered in low places by the rivers. A breeze in the upper altitudes was pushing the wall of cumulus to the south, followed by tufts of lighter cloud, opening a portion of blue sky. As the two men cycled leisurely up High Street in the direction of Centre Town, they lifted their faces to it, soaking up the welcome warmth.

Though they were forced to swerve more than once to avoid dogs, errant children, retired lady professors with walking sticks, and foreign tourists ignorant of the traffic laws, Alex began to feel a not unpleasant distraction from his worries. What might have been minor annoyances were now simply part of the liquid flux that flowed in many directions around the timeless architecture. Every detail impressed. He wondered if Whitfield experienced it quite the same way. Was it so familiar to him that it had flattened into ordinariness, becoming a vague backdrop?

Braking at the corner of a street named Worcester, they walked their bikes across the broad intersection toward Oxford Canal, a branch of the river Isis. Whitfield led the way onto Hythe Bridge Street and from there turned right onto a footpath that wound beside the canal in a northerly direction.

Side by side, they began to talk. Whitfield asked if Alex had learned anything from the students at Tyburne. Alex told him the little he had discovered.

"You say his closest chum couldn't tell you anything?"

"Nothing. Which strikes me as strange. I wonder if he was being entirely honest with me."

"It might be English reticence", said Whitfield. "North Americans frequently misinterpret us."

"I would have made allowances for that, except that he's from New Zealand."

"Oh yes, the Kiwi lad. A gregarious fellow by all accounts. He's not one of my students, but I do know that he was once apprehended walking across the cloister quad on his hands, entertaining members of the fairer sex. I would expect a young man like that to be rather forthcoming with whatever he knew, if he knew anything. And since Andrew is his friend, he is probably worried about your son's disappearance. Perhaps he has his own suspicions about these people Andrew is involved with but isn't quite sure. It may be that he doesn't want to alarm you."

Alex stopped by a low footbridge that angled over the canal, and stared down into the water.

Whitfield relit his pipe and puffed a few times to get it smoking properly.

"How's the jet lag? Did you sleep last night?"

"I had a very good sleep, thanks to you and your sherry. I feel more hopeful this morning, but it's frustrating not knowing where to look."

"Not knowing if any of a thousand paths will lead somewhere."

"The problem is, Professor Whitfield, I don't have the resources to check every possible road. I could knock on every door in this city, asking anyone who looks suspicious if he's seen my son. It could take a year, and I would still never know if I was being lied to. I'm not an entire police force. I'm just a man, and I'm running out of time."

Whitfield said nothing.

"I could hire a taxi and scour all the back roads between here and Cricklewood, go up every lane, hound every farmer in hundreds of square miles, and turn up nothing."

"Let's cross over", Whitfield interrupted, pointing to the bridge with his pipe stem.

On the other side, the path swung around to the south and veered in the direction of the Isis. The grade began to climb up to rail lines that ran alongside the river.

"Where are we going?" Alex asked.

"There's a route I like to follow that circles the lower part of the city and brings me back to Magdalen. About an hour's trek—less, if we cycle most of the way. Are you game for it?"

"I must do something to burn up this frustration."

"Splendid. Let's be off."

They half lifted, half roll-bumped their bicycles across the tracks. Pausing on the other side, Whitfield looked quickly at Alex and removed the pipe from his mouth.

"Do you like trains?" he asked.

"Yes, very much."

"So do I. I think the Birmingham express goes by in a few minutes. Let's watch it pass, shall we?"

"All right."

As they gazed down the track in the direction of Oxford Station, Alex recalled the song about Bobby on the railroad that had so delighted Andrew as a boy. He recited it for Whitfield.

"We sang one like it when I was a child", said the professor. "I suppose our parents encouraged it as a precautionary measure. Much more effective than nagging. Few little boys are scared off the tracks by harangues, nor are they known to be influenced overmuch by lectures about the dangers of human existence. It is danger, after all, which the young adventurer most desires—thinking himself immortal."

Alex had been a boy once, and though he had forgotten a lot about it, he recalled a major rule in the kingdom of boys.

"When shooed away by a grown-up, you must come back later in secret and accomplish what you set out to do."

"Precisely, Mr. Graham, precisely."

Yes, he remembered. But that was before a virus felled him.

"Your Andrew, I expect, is a lad who likes to accomplish what he sets out to do."

"Yes and no. He sets out to do many things and is often sidetracked."

"And that is what you think has happened?"

"Yes. I continually ask myself why has he proven so vulnerable to the lure of the sidetrack. I blame myself, Professor."

"Please call me Owen."

"Thank you. Please call me Alex."

"Right: Alex and Owen it is!"

"You see, Owen, I didn't give him enough—enough of myself, I mean."

Whitfield frowned. "Are you sure about that? I think most good fathers accuse themselves of failing their children—sometimes with reason, but mostly not."

"Well, in my case, I think there is reason to admit a certain guilt. I was too abstracted from my sons. I fulfilled my duty toward them, and I truly loved them, but—"

"And of course you would have died for them."

"Yes. Or at least I used to think so. I've begun to doubt a lot of things lately. Perhaps I wouldn't have after all. I mean, if I wouldn't live for them, maybe I wouldn't have died for them if it had come to that."

"What a horrid lie!" Whitfield erupted. "Don't believe it. I see plenty of evidence that you're an excellent father. You are here, aren't you?"

"Yes, after the horse is out of the barn."

"More accurately, after the *colt* is out of the barn and kicking its heels in the field. May I suggest, Alex, that you not put such a dire interpretation on things. What could you have done to keep Andrew safe?" He paused. "You're a Catholic, I believe?"

Alex nodded.

"I'm Catholic too. Doesn't our faith teach us that love costs everything? Love is always a risk."

Unable to find a rejoinder, Alex kept silent. When the professor continued, it was clear that his words were spoken from the heart:

"The believer is not a killjoy. He's in love with life, with all its comforts and all its troubles. The complete Catholic is a kind of romantic—but a very unusual kind of romantic, because he is also a realist."

"What do you mean?"

Whitfield relit his pipe and craned his neck in the direction of the station.

"I think our realist", he said, pondering, "knows that the laws by which the engine runs and the laws by which a child runs are not always compatible. He is like a man who long ago played on the tracks and narrowly escaped being crushed by the wheels of a locomotive. Many of his friends and companions did not escape. Now, in his old age, flocks of children have come to play on the tracks. In a kindly voice, he warns them of the danger, but they don't believe him. He speaks a little more authoritatively, and perhaps a patronizing note creeps into his voice, a sort of fatherly tone. The children, however, have heard a great deal about locomotives, and desire to see one. The tracks are signs that long ago some marvel occurred here and may well happen again. They are excited by them.

"The Catholic, breathing heavily from the weight of much experience and not a little worry, tries to tell them that the rumble on the rails and the wisp of smoke around the bend is perilous. The children gaze suspiciously at him. The old man smells of smoke and cinders. His clothing is rumpled. He is scarred. His voice is not calm. They ignore him.

" 'Please, get off the tracks', he says firmly. They turn their backs to him. Now he is frightened for them. He laboriously tries to explain why they must stand aside, but his anxiety for them handicaps his style. He looks and sounds extreme. Perhaps it is he who is dangerous, the children think. Is it not madmen such as this, they tell themselves, who spoil the great romance of the railroad? Perhaps the beautiful beast has not come for such a long time precisely because sour and critical men, scarred by their pasts and deformed by their negative thinking, have too long dominated the world!

"The rumble on the tracks is growing louder. 'Get off the tracks!' he shouts in a very unattractive voice. Now all credibility is gone, and the children turn toward the incarnation of their myth with great fervor."

Whitfield peered at Alex to see if he had gotten the point.

"What are you saying, Owen? That we should leave the children to their fate?"

"No, of course not. Common sense suggests that at this point any sane adult would lift the children off the track or try to stop the train. But, if we can continue the allegory just a bit longer, we are dealing here, in this age, with a mob of people who do not consider themselves to be children. Moreover, it is most difficult to stop this particular train, the engine of materialism and the cults that are churned up in its wake, because it is very big and very powerful and very fast."

Alex, wholly engrossed in deciphering the allegory, was startled by Whitfield's shout:

"Stand back!"

The professor grabbed his arm and yanked him away from the railbed just as an engine hurtled by with a roar and a clatter. When its last car had passed with squealing wheels, Alex exhaled loudly and stared at his companion.

Whitfield grinned fiendishly. "Let's proceed, shall we?"

Farther south they mounted their bicycles on Hollybush Row and made their way to Thames Street. Where it ended at Folly Bridge, they crossed over to a series of walkways and playing fields south of the city center and headed east. By the time they drew up to the front steps of Tyburne College, Alex was winded, feeling rather invigorated and ready for a meal.

"Would you care to join me in the refectory?" he asked. "I'm sure Mr. Groves will permit it."

"I would be delighted. John Groves is an old friend of mine, and a stout yeoman. I foresee no difficulties."

It was so.

Alex and Owen loaded their trays and found a quiet table near the windows. Mashed potatoes, green peas, and what appeared to Alex to be a baked pudding with three inches of fat sausage poking out of steaming crust made up the meal. After tea and tapioca, Whitfield lit his pipe and sat back, blinking, focused on unspoken thoughts. Still sipping his tea, Alex glanced about the room and saw the young New Zealander sitting alone at a table. He was eating with a fork in one hand, an open book in the other. Hunched over both enterprises, he seemed mesmerized by what he was reading. Food kept dropping off the fork before it reached his mouth.

"Yon Percival is not woolgathering", said Whitfield.

The boy closed the book, turned his attention to the meal, and consumed what remained of it with machinelike speed. Finished, he stood up and crossed the refectory toward the exit. When he spotted Alex, he changed direction and came to their table.

"Hullo, Mr. Graham. Hullo, Professor."

Alex stood and shook hands with him. Perce's grip was powerful. His short-sleeved polo shirt displayed unusually thick forearms, as tanned as his face.

"May I sit down, sir?"

"Of course", Alex said, drawing back a chair for him.

"I hope I'm not interrupting."

"Not at all, not at all", Whitfield said, eyeing him with amusement.

The boy laid his notebook and a copy of Aristotle's *Nicomachean Ethics* on the table in front of him.

"Mr. Graham, I hope you won't think I'm daft. Where I'm from we can be hugger-mugger if the wind's blowing the wrong way or we get short on rations. Yesterday when you asked me about Andrew's friends, my mind went blank. I couldn't think of anybody but the fellows he knows around here and over at Magdalen. Good sorts—fair dinkum—nobody that's teleporting up into space regularly, if you know what I mean."

"I'm not sure I do—"

"Mr. Graham probably understands teleporting," Whitfield interjected, "but he might be struggling over alien vocabulary."

Perce smiled sheepishly. Then, growing serious, he said, "I have thought of something. It could mean nothing, but I think I should mention it."

"You've thought of someone he knows?"

"Well, I'm not sure if *knows* is the right word. He might or might not know these people. After a debate at Oxford

Union last fall, there was a party. Andrew did well that night. In the final rebuttal he knocked down a big man on campus—with his points, I mean, not his fists. Anyway, this BMOC was so full of himself you could see even his own teammates were a bit sick of him. So when Andrew got the best of him and the adjudicator gave the debate to Tyburne, the whole house came down, lots of cheering, lots of fun. A great time was had by all. Afterwards, a mob of us went out to the Bird and Baby. Andrew and me and about ten others crammed into the alcove where Lewis and Tolkien used to sit."

"What is the Bird and Baby?" Alex asked.

Whitfield explained. "It's a pub called the Eagle and Child. The Inklings sometimes met there."

"That's right", Perce went on. "Anyway, we were having a few pints when this couple came up to our table and introduced themselves. Well, not quite introduced, because they didn't say their names. The girl was English and a real beauty. The guy looked like he was from the Far East, maybe India or Bangladesh. But not quite that either. He could have been from Egypt or Iran, maybe mixed race. Very pleasant chap. They wanted to congratulate Andrew on his handling of the debate. The guy told him they were really impressed by the points he'd made. The girl said they would like him to come over to their discussion group sometime and talk more about his ideas."

"Did they say where the discussion group was held?" Alex asked.

"Not that I heard." Perce paused, thinking hard. "The girl gave Andrew a card."

"A business card, you mean?"

"Yeah."

"Did you read the card? Do you remember anything that was written on it?"

"No." He shook his head. "Andrew put it in his jacket pocket. He thanked them, but then he just kind of blew them off—nicely, mind you."

Alex exhaled. "That's all you remember?"

"I'm afraid so, Mr. Graham. Like I said, it may mean nothing."

"What you've told me could be important."

"If I think of anything else I'll track you down. You're staying for a while, I take it?"

"Until I find Andrew."

"I'm sure he'll turn up soon."

"Thank you, Perce."

When he had gone, Whitfield leaned forward. "What is it? You look as if a fire alarm bell went off."

"Yes, one is ringing loudly. You see, the police told me that when the car in which Andrew was last seen stopped for gas in Cricklewood, there was a young English girl and a man from the Far East in it. I'm going back to his room to have another look around. That card could still be there."

"Right, why don't you do that, Alex? I have a lecture this afternoon, so I'll be on my way now. Would you care to call me if you find anything?"

"I will indeed. It's very good of you to be so concerned."

"I'm happy to do what I can. Speaking of which, would you be interested in a jaunt tomorrow? I don't have classes. I could take you down to Cricklewood for a scout around."

"That would be a help, Owen. I've been toying with the idea of hiring a taxi."

"A taxi! Good heavens, man, are you rich?"

"No, just desperate."

"Forget the taxi. I'll take you."

"That's very generous of you. It would be a great boost to have company. Uh, you aren't suggesting we go on bicycles, I hope."

"I have a car, such as it is."

They agreed to meet at nine the next morning, after Mass at Tyburne chapel. Alex walked him to the door, and then he stood for a few moments watching the professor go down the steps. Whitfield attached metal clips to his pant cuffs, waved good-bye, and pedaled away up Saint Clement's Street, the pipe in his mouth, a trail of smoke behind him. The professor seemed hearty for a man in his late sixties, but an aura of genteel decline was evident; his rumpled tweed jacket, his unpressed trousers, and his kind but troubled eyes testified to a long life that had contained many twists and turns.

After returning the bicycle to John Groves, Alex went directly upstairs to Andrew's room. A careful search through papers on the desk produced no cards. The various items on the bulletin board were innocuous, the usual mementos of college life: reminder notes, schedules, beer coasters from several pubs, pictures of his current heroes and heroines (a rugby star, the late Mother Teresa of Calcutta, the historian Christopher Dawson). There was also a blank postcard of the Stone Giant of northern Ontario, and a group portrait of the Graham family of Halcyon—Carol, Alex, and the two teenagers, taken a year or so before Carol's death.

The board was crowded, and Alex had to remove a few items in order to read everything that was there. Beneath a yellow sticky note, he found a photograph of himself. He was surprised, not so much by the sight of his own face, but by the fact that Andrew had put it there to look at every day. On a slip of paper taped to the bottom of the image was written:

"The Child is father of the Man"
Wm. Wordsworth, 1802

Who was the child and who the father? Alex wondered. Of course, he knew that the poet's intention was to say that a child forms, in part, his adult self. But there was a double meaning here. He pulled the photo from the cork and set the thumbtacks on the desktop. He sat on the bed and looked at himself.

This is what Andrew sees. But what does he see, really? Who is this man? Who is the child who fathered this man?

He tried to examine his face as a stranger might. And what he saw was a well-favored middle-aged man whose face was reposed, reserved, even guarded. The backdrop was a bank of books. The photograph had been taken by Jacob, more than a year after Carol's death. Alex remembered clearly how he had felt during that period, and he realized now that if he were to meet a person with such a face, he would instinctively draw back. The reserve was not offensive, but it was definitely there, definitely communicating something to the world:

"I mean you no ill, but you must realize that it is unnecessary for us to know each other."

Not conscious. But conveyed nonetheless. Was this the message that Andrew had read in his face?

He turned the photograph over and discovered handwriting on the back.

> Let us now praise famous men,
> Our fathers who begat us.
> Ecclesiasticus 44:1
> My Pa,
> King of Halcyon

He read it twice, then a third time.

If Jacob had written the inscription, there might have been an irony in it. But the scrawl was Andrew's.

Alex choked, his eyes blinded.

9. Ganymede and the Eagle

As he waited for Owen Whitfield to arrive, Alex walked up and down the sidewalk in front of Tyburne College in a mixture of drizzle and fog. He had just decided to go back inside to borrow an umbrella from John Groves when a little blue vehicle materialized from the blanket of gray and drew up to the curb. It was shaped like a box and did not appear to have ordinary signal lights. Instead, an illuminated mechanical arm flipped out of the right side and blinked.

Alex jumped into the passenger side. Whitfield did a U-turn, then eased back into the surreal maze of the city of mist. As they rumbled and lurched up High Street, Whitfield patted the dashboard. "How do you like the golden chariot?"

"Very quaint, Owen."

"Thank you. It's a Humber, more than fifty years old. Older than you are, but still able to putter about."

Whitfield turned west off High Street onto an avenue Alex could not identify, then navigated several more route changes until they entered a four-lane motorway. The fog began to dissipate, revealing fields of floating sheep on either side.

"I'm completely disoriented. Are we going in the right direction?"

"We're on A34, which takes us south. We should be at Cricklewood in half an hour."

The traffic was not heavy, but Alex noted that every other vehicle passed the Humber at high speeds, on the right. He forced himself to concentrate on the landscape that was now appearing as the fog slowly raised into a sheet of low-hanging stratocumulus. The day was lightening as well. Rolling hills, solitary farms, and the abiding hedgerows were dominant. Sheep touched down to earth on their delicate legs. A castle crept across the ridge of a distant hill. Alex turned in his seat and watched it pass.

"Is that a Norman castle?" he asked.

"No, it's a folly."

"What do you mean, a folly?"

Whitfield chuckled. "Like a Hollywood set for a cowboy film—a fake town in the Wild West. I believe that one was built by a wealthy eccentric sometime in the nineteen twenties."

"It looks authentic."

"That's the idea. Charming on the outside, empty on the inside. It's hollow."

"You mean to say it's purely decoration?"

"Yes, rather like a garden ornament. A very large ornament for a very large garden."

"For someone with a very large budget."

"Precisely. But then, one must have a hobby."

"Still, it is striking."

"Striking? Oh yes, it's that, all right. But what does it say about us? Are opulent illusions the defining art form of a people grown empty? Like Eliot's hollow men?"

"Maybe it's like boys building sandcastles on the seashore. You have to admit it was considerate of him to share it with passersby."

"You have a point. Trust a foreigner to see the good in our excesses."

On that note, Whitfield turned the wheel and eased the car into an exit lane. Leaving the dual carriageway, they veered in a southwesterly direction on a surfaced road that cut between hedge-covered embankments. An escarpment of hills rose before them. The road dipped suddenly and ran between a cluster of cottages.

"Isley Major. We're in Berkshire now."

The Humber made a right turn at the crossroads in the center of the village and continued due west along the baseline of the hills. Minutes later, Whitfield braked hard to avoid slamming into a horse-drawn cart that had wheeled onto their path. The farmer seemed oblivious to them, forcing the Humber to follow at a crawl. Alex was glad of this, because the professor had been hurtling down the narrow lane as if it were a major motorway. Now, to his credit, he did not try to pass, nor did he toot his horn.

Soon, the farmer turned off at a pasture gate, clearing the view directly ahead, revealing another village. Built upon the banks of a stream that drained the hills, it was larger than the one through which they had just passed, containing about two dozen homes, some roadside businesses, and a church.

"Cricklewood", Whitfield announced, coming to a stop in front of a public house.

The air smelled faintly of manure and winter hayfields as the two men got out and surveyed the surroundings. The post-and-beam pub with white stucco and a thatched roof stood beside a petrol station with computerized pumps.

"Look!" said Alex, pointing to the pub door.

The swinging sign above the lintel was a hand-painted brown and white pony prancing on a black background, above which was lettered in gilded script "The Bobbing Pinto". Below the hooves was written "Come in and have a pint-o!"

"Very witty", Whitfield mumbled dryly, trying to fire up his pipe against the light breeze.

"Owen, this explains something Andrew said to me during our last phone call. At the time I thought he was irrational. But I understand now."

"What did he say?"

"I had just told him about Darla, the handicapped girl I mentioned to you. I tried to bring him back to reality by reminding him how she used to give him pony rides. He said, 'Oh yes, the pinto. I was in the pinto last night.'"

"So, you're saying that it sounded quite mad at the time, but now it makes a certain sense?"

"Yes. He may have wandered, he may be on the wrong track, but he's still sane."

Whitfield looked as if he was reserving judgment.

"Let's go inside, shall we?" he said.

The pub was a humble watering hole for the country people of the region. It was poorly lit, save for a single leaded window and buzzing fluorescent lights in the ceiling. The bare plank floor and chipped furniture had been worn by generations of steady trade. On the wall above the bar, a second painting of a pony hung at an angle, more artful, crackled and darkened by years of smoke. Beyond the tap handles and barrels of ale, a stout woman flipped sausages on a grill as she listened to a radio comedy and canned laughter.

Since there were no other customers, Alex and Owen had their choice of tables. They sat down by the window and looked out at the Berkshire hills. Presently, a young fellow of about twenty years came up to take their orders. He was dressed in a white shirt with black pants stuffed into rubber boots. The boots looked none too clean.

Whitfield ordered two pints of draft beer. "Warm for me, chilled for my guest."

The waiter smirked amiably. "You not from around here, sir?" he asked Alex.

"I'm from Canada", Alex replied, puzzled.

"Poor blokes, they don't know any better", Whitfield apologized to the waiter.

"Drinks his own bath water, does he?"

"I'm afraid so."

When the boy went off to get their drinks, Whitfield explained to Alex with great seriousness that civilized people do not drink cold beer. Then he suggested that they order fish and chips for lunch.

"No thanks, Owen. I'm afraid that has unpleasant memories for me."

"How about bangers and mash, then?"

"Is it edible?"

"A feast surpassing excellence. I guarantee it."

The waiter returned with foaming glass tankards, took their food orders, and went off to the kitchen. Whitfield raised his glass and drank deeply from it.

"Aaar! Good for what ails you. Now, may I ask about the 'painful memories'?"

"Andrew was here only four days ago and ordered fish and chips. That pay phone in the corner is where he placed his first call to me."

"Hmmm. We should talk with the proprietor and see if he can remember anything he forgot to tell the police."

After the filling meal of sausages and mashed potatoes, Whitfield called the waiter over and asked if the proprietor was in the house.

"Dad's out back killin' chickens", he said. "I'll get 'im for you if y'like."

"Would you, please?"

Presently, a cheerful portly man came through the kitchen door wiping his hands on his blood-spattered apron.

"Help you, gents?"

Whitfield made the introductions and explained the reason for their visit to Cricklewood.

"Right, I remember", the proprietor said, looking out the window. "That lad missing from Oxford. I told the coppers everything I could—a thimbleful o' flyspecks is what it amounted to."

Alex repeated the questions the police had already asked. There was nothing new in the answers.

"Do you remember anything about the car or the people he was with?"

"Never saw them. You could ask my brother-in-law, Nokes. He has the petrol station next door."

"Did you notice anything unusual about my son's behavior?" Alex asked.

The publican shook his head. "Wasn't payin' much attention. That night we had a darts competition, and the place was packed. My wife had a better look at him than me. She served your lad, says he was just a normal-lookin' bloke—she told the coppers that too. He used the phone, paid for his takeout, and left. That's all we know."

Nokes, it turned out, was a less affable character, chary of words, and resistant to Whitfield's attempt at warm-up humor, but he was forthcoming with what he knew.

"Mercedes. Dark blue. That's all I can tell you. Same as I told the detective from Oxford."

"The people in the car—what were they like?"

"Driver was older, fifty, sixty. Just come from the barber by the look of him. Silver hair greased back like a toff, pricey suit. Paid for his tank-up with big bills. I'd say a German. But you never know these days. Could be Dutch or Austrian or anythin', now that they've pushed through this European Union. Against the will o' the English people, I might add. It's gettin' so there's no way a natural-born person can find a job or buy land in this country—"

Whitfield interrupted. "Can you tell us about the other people, Mr. Nokes?"

"Like I told the detective, there was three others. A young miss. Very pretty."

"How old was she?" Alex asked.

"Twenty-one, twenty-two. There was a colored bloke. Looked like a Pakistani, late twenties. Very proper, he was.

232

Minded his pleases and thank-yous. Then there was the lad they're lookin' for—your son, I take it."

"Did he seem troubled?"

Nokes shrugged. "He didn't say much but seemed all right. Just an ordinary Joe. I thought he was a Yank."

"Had you ever seen the car before?"

"Never."

"Nor since?"

"If I did I would've called the coppers."

"Is there anything else you can think of?"

Nokes shook his head.

They thanked him and were about to leave, when Whitfield paused.

"Do you know if there are any people living in the area who have a religious center or a retreat house?"

"Religious? Well, there's some nuns up Swindon way, but I don't think they're kidnappers. My wife takes 'em eggs and vegetables. They don't drive a Mercedes. I can tell you for a fact they don't drive at all. Other than that, there's nobody suspicious-like around here, and I know every freeholder and tinker between Isley and Lambourn."

"Thank you for your time, Mr. Nokes."

"Not at all. Good day." He tipped his cap.

Returning to the car, Whitfield and Alex sat in the front seats, leaving the doors wide open.

"These people are homely but honest, Alex. What they told us is the sum of what they saw."

"That was my sense also. It seems the Mercedes was passing through the village that night, coming from someplace else, going who knows where."

"This is a back road, but it's only a few miles from a motorway that runs down to Southampton, and another that runs west to Bristol. Those are both port cities."

"And aren't there other cities within an hour's drive?"

"Yes, quite a few. I would suggest, Alex, that we're not looking for a needle in a haystack but a flyspeck in a thousand haystacks."

"Then what do we do now?"

"We get out and walk."

"What? Are we going to search on foot?"

"No, we're going to clear our minds. Ordinarily, it's not a good idea to get too much oxygen in your system, but this is a special case. Let's go for a stroll."

For close to twenty minutes they walked around the village, and because there were so few streets they soon found themselves making the circuit a second time. Neither felt inclined to talk, but as they turned a corner by the churchyard, Alex stopped and gazed at the crop of headstones.

"You know, Owen, I have a feeling that we're coming at the problem from the wrong direction."

"I have the same feeling. But tell me what you mean."

"We've been picking about in the haystacks, and it seems to me it would be more profitable if we searched for the trail at the other end."

"Back in Oxford, you mean?"

"Yes. Back at the source. I suspect that what we're looking for is completely unconnected to Cricklewood. Its only significance to us is that we've learned something about Andrew's whereabouts, that he's alive, and that he's with a certain group of people. We're not going to learn anything more here."

"I think you're right."

Whitfield pointed to the church. "That's a Norman tower. Twelfth century. Care to have a look?"

"All right."

The square tower was about sixty feet in height, and its windows were vertical slits.

"Archer holes", Whitfield explained. "Excellent protection from attackers. Not even a child could get through from the outside, but I would guess that more than one arrow has been shot from them. Shall we go in?"

At the base of the tower, they came to a thick oak door studded with black bolts and other hammered ironwork, swinging on mighty hinges. Inside, the bare nave was chilly, the walls were composed of heavy gray blocks, and the flagstones were worn down by eight centuries of use. Even the pews were of great age, their plain boards rounded and buffed by the abrasion of untold generations of hands and knees.

"There was a tabernacle there once, long ago", said Whitfield, pointing to an empty recess in the sanctuary wall, above a rough stone altar. "For centuries men worshipped the presence of the living God in this hallowed place. These stones cry out."

A white pigeon flew up from an alcove and landed on a beam high above the altar, leaving an echo of flutters and a cascade of falling dust motes. Alex tried to imagine what the church must have been like when it was full of incense and chant, Baptisms and weddings...the sacrifice of the Mass.

He knelt down on the bare stones and prayed silently:

Lord God, I do not know if men still worship you in this place. But please hear my prayer. Out of the depths I cry to you. I do not know where to seek my son. I beg you, help me to find a key that will unlock this mystery.

Then, with greater fervor:

You have called us out of darkness into your own wonderful light. Nourish us unto eternal life! You are Father of us all. You are Andrew's Father. You have made him for light! Do not let him sink into darkness!

Rising to his feet, he made the sign of the cross, and Whitfield did the same. They went out through the door at the back of the church, and there they came upon an old man sweeping the walkway in tweeds and slippers, with a cigarette dangling from the corner of his mouth. He squinted at the visitors and stopped sweeping.

"Morning", he said.

"Good-morning", Whitfield replied. "We were just having a look around. I hope that's all right."

"It don't bother me none. I'm the warden here, so you have my permission. We get mobs of tourists down from the cities. Not many in winter. She's an old church, Saint Anselm's is. Historical folk is fitting her out again. Put on a new slate roof last year, cost a pretty penny, that. Look at the stone carvin', will you?"

He nodded at two recessed alcoves on either side of the oak door. They contained statues of pale yellow stone.

"Saint Mary and Saint Anselm of Canterbury", the warden said.

Alex and Whitfield inspected the images, which were flawlessly carved in Gothic style.

"They look new", said the professor.

The old man came over and stood beside them.

"That's right. They're only three years old. Artist feller from London did 'em. That cost us a pretty penny too."

"Where are the originals, the statues that used to be here?"

"Nobody but the angels knows. Under the mud at the bottom of the river is my guess. Cromwell destroyed 'em during the Civil War."

Whitfield shot a look at Alex. "That's *our* civil war—early seventeenth century, the Roundheads and the Cavaliers."

"Wasn't he the one who slaughtered the Irish?" Alex asked.

"Yes, he was," Whitfield answered dryly, "and butchered a lot of English too. Not to mention cutting off the king's head."

"That's right", the old man said. "Charles the first." He took a drag on his cigarette butt, squeezed out the ember between his thumb and forefinger, and flung the stub into the high grass of the graveyard. Then he pointed to the church door. "Oliver Cromwell stabled his horses right in there, gentlemen. When he came through the shire with his army, he stripped the churches and busted up the statues, he did. Put the Catholics to the gallows, and a few Anglicans too."

"Terrible", Alex blurted.

"Is this still an Anglican church?" Whitfield asked.

"Still is, but who knows for how long. I'm C of E, as was my father in his time, and his father before him. Some around here are complainin' we aren't true Anglicans anymore. We have a lady priest now. I call 'er Father Peggy. She doesn't like that much." He sighed. "Ah well, it's no use gettin' upset about it. Times are changin'. Times are changin'."

"Indeed they are", Whitfield agreed pleasantly.

Alex, however, was fuming. "Cromwell was a religious man", he said scornfully.

"Aye, a godly man. A Puritan, he was", the old man said, oblivious to Alex's contempt.

"Spreading terror in the name of God!" Alex burst out. "What a vile monster!"

The two Englishmen looked at him curiously. The old warden tilted his head.

"Aye, maybe he was. To tell the truth, he was an ancestor o' mine." He stretched out his hand, and Alex automatically shook it. "Howdja do. My name's Alfie Cromwell."

Alex was speechless.

Whitfield could barely contain his mirth. Smiling broadly, he said, "Well, it has been very nice talking with you, Mr. Cromwell. We must be on our way now."

"Nice t'meet you, gentlemen. Always glad to pass the time o' day."

And he went back to his sweeping.

Seated in the car, Alex stared through the windshield at the church tower while Whitfield gave full vent to his suppressed laughter.

"Tread softly, for you tread on my history!" he roared.

"What a thoughtless remark I made, Owen. I must remind myself to watch what I say. England is a minefield, it seems."

"Most of the mines are dead, Alex. Now and then you step on a live one, but no harm was done."

Whitfield turned the key in the ignition and added, "A little vehemence can be a pressure valve."

They drove back to Oxford without further conversation.

Later that day they made the rounds of the city. Whitfield pointed out famous landmarks, but Alex only half-listened to the running commentary. He was distracted from his anxiety for an hour when they went through sections of the Bodleian Library, and he even cracked a smile when he was asked to sign a form promising not to burn any of the books. Moving on to the Ashmolean Museum, he was absorbed for a while by the oddities housed there but could not really concentrate for long, though an eighteenth-century machine called a "man-trap" gave him pause. Made of black iron, it was designed much like an animal trap; when sprung by a human foot, its wide fanged jaws clamped poachers and trespassers, resulting in their deaths. Whitfield took pains to show Alex swords of every age, Cromwell's death mask, and an ivory bas-relief depicting the disembowelment of an English Catholic bishop.

"A green and pleasant land", Whitfield said.

After that, they happened upon a small watercolor by John Ruskin. It was a kingfisher flashing turquoise feathers and a fiery belly, its dignified tilt of head and regal beak expressing its pride in being itself. It intrigued Alex so much that he felt a rivulet of awe trickle into the stream of his worries. For a full minute all thought of his missing son vanished.

Whitfield said, "This seems to have caught your attention. Are you a bird watcher?"

"Not really."

"Pretty, isn't it?"

"More than pretty. In a way it's the transfiguration of what a bird is. A glimpse of... of what *birdness* will someday be like when all creation is restored in Christ."

"Birdness?" the professor said, taking a closer look. "Hmmm. I've never thought of it that way, but you might have a case there."

After that, Alex was in no mood for further sightseeing. They drove to the Oxford police station on Saint Aldate's Street, where they met with Detective Helm. Helm in the flesh was a short, stocky man with gap teeth and thick glasses, but behind the lenses was a set of sharp eyes that had spent many years inspecting the underbelly of English society. He was as courteous and sympathetic as he had been on the phone but had nothing conclusive to tell Alex.

"Just a bit of stale news, Mr. Graham, if news you could call it. I thought it best to send an inquiry to the Office of Missing Persons. And they've made an effort, it seems. Hospitals throughout the British Isles do not contain anyone matching his description. Unconscious men have been brought to various hospitals in major cities during the past month, but most have identification, and none of them are twenty-three years of age with a small wedge-shaped scar on the left temple. There was a young fellow in an Aberdeen asylum who had amnesia, but the scar was on the right temple, curved, not wedged, and when he was induced to speak, his accent was Orkney."

"That's all you've turned up, then?" Whitfield asked.

"I'm afraid so. The morgues have been similarly unproductive."

Taking their leave of Helm, they got back into the car and drove uptown.

"The morgues have been similarly unproductive!" Whitfield murmured. "Only in Oxford do police aspire to eloquence. Sorry about that, Alex."

Arriving at Saint Giles Street, they parked in front of the Eagle and Child and got out. The swinging sign over the pub's door was a scene from Greek mythology, the infant Ganymede being carried off to Olympus by one of Zeus' eagles. A classical abduction case. A missing son.

Whitfield tugged Alex from one side of the sign to the other, pointing out that the myth was painted in contrasting ways.

"Interpretation is the key, Alex", he said.

"What do you mean?"

"History is an art, not a science. It is largely interpretation. Do you know, my American students inform me that the United States won the War of 1812 in Upper Canada, and my Canadian students inform me that your country won it? Now, whom should I believe?"

"You should believe us, Owen."

Whitfield laughed. "Of course, you're being entirely objective."

"My origins, no doubt."

"Now look at young Ganymede here. On one side we see the poor child dangling from the eagle's beak, torn from his mother's breast by violence. On the other side he rides upon the eagle's back, having the time of his life. What sense do you make of that?"

"Perhaps one side shows the event from the baby's perspective, and the other is the bird's interpretation."

"Excellent! A penetrating analysis. Of all the students and colleagues whom I have guided to this very spot, you are the first to understand. The others were after beer and mystique."

Whitfield took him inside and insisted on buying two pints of warm stout, which they drank in the alcove where a small plaque indicated that here the Inklings used to meet. The benches were padded but somewhat stiff, the walls plain, the atmosphere freighted with memories. It was difficult to visualize the leading lights of twentieth-century Christian literature crowding together into this rather austere and somewhat run-down cubbyhole. Photographs of Tolkien, Lewis, Charles Williams, and the others confirmed its history but did not infuse the place with literary romance. Alex remained nervous and distracted as Whitfield extolled their writings. Eventually the professor saw that his monologue was having no effect.

"Had enough for one day? Shall I take you back to Tyburne?"

"Yes, please, Owen. I need to get my bearings. It's all a little overwhelming."

"Of course, it must be. I should have realized."

"I feel as if I'm hemmed in on every side, shut into a room with many doors, each of them locked. Yet something is nagging at the back of my mind, and I can't for the life of me figure out what it is. It's as if there's a key to the whole affair that I'm missing. Something insignificant. It's staring me in the face, but I can't see it."

Alex twirled his empty glass in the wet rings on the table, staring gloomily. Whitfield watched him.

"Let's call it a day", he said.

Whitfield dropped him at the steps of the college, and Alex went upstairs to Andrew's room. He liked Owen Whitfield very much and was grateful for the man's help, but he was glad to be alone. His greatest need at the moment was for silence and rest. A short nap might cure the physical ache in his chest that was intensifying his general anxiety.

He withdrew the key ring from his pants pocket and threw it onto the desktop. After removing his shoes, he lay down on the bed and closed his eyes.

A moment later he sat bolt upright.

The keys!

There were three on the ring. He fingered them one at a time. The first was for the room, the second for the front entrance of the college. What was the third for?

He put his shoes back on and went downstairs to the office on the main floor. It was empty. He knocked at the door beside it, and Groves answered. Behind him a television was broadcasting the evening news.

"Excuse me, John, but I've just thought of something. Can you tell me what this third key on the key ring is for?"

"That would be for his locker in the cellar."

"Do you know what's in the locker?"

"Yes, when the police came by to search, we went through it together."

"Did you find a card of any kind—a business card?"

"No. If there had been a card, it would have turned up. They were rather thorough. There wasn't much to see. Andrew kept a basketball and a pair of rugby shoes down there, plus some extra clothing that I suppose he seldom wore. The closets in the student's rooms are small."

"Can you show me the locker?"

Groves led the way to the end of the corridor and down a staircase to the lower level. On the street side of the building the cellar was below ground, but on the side facing the Cherwell the slope of the college property exposed the entire east wall. In this wall, windows illuminated a large room full of bicycles. Near the base of the steps, a door led to the back gardens. It was open, and a red-cheeked student wearing black cycling clothes was wheeling a bicycle inside. Behind him a stone path swung around the building.

"This is the mud room", Groves explained. "The lads often come in this way, more than through the front entrance."

Leaving the bicycle room, they passed ranks of coin-operated washing machines and entered a passageway along which several doors were set approximately four feet apart. Groves

242

unlocked one marked 3-12 and stood aside to let Alex look inside.

It was more a closet than a locker and contained what Groves had described: the basketball sitting undisturbed where it had been rolled into a corner; rugby shoes covered with dried mud; an umbrella; the two old suitcases that had once belonged to Alex's father. He bent and opened the suitcase catches. They were empty. Standing, he looked through the clothing that hung from a railing along the rear wall. Most of it was sportswear, some clean, some muddy. There was a blue hockey shirt emblazoned with the Toronto Maple Leafs crest; a new white sweatshirt printed with the insignia of an Oxford rowing club; a tan trench coat; an eiderdown parka, useless in the mild English climate; and a brown tweed blazer.

"That's all there is", Groves said. "Helm went through it with a fine-tooth comb, just as he did with Andrew's bedroom. He spent an hour sifting through every jot and tittle."

Alex sighed and shook his head. "Well, it was just a thought. There's obviously nothing here."

"Shall we lock up?"

"Not just yet. I'd like to stay a few minutes, if it's all right."

"Stay as long as you wish, Alex. I have to go upstairs and mind the phone, so I'll leave you to it."

When Groves had gone, Alex leaned against the door-frame, arms folded, mouth tight, unwilling to admit that once again he had come to the end of a false corridor in the maze.

"There's something here", he said aloud. "I know it."

Taking his time, he went carefully through all the clothing, pocket by pocket. In the parka he found a comb, a Toronto subway token, and an English shilling. When he came to the tweed blazer, he saw that it was torn at the elbow and guessed that Andrew had stored it in the locker until it could be mended. Perhaps he had purchased a better blazer and was now wearing it somewhere in the British Isles.

In one of the side pockets, he found a large cardboard beer coaster marked "Eagle and Child, Saint Giles Street, Oxford".

It struck him that Andrew would not have carried such an object longer than the short period between leaving the pub and arriving at Tyburne. This seemed to indicate that the last time he had worn the blazer was when he had been drinking at the Bird and Baby. Was it the night of the debate?

Penned on the back of the coaster was a bit of doggerel in his son's handwriting:

> In Oxford they say Maudlin,
> In Cambridge, Mag-da-len.
> A boy from dear ol' Canada
> Could lose his wits and ken.
> For spelling is most proper here,
> But speaking's not the same.
> In London it's called Tems;
> In Oxford it's called Tame.
> This says so much about the folk
> Who live beside me here:
> They owe a lot to mighty Thames
> But more to their mighty beer.
> A.G.

Alex poked his fingers into the inner breast pocket. It was empty.

There was nothing more to investigate. Yet the nagging sense would not go away, an insistent feeling that he was still missing the mark. He took the blazer down from its hanger and looked inside each pocket once more. When he came to the inner breast pocket for the second time, he discovered what he could not have known by touch alone: the bottom seam was torn.

He widened the rip but could not see if anything had slipped down into the lining. Then, abandoning all reticence,

244

he tore the seam open. And there, between the lining and the outer cloth, was a business card.

On it, Alex read the following:

Church of the New Advent
of the Divine Emanation
Worship Service: Sundays 10:00 A.M.
Discussion Group: Mondays 7:30 P.M.
Prayer Meeting: Wednesdays 7:30 P.M.

It was followed by an address and a telephone number. Penned on the back beneath a small logo was a personal note:

Dear Andrew Graham,
Tonight you spoke wisely in the forum of men.
Will you fear to speak before Angels?
Visit us soon,
Sarah S.

Alex raced up the stairway, taking two steps at a time. Beside the desk in Andrew's room there was a house phone hanging on a wall bracket. He dialed the digit for an outside line, then the number on the card. A woman's voice answered. He almost succumbed to the wildly imprudent impulse to blurt out a demand for his son's return. Instead, he hung up without a word.

Scotch-taped to the wall above the phone was a list of numbers. Below "Magdalen", "Pizza", and "Library" was the word "Taxi". When he reached the taxi company, he asked that a car come round to Tyburne as quickly as possible. The voice on the other end promised that it would be at the front door within ten minutes.

As Alex waited on the college porch, he looked more carefully at the logo on the card. It was a graphic of a winged angel with outstretched arms, holding a black tree in one hand and a tree of red flames in the other. He had no time to consider what it might mean, because promptly at eight fifteen the taxi arrived. He jumped into the passenger seat beside the driver and told him the name of the street.

"Any particular house, sir?"

"It doesn't matter. I just want to get to the street."

"It's a long street."

"That's all right. I need a walk."

"A walk it is, then", said the driver, doing a U-turn in Tyburne court. Accelerating, lurching, zigging and zagging, the car seemed to be exceeding the speed limit but maneuvered ably enough through the center of town. Alex was still not used to driving on the wrong side of the line, and it made him dizzy.

"Is it far?" he asked.

"Not very. Here we are at Banbury. That will take us up north end, past Jericho way and Walton Manor."

"Are those places in Oxford?"

"Suburbs, sir."

Fifteen minutes later, the car braked for a stoplight, then turned left onto a side street. The driver pulled over to the left-hand curb.

"Here we are at Merlin. Five quid, please."

Alex paid him and got out onto the sidewalk. The driver executed another U-turn and went back the way he had come.

"Merlin Road!" Alex murmured, shaking his head. "How predictable."

By the light of a street lamp he checked the card again and memorized the house number. The avenue curved away toward the river. Both sides were lined with three- and four-story brick houses that looked old, some of them very old, though young enough to be considered new. In Oxford the word *new* could mean anything from one year to three hundred years old.

He began to walk, pulling his collar up against a brisk wind that promised rain. Lamps were spaced one per block, and the window light from the houses did not reach to the sidewalk. Proceeding in the dark, he prayed for spiritual protection and, if necessary, physical protection. It struck him suddenly that he did not know what he would do when he arrived at the "church". Perhaps he would find Andrew seated in a nonthreatening room filled with earnest, spiritual people listening to a lecture. Or worse, Andrew might be giving one. Alex would walk in, seat himself in the back row, and wait for his son to notice him. He imagined the boy's voice falling silent, his face surprised, then lighting up with pleasure. He would run to his father and they would embrace. Doubtless these cult people would have influenced his thinking by now, and Alex knew he would have a difficult time convincing Andrew to return to Tyburne. But he recalled the inscription on the back of the photograph— "My Pa, King of Halcyon"—and felt certain that Andrew's heart contained much good sense that would reawaken at the sight of his father. And when he had his son safely back in Christian territory, the King of Halcyon, assisted by the King of Heaven, would untangle the falsehoods that had ensnared his mind.

He prayed for that, but his apprehension grew with every step.

We're going away, Andrew had said.

His footsteps rang hollow on the concrete, cats yowled and crisscrossed the street, the blue lights of television sets glowed behind muslin curtains in several houses. Three blocks farther along, the spire of a small church appeared on the north side of the street. Alex crossed over and proceeded more slowly. A single light bulb burned above the double-door entrance. In the wall to the left of the door, "Saint Swithun's Parish, Church of England, est. 1821" was engraved in a block of stone. On either side of the door there were recessed alcoves that appeared to have contained statues at one time but now were empty. Above the door, and beneath the light, was a finely lettered sign that read:

Church of the New Advent
Pastor Gustav Bloch, Ph.D., D.D.

Beneath the text was the angel graphic in gilt paint. The tree in one hand was an evergreen shape, solid black. The other tree was stylized flames, bright red. Alex stared at the sign with loathing. Precisely what kind of "church" was this? And what was a divine emanation? Was this the nucleus of all spiritual energy, this sad little building on a shabby street that had gone to seed decades ago? If so, why was it empty? Had the parishioners all ascended?

He walked a few steps farther and glanced up an alleyway to see if there were lights on inside. There were none. He turned and was about to retrace his steps back to Banbury, anticipating a long walk home, when he heard the front door open.

A woman came out and closed the door behind her, locking up with a rattling of keys. He stood on the sidewalk, watching her, wondering if she was Sarah S. When she turned to go down the steps, she spotted him and paused. Showing no surprise, she gazed at him for a few seconds.

Alex cleared his throat. "Excuse me, please. I'm looking..."

She was in her late twenties, pretty, but her face appeared severe, thrown into stark relief by the light over the door. Her unblinking eyes waited for him to continue.

"I'm looking for the Church of the New Advent."

"Apparently you've found it", she said without expression. "We're not open this evening."

"I had hoped—well, I had heard that there would be a discussion group tonight. Mondays at seven thirty. I realize I'm late, but—"

"Where did you hear about the discussion group?"

"I read it somewhere."

"Well, it has been canceled."

"Oh, I see. So there's no one here."

"No one but me."

"Uh, Dr. Bloch isn't here?"

"Dr. Bloch is away. Why are you looking for Dr. Bloch?"

"I'm searching for... I'm interested in what he has to say."

As she pondered his reply, her eyes flickered all over his face, down his coat, trousers, shoes, and up again.

"You're not English", she said.

"No."

"American?"

Alex nodded.

"Why are you in Oxford?"

"I'm here doing research."

"Oh, I see. And finding time long on your hands? Nothing to do in the evenings?"

"Yes, that's right."

"Which college?"

Alex knew that if he said Tyburne, he risked breaking the thread that might lead to Andrew.

"It's private research."

"What kind of research?"

Spoken with measured calm, clipped and penetrating, her questions seemed to be gathering a composite picture of the man before her. What for? Clearly she was not afraid of him.

"What kind of research are you doing?" she asked again. Her tone was not offensive, but it was pitched exactly on the borderline. A neurotic person might interpret it as coldly manipulative, a confident person would not—or should not. Nevertheless, he felt that he was being interrogated.

"Uh, poetry."

"Poetry. Which branch of poetry?"

"Not a branch, a poet."

"Which poet?"

Fear was now rising in Alex's throat. He began to wonder if he was completely transparent, if every time he evaded or shaded the truth she knew it. He had never before encountered a woman whose physical appearance spelled "vulnerable female" yet whose inner character emanated absolute self-control and, moreover, perfect control of the situation. Her manner was flawlessly correct and mild—yet inspired dread.

"Which poet?" she repeated.

"Hopkins. Gerard Manley Hopkins."

"Ah, Hopkins. I prefer Blake. Are you interested in religious poetry?"

"Yes."

She regarded him silently, considering.

"Well, I regret we won't be open again until May."

"May? That's more than three months from now!"

"Perhaps if you're still in Oxford at that time—"

"Oh yes, I would like to attend your sessions very much."

"When Dr. Bloch returns in the spring, we'll resume our Sunday morning worship service."

"At ten o'clock", Alex blurted irrationally.

"That's right. Ten o'clock", she said slowly. Then, arriving at some conclusion, she turned away in the direction of Banbury.

"I'm heading your way", he said. "May I walk with you?"

"If you wish."

Side by side they proceeded toward the intersection.

"Are there many people in your church?"

"Yes."

"Students?"

"Why do you ask?"

"I guess I'm curious about whether it's a young or old congregation."

"Young? Old?"

"I mean, do you have a variety of ages?"

"Yes, we're a mixture."

"Oh. That's...nice."

"Nice?" A flicker of humor appeared about the edges of her lips, unmistakably sardonic, fading quickly. "Yes, I suppose it's nice. You would have to see for yourself."

The small talk was becoming frustrating. Impulsively, he wanted to shout at her, to demand the information he needed, but stopped himself in time. He had no way of knowing, at this point, how cultish the group really was. Were they a group of high-class New Agers who respected a degree of human freedom, or were they something more sinister, intent on seducing minds and locking them up, and guarding their prey from other human contact? If it was the latter case, then demanding access to Andrew might prove to be the fast way of closing all avenues to him. She could deny any knowledge of his son and might report him to the police as a harasser. She looked hard enough to do just that.

How could he keep her attention, how to capture her trust long enough to find out where she lived? Maybe she lived with other members of this organization. Cult people usually lived with one another. And Andrew might be among them. Should he follow her home? No, that would be too obvious.

"It's rather a long way downtown", Alex said. "I think I'll hail a taxi. Would you like to ride with me? I could drop you at your home."

"No thank you. I have a car. I'm on my way to London."

"Do you live there?"

She turned and examined him coolly.

"I have a flight to catch."

"You're going away, then?"

"Yes." Her tone implied that he was an idiot.

"When will you be back?"

251

She stopped walking and turned to face him. "Why do you want to know?"

Alex stammered, "A-all I meant was, if you're part of the church, and if you're going away, then there might not be anyone I could talk with. May is such a long time from now."

She did not respond to this but continued to examine his eyes.

"Perhaps you have a group that meets informally—someplace I could visit now, before May?"

"You seem insistent."

"I'm sorry. I don't mean to push. It's just that I haven't met many people here in Oxford, and I'm a long way from home."

"You mean you're lonely."

"Yes, I suppose so. Though not in the way that sounds."

"How does it sound?"

"I just meant that I was lonely for human company. It would be so nice to meet like-minded people with whom one could discuss things."

They resumed walking.

"Religious things?"

"Yes."

They reached the corner.

"What is your name?" she asked without a hint of warmth.

"Graham", he said without thinking.

Her eyes glanced at him and probed.

"Graham, Alexander", he added. "And you are...?"

"My name is Shaw."

"Like the playwright?"

"No relation. Shaw is my first name. Shaw Cunningham."

"I'm very glad to meet you, Miss Cunningham. And I do appreciate your advice. I look forward to attending your services when they resume. And I am sorry not to have met Dr. Bloch. You said he's away?"

"Yes."

"That's unfortunate. I've been looking for a theologian who might help me with some religious difficulties."

"Personal difficulties?"

"Uh, academic. Hopkins—"

"Yes, well, that *is* unfortunate. I must go now."

"And you say he won't be back until spring?"

"That is correct."

"Where has he gone?"

Her face betrayed a moment's irritation.

"If you must know, he is in Helsinki attending a meeting of the International Society of Metaphysicians, an organization that he helped to found. Now really, Mr. Alexander—"

"Yes, of course, Miss Cunningham. I have detained you far too long. Thank you so much for your patience and your help. I will say good-night, then."

She nodded curtly and walked away north along Banbury.

For an instant he wanted to follow her to her car, to memorize the license plate. He checked himself, realizing that following her would arouse her suspicions again. He argued that she would almost certainly drive south on Banbury, since she was headed in the direction of London, and thus he would be able to catch the plate number as she passed. He watched as she receded into the gloom beyond a street lamp and disappeared from view.

He waited on the curb, expecting her to come. Five minutes went by, then ten. Finally, he realized that she had either driven north on Banbury or had taken a different route south. His hands clenching inside his coat pockets, he knew that the thread had slipped from his fingers, had been yanked away into the featureless dark. The walk back to Tyburne was very long indeed.

10. *Neuron Paths in the World-Brain*

The next morning, Alex met Owen Whitfield at the Oxford Oratory. After Mass, as they walked back to Magdalen, he told the professor what had happened the night before. Owen prepared a breakfast of coffee and sweet buns in his rooms while Alex elaborated on the conversation he had had with Miss Cunningham.

"It sounds fishy, Alex. The tone more than anything, the evasiveness."

"Yes, the strange combination of feminine wiles and icy calculation."

"I believe you've finally stumbled onto their trail. Or, to mix metaphors, you've caught the end of a thread that's tied to a string that's tied to a chain that's wrapped around Andrew's ankle."

"Yes, but the thread disappeared the moment I tried to grasp it."

"All is not lost. There are ways we can trace these people. You say they've left for a few months?"

"They won't be back till May, and who can say where they've gone?"

"It might be possible to find out. Helm could do some checking for us. We'll track him down after lunch. In the meantime, I suggest we make a list of everything we know so far, especially what has just come to light. Then we'll discern what steps to take."

For the next half hour they wracked their brains, the professor writing down on a large notepad every item that came to their minds. He spent another fifteen minutes silently collating the material, then writing it all down a second time, in different order.

He passed the notepad to Alex.

"First, we have a working model of the chronology—the sequence of events—correlating as many dates as we can remember. Now, here, on the second page, we have another model—this is the hypothetical structure of what we're up against—in other words, the organization of this group. Our information is spotty in that regard, but a picture is emerging. The third model is what we might call Andrew's profile. This is spotty too, but it's a portrait of a gifted, impressionable young man who is steadily being magnetized by an alien influence. Altogether it doesn't amount to a great deal of evidence, but the three models dovetail, and a larger picture is forming."

"Read the chronology to me, would you, Owen?"

"In early October he falls in love and quickly falls out of love, but he may have been left a little vulnerable because of it. In late October he wins a debate and is approached by these cult people. In November he grows silent, and in his writing he begins exploring metaphysical issues outside the requirements of his academic field. Also, he becomes lax in the practice of his faith. Over Christmas he drops from view and fails to call home at the very time of year most people contact their families. In early January, he's still missing. And we finish with his strange phone calls to you on the twenty-first and twenty-third of the month. That looks like a distinct pattern to me."

"This is helpful. Up to now, the details have been swarming in my mind, leaving me as confused as ever. But it doesn't really indicate what I should do."

"Well, let's take it one step at a time: First, the Church of the New Advent has to be legally registered, either as owner or as tenant of the property that was once Saint Swithun's Parish. This means names and addresses will be forthcoming. Second, the names Gustav Bloch and Shaw Cunningham might be listed with the Oxford or London telephone exchanges. If not, the operator would at least divulge the information that they have unlisted numbers. Although no number or address could be obtained if that's the case, at least we'll know Miss Cunningham isn't a phantom."

"I already know she's not a phantom, Owen."

"Yes, but I think it helps to know she's got a spot she calls home and isn't just flitting about the landscape like a will-o'-the-wisp."

"She was definitely not wispy."

"Our third objective will be to try to track down this Helsinki event. Maybe that's where their mothership is parked."

"Would you repeat that, please?"

"If they're aliens, poor Saint Swithun's is probably a beachhead, a mere scouting party, a baby flying saucer, if you will. The real source is the mothership, hovering far above our atmosphere."

Alex glanced at Whitfield.

The professor curled a smile around his pipe stem.

"A figure of speech, Alex. I expect these people are thoroughly human. But they may be aliens in another sense. Almost certainly this Bloch is, and there's half a chance that the supposed Pakistani is also."

"A society of metaphysicians", murmured Alex, rubbing his face with a trembling hand. "What in the world is that, really?"

"Hard to say. The name could mean anything from a coffee klatch of retired philosophy professors to some kind of brainy cult."

"But what kind of cult?"

"Obviously not the kind whose members go dancing in the streets in saffron robes."

Whitfield rang the Oxford police station, only to learn that Detective Helm was not on duty that day. He would be in the office the following morning. Another call to the county hall produced an answering-machine message telling them that the registry office would not open until the next day.

The telephone information operator advised them that there was no number listed for the names they requested.

Whitfield persisted. "Do you mean they are unlisted? It's very important, Madam. It's a matter of life and death."

"There is no registration for those names, either listed or unlisted. Sorry."

"Is it possible for you to check throughout the United Kingdom?"

She hesitated but agreed after a bit more pleading, and asked him to hold. After several minutes the woman came back on the line and informed them that she could find no numbers, listed or unlisted, under those names.

"Operator, would you please check and see if there is a listing for the International Society of Metaphysicians?"

A moment later she responded. "There is nothing under that name, sir."

"Madam, you are displaying admirable patience. May I tax your good nature just a little longer and ask you to check for a British or English Society of Metaphysicians?"

She punished him with a tone change but complied.

"Here it is. Under the British Society of Metaphysicians."

Whitfield jotted down the number. He begged her for the society's address, and once again she bent the rules and gave it to him.

"A thousand blessings upon you and all whom you hold dear, gracious lady", said Whitfield.

"Er...yes", she replied, and rang off.

Whitfield held up the sheet of paper triumphantly. "Eureka! They're in the fashionable district of Kew Gardens,

Richmond, Surrey. It's a borough of southwest London, not far from Heathrow."

"Eighteen Gallipoli Street", Alex read aloud. "That rings a bell, Owen. Where have I heard that name before?"

"The Great War?"

"Yes, but—wait a minute!"

Excited, Alex extracted a small notebook from his pants pocket and flipped it open. "My clue book", he explained. "Gallipoli, Gallipoli, where are you? Wait, here it is! Owen, the phone booth from which Andrew placed his second call is situated on Gallipoli Street in Richmond. The information operator told me it was on a block with house numbers between one and sixty."

"Double eureka! We've found our cult."

"And we may have found Andrew also."

"Let's try something."

Whitfield dialed the society's number. His face was expressionless as he listened; then he hung up.

"Blast! A recorded message. It says the society's office is closed until May."

"May? Another confirmation!"

"Not conclusive, but it does imply that the Oxford group and the London group are one and the same. But even if we're wrong on that, it looks as if they've closed shop for precisely the same period."

"And gone off someplace together?"

"Helsinki, perhaps."

"Which leaves us at an impasse."

"Not necessarily. We don't know what this place is really, do we? Perhaps only a few officials went away and some of their underlings are still at eighteen Gallipoli. The office is closed, but there might be a nonpublic aspect to this group, their life going on as usual behind the scenes. Andrew could very well still be there."

Alex leaped to his feet. "Then I'm going to find out right now."

Whitfield lit his pipe and leaned back in his desk chair, closing his eyes. He puffed and puffed, as if the restriction of oxygen to his brain helped him to think.

"I have nothing planned for today", he said at last. "Care for a drive?"

The Humber did its best to navigate the main superhighway M40 that cut diagonally across the south of England from Birmingham to London. All other vehicles passed the old car, and not a few of the drivers honked irritably and gestured at Whitfield. The professor did not seem to mind; whenever a passing maniac caught his eye, he waved back, beaming, clenching his teeth around the pipe stem.

"They're probably all taking their wives to the maternity ward", he said, smiling. "I would hate to have my baby born in a motorcar at a hundred kilometers per hour, wouldn't you? Don't mind the insults; it's not personal."

"It looks highly personal to me, Owen. And crude."

"Just a taste of our cultural lexicon."

Within ninety minutes they reached London.

Gallipoli Street was, as Whitfield said, fashionable. It was a quiet neighborhood full of stately Victorian homes set back from the street, surrounded by gardens and soaring elm trees. Parked in front of the houses were expensive automobiles, some vintage, others modern and foreign. As the Humber approached number 18, it passed a phone booth. Whitfield parked at the curb two car lengths down from it and got out. Alex joined him on the cobbled sidewalk.

"Our friends live in fancy territory", the professor mused. "Business must be good."

They opened a wrought iron gate in the brick wall that surrounded the yard, and walked uneasily to the front steps.

The windows of the ground floor were shuttered from the inside with wood louvered panels. The door was solid oak, windowless. Bolted into the brick beside it was a brass plate on which was inscribed the following:

British Society of Metaphysicians
Member, International Society of Metaphysicians
Founded 1969
London, New York, Hamburg, Stockholm,
Helsinki, Saint Petersburg

★

Europa Institute

★

Kosmos Corporation
Cultural Imports-Exports

"Do you think we've found the mothership?" Whitfield whispered.

Alex rapped the door knocker. He waited a minute and rapped again. Both men strained their ears, but not a sound came from within.

The professor lit his pipe and squinted at the brass plate.

"A lot goes on inside that one little mansion, wouldn't you say?"

"It sounds as if no one's home."

"They're probably hiding in the coal cellar."

They walked down the steps and backed toward the street, looking up at the windows on the upper floors.

At that moment a young woman, wearing a top coat and a nurse's cap, came out onto the front porch of the house next door. She was wheeling a baby carriage, singing to whatever was inside.

"Hello", Whitfield called. "Can you tell us if anyone's home here?"

She turned a bright face to them and said with an Irish accent, "I think they've all gone away."

"All of them? Are you sure there's no one home?"

"Not very, sir, but there haven't been lights on for days."

"Do you know the people who live here?"

"Not really. I see them coming and going, but they keep to themselves. It's an office. Mobs of people in and out usually, but I don't know them to speak to. It's been quiet since they left."

"Do you have any idea where they've gone?"

She shook her head. "Their gardener told me he was paid to keep the yard tidy until spring. They'll be back in April or May, I would assume."

"And he didn't know where they were going?"

"No, he didn't. Sorry."

"Thank you, miss."

She maneuvered the carriage carefully down the steps on its two back wheels and ambled away up the street in the direction of a park.

"Well, that's that", Alex sighed. "Once again the thread disappears just as we're about to grasp it."

"All is not lost. We're learning a lot, and we've narrowed the possibilities considerably. We're closing in on them."

"I don't think so, Owen. They've gone away. The last time I spoke with Andrew, he told me he was going away."

"To the nucleus of all spiritual energy, he said, didn't he?"

"Yes. When we learned about this place this morning, I had hoped it was the 'nucleus' he was referring to. But it's clearly not so. I think he's gone with them to Helsinki."

"The plate tells us they have an office in Helsinki. Which means an address and a phone number, unless they're a total sham. And they look too established and too public for that. I suggest we return to Oxford and make a few more inquiries."

"I guess you're right, Owen. That's all we can do for now."

They left Gallipoli and drove north in the direction of a major avenue that would take them back to the motorway.

Three blocks from Gallipoli, Whitfield slammed on the brakes and pulled over to the curb.

"Look at that", he said in a low voice.

"Look at what?"

"That shop window. It's a travel agency. See the sign?"

"Nordica Travel. Scandinavian and Baltic Tours."

The two men looked at each other and got out of the car.

They entered the shop and found a single agent sitting at a computer by the front door.

"Good afternoon", Whitfield began. "I understand you can arrange flights to Finland."

"Finland and anywhere else in the world", the woman said, smiling professionally.

"Yes, our friends told us you did. There are several of us going to Helsinki. Some of our party have already gone." He patted his pockets. "Oh dear, I seem to have misplaced the list. You didn't bring a copy, did you, Graham?"

Alex patted his pockets also and shook his head.

"Blast!" erupted Whitfield. "Someday I'm going to leave home and forget my head. Where did I put that thing?"

He rummaged through his pockets again, pulling out bits and pieces of paper, which he inspected with absentminded concentration.

"I hope I left it in the car", he mumbled.

The woman watched curiously as Whitfield stalked out the front door.

Alex smiled at her nervously. She smiled back.

"I'm just the same", she said. "Always forgetting my keys and pocketbook."

Within a minute Whitfield came grumbling back inside.

"Good heavens, I'm in for it now!" he exclaimed. "Dr. Bloch is going to be very irritated with me."

"You seem to be having some trouble", the agent said.

"Yes. You see, a number of our association went on ahead to prepare for a conference in Helsinki. They flew out earlier than the rest of us. I was to make a booking for those who were to fly later, but I seem to have misplaced the list of people I was supposed to purchase tickets for."

"Oh, that is a bother", said the agent. "Perhaps you can contact the gentleman."

"I'm not really sure where he is in Finland. But I do know the names of those who will be at the conference. If there were a way of finding out who went on ahead—"

"I might be able to check. You said the name was Bloch?"

"Yes. B-l-o-c-h. Gustav Bloch. Although he could have booked under the society's name—the British Society of Metaphysicians."

"Let me see", she said, typing on her keyboard. "No, nothing listed under Bloch. Now let's try the society. Yes, there it is! A group booking: seven passengers on British Airways flight 794 to Helsinki. I'll print you out a list of names if you like."

"Would you? That is frightfully kind. Thank you so much."

While the printer hummed, the agent smiled at them again and said in an amused tone, "You're not a very organized society, I must say."

Whitfield looked pained. "Alas, all too true! But you know what metaphysicians are like."

She laughed. "Forgetful?"

"Very."

She handed the sheet of names to Whitfield.

"Excellent, Madam. This is most helpful. You have saved my reputation."

"Now, would you gentlemen care to book your flights?"

The professor patted his pockets again. "Blast!" he said again. "My wallet! Where on earth did I put that thing?"

"In the car?" Alex suggested, wondering how far Whitfield was going to push this.

"No, I just looked through everything in the car. Oh dear, Madam, what will you think of me! I'm afraid I'm going to have to go find it. It's probably sitting at home."

Whitfield grabbed Alex by the arm and pulled.

The woman watched them curiously as they went out the door, and shrugged as the Humber rumbled away down the street.

Whitfield, controlling the wheel with his right hand, handed the paper to Alex with his left.

"What does it say?"

"They left last Friday. Four days ago", Alex replied in a subdued voice. "Andrew was with them."

"Do you recognize the other names?"

"Only Bloch, plus someone named Symington, whose first name is Sarah."

"Ah, the recruiter."

"Yes, the girl at the Bird and Baby."

"I wonder why our formidable Miss Cunningham isn't on the list."

"Remember, when I saw her yesterday she told me she was just about to catch a flight. I expect she was joining them late. So in that sense our tale was partly true. I must say, Owen, you are quite an actor."

"Thank you. I was in a Shakespearean repertory company when I was young and foolish. I also did some modern improvisation work during the sixties. Angry young men and all that."

Northbound on the M40, they lapsed into silence. As the seemingly endless boroughs of greater London gave way to a series of towns and then villages, Alex thought hard about what he would do next. The first task upon returning to Oxford would be to contact the Finnish telephone system. Beyond that, everything was blank. He tried to envision a variety of intensely dramatic phone discussions with Andrew, in which he pleaded or reasoned with his son to come home. But the present situation was so replete with unknown factors that he gave it up and in the process gave himself over to a dark melancholy. Depression or anger seemed to be the only responses that his temperament was capable of at the moment. Whitfield, sensing his mood, broke into his thoughts.

"I say, Alex, would you like to pay a visit to the nucleus of all spiritual energy?"

"Not really."

"It's not far, and I think you'd appreciate it."

"That's not very amusing, Owen."

Whitfield smiled and took an exit lane at a town called Beaconsfield.

"G. K. Chesterton lived here", he said.

At another time Alex would have been excited by this, as he was very fond of Chesterton and had an extensive collection of his books. But now he acknowledged the information with a dull nod. He wanted to get back to Oxford as quickly as possible and wondered why Whitfield was taking this unnecessary side trip and why he was indulging in humor at such an inappropriate moment.

From Beaconsfield they proceeded up-country on a secondary road, winding through agricultural land and arriving finally at the gate of an estate set in a miniature forest of holly trees. Alex asked no questions; indeed, he was so absorbed by his wrestling match with conflicting emotions that he scarcely noticed the sign on the gatepost as they entered the paved driveway:

Saint Alban's Home
Sisters of Mercy

The car went slowly up a low hill between shining hollies and clumps of heather and came to a stop in front of a four-story red brick manor house perched on the crest of descending terraces that leveled out at the bottom of a shallow valley. The view was to the east, and when Alex stepped from the car onto the pebbled surface of the parking lot, a pine-scented wind hit him from that direction. He saw on the far side of the valley a woods of sighing evergreens sweeping the underside of low clouds. Here and there, light burst through the overcast and spilled pools of silver onto the valley floor. Flower gardens flanking the front walkway contained bare rose bushes, and spears of crocus poking out of the black soil. The stripped branches of vines clung to the sides of the building, fingering the white frames of the many windows. Piano music came from inside.

Owen rang the doorbell, and within a minute a nun opened it for them. Her dress was functional: a simple pale blue habit, a little crucifix pinned to the lapel, a slip of white cap and veil on her head revealing wisps of gray hair. She was perhaps sixty years old, yet her luminous face seemed ageless.

"Owen!" she cried. "I'm so glad you've come. Philomena has been singing today, and I knew that was a sign you would turn up."

"How did she know, I wonder?"

"She always knows."

Whitfield introduced Alex to Sister Perpetua, who took his large hand in her own tiny one and shook it briskly.

"Well, come in, then, out of the cold, and let's see where she's got to."

There were many people in the halls of the ground floor, some in wheelchairs, some walking the halls arm in arm, others painting or working on handicrafts at tables. From there, they passed into a large salon that was walled on three sides by windows. In the middle of the room stood an upright piano at which another nun was playing a jaunty piece. Seated on cushions around the piano were at least a dozen residents singing contrapuntally and shaking tambourines, bells, and clackers.

Without interrupting the melody, the piano player waved at Owen with her left hand and pointed to a patio door. Sister Perpetua led them through it into a garden overlooking the terraced valley. Seated in a wheelchair beneath a statue of the Blessed Virgin Mary was a human figure that at a distance of twenty paces seemed to Alex to be an old woman bundled in woolen shawls and sweaters. Her back was turned to them, and both her arms were outstretched, as if she were embracing the valley, or invoking God in a silent gesture.

"Shhhh", whispered Sister Perpetua. "Don't frighten the jenny wrens."

Dozens of small birds—sparrows, wrens, tomtits—were alighting on the figure's hands, pecking at the seeds cupped in them, flitting away to safety, returning again to the hands, chirping and squabbling.

Whitfield went up to the figure and kissed her on the forehead. This was met by a cry of glee, and both arms were flung about the professor's neck, scattering his hair and collar with seeds. Alex, coming up behind, saw a round white face planting a wet smack on his cheek.

"Owyah, Dad?"

"I'm well, Philly. How are you, my darling?"

"Good, Dad. Singin'."

"I heard you singing. Did you know I was coming today?"

"Ah knew, ah knew, Dad! Feedin' a bird."

"Lots of birds came to see you today."

"Flyed away."

"Oh, I'm sorry. Did we scare them off?"

"Scare dem off, Dad. They come back. Where Mum?"

"She flew away, but she's coming back soon. She said, give my Philly a big hug and kiss and tell her I love her."

Kneeling on the damp grass, he enfolded his daughter and held her head against his chest. He kissed her forehead again. She was a grizzled pudding of a woman with tufts of gray hair on her semibald head. Her stubby fingers clutched and unclutched the arms of her father's jacket. The daughter exposed a toothless mouth in a broad smile, the professor smiling too. She began to croon tonelessly.

Alex stood off a few paces, watching. Moved, embarrassed, he remembered a time when he had embraced one of his own children.

Fourteen years ago, on an autumn afternoon fraught with anguish, he had followed a hunch that led him along the dirt road of a provincial park twenty miles north of Halcyon. Father Toby was driving, his car puttering along at low speed as they searched the ditches, hoping to see a living boy and a bicycle. In the flaming red woods, all possibilities became real and present: both exultation and disaster. The most terrible imaginings had been flashing through Alex's mind during the previous two days, and he was now frantic with worry. The road ended at a forest stream, beside a natural landmark that was known locally as the Stone Giant. Viewed from a certain angle, this low cliff of shattered and tumbled Precambrian rock presented the image of a man seated beside the rushing stream, the man's axlike head on his chest, knees drawn up, toes dabbling in the water. The legs were two buttresses of stone between which was a sandy gap about a yard wide. They found Andrew asleep between the feet. All thoughts of recrimination or punishment evaporated. He scooped his son into his arms and held him, rocking him, groaning, breathing prayers of relief. And Father Toby had stood off a few paces, watching, embarrassed.

During those few moments, while the boy babbled out the tale of his personal odyssey, Alex had not listened to what he was saying. He heard only a language that was beyond words, that was the fluid convergence of soul and soul, of progenitor and child.

Now, all these years later, he was observing another man experiencing the same. Yet not the same, for Whitfield's child was in a safe and loving environment, a place from which she never strayed. He asked himself why Andrew had taken that long and perilous journey to speak with a stone giant. Was it because his human father had been all too often like a stone man?

It was just as likely, Alex told himself, that Andrew had simply desired to see what lay beyond the safe havens of the Clementine. He was a sweet-tempered, lovable child but also strong willed, imprudent, unwise. And though Alex had not expected prudence or wisdom from a ten-year-old, he had felt a keen stab of fear for the vulnerability of his son—this venturing spirit within such frail and untested flesh.

A bird landed on Whitfield's head and began to pick at the seeds in his hair. Another joined it, then another. More birds landed on his shoulders and arms. The professor and his daughter sat back and laughed together. The birds all rose in a flutter of alarm.

Whitfield called Alex over and introduced him to Philomena.

"This is Alex, Philly. He's my friend."

"Hello, Philly", Alex said.

"Owyah, Ayix?"

"I'm well, Philly. How are you?"

"Good, Ayix. I singin'."

"I heard you singing. I saw you feeding the birds."

"Feedin' a bird. My fren'."

"Lots of birds came to see you today."

"Flyed away."

"But they came back."

"They come back, see me."

Whitfield stood and said, "We have to go now, darling. I'll be back in a few days. Mum will fly home next week, and she'll come right away to see you."

"Jollie!" Philomena giggled.

Her father kissed her one more time.

"You come back, Ayix?" she asked.

"I will try to, Philly. Good-bye for now."

"Byee. Bless, Dad."

Before the two men had crossed the lawn, Philomena had extended her arms to welcome her many friends.

The Finnish telephone company informed Alex that the International Society of Metaphysicians had a number in Helsinki, but the listing contained no street address. He placed a call to the number and received an answering machine message in Finnish, Russian, German, and English, informing him that its offices were closed until the first of May.

Detective Helm did some checking and told him that Saint Swithun's Church had been sold the year before to a German company, which had leased it to the British Society of Metaphysicians. The Oxford city tax records revealed that the names listed as legal officers of the church were Bloch and Cunningham. The address given for both was Merlin Street, Oxford—the Church of the New Advent. Using his detective status, Helm went farther afield and netted the information that the society's headquarters on Gallipoli Street in the Richmond borough of London was also owned by the German company. The society's officers were listed on the Richmond tax records as Bloch and Cunningham. The company was Krueger-Kiel Pharmaceuticals of Hamburg.

After supper at Tyburne, Alex walked up the street to Magdalen and met with Whitfield in his rooms. Alex told him what he had learned, and as usual when receiving undigested information, the professor lit his pipe and gazed at the ceiling before responding.

Alex poured the tea for both. Whitfield offered a plate of biscuits. Then, without explaining, he picked up the phone and dialed a number. He conducted a friendly chat with the person who answered—someone named Patrick—then asked him if he knew of a company by the name of Kreuger-Kiel and a nonprofit foundation called the International Society of Metaphysicians. He asked several more questions of a technical nature, jotting information on a notepad, then hung up.

"That was my son", he explained to Alex. "He's in investments in London. He says he's never heard of the metaphysicians, but he's going to do some checking. Kreuger-Kiel, apparently, is quite well known. It's a reputable pharmaceutical firm, not the largest in Germany, but very big. It's owned by a consortium that's comprised of a dozen companies. It has a lot of influence in western Europe and is spreading into eastern Europe as well. Typical Eurofinance, clean as a whistle, boasting an annual profit greater than the budgets of many a small nation. He says he can locate the names of chief executives and directors, et cetera, but it will take some time." Whitfield paused and puffed on his pipe. "That might be of some help, Alex, but my guess is it will prove futile."

"Why do you think so?"

"Because typically these transnational corporations are very good at what they do."

"What do you mean? They manufacture medicine, don't they?"

"Yes, and many other things. As far as Patrick knows, none of it's illegal. Like all big companies, they're very good at image making. Benevolent foundations funded by interlocking holding companies that are stacked inside other companies, inside consortiums—"

"But who's behind Krueger-Kiel?"

271

"Theoretically, if you could trace every avenue back to its sources, you could end up with hundreds of names and addresses. If what they're up to is shady, you would be met by intractable diplomacy and a dearth of information. It could take years and would probably produce nothing."

"I see", Alex said gloomily.

"All I can tell you is Krueger-Kiel is big, it's complex, and it wields a lot of influence. If they're the kind of people who don't want outsiders probing into their affairs, they would spot you on their trail after your first inquiry."

The phone rang. Whitfield picked it up, listened, grunted a few times, jotted down notes, and hung up.

"That was Patrick", he said. "He's found an interesting bit of information. Bloch is on the board of Krueger-Kiel. He's given me a list of names of all the directors."

"At last we have something solid to go on!"

"There's more. He's also tracked down the names of the board of the International Society of Metaphysicians."

"How on earth did he do that so quickly?"

"The Internet", Whitfield said, smiling crookedly. "It's all in the world-brain. You just have to find the neuron paths."

"That's beyond me, Owen. Can I see the list?"

Whitfield handed it over, and Alex read the following:

Pat says International Society of Metaphysicians has offices in London, New York, Hamburg, Stockholm, Helsinki, Saint Petersburg.

Board members are:
Dr. Gustav Bloch, Ph.D., D.D., D.Sc.
Dr. Helen Ramsey-Scott, Ph.D., D.Sc., D.D., R.A.Sc.
Dr. Vasily Yefimovich Dubrovskoy, M.D., D.D.
Dr. Constance Von Arnow, D.Litt., D.D.
Dr. Iain Krishnamurti, D.D.

"Notice anything?"

"Some of these names are people who flew to Helsinki with Andrew", Alex said, looking up.

"Confirmation, Alex. Confirmation."

"Can I keep this?"

Whitfield nodded, and Alex inserted the paper into his clue book.

"Rather a lavish bouquet of doctorates", said the professor. "They obviously aren't shy about their degrees. How do they get along together, I wonder?"

"Are there addresses for their offices? What about the one in Helsinki?"

"Patrick says the addresses for Helsinki and Saint Petersburg are just post office boxes."

Alex shook his head and muttered, "Another dead-end street. It looks to me like I'll never get into their maze."

"I rather doubt you will." Whitfield pondered a minute. "I expect your search doesn't lie along the much-traveled high roads."

"What do you mean?"

"I mean you don't go marching into the front office and make inquiries. Your best route is to strike cross-country, avoiding the obvious, keeping your nose at grass level, jumping hedgerows and swimming rivers, if you will. By that method you might come upon them unawares."

"Maybe I should go home and return in the spring."

"Well, you could. But wouldn't you worry yourself to an early grave wondering what's happening to Andrew during the interim?"

"I could wait for him here, on the chance that he returns early. It's possible he'll try to pick up his belongings at Tyburne."

"Can you sit in that student residence for three months, watching the clock, waiting for a key to turn in the lock? What would you do with yourself during that time? If I were

273

in your shoes, I would go quite mad waiting around for a reunion that might never take place."

Alex stared mutely at the floor.

"It's entirely possible that he's not coming back to Oxford. They seem to have several centers of operation. And they could have plans for your son. With his attractive nature and capacity for dedication, they may have marked him out as someone to develop. He might very well become one of their recruiters."

Alex's face went dark with foreboding.

"It's only an hypothesis, and it pains me to say it. But perhaps it should be a factor in your decisions."

"I don't know what to do", Alex said, forehead in hand, rubbing his brow distractedly. But even as he said it, he realized that it was not so.

"I'm going to Helsinki", he said with finality. "I'm going to find him."

Whitfield nodded, his eyes searching Alex's face.

"Need a ride to the airport?" he asked gently.

Throughout that night, Alex tossed and turned on Andrew's bed. What had drawn his son and the metaphysicians to Finland, of all places? And what was the exact nature of their neopaganism? Oriental meditation? A covert or an explicit adoration of evil spirits? What was Andrew doing now, at this very moment? Was he on the borders of this cult, or was he already involved in some horrible act? Were they inducing him to do evil things, or had he realized that they were deceivers? Was he their star recruit, or was he their prisoner?

Alex examined all the possibilities, his mind tumbling with irrational thoughts and revolting scenes—more general than specific, yet capable of instilling in him a terror he had never felt before. And after terror there came feelings of despair, then anger, followed by a collapse into a sense of utter helplessness.

Finally he fantasized his own fist striking the face of Bloch again and again, the face a blur without identity, a specter or spirit rather than a person.

Arriving at this stage of descent, Alex threw back the blankets and got out of bed, his feet bare and cold on the floor. For some minutes he paced back and forth in that state, his hands trembling, his teeth bared. Finally, he turned on the desk lamp, dressed, and went down to the chapel, where he prayed fitfully until dawn.

Early the next morning, he went to an Oxford travel agency and bought a ticket on a Finnair flight leaving Heathrow that afternoon. The agent also booked a hotel room for him in Helsinki. He spent his final hours in Oxford praying, walking the streets, worrying, and going over in his mind everything that had happened.

Whitfield drove over to Tyburne after lunch to pick up Alex for the drive to the airport. Father Turner and John Groves came down the front steps with him and made their good-byes, promising to pray for guidance and protection for every step of his journey. When he tried to thank them, he choked and found himself unable to say anything. Understanding his emotion, the priest merely looked him in the eye and blessed him.

At the airport, Whitfield seemed lost in thought. When they shook hands at the security gate, the professor said, "Bring us back a star."

Then Alex was in the air, flying north into the unknown.

PART TWO

11. *The Winter World*

From an altitude of thirty thousand feet Finland was a sheet of white, blanked off the map by an Arctic storm that had howled down from the frozen Barents Sea the day before, passing to the west over Sweden and Norway. The jet landed on the plowed runway safely enough, and Alex went numbly though a series of gates, rituals, and vehicles that brought him finally to the eighth floor of Hotelli Suomi in the core of Helsinki.

From the window of his room he looked down upon the plumes cast up by snow removal machinery trying to clear city streets half-buried under drifts. He turned off the lights, lay down on the bed, and stared out at the star-filled sky. Feeling for the first time the full impact of his solitude, he saw that he was now alone in a strange land, ignorant of its language, and uncertain about what he should do. He was seeking a person who might well prove to be as elusive as a snow star spinning into a featureless white universe. His son could be practically anywhere—or nowhere.

Alex wondered how much longer he could maintain the chase. His money was dwindling, as were his brief infusions of optimism. And he was beginning to doubt that, even if he found Andrew, their reunion would solve the real problem. His son had abandoned the extraordinary privilege of an education from one of the great universities of the world, and this surely revealed something about his state of mind. Perhaps no ordinary approach, no amount of reasoning, would touch him. What could Alex possibly say that would reverse the downward spiral into the fearful asymmetry, as Owen Whitfield had called it? Would a hug and a few small birds twittering in his hair dispel the lies that had ensnared his mind?

Alex knew that he was suffering a temptation; he realized full well that discouragement spun a web of futility that blinded perception. He reminded himself that men all too often gave up their efforts just as they neared their goal. Some, however, persevered to success by exerting, at the last, more intense effort than before. But they could not do so if they allowed themselves to lose heart.

He went down to the restaurant off the main lobby. It was full of customers chattering in Swedish and Finnish, the latter executed with a peculiarly rapid, clipped monotone that appeared to be a national characteristic, easily distinguished from the more melodious inflexions of the Swedes. A waitress approached, and after a certain linguistic fumbling, discovered that Alex spoke English and Russian. Russian presented no problems for her, and they proceeded to the ordering of a meal. Alex asked her to bring whatever was the special of the day. It turned out to be smoked reindeer.

Afterward he returned to his room, feeling somewhat revived by the food. A perusal of the bedside telephone book produced no listing for the Europa Institute or the Kosmos Corporation, or any variations on the names. The number for the metaphysicians' society was listed, but it was the one he already had. No street address was given. He called the number and listened to the same message he had heard the day before. Hoping to find the address by another method, he went down to the lobby and asked the staff at the desk if they had heard of the society, but they had not. At a loss for what to do next, he decided to walk the downtown streets on the chance that he might catch sight of the metaphysicians' window sign. Seeing Alex heading for the exit, a desk clerk informed him in English that the temperature was minus thirty degrees Celsius and that it was not wise to go outside without a hat. Alex admitted to himself that the man was right. Moreover, in a city of a million people, to venture forth on a random search was a return to the logic of the haystacks—or the snowfields, as he now thought of it. It would be a waste of time.

The desk clerk suggested that he might enjoy a sauna in the recreation floor of the hotel. Not knowing what else to do, Alex took the elevator down to the lower level and discovered that it contained exercise rooms, a swimming pool, a squash court, and the sauna. An attendant took his wallet and the computerized card key for his room, put them in a safe-deposit box, and gave him a brass key pinned to a large white bath towel. Alex tried to communicate by hand gestures his desire to borrow or rent a bathing suit but did not succeed in getting this idea across. Knowing no English or Russian, the attendant pointed in the direction of the men's door.

The room was entirely lined with white and blue tiles, and practically deserted, save for a few large-bellied men who were stripping themselves. When Alex was himself reduced to his essential form, he wrapped himself in the towel and went through a door marked "Sauna". Inside, at least a dozen men of various ages were seated on the bleachers of a wood-lined room that could have seated sixty. They had all dispensed with their towels. The air was oven hot. In the center was a container of round stones suspended above glowing electric elements.

Alex sat down on the lower tier of benches and began to sweat. It was a pleasant feeling, and he was surprised to learn that he had been chilled for a long time, that it had become so abiding a condition that he had ceased to notice it. Perhaps he had always been cold and had not known it.

Now and then one or another of the guests would stand and beat himself with a leafy sapling, then saunter through swinging glass doors to an outdoor pool that was exposed to the night air. Beyond a guardrail the lights of office buildings towered all around. The water steamed with the cold, and a skim of ice clung to its edges. The hardy Finns plunged in without hesitation, sputtering, kicking, and blowing whale spumes with obvious enjoyment. As much as he admired them, Alex decided that this sport was not to his liking.

After ten minutes of roasting, he felt the deep pleasure of total warmth, a relaxation of all his muscles, and a blessed drowsiness. He was about to lie down flat on his back when a door opened and three women sauntered in. They were in their thirties or early forties, heavily made up with crimson fingernails and blond hair of an unnatural hue. They were carrying drinks in their hands, they were talking loudly, and they were stark naked.

Alex decided not to lie down.

The other guests appeared not to notice the new arrivals. The women sat together on the bench opposite Alex and continued their discussion, which he now realized was being conducted in German. They eyed his towel as if it were obscene. The situation was so completely alien to his experience that Alex was for a moment paralyzed with astonishment. In the aftershock of the total inversion of cultural norms, it took him a second or two to regain control of his eyes. He got up and left.

After an icy shower that restored his equilibrium, he returned to his room, opened the sliding window, and sat down on the bed facing it. Gusts of cold air wafted in, billowing the curtains, carrying with them a shimmer of frost particles.

He blew a few puffs of breath against the draft and watched the colors of the city lights materialize in their crystals.

"*Matto-pazzo*", he said aloud. Then he laughed, throwing himself back on the bed, shaking with the crude humor of it. The meaning of what was funniest lay beyond his grasp, and so too any ability to explain to himself why he was so convulsed.

He sat up, still chuckling, staring out at the bleak landscape of this liberated Nordic void, and shook his head in disbelief. The scene in the sauna had taken him totally by surprise and was now indelibly imprinted on his mind. Yet the sight of the red-taloned Valkyries had little power to inflame him, for what he had witnessed was absurd and sad, a symptom of a society that had lost its sense of mystery. If it had been merely a three-dimensional pornography, a kind of virtual reality of hot cavorting pagan flesh, he would have been morally offended. But now, in retrospect, he was most disturbed by the banality of the women's demeanor. The situation appeared to be, for them, completely normal. Strangest of all, it was asexual—or at least the Europeans in the sauna had treated it as such.

Alex's desires had always been well within the range of the natural. Yet he now felt an inexplicable disgust, for the sudden and unexpected cornucopia of female bodies was not in essence feminine, not womanly in any way that awakened the heart's deeper longings. Why all this pink flesh? he wondered. Why the desperation to return to the bacchanal in the forest glade? Did these women think their overexposure was attractive? If they had ever known real love, would they have unveiled themselves to strange men? The sensation of attracting male eyes would have been revealed to them for what it was: an adolescent concept of sexuality, bereft of love, and in the end bereft of genuine passion. Then it struck him that perhaps they did not think about it at all.

He laughed again, remembering his first dance. The gymnasium of Clementine Valley Regional High School. It was April 1974. D-Day. Dance day. Dragged by his pal Toby from the chrysalis of introversion, he had attended the mating rites like a sacrificial victim. While two hundred of his peers gyrated to the blasting rhythm he protected himself by sipping from a soft-drink bottle with a bored look as he leaned against a wall in the corner farthest from the sound amplifiers. He was also protected by a newly cultivated sardonic veneer, protected most of all by analyzing what was happening out there on the dance floor beneath the coiling streamers and the whirling colored lights. The sensation of floating above mayhem was a form of transcendence. Reason asserting itself over irrationality.

Nevertheless, he was drawn by the fascination of sensual chaos. Cavort, thrash, plunge, fling, scream, yowl! Demolish harmony and feel the thrill of it: testosterone and estrogen surging to the thump-thump-thump of the deafening drums and squealing guitars. He recognized the ethos of Nietzsche. Definitely *nyet*.

"Kill romance and watch what rushes in to take its place", he said, aloud, to no one. No one could hear.

Not that he had ever had a romance with a real girl, he reminded himself—sardonically, analytically. The surges of testosterone-fuel were burned up by winter runs along the height of the Clementine's ice-covered bluffs. Beating his ribs against the cold, puffing frosts of breath, he always sprinted harder as he passed the crest of a hill where one could so easily be mesmerized by natural vistas, the white satin dresses of impossibly beautiful women, the distant feminine principle, the utterly mesmerizing, the unobtainable. These winter landscapes, he told himself, were the solid metaphor of the semidomesticated and sometimes savage wilderness of the soul. Though he did suspect in candid moments that his impervious solitude was the mask of loneliness.

He checked his watch and hoped the dance would not take too long. Toby had borrowed his father's rusty 1958 Pontiac, and Alex was dependent on it for a ride home, unless he wanted to hoof it all the way back to Halcyon in the dark. But Toby was in a fit of creative dancing out there in center place. Massive, muscular Toby, the hockey captain with a bevy of maidens vying for his attention.

And so, the incredibly intelligent and incredibly distant Alexander Graham, failing everything in grade 12 except Literature (A+), destined not to graduate but content with this form of failure, remained where he was, immobile, uncommitted, risking nothing.

Among the lovely girls who were dancing that evening was one who drew his eyes again and again. Easily the most beautiful in the Clementine Valley, she wore a long white gown that seemed out of place among girls squeezed into tight jeans and tighter tops. Toby was zeroing in, but she seemed indifferent to his desperate attempts to make eye contact. He was just one of the many who were entranced by her presence. She floated around from one partner to the next, friendly but detached.

What was it about her? Something in the expression of her face. There was goodness in it, combined with self-respect. She wasn't vying for anyone's attention. She danced somewhat woodenly, which endeared her to Alex—endeared her at a distance, for he knew that he had no hope of meeting her. But from that moment on, he could not take his eyes off her. He noticed that she laughed at her mistakes, did not seem to mind that she was inept at the art of controlled frenzy, that she was uncool. And that made her very cool in Alex's estimation. She was protected by her beauty, of course, because beautiful women are forgiven just about anything. But her laughing eyes were also full of character. Alex saw by this that she needed no protection. And that was her protection.

During a break, Toby sauntered over to the corner, sweating, grinning, his chest heaving.

"Having fun, Worm?"

"A fabulous time, Toffee. Simply fabulous."

"Danced with anyone yet?"

"Nope."

"Why not, dummy?"

"An act of charity on my part. People have been known to die of boredom, and I don't want that on my conscience."

Toby shook his head and shot a look of chagrin at his friend.

"Weird, Worm. You're weird."

"You too, Toffee. When do we go home?"

Toby rolled his eyes. "Two hours from now. Hopefully three hours. Look, instead of torturing yourself, why don't you just jump in, cheer up, and have fun?"

"That's a really inspired suggestion", Alex drawled. "Why didn't I think of that?"

Toby, who at that stage of his life was practically immune to ironies, nodded enthusiastically.

"Yeah! Now you're getting the idea", he said, casting a glance about the room in search of a suitably boring partner for his boring friend.

At that moment, the most beautiful girl in the Clementine Valley walked over to them and said, "Hi! Crazy, isn't it?"

Toby instantly turned on the charm—facial expressions, body language, and repartee. Alex knew that he was about to become an unnecessary third party. He said nothing as Toby and the girl chatted. Toby asked her for the next dance. She replied that she wasn't a good dancer and was kind of worn out. Would he mind if she said no? Toby was crestfallen but said he didn't mind. The girl did it nicely, kindly. She seemed devoid of the subliminal messages and controlling devices that girls usually employed when dealing with transparent males.

So removed was Alex from the possibility of knowing her that he did not bother to make his presence felt. But he did notice that she looked tired. He crossed the gym and found three empty stacking chairs, brought them back to Toby and the girl, and pushed one toward her. He bowed slightly as he did this, his face as somber as a butler. She looked at him and smiled. She sat down.

The music started up again, and further conversation became impossible. Because Toby was unable to endure immobility for long, he quickly found another partner and dived back in, his creativity exploding with renewed force.

Alex and the girl sat side by side watching the anarchy. Rather, Alex stared at absolutely nothing, completely overwhelmed by what another people, in another time and place, might have called an illumination. He was stunned; he had become pure consciousness raptured before a tree burning bright on a mountain top, revelation and awe combining in an ineffable moment of encounter.

The music ended.

The girl turned to him and said, "I saw the most beautiful thing today."

Alex cleared his throat. "Uh, you did?"

"I was walking in the woods above our school."

"Where do you go to school?"

"Holywell."

He remembered vaguely that Holywell was a girl's boarding school in a town thirty miles south. He had never been there. Even more impossible, he told himself, she lived far beyond the limits of his world. Hopeless, utterly hopeless. Life is not fair. But in a split second of analysis, he thought that however pointless their conversation might prove, it would be a bright memory that he could cling to in the future, mingling exultation and permanent disappointment.

"Are you here with someone?" he asked in a tone that he regretted, for it sounded both boring and boorish.

"I came with a friend from school. She's from Halcyon."

"Where are you from?" he said.

"Northern Alberta. We have a farm near Peace River. Dad raises buffalo for the government."

"Oh."

Oh. What could he say? Buffalo gal, won't you come out tonight? More and more impossible!

He glanced at her hands, half expecting to see calluses and blunt digits, but they were slender, the fingernails well manicured, unpainted.

"Are you interested in farming?" he asked lamely.

"Not really. I hope to study library science after I graduate. I want to be a librarian."

"Oh."

Again with the stupid *Oh!* As if someone had hit him between the eyes with a two-by-four.

"Uh, do you like books?"

She laughed and nodded.

Dumb, Alex! Of course she likes books!

"What kind of books?"

"All kinds of books. I love poetry especially."

"What kind of poetry?"

"Every kind. Emily Dickinson's my favorite. Have you heard of her?"

"American. Nineteenth century. But I haven't read any."

She looked at him curiously. Then, in this most improbable place, in the midst of the rites of pandemonium, the impossible girl recited a poem in a voice full of feeling and sensitivity to the meaning of words:

> I'm Nobody! Who are you?
> Are you—Nobody—too?
> Then there's a pair of us!
> Don't tell! they'd advertise—you know!
> How dreary—to be—Somebody!
> How public—like a Frog—
> To tell one's name—the livelong June—
> To an admiring Bog!

Alex smiled at her. She smiled back.

"Would you like to hear more?"

"All right."

> I thought that nature was enough
> Till Human nature came
> But that the other did absorb
> As Parallax a Flame—

Alex saw trees burning with holy fire, unconsumed! Holy ground! Holy wells!

Now their eyes met, and neither he nor she was capable of glancing away.

"Can you tell me another?" he asked.

"Are you sure I'm not boring you?"

"You're not boring me."

And so in a wistful voice that totally demolished his heart, she recited the following:

> Oh Sacrament of summer days,
> Oh Last Communion in the Haze—
> Permit a child to join.
> Thy sacred emblems to partake—
> The consecrated bread to take
> And thine immortal wine!

She fell silent, gazing pensively at the floor.

"You said you saw something beautiful today", Alex prompted.

Her face became suddenly serious, and she leaned toward him with an earnestness so at odds with the customs of his era that he suspected she might have come from another century. Was she from the nineteenth? Was she, perhaps, Emily Dickinson herself?

But the music broke out again, obliterating any possibility of a reply. They sat together making a little pool of silence in the maelstrom of noise. When there was another intermission, the girl turned to him.

"It was like the last poem", she said. "Like a sacrament of summer days. This morning, I was walking in the hills above the college. There's a maple woods up there, and it's full of damp hollows covered with last year's leaves. I love the rustling sound they make when you walk through them, just when the new green leaves start budding. I stopped to listen to the warblers. The warblers are back now, did you know?"

"Yes, I knew."

"Warblers, and bobolinks for choristers. And the woods a dome of light. Hope, a thing with feathers that perches in the soul. It was so lovely, that feeling. I was so happy. Then something more wonderful happened."

"What was it?"

"I heard rustling on the other side of a little hill, as if people were walking there. I wanted to be alone, so I hid in the trees hoping they'd go away without seeing me. But they didn't. The sound of the leaves just got stronger and stronger. It was a rhythm, like poetry. I crept closer to the brow of the hill and peered over. And there I saw, down in a little bowl of a clearing, three deer."

"Deer?"

"Yes, and they were dancing."

"Do deer dance?"

"Yes, they do. Until this morning I didn't know it, but now I know." Her eyes brimmed with emotion. "They *do* dance."

"How do they dance?"

"The bowl was about thirty feet across. The deer were springing—you know the way they spring on all four feet. Round and round they pranced, spaced equally apart, round and round on the sides of the bowl, in a perfect circle..." Her voice trailed off. "Why were they doing that?"

"Maybe it was a mating rite."

"No, I don't think so. Deer mate in the fall. Besides, it was a doe and two yearlings."

"And that's what you saw."

She glanced at him uneasily. "Yes."

"That's very beautiful", he said.

"You think so? You really think so?" Her question was asked with the intensity of a child begging permission to join in a last communion.

"But what does it mean?" he asked.

"I don't know. Maybe we don't need to know what it means. Maybe we just have to see it and let it live inside us, like an emblem."

The music began again, this time slower, closer to what in another age would have been called a waltz.

Alex stood up.

"Would you dance with me?" he asked.

"Yes, I would very much like to dance with you", she answered shyly.

And during the dance, as he held the impossible, the ineffable, the miraculous in his arms, he said to her, "My name is Alexander."

"My name is Carol", she said. "Don't tell. They'd advertise, you know."

Then the long courtship full of hand holding and brief, discreet kisses. The thrill of praying beside her at Mass, knowing that their souls were uniting, knowing that the reined passions would be released on the wedding night, when they, like two deer maddened by love, would dance in the holy forest under skies crammed with singing stars. A great joy was hidden in their longing. He and Carol discussed it often, murmuring consolations and reminders, waiting together for the sacrament, as love deepened and deepened until it seemed there was no bottom to the reservoir. When the reservoir fountained at last, there was no holding it back; it became a river, became a flood, then spilled into the oceanic cosmos of supernatural love, natural and supernatural flowing together in potent-fertile joy. They drowned in it and were born.

How poor were the tumbled metaphors with which he had sought to express something that was—was everything: the mystery of love. The dance of love. The sea of love. The kingdom of love. The night Jacob was conceived, the night Andrew came into existence. The countless tender moments. The fire that burned but did not consume, two small flames that filled the whole realm of their covenant, uniting into a single flame that was greater than the sum of its provinces. They had no need for lands, or money, or power. Their bed was consecrated and joy filled; its four posts were the quadrants of the world's compass, their quilted blankets a domain spreading from horizon to horizon.

Prayer was the atmosphere of their kingdom. Their children were conceived in prayer and born in prayer. Carol had died praying, held in his arms and enfolded in his prayers. Birth and death had been suffused with grace. And because that was true, Alex now reminded himself, even the darkness was enfolded, even the loss and the abandonment, and the falling through the ice of the solid world into the desolation beneath.

Prayer! He now realized that in his anxiety he had been neglecting it again. Bowing his head, he invoked Christ's peace upon his mind and heart—and flesh. Eventually the turbulence subsided, and lying down, he fell into a profound sleep.

In a dream, he knelt in the snow of a winter garden, raked with the purple shadows of naked trees and bushes. Shriveled orange berries clung to the bare branches. The mint-green moon rode high, and the garden was silver under the orb.

A woman appeared, standing on the moon. She descended toward him, her face so radiant that he could not look at her. He glanced down at his feet, which were bare, scarred, dirty. Ashamed of his mortality, he shivered in the numbing wind.

"I bring a gift for you", she said.

Overwhelmed by awe, he could not speak.

"Will you open your hand, Alexander?" she said.

He opened his right hand and saw that it was scarred and unwashed, red with the cold. Red, also, with blood. Whose blood? He clenched it swiftly and withdrew it.

"It is for you to decide", she said. "You are free to open or not to open. I ask you to open."

He opened his hand. She cupped his hand in hers. It was warm; his was cold. Hers was a small temple, his a cage of bones.

"Who are you?" he whispered, unable to look at her.

"I am the one who serves", she said. "I am the one who believes when all hope is lost. I am the sweetness of the tides and the cloak of stars."

All around him the snow melted, the air grew warm and fragrant, the trees budded and flowered, and their fruits swelled as the leaves turned red and gold. The sounds of children singing and calling arose in the distant woods.

The woman placed into his hand a single object: a carved piece of blue stone embedded in a chunk of ice. It was a kingfisher, immobilized in its beauty. Within the stone a tiny heart ticked rhythmically.

She closed his fingers over the gift.

"Now the greater gift", she said. Extending her hand toward a cupola of white ivory above a line of cobalt trees, she drew forth the form of another woman. As this second figure approached, the first said to him, "Here is the heart that is on your path. You are free to choose or not choose. But understand that not choosing is a choice."

He could not see the face of the second woman, though love and sorrow were in her. He stepped toward her. Then she came to him and took his hand, and did not let it go.

"Now you must sleep again", said the first.

He was taken away from that place and awoke in the dark.

Helsinki's sixteen-hour midwinter night stretched far into the morning. When Alex got out of bed he felt revived a little, still pondering the meaning of the dream. It was symbolic, he concluded; it was his subconscious creating images of the feminine to correct what he had seen last night in the sauna. It was also about hope, about spring and summer and autumn after the winter of his current condition.

He spent two hours on the phone calling every major hotel in the city. None had a guest registered under the name Andrew Graham, and none had heard of a meeting of a society of metaphysicians. One clerk was willing to check for Finnish translations of the society's name, but her efforts produced no results.

In the lobby gift shop, he purchased a fur hat and fleece-lined gloves with a fistful of *markkaa*. Then he went out onto the street, where the rays of low-hanging sun hit him full in the face. Wondering if he should turn to the left or to the right, he closed his eyes, prayed, and walked to the left.

His ramble seemed directionless, yet by late morning he realized that on some semiconscious level he had paced a route of concentric squares, extending farther and farther from the center of the city, moving gradually out from Mannerheimin-tie, the great avenue that split the downtown core. He examined all the buildings that he passed, scanned a thousand signs, fighting off a glut of sensory overload, the result of hyperfocus. There was, as well, the growing sense of discouragement, a feeling that despite his methodical search, he was once again looking for a microscopic crystal in a galaxy of snow.

At lunchtime, he ventured down to the harbor front, searching for a place where he could purchase inexpensive food. Walking along the stone quayside, he saw tugs breaking up the ice that threatened a passenger liner docked a hundred yards along the quay. Gulls screeched and wheeled. Grandfathers walked small children whose excited babbling competed with the birds; they were happy despite the numbing cold, bundled in white woolens shot with red, blue, and yellow braiding; silver bells tinkled on their elf hats above red-cheeked Caucasian faces with Mongolian eyes.

Ferociously hungry after his hours of walking, Alex finally found a covered market on the harbor front. It was relatively warm inside, and he chose one of the many food stalls that were strung along both walls. Neither he nor the serving girl had any language in common, but the message of hunger, and the exchange of money, proved to be universal. He pointed to a number of items in the glass coolers, and she understood. He took the food to one of the high tables at which manual laborers and office workers stood eating their meals. They glanced at him and returned to their conversations, which were unintelligible except for occasional words such as *Brussels* and *California*. Alex wondered what was happening in the world.

He ate slabs of cheese on brown bread, a pickled egg, a piece of sizzling sausage, and chocolate-covered rusks. Then he turned his attention to a platter of smoked herring.

"Speak to me", he murmured to a coppery fish that glared at him. "Grant me a wish."

He finished it off with a mug of coffee so dark, so sweet, that he was somewhat revived. Still, he sipped the dregs with a heavy heart, feeling keenly the loneliness that had grown with each passing hour. After a second cup of coffee, he resumed the search.

All afternoon he continued to pace out his expanding squares, forcing himself to go slowly, to ignore the sensation of panic that lurked on the perimeter of his feelings, which could easily sabotage his efforts. He purchased a yellow highlight pen and a city map at a grocery store and marked off the streets he had already covered. They seemed pathetically few compared to the area he had yet to walk. A riot of protest broke out within him as the background sense of futility worsened, yet he pushed it away and continued on.

The sun set. Through the dusk he investigated a final long street, forcing himself not to hurry, not to speed toward a hasty completion for fear of missing that single vital sign that could be so easily overlooked in his fatigue. At six o'clock he gave up and turned back toward the hotel.

Upon arrival, he ate a meal in the restaurant and returned to his room for a hot shower. After that he tried to pray, but he was mentally exhausted, garbling memorized prayers, mixing the words crazily as behind his closed eyes he hallucinated a continuous stream of signs in foreign languages. He longed for sleep, but his muscles ached; he felt like weeping but couldn't. His mind was a tumult of everything he had seen since his departure from Halcyon. He began to groan soundlessly.

The following two days were spent much in the same way, and though he later tried to recall the chronology of that merciless trek, it would ever after elude his memory. Swirling about the axis of manic determination were disconnected fragments: a carved sailing ship in a shop window, a doll's house filled with miniature eighteenth-century furniture, the bass boom of a ship's horn, an old woman feeding pigeons in a park, a drunk declaiming at a street corner, children skating on a rink under arc lights, a Laplander couple in fabulous parkas and fur boots, staring into a department store window that displayed designer clothing. Once he passed a bronze figure on a pedestal in front of an art gallery—a runner nearing the finish line like an exhausted beast, ice in the crevices of his torso, snow filling the sockets of his blind eyes.

All such details were subsumed in the endless snow-filled avenues, the short gray days, and the looming cloud of despair. Still he would not give up and continued to mark off the streets on his map, one by one, as if they were not the mileposts of a descent into nether regions of the hopelessly obsessed. There were times when he had to stop and shake himself, groping for the memory of why he was doing this. In one frightening moment, he could not remember where he was or what he was looking for. He sat down on the curb and strained for a clear thought. For a few seconds he could not even recall his name. It took a bit longer to locate, in a numbed zone of his mind, the name of the city. This was followed, with effort, by the name of his son.

"Andrew", he said. "Yes. This is for him. For my son. Who is lost."

Then came the certainty that he was now, for today at least, beyond the point when further walking would be of use. He struggled to orient himself on the map and trudged back to the hotel.

12. *The Hollow Men*

That night, the accumulated strain of overexhaustion produced a form of sleeplessness that was only half-conscious, a state in which images and memories blended into fitful prologues of uncompleted dreams, then shattered in every direction. Feeling more desolate than he had felt for many years, he forced his aching body out of bed and sat in a chair in the dark, staring at the silent riffling curtains of red aurora borealis in the northern sky.

Empty, he said to himself. *I feel so empty.* He was a void around which the fragments of his life circled without apparent meaning: Andrew's face, Jacob's, Carol's; his father, his mother; Father Toby; Charles; Oleg; and Jamie and Hannah Colley, surfacing between the ice floes, then sinking again. Of the many elements swimming before his mind's eye, memories from the past began to assert themselves. Some of these were scenes of sadness, and thus Alex pushed them away and tried to think about his first love—books. Facets of many tales leaped out of the shadows: Karamazov's four boys, Tolstoy's princes and serfs, Lermontov's heroes and killers, Turgenev's fathers and sons—materialists breeding nihilists and nihilists breeding anarchists, saints breeding sinners and some of the sinners breeding saints, and all the weltering masses of mankind who swam between the shores of birth and death.

But where was he in this continuum? Somewhere in the crowded waters he was a man adrift, tethered to shore only by the fading memory of his home valley, his safe shop, and, of course, the faith. That he believed in God was without question. This had always been true of him; it was the objective fact of his life. But there were gaps in the makeup of his personality, and he now saw that these were not inconsiderable. When his wife died, for a while it was the end of the world, because part of him had died with her. As the long, slow recovery proceeded, he had gratefully and guiltily accepted the return of equilibrium. But he had not paid attention to a parallel phenomenon: his reversion to what he had been before his marriage. Though changed by whatever he had learned during their years together, and by whatever healing had taken place, he had fallen back into the old pattern of withdrawal. Nursing the dreadful wound of her absence, he had failed to notice the subtler void opening up within himself.

As a boy he had loved to sit by the Clementine River on the outcropping of rock that jutted into the current half a mile upriver from Halcyon. There he would remain immobile for hours, staring at the water, simply content to observe and to listen. At that period of his life he had not yet begun to examine his motives, had not reflected on why he should waste large quantities of time merely looking at something that was completely ordinary. Now, more than thirty years later, he wondered at himself. Other boys would have taken a fishing rod and done what was necessary to pull a fish triumphantly from the water. Or would have thrown themselves into it. Or would have heaved stones and made a fort beside it. None of these had Alex done. Yet in that solitary and isolated place, he had experienced extraordinary calm. He had fallen in love with *being* itself.

What kind of child had he been, and what kind of man had the child fathered? Was not a man defined by what he loved? It was there by the Clementine, after all, that he had met Leonid Vozhinsky. He had surely loved the old man. It had seemed to him, and still seemed to him, that Layo was not so much a messenger as he was the message itself, cast up on the shore by the moving waters. That intrusion, that singular distraction, had altered Alex's life forever. But he now wondered why the people he had loved were always taken away from him. As they passed into memory, or abstractions, did he fade along with them?

In the three areas of life that mattered most to him—faith, family, and culture—he was practically a nonentity. Subtract him from the social equation, and few, if any, would notice. Within his parish he was an anonymous layman, and desired to remain so. Within his community he was a recluse, and clung to his privacy ferociously. Within his family he was a function that had outlived its purpose.

He now asked himself if he had become one of Eliot's hollow men. If so, he was unlike other hollow men in that he was burdened with the curse of sensitivity, observing the slow-motion catastrophe of his times with horrible clarity, helpless to stop it, capable only of saving the literary debris that floated to the surface.

He recalled a conversation that he had had with his father shortly before his death. Unable to sleep one night in early spring, Alex had lain awake for hours, hands folded behind his head, legs stretched out, the sinuous bow of his body happy with recent growth. He was eighteen years old, and the night whispered with budding maple leaves outside the open window of his bedroom. Fully recovered from his near-fatal battle with rheumatic fever, he was growing lean and muscular from daily walks in the hills. He now understood that he was capable of pushing back death with his own small powers. Moreover, he had danced with a girl the night before. Carol was her name, and he was flushed with the awe of unexpected joy.

His mother was away visiting her family in the Maritime Provinces, and thus he was alone in the empty house with his father. At about two o'clock in the morning, he heard faint strains of phonograph music coming from below. Getting up and going downstairs to his father's office, he opened the door and found Angus Graham seated in the armchair beside the record player. The melancholy strains of an Italian opera filled the room.

His father's eyes were closed, but he was not asleep, for clasped in his right hand was a glass tumbler with which he was keeping time to the music as if it were a conductor's baton. On the desk stood a large bottle containing only whiskey fumes. His silver hair was askew, and his face was flushed. His suit jacket lay on the floor where it had been tossed. He was wearing his crackled World War II bomber jacket. Angus Graham never wore that jacket. Never. It always hung in the attic closet, packed in naphthalene.

"Father?" Alex said hesitantly.

His father's eyes opened suddenly.

"Ah, my scion!" he mumbled.

"Father, are you all right?"

"Never been better."

That his father sipped occasionally from a bottle that he kept in the armoire beneath shelves of statute books was no secret. But those sips were few and far between, taken in the company of juridical, if not judicial, peers. Never before had Alex seen him drunk.

"Siddown, my boy."

Alex sat on the footstool, three paces away, clasped his hands tightly around his knees, and regarded his father with an anxious expression.

The scratchy disk of Enrico Caruso singing *O mio babbino caro* came to an end, and the machine turned itself off.

"It's late, Father", Alex said. "Maybe you should think about going to bed."

"Exshellent idea!" Angus replied, waving his glass. "To shleep! To shleep! Full fathoms five my father lies!"

"Is something wrong?"

Angus Graham straightened himself, snorted, and drank the last drops of whiskey in his glass.

"Bring me that bottle, there's a good lad."

"It's empty."

"Then bring me another!"

"I...I don't think there is another."

"Oh? Well, no matter. It's far too late!"

"Something's the matter, Father. Can't you tell me? Is Mother all right? Have you heard from her?"

"Your mother?" he drawled. "She is my consolation and shall return forthwith. She has called, and we have spoken together of many things—of the jabberwockied world, of string and sealing wax, of the view from the wrong side of the looking glass, and finally we spoke, with circumspection, of the ligatures that bind men's souls."

Angus smiled bitterly, and Alex felt the sinking feeling that children feel when they discover for the first time that their parents are not invulnerable.

They stared at each other in silence.

"I have killed", his father said at last.

"The war?"

"No, not the war. Though I flew the infernal machines that laid the death eggs, it was not my lot to drop any upon the cities of man. Subhunting. Atlantic. Coast duty, cracked the seal of a few, made them rise, sent the crews off to POW camps. That was my best and worst. Killed nobody, not for lack of trying. There by the thundering sea I met your dear mother. Good lass, good woman. A toast to her! Halifax girl. Happy. Happy marriage. Hail thee, good wife, good marriage! Hail thee, good son, good scion!"

"Father, you should go to bed."

"To sleep full fathoms five? What of the victim, Alexander? What of her? Does she sleep the sleep of the happy brides?"

Confused and suddenly frightened, Alex said nothing. When he was able to form words, he said, "Who?"

"Who, you ask? I will tell you who. I will tell you two—though the first was beyond my reach and could not be protected. It is the second who died because of me."

"Died?" Alex stammered. "Who died?"

"The details of this horror are not germane to our discussion. But the souls, Alexander, the souls whom we the wise did not protect—of that I speak. Along with sealing wax."

He sucked at his empty glass.

"Who died?" Alex insisted.

Ignoring the question, his father asked, "What do you want to do with your life?"

"I don't know. I'm not sure."

"Any ideas?"

Alex shook his head.

"A lawyer like your beloved father?"

"I...I don't think so", he whispered, fearing to offend.

To his surprise, Angus leaned forward with an exuberant grin.

"Good!" he roared. "Never—I tell you, *never*—become a lawyer!"

"Why not?"

"Because for every Thomas More there are a hundred Henrys, a thousand Cromwells, and ten thousand Richard Riches. At worst, cynical corruption; at best, blindness, indifference, compromise!"

"You're like Saint Thomas, Father. I know you are."

"I?" he snorted. "Thank you, loyal son. But 'tis not so. I, fool that I am, succumbed to the *spiritus mundi*. Gradually, gradually. Gradualism is the pervading *modus operandi* of our times. My peers' pressure is subtle but relentless. Who can hold it back? A lawyer, a magistrate, a judge—ho! A personage to be reckoned with, am I not?"

"I don't know what you're talking about."

"Of course you wouldn't. Which is as it should be. Never mind; you haven't missed a thing. The century creeps on at its weary pace with nary a change. There is nothing new under the sun. No edifying thing is there to be learned about our species!"

The word *species* was uttered with loathing.

"You can teach me", Alex said gently.

"I? I can teach nothing to anyone."

"That's not true."

"It is true. I am not worthy of the name *judge*. Lo, I am no different from the leering old judges who tried to condemn brave Susanna. Saved by Daniel, a true man, in the nick of time. There are no more true men. Old Daniel could have taught us a thing worth knowing. But there are no more Daniels."

"What can he teach us, Father?"

"To respect no man, despite his office, until the man has proved he will lay down his life for the truth."

"You're that kind of man. I know you are. I respect you."

"Do you? Tonight you are the only one in the Clementine Valley who does."

Alex reached out and clutched his father's forearm—an unprecedented act. Angus stared at his son's fingers clamped about his wrist. He laughed.

"Tell me what happened, Father. Please."

"All right, then. I'll tell you."

Angus dropped his eyes. He looked up sharply and resumed. Though a few of his words were slurred, and the delivery was slower than was usual for him, under the influence of alcohol he waxed loquacious.

"Two years ago, an ugly case came before my bench. A monster, just days away from his eighteenth birthday, had killed a girl. I will spare you the details of his crime, which was the outcome of a life devoted to self-indulgence, dominated by lust and other drugs. If he had committed the act a few days later, he would have been sentenced to life imprisonment. Yet, because the ethos of sentiment reigns, the scientists of the psyche insist that no one is guilty of anything; these hollow men have infested every level of public life and thus have affected the legal system as well. The culprit's lawyers and psychologists maintained that he was quite disturbed and needed therapy. Thus far has justice fallen in our fair land.

"I was constrained to send him to an institution for the unhappy and maladjusted. If I had given a harsher sentence, his lawyers would have moved for mistrial. He easily could have walked away. And so I gave him the maximum for a juvenile, and off he went merrily for a rest in a rehabilitation center, where he enjoyed the attention of psychologists and counselors, and unlimited films and television and other luxuries. A month ago he was released with a clean bill of health. This morning he was arrested in Toronto for repeating his first crime. Now two young women are dead."

"But what could you have done! The law—"

"Oh, the law! The law! Is it the standard of human justice and the arbiter of human grievance any longer? Nay, the hollow men have made it a cunning tool of social and political manipulation. But I serve the law, don't I? It struck me tonight, Alexander, that I am a judge in nothing but the name, for the word *law* has come untethered from the source of Truth. I am an instrument in the hands of a revolution. I am Richard Rich. I should have raised a public hue and cry when that monster got off with a vacation. But I kept silent. Do you know why?"

Angus Graham bent forward until his bloodshot eyes were inches away from his son's.

"I'll tell you why. I had nursed a secret longing for a seat on the superior court of this province. And after that, well, who knows, maybe the supreme court of the land. Ah, what good I would do, if I were to arrive at the summit, I told myself. Yes, I would do my part to shift the legal system back in the direction of justice. *Iustitia! Veritas!* Just a little silence, a little complicity, a little good-old-boyism and I would be there. Then, by gum, we'd turn things around. How would you have liked to live in Toronto, Alexander?"

"Not much, Father."

"How about Ottawa?"

"No."

"Well, we can still go there if I keep playing by the rules of the game. The high benches are crowded with ambitious lawyers bloated with the ambience of their weighty responsibilities, their magnificent egos, and their exalted reputations. Idealists, the lot of them. Not one of them fails to consider the meaning of justice, to discuss it soberly like philosophers, and to betray it at every turn. The more betrayal, the more advancement, you see."

"Is this true?"

"Well, not entirely. I am suffering a momentary disillusion, as you can probably tell. I am sick of precision. I am speaking in broad and unfair generalizations that underline a truth: Why do the wicked prosper, my son? Why do they prosper? Can you tell me why?"

Alexander shook his head.

"The prince of this world. That is the reason. The prince of this world. The devil in a three-piece suit."

"Hasn't God conquered the world?" Alex argued.

Angus Graham tilted his head and pondered the problem. "Yes and no."

"What do you mean?"

"Ask the theologians. As for myself, I am sick to death of maneuvering, of strategies, and of reputation. If you talk with the devil every day, some of his soot clings to you. I need a bath."

"A bath?"

"I will resign."

"But you can't resign. Good men have to stay in the system, to work for change."

"Thank you for your loyalty. It does a father's heart good. Where is that whiskey bottle?"

"It's empty."

"Find me another."

"There isn't any."

"Well, no matter. Find me my violin."

Alex's father was an undistinguished musician. In his youth he had studied violin, and played moderately well. But for many years the instrument had sat on the top of the office safe gathering dust.

Alex brought it to him and opened the case.

"Ah, my beauty", Angus said, withdrawing the violin carefully. He tucked the curved base under his chin and plucked a string with his forefinger. Positioning the bow, he drew it across the strings. The squeal was unpleasant.

"I am", he said, "an instrument in the hands of a state that is no longer able to read the composer's score. What, then, should a man do?"

"He should return to the composition, shouldn't he? He should make music the way it was written."

His father smiled at him sadly.

"Alexander of Halcyon, such a response comes from a good but naïve heart."

"Am I naïve, Father? Are things really as bad as you think?"

"Oh yes, they are indeed. And you will see worse."

Alex looked at his father dubiously.

Angus fingered the strings and drew the bow back and forth. He stopped, twisted the tuning pegs, and tried again. The squeal softened and issued into a bar of halting music.

"Never become a lawyer, Alexander. Promise me?"

307

"I promise."

"Then it is done. Contracted, sealed, witnessed by heaven."

"Why did you become a lawyer?"

"Because I was confused. Aside from a simple trust in civilization and a rudimentary faith, I did not know what was of value in this world." Angus stumbled abruptly to his feet and began to play. The piece was imperfectly executed, but as the violinist's hand steadied and his memory stirred, the score began to flow.

"What's that you're playing?" Alex asked.

"Niccolò Paganini."

"It's beautiful."

"Thank you."

Angus sat down and laid the violin on his lap, the bow slicing the air like a lecturer's pointer.

"It was more than ignorance and confusion. It was loyalty."

"Loyalty?"

"Loyalty to my father. Your grandfather, as you know, was a lawyer, and his father before him. For a clan of Catholics in Orange Ontario, these were no mean accomplishments. Even so, despite the Lodge and the pork-barrel politicians who ran the county, and still run the county, it was a comfortable life. The worst my grandfather had to contend with were wills, boundary disputes, snake-oil salesmen, and town drunks."

Angus paused and sipped at the empty glass. Though his eyes were red and his words slurring more and more, his speech was in no way incapacitated.

"Father," Alex pleaded, "it's late—"

"Late? Yes, the hour is late. Far, far too late. *Kronos* kills us all in the end. Father Time is a consummate democrat. Now where was I?"

"You were telling me about Great-grandfather Graham."

"Oh yes. Well, my father in his time was presented with much the same, though an occasional murder and that rarest of events, a divorce, began to appear in our placid village. By the time I began to practice law after the war, the waters were muddying. By the sixties, madness entered. Not good old-fashioned insanity but social madness—widespread cheating and myriad forms of slick, avaricious dishonesty; drugs; domestic battering; rape—all rising from the fever swamps of the apostatizing human community. And let us not forget the inauguration of premeditated, state-sanctioned murder. Litigation became a way of life, a cultural norm. What do you think the next generation of lawyers and judges will inherit?"

Alex shook his head.

"Unthinkable evil entwined with unimaginable stupidity. Wisdom is departing from the land, my son. And where there is no wisdom, the people will perish."

Alex's doubts were expressed clearly on his face. Angus paused and scanned him with his old judge's eyes.

"I wanted to be a concert violinist when I was young", he went on. "Instead, I succumbed to pressure, to the lure of position and status. I was afraid."

This last admission was mumbled, and Angus' eyes looked away.

"I was afraid", he repeated. "I had been told from birth— no, soaked it up with the atmosphere in these rooms—that money and influence are the substance of our society. Knew that while my grandfather and father had not always been liked, they had always been respected. I wanted that too. So I wrapped my cowardice in idealism, and now these many years later a monster whose fate I held in my hands has killed again."

He put the violin and bow into the case and returned it to the top of the safe.

Standing with his back to Alex, he said, "I did not listen to my heart."

There was no further conversation. They both went off to their bedrooms, and shortly after, Alex heard his father's snores. He lay awake in the dark wondering what his father had meant by the "heart". He determined to ask him for further explanation, but in the cool light of dawn, deferring to his father's embarrassment, he hesitated. Shortly after the exchange—the next day, in fact—Angus Graham resumed his robes and his bench and went on as usual. The question remained unasked and unanswered. Angus recovered. Dignity was restored. During the following years, however, Alex or his mother would sometimes find the door of the office locked, and they knew that behind it Angus was sipping whiskey and fingering his violin. On occasion he would burst forth from the room to deliver slurred renditions of cathartic verse, swaying and emoting and declaiming in the hallway while mother and son kept him from toppling and pushed him up the staircase to bed.

"Prospero the sorcerer has seized my land!" Angus shouted during one of those sessions. "Here be Caliban, judicious murder in his hand!"

"Come to bed, Angus dear", Alex's mother soothed. "You're overworked and very tired."

"The state totters! Drink, servant monster, for it shall come to pass; do not seek thyself in a looking glass!"

"Hush now, hush."

And Angus allowed himself to be hushed.

He drank rarely, and never was he a mean drunk; always he was the quintessence of genteel inebriation, waxing eloquent and melancholic to such a degree that his outpourings approached the level of poetry or primitive music. Because of Alex's and Angus' habit of mutual detachment, they never referred to their most intimate conversation, but Alex remembered every word of it. He respected his father, and pitied him too, and when Angus' car skidded off the icy road on the bluffs above the Clementine three years later, he grieved for him.

Sitting in the dark thirty years later, Alex heard the squeal of the violin afresh. Hoping to distract himself, he turned on the television set and watched a Finnish network, then switched to one from Stockholm, and finally to a satellite channel that offered the English-language CNN. The news informed him that another high school massacre had occurred. Two boys had shot and killed a dozen schoolmates and teachers, while wounding dozens more, then committed suicide. It had happened in a prosperous, middle-class town in America. He turned off the television and slept fitfully for a few hours.

After a solid breakfast the next morning, he felt somewhat revived, and realized that the habit of skipping meals had contributed to his dissociation and inability to think. As he lingered over coffee in the hotel restaurant, planning his route, he adjured himself to set a more realistic goal for the day, to walk fewer streets. By now he was beyond the issue of whether or not the search would prove fruitful. It was his task merely to continue until he had looked at every sign in the city. If it took years—well, he turned away from that thought.

Had he become unbalanced? Yes, he had, but just a little, he told himself. He must not give up, must not turn aside when a bit more effort might lead to success. Though success was also beyond the issue of the real.

What, then, was real? To walk was real. To root and poke, to grope and fumble, to look, to seek—these were real.

He got up from the table and with map in hand went out into the streets for the fourth day of the search. The temperature, thankfully, was not as cold as it had been. Indeed, it had risen close to the thawing mark. This, combined with the light of the pale sun struggling out from behind a sheet of overcast, reduced the strain of the trek. Alex moved carefully along at an old man's pace, guarding his energy, reducing the visual stimuli to proportions that did not produce burnout.

He tried to pray and found that the words of his prayers, and even the interior sense of prayer, were once again flowing with coherence. He also experimented with linear thought; the experiment did not fail, the thoughts made sense. He breathed deeply and quickened his pace a degree, keeping a cautious eye on what this increased output of energy cost him. He was relieved that he could maintain a normal speed without losing his sense of mental balance. It was not exactly vitality, but on the other hand it was no longer dementia.

Checking the map, he saw that he had come to the edge of a district called Eira, situated on a promontory that capped the southwest corner of the city, overlooking the shipbuilding docks in a bay to the west with the broad expanse of the Gulf of Finland to the south. On its half dozen circuitous streets were the homes of the wealthy, mansions and luxury townhouses. Most of the buildings had been constructed in the previous century, but their elegance had been maintained fastidiously.

As Alex climbed the hill, he noted a few signs on gateposts and doors announcing mainly the embassies of small nations. He considered the possibility that he was wasting his time exploring this enclave and was on the point of turning around to go back down into central Helsinki when he was struck by the thought that Eira was the ideal spot for moneyed metaphysicians.

If it's anywhere, it must be here, he told himself.

At the very crest, he entered a square named Engelinaukio and ambled slowly around it for five minutes, distracted by the cumulus clouds that were now scudding across the frozen sea and by the welcome intrusion of blue sky. When he passed a small sign affixed to the gatepost of a castlelike building, his eyes were already going numb with the influx of too much random detail. He only half saw it and walked farther along the street before the word *kosmos* registered in his brain. He stopped and retraced his steps.

The "castle" was neither very ancient nor modern. It appeared to be one of those ornate eighteenth-century buildings that had once been residences for the aristocracy but that had been turned to other purposes during the postwar period. It was a handsome edifice and the largest building on the block. Its stones were yellow; the woodwork around the windows and doors was enameled white. Alex went up the granite front steps and looked closely at the brass plate on the green door.

Kosmos Yhteistyö

Kosmos Oy

Kulturin Tuonti ja Vienti

He flipped through his Finnish-English phrase book to confirm what he already knew, then twirled the bell key in the center of the door. A chime echoed distantly within. He waited, then rang again. Stepping back, he looked carefully at the leaded glass windows on each side of the door, but they were shaded by closed venetian blinds.

He rang the bell once more.

Finally, the sound of a muffled human voice came through the door, accompanied by rattling chains and latches.

The door opened a foot, and a gnome peered outside.

He was no more than four feet in height, his skull completely bald, his eyes two wrinkled slits that gazed up at Alex with a mixture of natural openness and professional caution. He said something in Finnish, of which Alex understood not a word. He tried a response in English, but the old man merely shook his head and closed the door an inch. Then Alex tried Russian, and the eyes crinkled, the door opened an inch, and the man said, "*Da! Da!*"

"Is the Kosmos Corporation open for business?" Alex asked.

"No, there's no one here."

"But I see that you are here, sir", Alex replied.

"Are you a Russian?"

"No, I'm from Canada."

"That's in the United States, isn't it?"

"Not exactly. May I ask you some questions?"

"Ask me what you will, but don't be disappointed by the answers. I'm only the caretaker." He cackled with merriment. "I am Ooski."

"Mr. Ooski, can you tell me when the people who work here will return?"

"It will be a long time. Next month, the month after, or the month after that. Why do you seek them?"

"I visited the Kosmos office in England, and now that I'm visiting Helsinki, I would like to meet with them here."

"Oh, I don't know anything about that. You'll have to come back after winter."

"I won't be able to. I must meet them now."

"Impossible, impossible."

"Please, sir, it's an urgent matter. Isn't there another address in the city where I can reach them?"

"If they have one, they haven't told *me* about it. These people come and go. Poor Ooski sweeps up, keeps the furnace going, empties the mousetraps. That's all he knows."

"I see. Do you know Dr. Bloch?"

"Dr. Bloch? I don't recognize the name. It's not *suomen kieli*."

"He is a German."

"Ah! There's a German who comes here sometimes. But I don't know him. He's one of the bosses. He flies here from Hamburg."

"That's right—Dr. Bloch is from Hamburg. Tell me, is there an office for a society of metaphysicians in this building?"

"A society of what?"

Alex repeated the word slowly, but the Russian term lost something in the translation. Ooski shook his head.

"Is there a Europa Institute here?"

Another shake of the head. "So many comings and goings, so many foreigners—pardon me, I don't mean you. You're a good foreigner; this I can plainly see."

"Thank you, Mr. Ooski. Tell me, did you recently meet in this house a young man who spoke English?"

"English? Yes, I heard English and many other languages. There were several from England who came—a week ago last Friday it was. They came for a meeting."

"Where was the meeting held?"

"In the ballroom upstairs. What a mess they left. I worked for hours cleaning up the wine spills and the caviar on the parquet floor. Smart people have bad manners, I always say. They never give a thought for the little people."

"Did you hear the name Graham mentioned? Or Andrew?"

"I heard much, but not that. Foreigners have strange names. This house has seen many in its time. It used to be the residence of a Swedish lord, before the czar of Russia kicked them out. Then we kicked the czar out, then those Hitler troops, then that Stalin bastard. Then in '56 the Russians took their stinking naval base off our soil, ran away, and never came back." He gave a single ferocious nod. "Nobody beats the Suomi folk for long!"

"So, you don't remember the names of the people or the names of the organizations?"

"I hear things all day long, but it's in one ear and out the other without a pause in between, as I tell the bosses. Euro this and Kosmo that, meta this and meta that. What do these things mean to me? Nothing! Ha! Don't worry yourself about the big people, I always say. Soon, they too will be gone."

"I'm sure you are right, Mr. Ooski. Are you certain there will be no one returning here for some time?"

"Ooski is sure. They all went off to the land of the Russians."

"When did they go?"

"The Monday after the party, I think."

"Eight days ago?"

Ooski made his face more gnomish than ever. "Maybe it was eight days ago. But then, they never tell me their business."

"Did they say where they were going in Russia?"

"To Saint Petersburg. I overheard it. That's the old name for Leningrad, but now it's the new name again."

"Can you tell me where they will be staying?"

"No."

"But surely you have a number where they could be contacted?"

"What for? So I can call them and tell them how many mice I caught this week?" His face went red with hilarity.

Alex forced a hollow laugh. "Yes, I see what you mean. But I would wager that in the office there is a paper that would tell us where they are staying in Saint Petersburg."

Ooski's face resumed its first caution.

"I doubt this."

"Would it be possible for you to check?"

Now the caution became suspicion. The door closed another inch.

"I cleaned the office. I saw no paper like that. You should call on the telephone. The message machine will tell you."

"I have already called. It tells me nothing. I'm greatly disappointed by this, for the matter is urgent."

"What kind of urgent?"

"It's a question of life and death."

And eternity, and the destiny of a soul, Alex added silently.

Ooski relented a fraction, his face screwing up as if a thought were pausing between his ears.

"Why don't you call the Russians?" he said. "A person needs papers to get into Russia. They can tell you, down there at the bottom of the hill."

Realizing that this was a useful suggestion, Alex thanked him and turned to go.

"And write the bosses a letter", the old custodian called after him. "Mail it to this address. They'll write back to you. They're nice people, except for the sloppy table manners."

Later that day Alex located the embassy of the Russian Federation on Tehtaankatu Street, below the hill of Eira. There a secretary listened while he explained that he needed to contact his son who was traveling in Russia. An important family matter made it urgent that he speak with him immediately. It was a matter of life and death, he added. She peered at him carefully, then consulted her computer.

Fifteen minutes later he left the embassy with the information that Andrew had indeed gone to Russia on a three-month tourist visa, in a party of fourteen people. They had departed by the regular Aeroflot flight on the twenty-sixth of January and were registered with the state travel agency, Intourist, at the Hotel Peterhof in Saint Petersburg.

Groaning inwardly, Alex realized that Andrew had left Finland on the day he and Owen Whitfield were drinking ale in the Bobbing Pinto in Cricklewood. And that night Alex had had his chilling encounter with the lovely Shaw Cunningham, who was about to catch a flight. A flight to where? Until now, he had assumed that her destination was Helsinki, but clearly the metaphysicians had already left the city by that time. If she was joining them, she had probably flown directly to Saint Petersburg. What was the reason for all this convoluted travel? Where were they going?

Alex hoped that they had come to ground permanently in the old imperial capital and that they intended to go no farther. The trail was now nine days old, and it was crucial that he narrow the gap as swiftly as possible.

Back in his hotel room, he placed a call to the Peterhof and asked if an Andrew Graham was registered. He was. Trying to suppress his growing excitement, Alex stammered out a request for a connection to the room. A few seconds later the call was answered, and a heavy voice said, "*Ja?*"

Speaking in as natural Russian as he could muster, Alex asked for "*Andrei* Graham".

"Who is calling?" the voice asked in Russian.

"An acquaintance", Alex replied calmly.

"What is your name?"

Groping, he blurted, "Serov—Alexei Serov."

"Serov? Who are you, Serov, and how do you know Graham?"

"I met him once. I wish to speak with him again."

The phone's mouthpiece was covered by a hand. Muffled conversation filtered through.

"He does not recall your name. Where did you meet him?"

"In Oxford."

"You met him in Oxford", the voice repeated dubiously. "How did you know where to find him?"

"He told me."

An ominous silence came back over the line. Then the voice said tonelessly, "I do not think so."

The line went dead.

With a stab of fear Alex realized that he had acted precipitously, that he had naïvely overlooked the nature of the people Andrew was with, had forgotten that their organization was inextricably bound up with deception. They would, of course, be extremely sensitive to contact with anyone who was not on intimate terms with their beliefs and goals. Andrew was a fresh recruit, and they would guard him against exposure to anything that might pull him from their web.

Beating his head softly with his closed fist, Alex groaned in exasperation.

What should he do? If he called back and demanded to speak to his son, they would probably hang up again. But if Andrew had a room of his own, or if he was sharing it with another person, there was a chance that at some point he would be alone. If Alex called at that moment, he would be able to speak with him, plead with him, beg him to run from these people with all haste.

He tried three more times that day, but each time the same deep voice answered, and each time Alex replaced the receiver on its cradle without saying a word. He had an intuition that it was Bloch on the other end, for the voice was very like the voice that had terminated the call Andrew had made from the phone booth on Gallipoli Street.

He wondered if he should contact the police in Saint Petersburg and ask them to investigate. This was a possible solution, but after weighing it, he knew that it would be counterproductive. Andrew was not a physical captive. At any time he could walk away from these metaphysicians, if he so wished, and come back to reality. But he was choosing not to do so for reasons that were wholly mysterious. Alex guessed that he was convinced to some degree by the group's religious beliefs; or at least he was intrigued by them and was on a quest for more knowledge and experience. No doubt he was excited by an adventure of cosmic proportions. Step by step they were taking him to increasingly exotic places, and added to the lure of the transcendent aspects of their philosophy, this would make a powerful intoxicant. He was riding on the back of Zeus' eagle and having the time of his life.

Alex saw that his only choice was to narrow the gap physically, geographically, to seek a way of meeting his son face-to-face.

Then followed days within a labyrinth of bureaucracy. This included calls to Charles Findley for additional funds. The money was wired to a bank in downtown Helsinki, and that too entailed negotiations. There were applications at the Russian embassy for a rushed visa, which required photographs, identification papers, and interviews. There were arrangements through a travel agent, which was necessary for the satisfaction of Intourist requirements: a hotel license number, booking confirmations, more faxes. A rail ticket from Helsinki to Saint Petersburg. The costs were mounting rapidly, and for that reason it was necessary to forego an airline flight. The trip by rail would take only six hours, and the ticket for a coach seat was relatively inexpensive.

It was a week filled with frantic worry and the ever-present battle against discouragement. There were taxi rides and more walking; there were documents and more documents. It was the documents especially that eroded his peace. The whole world lived, breathed, and ate documents, it seemed. Documents were not made to serve man; man was made to serve documents. At the end of this complex test of endurance, Alex found himself fuming against European bureaucracy and feeling more lenient toward his native country than he had in the past.

He tried several more times to reach Andrew's hotel room, hoping against hope to get past the barricades. The Peterhof lobby desk divulged the information that the party that included Andrew Graham was still registered and would continue to be in residence for an indeterminate period. Alex dictated a message for Andrew. But when he spoke with the clerk the following day, the man could not say if Andrew Graham had received the note; he suggested that perhaps one of the party had picked it up for him. Alex dictated a second note and asked the clerk to seal it in an envelope to be hand-delivered to Andrew alone. The day after, the Peterhof switchboard began to automatically terminate Alex's calls. Obviously the hotel had call-recognition technology, and someone had asked the switchboard to abort any calls from Alex's number in Helsinki. His attempts to reach the hotel from public phone booths got a little farther, but only as far as the front desk. When he asked for Andrew Graham, he was met with a clerical wall of noninformation and abrupt terminations.

Hoping to boost his spirits, Alex tried to contact Owen Whitfield by phone, but there was no answer at his rooms at Magdalen. The college receptionist said the professor was at a conference in Cambridge and would not return until the following week. She offered to take a message. Alex asked her to tell Whitfield he was on his way to Russia and would try to call him from there. Then he phoned Jacob in Toronto, only to connect with the answering machine. After the beep he left a message telling his elder son where he was and what had happened and asking him to return the call. He tried Father Toby as well, but another answering machine informed him that he was away at a retreat for the week. The whole world was away, it seemed, leaving Alex feeling very much alone with the greatest crisis of his life.

He spent an afternoon wandering about the Ateneum, the Finnish national art gallery. It helped to fill the hours of waiting that had become a torture. Wandering aimlessly around a room that hosted a visiting exhibition of works by the German artist Ernst Barlach, Alex saw a number of sculptures embodying a sense of man's exposure and isolation. For the most part these were human figures, solitary forms wrestling with mythological presences and the human condition. There were many bronze and wooden angels in the room, and among them were works for which Barlach was famous. Alex noted their technical mastery, but due to his worried state he remained untouched until he came at last to a bronze angel with upraised sword, standing upon the back of a wolf. The angel was triumphant, sword raised high in his hands. The wolf cringed, crushed beneath the angelic feet that barely touched its back. The sculpture's title was *Warrior of the Spirit*.

On the Sunday before he was to leave for Russia, he located a Mass at Saint Henrik's Parish down the street from the Russian embassy. There was a scattering of Finns in attendance, plus a few Swedes, but for the most part the congregation was from the diplomatic corps and the community of Asian and African immigrant workers. Alex was grateful for the sacrament but could not concentrate.

The next day, he walked from Hotelli Suomi to the railway terminal at the far end of Mannerheimintie. It was an ugly stone building, its outer walls girded by sixty-foot-high statues of giants holding illuminated globes. Whether this team of *Übermenschen* included Atlas, Prometheus, or Antichrist himself, it was hard to tell. They looked like so many gargantuan bowlers about to hurl their globes into the maze of the city, to topple the pins of the architecture in a frenzy of superior destruction. Alex boarded the train and was glad to see the last of them.

13. *Cabins and Palaces*

From the window of his coach, Alex stared out at mile after mile of Finland. The ingenious constructions of steel, glass, and white concrete declined in size and number as the West fell behind, giving way to orderly farms, neat villages, finely surfaced roads, and colorful cottages—all in a state of excellent repair. It was a country that exuded prosperity. And it was also strangely familiar. Alex had to remind himself that he was not in the northern regions of his own native province, that armies had swept back and forth across these fields. White-clad Finns on skis had shot Russian invaders from the shelter of these rock formations and stands of pine. Here, Swedes on horseback had plunged lances into the breasts of youths, and there, motor-mounted Germans had blasted their pathway through to the unknown country: *terra incognita*, Holy Russia, Mother Russia.

For two hours the Finnish train, clean as a newly fletched arrow, fleet and almost silent, pierced this multilayered zone toward the eastern frontier. Forest thickened. Frozen bogs began to appear. Snow flurries dropped from a sky haunted by a sense of absence.

From time to time distinctive strokes relieved the void: a white fox pranced up an embankment on dainty legs, stopping to glare at the train over its shoulder. The flag of Finland flapped on a pole in a farmyard—white banner on white field under white sky, its blue cross dancing. A gold-brown horse rubbed its side against a whitewashed barn. A child in a yellow snowsuit stood on a white stone fence with his red scarf blowing sideways and both arms shooting up in greeting. *I greet, I greet, I greet you!* The little face flashed past, apotheosis of childhood, of confident joy, of exultant admiration. Alex raised his arm in response, too late. Then more trees, the endless dark kingdom of the taiga.

The coach was practically empty, save for a half dozen people scattered throughout. Across the aisle sat two men dressed in charcoal gray suits, their shoes black alligator, their overcoats black leather, their wristwatches gold. An electronic instrument of some kind beeped a musical tone, and one of the men put a cell phone to his ear.

"*Da?*" he said loudly in Russian. "Yes, Vasily, yes. It went well."

Silence.

"Of course they signed the contract. They can smell money upwind."

Silence.

"An interesting encounter. Finland is a nation of engineers. They have no passion—a very strange people. We'll arrive in Petersburg by three o'clock. Can you meet me at Finland Station? Good."

Pause.

"We settled at three million euros. Yes, yes, of course I offered payment in rubles, then *finnmarkkaa*, but they weren't interested. I had to give in."

Silence.

Now the Russian's voice increased in volume and irritability. "What did you want me to do, walk away from the deal? Listen, listen, Vasilinka, I am bringing you a prize. The containers will be shipped to Petersburg on Monday. Why do you complain? This is Sony, Panasonic, Nokia we're talking about. Not that garbage from Minsk."

It went on for some time, and as Alex listened—he would have had to plug his ears to block it out—he wondered at the man's lack of concern for eavesdroppers. What was the implication in this? That Russia was a global force, powerful in commerce, and the speaker an instrument of that power, indifferent to whoever knew it? Or was it the contrary: the insecurity of the new rich, who were only too eager for an opportunity to strut in public? If that was the case, it was not much of a public.

The telephone conversation ended. The Russian popped the instrument into his breast pocket, then looked across the aisle at Alex. With an apologetic grimace, he said:

"Business, business, business!"

"Business is good?" asked Alex politely.

"Yes, very good. And for you?"

Alex cast about for an appropriate reply. "Not so good", he said noncommittally.

"Your first time in Russia?" asked the other with a tone of personal interest.

"Yes."

"You are, I think, in telecommunications. Many foreign companies come to Russia now."

Alex shook his head. "I am traveling for personal reasons."

"Ah, personal", said the man with an inquisitive look.

But Alex felt disinclined to tell the whole sad story. He returned to observation of the passing landscape, and the man across the aisle lost interest. The forest of fir trees was now uninterrupted, broken only by outcroppings of frost-covered stone and desolate frozen lakes.

The train slowed as it approached the frontier.

Alex's heart accelerated with excitement and mild apprehension. At last he would enter the country that had preoccupied his imagination since boyhood. In a sense he knew this land, or rather, he knew a great many things about it. He was well aware that the reality had been filtered through literate assumptions and secondhand images—a montage of firebirds and cossacks, missiles and death squads, circus bears and fur crowns, taiga-dwelling hermits and ranting revolutionaries. He understood that one could know Russia and yet not know it, just as he had strained to see through the mask of Layo, to decipher the spirit of his homeland beneath his laughter and his snarls, his adamant proclamations and his silences. Or was it more like falling in love with an unreachable woman? One could observe her appearance and infer her qualities, perhaps even love her more than she had ever been loved by another human being. Yet this was not the same as the knowledge that her spouse or her child had of her, or her own self-knowledge.

Decelerating to a crawl, the train penetrated a series of barbed-wire ramparts flanked by wooden watchtowers. These were followed by cinder-block guardhouses, rusting girders, broken concrete, metal refuse flung this way and that, and a row of ten young soldiers in green uniforms marching out of step along the railside road, which had spontaneously turned from pavement to rutted gravel as it left Finland. Although he could hear nothing, he saw that they were joking with each other, engaging in horseplay, laughing, and tossing their hats in the air. The Russian Army.

A loudspeaker announced the approach of the border town, Viborg. Beyond the coach windows, a dismal gray burgh emerged from groves of willow and pine. At one time it must have been a charming place built upon compact hills surrounding a narrow inlet of the Gulf of Finland. Church spires and old stately homes capped the heights, but even at a distance Alex could see that they had suffered from generations of neglect. The town was now dominated by low, dull postrevolutionary buildings that appeared to be in an advanced state of disrepair. Their very lack of character was their character.

The train drew alongside a cement quay in front of a station block. It squealed to a halt, and uniformed officials entered the car. There were three levels of officialdom among them: passport controllers, import-export agents, and currency inspectors. They were dour, grave to a fault, imbued with the mystique of the Russian state. Whatever threat Alex felt was largely in his own mind, for if they lacked warmth, they were at least courteous.

When the paperwork was completed, passengers were told by the conductor that they were free to take the air outside; the train would depart for Saint Petersburg in fifteen minutes. Alex hastened out onto the quay, relishing his first step onto Russian soil.

Because the station blocked the view of the town, it was necessary to go inside the building and out the street entrance on the far side. A heavy iron door opened on resisting hinges, admitting him to a different world, a different time in history. The Stalinesque interior was painted in dark green peeling paint, poorly lit, smelling of decaying wood. A scowling woman of indeterminate age stared from the window where tickets were sold. At a makeshift kiosk by the odoriferous public washroom, a dowdy girl sat on a wooden chair polishing her fingernails, waiting for customers to buy tiny squares of soap and a swatch of toilet paper, or sad little sandwiches and bottles of orange-colored drink. An old woman swept the floor with a twig broom. Although it was the middle of the day, there were two school-age children, bored and burdened with fate, selling cigarettes from trays. There was, as well, an assortment of passengers, all of whom were dressed in worn clothing. Old men and women with plastic handbags stood along the bare walls with drooping arms, waiting, gazing at Alex mournfully.

A frowning youth was propped in a corner, one leg thrust forward, a battered violin case under one arm and a tortoise shell cat in the crook of the other. He was smoking a cigarette without the aid of his hands, his face inscrutable, his thoughts churning but unreadable, perhaps secretly hating poetry killers. Oleg must have stood here before his flight to the West, and he would have resembled this boy.

Within the station's enclosed interior, Alex felt a sense of looming existential events, as if he were in the center of an indecipherable symbolic choreography or had stumbled by accident upon a crew of actors attempting a stylized pastiche of prerevolutionary Russia. Yet it was neither Chekhovian nor Dostoyevskian. Neither was it Orwellian. It was, if anything, Kafkaesque. The feeling, whatever its cause, was prompting misinterpretation. He reminded himself that it was useless to define the mood by appearances, or by history itself. This place was no more than an ordinary small-town scene: people going about their random business, and the business of the moment was to wait in a dingy holding tank for the train to depart.

The scene would be practically indistinguishable from those that had occurred here under the czars, the Bolsheviks, or the late Soviets. The state, for all its heavy weight, a weight that had pressed down without interruption for more than a millennium, was experienced as a necessary evil. And though each form of government had left scars on the people, it had not succeeded in destroying their essential spirit. For beneath a veneer devoid of surface charm, there was a brooding heart, stolid, enduring, containing undisclosed passion and courage.

Pushing open the second set of iron doors, Alex exited the station onto a street filled with diesel exhaust, cars without mufflers, and a few pedestrians hunched against the cold. The buildings around the square were uniformly in need of repainting. The patchwork pavement was riddled with potholes and hedged by banks of dirty snow that workmen were shoveling by hand. Yet the remnants of Viborg's lost grandeur on the hills above, and the port on the far side of the square, offered the promise of larger worlds.

"This is where Oleg and his friends wrote their poems", said Alex.

What kind of poetry would they have composed in such a place? Perhaps the things that the intelligent young always wrote: nature's beauty unlocking the passions of the heart. Love poems, surely. And political thoughts in the form of verse, release valves for frustration and black despondency. It would not be difficult to feel despair here. Nor impossible to convert the despair into muted hope by the magic of adolescent art. Alex regretted that he had not asked Oleg to write out a few lines. Oleg, with wife and daughter in an alien land, Oleg in another kind of underground, deep in a mine, thinking of his lost home, the very place in which Alex now stood. The oddness of it altered his perceptions yet another degree. But he had no time for further musing because the train horn hooted and he had to run, leaping onto the moving steps of the coach at the last moment, reeling down the aisle on unsteady feet as it drew away into the East.

Two hours later the forest began to break up into sporadic woods, fields in which snow and dead weeds fought for supremacy, and a few rustic villages. The latter were clusters of shabby huts, unplowed streets, and unpainted fences around small backyard gardens, some made of pickets, others of woven willow saplings. As in Viborg, all structures were in steep decline. Every roof was constructed of tin rusted to a uniform brown. Yet, despite the poverty, there were signs everywhere that villagers strove to make a human life in the midst of deprivation. A cat slept alongside a geranium in a cottage window; an old woman, in kerchief, pants, and quilted jacket, removed slabs of frozen laundry from a backyard wire; an old man, bending over a neatly stacked cord of firewood, straightened his back and turned to watch the passing train.

A child, standing on the cross-slat of a sagging fence, swayed forward and backward, unsmiling.

Another half hour, and large prerevolutionary manors appeared, separated by woods and an increasing number of hamlets. The great houses were now eyeless and crownless, porches crumbling, pillars toppled, gardens overgrown with unpruned trees, iron fences bent as if rammed by tanks or crowds of angry proletarians. Everything that had gone into the manors' former life—prosperous days followed by revolutionary storm and the long, slow collapse into disremembering—was now irrevocably locked in the past. Yet it took little imagination to see what they once had been: phantom horses trotting about the estates pulling lacquered carriages; cavalry officers galloping along the road to the capital, dreaming of careers at court, scabbards clattering at their thighs; pilgrims coming to the gatehouses begging and going away with baskets filled; giggling children spinning hoops and playing tag on the grass beneath the blossoming cherry trees as the faint arpeggios of *Swan Lake* and the *Nutcracker* wafted through the open windows of the parlors, borne on billowing muslin curtains. There was courtship between man and maiden walking beside the streams of the *barin*'s manicured parks while beyond the hedges sweating serfs piled perfumed hay in the fields. And ladies read to each other on lawn chairs, quoting in French from the very daring Molière and the absurdly gloomy Turgenev.

Alex felt a wave of longing for that vanished world even as he reminded himself that its halcyon days had been brief and only for the privileged few. The few were gone, by flight or by violence, and the only remaining traces were these crumbling monuments to gentility.

The northern suburbs of the city now began, dreary vistas of factories and three- and four-story apartment blocks, cemeteries, webs of electric wires, and little traffic jams of a half dozen rusting cars at every rail crossing. The winter afternoon was waning, and here and there on the side streets could be seen many a grandparent walking a child home from school. Like children everywhere, they were chattering their news, looking up at the adults in whose care they lived and dreamed without fear. For if life was still difficult, the days of absolute fear were now submerged in the past, and ordinary worries had taken their place—health; food; debts; a little money for a new set of boots, an umbrella, a book, if we can save enough rubles. And seeds to plant in *chernozem*, the black earth in the window box of the apartment, for flowers when winter is over.

On every hunched shoulder was the message: Endurance. Endurance was engraved in the genetic code of all those who had survived. And with it the patient, mute, recurring cry: Come quickly, spring! Come quickly!

Snow flurries blew sideways.

Suddenly Alex was blinded by a cement wall sliding past, startled back into the interior of the carriage as the train came to a squealing halt.

"Pietari—Petrograd—Saint Petersburg!" the electronic voice announced. "Finlyansky Vokzal—Finland Station!"

"I'm here", Alex breathed, standing, struggling into his overcoat.

The rail platforms were crowded with milling passengers and ranks of onlookers. Alex, travel bag over his shoulder, gym bag in hand, walked to the main entrance past rows of vendors, idlers, beggars, and military travelers of several kinds. Police surveyed the scene, batons in hand, their grim faces reminders of an era that had ended little more than a decade ago. Inside, the station was a larger version of Viborg, though more crowded. Alex bought a city map at a kiosk and went outside into the lowering dusk. It was deathly cold. Passing through the bleak square in front of the station, he noticed a large marble bust of Lenin, the face turned toward the entrance as if to greet all those arriving in the workers' paradise. More than eighty years ago, Lenin had arrived here from his years in exile. Greeted by cheering crowds carrying red banners and torches, he had shouted his famous slogans and swept through the city on the top of an armored car, conquering the divided revolutionaries by the sheer force of his will and galvanizing the Revolution.

The two elegant Russians from the train swept past him, went down the steps, and got into a black BMW that was waiting for them at the curb. Alex waved away the several solicitations from taxi drivers and decided to walk in order to save money.

His first task was to find his hotel. Intourist had offered him a number of hotels to choose from. Andrew and the metaphysicians were registered at the five-star, American-class Peterhof Hotel on Nevsky Prospekt, a few blocks south of the Winter Palace. Alex had avoided it, not only because of the astronomical price of a room, but because he thought it might be important to have a base of operations removed from the influence of the group, a place to which he could take Andrew without interference.

Farther south on Nevsky was the hotel where Alex was registered, the Moskva. A glance at the map indicated that it was a short walk from one to the other, with sufficient distance between the two to offer a safety zone. Saint Petersburg was a city of six million, and the number of people would help guarantee anonymity. He told himself that it would be a mistake to go directly to the Peterhof for an immediate confrontation; he would be better prepared if he first checked into his own hotel, had a nap and a meal. He estimated a twenty- or thirty-minute stroll between Finland Station and the Moskva.

Five minutes walking along a broad traffic-choked avenue brought Alex to a bridge over the Neva River. He turned south onto the pedestrian walkway, facing into a blast of wind that made his eyes water. In addition to slippery footing, the going was made more treacherous by frost-heaved slabs of concrete. The few people who passed him coming from the opposite direction were huddled inside their coats and did not meet his eyes. Casting a glance to the left, he saw the great river that drained the Russian heartland and spilled into the ocean only a mile downstream. The surface was frozen solid.

As he trudged across the span, Alex looked about at a city that was not nearly as ancient as Moscow or other capitals of Europe but that displayed old-world grandeur at every turn. Founded by Peter the Great in 1703, enriched by Catherine the Great in the mid-eighteenth century, it resembled Paris in its wide avenues, its bridges, and its vast numbers of ornate apartment blocks, many of which contained palaces where the nobility had lived. Like Venice, it was built upon the canals and islands of an estuary, but it resembled nothing but itself in the general atmosphere of decay.

Alex knew this was not an accurate first impression, for the tourist booklet that he had picked up in the station showed photographs of the city in summer, softened by parks, warmed by the resplendent colors of palaces and cathedrals. A city of culture, Russia's "window on Europe" boasted numerous theaters, museums, concert halls, universities, and institutes, as well as throngs of happy pedestrians strolling past glorious monuments.

All of this was invisible at present, as the wind veered and snow flurries changed to a genuine Arctic storm blowing viciously down the Neva, battering Alex sideways and forcing him to cringe within his inadequate winter clothing.

Reaching the other side of the bridge, he continued on Liteyny Prospekt into the core of Saint Petersburg. Rusting trolley buses packed with people lurched up and down the street, blue sparks crackling from their radial arms, circumnavigated by swarms of equally rusting automobiles and trucks. Here too the sidewalks were in a state of interrupted repair. Manholes gaped open every few blocks, their lids tossed aside, most of them unbarricaded, leaving little to warn pedestrians. Unconcerned, people instinctively swerved to avoid these man-traps. Alex picked his way through the rubble more carefully.

Block after block of apartment buildings flanked him on both sides; the stonework was chipped, every window frame was rotting with age, glass was cracked and dirty. Although a great deal of the city had been ruined by German bombardment during the Second World War, it had been rebuilt. Evidently, the ravages of weather alone had worn it down to its present condition.

Liteyny ended at the intersection of Nevsky Prospekt, the great central artery that traversed the city from the former imperial palace at the northwest end to the great monastery of Saint Alexander Nevsky at the southeast. A study of the map showed Alex that he had badly underestimated the distance. It had taken him forty-five minutes of brisk walking to reach a point that was only halfway to his destination, the Hotel Moskva, situated across the street from the monastery.

With a start, he realized that he was standing beside a wall of the Hotel Peterhof on the corner of Nevsky and Liteyny. Only three years old, this twelve-story giant filled a city block between Liteyny and the Fontanka Canal. Alex glanced at the flags of several nations snapping along the granite balconies, and at the purple carpeting and white marble steps under the hotel's entrance canopy. Standing at attention beside massive glass doors engraved with crystalline double-headed eagles, six attendants in black and gold livery were poised to serve. They sprang into action to receive guests as white limousines and smaller luxury vehicles with antennae and bodyguards drew up, discharged their sable-clad passengers, then sped away. Whenever the hotel doors opened, symphonic music drifted out and was lost in the roar of the streets.

Was Andrew in there? Yes, surely he was. Alex took a step toward the entrance. The doormen eyed him without expression.

Careful, he told himself. *Don't make the same mistake twice. Don't hurry, don't rush in, and above all do not spend your ammunition before the right moment.*

Tense, fists clenched, he turned away from the Peterhof and went deeper into the bleak canyons of Nevsky. Another forty-five minutes passed, during which the appearance of the streets changed little from what he had already observed. The snow kept falling, though the whistling wind seemed to have been broken somewhat by the maze of buildings. Around five o'clock, under a black sky and battered by the storm, he came to the end of Nevsky, rounded a corner, and saw the massive curved wall of the Hotel Moskva. It seemed to dwarf the monastery across the street.

He entered the lobby with relief. Warm, brightly lit, jumping with recorded pop music and the jangle of casino machines, it was a welcome change from the storm. The registration desk was not busy, and he approached it fully expecting to be immediately served by one of the three clerks on duty. All three cast a glance at him with bored expressions and flicked their eyes down to their computer screens.

A minute went by, two minutes. A phone rang, and one answered it. The second began to shuffle through a stack of papers before her. The third tapped lazily on her keyboard.

Alex cleared his throat.

No one looked up.

"Excuse me", he said in English. "I would like to register."

"One minute", the clerk before him said in a sour tone, as if the world were full of overeager guests and they were the bane of her existence.

He suppressed his irritation and waited another five minutes while they conducted little conversations about this and that, mostly concerning the minute details of paper-filing procedure. Unfortunately, Alex had already paid for his room through the travel agent in Helsinki and was not in the financial position to walk out. Nor was the weather outside appealing.

He leaned toward the clerk in front of him and, speaking to the crown of her head, said in English, "The petty tyranny of minor public officials!"

The woman looked up suspiciously. "I do not understand", she drawled in Russian, and returned to her paperwork.

"I have spent a lifetime being patient with them", he went on in English, using a pleasant tone. "I have fed their vain-glory, cringed before their malice, their endless resentments, the incestuous entanglements of their damaged egos, and the arrogance of their false personalities. Their name is legion: ticket sellers, county tax clerks, customs agents, the officious and mean-spirited of the earth, the nabobs of microscopic cantons who derive loathsome pleasures from exercising their powers."

Trying to ignore him, the clerk to whom he had spoken bent an extravagantly swanlike neck in the direction of the clerk on the left and said in the driest tones of bored irritation, "Tamara, you take him. I have too much to do. Besides, he speaks only English. I can't understand him."

Alex bowed to her in a manner that was in no way sardonic. She eyed him doubtfully, with a spark of curiosity.

"Madam, I shall transfer myself to Tamara", he said. "Yet I thank you. For our meeting, though brief, has been most profitable for me—a taste of old Russia, though I am as yet uncertain about which era. Did you study at the Institute for Human Relations, perhaps?"

"Check him into his room, Tamara! And shut him up if you can. He's driving me crazy."

"What's he talking about?" Tamara said.

"Don't ask me. You're the one who speaks English."

"Not that kind of English."

Then Tamara—exotic Tamara—gave Alex the most patently false smile he had ever received and said, "*Pazhalusta, Gaspadin*—Please, Mister, you want hotel room?"

"Yes", Alex said, smiling back. "That would be nice."

A half hour of further technicalities ensued before he was given a key and was able to let himself into a small room at the back of the hotel. A room with a view. A view of a junkyard, a deserted school playground, and the service alley of the hotel, above which a smokestack belched black exhaust.

The bit of fun he had had at the lobby desk, though it was self-indulgent, left him feeling as if he had won a minor victory, had delivered a rebuff to the forces that had engulfed his life. Then it struck him that these poor functionaries were not his enemies; in fact, they were as much victims as anyone else. He felt suddenly ashamed. Fatigued, muscle-sore, and chilled to the bone, he stripped down to his shorts and hung his damp clothing on a chair back. There was a sink in the bathroom, a toilet that could be flushed only after its engineering had been studied, a piece of brown soap the size of his thumb, a clean drinking glass, and a deep tub. When he turned on the taps, rusty water spurted out. He let it run for a few minutes, and while it was gradually clearing, he inspected the bedroom. The furniture, including a television set, a low bed cot, and a hard chair, was cheap and worn. The rug was stained. Yet on the whole the room looked clean, the linen on the cot fresh, the pillow plump and comfortable.

When the tub was full, he let himself slowly into the steaming water and lay back, trying to ignore bits of sand and gravel on the bottom, simply glad for the primal element of heat. He fell asleep for a while in the tub, waking when the temperature had become lukewarm. He washed his socks and underwear in the sink and hung them to dry on the hot-water pipe that fed the bathroom appliances. Afterward he dressed in his only change of clothing and put on his brown tweed blazer.

On the ground floor he located the hotel restaurant, and there he treated himself to blintzes, cabbage rolls, boiled fish, and a basket of breads and cheeses, topped off with a bottle of dark brown Baltika ale that arrived automatically with the meal. He hesitated over it, then took a few sips. It was strong, very calming to his frayed nerves. The entire feast was ridiculously inexpensive, instilling mixed emotions of gratitude and shame that he was profiting by the devaluation of the ruble. The Russian poor were paying for this meal, but he did not know how he could compensate them for it. He reminded himself that practically everything in Russia was compromised by the confusion that existed during the transition stage between the old and new orders and that he was wandering in this moral maze without an accurate compass. Sipping the last of the Baltika, he mumbled a line from a Hopkins poem:

"'O pity and indignation! Manshape that shone...'"

A waiter standing nearby mistook his meaning and put another bottle in front of him. Alex did not argue. The potent ale made him light-headed, but under its influence his wretched emotions subsided to their proper seabed; equally, the influence of mystical poetry reoriented him to the hierarchical universe, if only for a moment. A desperately needed moment.

"All is not compromised!" he said to the waiter. "All is not in unfathomable, enormous darkness drowned! Sparks shine here and there! Light that shone—light that is shining—light that will shine again!" But the waiter, who had served many strange foreigners in his time, merely bowed and went away.

Alex checked his wristwatch and saw that it was after eight o'clock. There was no telling how long the metaphysicians would remain in the city. He had to contact Andrew as soon as possible.

Back in his room, he placed a telephone call to the Hotel Peterhof and inquired in his best Russian accent if the Bloch party was still registered there. It was.

By now his coat had dried a little, and he bundled himself in it, along with the Finnish cap and gloves, and went back down to the lobby. The street map marked the underground metro stations, and thankfully there was one around the corner from the hotel. When he went outside, gusts of cold air cleared his mind, without negating the good effects of the meal, the ale, and the poem. Within a minute he was riding the longest escalator in the world far down into the earth. A screaming train arrived, and he shuffled inside a carriage along with dozens of other people. Two stops farther along, he got out, rode another escalator up to the street level, and exited onto Nevsky. He was now four short blocks from the Hotel Peterhof and hastened toward it, arriving at the lobby entrance within minutes.

None of the doormen gave him more than a cursory glance, and the glass doors opened automatically. Inside, however, there was an armed security guard standing beside the arc of a metal detector, through which all guests had to pass. Alex did so without any problems, save for a harmless blip caused by the crucifix hanging on a cord beneath his undershirt. The guard stepped forward, pointed a detector baton at the center of Alex's chest, and said, "What is this?"

"A cross", Alex replied. *"Khristos voskrese!" Christ is risen!*

The guard seemed momentarily startled by this liturgical exclamation. Lowering his voice, he whispered the traditional response, *"Voistinu voskrese!" Truly he is risen!*

With a noncommittal expression, he waved Alex through.

He crossed the lobby slowly, gazing at the Oriental carpets and crystal chandeliers, the pink marble grand staircase, alabaster carvings of classical gods and goddesses, white leather sofas and easy chairs. The music of a string ensemble issued from a ballroom to the right, where liveried attendants were welcoming a steady stream of elegant guests in evening dress.

At the front desk, Alex stood and waited behind an American couple attired in denim-chic. Both wore heavy amber jewelry. Their ginger poodle tugged at its leash. They seemed bored but kept eyeing the ballroom curiously. The duty clerk spoke with them in flawless English and handed them a computerized card key. When they left with a porter and a cart full of luggage in the direction of the elevator, the clerk looked up at Alex. He stepped forward and addressed the woman in Russian, asking for the room number of Andrew Graham.

She checked her file and said, "In the Bloch party?"

"Yes, in the Bloch party."

"I regret, sir, we cannot divulge room numbers without the permission of the occupants, but I can ring the room and ask."

"Yes, please call the room and ask for Andrew Graham. *Only* Andrew Graham."

"I must give the name of the person who is calling."

"Do you? Why?"

"It is policy."

"The hotel's policy or the policy of Dr. Bloch?"

She glanced at him uneasily. "It is the hotel policy if a guest requests it."

"I see. And Dr. Bloch has requested it?"

"Yes. All calls must go through his room. Your name is...?"

Once again the quandary arose. His own name was worthless in this situation, for Bloch would terminate any attempt to reach Andrew if he used it and would probably call house security and have Alex thrown out. His face now recognizable, there would be no further possibility of entering the hotel.

And if he said that his name was Alexei, thus avoiding a lie, he might also be recognized. It was uncertain whether or not the metaphysicians had seen through this thin disguise, but the name was now known to them, and they knew that Alexei, whoever he was, was on the trail of their recruit.

Alex pulled the paperback Hopkins from his pocket.

"My name does not matter. I have a book that belongs to the young man. I wish to return it."

"Ah, then you know him?"

"Yes", Alex replied, trying to control his nervousness. "I know him very well."

"Then there should be no difficulty if you give me your name."

"Unfortunately, Dr. Bloch and I are at odds with each other. He is not a fair man, and he does not wish me to speak with Mr. Graham."

Suspicious but undecided, she did not know what to think of the situation. Making up her mind, she said, "I will ring to see if they are in. In the evenings they frequently go out."

She punched the room number into the desk phone, below Alex's line of sight. After a minute she hung up.

"They do not answer. Possibly they are away for the evening."

"Perhaps only some of them have gone. Did you call Andrew Graham's room?"

"No, I did not", she replied coldly. "I called Dr. Bloch's room. It is policy."

"Yes, you said that."

At a loss for what to do next, he prayed silently for an inspiration. Should he tell her that Andrew was his son and that he had been brainwashed? How believable was that?

Then it struck him that there was another way to connect. He opened the front cover of the book and wrote on the flyleaf:

The child is father of the man: To a boy who slept in
the arms of a giant, from a king of Halcyon

Below this he wrote:

Hotel Moskva, 2 Ploshchad Aleksandro Nevskovo,
Room 611

He asked for an envelope large enough to contain the book,
and when she went away to find one he removed a thousand
rubles from his pocket. Upon her return, he inserted the
book into the envelope, sealed it, wrote "Andrew Graham" in
Cyrillic letters on it, and slid it across the desk with the money
tucked underneath, where she would find it the moment he
was gone.

His hand palm down on top of the envelope, he said, "I
beg you to believe me and to trust me." She glanced from his
hand to his face and back again, her eyes retreating into the
cool gaze of neutrality. "It is of utmost importance that this
reach him without anyone else knowing about it. Andrew
Graham would want it this way, and he will thank you for
it when he receives it." Alex read her name plate. "I realize
you are suspicious, Olga Andreyevna, and that is because you
are a dependable employee and a person of integrity who has
the interests of your guests at heart. But I appeal to a greater
integrity. This envelope contains a book of poems. It is not
illegal material. It will do no harm but only good. It is a
matter of personal relationships. Thus, I would be grateful if
you would give it to the young man as requested."

He withdrew his hand. She reached forward and pulled
the envelope across the desk.

"Is it possible for me to wait in the lobby?" Alex asked.

"Security would not like it", she replied with a cautious
look. "If you do not have a proper explanation, they will
interview you in the office and then eject you. You would

be refused permission to enter again. The watchers—" She glanced at surveillance cameras in the corners of the lobby ceiling.

"Well, no matter. I will go now", said Alex, tapping the envelope. "I beg you also to accept a small gift of thanks, as a token of my respect."

Without waiting for a reply, he bowed his head to her, turned, and left the hotel. For more than an hour he walked up and down the street in front of the Peterhof, keeping his eyes constantly on the entrance. But Andrew did not come. In the end his toes were beginning to freeze inside the thin boots, he was shivering, and numb spots of frostbite were forming on his cheeks. He hurried to the metro and went down into the bowels of the earth.

At the base of the escalator, he noticed two small boys, about six and eight years old, sitting on a dirty blanket by a wall. They appeared to have no adult guardian. At their rag-bound feet was a cup containing a few coins. The older boy played a hand concertina; the other jangled finger cymbals. They were singing a rousing folk song in high-pitched voices that veered back and forth between unified chant and astonishing harmonics. Alex stopped to listen.

Their bodies weaved and bounced to the rhythm, their eyes danced, their mouths mimed the swinging moods of the sung tale, which was about a lad who was hatched from an egg and ran away to the taiga to seek his fortune. The little boy's name was Puny. In the forest he met a witch named Baba Yaga who snagged him and locked him in a cage in order to fatten him up.

> O Baba Yaga, Puny cried,
> Bring me another dish
> Of piggy fat and beefy dried
> And sizzly sturgeon fish.
> I'll make a meal for you one day

If I could only wed
Your fairest daughter over there
Who's weeping in the shed.
She's lonely, Baba, can't you see?
I'd make a lovely mate!
Please don't eat me, Baba dear;
The taste of me you'd hate.
Let me out and I will cook
An om-e-lette so fine
With onions for your breath,
And salt and bread and wine....

Baba Yaga, unable to resist the lure of romance, let Puny out of the cage. Instantly, he leaped upon her and killed her, killed her fair daughter, killed her less fair daughters (all of whom were witches), and, seizing a bag of gold, ran away into the endless steppe, where he lived happily ever after, taming wild horses.

This country! thought Alex, shaking his head as he dropped coins into the boys' cup.

Later, resting on the cot in his hotel room, he realized that his attempt to engage the clerk's assistance had been a gamble. She might be offended by the rubles, or she might be pleased. In either case, she might or might not comply with his request. There was nothing he could do about it but wait for Andrew's call. The phone did not ring that night.

14. *Surely We Have Met Before*

Alex waited half the following morning, edgy, pacing the small room, calling the desk from time to time to see if anyone had left a message. No one had. He tried to read the poetry of Hopkins in the little hardcover edition but could not concentrate. He switched on the television, but watching it was an exercise in nausea, and he turned it off after ten minutes.

After a late breakfast in the hotel restaurant, he retraced his route of the night before. The storm was over and the sun was breaking through fleets of boiling gray cloud. It was somewhat warmer and windless but was still Russian winter.

Shortly before noon he reentered the Peterhof and inquired of a male desk clerk if the Bloch party was in. They were not. He asked for Olga Andreyevna, but she was off duty. He also asked if the envelope that he had left for Andrew Graham had been delivered. The clerk checked the message boxes and told Alex that he saw no envelope and that it must surely have been delivered.

Alex hurried back to his hotel, but when he arrived he found no messages. Early that afternoon, feeling half-crazed with waiting and claustrophobia, he caught the metro and took it to the upper end of Nevsky, near the Winter Palace. There he entered a great square through a triumphal portal and walked slowly across its snow-filled expanse toward the last official residence of the czars. Its capitals and ornamentation were radiant gold in the bright sun. Stopping beneath the Alexander Column in the center of the square, he gazed about, finding it hard to believe that in this very place Nicholas II's troops had shot demonstrators in 1905. Bloody Sunday—the January day a crowd of Saint Petersburg working men and women had gathered to present their petition to the czar, demanding representative government. After the slaughter, workers had turned to more radical protests, strikes, and isolated acts of terrorism that culminated in the Revolution of 1917.

Alex had read many books about the chain of events leading to Communist rule and knew that it had not been a massive uprising of the poor but a carefully timed series of maneuvers. The masses did not make history; no, it was made by a few individuals reading the temper of their times and exploiting it to their advantage. Three generations had now passed, and change was once again in the wind. Tanks had given way to luxury cars, bullets to bank bonds, and missiles to fast-food restaurants. Yet the new politics and its new economy were no friend of the poor. The masses remained as they were.

His musing was a feeble exercise, he knew. The compression of history into a concept no larger than a Fabergé egg was unrealistic. As Owen Whitfield had told him, history was an art form, not a science. And so it seemed at this moment, for here at the site of monumental historical events Alex now understood that the senses insisted on being fed before the mind. He tried to imagine the screams and gunshots, straining unsuccessfully to see through the barricades of time, to grasp what had only been approximated by information in books.

The palace was now one of the world's foremost art galleries—the Hermitage. The main entrance was on the far side of the complex, facing the Neva River. Alex walked around the west end of the building and turned right along the riverside esplanade, feeling the grandeur of what prerevolutionary life in Saint Petersburg must have been. As he stared across the

Neva to the soaring gold spire of the Petropavlovsky Sobor in the Peter and Paul Fortress, it seemed that his imagination came to life. Winter became spring, and the infernal roar of the city's automobiles faded out, replaced by the clean salt wind from the Baltic and the cries of swooping petrel birds. It was a city of high-stepping horses, flowing water, sleeping cannons, and contrapuntal bells that were ever awakening the populace to prayer. The quality of the air itself was hushed, for the demoniac rumblings and volleys of the age to come were as yet unknown. All around the palace the rosebeds budded their first tentative pink and yellow and peach, and the privet hedges sliced into geometric perfection lawns and gardens as elaborate as Parisian sweet cakes and Viennese pastries.

A sailing ship drew up to the quay in front of the palace, and the royal family was conducted toward it by admirals and courtiers, the princesses skipping down the steps in eagerness for their first voyage of the season, the young prince held back by his mother's hands, for fear of bleeding.

Bang! Bang-bang! A decrepit army truck backfired as it lurched along the avenue between the river and the palace, jolting Alex forward in time. Slowly, he climbed the steps to the entrance in the rearguard of schoolchildren and their teachers. The children were animated, laughing and chattering—like children everywhere. The teachers, who were for the most part bright young women with wholesome faces and large, expressive eyes, were trying to keep them in orderly bunches—like teachers everywhere.

"Vasya, if you don't stop pushing Ivanka, you will go straight back to the bus and sit there for three hours. Would you like that? No? Then be good."

"Masha, you chatterbox, put a little cork in your mouth! Yes, you too, Stassya—you're the worst. Now, shh, shh!"

Standing behind them in the line to the ticket desk, Alex felt heartened by the variety of antics and thought how absurd it was for states to attempt the engineering of human souls. When the teachers, like clucking hens, herded the children toward classical antiquities, he stepped forward and bought his ticket. He then strolled in the other direction, not knowing where he was going or what he wanted to see. Hardly an item in the vast collection would fail to draw his mind away from his troubles, even if only for an hour. Three hundred thousand pieces, the guidebook said, displayed in a labyrinth of 350 rooms.

He wandered at random, astounded as gallery after gallery revealed marvels that no art book could ever encompass. In all directions he saw apparitions, incarnations, transfigurations of raw matter into the language of mankind: beauty and terror; love and desertion; pomp and humility; horror and holiness. Ivan the Terrible's crown and four stuffed horses bearing black-armored Austrians. Coins and goblets from Byzantium, and squat Stone Age idols. Greek nymphs singing siren songs, imbroglios of lusty baroque maidens, and chopped Picasso women. Icons bursting with presence—the Savior, the Mother God-bearer, the saints, the angels, all hovering over Russia.

There were chapels in which the czars had worshipped, grand ballrooms in which they had danced, and ateliers in which they had made complicated and compromising negotiations. There were thrones on which they had sat uneasily, yearning for absolute security or at least for a brief diversion at picnics beside the ponds of the summer palace, desks at which they had made decisions affecting the fate of millions, and beds in which they had slept and dreamed the innocent dreams of the elaborately isolated, in which they had conceived their royal lineage, in which they had died of old age or poison.

Everything was freighted with age, with histories that evoked the theosis of man and the betrayal of man. Golden light poured through the high windows. Waxed wooden hallways glowed, echoing with the exuberance of children who laughed as they leaped over that old monster, *kronos*: Alexis the little czarevitch skipping down these corridors as he yearned for fast horses upon which he would never be permitted to gallop; his sisters the doomed czarevnas dreaming of parties and princes of royal blood to whom they would, surely, one day be engaged. Hand in hand they ran with the children of a later age who dreamed of jet planes and automobiles of their own, and to whom the dim memory of angels might be returning.

Saturated, mentally numbed, Alex climbed a marble staircase and entered a gallery full of Rembrandt paintings. Recognizing some from his art books, he felt nothing and merely moved without purpose among the self-portraits, the biblical scenes, and the hamlets of Holland. He realized that he was viewing the images superficially and that this was probably due to mental exhaustion. Too much had happened to him in too short a time, aggravating the ever-looming anxiety of his search. Few were the minutes that passed without a recurring pang and the interior utterance of his son's name.

Aside from the room guard, who sat beside the entrance with hands folded on her lap, watching him, there was only one other person present, a youth moving slowly from painting to painting at the far end of the hall. Alex was glad for the near solitude. He felt a need to be still, to rest in silence. His natural habitat of order had been swept aside, and his temperament, reflective and withdrawn, had been forced into the open in strange situations among alien peoples. Never in his life had he been compelled to navigate through such large numbers of people, and this was taking its toll. At the worst moments he had even dirtied his lips with untruth. Exhausted by the tension of artifice and deception, which for many people in this world was effortless, he reeled with sudden dizziness. He stopped and covered his eyes with his right hand. Remaining in that position for some minutes, he tried to quiet the inner turbulence. When his head cleared a little, he looked up. Before him was Rembrandt's *Return of the Prodigal Son.*

At first glance, the painting seemed to be immense, because he was standing only a few feet from it, and he was forced to crane his neck as he looked up from the battered feet of the son, through the tender hands that embraced him, to the face of the father.

Alex stepped back a few paces.

Red, umber, and sepia bathed the image in warmth. The son knelt before the father with his head on the old man's chest, as if seeking refuge in the folds of his garments. The father bent over him, both hands on his son's back, the fingers splayed slightly, palm to the flesh that had come from him, that had fled from him, and that was now returning to him. The hands protected and comforted. The tilt of the aged head and the half-lidded eyes conveyed infinite compassion, a wisdom that was in no way naïve about the sins of the son but that submerged all wrongs in mercy. The dignity of the father embraced the degraded son in a communion that would restore him to his lost dignity.

To the right, robed in a different kind of dignity—that of the righteous, the good, the responsible—was the elder brother, who regarded the scene dubiously, and with resentment. His upright body was unbending, his hands clasped tightly around the staff of his authority.

Alex could hear the words of protest muttered by the elder son: "This *son* of yours..."

And the words of the father's answer: "This *brother* of yours..."

Was lost and is found.

Alex closed his eyes for a few moments. When he opened them again, he noticed that the youth who had been going slowly from picture to picture at the far end of the gallery now stood a pace to his left. Oblivious to Alex's presence, he gazed solemnly at the image, his arms hanging by his sides.

Alex regretted the interruption but stepped aside to allow the other a central place before the painting. He expected the interloper to move on quickly, but minutes passed. How long they remained like this was impossible to tell. The boy's stillness and rapt attention to the painting were inexplicable. He was in his late teens or early twenties, and Alex wondered how one so young could be capable of such concentration, if concentration it was. Why was he not at school? Why was he not tinkering in the innards of a car engine, or pounding around an athletic field?

His face in no way displayed typical Slavic features. It was quintessentially primitive, the forehead slanted, brow ridges heavy, eyes small and inexpressive, cheeks hollow. His thin lips were parted slightly, and his chin was unevenly shaved. Brown hair was cropped close to the skull. His hands were large and his fingernails dirty. His blunt and muscular body was a peasant's torso with slightly bowed legs hinting at malnutrition. He wore a dingy green coat full of holes, and baggy workman's pants with cuffs suspended inches above wet, down-at-heel shoes.

Heaving a sigh as old and as freighted as humanity, the youth caught himself, perhaps becoming fully aware that there was another person beside him. He shot a swift glance at Alex and shifted his body away. His face, which had been open and defenseless while absorbed in the painting, now closed in on itself, guarded and anonymous.

Alex too retreated into himself, wishing the other would depart.

Eventually the youth turned a few degrees in Alex's direction and murmured, "*Zto horosho.*" *It is good.*

"Yes," Alex replied in the same tone, "it is good."

Now it was possible to attempt more.

"The father...", said the youth.

"Yes, and the son...", Alex replied.

"And...you see...the hands..."

Each sentence was left unfinished with spaces of many seconds between the responses. It was neither interruption nor inarticulation; it seemed to Alex that it was a necessary reduction, so that speech would not ruin what was now flowing back and forth between them.

"The boy...he came home", said the youth.

"And the father ran out to meet him", Alex replied.

A sudden tension crossed the youth's face. "If the father had not, what then?"

"But the son trusted."

"He risked..."

"The father also risks."

The youth turned to face Alex. He crossed his arms as if holding himself, as if he were cold.

"I...my..." He looked down at the floor, his eyes haunted.

For a moment or two, Alex could find nothing to say, and when he spoke he did not know where the thought had come from:

"The son should return to the father", he said.

"But what if the father does not want the son?" replied the youth.

"If he does not, then the son must remember." Alex pointed at the old man in the image. "Remember this face. It is a window. Through it you see the hidden face."

"The hidden face?"

"Yes. He is looking at you."

The youth glanced up at the painting again. Then back at Alex.

"How...this speaking...you and me speaking?"

"I seek..."

352

"You seek your son?"

"Yes. He is lost."

"I think maybe you will find him. A father such as you will find him."

"Will he want me?"

"I do not know. But I think it will be so."

"And your father?"

Once again a spasm of pain crossed the boy's face. He did not answer.

"Have you lost him?" Alex asked.

"I have run from him."

"You must return to him."

"Will he want me?"

"I hope it will be so. He should want a son such as you."

"But..."

"It may be he does not yet know you."

"Who are you?" the youth asked.

"You know me."

"Do I know you, sir?"

"Yes. And I know you."

Strangely, this did not disturb the other, though he spent a minute pondering it.

"Surely we have met before?"

"No."

"But tell me, who are you?"

"I am you."

The boy uncrossed his arms. He opened his mouth but said nothing.

"As you will be, in time", Alex said.

"I..." The eyes blinked rapidly, withholding tears.

"The child is father of the man", Alex said, looking up at the father in the painting. "Remember his face, for he too is your father. Remember my face also, and the words we have spoken to each other."

The boy looked into the man's eyes and nodded. Unable to speak, he walked from the room.

Alex left the Hermitage soon after, overcome by this inexplicable exchange. It was by now late afternoon and growing cold. The rush hour traffic had begun in earnest along Nevsky, but despite the roar he decided to walk the entire length of it to the Moskva. It took more than an hour, but it seemed to him that time had continued to alter its nature. He looked into many hundreds of faces on the way, and in all of them he saw what he had seen in the face of the peasant youth.

All men are my son, and all women are my daughter.

He arrived at his hotel room after six o'clock. There were no messages. He lay down on the bed and covered his eyes with a hand.

In the morning he awoke to the sound of screeching wind rattling the windows. He felt certain that this was the day he would finally meet Andrew. It was possible that by nightfall they would be on an airplane together bound for home.

There were no messages for him at the desk. He telephoned the Peterhof and learned that the Bloch group was still registered but was away for the day. The clerk could not tell him where they had gone but suggested they might be at a conference somewhere in the city.

This precipitated a hunch on Alex's part. He recalled that the plaque on the group's house in London had listed Saint Petersburg as one of its stations, which indicated they had an office in the city. He called telephone information and asked for a listing under Russian variants of the society's name, and also for Kosmos Corporation and the Europa Institute. There was nothing.

This left him no option but to go back to the Peterhof and attempt a penetration of hotel security. Another metro ride brought him to the lobby desk of the Peterhof, where the day clerk repeated what he had already told Alex. He accepted a second note in a sealed envelope and promised to hand it personally to Andrew Graham. The note said simply:

Andrew,

I beg you, please call me at the Hotel Moskva or come to me there as soon as you can.

I love you.
Dad

Followed by the address and phone number.

That Andrew had not yet called suggested two possibilities: the first, that Bloch had intercepted the Hopkins book; the second, that Andrew had received it but was so immersed in the cult that he did not want to respond. The latter was the more disturbing, for it meant that Alex's task would be more difficult than it already was. He prayed that such was not the case and that the message would get through.

He spent a frustrating hour walking back and forth in front of the hotel. The doormen had now developed a habit of watching him, their poker faces turning in unison whenever he passed, back and forth. Back and forth. Back and forth. No matter how much he extended the walk in either direction, no matter how convincing the air he affected of a harmless fellow busy about a legitimate task, they had noted him well, had observed his odd behavior, and were doubtless analyzing the degree of threat. Whether he was a madman, a hustler, a parasite, a gatecrasher, or a pesterer of valuable guests, he was definitely a man to be watched.

Thinking that the group would probably not return until later in the day, Alex decided to go north along Nevsky to the Hermitage. He walked quickly, head down, across the wind tunnel of the Fontanka Canal. Beyond, the wind was broken up by the buildings but was still formidable. He kept as close to the walls as possible, sidestepping gaping manholes and tilting slabs of pavement. Five blocks farther along he came to a second and narrower canal. A short way east along this icebound channel was a church that resembled the famous Saint Basil's in Moscow. He was intrigued but decided against any unnecessary detours. He was about to proceed on his way when he noticed a street sign affixed to the wall of a building on the north side of the canal. It said "Kanal Griboedova".

The name was vaguely familiar, but he could not recall its significance. Following an intuition, he found temporary shelter in the alcove of a shop door on the corner of Nevsky and Griboedova and leafed through his pocket address book. There, under the name Serov, he found "Petrovsky Rare Books and Manuscripts, 38 Kanal Griboedova, Saint Petersburg".

More than a year ago, on the advice of the Berlin dealer, Alex had tried to contact Serov in order to offer him the Russian collection of Kingfisher Books. His letters had prompted no replies, and his inquiries had failed to turn up a telephone number. Yet here it was—Griboedova—apparently real.

The section between the Nevsky bridge and the ornate church was a block long, bordered by narrow streets on both sides of the canal. Under the shadow of the church, which was a stone's throw across the canal, he found number 38, a five-story structure of pink brick and stucco. A line of buzzers beside the locked front entrance listed about twenty names, most of them offices of small enterprises and professional people, in addition to a few private apartments. No Serov was listed, but there was a "Petrovsky Firma". Alex pressed the buzzer, and a moment later a voice said, "Yes, what is it?"

"May I speak with Viktor Serov, please?"

"This is Serov. Who are you?"

"My name is Alexander Graham—from Canada."

There was no response to this.

"Do you remember my letters to you of last year, sir?"

The voice when it answered was vague, as if trying to recall something of minor importance.

"Regarding my collection of Russian books", Alex prompted.

"Ah, books. You want to talk books!"

"Yes, that's right. May I come in?"

"Well, I am very busy."

"I won't take much of your time."

"All right. Come in."

The buzzer went off. Alex pushed the door open and entered a narrow hallway. At the end of it was a staircase. At its foot stood a policeman, or what appeared to be a policeman, carrying a machine gun. His eyes stripped Alex and pronounced him harmless. "*Da!*" he said into a microcommunications apparatus clipped to his collar, and nodded to the staircase.

"Third floor, to the right. He's waiting."

Upstairs, Alex was met in the hallway by a man in his early sixties. No more than five feet tall, well barbered with sleek silver hair, burly and smartly dressed, he was smoking a cigar and squinting at Alex. He offered a hand that bore many rings. Alex shook it.

"So, you're Graham, are you?" he said in English. "Well, come in, come in."

Serov led him into an office furnished in Scandinavian modern. The walls were completely covered by shelves full of old books, and the spacious room was crammed with worktables, chairs, designer lamps, and a single teakwood desk that appeared to be Serov's center of operations. Crowding its surface were three computer screens, a fax machine busily churning out paper, two telephones, and stacks of documents. Alex thought it a rather strange bookshop.

"You like my perspective, Graham?" Serov asked, waving his hand toward the windows. The view was splendid indeed, for it overlooked the canal and the multicolored domes of the church on the opposite side.

"It's beautiful", Alex said.

"Yes, beautiful", the man said with a faint note of irony.

"What is the church?"

"It is the Church of the Resurrection, sometimes called the Church on the Spilled Blood."

"In honor of the Blood of Christ", Alex said to show that he was not an ignorant Westerner.

"Actually, no", Serov replied. "Czar Alexander II was assassinated on that spot."

"Oh yes, now I remember." Alex leaned forward eagerly. "A bomb. In 1881. He was killed by the revolutionary organization Narodnaya volya—the People's Will."

Serov smiled archly.

"I see you know a little Russian history, Mr. Graham. Congratulations. I salute you." The irony now became fully visible. Behind it was a sneer. "Perhaps you also know that the title has become more appropriate in recent weeks."

"What do you mean?"

"Did you not hear? Ah yes, but you are a tourist. Such matters would not concern you."

"Which matters?"

"A few days ago Tuganov, the boss of Saint Petersburg Oblast, the number two man in Zhirinovsky's party, was gunned down on the street out there. Seven bullets in the head." Serov considered the glowing end of his cigar and blew a long stream of smoke at the ceiling. "A terrifying incident. And last year, just over there on the other side of the canal, state deputy Galina Starovoitova was brutally murdered. A tragedy."

"The new politics are complicated", Alex said cautiously.

Serov shrugged. "It is always complicated. But I think in the Tuganov case, money was involved. Who knows? Now, how can I help you?"

Serov sat down in a leather swivel chair behind his desk and gestured Alex to sit across from him in an equally comfortable one.

Alex cleared his throat, trying to shift from assassinations to antiquarian books.

"Do you recall the letter, Mr. Serov, regarding my collection?"

Serov looked bored. "Vaguely. You're the one Marcus Schlel referred to me, aren't you? That man is definitely *ein Berliner*. He shouldn't have done it."

"Why is that?"

"Because this is not a pastry shop. My business is a private brokerage of cultural materials. I import and export under license from the Ministry of Culture. We buy, we sell; but we are not interested in street trade, you understand. Collections are being offered to me by people all over Europe. You did not state in your letter what distinguishes your collection from the others."

"I have some first editions."

"So do they all."

Serov smiled, waving at the wall behind him. "Behold— shelves full of first editions."

"I see", Alex said, his heart sinking.

"And I assume you have a lot of Soviet dissidents?"

"Yes."

"Bound copies of *Grani*?"

"Yes, those too."

"As I thought."

"I do have a very special book, a copy of *Dead Souls* signed by Gogol."

"I have three of them. Take a look."

So he did. Three copies, all in better condition than Alex's great treasure.

And that was that.

Serov leaned forward, his face sympathetic. "Mr. Graham, on behalf of the peoples of the former Soviet Union, and those of the new Russian Federation, I thank you for looking after our literary heritage during the brief period of our discomfort. For us, seventy-five years is the twinkling of an eye. I appreciate your sentiments, and really, I do not want to appear ungrateful, but you need not trouble yourself about us any longer. Our culture is emerging from the rubble; indeed, it is strolling around in the sunshine."

Dismayed by his thirty years of romanticism, Alex said nothing.

Serov leaned back and flicked cigar ash into a crystal bowl.

"So, is there anything else you wish to discuss?"

Alex shook his head.

Serov stood and offered his hand once more.

"A pleasure meeting you, Mr. Graham."

"Thank you for your time, Mr. Serov."

"Do not mention it. The man at the bottom of the stairs will see you out."

"Good-afternoon, then. *Dobry dyen*."

"Good-bye. *Da svidaniya*."

Ejected peaceably onto the street, Alex stood for a moment collecting his wits. Against his will his eyes darted up and down Griboedova in search of spilled blood. A little dazed, he turned in the direction of Nevsky, bumping into the front fender of a car parked a few paces from Serov's building.

"Sorry", Alex mumbled. "Pardon me."

The driver, who was perusing a newspaper, eyed Alex coolly and went back to his reading.

Dispirited, Alex decided against a second visit to the Hermitage and returned by the metro to his hotel. There, to add to his woes, he found there was still no message from Andrew.

After a supper in the Moskva's restaurant, he downed a bottle of Baltika and wondered if he was becoming overly attached to the effect it had on him. An estimable drink, this—inducing rosy feelings in the pit of disaster. He ordered another.

Back in his room he dialed the Peterhof and asked for Olga Andreyevna. When she came on the line, he identified himself as the man who had left the envelope for Andrew Graham, and asked if she had been able to give it to him.

She replied coldly: "I will return your call, sir, when I have the information. What is your telephone number, please?" He gave it to her and she hung up.

Alex stared at the receiver.

An hour later his phone rang.

"This is Olga", she said. "I am sorry to have spoken with you improperly. But it was difficult to have a conversation when you called. I am on my break now and am calling from a pay phone."

"Thank you for your help, Olga Andreyevna. I realize it is unusual."

"Yes, it is unusual. You must understand it is not because of the money."

"I understand."

"I gave the envelope to Andrew Graham when I saw him yesterday."

"Was he alone?"

"It seems he is never alone. Or, if he is, I am not there to see it."

"Was the German, Dr. Bloch, with him?"

"No, it was a woman."

"A woman from England?"

"Yes, that one."

"Did she say anything?"

"She was curious but did not ask what was in the envelope—not in front of me. Your son put it into his pocket, and that is the last I saw of him."

"This is very good news. Thank you." Alex paused. "How did you know I am his father?"

"It was not a great difficulty. You look like him. Is he in trouble?"

"In a sense, yes. Spiritual trouble."

"I do not understand what you mean by spiritual trouble, but I think he will come to no harm."

"Why do you think this?"

"Because he is a nice boy. That is easy to see. The others—the ones he is with—they are not so nice, I think."

"Please, would you ask him to contact me immediately?"

"If I see him, I will do it."

"You must try to speak with him when there is no one else with him. Is it possible?"

"Possible, but difficult."

"I am going to the Peterhof tomorrow. When does he usually come through the lobby?"

"It depends—in the morning they all go out and stay away for the day. They return at different hours—sometimes for supper, at other times close to midnight."

"Where do they go?"

"This I do not know. Perhaps they go to the ballet or opera, like many guests. Maybe they go to meetings elsewhere in the city."

"Can you arrange permission for me to wait in the lobby? I have been freezing out on the sidewalk."

"That is the other reason I am calling you. I regret to tell you that all desk and security staff have received a copy of your photograph. We are warned to report immediately if you come here."

"What! Where did they get a photograph of me?"

"That is nothing for them. It is from the watcher cameras—a computer printout from the video image."

"But why? Who ordered this?"

"A guest complained. The manager says that you are trying to harass guests. He says that if you come again to the hotel, even to the sidewalk outside, we are to call the police. As for entering the Peterhof, that is now impossible. I am sorry."

"But what am I going to do?" he said, more to himself than to her.

"Perhaps you should remain in your hotel", she offered timidly. "You should wait for your son to telephone you there. Good-bye, Mr. Graham."

She hung up.

The next morning was a Friday. Alex awoke, checked for messages, and as usual found none. Disconsolate, he wandered out onto the walkway in front of the Moskva with no particular intention. Across the avenue, people were streaming on foot through a gate in the monastery walls, heading in the direction of bells ringing in the church tower. Police were setting up blockades in the street, and workmen were erecting a stage and a bandstand.

Alex crossed over in a crowd of pedestrians and followed them through the gate. Beyond it was a narrow cobblestone passage that crossed a moat. On both sides of the passage beggars stood silently, hands held out before them, their lips whispering prayers. More than a few people dropped coins into the open hands, yet the givers were as poorly dressed as the beggars. For the most part the crowd was composed of elderly women, with a smaller contingent of old men. There were, as well, a surprising number of adolescents. All were progressing toward the Trinity Cathedral of the Saint Alexander Nevsky Monastery.

At the far side of the moat, Alex slowed his pace before an old woman in rags who was kneeling in the snow. Propped up on her lap was an icon of the Mother of God and the Christ Child. She rocked slightly, her right hand held out

363

before her, the bare skin chapped and red. Her face was thin, very wrinkled, her head covered by a dirty kerchief, her feet bound in rags.

Alex fumbled in his pocket, found some coins, and poured them into her hands.

"*Da kranit vas Gospod!*" he said. *May God keep you!*

"*E tebye*", she said, nodding. *And you.*

"Please pray for my lost son, grandmother."

"You will find him", she said, making the sign of the cross with three fingers joined to signify the Holy Trinity.

This was strangely calming—and authoritative—for the holy beggars of Russia were a class considered to be closer to God than the priests. He had seen few such beggars so far, no more than a dozen scattered throughout the city, all kneeling on the streets, all praying, all making the sign of the cross when any passerby happened to place a coin into their hands. By contrast, the professional beggars were identifiable by their aggressive technique and predatory eyes—none of the latter were in the monastery grounds. The beggars whom Alex now passed were patiently awaiting a shower of providence.

Within the Trinity Cathedral, the Divine Liturgy of the Orthodox Church was being celebrated. Mitered priests and archimandrites were solemnly intoning the prayers, incensing the sanctuary in a ritual more than fifteen hundred years old. Unlike in Roman Catholic churches, there were no pews, and worshippers moved about in the central nave and side alcoves, lighting candles at shrines, praying private devotions to the saints, to the Mother of God, and to the Savior himself. Clusters of women whispered together, parents bought snacks at a counter by the entrance, people arrived and departed at random—bowing, making the sign of the cross with great formality, bowing again before leaving. The men, especially, prayed with a physical stance that seemed curiously familiar to Alex. When they turned their faces to the mysteries being enacted on the altar, or to an icon, a stillness overcame them, their arms dropped at attention, hands to their thighs. This gesture was maintained throughout their prayers in a manner that was formal but not rigid. Alex suddenly remembered the incident at the Hermitage when he had stood with the young stranger in front of *The Return of the Prodigal Son*. He now realized that the youth had been praying.

As he silently pondered this, he remained unobtrusively in a shadowed alcove. A few steps away, a young man approached an icon, carrying an enormous cloth bundle in his left arm and leading a five-year-old girl by the hand. The bundle contained a baby with only its tiny face exposed in the cocoon of swaddling bands. Father and daughter bowed from the waist before the image of a woman saint. The little girl observed her father, copying his gestures. He straightened, made the Orthodox sign of the cross, then bowed again. The girl did the same.

"Light the candle, Ksenia", he whispered. She went forward with a thin beeswax taper, lit it from a flickering candle in a brass tray, and placed hers in a slot beside it.

"Now you can kiss her", said the father.

"I'm too shy, Papa."

"Oo-oo, too shy!" he chided. "Look, just do it like me."

He bent over, still holding the papoose to his chest, and kissed the painted hand of the saint.

"You see, it's easy. Come; don't be afraid. You are named for her."

The little girl stepped forward, one hand holding onto her father's sleeve. She kissed the icon and looked up into the face of Saint Ksenia.

"She's smiling at me, Papa. Before she was sad, but now she's happy."

"Yes, sometimes it's like that. She's saying how fine it is that you've come from Pskov to see her. Now she will never forget you."

"What do I say to her?"

"Ask her to pray to our Savior for us. For a good harvest in the garden, for Sima's eyes to be fixed by the doctor. For Baba's heart. For faith."

"What is faith?"

"Everything is faith, Ksyusha. But mostly it's to see what the eyes cannot see."

The girl stepped forward and kissed the icon again. Then she stepped back, gazing up at it in wonder.

"I asked."

"Good. Now, see there at the front, it's almost time for the Holy Gifts. After, we will go and buy bread."

The father lifted the baby high on his chest so that its chin rested on his shoulder. As they turned away, Alex saw the baby's little face beaming like a ripe peach, large black eyes smiling at him. The eyes were badly crossed.

At that, a volley of voices raised an acclamation in praise of Christ the Savior. Conversations and private prayers ceased, and from every direction people streamed toward the altar. Alex held back, a stiff foreigner, a Latin, a stranger in a strange land. In deference to the divisions that still existed, and to the laws of this Church, he did not press forward with the crowd to receive the Sacrament.

After the liturgy, a double line of priests, deacons, and acolytes came down from the altar. Robed in lavishly embroidered vestments of gold and red, accompanied by icon tapestries held high on poles, by lamps and incense burners, they processed out through the great double doors of the church, parting the congregation, which closed in after them and followed. All sang a soulful hymn in honor of the Bogoroditsa, the God-bearer, the humble virgin of Nazareth who had become Mother of the Savior. Swept up in the polyphony of celestial beauty, Alex fell in with the last of the procession.

They moved out into a fall of snow that carpeted the grounds of the cemetery where hundreds of monks were buried. The bare branches of linden trees swayed in rhythm. At the moat the beggars joined in with the others, and all poured into the jarring nouveau architecture of Nevsky Prospekt. The archpriest crossed to the center of the avenue and mounted the stage, followed by the other clerics. Hundreds of people crowded around. Loudspeakers squealed, and were adjusted.

Alex watched from the gate. Traffic was backed up in all directions by the police barriers. The police removed their caps. Automobile drivers got out of their vehicles and stood facing the stage, some from curiosity, a few with heads bowed and hands held to their thighs. On one side of the stage a corps of youths in military garb doffed their caps also. Among them Alex saw three contingents arranged in disciplined ranks: army, air force, and naval cadets.

The archpriest prayed aloud, his words and chant echoing against the wall of the Hotel Moskva. At the end of the prayers, a military brass band struck up the national anthem. This was followed by more prayers, a homily, and a final hymn.

When it was over, the crowds dispersed in all directions, and the procession returned to the monastery amid the ringing of cathedral bells. The soldiers, most of them adolescents, scattered toward waiting buses, upright in their smart uniforms—joking, shoulder tilted to shoulder, some arm in arm, lighting a surreptitious cigarette here and there. Their officers, looking scarcely older, scolded them humorously. Sailors, some wearing the insignia of submariners, mounted the bus closest to Alex. He watched their faces, trying to grasp who they were, and noted a few among them who could have been Andrew or Jacob.

In the afternoon he stayed in his room and waited for Andrew's call. He read from the Psalms, dug his rosary out from the bottom of his shoulder bag, prayed the sorrowful mysteries, and napped. At three o'clock the phone rang.

"Mr. Graham?" A woman's voice. Olga. "I have wanted to call you for two hours, since I came on duty. But there has been no opportunity until now."

"Do you have news for me?"

"Yes. I must speak quickly, for I have taken a short break and am at the pay phone in the restaurant. When I arrived for the afternoon shift, I learned that your son and the others are no longer here."

"Do you know where they have gone?"

"They have checked out of the hotel. They went to Pulkovo at eight this morning with all their luggage."

"Where is Pulkovo?"

"It's the airport."

"Do you know their destination?"

"Moscow."

"Where in Moscow?"

"I checked with Intourist. They are booked into rooms at the Troika Kiel."

"I see", Alex said, his heart sinking.

He paused, thinking, trying to make sense of this further complication.

"Are you there, Mr. Graham?"

"Yes. Can you tell me where the Troika Kiel is?"

"I think it is near the Kremlin."

"Do you know if there is another hotel near the Kremlin, a place where I could stay?"

"I have been to Moscow only once, but I remember a very large hotel across from Red Square. The Rossiya, I think. Yes, it was the Rossiya."

"I am in greater debt to you than ever, Olga Andreyevna."

"It is nothing. I must go now."

"First, let me say, I thank you from my heart. You are a fine young woman."

"*Nichivo*. I do not know why I am doing this."

Alex searched for a reply.

"You will tell no one about our conversation", she said firmly. "I would lose my job."

"I understand. I will tell no one."

"We have not spoken. We have not met. Good-bye."

15. *Around the Great Wheel*

The next morning Alex checked out of his room and took the metro to Moskovsky Vokzal—Moscow Station, which was situated on a square just off Nevsky, about halfway between the Peterhof and the Moskva.

He arrived at nine, which left him an hour in which to buy his ticket and get a cup of coffee at a kiosk. That took fifteen minutes. Looking for a place to sit, he saw that the station was a vast echo chamber where many people went to and fro as if they were in a cathedral, searching for points of ultimate departure and arrival. A bronze bust of Peter the Great overlooked all.

Alex entered a crowded waiting room and found a spot on a wooden bench beside an old woman who was knitting a sweater, across from a young couple whispering intensely in a heated quarrel. A one-legged man in an army camouflage jacket hobbled past on crutches and sat down in the only remaining place. Presently, those who were stretched out asleep on the benches were roused and asked to make space for other travelers. Though he had spent only four days in Russia, the rich variety of human life was beginning to seep into Alex's blood, and as the seats filled, it seemed to him that he recognized every face. Many resembled Oleg and Olga, Serov, the beggar woman from the monastery, the peasant father and his daughter Ksenia, the youth from the Hermitage, and even the man whose car he had bumped into on Kanal Griboedova.

At 9:45 the loudspeaker announced the departure of the Moscow express on track 6. The old woman packed her needles; the one-legged veteran heaved himself up unsteadily, struggling to get the crutches under his arms; the couple ended their argument and kissed; the doppelgänger from Griboedova closed his magazine; and all of them made their way toward the platform without a glance in Alex's direction. The veteran stumbled once, and Alex flashed out a hand to steady him.

"*Spasiba*—thanks!" said the veteran, his eyes meeting Alex's for a split second before he struggled on alone.

South of the city, the land was flat. The last of the outlying suburbs disappeared, giving way to the normative expanse of the great Russian earth, sleeping now. Mile after mile the passing scenery remained unchanged, white fields bordered by uneven stands of trees, a few evergreens and the more numerous skeletons of birch, followed by a village, fields, forest, village, fields, forest...

The villages invariably contained no more than fifty to a hundred small wooden homes, most of them constructed of clapboard, a few of logs. Some were painted, but of these the dominant colors were dirty mustard, pale blue, and a green that resembled verdigris, the hue of death. This effect was worsened by the low-hanging overcast, which seemed backlit by flashes of photographic silver, as if the clouds screened a clash of arms between titans who fought hand to hand over the unheeding souls below.

The entire atmosphere was infected with dread. Was it a mood imposed by low air pressure, by history, by the bare facts of poverty, or by a combination of these? Alex did not know, and he reminded himself that he might be projecting his sense of personal helplessness upon the actual geography. Yet he could not dismiss the growing suspicion that he was locked into a Sisyphean ritual that would have him trailing his son all over the world, always a step or two behind, never quite catching up to him, condemned to an eternity of increasing weight—his own heart the stone that he must roll up the mountain.

He shook off the pagan myth. He prayed for courage and perseverance.

About an hour into the journey, the train rattled onto a trestle bridge. So familiar did it seem to him that he had to grope for the certainty that he had never seen it before. No doubt it prompted residual memories, especially of a summer day, years ago, when under a cloudless Ontario sky he had passed into manhood. At the age of seventeen, fully recovered from his heart disease, he had walked three miles along a deer track to the Algoma rail line that cut through the bush toward the mines of the north. And there he had come upon a bridge spanned by two high arcs of gossamer steel. Stripping down to his shorts, he had climbed the metal grid, hand over hand, fighting fear more than he fought vertigo. The nervous tension of a million observing insects burst into dizzy symphonies of praise and protest. Higher and higher he went, until finally he arrived at the top and stood slowly upright. The view in all directions was of uninterrupted forest. Looking down, he saw the water flow deep and dark beneath the bridge.

There was a moment when he was about to revert to a primate form, to cling with his fingers to the bolts and rivets and to crawl back down to the floor of the planet. But he grew angry at this impulse, and using every shred of willpower, he forced his trembling limbs to straighten again. Squaring his shoulders, he extended his arms until they were parallel with the rails below, felt the last burning strokes of sun on his naked back, and bent his knees, steadying himself for the single springing leap that could easily be his last. With a sharp intake of breath he hurled himself off, out, over, into the abyss. At first it seemed that his body rose, or was held suspended between one world and another, and between past and future. Then the force of gravity took him in a long, slow curve down into the mouth of the water. His hands and arms split the surface and drove a wedge for his body, deep, deep, deeper, until his fingers touched the stony bottom. He coiled, somersaulted, and drove for the surface.

As he sat shivering on the riverbank, a streak of blue shot past him, a kingfisher diving for a fish.

Now, thirty years later, the train crossed a remarkably similar bridge, and then passed through a village clinging to the bank of the frozen river. Pale smoke rose from a thicket of stovepipes. Among them, surrounded by hundreds of shacks, a church was being rebuilt. Webbed with timber scaffolds around yellow brick, capped with a golden dome, it was rising again at the heart of the community over which it had once presided.

Another hour passed, during which Alex, speeding past a copse of pines, saw his second rural church, a red-brick Byzantine structure topped by a silver dome. It too was being restored. Then a dozen smaller hamlets flew by, churchless. The uneven tracks clattered incessantly, and from time to time they jolted the carriage, refusing passengers the luxury of mesmerization.

About halfway to Moscow the land began to undulate, the clouds thinned, and a feeble disc of sun appeared. Now the snow displayed a surprising range of colors, pale blue, mauve, yellow, and ivory. Every so often the track crossed the meandering paths of frozen rivers, outlined by purple where the waterway met the flanks of land. Clinging to the steep banks were small villages of great beauty, their charm no doubt magnified by the benefit of distance. They were as old as others the train had passed, but their buildings were fewer in number, and footpaths linked every house. Alex wondered what would it be like to live in such places. Had they been poisoned by memories of betrayals and denunciations; did they seethe with generational resentments? Or were they islands of private life, far enough removed from the politics of the great cities to retain their humanity?

Mile after mile, the alien world ceased to be a homogeneous mass. As the train approached the next village, it slowed to a crawl. On a hillock beside the tracks, six young men sat together on a wooden sledge, their heads bent toward each other in conversation. Above them was a log barn from which a seventh was leading a white horse, the boy leaping through the snowdrifts, luring the animal toward the sleigh with a handful of hay. Among the six were two who carried bow saws slung over their shoulders. Were they speaking of the day's task, of wood cutting, or of plans for their lives, of going someday to Moscow, where the riches of the world were now pouring in? Whatever the subject was, they dropped it and turned to look at the train as Alex's carriage drew past.

A minute later the hillock plunged toward a river bed, and the train rattled onto another bridge. Along the riverbank the snow-covered hulls of small boats were ranked. Nearby, six old men were seated in a circle on boxes with handheld strings threaded through holes in the ice. Men whom Alex would never meet, would never know. And yet he seemed to know them, for they were doing what Leonid had done. Like his old friend, they contained loves and hatreds, greatness and sin, prejudice and truth, songs and poems and tales. Perhaps they were waiting for golden fish to speak, to grant wishes, to reenchant the world.

With a start, Alex realized that here was the valley of the Clementine as it must have been a hundred years ago. It was a view into the lives of his ancestors, a microsecond of exposure that was now printed indelibly on his mind. *There is my grandfather a boy again*, he thought. *He is fishing through the ice, and my father has not yet been born.* Years pass like flowing water—winter, spring, summer, fall—year after year, century after century. Now it is spring with its resurrected hopes.

Now it is summer, and the people long in their graves are strolling in the hot hayfields, sweating and happy, yearning for spouses they have yet to meet, building their strength, glowing in their limited and healthy powers, making grass mountains on the horse-drawn wagons. The buzz of flies and the creak of leather traces, the singing of crickets in the falling red sun. Then comes autumn with its bountiful harvests. And here is the winter again, with its burning woodfires that hold back death.

On the far side of the river, the land heaved upward and thrust a pine forest toward the spreading sky. Wind blew snow from the tossing branches. Was this the youths' destination? Would they cut timber here? Logs for a cabin? Stovewood? Willow switches for their grandparents' gardens? Wedding beds, cradles, and coffins? Alex wondered what his own sons had gained by their success in the modern age. Freedom from terror of the concentration camp and the knock on the door in the middle of the night? Yes, they had been spared that. But had they been protected only to be locked into something else? For Jacob, was it the security that money and prestige would bring? For Andrew, was it the adventure of dangerous mysticism?

By midafternoon, the train had passed about forty villages and half a dozen larger towns. Near the latter were fields containing countless crosses of blue ironwork. One crowded cemetery seemed to stretch for more than a mile. It struck Alex that he had seen no children on the journey from Saint Petersburg, but he reminded himself that Russian parents, like parents everywhere, would warn their children against playing near the tracks. Moscow was close now, for the villages were larger, followed by towns that were closer and closer together, until the woods were mere patches between them. Now the train passed scattered industrial settlements, and the sun fell toward the horizon, tinting the land pink, then dusky rose, then violet. In the east a radio tower came up over the low hills, its warning lights blinking. As it approached with infinite slowness, Alex saw that it was more than an ordinary metal spire; it was a concrete structure of staggering height, containing lighted windows, floors of offices, and a lance soaring far above the entire plain. After that came suburbs clogged with mile upon mile of apartment blocks sharing grudging space with a sprawl of factories, succeeded in turn by more ranks of tenements, and a final glide into the bay of a railway station.

"Moskva, Leningradsky Vokzal", a loudspeaker proclaimed as the train halted, thus ending Alex's voyage between two worlds. His body ceased to float more quickly than his dreaming mind, for the flesh was now rooted at a fixed point of the compass.

Moscow! The Kremlin fortress was the axis of a great wheel, around which revolved the city's concentric ring roads connected by spokes of wide boulevards, containing over three hundred square miles and ten million people. At the hub of this circling foment, across the street from the Kremlin, the Hotel Rossiya towered above the north shore of the Moscow River.

When his taxi pulled to a stop at one of the hotel's four lobbies, the driver told Alex with enthusiasm that it contained more than three thousand rooms and that in order to build it, the Soviet government had razed sixteen churches and chapels that had once stood on the site. They had left the seven cathedrals of the Kremlin and the half dozen other domes in the surrounding streets—more than enough religion for one city, he said.

Alex paid the man and got out onto the sidewalk, where he paused for a moment. The building was a featureless block of concrete, impressive only by its perverse mass. He passed into the lobby, navigating a phalanx of serious-looking men standing about the entrance with their hands in the pockets of their leather coats. They eyed him carefully, then ignored him. The lobby was noisy with electric casino machines and the tinkle of glasses at a bar. More men in leather jackets were seated here and there on couches, some of them in the custody of very beautiful women whose winter coats were cast lazily over the shoulders of their evening dresses. They all stared at Alex.

He was not fool enough to think that the women were interested in him for purely natural reasons. The air was heavy with the unmistakable odor of commerce and its clandestine offshoot, organized crime. He did not know how he arrived at this certainty but attributed it to some primitive faculty of discernment. Obviously there was a different class at work here than the petty tyrants of officialdom that he had encountered in Saint Petersburg. There was something controlled and sinister about the atmosphere of the Rossiya.

Alex checked in, and because it was a three-star hotel, the desk clerk offered no welcome and inflicted the customary wait. He was given a hotel passport that got him past the security guard and into an elevator to the ninth floor. Exiting the elevator, he found his way into the main corridor and began a heroic quest for his room. More than once he passed women dressed in the uniforms of expensive seduction, and he tried with some success to ignore their attempts to make eye contact.

His room left a few things to be desired, but on the whole it was comfortable. He opened the window, which overlooked an interior courtyard, and the thumping of a dance band and the loud wails of Russian pop songs crashed in. He closed the window, blocking most of it out. Clinging to the hope that he and Andrew would soon be flying home, he expected to spend no more than a day or two in Moscow. His first task was to try once again to make contact. He took a hot shower, dressed, prayed for spiritual protection, and placed a call to the Troika Kiel. As he waited for the connection, he flipped through a tourist magazine and noticed on a map in the centerfold that the Troika was directly across the river from the Rossiya.

When the desk clerk answered, Alex asked for Andrew Graham, a member of the Bloch party.

There was a pause before the clerk asked, "In the Bloch party?"

"Yes", Alex said indifferently.

"Your name, please?"

Once again the ramparts loomed; once again he had forgotten to plan ahead.

"A friend", Alex said firmly.

"We shall need a name, sir", the clerk insisted.

"Why do you need my name? Mr. Graham and I are closely acquainted. There is no need for this formality."

"I am sorry; all calls must go through the proper channels."

"You mean through Mr. Bloch's room?"

"That is correct."

"Then you may say that Mr. Wordsworth is calling. Mr. William Wordsworth."

Alex waited impatiently, listening to the bird noises of a Viennese musical confection that came through the wire. He was quite sick of it by the time the clerk came back on the line.

"Regrettably, Mr. Wordsworth, the party is not available to take your call."

"Did you speak with him?"

The clerk did not reply.

"Are they refusing my call?" Alex insisted.

"If you wish, sir, you may leave a message."

"Please answer my question: Are they refusing my call?"

"I am not in a position to say."

"Do you speak English?"

"Yes", the clerk answered in a distinctly dry tone.

"Mr. Graham does not speak Russian. Please tell him the following in English: 'The child is father of the man. The kingfisher is waiting for you in the Hotel Rossiya, across the river from the Troika.'"

"There is a misunderstanding, I think. There is no Mr. Graham registered at the Troika Kiel."

"What! Don't tell me that! I know he's there."

"Sir, he may or may not be here, but he is definitely not registered as a guest."

"Why are you lying to me!" Alex shouted.

The clerk abruptly terminated the call.

When the phone rang twenty minutes later, Alex leaped to answer it, knocking an ashtray to the floor, forgetting to say hello. It was a woman. Speaking in broken English, she offered "companionship" for the evening. Alex said that he was not interested. She repeated the offer more explicitly. Very good rates, she added. He told her to think of her mother and to leave the trade that was destroying her soul. He searched hastily in his memory for the Russian word— *dusha*. She swore at him and hung up. He wondered how she had gotten his room number (one of three thousand) and how she had known to speak English.

During the next hour or so, Alex received three more calls, each of them from different female voices, each offering, with various levels of sophistication, a single commodity. By now, his disgust was giving way to conflicting feelings of pity and—he had to admit to himself—attraction. Exasperated, he called the front desk and protested. The desk clerk pretended not to understand. When Alex spelled it out, the clerk said, "Those girls! But what can I do? They use the house phones. There are so many guests in the hotel, we cannot keep track! Why don't you unplug your phone?"

Alex did not want to do so for fear of missing Andrew's call. Maybe—just maybe—the clerk at the Troika Kiel had

had second thoughts and had delivered the message. He sat in the armchair beside the phone and waited. It was now about ten thirty. He recalled that in Saint Petersburg the metaphysicians had frequently stayed out until midnight. He decided that if Andrew had not contacted him by one in the morning, he would unplug the phone.

Not long after, it rang again. The voice on the other end was calling about the usual business, but she spoke in Russian and sounded timid, as if she was unused to the procedure.

"Miss," he said in as patient a tone as he could muster, "what are you doing to yourself?"

She did not answer, and she did not hang up.

"Please—explain", she said at last.

"Why are you degrading yourself? Why are you selling yourself?"

"I must."

"Why must you?"

"It is personal. I do not discuss personal matters with clients."

"I am not a client. Besides, is there anything more 'personal' than what you are offering for sale?"

Again the pause.

"Think of your mother."

"My mother?"

"And think of your father."

"I do not have a father", she said without emotion.

"Surely there is another way to make a living."

"I need money quickly. I have children. I must feed them."

"Where is their father?"

"Gone."

Alex sighed and searched for a reply. "I am sorry", he said.

"*Nichivo!*" she said, but the verbal shrug lacked conviction.

"But it does matter", Alex said. "You suffer because of it."

The silence stretched uncomfortably. He wondered why he was talking to a prostitute. Were his motives as pure as they seemed? Was his righteous talk only to ease his conscience as he inched toward the edge of the precipice? Was his loneliness driving him, or was it compassion? Christ talked with prostitutes, after all. Yes, but he was not Christ. He wondered, moreover, if her story was a clever ploy, plan B for a slow night at the Rossiya, or possibly a methodology that worked well on the reluctant and the guilt ridden. Would she in the next breath tell him of her miserable straits, of her hungry children exploited in hostile surroundings?

"Why do you ask me such questions?" she said, breaking the silence. "Are you not a normal man?"

"I am a normal man, miss. Normal men do not turn women into things that they purchase."

"I do not care about that", she said sullenly.

"You are a person."

"A person? What is a person? A person must eat. Children must eat."

"What are the names of your children?"

"That is a private matter."

If she had told him their names and added a convincing tale of woe, Alex would have thought she was inventing it, or that, if the tale was true, she was simply using it to warm up a cool customer. But she did not. Her reticence, he sensed, was a defense against total dehumanization.

"Are you from Moscow?" he asked.

"No."

"Where are you from?"

She hesitated. "Smolensk."

"Can you not return there?"

"With money I could. But I have no money."

"Why did you come to the city?"

"It is rich. A person can advance. Make a fresh start."

"Could you not make a fresh start in Smolensk?"

"You are a foreigner. You do not know. Moscow is not Russia. Moscow is Moscow. Outside of it there is much hunger, jobs are few, money is difficult to find. Month after month many people do not get their pay."

"Are there no jobs here?"

"I have a job, as you can see." It was the first hint of irony, but tinged with sadness.

"I meant—"

"I know what you meant. You are not a bad man. But you do not understand. The government no longer demands passports to move throughout the country. If a person can get money for a train ticket, he can come to Moscow. For that reason the city is now full of people like me, and there are not enough jobs for everyone."

"Would you let me help you?"

"How can you help me if you are not interested in what I am selling?" This was said with the dead calm of an old bitterness.

"I will give you a gift."

"What kind of gift?"

"Money to help you make a fresh start."

"Are you that rich?"

"I am not rich."

"You are a foreigner. You are rich, even if you think you are not."

"Maybe this is true. It is also true that I can help you a little. Let me at least give you money for a train ticket to Smolensk."

Even as he said it, Alex groaned inwardly, watching his meager resources begin to pour through a hole in his pocket.

"*Nyet!*" she said firmly. "I do not want this money. I work for what I earn."

"Does the one who rules you get part of the money?"

"Him? Yes, but he clears the path for business."

"He is a parasite. He is using you."

"And I use him."

"You do not sound like a person who is happy about it. I think you are a good person. I think you have the soul of a mother."

"A mother? Do not speak to me about *mother*. I am a terrible mother. I do this…"

Her voice choked, and she could not go on.

"Please, let me help you."

"No! Good-bye!"

Alex sat brooding for several minutes, wondering about her. She was not a predator. She clung desperately to her tiny scrap of misplaced honor, her refusal to take money without an exchange of services, and this, though its logic was inverted, prevented her from losing everything—losing herself. He had not seen her face, but strangely he felt that he knew her, felt her fear and pride as if they were his own, her helplessness adding to his own growing list of failed hopes. He sighed. The gulf between them was vast, and she had not found the strength to hurl her true self toward his outstretched hand.

Shaking off a looming paralysis, he called the Troika once more. When the clerk answered, he said, "I am a foreigner visiting in Moscow. I am interested in booking a hotel room. How many stars are you?"

"We are five stars."

"Oh, that's very good. Are you owned by Hilton?"

"No, the Troika is a hotel of the Kreuger-Kiel line."

"The German company?"

"That is correct, sir. Would you care to book a room now?"

"Yes", said Alex, making an instant decision. If hotels containing Bloch were impenetrable by unwanted visitors, they could at least be entered by registered guests.

"Your name, please?"

"Uh, Halcyon."

Alex told the man that he would come to the Troika in the morning and would register then. After he hung up it struck him that Russian hotels demanded a guest's passport at check-in and that there would be no reservation for Alexander Graham. But he thought it would not be too difficult to bluff his way through the discrepancy. After all, Halcyon was the address on his passport, and he would explain that he had misunderstood the clerk's question.

He unplugged the phone, got into bed, turned out the reading lamp, crossed his arms behind his head, and stared at the darkness. Tomorrow he would close the gap for good.

At dawn he dressed and went down in the elevator to the restaurant, a room that could have seated several hundred. There were about two dozen people scattered throughout, most of them eating alone. At the buffet table he filled a plate, choosing from the selection of biscuits and boiled eggs, cabbage rolls, and yogurt. A samovar was steaming with tea, but he filled a cup from a small urn of coffee.

A cluster of British men were talking loudly at one end of the room, their every word voluble enough to broadcast details of their romantic conquests from the night before. Alex went to a table at the opposite end, turned his back to them, and sat down. He prayed a silent grace and glanced out the window, realizing with a start that he was only a hundred yards from the golden domes of the cathedrals inside the Kremlin walls.

He ate slowly, with a curious mixture of fearful pleasure— pleasure that he was here at this axis of history, fear that within the hour he would once again try to enter the kremlin that the metaphysicians had erected around his son.

He was sipping the last of the coffee when a shadow fell across the red tablecloth. He looked up to see a woman in her early twenties staring at him uneasily, as if she was uncertain what to make of him. He thought at first she was a waitress, then realized she was not in the white uniform of the matrons at the buffet. She wore a tight black miniskirt and an equally tight sweater of pink angora. The strap of a shoulder purse crossed her thin chest. Her face was small, heart shaped, framed by short blond hair. She was very pretty. Her eyes were green and troubled.

"May I sit down, please?"

He stood and gestured with an open hand to the chair opposite.

"Smolensk?" he asked.

She nodded and her face reddened.

"How did you recognize me?" Alex said. "How did you know I am the man you spoke with on the telephone?"

She shrugged and put on a Russian poker face. "It is no great difficulty." She pulled a cigarette from a package of Camels, tamped the end on the back of the package, and lit it. She inhaled deeply and blew the smoke sideways. Alex thought it was very much the way teenage girls in his hometown smoked, affecting an air of sophistication that did not suit them.

"Were you serious about the money?" she said, trying to appear hard and businesslike. But it was not a convincing performance. Her lower lip trembled.

"I was serious, yes. I am willing to help you."

"Why? What are you after?"

"I am after nothing."

"Don't fool yourself. Everyone wants something."

"Not me."

"You pity me, then?"

"No, I feel sadness that a woman is forced into this way of life. When we talked last night, I sensed that you were my daughter. Does that sound strange to you?"

"It sounds insane to me." A smile flickered at the edges of her lips, but her eyes remained the same—haunted.

"Would you like some tea, miss?"

She glanced nervously about the room. "No. I don't have much time."

"Is the parasite watching you?"

"He is sleeping. The other women—the business women—they come to the hotel later in the day. Even so, I am known in this place. There are dangerous people here."

"Here?"

"In the lobby. Powerful people. They would not be happy if I returned to Smolensk. So, if you please, I wish to speak with you—privately."

Alex frowned.

"We will go for a walk outside. You will take my arm. But first, you will lean across the table and kiss me."

Alex stared at her.

"It is only for show", she explained. "To avoid suspicion."

He leaned across the table and kissed her, a little woodenly, bumbling. Most of the kiss went to her cheek.

"That is good", she said in a low voice. "Now we go for a walk, a girl and her client."

They stood, she took his arm, and they walked out of the restaurant into the wide avenue of the hallway. In the vestibule she found her winter garb, an ankle-length black coat, high leather boots, and a molded black hat on which was sewn, incongruously, the insignia of an American sports team—the Chicago Bulls. It looked hideous, and Alex hated it. From there she led him along a side hall, through a service door, and down a flight of back stairs.

"We go to the employee entrance", she explained.

On the ground floor, they came to a nondescript glass door, nodded at a security guard in passing, and went out onto a street named Varvara. The sky was blue and the air very cold. The woman from Smolensk held her collar over her chin and proceeded with Alex down Varvara to the base of Red Square. As they passed Saint Basil's Cathedral, Alex could not take his eyes from it.

"You are here for the first time", she said.

"Yes. All my life I have seen photographs of it, but to see it face-to-face..."

She observed him from the corner of her eye as he stopped and turned in a slow revolution, taking in the surrounding architecture. Last night the city had seemed to be in the grip of a spirit that had held it in bondage for three quarters of a century—the very core of Satan's political territory on earth. Yet in the daylight its fuller face, indeed its truer face, had emerged. The downtown buildings were in much better condition than those of Saint Petersburg, the atmosphere more cosmopolitan, the streets well paved, new paint everywhere. And in all directions the domes of magnificent churches were blooming like an old garden that was being restored to fruitfulness: Saint Basil's with its multicolored fantasia of oriental blossoms, others capped by black bulbs appointed with gold stars, dark green bulbs with silver stars, light and dark blue bulbs with silver and gold stars, or totally gilded bulbs. They were of diverse shapes and sizes. All were surmounted by crosses, dazzling the eyes beneath the February sun. Alex wondered what this part of the city would have looked like before the sixteen churches had been razed for the Rossiya.

"Everywhere one looks, so much beauty", he said.

"You see with a foreigner's eyes", she replied evenly.

They proceeded through the cobbled square and turned onto a sidewalk leading down to a bridge over the Moskva. As they began to cross it, the wind gusted in fits and starts, increasing in velocity as they approached the exposure of mid-river. At the halfway mark she slowed her pace, stopped, and turned to face the west. Alex joined her, and they stood side by side, leaning against the bridge's waist-high stone wall.

Downriver, past the farthest guard tower of the Kremlin walls, an immense Byzantine cathedral arose over the city skyline. It was the largest of all the surrounding churches, and the color of the dome was unique—a coppery bronze.

"What is that building?" Alex asked.

"That? Do you not know it?"

She made a surreptitious sign of the cross, and inclined slightly toward the building.

"That is the Cathedral of Christ the Savior", she said.

"Do you go there sometimes?"

"Me?" she said without emotion. "Do you think I am a holy harlot? Like Saint Mary of Egypt? Of course I do not go in there. I stand outside and pray."

"You pray?" he said in a disingenuous tone.

"Yes," she snapped, "even prostitutes pray sometimes."

"I'm sorry. I didn't mean—"

"Forget it."

"Who built it?" he asked, trying to move the conversation onward.

"The Church, the patriarch. He had a lot of help—the city of Moscow gave money, and even the Kremlin contributed, people say."

"That is a great sign of hope. Life is changing."

"Changing?" she said doubtfully, glancing up at him. "Many things have changed, some for better, some for worse." She pointed at the cathedral. "Maybe this is one of the better ones. Do you know its story?"

"No, tell me."

"Many years ago, the Communists tore down the cathedral that once stood there. It was just like this but smaller, and the dome was a different color, more like the others you see around here. They planned to build a big monument to Lenin where the church used to be. It was going to be so big that it would be the highest thing on the Moscow skyline. The statue of Lenin would be huge. His arm raised over the city, his finger pointing. His finger alone was to be three meters long."

"Did they build it?"

"They tried to. But every time they did, the foundations crumbled and filled with water. After years and years they finally gave up and built a swimming pool and a park instead. Then after the Communists were no longer in control, someone decided to rebuild the old cathedral. This, as you see, did not crumble."

The central dome was flanked by four smaller domes, each containing bells of many sizes. As Alex and the girl watched, tiny human figures in the open belfries began to move, and the bells resounded. There was a single deep bass, its sonorous boom joined by a great assortment of higher pitches and lesser volumes, spreading across the city in wave after wave. The ringing continued steadily for several minutes, then ceased.

The girl shivered. She turned to Alex and said, "You offered to help me."

He opened his wallet, extracted ten thousand rubles, and handed the money to her. She took it, counted it, and stuffed it into her pocket.

"That is two months' wages", she said, staring at the ground.

"Will you go to Smolensk?"

"I will not lie to you. I tell you only this: I will try to go home as soon as I can. It may be tomorrow, it may be a month from now." She patted her pocket. "This makes it possible."

"Go soon", he said.

She shrugged but could not quite manage the dour indifference of the Russian mask.

"What is your name?" he asked.

Bitterness contorted her face. "My name? My name is Interdevushka."

Interdevushka—International girl.

She pulled a paper and pencil from her pocket.

"Give me your address", she said abruptly. "I promise nothing, but one day, if I am able, I will return your money."

"It is not necessary to return it."

Nevertheless, she insisted. To confirm her sense of self-respect, he wrote down his name and address and handed the paper back to her.

"Consider the money a gift from Saint Mary of Egypt", he said.

Her face crumpled. She turned and walked quickly away, head down, hands in her coat pockets. He watched her until she reached the far side of the river and disappeared into the maze of the city.

16. *In the Underground*

Alex gathered his belongings from his room and returned to the lobby, where he asked the desk clerk if there were any messages for him. As usual, there were none. He checked out and hired a taxi for the five-minute ride to the Troika. As the car crossed the bridge, he scanned the sidewalks, half expecting to see the woman from Smolensk, but of course she was nowhere in sight. He tried not to think about her, because the car was now descending a ramp from the bridge and entering the driveway of the hotel.

Liveried men hurried to open the doors of expensive vehicles that drew up before and behind the taxi but ignored the little Volga. Alex paid the driver and stepped out onto the marble reception area beneath a gold-colored canopy. As the taxi drove away, he hastened up the front steps, whispering a prayer that he would be able to get into the hotel and register without any problems. It was not to be, for two security guards in plain clothes stepped in front of him before he reached the doors. They told him to leave the premises. An argument ensued in which he insisted that he had preregistered and had a room in the hotel. They scowled at him and said this was no longer so, and that if he, Alexander Graham, did not wish to be arrested, he would leave now—immediately!

Alex demanded to know how they knew his name.

"We have a photo of you. You are a troublemaker!" one said.

"At least let me leave a message at the desk!" Alex protested.

"*Nyet!* No message", the other said. "Go, or I call the police. You would not enjoy our Russian prisons."

They each took one of his arms, hustled him down the staircase and along the entrance walkway, and then pushed him onto the public sidewalk.

"Do not come back. If you show your face here again, we will hold you and hand you over to the police."

"You would not have a nice vacation", the other sneered.

Breathing heavily, Alex stood for several minutes staring at the hotel entrance, mentally begging Andrew to come out. But he did not. After that, Alex walked the entire circumference of the Troika searching for other entrances, of which there were many, but at each glass doorway a man in a black suit stood inside glaring at him. None of them failed to put a cell phone to his ear and speak into it as he passed.

Short of standing all day on the public sidewalk, Alex could think of nothing more to do. He would freeze if he waited outside in the elements, and within the near proximity of the hotel there were no safe warm places where he could watch the main entrance. He hailed a taxi and returned to the Rossiya, where once again he went through the laborious registration process and was given a room. It was more forlorn than the other one, and the view even more depressing, for the window looked out upon a row of chimneys that belched black clouds over the Moscow skyline. He stared at the scene bitterly, alternately boiling with frustration and heartsick with dismay.

The desire to give up was overwhelming. He felt certain that some of the messages he had left for Andrew had been intercepted but surely not all of them. There was the Hopkins book, wasn't there? Andrew had put the envelope with the book into his pocket. How could he have failed to understand its significance? How could he have failed to decipher the message inside the cover? Why had he not responded? Was there a reply in the silence? "Stay away from me. I don't want to see you. Go home."

If that was the case, what did it say about the state of his son's mind? Moreover, the state of his soul? What kind of son would refuse to meet with his own father when both of them were only minutes apart in a city half a world away from their home? Was it possible that Andrew now regarded him as a wholly unwanted pest, or worse, a threat? If so, the boy was truly in bondage, and nothing Alex could say to him would make any difference. Was this true? Perhaps he was being too pessimistic. Perhaps Shaw Cunningham had confiscated the book before Andrew had a chance to read the message.

Alex argued with himself, now this way, now that. But in his heart he was shaken by a great dread, feeling that no matter what he did to retrieve his son, *they* would always be one step ahead of him, always stronger than him. He told himself that this was not so, that they were the weak ones because they dwelled in the shadow world of lies. On the other hand, if they were truly evil, they had dark powers on their side. And what was one man against all of that?

Shamefacedly, he reminded himself that it was not a case of one small man against a host of adversaries. The powers of truth and love were on his side. God was with him, and in the end the darkness could not overpower the light. He hoped this was so. Indeed, he had nothing else to rely upon. Yet there remained a nagging fear that while it was true that light would eventually win the great cosmic struggle, there would also be many casualties. His son could easily become one of them. This doubt was further aggravated by the practical problems of money and time. His money was dwindling rapidly. If he did not soon return to Halcyon, the bookstore would remain closed, and there would be no income to repay the loans. He could lose the Kingfisher.

He phoned the Troika that morning, using an assumed name, and succeeded in reaching Bloch. He tried to get past the now-loathsome *"Ja?"*, pretending he was a Troika employee who had found—Alex groped quickly for this detail—a scarf with a name tag on it. The name Graham. He asked to speak to the guest.

"Graham has not lost his scarf", said the German voice. "Don't you ever learn from your mistakes?"

This was followed by a short, ugly laugh, a click, and a dial tone.

It was the laugh that did it. When Alex had placed the call, he had resolved that this would be his final attempt. But the laugh reached down into some recess of his paternal instincts and also to the root of his self-respect, stabbing him as he had never been stabbed before. That little laugh had revealed a man so arrogant that he had indulged in cynical pleasure over Alex's predicament. *I am more powerful than you*, the laugh said. *I have your son. And you cannot have him back. I have decided this is the way it will be. I am in control.*

So it was settled. He would not give up. He would not turn tail and run home to the comfort of his books, home to the safety of his Halcyon world, resigned to meditation on unaltering domestic landscapes, condemned to a perpetual flight without leaving his fixed position.

"I'm not going away", he muttered into the buzzing phone, to the walls, to the encircling dark. "Even if it costs me everything. Everything!"

Although this utterance was sufficient for a temporary energizing of the will, it did not really solve the actual problem before him: what to do.

Realizing that it was Sunday, he flipped through a tourist guide in search of the location of a Catholic church. There were two in the city, and the closer was several blocks to the north of the Rossiya, near the Lubyanka prison. Grabbing his coat and hat, he went out to find it. Ten minutes of brisk walking took him to the yellow KGB building that backed onto the prison. He passed it uneasily, despite the fact that the KGB was no longer what it once was, glancing at the barred windows, remembering that Solzhenitsyn had been stripped and interrogated there. Remembering also that untold numbers had been tortured and killed inside its cells.

A few more minutes of walking brought him to a street on which the old foreigners' Church of Saint Ludovic's still functioned. It was no larger than a moderate-size parish church in small-town North America, its exterior nondescript. Inside, it was in a state of disarray, dusty, tangled by scaffolding, piles of brick, and other signs of restoration. The faded murals on the ceiling were post-Renaissance, and Alex thought that they were probably Austrian baroque of the nineteenth century. The pews were three-quarters full of worshippers. A Mass was just beginning.

Alex found it difficult to focus, though as the Consecration began, his inner turbulence subsided a little. After Communion he felt peace. He tried to pray, but no words would come. Seeing the full extent of his helplessness, he felt certain that any further attempts to reach Andrew would indeed cost everything.

After the recessional hymn, Alex left the church, intending to return to his hotel room, where he hoped to spend the remainder of the day trying to think of various strategies. The future was a blank wall, and unless a breach opened, he was condemned to an endless round of futility. Strangely, this did not provoke a return of anguish. That in itself was miraculous, he told himself, and perhaps it was a sign that a breakthrough was coming.

The sky above the city was cloudless. Ordinarily such weather was typical of Arctic fronts accompanied by numbing cold. On this extraordinary Sunday, however, the temperature was rising toward the thawing mark. The sting was gone from the air, and wherever the sun struck full force, meltwater began to flow down roof drains and to trickle onto the sidewalks. When Alex crossed a park near the Lubyanka, he saw many people sitting on benches talking with each other while around their feet pigeons pecked at bread crumbs in the snow and strutted with humble pomposity.

Unable to endure his hotel room, he continued to walk for the remainder of the afternoon. He merely looked at the faces: in parks, on streets, in café windows, and emerging from the weathered doors of churches and shops.

He recalled something the old Russian professor from Toronto once wrote to him in a letter.

"I think you love us, Mr. Graham, but you do not understand what you love. You will forgive me, I hope, if I say that such love can easily grow bitter—at a stroke, at a single blow. You know us, yet you do not know us. It is true that we are people of the heart, of the great passions. If you are hungry and you ask a Russian for a piece of bread, he will take his last piece of bread and tear it in half. He will give you the half. He may even give you the whole piece. Fifteen minutes later, if some official comes along and tells him to shoot you, he will shoot you."

Of course, she had been a bitter expatriate. He knew that generalizations about races were flawed, often deeply flawed. Yet there was a unique genius or spirit to each people, and if the definition of its character was elusive to foreign eyes, the foreigner at least learned that the spectrum of human existence was larger than he had supposed. The fracturing of his internal compass—an instrument with its arrow locked permanently in one direction—was necessary for a true reorientation. Without his compass he would feel lost for a time, but he was now freed to look in all directions.

People of the heart, the professor had said.

Her compatriot Solzhenitsyn had written, "Gradually it was disclosed to me that the line separating good and evil passes not through states, nor between classes, nor between political parties either—but right through every human heart."

There were still harder words: "The line shifts, oscillates....Even within hearts overwhelmed by evil, one small bridgehead of good is retained."

Bloch? Even odious Bloch, with his false *ja* and his existential *nein*—was there a bridgehead of good within him?

"And even in the best of hearts, there remains an unuprooted small corner of evil."

"What about me?" Alex asked. "Where within me is the small, un-uprooted corner of evil?"

Now the streets were filling with thousands of people, striding and strolling in all directions, eyes dark with winter brooding, the skin of their faces as white as the void that had defeated Napoleon and Hitler. Though the atmospheric fear was now largely evaporated, and the people were emerging from their long winter into the warmth of an unexpected spring, their countenances seemed to deny it. Do not be deceived, their eyes insisted. It is not true spring. We must not put our hope in it, for then we would lose our endurance.

Feeling more aimless than ever, he continued to stroll in no particular direction, moving among the large number of pedestrians on the sidewalks as if he possessed no identity, no past, and no future. Hoping to escape the jostling and the noise of heavy traffic, he went down a ramp into an underground corridor that cut beneath an avenue, passing rows of people selling pets: old women with cats, boys whispering into the ears of pups, girls kissing beloved kittens, an old man with a fox in a cage. "Fox Mykyta! Only a thousand rubles for Fox Mykyta!" And farther down the line, a round country woman who piped, "Sonia's a fat one. She cheated the fox; she cheated the wolf! Five hundred rubles for Sonia!" At her feet, tied to her wrist by a leash, an emerald duck quacked and pecked in the slush. But these, the vociferous and the talented, were a minority, for most of the thirty or forty vendors seemed downcast, staring into space, transfixed by the dilemma of needing to sell and hoping that no one would buy.

Deeper in the underground where hundreds of people were passing to and fro, the walkway branched in four directions, and a fifth led to the metro. In this dimly lit labyrinth, the compacting of limited space beneath a low ceiling added to the reduction of dimension, as if cutting off all hope of transcendence. This was the horizontal universe, the suppressed universe. Yet within it there was no end to the complexity that Alex had come to expect from the Russians.

He rounded a corner into a branching tunnel and came upon an elderly man seated on a wooden crate. At his feet was a small cardboard box containing paper rubles. Dressed immaculately in a black wool coat and a homburg hat, shiny shoes, a crisp white shirt, and a black tie, he was dignity incarnate. His face was distinguished, and it took no stretch of the imagination to think he might be a composer of vast reputation. In his arms he held a banjo, which he played as if it were a Stradivarius violin.

Twenty paces beyond, three teenagers with numerous rings piercing their faces wailed a pop song, hammering on small drums, thrusting their pelvises to the beat, and snarling insults at any well-dressed passersby who failed to drop money into their outstretched hands. A young man hobbled slowly by them, his legs clamped in metal braces, pushing the skeleton of a baby carriage as his walker. His face, strained with the effort to avoid collisions, contained pain and dignity. The teenagers fell silent, then resumed their performance when he had passed.

Farther on, another musician blew into a saxophone, wailing a melancholy jazz piece. He wore white cotton peasant garb, his feet bound in traditional *bast* shoes. At his feet a tin can contained donations. He was about fifty years of age, clean-shaven, the face of a philosopher or mathematician with eyes closed over an internal score that was released only through the reed.

Then came an elderly woman with amputated legs. She was being pulled along on a low cart, two children tugging its ropes. "Slower, Masha!" called the woman. "Oy, Mitenka, watch; don't hit the people!" she shouted. "Don't worry, Babula!" they replied with great cheer.

A policeman in a bulletproof vest strolled past with precise nonchalance, hand to his pistol holster. An old woman carrying an empty bird cage came up to him and asked for directions to the metro. He took her arm gently and escorted her to the entrance, opened the door for her, and with a final bow saw her onto an escalator.

Hundreds of faces flashed by Alex, masked with anonymity, lives that he would never engage, that would never enter into his own save for the split second when they imprinted themselves in his memory. For more than forty years his mind had been shaped by life in a small, remote town, where connection with others was limited. Until his journey east, his knowledge of crowds had been entirely theoretical, and though he was growing accustomed to them, he did not possess the subconscious screening that protected the mind from being overwhelmed. His eyes now began to blur and his head to swim. He stopped and leaned against a wall. When he closed his eyes, the images became a near-visual hallucination of endless faces that looked at him but did not see him.

Alex rubbed his eyes, pressed on, and arrived at the branch of an underground passage that he thought might lead him closer to the Rossiya. As he turned into it, the sound of classical music greeted his ears. At the far end he came upon a string quintet composed of three young women and two young men. Their faces expressed a rare form of intelligence, a *gravitas* drawn not only from the Russian character but from the universal music of man. Alex stopped a few paces away and listened. They were playing Mozart with great earnestness. Two violins, two violas, and a cello. An open violin case at the feet of one of the women contained coins and paper rubles.

All who went by heard the music, and though most displayed no interest, their conversations ceased so as not to interfere. A few dozen people had stopped to listen, their backs to the opposite wall, leaving space for people to pass between. Among them were housewives with raptured eyes, children momentarily halted with fascination, old men with tears brimming, young men leaning forward earnestly in studied appreciation, and girls nodding to the beat. All were silent. Poor and rich, European and Asian, Old Russian and New Russian, intelligentsia and laborer. Cutting across the class lines was a gesture that Alex had come to recognize: many of them held their hands to their sides as if in prayer. Was it prayer? It did not seem so. If not, then what was it? Perhaps it was a gesture for all forms of reverence, for submission to anything great that fed the soul.

Having completed a Mozart piece, the musicians turned the pages of their sheet music and adjusted the tuning pegs of their instruments. During this brief intermission, a tiny Mongolian boy pulled away from his mother's hand, dropped a kopeck into the violin case, then danced back to safety. One of the violinists smiled at him.

After that, Beethoven. The piece throbbed with unaccountable force, the power of purified music as spirit, played in a confined space, amid slush and the shuffling of a thousand feet. It penetrated the barriers of the soul, poured in on a current that filled and inebriated a person's interior until he became the music itself and the flesh was revealed for what it was—the instrument played by the music. And though it was performed in a dingy spot as filthy as a public toilet, complete with puddles of spilled beer and urine, the music transformed the gloomy tunnel into a place of worship.

The music ended. The musicians packed up their instruments and went away, the audience eased into the flow of pedestrian traffic, and Alex continued to wander without aim.

Along the river of man, many faces continued to bob and sink and rise: the dreaming young, and the aged becalmed on the Sargasso of memory—old women containing sagas, old men containing the movements of armies. Children crawling forth from the fractures of history, and babies containing the future.

Streams dividing and subdividing.

A little girl with a face of fragile beauty, her small hand tucked in her father's large hand. She stumbled, righted herself without concern, and danced on. A deranged youth lurched into view, babbling the litany of madness, alone, alone, alone. After that came two Orthodox nuns whose faces were still warm with traces of fervor and the golden words of Saint John Chrysostom. Then the doppelgänger from Kanal Griboedova stared at him and turned swiftly away. Now the warrior-prince Andrei Bolkonsky and his Natasha appeared, followed by the idiot-prince Myshkin and his doomed Nastasya.

Alex passed kiosks selling souvenirs, magazines, cigarettes, chocolate, and music. Fragments of recorded sound leaped out to him as he walked, blending balalaikas and electric guitars, piano classics, army choruses, violin concertos, barbarian drums, and the roar of trains passing beneath his feet.

Suddenly, there was Carol walking toward him, arms outstretched to him. His arms flew up to greet her and he lurched forward, but she melted away into the flow of moving masses. Confused, paralyzed with longing, he could not follow. Then, without warning, an Italian aria poured from a nearby music kiosk, sweeping him into an upsurge that carried him higher and higher, his eyes streaming tears that contained both agony and joy, until the wave curled into a downward gyre and he pitched back toward the earth.

As the kingfisher plummeted like a bolt, the sun shimmered on his back, and the holy cobalt, the sacred silver of his feathers, caught fire. He plunged beneath the surface of the waters—where all currents crossed, ebbed, flowed, the swimmers trailing ribbons of affirmation and denial like the seaweed that clings to those who drown in deep waters. And when he could see again with his eyes, it seemed to him that he swam among them not as a man apart, but as one of them.

Alex found a staircase and emerged from the underground into the late afternoon sunlight. Reorienting himself, he saw that he was on a street in the shadow of the Kremlin, beside a broad plaza outside its north wall. Here too there were thousands of people milling about, many heading toward the entrance of a one-story commercial enterprise of some kind. It appeared to be of recent construction. The materials of the outer structure ranged from bronze adornment and polished marble walls to glass skylights. Following a stream of people, he went into the building and found himself swept onto a shining new escalator descending into the earth. As he passed floor after floor of an open mezzanine, he realized that he was now in an underground shopping mall of dazzling opulence, containing hundreds of businesses selling electronics, sable coats, imported culinary delicacies, and designer clothing from western Europe and America. A giant mechanical bear gestured and sang a love song. Synthetic music blasted from every shop door and was subsumed in the mall's sound system, which was playing Russian elevator music. Reaching the lowest level, Alex stopped and stared, trying to take it all in.

Suddenly, from an alcove, an old woman in rags approached him, her back bent, her eyes squinting with determination.

He drew back, but she stepped forward and grabbed his sleeve with a wrinkled paw. Alex fished in his pocket for some coins to give her.

"Not the rubles!" she squeaked. "I do not want the rubles!"

"What then, grandmother?" he said.

"Flee from this place! This is Mammon Mall. It will destroy you if you do not repent!"

"Why do *you* not flee?" he asked.

"This is the station of my task. I am the warning one. I am the sign of rejection. See these pitiable young people worshipping the demon. They look but do not see. They hear but do not listen. I am the voice. I am the most low. I weep for them." She thumped her chest, making holy medals jingle inside the rags. "Go, now, before it is too late."

Alex felt he was in no immediate danger—least of all from the lure of consumerism.

"What do you mean by too late?" he asked.

She raised a finger in warning. "The black fire of the soul! The worm that does not cease to devour! The bomb of corruption that is not seen with the eyes!"

"Why do you speak to me, grandmother?"

"Your face."

"My face?"

"Yours is the face of the half-purified. Yours is the heart that is half-broken."

Then she bowed before him—like Father Zosima bowing before Dmitri Karamazov, because the priest saw with the eyes of prophecy that Mitya was going to suffer. But the old woman's gesture seemed too quaint, an unconvincing parody of countless half-remembered Russian stories.

Straightening, she made the sign of the cross slowly on her chest. Then, peering into Alex's eyes, she said with absolute conviction, as if she had read everything inside him, as if she possessed some incontestable authority:

"I tell you, your heart *will* be fully broken, and then only will you find your true heart."

"All right," he said, "I will go."

If only to comfort her, he thought, *only out of respect for her hard calling.*

"Do not return", she admonished, pushing him in the direction of the escalator. Somewhat dazed, he rode up toward street level. As he ascended he looked back to the floor below and saw her standing like a tiny island around which surged the streams of shoppers, a single node of stillness, watching him go.

Outside, he turned in the direction of the great north-south artery of Tverskaya. It was a wide avenue of many lanes and roaring traffic. He traveled along it for several blocks, seeing little, mentally replaying the scene in which he had just been appointed a significant role. Was she a prophetess, or a holy fool, or simply one of the city's many destitute old people who clung to exalted images of themselves? There was no way of knowing which of these she was. He was struck, however, by the fact that she had refused his money.

The half-purified, the half-broken, she had said. *Your heart will be fully broken.*

Mother Russia, he whispered, why did you speak to me? In what way does the speaking help? I am alone with my heart. I have empty spaces within me, steppes and taigas of the soul. O woman, you did not tell me enough. You spoke words that disturb, but no words to guide.

"I am lost in an alien land", said Alex aloud. "And I have lost my son!"

Several passersby stared at him, then looked away.

On Monday morning Alex awoke with the usual ache of anxiety. He got up, dressed, and plugged the phone into the jack. After praying, he went down in the elevator and entered the lobby pharmacy. There he purchased a packet of hair dye and some makeup. In a clothing shop in another wing of the ground floor, he bought a Russian-style fur hat and a cheap leather coat. Then he returned to his room and attempted a transformation.

First he used his safety razor and scraped back his hairline an inch. Fortunately there was no discernible tan line. After that, he dyed his hair blond. In sharp contrast to the advertising on the package, the color did not look at all natural; it seemed to be a shade of bright yellow. However, he reminded himself that the hair on the heads of many young Muscovites was similar. With the help of a little makeup, subtle hollows appeared under his eyes, his lashes darkened, and roses bloomed on cheekbones that had magically widened. A few more touches here and there and the Anglo-Saxon Celt had become a Slav. Staring at the final effect in the bathroom mirror, he uttered a pained laugh. The disguise seemed to him to be as convincing as a clown mask. He hoped that his appearance would be ridiculous only to himself, that it would be taken at face value by others. People rarely looked with attention, were habituated to cursory sweeps of the eyes, their brains registering only familiar-unfamiliar, known-unknown, harmless-dangerous.

Donning the leather coat and fur hat, tucking a large manila envelope under his left arm, he left the hotel determined to crash through the impenetrable fortress at last. As he walked across the bridge, he practiced his mask—dour, noncommittal, interiorized. The Russian walk—winter version—was not difficult to mimic, for it was similar to the Canadian: head down, shoulders hunched, the pace fast and tense—the subconscious stance of flesh bludgeoned by annihilating weather. He commanded every muscle of his body to exude endurance.

Arriving at the Troika, he went up the front steps with just the right mixture of confidence and deference, as if he were a typical Russian businessman, modestly successful, on a legitimate errand, entering a hotel where he would never stay but where he might have a meeting with very important people. The two guards who had hustled him out the day before merely eyed him and looked away. The metal detector at the entrance registered nothing, and Alex arrived at the lobby desk without interference.

There, he caught the attention of a clerk and said, "I am late for a meeting. Can you direct me to the room of Varvara Morozova?"

The clerk examined his face judiciously. "Is she a guest here, sir?"

"I believe she is a guest, or at least she is staying here with a...a patron."

"A patron?"

As the clerk scanned the hotel registry, his brow furrowed. He raised his eyes to Alex and said, "There is no Morozova registered at the Troika Kiel."

"Perhaps she is not registered. Yet I was to meet her here."

"Varvara Morozova, you say?"

"Are you not familiar with the great Morozova?" Alex exclaimed. "The prima soprano of the Mariinsky Theatre in Saint Petersburg! Surely you have heard of her!"

"I regret that I have not, sir."

Alex shook his head. "Well, then, how am I to find her in this hotel? Really, it is most urgent."

"She is expecting you?"

"Of course! So is her patron."

"And what is the name of her...patron?"

Alex shrugged his shoulders Russian style and said in an irritated tone, "I do not remember!" He waved the manila envelope in front of the clerk. "She is waiting for these. These are the costume designs for *Boris Godunov*. Maybe I should go upstairs and look. I was there yesterday. If I recall correctly, the patron's room was on the fifth floor. No, maybe it was the sixth. But it might have been the tenth. Oh, I cannot remember!"

"It is possible she will seek you here in the lobby", the clerk said. "You can wait." He pointed to a sofa beside a fountain. "That is all I can suggest."

Alex frowned, wracking his memory. "Yes, yes, now I recall. The room was next to a group of Americans or British people. There was a German with them, talking loudly in the hallway! And a dark man—a Pakistani or Indian, I think. They had the suite next door."

"Yes, I know whom you mean. That would be on the twelfth floor." He checked the registry again. "The suite on one side of that party is occupied by a couple from Riga. Would that be your patron?"

"It is possible. I did not meet them."

"On the other side is a Dr. Brenner from Switzerland. Perhaps he is the one?"

"It is possible. Can you tell me the room numbers? I will go up and inquire."

"That is not permitted. I will ring both rooms to see which one is expecting you. Your name?"

"Just tell them the designer from the Mariinsky Theatre is here."

The clerk rang the first. "No one home." He rang the other. "No answer."

Looking up at Alex, he said, "I regret, these guests are not in their rooms."

Alex offered a silent prayer of gratitude. Feigning suppressed frustration, he said, "Then what am I to do?"

"You could leave a message."

"Yes, then please do it. Tell them I will wait in the lobby. That woman! She is always late, always the irresponsible artist!"

The clerk cracked a swiftly passing smile and scribbled notes that he placed in the message slots for both rooms. Alex saw that the room number between the slots was 1228.

"If you wish, sir, you may wait in the restaurant."

"Thank you. I need tea—badly."

The clerk smiled again, and Alex strode with a brooding face into the restaurant on the far side of the lobby. There he went to a corner of the room where the washrooms were situated, on a narrow corridor that ran between the kitchens and the main dining hall. At the end of the corridor, he found a door on which was posted an Employees Only sign. He went through it unseen into a barren hallway that appeared to be part of the hotel's service wing. Midway along this, he came to an elevator. He pressed the button, and its doors opened. It was empty.

His heart hammering, he rode up to the twelfth floor and exited into a carpeted hallway. Within a minute he located the annex for rooms 1220 to 1250. When he came to 1228 he saw that a service cart was parked beside the open door and that the sound of a vacuum cleaner was wailing inside. He entered the room and looked about. A woman in a maid's uniform turned off the machine when she saw him.

"Who are you?" she said, uncertain if he deserved the respect due to paying guests.

"Is this Dr. Bloch's room?" Alex asked.

"I don't know. We don't know the names."

"The German."

"Oh, the German. He had the room down the hall. This was for the men who were with him. The others—"

Alex waved the envelope. "I have a package to deliver."

"It's too late. They left this morning."

"All of them?"

"Maybe all of them. Their rooms are bare."

"Do you know where they have gone?"

"No. Ask at the desk."

Wheeling, Alex raced to the elevator and counted the seconds as it carried him down to the ground floor. Thinking hard and fast, he approached his old friend the desk clerk and said, "I think Varvara Morozova went with the German."

"The German?" said the clerk, peering at him curiously.

"Yes, and the man from Pakistan."

"What man from Pakistan?" the clerk said suspiciously. "There is no man from Pakistan here."

"India, then! I must see her. She will be furious if I don't give her these designs today. Can't you tell me where they have gone?"

But the obtuse face before him was impenetrable. He shrugged inoffensively. "They have checked out. The opera singer will return, no doubt, and then you can give her the envelope. Judging by her behavior, she does not seem overly concerned about it."

"Artists!" Alex growled. "They're all alike."

This time the clerk did not smile. He merely regarded Alex with a probing, unwavering stare.

"Where has Dr. Bloch gone?" Alex said.

"How do you know his name?" the clerk parried.

"I..." But Alex could not think quickly enough.

"I do not know where the party has gone", the clerk said with dangerous finality. "They are no longer guests of this hotel."

17. *The Vault of Degradation*

As he made his way back to the Rossiya, surrounded by a cloud of absurdity in which his disguise appeared more bizarre than ever, his feelings veered wildly back and forth between a desire to weep and an alien fury. He stopped at the midway point of the bridge and yelled. The traffic, louder than Vulcan's forge, permitted him full vent to his frustration. Turning to face the Kremlin, he shouted a number of things, though it was unclear even to himself whether he was raging against it as the nearest personification of power or if he was uttering a more animal scream of protest against the unfairness of life.

Who or what higher forces were playing with him? Why had they drawn him deeper into a futile effort, tantalizing him with bait, then always whisking it from under his nose at the last moment? Were they omniscient? Did their guardian demons whisper in their ears as they saw what no man could see, saying, "Go now, the pursuer is approaching"? And if so, where was God? If he who saw the sparrow fall and numbered the hairs of man's head was so easily outwitted by his adversaries, what hope was there? Why did there seem to be so little strength, so little power to oppose them?

Alex knew that this thinking was distorted, that he was ignoring the many graces and extraordinary human help he had received since his departure from home. Indeed, the humble messages and signs written into the flow of events and uttered through incarnate things had been continuous. But he was tempted now in a way he had not yet been. Blackest bitterness threatened to overwhelm all sense of proportion and was very close to sprouting its poisonous fruit. Alex had never hated anyone before, though like all men, he was no stranger to the sentiments of preference and aversion. Only once had he felt a dislike so intense that it had erupted into an action, the punch that had knocked Charles Findley, age twelve, from his small throne. Alex now recalled what he had felt during those few seconds—a flash of murderous rage hidden beneath the veneer of righteous indignation. Swiftly come, swiftly gone. Yet the feeling had so horrified him that he had taken it to confession immediately and regretted his single act of violence ever since. He had experienced no repetitions during the ensuing thirty-five years. That is, until this moment, when, standing in a blast of wind on a bridge under an overcast sky, his fist smashed into Gustav Bloch's sneering face, wiping the ugly laugh from it, proving that the guru was very mistaken in thinking he had an absolute right to someone else's life, proving most of all that his cosmos-size ego was not in perfect control.

Raw, ugly hatred. A hatred springing from his sense of being mocked by an overpowering force, that he was a cornered mouse defending his little scrap of being. Alex bent over the balustrade, held his face in his hands, and prayed for help—help against the malice swelling within him.

Words of Scripture arose from memory: *Pray for those who do you harm. Do good to those who hate you. Forgive your enemies. Love your enemies.*

Love Bloch and his pack of lethal metaphysicians? Why? Why should he do that? What good would it do?

Then an angel warrior thrust his sword, and a wolf cringed.

So that hatred will lose its power over you. So that hatred will not breed more hatred. Alexander, do not give in to it!

Slowly the mood receded. But where did it go? Back into some un-uprooted corner of evil in his heart? Did evil reside there like a corrupt substance, a melanoma that he carried about within himself, sometimes growing, sometimes in remission? Or was it more true to say that within himself was a zone where good did not fully reign? In any event, the worst was over now. Anguish remained, but the rage was gone.

Back in his hotel room he threw the manila envelope and the leather coat onto the floor. For some minutes he paced back and forth, feeling the room shrinking, closing him up inside a box filled with impending madness. Hastily he donned his grandfather's greatcoat and the fur hat and left the hotel in search of some relief. During the next few hours he walked aimlessly through the streets of downtown Moscow, his eyes riveted to the sidewalks. Clearly, all hope of picking up Andrew's trail was gone. He was condemned once again to a random search among the infinite snowfields. And although he was willing to continue the search, he now felt that it was truly an exercise in futility. At best it would be a symbolic journey, without any promise of resolution; its only merit would be that he had not given up, that he had spent everything. Almost certainly, he would lose the Kingfisher if he went on any longer. If he was to ask Charles for another loan, he would be taking a debt upon himself that could not be repaid. And that was self-defeating. Had he not expended every reasonable effort to reach his son? Surely to persist in this line was deliberately to destroy all that had been his life until now. In the beginning he had risked it because he had been able to say to himself that it was for Andrew's ultimate good and that his efforts would restore their lives to what they had been. But now it was obvious that the boy did not want to make contact, was in fact fleeing him. Was there any longer a point in pursuing? No, there was not. Reason dictated that it was time to admit defeat.

Trudging with heavy feet throughout the city, he unconsciously paced concentric circles that were crossed again and again by the coils of the Moskva River. North on a bridge, south on a bridge, away from the sun, toward the sun, sun on his left shoulder, sun on the right. If he had asked himself where he was going, he would not have been able to say. He merely clung to the sensation of motion, driven by the need to avoid immobility, to seek even the illusion of progress. The lure of hatred on one hand, and despair on the other, were held at bay.

About three in the afternoon he heard bells ringing and looked up to find that he was passing a small church, a white building capped by a pale green dome. In its open belfry a human form whipped a rope back and forth, making the little bells do his bidding. Alex listened for a while, until the man, or child, or angel, came to the final notes and let the bells swing into silence as he stood with his arms dropped to his sides, gazing out over the Moscow skyline. Noticing Alex on the sidewalk below, he waved. Alex returned the gesture wearily. For a minute they regarded each other; then the figure went down inside the bell tower.

Alex remained there long enough to utter a bleak prayer asking for God's mercy on himself and on his doomed venture. Casting his eyes to the ground once again, he continued walking, turning a corner at random, indifferent to where his feet led him. Within five minutes he passed a gate on which was posted the sign "Tretyakov Gallery". His mind was now so fogged with fatigue that the words meant nothing to him, though they sounded vaguely familiar. He supposed that the large building before him housed an art collection of some kind.

"Art", he said aloud. "Was it in Oxford I saw the sculpture of the angel and the wolf, *The Warrior of the Spirit*? No, that was in Helsinki."

He entered the museum and ambled through the foyer without direction. Wholly engrossed in his troubles, he was dimly aware that he was passing into a wing that housed nineteenth-century portraits. But he could not concentrate on them for more than a few moments, and moved on into a wing that contained ancient icons. He had seen many icons during his time in Russia, in museums, churches, and shops, and in the hands of beggars. But nothing equaled what was now before him. Waking fully, he saw that this collection spanned many centuries, room after room of the most famous examples of Byzantine art in the world. He was familiar with some of the images, for he had marveled over them in the pages of art books in the Russian room of the Kingfisher, somewhere in the distant past.

But now the effect of seeing the originals arrested him in a way that was, for him, a shock—moreover, it was a spiritual shock. First, he saw that the icons bore little resemblance to the small, poorly colored reproductions. They were very large, the figures in some of them two or three times larger than life-size. The colors were brilliant, creating an effect that seemed to bridge earth and heaven, mundane and sublime, immanent and transcendent.

In one small annex he came upon the icon of the Virgin of Vladimir—the *Vladimirskaya*, the East's most famous image. It was not a Russian icon, for it had been painted in Constantinople more than eight hundred years ago. Tradition held that it had been copied from an icon painted by Saint Luke himself. The Virgin of Vladimir was the guardian of Moscow, and legend attributed to her intercession the salvation of the city from two Tartar invasions. She was also the Mother of Russia.

Alex knew these details from his reading of art books. Now, however, the reality revealed to him the extent of his ignorance. The icon was about two and a half feet wide by three and a half high. The wood was badly corroded, yet the patina of age had created a general aura of amber light. In the center of the image, the Mother gazed out at Alex with profound gravity as she held the Child close, their cheeks pressed together. Standing a pace away from it, he began to doubt his senses. His eyes blinked again and again, trying to dispel the optical illusion of a three-dimensional face floating on the surface of the board. But it would not retreat into two dimensions. Whether this effect was an illusion of purely physical origin, or a spiritual grace, a subconscious influence, or a combination of these, he did not know. He understood only that of all the images he had looked at on this bleak day, none had been so like an open window.

His arms had dropped to his sides, and now, almost of their own will, they lifted toward the image in a mute gesture of beseeching that was beyond all emotion. His mind was without thoughts of any kind, but it seemed to him that the Mother was calling him. Her eyes looked deeply into his soul, at one moment grieving, the next full of tenderness, desiring that he understand the necessity of all that was happening.

At that moment a group of tourists brushed up against Alex and in loud voices began to speak about the image. He moved on.

The next room was one of the most spacious in the museum. Here were the largest icons, towering works borrowed or long ago stolen from the iconostases of cathedrals throughout the land. As Alex walked slowly past them, he became aware of a peculiar feeling that something was waiting for him here. As he glanced about, he saw nothing that appeared to be more significant than the rest, for all the images were beautiful. But when he stood completely still in the center of the gallery and closed his eyes, he sensed an invisible radiance pouring from the far side of a wall panel that bisected the room. He followed it to its source.

It was *The Trinity.*

Speechless, he stood before Andrey Rublyov's masterpiece in a state of absolute attention, a small creature contemplating the limitless glory of his Creator. It was the transfigured light of Mount Tabor, the fiery radiance of Sinai's burning bush, and perhaps also the blinding flash on the road to Damascus. The icon was about four feet wide by five feet in height. Like the *Vladimirskaya*, it floated in three dimensions; it was so much a transfiguration of light itself that everything else seemed dark by comparison. But if the *Virgin of Vladimir* was a window, *The Trinity* was a wide-open gate.

The image portrayed the three angels of the Old Testament who had come to Abraham, a prefigurement of the fuller revelation of the New Testament. Who could see the face of God and live? To see his hidden face was to die. Was this because the fire of love in that face was so consuming and freeing that a human vessel could not contain it? Could the face be apprehended only in symbolic form? The three angels, representing the Father, the Son, and the Holy Spirit, were so composed on the board that they formed an equilateral triangle within a circle of contemplation—the contemplation of each other. Within this relationship, love flowed eternally between the Three-in-One. They were the source and the fulfillment, and man was the fruit of their love.

Now in his soul he saw three deer springing about the rim of the chalice in the icon, dancing a perfect trilogy within the perfect sphere of expanding creation, singing in perfect harmony, loving in perfect joy.

Alex dropped to his knees and put his forehead to the floor.

O save us, save us, Savior of the world!

For we are blind and poor and do not know what we are doing!

Three dancing in the marriage of man and woman and God. Man and woman he made them, dancing in the ecstasy of *sobornost*, the burning unity of grace, a son issuing from the consummation—the son embraced, face-to-face, heart to heart. A son, a son!

O Andrew, my son, my son, my lost son!

Then he saw two sons: the prodigal one and the righteous one. The righteous prodigal and the prodigal righteous.

Andrew! Jacob!

"I love the rustling of leaves when you walk through them, just when the new green leaves start budding. I stop to listen to the warblers. The warblers are back now, did you know?"

"Yes, I know."

"Warblers, and bobolinks for a chorus. And the woods a dome of light. Hope, a thing with feathers that perches in the soul. It was so beautiful, that feeling. I was so happy. Then something more wonderful happened."

"What was it?"

"I saw."

"What did you see?"

"The Holy Trinity is love, Alex, love!"

I love you, Carol! I love you!

Why did you leave me?

Why did you die?

Why am I losing everything?

Then it ceased, and in the stillness of the suddenly material gallery, footsteps echoed on the wooden floors. Alex now became fully aware that he was prostrate before an icon in a foreign land, confused and a little crazed.

As the footsteps came closer, he looked up. An old woman stood beside him, one of the room guards, with an identification badge on a chain about her neck. Looking down at him with a puzzled smile, she said, "Stand up, *gaspadin*, sir. You might get in trouble. You might have to leave."

"Because I am praying?" he sighed.

"Praying is permitted. People sometimes bow before the icon." She turned to *The Trinity*, bowed at the waist, straightened, made the Orthodox sign of the cross on her chest, bowed again, then straightened.

"You see. But you cannot lie down on the floor. It is disturbing to the other visitors."

He nodded, got up, and left.

Alex went out of the Tretyakov into the dusk of late afternoon. The city lights winked on, and night was near.

Now, said a voice that is soundless. *Now is the beginning.*

"The beginning of what?" he asked, presuming that his subconscious mind was throwing up irrational thoughts.

Reorienting himself by the street map, he saw that he was at least a mile south of the Rossiya. Should he return to the hotel? He had neither eaten nor properly rested since early morning. He turned east and came to a street named Novokuznetskaya, turned north, and crossed the river onto Pokrovskiy Boulevard, one of the inner ring roads that circled the city core. As he walked, he began to debate with himself:

"What is happening to me?" he murmured. "I'm not mystical. Whatever that was, whatever I felt when I was with those icons, was caused by fatigue and hunger."

"But what about the peace?" he argued. "Where did that light come from?"

"It was my imagination."

"No, never in my life has my imagination produced such an experience."

"But what does it mean? Maybe nothing."

"Nothing? Was that nothing?"

As he trudged onward he continued to debate, trying to understand what had happened. But he could not. Afraid for his mind, saddened by the fact that whatever consolation he had received through the icon was now dissolving, he thought it better to walk for another hour or so before returning to the sterile cell of his hotel room, where a backslide into despondency might await him.

Now, said the voice again. *Now is the beginning.*

"It's over", he kept repeating to himself. "There's nothing more I can do."

Just ahead, a sign indicated a staircase leading to an underground public washroom. He went down the slippery steps and entered a dimly lit hall that might have doubled for a Nazi gas chamber, except that the sound of running water was real. The temperature was just above freezing and the floor wet with melting snow, mud, and other liquids of unknown origins. He was alone in the room with a choice of dozens of cubicles. More accurately, they were stalls, separated by waist-high barriers that offered a privacy more symbolic than actual. Furthermore, they contained no porcelain toilets, only holes in the floor, each of which was continuously flushed by jets of water spewing from rusty pipes. The smell of the place was nauseating. Trying not to breathe, he told himself that he had no other options.

As he entered one of the stalls, he heard a bestial wail, or a snort, or the gurgle of a cut throat. Leaping back into the center of the room, he turned in every direction but could see no other person. Then the sound came again from the farthest corner, this time followed by groans. Creeping warily along the row of cubicles, Alex stopped suddenly and remained motionless as he stared into the last stall. The scene was so completely beyond his experience and normal categories of thought that he was momentarily paralyzed.

Lying on the wet floor was a young man in fetal position, reeking of alcohol, body fluids, and human befoulment. His shoes were soaked, torn, sockless, laced with string. His thin cloth coat was flung open, revealing a cotton undershirt stained with blood and vomit. But his face was the worst, for it was bruised and lacerated with cuts, scabbed with dried blood. His nose was broken, though this seemed to be an old break that had healed badly. His lips were swollen and cracked, opening and closing with shallow breathing that came from his mouth. His chin was dark with several days' growth of beard. By what chain of follies he had come to this end, Alex could not begin to guess.

He knelt down and reached out to shake the man's shoulder, but there was little response, only a resuming of mute cries that seemed to come from the pit of the soul. His glazed eyes managed to swivel toward Alex but could not maintain their focus and returned to a sightless gaze at the floor. His arms were locked in an X across his chest, with large hands clenched tightly. His body convulsed and shook with chills. Alex put his hand on the man's forehead. It was ice cold.

He now realized that the man was lying across the drain hole and that spray from the water pipe was soaking the entire length of his back. Fighting overwhelming disgust, he grabbed the inert form and dragged it out of the cubicle into the dirty slush of the main section of the washroom. An empty vodka bottle skidded out with him and spun in circles. Alex closed the front of the coat over the man's chest and bound it with strings that were knotted in the buttonholes. After a quick search, he found a weak heat source farther along the wall, the ventilation shaft out of which warm air was rising, accompanied by the faint roar of the subway many meters below. He dragged the man's body over to it and propped it up in sitting position.

Removing his own scarf, Alex soaked it in the water spurting from one of the nearby sinks, then used it to clean the man's face and hands. The rest of his body was in a condition that was beyond any help he could offer.

The man's eyes opened and tried to focus again.

"Little brother," Alex said in a low voice, "what has happened to you?"

The answering groan was an attempt at articulation, but it failed.

"What is your name?" Alex said.

"No name", slurred the voice.

"You have a name", Alex said firmly.

"No name", the voice cried with sudden volume. The head lurched sideways, the eyes rolling.

Alex removed his fur hat and put it onto the man's head, pulling down the flaps about the ears.

"Where do you live?" he asked.

"No live, no place, no live, no place, no nothing, no..."

The chorus of *nyet, nyet* went on for some time until the man's eyes glazed over and his teeth began to chatter violently.

"But you must live someplace. Tell me, where? I will take you there."

The eyes struggled to focus again. The blue lips parted to reveal an insane grin.

"Live here. Die here. Live, die, live, die—"

"You cannot stay here. You *will* die if you stay."

"I *am* dead. I live in the drain hole—"

"You must try to get up!"

"—the drain hole of the universe."

"That's not true! You must get up!"

"I die in the hole. I *am* the hole. I am the *nyet, nyet, nyet, nyet*..."

Alex's face went hot with shame and pity. He seized the man's coat lapels tightly, pulling his loathsome body, trying to lift him. But it was no use. The man's head flopped back and banged against the wall. Alex put his hand on the back of the man's skull, sticky with blood and the detritus of the hole of the universe.

"Fifty rubles for me", the man babbled. The eyes wept and laughed. "Cheap."

"What is your name?"

"A bottle. A needle."

"Your name?" Alex shook him.

"One sip."

"You must remember. Try to remember."

"No name."

"Tell me your name!" Alex cried.

"I...I..."

Now the man's mad mouth fell slack, and the laughing-weeping eyes turned to pure weeping.

"I once was Alexei", he sobbed.

"Alexei? Your name is Alexei?"

"Alexei Andreivich, who has become a hole."

Alex jerked back, holding the other's body at arm's length, staring into his eyes with uncertainty.

"Get up", he said.

"*Nyet.*"

"Get up, Alyosha, get up!"

"Alyosha?" The eyes strained to focus, filled now with puzzlement. "You call me Alyosha?" he whispered.

"Please, get up!"

"I cannot. My legs."

Alex stood, dragging Alyosha's body up with him, straining every muscle. Shifting the weight of the other to his right hip, he gripped the man's chest under his arm and hobbled with him to the entry stairs. Climbing-dragging him up to street level took an eternity. When they finally emerged, Alex lowered him to the pavement and propped him against the post of a street lamp. A search through the man's pockets produced no identification papers, nothing to indicate a home address.

Alex dashed to the corner, hoping to spot a policeman. A few minutes later a taxi wheeled around the corner and barreled along the street in his direction. He flagged it to the curb.

"I have a sick man here", Alex said. "Can you take him to a hospital?"

"Yes, for two hundred rubles."

Alex rummaged in his pockets and hastily gave him the money.

"Can you help me carry him?"

The driver shrugged, got out, and walked with Alex to the street lamp. When he saw the bundle of groaning rags, he took a step back and said, "He's filthy. He's a hotel for lice."

"He will die if he stays here."

"So? What is he to you?"

"He is...", Alex said slowly. "He is my son."

"He's your son? All right, let's get him. You take his shoulders; I'll take his feet."

The driver reached down to grab the ankles, then drew back.

"Forget it", he said. "He'll make a mess in my car."

Alex unbuttoned his coat and threw it over Alyosha. He removed the wallet, passport, and papers from his tweed jacket and stuffed them into his pants pockets. The jacket went over Alyosha's legs and feet.

"There, we'll wrap him in this. Now he won't soil your upholstery."

"This is not your son", the driver said. "You're a foreigner."

"Yes, I am a foreigner. And you are right, he is not my son." Alex shivered in the night wind. "He is my father."

The driver stared at him suspiciously. Alex handed him another hundred rubles. This finalized the deal, and without any further discussion they loaded the body into the back seat of the car. Ten minutes later they carried Alyosha into the emergency ward of a hospital.

The driver took off immediately, leaving Alex on a hard wooden bench with Alyosha propped against his shoulder. For an hour he watched the frantic comings and goings in the ward, amazed that the city contained so many tragedies, even more amazed that he was sitting in the midst of it with a stranger's body leaning against his. Wondering why.

Wondering if he had fallen through the thin ice that separated all men from the suction of the void.

With his eyes closed, Alyosha rolled his head back and breathed noisily through his open mouth. His teeth stopped chattering, he was no longer shaking, and a great heat now emanated from his body. When at last a doctor approached with a clipboard, Alex explained what had happened. Frowning, she jotted down pertinent details, then put her hand to Alyosha's forehead.

"He's burning up", she said in a monotone. "Does he have papers?"

"I think he has been robbed of his documents."

"There's not much we can do for him."

"Is there no place for a Russian citizen who has suffered this misfortune?"

She shrugged. "We look after all our citizens."

"I can help with expenses", he said.

She put her clipboard under her arm and gave him a stern look.

"Sir, though you speak Russian very well, it is obvious that you are not from this country. It is a foolish thing you have done. There are very dangerous people in Moscow, flooding in from all over, criminals who would not hesitate to cut your throat for a ruble. In the future you must remember that it is better to avoid trouble. Do not make eye contact with strangers. Do not answer them if they speak to you."

"This is most helpful advice, madam", he replied politely. "Still, I do not think this man is dangerous. He is just a lost soul."

"I can see that you are a person of considerate nature. However, people from the West are naïve. It would be better for you to keep to the hotels and the tourist places. We do not want incidents."

"Of an international nature?"

She flashed him a look and returned to writing on her clipboard.

Calling two orderlies, she instructed them to take Alyosha away. "To DT wing. Shower and disinfect him there. I will call the chief of detox to register. If anyone makes problems, tell them I will take personal responsibility."

They carried Alyosha to a gurney and loaded him onto it. The doctor watched them go through a set of green double doors, and then she turned to Alex.

"Do you know how many of those I see every night?"

He shook his head.

"On a good night, three or four. On a bad night, ten or twenty. Most of them die within a few hours. Most of them crawl here or are dumped at the door by the police. The morgue is full of them, and most are either very old, or young like this one. Never has a tourist brought me one. Why did you do it?"

"He is my son."

"He is Russian. He is not your son."

"He is my father."

"Are you insane, or are you a poet?"

"Neither."

"Religious, then. The Good Samaritan?"

"Are you religious, Doctor?"

"Not in the least. Answer my question."

"I am a father who has lost his child, and he is a son who has lost his parents."

"Perhaps he has no parents. These street people often don't. He might have killed you."

"Well, the risk was mine."

Scrutinizing him with an expression of disapproval, she said, much to Alex's surprise, "Would you like a cup of tea?"

"No thank you. I will return to my hotel. But first may I leave a message for Alyosha?"

"Alyosha, is it?"

"Alexei Andreivich is his name."

"All right, you can leave it with me. I'll see that he gets it, if he survives the night."

While she went to get an envelope, Alex wrote the following on a page in his pocket notebook:

Alexei Andreivich,

You do not know me, and I do not know you. You have a name that is beautiful in the sight of God, who is your Father. You have a Father, Alyosha. You are not alone. Though you say you are dead, you are alive. Though you think you are destined to fall down into the drain hole of the universe, it is not true. Do not believe that lie. You are more than you think you are.

Life demands that we part, but I will not forget you. We are united in a bond that nothing can break. Take this gift, and when you have recovered your health, begin again.

Aleksandr Graham

He tore the page from the notebook and folded it around two five-hundred-ruble notes. Examining the rumpled bills that remained in his pocket, he saw that he now had less than a thousand. He kept enough for a taxi ride back to the Rossiya and added the balance to the gift. When the doctor returned, he put the note and money into the envelope she gave him, sealed it, and wrote Alyosha's name on it.

"You are mad", she said, shaking her head. "Why do you throw away your money?"

"Will you give it to him?"

"If he lives", she said without emotion. "But what if he dies?"

"If he dies, give it to someone like him, someone who survives."

"What about your hat, your coat, and your jacket?"

He hesitated only a moment, then bid farewell to his grandfather's overcoat.

"They are now his."

"And if he dies?"

"Give them to someone like him."

Her frown intensified, as if she was deeply offended by all that had occurred.

"Wait here", she commanded, turning on her heel. A few minutes later she returned bearing a huge old greatcoat of dark blue felt, and a leather cap lined with dirty sheepskin.

"Take this", she said, thrusting them upon him. "No one needs it."

"Who does it belong to?"

"I took it off a dead man earlier this evening. A man with no name. He was not diseased. He died of heart failure."

Alex put on the coat, which fit well and smelled of dried sweat. He wrapped his beloved tartan scarf around his neck.

"Thank you", he said.

And so he left wearing the garb of the nameless, aware only that he was moving ever closer to the loss of everything, unaware that the doctor stood motionless in the center of the ward watching him go.

18. *Millennium Angel*

The next morning, Alex awoke with a cough and a light fever. He showered, dressed in the last of his clean clothing, and went down to the lobby. There he handed his soiled clothes, including the dead man's coat and cap, to the laundress in the service bay, asking her to have the fee put on his bill. She told him that the clothes would be delivered to his room by midafternoon.

Returning to his room, he sat by the phone, head in hands. He did not have a kopeck now, and his only choice was to plead with Charles Findley for another loan. He cringed at the thought of it, feeling certain that Charles had been pushed as far as he could be pushed. By now it should be time to start repayment, not time for more handouts.

First, Alex placed a call to Saint Mary's parish in Halcyon. Father Toby himself answered the phone, and the sound of his voice was so wonderful that Alex could not at first speak for gratitude.

"Hello! Anyone there?"

"It's me", said Alex.

"Worm!" Father Toby yelled. "Thank God! I've been worried out of my skull. Nobody's heard from you for weeks. Where are you? What's going on?"

Bumbling over the English words, surprised that he had to grope for his native tongue, Alex briefly recounted the stages of his search. When he had finished, there was a moment's silence on the other end. Then:

"It's time to come home, Alex."

"I can't."

"What do you mean you can't? Of course you can. You just have to admit that it's out of your hands now."

"It's been out of my hands since the beginning."

"My point exactly."

"That's all the more reason to keep going."

"I don't follow you."

"Even if it's hopeless, it would be a mistake to give up now."

"It'd be a mistake for you to beat a dead horse, Alex. Get home now, fast. Regroup, get your reserves together. There are other ways to reach Andrew. And if my guess is right, he's going to drop this wild scheme, just as he's dropped things all his life. I'm sure of it."

"I'm not so sure. What's happening isn't like anything he's done before. There's more involved here than I thought at first. These people—"

"The cult people?"

"Yes, these people are operating on a level I don't understand. They have power, very big worldly power. And even supernatural power—"

"What are you taking about, supernatural power?"

"I don't think they have any supernatural power of their own. But there's a darkness around them, and uncanny things are happening. It's as if something is watching everything that's going on—observing in a way that no human being can observe—and it pulls their strings, saving them from any contact with me. The timing is bizarre. This power doesn't want me to find Andrew. It wants him. It wants to keep him forever."

"So, are you saying you have to keep jumping after the carrot they dangle in front of you?"

"No. They aren't dangling a carrot, if by *carrot* you mean Andrew. They're definitely trying to avoid me. At least they're forced to maneuver around me, and maybe it's complicating things for them. I may be just a gnat biting their ankles, but I am becoming a bother. And if I bother them enough, they're going to slip. They're going to say something or do something that will expose the secret malice beneath their dreamy metaphysics. If they do it in front of Andrew, it could open his eyes."

"And you could get hurt."

"I'm already hurt."

"How's the money holding out?"

"That's why I'm calling."

"How much do you need?"

"I don't know."

"That's not very specific, pal. I've got eight hundred bucks in my account. Will that do?"

"It's...it's a great help. Thank you."

He told the priest the money should be wired to him at a branch of Mosbank in the GUM shopping complex across from Red Square.

"Consider it done. Anything else I can do?"

"You can pray for me during the next hour. I'm calling Charles Findley after we hang up, and I'm going to ask for another thousand, just in case I have to stay in Russia a bit longer. I may have to move around the country. Anything could happen, you see. It's a long shot. I doubt if Charles will give me any more."

"Don't be so sure about that. He fakes grave concern whenever he asks if I've heard from you. But he's looking ever so much like the cat who swallowed the canary."

"I know. He wants my house and bookshop. He's probably going to get it."

"Look, Alex, I'll say this one last time. Come home now."

"Can't do it."

"Explain it to me again."

"It's not just the fact that I'm trying to get my son back. It's something deeper and stranger."

"Deeper and stranger?"

"I think there's another power at work in this mess. I don't understand it, and it's definitely the craziest thing that's ever happened to me, but way down inside, underneath my fears, there's a knowing."

"What do you mean, *a knowing*?"

"Call it a sense, Toby, or a quiet voice. It's telling me—not with words, so don't ask me how I know this—it's telling me that God has his hand on it all."

Alex paused and replayed his own words in his mind. Where had the thought come from? Yesterday he had plunged close to despair. Then he had encountered Alyosha. Alyosha was in it somehow, but he did not know why.

"In what way does God have his hand on it all?" said Father Toby.

"He's letting these guys, the gurus with their dark little secrets, do what they think they have to do. But this is about something bigger."

"Bigger?"

"I don't even know what I mean. But maybe God is bringing some kind of good out of it that only he can see. Today it's as if I can taste it, and that's strange, because in my lowest moments all I want to do is jump onto a flight for home. Remember the Alex who hides in his nice little shop so he won't get hurt? Remember him, Father?"

"Uh...do I have to answer that?"

"Well, that guy is still very much me. But maybe there's another me inside of him that I didn't know was there."

"Maybe you just forgot he was there."

"In any event, I can't run. Something is going on, and I have a part in it, but I just don't know what it is yet."

"And that's what your 'knowing' is telling you?"

"For better or for worse, it is."

"Okay, I'll take your word for it."

Alex promised to call him again if there was a breakthrough in the search. After they hung up, he collected his wits for a few minutes, said a prayer, then dialed the number of Clementine Valley Credit Union.

The conversation with Charles was stilted, a little jig that both he and Alex performed with full knowledge of each other's motives. When it was over, Alex breathed a sigh of relief. A thousand dollars would be sent by electronic transfer and could be picked up the following day at Mosbank.

That accomplished, Alex was left with himself. There was nothing to do until his clothing was ready later in the afternoon, so he sat on a chair by the window, staring out, wondering about Alyosha and the girl from Smolensk, offering prayers for them both.

He tried not to think too much about what lay ahead, and this was aided by the fact that as far as he could see, nothing lay ahead. If the *knowing* was not an illusion, then a crack would open in the barrier that loomed before him, even though it was featureless, offering no handhold. He had no means of advancing, yet he wondered if this further state of reduction was a hopeful sign, despite what his rational mind told him. If he was completely powerless, was it not an invitation to a greater outpouring of God's assistance? From this time onward, surely, the help would have to be miraculous, because all human effort on his part had now brought him to a dead end.

He knelt down beside the bed, self-consciously. It struck him definitively that he was ridiculous, a burdened, aging man in an alien territory, an insignificant man, smaller indeed than he had imagined. A fool, a clown with dyed hair! At first he wanted to shake off this image of himself and reassert his dignity, but he had no strength to do so. He lay down on the bed and closed his eyes.

"O God, where am I going?" he murmured as he drifted into sleep.

You are falling, sang a voice in music that was soundless, *from what you think is above. You are rising as you fall.*

With a stab of fear, he slipped into the gurgling drain hole of the ultimate *nyet, nyet, nyet*, sucked downward, downward, until at last he was spewed out into a dark ocean, where he sank and drowned. Then, struggling frantically upward, he broke the surface, coughing water from his lungs, crawling out onto a barren shore.

"Help me, Layo, help me!" he cried.

But the golden fish that swam in the sea did not always grant the wish one most desired.

"Where are you, Layo?"

And suddenly, there was the old man, pulling a golden fish from the sea. Turning to Alex with archangels in his eyes, he said, "*Vada*, Alyosha."

"I don't care, I don't care! I just want to go home!"

"*Nyet*, little boy! Do you want me to destroy the *kosmos* rules, the *kosmos* tradition, just to make you happy?"

"No", though he meant *yes*.

"Good. Now tell me why you like this Alyosha name so much."

"I don't know."

"Is it the fairy tale? Is it because of *Alyosha the Fool and the Firebird*?"

"No."

But, in fact, it was. Alyosha the crippled orphan grew tall, strong, and handsome after capturing the magic firebird and presenting it to the king, who adopted the boy and rewarded him with a palace and a mountain of gold. And thus he became Prince Alyosha the Wise.

Relenting, Layo gave him a look of pity and said, "See the light refraction."

433

"What do you mean?"

"I mean, our eyes deceive us. The optical distortion of a fishing line tells us that its trajectory is broken."

Little Alyosha, frantic with the desperate need to understand, jumped up and down, shouting, "You make no sense!"

"The thin monofilament—finer than a thread—is the line connecting two dimensions, two worlds. The eye on a good day sees the distortion; on a bad day it sees nothing under the surface of the water. Yet the line vibrates. And soon—yes, soon—a force will seize the other end and pull on it. You will resist. You will fight it, Alyosha; you will fight it hard, though you cannot yet know what it is you fight."

"Then tell me!"

"Ah, ah, it is not my place to say. You are too young, little boy."

"I am not a little boy!"

"No? All right, then. You will find out in the end anyway, so why not I tell? It is this: every fish that breaks the surface tension reminds us that we too are caught."

"Caught? By who?"

Layo would not answer.

"But what do you *mean*?" Alyosha wailed in despair.

"The golden wish is already within you. It is you. It is what you will become."

Layo dissolved into the darkness growing over the sea.

"Come back, Layo! Help me!" he screamed.

Loud rapping on the door startled him fully awake. His eyes flew open. He got up and went to answer it. It was a maid delivering his clean clothing.

Later, he dressed in a fresh shirt and trousers and donned the greatcoat, smelling the scented wool. The cap too seemed almost reborn, its leather shining and its fleece giving off the faint aroma of soap. Who was the dead man who had worn it?

Alex remained in his room for a day and a half, resting, praying, growing accustomed to the sensation that all avenues leading to his son had now come to dead ends. There was simply no place to go. The money arrived, and with part of it he paid his hotel bills. It did not bring a sense of restored self-sufficiency, but this no longer mattered. Knowing that the trail was growing colder hour by hour did not drive him to frantic worry. It was *all* out of his hands now. In the event that a door opened, he would go through it. If a thread drifted down across his path, he would take its end and follow it to the source. Until then—well, until then there was the purgation of immobility.

On the morning of the twentieth of February, he awoke to the sound of furious winds battering the window and thick snow cutting obliquely across the pane. The factory smokestacks were spewing out a black gurge that could not rise above the overcast. It spread and dropped until the entire world became a uniform charcoal gray. Alex rubbed sleep from his eyes with the heels of his palms and knelt beside the bed to say his morning prayers. When his customary devotions were completed, it came to him that heaven might be waiting for him to ask for something more. Heaven always respected human freedom, and it now occurred to him that answers to prayer often came more swiftly when the prayers were specific. He was in the habit of crying out several times a day, "O God, save my son!" He felt it was a worthy prayer, yet he wondered if God now wanted another investment of the self. What if the Lord desired that he and Alex work together more directly, step by step, giver and receiver talking together about specifics?

"Father," he said, head bowed, hands held out before him, "what am I to do?"

Silence.

"If you want me to go on, please show me the way. Where should I look?"

Silence.

"Father, I hear nothing." Though this might not be exact, for the peace that filled the exchange was, perhaps, a kind of language.

"Am I not supposed to know?"

More peace, more silence.

But he needed answers, directions, maps! Even a nudge would suffice. Why did God not wish him to have them? Why was there no answer in a language he could comprehend?

"Father, I'm asking for a gift. I ask that you open a door before me. I'm not seeking to know where it's leading, or to understand it. But I do beg you to open it, so that I can begin to move."

Silence and peace.

Alex prayed fifteen decades of the rosary, asking the Blessed Virgin to intercede for him. And as he meditated on the life of Christ embedded in the mysteries, a light seemed to grow in his mind, bathing a scene from the Gospels with particular significance. It was the flight into Egypt—Joseph and Mary rising in the night and taking the hunted child with them out into darkness and exile, into radical insecurity. They knew next to nothing of the reason why. They simply obeyed.

Was this what God wished to show him?

Alex straightened slowly, unbending his aching joints. He sat on the bed and stretched, and in doing so inadvertently knocked his pocket notebook from the night table. When he picked it up from the floor, a piece of paper came fluttering out. It was the note on which Owen Whitfield had jotted down the names of the metaphysicians weeks before. And there, now staring him in the face, was the name Dr. Vasily Yefimovich Dubrovskoy, M.D., D.D.

Of course! Dubrovskoy, like his colleagues, was a "doctor of divinity". But he was also a medical doctor. And he was Russian. Moreover, if he was an influential Russian, he probably lived in Moscow.

It did not take Alex long to obtain the address from the telephone directory, and when he had it, he moved at once. A hair-raising taxi ride brought him through a howling blizzard and traffic lanes littered with stalled cars and into the Sparrow Hills on the southwest borders of the city. He arrived at a modern three-story clinic situated in a grove of pines between the mansions of the defunct Communist elite and the up-and-coming nouveaux riches. With his heart skipping beats, he climbed the wide front steps to glass doors against which snow had drifted inches deep.

Were the metaphysicians here? Was Andrew with them?

Inside the front door, he glanced at an engraved metal plate on the foyer wall. Scanning it, he saw that the building was occupied solely by physicians and contained no institutes or corporations. Dubrovskoy's office was listed on the second floor. He was an oncologist.

For the most part the building seemed deserted, though some of the doors were open in the first-floor hallway, and beside them a patient or two sat waiting on benches for appointments. Taking the emergency staircase, Alex arrived at the landing of the second floor, and checking up and down the corridor, he saw that it was empty.

Though he feared a confrontation with the doctor, he reminded himself that he no longer resembled the photo possessed by hotel security at the Peterhof and the Troika. When he came to Dubrovskoy's office, he found that it was closed. He hesitated, then knocked. The door was opened by a woman in her thirties, wearing a white uniform and her red hair in a pixie cut. Her fingernails were metallic purple, and it was apparent that she had been interrupted in the act of filing them with an emery board.

"There are no appointments", she said.

"I am not seeking an appointment", Alex said with a slight bow. "Is Dr. Dubrovskoy here today?"

"No", she said without further explanation.

"I thought not. But as I was passing by, I decided to take a chance and drop in to see Vasily Yefimovich."

"Is he a friend of yours?" she asked, shifting to a slightly less officious tone.

"Not an intimate one", Alex shrugged. "We have a close mutual friend."

"A terrible day for a surprise visit", she grimaced, nodding toward the window. "I really shouldn't be here. But I have to catch up on paperwork."

"Ah yes, there is no end to paperwork, is there?"

"*Nichivo!* You look cold. Would you like to come in and warm up for a minute?"

"Thank you, that is most kind. Also, may I leave him a message? Would you give it to him?"

"Then you haven't heard?"

"Heard?"

"He's away. He won't be back for some time."

"Oh yes, but I didn't know he was leaving so soon."

"He's terrible, so forgetful! Never telling people what they need to know. Imagine my situation, a secretary to such a man! Still, he is a great man. He saves many lives, impossible cases that other doctors will not touch."

"It is the spiritual element in his practice, I expect."

Warming to his comment, she leaned forward earnestly and said, "Exactly. He is breaking new ground. The integration of the physical and the spiritual energies."

Alex nodded solemnly. "Men such as Vasily Yefimovich are visionaries. It seems to me that he is one who forges ahead in the vanguard of mankind."

Her eyes blinked with feeling. "I see that you admire him." She lowered her eyes. "As I do."

She opened her arm, indicating that he should sit on a chair. "*Pazhalusta.*"

Seated, Alex asked, "If he has gone, who is caring for his patients?"

"They have been taken by colleagues during his absence. Vasily Yefimovich regrets the inconvenience, but the other doctors are very much in line with his philosophy of healing."

"Are you part of the group?"

"Regrettably, no. But I do appreciate their ideas. And I've been reading their books. They are so *spiritual*! I would have gone to the conference, but my poor mother is ill."

Alex buttoned up his coat collar. "Well, I am sorry to have missed him. When will he return?"

"The end of April. Did he not tell you?"

"He is not the only forgetful one", Alex said, smiling. "I'll tell him I met you when I see him at the conference."

"You're going to Novosibirsk?"

"Yes, of course."

Novosibirsk? In Siberia? Alex's heart sank.

"Well, I suppose you aren't too late. He said they begin on Saturday. You're flying out tomorrow, then?"

"Yes. I'll probably stay at the same hotel."

"The Ob? I hope you made a reservation; it could be full."

"No matter—there are other hotels."

He made a mental note: *The Hotel Ob!*

"If you can't get into the Ob, call him and tell him where you're staying, because they're planning to go on from there as soon as everyone arrives. The delegates are flying in from all over. They're supposed to meet at the Ob, just so no one gets lost on the first day."

"Where are they going after that?"

"I'm not sure where it is. He said something about their special place. The Dacha, he called it, but it must be much larger than a dacha. Didn't he tell you about that?"

Alex tapped his forehead and smiled again. "I'd better go home and check his letter. The details are all there."

Another mental note: *The Dacha!*

"First, will you take a glass of tea?" she asked solicitously.

"Please. I would be grateful."

She went through a doorway behind her desk and began opening cupboards and rattling spoons. While he waited, Alex sat in the reception area looking about. He saw that the doctor was not suffering from financial difficulty, for he employed a friendly if somewhat naïve secretary, his portion of the clinic was a suite of rooms, the carpet was thick, and the furniture was elegant avant-garde.

A painting on the opposite wall refused to be ignored. Approximately six feet square, it seemed to emanate a strange power, compelling the eye to seek its message, or passively to receive it. Dominating half of the canvas was an armored warrior. In his right hand he held a bow with its string vibrating. A quiver full of green-fletched arrows hung on his back. He knelt in the ruins of a modern city, and so great was his size that his knee rested on the rubble of several buildings. All around him a maze of shattered habitations and fallen office towers stretched toward the horizon, the buildings split open to reveal countless rooms shaped like wasp cells.

Alex got up and went over to look more closely.

Within the wasp cells were human bodies, some dead, some living but hypnotized with despair. Each forehead was stamped with a miniature bar code. In the foreground, a tree grew up the left side of the frame, and on it a few branches sprouted sickly leaves. In the crook of a branch sat a bird's nest. In the nest, a broken eggshell. On a piece of shell, a computer bar code.

Alex returned to his seat and examined the work from a distance. At first glance it appeared to be a protest against the dehumanizing aspects of modern life. Man alienated from nature would destroy himself and in the end would also destroy nature. The bar code expressed the commercialization of existence. Every created thing, from man to bird to tree, had become an object for sale and for consumption. And in the end all was consumed.

Did the giant warrior represent the ecology movement—armored for battle because the war against nature was especially bad in Russia? Was he an angel? Yes, perhaps that was it, for a splay of wings sprouted from his back, dissolving into boiling clouds of factory exhaust in the background. Range upon range of dark Satanic mills. Among them was a burning nuclear reactor, which Alex had first supposed to be the setting sun but which he now thought was Chernobyl. There were other Chernobyls strung along the horizon.

Was it saying that existence was perpetual war, inexorably leading to an ultimate climax—to the catastrophic end of things? If so, it was a world view that had been continuously reinforced by Russia's history. Indeed, the image could not have emerged from any culture other than Russia's, for the armor was Russo-Byzantine, as was the sense of spiritual presence and brooding northernness.

He looked more closely at the face of the warrior. So far, he had regarded the figure as a "he" because of the masculine iconography of armor and weapon and the muscular torso. Now he saw that the face—an extraordinarily beautiful face—was feminine, or more precisely neither masculine nor feminine but completely androgynous. The features were a combination of a da Vinci angel and a Botticelli satyr. It was this dissolving of identity that was most disturbing. Moreover, keen intelligence seemed to shine from its eyes, cunning, cold, redefining good and evil, and perhaps reconciling them, as if they were equal forces that maintained each other in a great equilibrium.

Who was this warrior? Was he grieving over the city, or was he its destroyer?

Alex scanned the ruins in search of a clue. With a start he came upon a tiny church in the center of the city. It was shattered, its minuscule cross bent sideways, its dome split by a notched arrow shaft. It was only one of hundreds of fascinating details—so small as to be practically unnoticeable. Alex's vision dropped along a line of pictorial design—a black crevasse in the earth that led directly from the broken church to the warrior's left hand. The hand was holding something it had picked up from beneath the nest, the fingers clenching a tiny form, crushing it. Oozing from the fist was a trickle of blood and feathers. The feathers were cobalt blue.

Examining the artist's signature at the bottom of the page, he noted small trees flanking the first and last letters—one black and the other crimson.

At that moment the secretary returned to the room with two mugs of steaming tea. She handed one to Alex and nodded toward the painting.

"Tremendous, isn't it?"

"It is powerful", he replied and took a sip of tea.

"It's by a friend of Vasily Yefimovich. Its title is *Millennium Angel*."

"An angel of the Apocalypse?"

"Apocalypse? I don't know about that. Anyway, what it says is so true, don't you think?"

Alex suggested that it was a work of genius. She enthusiastically agreed.

When he had finished his tea, he stood to go. She reached out her hand, and he shook it. She told him her name, and waited for him to respond with his.

"Aleksandr...", he murmured. "Aleksandr Strannik."

"Pilgrim? An unusual name."

"Yes, I suppose it is."

She smiled at him demurely. "It's very spiritual."

He asked her to phone for a taxi, thanked her for her help, and went down to the foyer to wait. It seemed that the anti-icon came with him, embedded like an arrow in his mind.

"Sibir", he said, staring out into the darkening storm.

19. *Scenes of Historical Importance*

In preparation for his departure from Moscow's Yaroslavsky Station, Alex purchased a used wool blanket from a street vendor, anticipating that Siberia would live up to its reputation for brutal winters and that even in a train carriage he might find himself chilled to the bone. Moments before boarding the Trans-Siberian Express, he added to his pack a loaf of black bread, a packet of smoked fish, a half dozen hard-boiled eggs, and a bottle of Baltika beer.

His first-class ticket provided him a spot in the "luxury" carriage of a long powder-blue train pulled by a diesel engine. His room contained two cots and a table beneath the window. The walls were lined with fake wood panels, the floor covered with imitation Oriental carpet. The room was superheated, and this, added to the rhythmic clatter of the tracks as the express rolled into the east, induced a drowsiness that Alex could not resist. He fell asleep frequently, waking every hour or so to brood on his problems and to renew, by an effort of the will, his resolve to persevere. From time to time a woman conductor knocked on the door, bringing him a tray of biscuits and a pot of tea stamped with the insignia of the train—the Petrel.

For a day and a half he stared out the window at the passing landscape, frosty birch forests, villages of log cabins, and scenes nearly identical to those he had observed between Saint Petersburg and Moscow. Yet he saw that in all places there was originality, resulting from the human efforts at decoration and ingenious methods of survival. Occasionally he sat up straighter and peered closely as larger towns and cities raced past the window—Yaroslavl, Perm, and on the eastern side of the white hills of the Urals, the famous Yekaterinburg, where the last czar and his family had been imprisoned under house arrest and executed in July of 1918. As the train rumbled through these scenes of momentous historical import, Alex stared numbly at the domed churches, suburbs, and factories, unable to connect what he was seeing to the dramas of the past. It was picturesque but ordinary, as if all significance had been suffocated under the pall of dull, gray winter.

In the afternoon of the second day, the train slowed in jerks and hobbled onto a siding, where it came to a halt in a wilderness of frozen swamp. There was no sign of human habitation in any direction. The Petrel sat for an hour, vibrating, chugging diesel exhaust that drifted in through the doors connecting the carriages. Alex went into the corridor and asked a conductor why they had stopped.

"Trouble in the engine", she said.

"Will it take long to fix?"

"Maybe a day", she shrugged. "Maybe a week. Maybe never."

Alex knew that a single breakdown would never be permitted to interrupt the heavy flow of rail traffic that was the lifeblood of the country.

"So, we wait here?" he asked.

"Another train is coming from Tyumen. It will arrive in a few hours, and then you will transfer."

"Will it take me to Novosibirsk?"

"Of course."

Alex stepped down out of his carriage onto the track bed and looked toward the tail end of the train, beyond which the orange sun was dropping into the Urals. There was no wind, but the temperature was close to twenty degrees below zero. He jogged up and down the track, breathing great clouds of frost, trying to ignore the sting that came through his thin trousers, very thankful for the Russian greatcoat. The air bit into his lungs and brought him fully awake. His thoughts were clearer than they had been for days.

As the sky darkened, stars began to emerge. Alex spent close to an hour outside, no longer jogging, merely pacing the length of the train several times. When he realized that he could not feel his toes, he hastened back into the carriage, where the blast of heat and a fresh pot of tea welcomed him. The rescue train arrived at about nine thirty, and all the passengers were transferred to it. It was clearly of lower quality than the Trans-Siberian Express, for it had no name, only a number, and its exterior was dirty green. The engine was electric, hauling fourteen weather-beaten coaches. There was no first-class carriage, only a single *coupé* or second class, and this was already full. Alex found his way to a *platskart*, or third-class carriage. Pulling open the door to enter, he drew back from the stench of human sweat, disinfectant, and vodka that greeted him. Then, because he had no choice, he went in. The wooden benches were crowded beyond capacity. Reluctantly, the few children in the carriage shifted onto their parents' knees to make space for the transfer passengers.

Alex found a spot at the very back, beside a man who seemed to be asleep, his body compacted into the corner by the window, legs crossed at the knees, hands clasped on his lap. As he sat down, Alex breathed a sigh of relief, for the train had begun to roll and was quickly gathering speed. It wheezed and creaked and squealed and bounced, transmitting not only the sound but the vibration of every flaw in the tracks. He estimated that Novosibirsk was still several hundred miles ahead. This last stage of the journey would be uncomfortable, but it was night, and he expected that he would sleep through some of it. No doubt everyone else on board felt the same.

But it was not so. The atmosphere in the carriage was quite different from that of the express, for here there was no effort to pander to the tastes of Western tourists or wealthy New Russians. No, this was a conveyance for human freight, and the freight knew it all too well. There were several drunks on board, shouting and singing loudly, but not otherwise offensive. No one else seemed to consider this behavior out of the ordinary. Most of the passengers paid them no mind and contented themselves with quiet conversation or staring at nothing, thinking private thoughts. A few heads were bobbing off to sleep.

Alex glanced across the aisle and saw two old men seated side by side, engaged in a discussion that he could not hear. From time to time one or the other would nod or make a point with an index finger. Whatever the subject was, it was a serious one. In the seats in front of him were several grandmothers bearing bundles of cloth on their laps, chatting in a spirit of acceptance or grumbling about the overcrowding.

Examining his own seatmate circumspectly, Alex noticed that the man was gaunt, late middle-aged, face and body set in a mode of permanent tension. Intelligence seemed to be written in the large frontal dome of the skull, the furrowed brow, the wide cheekbones with a hint of Tartar in them, the tangled reddish-gray beard, the mouth a line of nervous strain, the entire visage marked by a history of wrestling with grave ideas. Alex thought it a stroke of good fortune to have found a seat beside the sort of Russian he would feel most at home with. The man looked as if he had wandered out of the nineteenth century by mistake and had by some freak of *kronos* or by a dispensation of providence arrived in the modern age with quill-penned manuscripts bulging out of his pockets.

Later, when the man awoke, he shivered, opened his bloodshot eyes, and removed from his pocket not a manuscript but a liter of vodka. It was half-full. He uncorked it and tipped it to his mouth, taking it down to the quarter mark in one long pull. Then he smacked his lips and looked out the corner of his eyes at Alex. Though the eyes contained a flicker of intelligence, behind them an unruly and possibly dangerous personality seemed ready to erupt. Once again Alex was forced to meet his presumptions, and his Russophilic romance, face-to-face.

He realized suddenly that he was staring at the man. The man, for his part, was glaring back with his head hunched down into his shoulders, assessing Alex with a hostile expression.

"Why don't you ask", he growled.

"Ask what, sir?" Alex replied, thinking, *Manuscripts? Political insights? Spiritual prophecy?*

"For a sip, if you're so desperate. Here!" He thrust the bottle at Alex.

"No thank you, sir", said Alex. He rummaged in his pack and withdrew the bottle of Baltika. "I have this."

"Pew—beer!" said the man with disgust. "Why use horse piss when you can get rocket fuel?"

A coy look came over his face. He uncrossed his legs and offered his right hand for a shake, peering into Alex's eyes with no effort to conceal his curiosity, pressing too close. Alex shook the man's hand and suppressed a nervous laugh, not wanting to give offense by any outward indication of amusement, for his seatmate was a parody of the Russian eccentric—the fellow was a "type" well examined in the literature of this land.

"How do you do? I am Alexander Graham."

"Aha, a foreigner! I thought so."

"And you are...?"

"I am Kolya the Water Skimmer", the man chuckled in a wicked tone.

"Water Skimmer? Really, is that your name?"

The man cackled, making little clickety-clickety-clicks in the back of his throat.

"Of course that's my name! I baptized myself with it." He tilted the bottle over his brow and let a few drops of vodka fall onto his forehead. They ran down his face, and he caught them on his tongue. Alex eased away from him a few inches. A man under the influence of alcohol was one thing, but several hundred miles in the company of the deranged was another thing altogether.

"I am one of those spider bugs that scuttle across the surface of ponds without sinking", his seatmate continued. "Their delicate little toes merely dimple the surface."

"Why do you call yourself that?" Alex asked.

"Because then I'm so light they can't catch me."

"Who wants to catch you? Are you being chased?"

"Didn't I say I was? Yes, yes, I'm being chased."

"By whom?"

"By them."

"Them? Who are they?"

"You don't know?"

Alex shook his head.

Kolya the Water Skimmer leaned so close to Alex that their foreheads touched, and lowering his voice he whispered, "We're watching you too."

Alex realized now that the man was quite mad. Inside those eyes were all the characters that dwelled in the tiny cage of his mental universe—both chasers and chased.

Alex opened his bottle of Baltika and took a long sip, hoping that it would anaesthetize his discomfort and hasten his arrival at Novosibirsk.

"I made that", said Kolya, pointing at the bottle.

"I don't think so", said Alex, resolving to waste no energy confirming the man's delusions. "I bought it at Yaroslavsky Station in Moscow."

"*Nyet, nyet, nyet*, I don't mean *that* bottle. Do you think I'm crazy? I mean when I was in the bug cage I used to make it—beer, that is. Not that they ever let us have a sip."

"The bug cage? When were you in a bug cage?"

"Shh! Not so loud. They listen. Always, they listen."

"Who?"

"The listeners."

This frustrating game went on for some minutes. Just when Alex was ready to abandon the useless exercise and feign sleep, Kolya grabbed his arm.

"All right, I'll tell you. I can see you know nothing. Therefore you can't be one of them."

"I'm not, sir. Truly, I don't know what you're talking about."

"I used to be smart. I used to be brilliant. I used to write."

"What did you write?"

Kolya frowned and pondered the question as if he was searching his memory.

"Short stories. They were published. Now you understand?"

Alex shook his head.

"Stupid!" Kolya shouted. "Are you stupid? Do I have to spell it out? I wrote what must not be written. Stories they didn't like. Then the drugs."

"Ah, I see", said Alex sympathetically. "You struggled with drug addiction."

"No, it was *state* drugs."

He slapped both sides of his head, making *psst-psst* sounds with his mouth.

"My wife taken away, my Lyda. My daughter, my Tatya, taken away. I am taken away. Everything is taken away…"

The tone of this recitation slid into a chanting singsong. Alex leaned closer with sympathy.

"Now I understand. You were a writer during the Soviet era. You were in prison."

"Not just any prison. Psychiatric prison, where they pump your brain empty and fill it up with chemicals."

"I am sorry, sir."

"Call me Kolya—we're comrades."

"I am sorry, Kolya. You have been through a great suffering."

"Suffering?" he said in a tone of amazement. "Yes, I've had my knocks. But I'm happy enough. I've learned the most important thing in life. Whenever trouble comes, I just skim away on the surface of the water. The stupid guards can't catch you. They're too heavy. Everyone on earth's heavier than me. Even you—yes, you—you're too heavy."

This tragic reduction of all thought to the rationale of the bug cage was a challenge too big for Alex. He let it be.

"When did you leave prison?" he asked.

"In 1979 they let me out. My youth all gone. Ten years I was a *zek*. After the hospital, I was in many camps, some I can't remember. Big ones, little ones, but always hard work. I got beat up sometimes by the *ugolovniki*—those regular criminals, those foxes. They said I used too many big words. After a while I couldn't remember the words, so it didn't matter. The guards were bad in those days, a little better in the last years. Still, I spent lots of time in the *shizo*."

"What is the *shizo*?"

"A hole in the wall. An isolation cell."

"What do you do with your life now?"

"I skim. I read the papers. I try to remember what I can."

"Where do you live?"

"Omsk. With my wife."

"So, you found her again."

"No, I never found Lyda. I never found Tatya either. Maybe they didn't want to be found. This one is my third wife. She pays the bills. She's got a good job in a repair shop for the engines. I have a rail pass. See." He held up a card inside the cover of his Russian internal passport.

Kolya rambled on for a time, while Alex withdrew into his own thoughts. Stricken by the specter of the man's life, he wondered what he had been before his arrest. While the Soviet state was pumping his brains and filling him with chemicals, a certain Alexander Graham, an overheavy romantic from another world, was studying the great, the mighty, the true and free Russian tongue, the strength and staff of those who were falling into despair at the sight of all that was taking place in their homeland.

Alex turned his attention back to Kolya's monologue, which during his absence seemed to have improved in quality:

"—the state must catch criminals in order to prove it's in control. Right? So by maintaining law and order, the state provides security and peace. Right? Thus, the number of prisoners should match as closely as possible the number of crimes committed in the country, you see. If by chance a few innocents get caught in the net, that's regrettable. Even so, the good of the people is fostered by the mistake. Why should a citizen complain if he's condemned for a crime he didn't commit? After all, in time of war he offers his life as a sacrifice. Why shouldn't he do so now for the good of his country? Eh? Tell me if you disagree."

"I'm afraid I do disagree. Such a government is an evil government. It devours its own people."

"Ha! When have governments been any different? Certainly not in Mother Russia!"

"Are you saying that we must accept what governments do to us?"

"Stupid! Stupid! You don't understand me at all!"

Alex groaned inwardly as his seatmate launched into yet another tangent. It went on interminably, Alex not daring to interrupt because the logic of madness is irrefutable. He listened out of respect for the man's suffering, and also because the bottle of Baltika was in his hands, warm now, as warm as a civilized man should drink it. He wished Owen Whitfield were here at his side. What enlightening conversations they might have had. What a support he would have found in the professor. But as luck or providence would have it, he was continuing his downward plunge into the zone of the dispossessed, unaccompanied by rational man.

He began to pray silently for Kolya the Water Skimmer.

Strangely, as Alex prayed, the babble of Kolya's speech sputtered and stopped in midsentence.

"What are you doing?" Kolya snapped.

"I am doing nothing."

"You were, you were", came the accusing reply. "I felt it. The surface of the water trembled. There was fire. It hurt."

"What hurt?"

"The thing you were doing. Inside you. Stop it! Stop it!"

Completely puzzled, Alex could only stare in amazement.

"You know what I mean. You know."

"I was praying. Is that what you mean?"

Kolya shot him a furtive expression.

"Do you believe in God?" Alex asked.

"Don't say it!"

"What is the matter? Why are you afraid? You have nothing to fear from God."

"Then why does it hurt?" Kolya screamed. With that, he began to weep, the clickety-clicks resuming their strange repetition in the back of his throat.

"What is the matter, what is the matter?" Alex said in the voice of a father trying to console a frightened child who will not tell what is wrong.

The weeping went on for several minutes. Eventually Kolya choked back his sobs and cried, *"Khamstvo! Khamstvo!"*

Alex knew that the word meant "boorishness" and also "shamelessness", but what it meant in this context was beyond him.

"What has happened to you?" he said, gripping the man's arm. "Tell me."

When Kolya was able to speak again, he turned his haunted eyes upon Alex and said:

"If the ax splits the skull, we die. If the ax splits the mind, we do not die, we live—we live in hell."

Realizing that words would have no good effect, Alex was paralyzed. He continued staring at the man, afraid to speak, afraid to invoke heavenly aid. Kolya turned away and stared out the window. He pulled a small flask from his coat pocket, put it to his lips, and emptied it in a long swallow.

"Go away, idiot", he said, wiping his lips. "You know nothing. You understand nothing."

"I . . . I . . .", Alex stammered, then fell silent.

"Go away, go away. Go back to your pampered life."

Alex looked about the carriage in search of an empty seat. There were none. He noticed that across the aisle the two old men were watching him. The nearer one nodded sympathetically.

"Would you like to exchange places?" he asked.

"If you wish", Alex said.

They got up, and the old man sat down beside Kolya, who did not at first notice the presence of his new seatmate. Alex sank with relief into the spot beside the other. He sighed and withdrew into his own thoughts. It came to him that his empathy for suffering people, however laudable it might be, had proved too small a thing in the face of Kolya's condition. Now a mood of discouragement took hold of him, along with renewed anxiety for Andrew. Where was he? And what would *they* do to him?

Presently he noted that the man who had replaced him was talking quietly with Kolya and that although the crazed look had not disappeared entirely from the Water Skimmer's face, he seemed less agitated. The conversation between the two was conducted in low voices. The old man made small comments as Kolya gestured, scowled, or spoke at length. But what either of them said was drowned by the noise in the carriage.

The man seated beside Alex had so far said nothing to him. He wondered if the two were brothers, for though their appearance was different in some aspects, they were oddly the same. The man sitting with Kolya had blue eyes and was short in stature, clean-shaven, and fair skinned, with trim silver hair and a thin mouth. The man beside Alex had swarthy skin, a wide, full mouth, and gray hair parted in the middle and tied in a bun at the back of his head. His bushy beard reached nearly to his waist. He had suffered an accident sometime in the past: his nose had been broken, and there were scars on his forehead, cheeks, and upper lip.

But the expressions were curiously identical: strong, reserved, yet open. There was kindness in both sets of eyes. On neither of their faces was there the brooding interiority he had come to expect from the *kremlin* of the soul. These were unusual men. But who were they? Yes, brothers, Alex concluded.

His new seatmate seemed to fall into a light doze, though his lips continued to move silently as if he was articulating a dialogue in his dreams.

As Alex observed the conversation across the aisle, it looked as if the other old man had succeeded in calming Kolya. The Water Skimmer was now whispering into his ear. He in turn nodded frequently and patted Kolya's arm. Eventually, the madman closed his eyes and seemed to fall asleep, as if he too was drifting into dreams.

An hour or so later a conductor came through the carriage, calling in a loud voice, "Omsk, Omsk, Omsk."

The train began to pass lighted buildings. Alex checked his watch. It was past one in the morning. He was distressed and very tired, but glad that he was still progressing into the east.

At Omsk Station, Kolya fluttered his eyes and sat up straight. He seemed as bright as a new kopeck, none the worse for his arduous emotional outbursts. The old man got up and let Kolya into the aisle. Then, without a by-your-leave or a word of farewell, the Water Skimmer left the train, whistling to himself. From the carriage window, Alex saw him embracing a woman on the platform. He noted also that the man had a blanket—Alex's—tucked neatly under an arm. Moreover, he pulled a blue-green tartan scarf from his pocket and wrapped it lovingly around the woman's neck.

Well, no matter—*nichivo*, as the Russians said—he could do without it. He was warm enough. He could afford to suffer a little thievery. What was the loss of a scarf compared to the theft of a mind?

The train rumbled, clackety-clacked, gathered speed, and continued on its journey. The brothers remained where they were; neither of them made a request for a repositioning of seats. The dark one fell asleep, and the fair one soon drifted off into the same state.

Alex was awakened by the rising sun that burst above a ridge of taiga as the train rounded a bend. He stretched his limbs and eased his aching joints. Gazing across the aisle, he said to the fair one, "Thank you for your help last night. Would you care to have your seat back?"

"Please", the man said.

Alex slid into his former place and occupied himself for a time by gazing out at the white land, which was flatter than it had been the day before, a uniform texture of bare deciduous trees interspersed with frozen swamps. There were no signs of human habitation.

"Sibir", he whispered, his breath adding to the frost on the lower part of the window.

He nibbled at a hard crust of black bread, slowly chewed the last sliver of smoked fish, and washed it down with the dregs of the stale Baltika. For the next few hours he alternately dozed and watched the passing landscape, indifferent to what was occurring inside the carriage.

Close to noon, he roused himself and leaned across the aisle.

"Excuse me", he said to the fair one. "Do you know how far we are from Novosibirsk?"

"About three hundred kilometers", the man replied.

"Perhaps four hundred, Sergei", said his companion.

"Yes, you are right, Serafim; it is closer to four hundred."

"Thank you", Alex said. "Are you traveling to Novosibirsk?"

"No, we leave the train at Obsk", Sergei the Fair responded. "We arrive there shortly—five or ten minutes."

"Obsk? I have not heard of it."

"It is not on many maps of western Sibir. Only local maps of our region. Even so, it is frequently overlooked."

"This is a blessing", the dark brother said, as if speaking to himself.

The use of the word *blessing* gave Alex pause, for it had religious connotations. The man had not said *fortunate* or *good luck*. And he had indicated that obscurity was beneficial. Why did he think such a thing?

"Are you traveling to Novosibirsk as a tourist, sir?" the fair one asked.

"No, I am—"

He was unable to finish the sentence because the train suddenly screeched, gave a sickening lurch, screeched again, lurched once more, corrected itself, then in a series of violent jolts ground to a halt. Alex found himself tumbled forward against the seat in front of him. All around, passengers were groaning, complaining, readjusting their clothing and baggage, shaking fists in the direction of the engine. But no one appeared to have been hurt.

"What now! What now!" cried a grandmother in the bench immediately ahead of Alex. "In the old days the Railway Ministry was efficient. Now it's falling apart!"

"It's about time we got back to the way things used to be", said another.

"No, no, we can never go back."

"You'd think they could at least make the trains work properly."

"Quiet!" shouted the woman conductor, her voice capable of astonishing volume. "Keep your heads down. The train is under attack."

Laughter and taunts greeted this warning: "Who is attacking us? The Chinese? The Americans?"

Forward in the coach, a window cracked and bulged inward. Gasps came from the passengers, who as a single entity fell silent and stared at it.

Another window cracked under a blow.

"It's the Germans! They always hated us."

"No, it can't be them; we're too far from Europe!"

"Oy, oy, *Rodina, Rodina,* Mother Russia!"

A third window cracked. Whatever projectiles were striking the carriage did not seem to be very strong. The glass panels fractured but did not collapse.

Peering above the ledge of his window, Alex saw thick smoke boiling ahead, to the right of the train. It was near enough for him to observe that some kind of wooden structure was burning, but far enough away that he could not discern what it was.

He turned to the brothers, who were staring out their own window.

Another glass cracked. A woman screamed.

"Keep calm, keep calm, everyone!" the conductor shouted.

"Who is it? Who is doing this?" people shouted back.

Furious, the conductor stomped up and down the aisle, talking into a pocket phone.

Another missile hit the train, on the left. Now, instinctively, everyone ducked.

"What is happening?" Alex asked the brothers.

They looked at him calmly and shook their heads.

Alex surveyed the scene outside his own window, which was as yet untouched. A head popped up from behind a snowbank, hurled something at the carriage, then ducked down again. Three seats ahead, another window fractured.

Now more and more heads appeared from the snowbanks as the attackers realized that no retaliation was forthcoming. All along the track bed, men stood up and raised their arms in menacing gestures. They were dressed in the strangest array of clothing that Alex had ever seen, a mixture of multicolored ethnic Russian garb and the animal hides of primitive peoples.

Passengers sat straighter and grumbled:

"This is ridiculous!"

"Who are these crazy people?"

"Where are the police when you need them?"

"Where are the train guards?"

Another window shattered.

"Oy, if I had Gorbachev here, I'd give him a piece of my mind. He's the one who started this whole mess!"

"Yes, and Yeltsin made it worse!"

"And those ice-heads who run things now!"

None troubled themselves to agree with the last comment, because ice-heads, as everyone knew, were as dangerous in a democracy as they were in a tyranny.

"Why aren't we moving?"

"Why doesn't the engineer just get going?"

"Why doesn't someone shoot them?"

"Why shoot them? They're harmless!"

"Harmless? I say shoot them!"

"Shut up! Shut up, everybody!" the conductor bellowed. "I can't hear!"

Everyone shut up.

As the woman strained to hear the message on her mobile phone, the passengers watched the attackers to see what they would do next. Alex noted that there were about twenty or thirty on his side of the train and about the same number on the left or north side. Most were young or middle-age men, but some were older, and a few were women. All of them were shaking spears and hurling rocks. One fired a real arrow from a real bow. It struck the side of the train and bounced off. Four men on Alex's side unrolled a long cloth banner and held it up for the passengers to see. Painted on the white sheet in green Cyrillic script was the message:

WHEN WILL THE MADNESS END?
CEASE THE ECO-RAPE OF SIBIR!

Then they began to dance a kind of bastardized war dance they must have learned from American films about the Wild West. From the snowdrifts a few more men emerged, riding ponies of the kind that drew troikas on the steppe or taiga. The ponies were shaggy little creatures, trotting stoutheartedly alongside the track, the feet of their riders almost touching the ground. More bows were fired by the attackers mustering on the south side of the train near Alex's window. The sound of steel-tipped shafts made clink-clunk sounds as they dented the metal siding. The entire scene was videotaped by a blond Tartar. The banner was rolled up. Turning as a herd, they stampeded away over a low rise and disappeared.

All the passengers sat up, some straightening their hair and clothing, others inspecting the bulging glass of the windows. Although a few were chuckling and making comments about the Golden Horde and Tamerlane, the general mood in the coach was one of irritation.

The brothers caught his eye and smiled.

"No one was hurt", said the fair one.

"Thanks be to God", said the dark one, making the Orthodox sign of the cross on his forehead, chest, and shoulders.

Alex raised his eyebrows and said, "Does this happen often on the Trans-Siberian?"

"It was", said the fair one in an amused tone, "a singular event."

Ten minutes passed.

"Well," someone called, "why aren't we moving?"

"Shut up! Be patient!" shouted the conductor.

She babbled into her phone, and it babbled back at her. She mumbled "*Da!*", clicked it off, and pocketed it. Her morose face fell still further into an expression of utter fatalism.

"The idiots have burned three bridges between here and Novosibirsk", she explained to the passengers. This was greeted by groans and curses. "The Ministry is sending help. They'll have the bridges repaired by tomorrow, maybe the day after. But it looks like we sit here until it's fixed."

The ensuing uproar was truly impressive.

"Don't worry, don't worry", she snarled. "We have electricity. It will be warm. Food will be distributed free of charge."

The brothers stood and slung packs over their shoulders.

"Are you leaving?" Alex asked.

"Yes", said the fair one. "Obsk is not far. An hour's walk. We will cross the river on the ice and connect with the road on the other side."

"Is there a hotel in Obsk?"

"I am sorry, no. It is a small village. If you need to go to Novosibirsk quickly, I suggest you stay on the train."

By now, Alex had spent one night on hard seats and did not relish the prospect of another. Hoping to find more comfortable accommodations, he asked if there was a private home in Obsk where he might rent a room. Sergei the Fair explained that in Obsk the houses were small and very poor; it would be difficult to find a spare bed, let alone an entire room.

"But...", he hesitated, glancing at the dark one. "Perhaps there is a place on the sofa."

Serafim the Dark furrowed his brow and nodded.

Alex hastily donned his greatcoat, slung the shoulder bag around his neck, and grabbed the gym bag from under the seat. He looked about for his fleece cap, but it was missing. Kolya, again!

They detrained onto the track bed and faced into a blasting wind that carried with it the smell of burning creosote. The two older men led the way, surprisingly agile for their age, bending before the weather with archetypal endurance. Alex hunched along after them, trying to hide from the wind behind the shield of their bodies. Soon they came to the source of the smoke, a wooden bridge in flames. It traversed a narrow frozen river that in summer flowed between low banks. Most of the bridge timbers were crackling and roaring, churning up a fume of oily black clouds. The beams nearest the west bank had collapsed. The rails sagged dangerously, and even as Alex and his two companions approached, one ripped away and dropped with a loud boom onto the ice below. Trainmen stood by, their hands on their hips, muttering, cursing, and smoking cigarettes.

The two old men turned aside and began to forge their way down the incline toward the riverbed. The snow was deeper on the slope, and Alex was thankful that he was following in the trail broken by these seasoned Siberians.

20. *On the Little-Little Ob*

It took a minute to cross the ice, and another to climb the other riverbank. Arriving at its height, they came to a footpath that ran along the east side of the river, and they turned north on it. As they continued to walk, the wind now blasted them from the right. The route was clearly not one on which motor vehicles regularly traveled. Sergei explained that it was a summer road, passable by truck only between the months of June and September. Alex ventured to ask where, precisely, they were. Sergei told him they had just crossed a river called the Little-Little Ob. That was not its proper name, he said, not the name on maps. It was a tributary of the Little Ob that flowed hundreds of kilometers northward to join the great Ob itself, the mighty artery draining western Siberia. Along these far-flung waterways, lost in millions of square kilometers of wilderness, were countless villages whose residents scratched a living from the taiga by trapping, logging, and subsistence farming. Summers were short, winters long, and the transitional seasons brief. Obsk, however, was close to the railroad, about five kilometers north of it. This, combined with its position on a water route, increased its importance in the region, an elevated status acknowledged only by the residents of the surrounding settlements, who once or twice a year passed through on their way to larger places.

As Alex followed his guides, the woods thickened. Poplar and birch predominated, though other species unknown to him were also present. All the trees were as thin as rails, bowing, swaying, the wind blowing snow from their branches. His right cheek was beginning to ache with the onset of frostbite when he saw the roof of a church rising above the tips of the trees. The dome was a traditional onion shape, covered with wood shingles rather than gold leaf or enamel paint. On the peak, a metal cross wobbled in the wind, flashing intermittent reflections from the sun. As they came to the border of the trees and entered a clearing, Alex saw that Obsk was as it had been described—primitive. It was a collection of no more than a dozen log cabins perched on the brink of a loop in the river and surrounded on all sides by unending forest.

The dark one, the man named Serafim, made straightway for the church, which was merely a larger cabin surmounted by the distinctive dome. He led the two others around to the far side of the building, where they navigated through heaps of firewood, and he unlocked a door in a shed attached to the wall of the church. As they entered, Alex realized that the shed was a home. He was also confirmed in what he had already begun to suspect—that Serafim was a priest.

Serafim and Sergei turned in unison to one of the corners, bowed at the waist, and made signs of the cross. Then Serafim lit an oil lamp and Sergei got a fire going in a barrel stove in the middle of the room. As the two older men busied themselves with the primary task of securing warmth, Alex sat down on a bench by the door and began to survey the character of this habitation. It was about twelve feet square, the air scented with wood smoke and liturgical incense. Sunshine came through a small four-paned window, providing barely enough light to illuminate the interior. As his eyes adjusted, he saw that the room contained a plank table flanked by benches, a bookshelf made from a wooden crate suspended on wires from the rafters (this contained exclusively black-bound volumes), and two beds, one on each side of the stove. These were narrow wooden platforms covered with layers of blanket cloth. The "sofa", Alex suspected, was the rough pine box lying against the middle wall, in which were stacked blankets and a pillow. It was, in fact, an empty coffin.

The corner to which the two Russians had bowed was, he now saw, the traditional *krasny ugol*, the "red corner" or "beautiful corner" in which icons were enshrined on a shelf. The priest lit a crimson vigil candle before them and stepped back, bowing again. Father Serafim's possessions were few, and his icons were consistent with this. There was a small Mother of God, a painted Byzantine crucifixion, and a bearded saint in a white robe kneeling before a bare Orthodox cross. Alex supposed that the saint was Serafim of Sarov.

Sergei lifted a tin pail from the floor. Looking inside, he blew into it, causing a flurry of black specks to fly out. He put it on the stove.

"The mice again, Serafim", he said. "We leave for three days, and they take over."

Father Serafim grunted an acknowledgment, or possibly his disapproval.

The bucket contained ice, which began to hiss as it melted. Alex wondered nervously about the mice feces, until Father Serafim stood up, saying, "We all need tea, especially this weary traveler from a distant land. I will dump this and go to the river."

"Here, let me do it." Sergei took the bucket from the stove, and an ax from the woodbox.

"If you're going for water, may I accompany you?" Alex asked.

"Of course, of course, come along. You can carry the ax."

Outside, the old man upended the bucket beside the entrance, and an oval of ice slid out onto the snow. Then he led the way by a footpath to the edge of an embankment and down through willow scrub to the flat of the Little-Little Ob. A few feet from shore, he scooped away a mound of snow and exposed a wooden box, beneath which was a stack of old copies of a Siberian newspaper—*Krasnoye Znamya*—the Red

Banner. Beneath these coverings was bare ice. Kneeling in the snow, Sergei put a pair of reading glasses onto his nose, squinted, and began to chop at the ice with the ax.

"Isn't the ice too deep?" Alex asked as he squatted beside him.

"The river is frozen down three or four feet. We keep a hole open, and if we come every day, just the surface freezes— a few inches. But we have been gone for three days, so the ice will be thicker, harder to break through."

"Can I help?"

"You have to know how", Sergei said in a bantering tone. "Otherwise you get a splinter in your eye. And we don't want to wound a visitor from the outside world before we show him our hospitality."

Alex smiled in appreciation. "You have already shown me great hospitality. To take a stranger into your home is uncommonly generous."

"It is not much, Aleksandr."

Alex glanced at him curiously.

"How do you know my name, sir? We have not made introductions."

"Yes, yes, we're a bit distracted, Serafim and I, what with the attack upon the train." He chuckled to himself.

"But my name—how do you know it?"

"We could not help overhearing your conversation with the man from Omsk."

"Kolya."

"Yes, Kolya who calls himself a water skimmer."

"An eccentric fellow", Alex said, shaking his head.

"A suffering man", Sergei said in a tone of finality. "Look, we have found water!"

Indeed, there was now a gurgling deep in the hole. Alex handed the pail to Sergei, who dipped it in and withdrew a bucketful. He swirled it around and threw the water out.

Twice more he did this. When satisfied the pail was clean, he dipped it into the hole again and brought forth clear river water, reflecting rings of gold in its depths. Then the man methodically replaced the hole's protective coverings.

"Soon we will have tea", he said with much satisfaction.

"Please allow me to carry it", Alex insisted. Sergei let him take the pail by the wire handle, and together they walked side by side up the trail in the direction of the church.

"So you know my name", Alex said. "But I know only that yours is Sergei. Are you the priest's laborer?"

"I am a laborer," Sergei replied with a nod, "but I labor in a different part of the vineyard. I am Father Sergius."

"You are a priest! I should have guessed. But Obsk is a small village for two priests. Are you from another parish?"

"Siberia is my parish."

"Siberia is your parish?"

"I am not a Russian Orthodox priest", Father Sergius said carefully.

"No? What sort of priest are you, may I ask?"

"I am a Catholic priest", the man said, keeping his eyes on the trail.

"I too am a Catholic", Alex said.

The other paused and examined his face. "I knew you were a Christian. Yes, both Father Serafim and I knew this about you, even before you spoke. But what kind of Christian— well, it was not clear. You see, these are confused times. And in Russia it can be especially confusing."

"Then the days of mistrust are not over?"

"Far from over. The nature of the struggle is changing, but it is no less intense than in former times. Now the threat is primarily spiritual. But we shall say no more about that for the time being."

Arriving at the yard in front of the shed, Father Sergius gathered in his arms a few blocks of birch from the woodpile.

"Here we are. Serafim is eager for his tea, as am I. Let us go in and get warm."

In their absence, the Orthodox priest had concocted a lunch of hard black bread and slices of white cheese. Taking the pail of water from Father Sergius, he poured some of it into a kettle on the stovetop. Father Sergius opened a paper bag, withdrew a handful of powder from it, and dropped it into the kettle.

"I apologize, Aleksandr Graham", said Father Serafim, addressing him directly for the first time. "I do not have a samovar."

"You are far from home", said Father Sergius. "What is your native land?"

"Canada."

Both men raised their eyebrows.

"You thought I was an American", Alex said, smiling.

Both men nodded seriously.

"We are not unsympathetic to America", said Father Sergius. "But Canada is more like Russia."

"Yes, its geography and its climate are very much like those of Russia", Alex replied warmly. "Where I come from is similar to European Russia, especially around Saint Petersburg. A little north of my home, however, the land is total wilderness, much like this. The forests are thicker and the hills higher, and it is less populated than Sibir. But one could easily mistake the one for the other."

"I have read of it", said Father Serafim. "A very interesting country."

"Exotic", said Father Sergius with the now-familiar note of whimsy.

At once, it seemed that they were looking at each other through reversed lenses—the familiar and unfamiliar flipping around so completely that Alex suddenly saw himself as they were seeing him. They too, perhaps, were intrigued by the perspective of how their lives must appear to him. The three men laughed simultaneously, and between them there was formed an instantaneous bond. This was cemented by the arrival of the tea, which Father Serafim poured into three chipped cups. There was no milk. Father Sergius offered a pot of sugar and a jar of red jam. Alex spooned some sugar into his cup and sipped. His hosts stirred tablespoons of jam into their own cups and sucked at the tea enthusiastically.

"Ah, ah, ah", they all sighed, feeling the chill withdraw.

By then the room was also warming, and they took off their overcoats. Neither of the two Russians wore priestly dress, only rough work shirts over woolen trousers. On a chain around Father Serafim's neck, poking out from under his ample beard, there hung an embossed Orthodox cross made of dull brass. Around Father Sergius' neck hung a small wooden crucifix with a silver-hued corpus.

Father Serafim cut a slice of bread from the loaf, sprinkled it with a pinch of salt, and handed it to Alex.

"Welcome", he said.

"'Eat bread and salt, and speak the truth'", said Father Sergius. "That is one of our old proverbs."

"Yes, I know it well", Alex said before taking a large bite.

The priests regarded him with reflective expressions as he ate.

"Why are you here?" asked Father Serafim.

"In Russia", Father Sergius added.

Alex told them about his missing son and his seduction by the cult and concluded with a brief outline of his journey thus far. He explained that the search was not yet over and that he hoped the trail would end in Novosibirsk. When he had finished his account, the priests remained without speaking for some time. Father Sergius poured Alex another cup of tea.

"Is it discouraging?" he asked.

"At times it is discouraging", Alex said. "But, strangely, I am growing used to it. As if I have come through a barrier and am breathing an atmosphere I did not know existed. This new world is dangerous—but it is alive. It's like a leap from a bridge. Yes, like that. I feel as if I am falling—falling in a slow arc through the sky. Below me is a river, swift and deep. What awaits me beneath the surface, I cannot say—either life or death, I do not know. It is not for me to know. It seems this is what God wants for me now."

The priests continued to gaze at him with sober compassion.

"You speak in poetic form," said Father Sergius, "but the mystery you describe is not unknown to us."

"Kenosis", said Father Serafim. "One becomes empty and poor, and in that state the Kingdom of heaven is given to you."

"Ah, yes", Alex replied, eager to prove that he understood.

The priests exchanged a small smile.

"Have you had enough to eat?" Father Sergius asked Alex.

"Thank you, I'm full."

After a long, probing look into Alex's eyes—into his soul, Alex felt—Father Serafim stood.

"I must go to visit the people", he said. "Please be at rest, as if you are in your own home. I will return toward nightfall, and then we will have a supper."

He took an ankle-length black cassock from a wall hook and put it on over his clothing. This, combined with the cross and the beard, made him look every bit the image of a Russian Orthodox priest. He was a tall man, thin as well, and sturdy despite his age, which appeared to be somewhere in the seventh decade of life. His broad, scarred face was wrinkled, the eyes deeply set, grave, and full of thoughts. It struck Alex as odd that such an impressive figure was not the pastor of a prestigious parish in Moscow or Saint Petersburg, or the head of a monastery. Perhaps the man desired the blessedness of obscurity. Perhaps he was a saint.

Father Serafim bundled himself in his greatcoat, donned a fur cap with long earflaps, and slipped his feet into a pair of knee-high felt boots. He said good-bye to Alex and asked Father Sergius to step outside with him for a moment. The Catholic priest returned shortly, sat down at the table, and poured two more cups of tea.

"Are you feeling warmer, Aleksandr?"

"Yes, much warmer, thank you. I am sorry for the imposition. My presence must be an inconvenience for you."

"It is no imposition. We have a saying in Russia: Every visitor is to be received as Christ."

"As Christ?" said Alex, uncomfortably.

Father Sergius nodded.

"I won't be staying long. If the train is running again within a day or so, I will proceed to Novosibirsk. Before I go, however, I will make a contribution for your trouble."

"That is not necessary."

"But I see that you are..."

"Poor? Yes, we are poor in rubles. Yet we are the wealthiest men in the land."

Humbled by the priest's goodness, Alex fell silent.

"Aleksandr, what do you hope to achieve if you should reach your son in Novosibirsk?"

"I will try to reason with him, to warn him about the deceptions of the cult. And, God willing, he will be convinced to come home with me."

"I will pray for this. Father Serafim too will pray. He is already praying for your mission."

"I had not thought of it as a mission."

"You have traveled long and experienced much in your journey", the priest mused. He sipped from his cup and seemed lost for a moment in some private question. Looking up at last he said, "Father Serafim said to me as he was leaving that he hears a word in his heart about you. He says God may have brought you to Russia for reasons you cannot see. There is a mystery here that involves more than your son, I think."

"I doubt if one man can do much about this group that has taken my son. Maybe I can warn a few Russians about the danger."

"Possibly. Yet I sense this is not God's only purpose for your journey. You cannot stop a tide. Russia is filling quickly with aberrations of various kinds. We have our own indigenous cults, which are very dangerous, really. Then there are the philosophical Westerners who come here to borrow from the mystique of old Russia. And of course the God seekers looking for spiritual experience, and importers of oriental and Western sects." He paused. "And the people who attacked our train this morning."

"Yes!" Alex sat up straight. "Can it really have happened, and only a few hours ago?"

Father Sergius smiled. "Even *we* are endlessly surprised by this land's capacity for producing the irrational. Indeed, our history is spilling over with such aberrations."

"You are a passionate people."

"Yes, we are passionate. What kind of passions rule us, do you think?"

Recalling his experiences in Moscow, Alex saw at once so many dimensions of passion that he could not at first reply. It had seemed to him at the time, and did now, that these could be neither understood nor expressed in rational terms. Why, then, had they come to mind instinctively in response to the priest's question?

"What is passion?" Alex thought aloud. "Is it the intensity of feeling that seems to be everywhere in this country? Is it something deeper, beneath the surface waves of the emotions? I really don't know. But I do know that it's here, in a way that it's not there in my homeland."

"Perhaps you simply have not experienced it there."

"Perhaps."

"But you don't think so?"

Alex shook his head uncertainly. "There's something asleep in us, or drugged. You can't see it until you step outside of it."

He went on to describe his new consciousness of the tragic beauty of mankind, the totally confounding mixture of grief and joy he had felt in the underground mazes and sewers of Moscow.

Father Sergius listened, making no comment.

Alex concluded by saying, "I wouldn't call it a mystical experience. I don't know what it was. But it was unlike anything I had ever experienced before."

"Perhaps it was a moment of seeing."

"Yes, but I had already seen many thought-provoking things since crossing the border. This was another kind of seeing. It was..." He threw up his hands, exasperated by the lack of a vocabulary to express it.

"It was seeing with the heart?" Father Sergius suggested.

"Yes, maybe that was it."

"For the heart to see," Father Sergius added in a quiet voice, "it must be broken open."

It began to dawn on Alex that among the several unexpected events of this day, his meeting with the two priests was one of the more unusual.

"Father," he asked in a tone of tactful interest, "I see that you and Father Serafim are friends. Do you live here with him?"

"No. Like you, I am a visitor."

"You seem to know him well."

"We have been brothers under the cross for many years. We met in the camps. We are both zeks."

Alex absorbed this, then asked:

"Where do you live now?"

"For the most part, I travel. As I go, I preach, I offer Mass, I baptize and marry and hear confessions. I have no permanent home."

"But how do you live?"

"By the generous hearts of God's children. Some Catholic, some Orthodox, and even those who believe in nothing."

"You must have had an interesting life", Alex prompted. Having said it, he immediately regretted the facile word. Of course the man's life would have been *interesting*. As interesting as a wrestling match with a maddened bear.

After a few sips of tea, during which Father Sergius continued to stare at the floor, or at a panorama of memory, the priest looked up. Slowly, as if fighting some natural reluctance, he told this story:

"My ancestors were Russian Germans settled in Ukraine by Catherine the Great in the eighteenth century. I was born just prior to the war with Germany, in Astrakhan, a city on the estuary where Mother Volga flows into the Caspian Sea. My parents had fled there from a village near Odessa, during the time when Stalin was destroying the people of Ukraine. The Catholic villages and the Mennonite villages along the Black Sea were being wiped out, the people starved or shot, their houses bulldozed under the soil, so that not a stick of wood remained in memory of them. Our family escaped into the east.

"But then came Hitler. Stalingrad to the north of us was in torment, people dying everywhere. I cannot remember anything about that time, but my father later told me much, and even now I tremble to recall his words. Hunger, hunger—parents eating their dead children, children eating their dead parents. Horror. Horror unimaginable.

"My parents were people of limitless faith. They were God fearers. Even after the war, when everything was confused and no less bitter, they prayed for the grace to resist the temptation to hatred. They were saints, Aleksandr Graham. True saints. How beautiful they were, how full of kindness and peace, even when the worst was all around us. I know now what a terrible struggle it was for them to protect us from the evil temper of the age. What effort it cost them to overcome their own terrors! Not a hint of this did they let us see. Instead, they taught us to pray and to trust. They instructed us from the catechism they remembered, they worked hard, they waited, and they hoped for the coming of our Savior. 'Christ is coming', they whispered into our ears each night as my brothers and sisters and I fell into untroubled dreams.

"We lived in a chicken shed, on a farm run by a Kalmyk. We survived because my father was willing to work as a slave for him. He thought my father was a fool. They were uneducated people, my parents, very simple, but their faith was monumental. Though the Soviets tried to destroy the Catholic faith in Ukraine, and everywhere, there were priests who traveled back and forth through the net, hidden from the eyes of the state. Now and then a bishop. But many Catholic priests and bishops were caught and destroyed, sometimes betrayed by the very people they served. It was a time when hopelessness was a more constant enemy that our human adversaries.

"I will not tell you all the details of how I became a priest, for there is much that must remain hidden. The times are better now in some ways, but still unstable. This new government is trying to make democracy, they say. Will it last? Will we be cast back into the evil times? I do not know."

"Were you trained in an underground seminary?" Alex asked.

"Yes, though it would be incorrect to think of it as a building or a place."

"Are there many like you?"

"Most are dead. A new generation of priests and bishops is springing up like the first buds after a long winter. The Catholic Church is now permitted to function above ground. But we are small in number and greatly in need. There is still only one privileged religion in this land, and that is Russian Orthodoxy. At any time all ministers of religion who are foreigners can be deported. There is some harassment, of course, but these are technical things, paperwork mostly. Compared to what we suffered under the Soviets, the situation is mild."

"You say you met Father Serafim in prison. How were you arrested?"

"My arrest was a quiet and very common affair. I was offering Mass in the apartment of a Lithuanian family in Magadan. Do you know about Magadan? No? It is a city on the sea, in the Kolyma region of eastern Siberia. This family and some of their friends were Catholics, internal exiles who had been imprisoned during the 1930s and had been slave laborers for decades. When Stalin died, a lot of people were released from the Kolyma camps, but they had nowhere to go, so they stayed in Magadan.

"With us that day were some older Slovaks and a Ukrainian as well—all former zeks. Someone in their building must have notified the police, and they broke in during the Mass. It was a great blessing that we had received Communion at that point—the last I was to experience for many years to come. We all went to prison for a long time. I do not know where any of them are now.

"Serafim and I first met in a camp near Kuybyshev, where we noticed each other but did not have a chance to speak. Years later he told me that he knew immediately I was a priest of Christ. And I had recognized the same about him. Four years passed before we met again, when at a camp in the Perm region, close to the Urals, we found ourselves together in the same work brigade. There for the first time we were able to

475

speak. He heard my confession. I heard his. During that time many blessings came to us—very great blessings.

"One of the guards was a secret believer and brought me a little jar of wine. I was able to give half of it to Serafim for his Divine Liturgy. He had made bread for himself, secretly. My own Mass—well, for years I had been unable to say the Mass. My hands were broken, you see."

Alex glanced down at the priest's hands, noticing for the first time the misshapen joints and slashes of white scars.

"That was a long time ago", said Father Sergius with a reassuring smile. "I have a little arthritis now and then. After my hands healed, the guards watched me closely, because of all the classes of religious prisoner, none was considered more dangerous to the state than the Catholic. How good Serafim was to me! You cannot imagine how good. He was Christ to me. He, an Orthodox priest. I, a Catholic priest. He, an ethnic Russian; I, a German from Ukraine. He taught me forgiveness.

"You must understand how unusual he is, Aleksandr. In Russia, generally, a person's first loyalty is to his ethnic origins. Think of our numerous languages and tribes, our states within states. Add to this the religious and political loyalties, and you have an atmosphere of suspicion, or at least cautious insularity."

"You say he taught you forgiveness."

"I did not love Russia when I was younger", Father Sergius replied. "Russia crucified my Church, crucified my people, crucified my parents' homeland. Yet I have come to love her greatly. For she is not only the power of evil men, she is the humility of good men—and such goodness I have not met elsewhere."

"Nor such evil?"

Pain crossed Father Sergius' face. "Poor crucified Russia! Crucified by her enemies and crucified by her own children!"

"It seems that men such as Serafim are a sign of hope for the country's future."

"Yes, he is a sign. But Serafim is not typical. Though there are others like him, perhaps more than we realize, he represents a minority."

"Why was he in prison?"

Leading Alex to the "red corner", Father Sergius bowed before the icons, made small signs of the cross on his forehead, lips, and chest, and took a piece of paper from the shelf. He handed it to Alex, who read the following:

I have known gladness and sorrow. I have rejoiced and I have wept. The same happens to me now, but as the days pass, sorrow and gladness, joy and tears, pass with them. I have been praised and exalted. I have been criticized and abused. The same ones who praised me, have cursed; and the ones who abused me have turned to praise me—such is human constancy!

Poor is man from his mother's womb unto his grave. Born with a cry, he lives tossed up and down as a ship on the sea, and dies with tears. Once I lived in a house of plenty, now I live in a hut. And this too will pass. I had friends—some have become enemies, some have become false brothers. Where are the times when I was driven in a coach-and-four? Where are the days of reproach and unhappiness? These too pass away. Such is our existence in this world. Not so will be our life to come, of which the Word of God and our Faith assure us. Once begun, that life will never end.

"These are the words of Saint Tikhon of Zadonsk, an eighteenth-century bishop and ascetic. Father Serafim reads them every day. Did you know that Serafim was once the hegumen, the abbot, of a monastery here in Siberia? It was a humble place, named in honor of Saint Peter and Saint Paul. Very small, very poor, housing only a handful of men, it was left more or less in peace by the government because the monks were for the most part simple folk, and the monastery remote.

"One day in the year 1961, a visiting priest from Moscow took Serafim aside and confided to him that for some years, while functioning as a priest and later as a secretary to a bishop, he had operated as a KGB agent. He explained how he had been tricked into serving them by a combination of personal sin of a scandalous nature, by desire for advancement, and by the hope that his family would benefit. Furthermore, he told Serafim that some of Russia's bishops were colonels of the KGB. Of course, rumors of this were widespread—and certainly known by all the clergy. Until then, however, Serafim had reserved judgment.

"The former agent had repented utterly and begged to be sheltered in the monastery, where he hoped to live out the remainder of his days anonymously, making acts of reparation. Serafim agreed. Sorrowing over what he had learned, and praying throughout the night, he recalled a saying of Saint Tikhon that the great bishop had delivered to his own clergy: an exhortation that they must stand up and speak out against any form of injustice, wherever and whenever they encountered it. Tikhon's own life had borne witness to this ideal.

"Serafim fasted and prayed throughout the Great Lent. During that period, he dwelt alone in a forest hermitage, and there on Good Friday it came to him that he must make a pilgrimage to Moscow with the purpose of speaking to the patriarch. He did not know whether the patriarch was involved in the compromise, but he was given a spiritual understanding that he must go to him and speak a word of truth. The word he heard in his heart was this: 'He who would save his life will lose it.' This and only this, would he say.

"And so he departed on foot. It was a long and arduous journey. Throughout the spring and summer, he walked to the west. On occasion, he accepted short rides on horse-drawn carts. His health failed along the way, and he was often detained by sickness, and by officials, but each time he was miraculously freed to continue his journey. He arrived in Moscow on the thirteenth of August, 1961, a hundred years to the day since the canonization of Saint Tikhon.

"He went straightway to the palace of the patriarch, but he was refused admission. Again and again he went, day after day, praying and fasting, knocking on the door, but each time he was refused a meeting. Finally, he sent a written message through a bishop in the outer office. On a piece of paper he wrote the word the Lord had given to him to deliver. He signed his name and left, proceeding from there to Red Square. He was dressed in the robe of hegumen. In his right hand he bore a small icon of the Mother of God of Vladimir, and in his left he carried a knotted *chotki*.

" 'Lord Jesus Christ, have mercy on me, a sinner.' With this prayer on his lips and in his heart, Serafim stood before Lenin's tomb and begged God to end the reign of unrighteousness. Then, because the gates of the Kremlin were closed and he was unable to enter the great cathedrals within the walls, he crossed the square and stood in front of Saint Basil's. There he prayed for the reconversion of Russia and the purification of the Church. It came to him also that he must cry out the words 'He who would save his life will lose it.'

"This he did in a loud voice, holding the icon aloft, facing the Kremlin. A small crowd gathered about him. A few, mostly old people, bowed and made the sign of the cross and prayed with him. Then the KGB arrived. He spent the next fifteen years in the Gulag."

A long silence ensued, during which Father Sergius got up and threw more wood into the stove, then seated himself again. He seemed momentarily lost in his memories, and Alex did not want to intrude on them with the many questions that came crowding to his lips.

At last the priest glanced at the visitor.

"So, you see," he said, "it is complicated."

He stood abruptly and put on his coat. "Would you like to see the village?"

They went out and walked slowly around the cabins on lanes that had been pounded firm by the comings and goings of the villagers. That people were busy with their lives inside their homes was evident from the smoke rising from all chimneys, the sound of a woman's voice complaining about something, a laugh, a baby's cry. A few dogs followed them in a friendly way, grinning when the priest patted their heads. An old man loading his arms with firewood smiled and nodded when he spotted Father Sergius. The priest bowed slightly in return and greeted him. The old man then asked about the rumor he had heard of barbarians destroying the railroad. Father Sergius explained what had happened and introduced Alex as a traveler from the train. After a few minutes they walked on. It did not take long to circle the village, and they soon found themselves back at the church.

"It is consecrated to Saints Peter and Paul", said Father Sergius. "Shall we go in?"

Stepping inside it, they entered a dark space that seemed filled with whispers and the shadows of long-departed souls. There were no benches or kneelers. The walls and rafters were black logs, and the floor was made of wooden planks that glowed deep gold wherever a sunbeam entered through the small windows. Though they were the only people present, it seemed to Alex as his eyes adjusted to the dim light, that the images on the icon screen separating the nave from the sanctuary were a cloud of witnesses. Father Sergius bowed toward the iconostasis and made the sign of the cross. Alex did the same. For a time they stood side by side in silence.

"East and West must avoid cultural nostalgia", Father Sergius said at last. "Each must seek the true source in a way that has not been done since the very first centuries of the Church. We must seek the heart of Christ himself."

Alex nodded in agreement.

"Tell me, Aleksandr, what do you really see when you look at us? At Russia, I mean."

Alex gave this question some thought before answering:

"I came to this land with one purpose, and this you already know—to find my son and return home as quickly as possible. I arrived in your country anxious and distracted. I came here with a certain Western concept of a society in crisis—organized crime rising, political instability, poverty. It seems to me that these are elements of the situation, but when I prayed before the icon of Our Lady of Vladimir in Moscow, I felt her great love for your people."

"Yes, she loves us. But we are ever abandoning her. This is our condition, this is our *khamstvo*, our shame."

"Would she ignore the prayers of the saints and the countless martyrs who have shed their blood on this soil? How your springtime will come, I cannot guess, but my heart tells me it will."

"It is interesting to hear the word *heart* from the lips of a foreigner."

"Do you think Westerners don't have hearts?" Alex asked.

"You have hearts. You are human, so you have hearts."

"Yes, but sleeping or drugged hearts, aroused only when there is a new pleasure to be had."

"We tend to think of the West as all mind, all rational thought."

"Far from it."

"What you must guard against, Aleksandr, is your own nostalgic feeling for us. What you fail to realize is that our situation in Russia can go either way—to God or to Satan, to Holy Russia or to Gog and Magog."

"I'm sorry if I'm superficial, but I can't help believing that Russia will find her soul again."

"You love Russia, even though, as you readily admit, you do not understand her. Why is this?"

Alex shook his head. "I don't know."

"Do you see something of yourself in us?"

"We are very different. We haven't suffered as you have."

"You have suffered. The West suffers from the same beast that is devouring our soul."

"I once thought so too. But now I see that your sufferings are catastrophic. Ours are small by comparison."

"Smaller, but relentless."

"Yet we have freedom."

"Freedom? Yes, but what exactly is freedom?"

The answer seemed so obvious that Alex refrained from saying it.

"Well, my eyes are Eastern eyes, and yours are Western eyes", the priest sighed. "Eyes are always translating, always interpreting according to their own preconceptions, filtering out important things."

The discussion had taken its toll on Alex. Though he would have liked to continue, no more thoughts came to mind. Sensing this, the priest bowed to the iconostasis, and they left the church.

It was now late in the afternoon, and dusk was upon them. Entering the little rectory at the back of the building, Alex welcomed the warmth and noted that the oil lamp and candle in the corner seemed more radiant. The charm of the room was augmented by this soft light: the subdued colors, the glowing icons, the quaint log walls, the atmosphere full of

incense and birch smoke, the soulful priest gazing thoughtfully at him—all of these contributed to his sense of having
stepped back in time. It was as if the air itself was filled with
an unobtrusive grace, yet one so tangible Alex almost reached
out to touch it.

Not long after, they heard Father Serafim stomping the
snow from his boots outside the door. When he entered the
room, Alex stared at him solemnly, trying to absorb all that
Father Sergius had related about the man's past. For his part,
Father Serafim nodded a greeting, rubbed his hands together,
and said, "Well, my friends, let us have a little supper."

21. *Petropavlovskaya Poustyn*

Despite his extreme fatigue, Alex could not sleep. He lay awake on the coffin-sofa listening to the sounds of two old men snoring on their cots, wind humming in the stovepipe, the fire quietly crackling in the stove. The icon candle flickered red and gold, making the stripes of the logs and their chinking extend and contract as the wick performed its tiny dance. Strangely, his anxiety over Andrew had withdrawn for a time, and as he gazed at the *krasny ugol*, he was at peace. Beneath the blankets and a fur coverlet, he felt safer than he had for a long time. All his muscles relaxed, and he realized that for more than two months he had lived in a state of constant tension. He began to breathe slowly and rhythmically, as if he were inhaling and exhaling the very streams of the Holy Spirit. This was without emotion of any kind. It was a sense of profound rest.

How long he remained in this state he did not know, for he was only half-awake. He became fully alert when the door of the cabin scraped open and a vertical strip of stars appeared. A shadow figure crossed it, bent over, threw something inside, then pulled the door shut. Whoever it was had not entered, for Alex could hear the sound of footsteps crunching faintly on the hard-pack snow in the yard. The steps faded, and all that remained was the wind.

From the direction of the door came pattering footsteps and a low rumble like a miniature motor.

Although on the whole Alex was not overly fond of cats, he supposed they had their purposes. By the light of the vigil candle, he picked out its small form near the stove. When he made imitation purring noises with his lips, it ceased prowling about the room, turned, and moved on stealthy feet toward him. Stopping in midstride, it sniffed the air, came to some conclusion, and leaped onto his chest, where it began to purr loudly, nosing his face in an investigative manner.

"Shh, shh", he said, stroking its back.

Satisfied that Alex was no more than an ordinary fixture, the cat curled up on top of his chest and settled itself for sleep.

"Sasha," he whispered into its ear, "would you mind removing yourself?"

But the cat did not understand English. The same message repeated in Russian failed to make an impression. Then he spoke to it in a universal gesture, pushing it off his body. The cat promptly jumped back up again, though it seemed to have gotten the point. It contented itself by curling into a ball by his pillow. Its purring was thunderous.

Not wanting to disturb the priests by an open struggle with the creature, Alex accepted a truce, put his hands behind his head, and continued to look up into the darkness above until he fell asleep.

The lid on the stovetop clinked, and Alex opened his eyes to see Father Serafim feeding wood into it. Birch smoke hazed the air, and the sunlight pouring through the window transformed it into a luminous cloud. Father Sergius was nowhere to be seen. The cat sprawled beside the stove, chewing a fish head. The cat's fur was white, and it had a black smudge across its nose.

Coming fully awake, Alex sat up, stretched, and yawned. He rubbed his eyes and squinted.

"Tea, soon, Aleksandr", the priest said, without looking at him.

Alex put his bare feet onto the floor and instantly regretted it. The floor was like ice. He pulled on his socks, dressed quickly, and stood.

"Did Katusha bother you?" the priest asked. "Did you sleep well?"

"I rested well and slept a little. Is this Katusha?" he said, pointing at the cat.

"Yes. She comes to visit sometimes. She belongs to a neighbor. He is lending her to us for the mice."

"A nice cat."

"The mice do not think so", said the priest, setting a pot of buckwheat porridge called *kasha* to boil on the stove. "Her master left early this morning for the rail station in Barabinsk, a town to the east of us. There is a post office and telephone there. When I spoke with him yesterday he promised he would try to learn whatever he could about the condition of the bridges. He will return this evening with news, if there is any."

"Then I am forced to accept your hospitality for the day", Alex said.

"Forced?" said the priest, turning around with a look.

"You are very generous to a stranger", Alex tried to explain.

"Do you fear that you are a burden?" said Father Serafim, turning back to his cook pot, stirring the kasha with a wooden spoon.

"Yes, I do."

"You are not a burden."

Alex accepted this at face value and admonished himself. He must stop this Western thinking! This endless projection of his isolationism!

"Where is Father Sergius?" he asked.

"He has gone to a cabin farther down the river—the *poustinia*. It's a place where we go sometimes to pray."

Poustinia, the "little desert", thought Alex.

Father Sergius returned not long after, and the three men sat down to a simple breakfast: hot kasha, tea, and a few salty slices of smoked fish. The food energized Alex and made him eager for whatever the day might bring. He had many things to ask the priests but decided to wait until the meal was over. Aware of his noisiness—yes, he, Alexander Graham, the most silent of Westerners, was full of noise—he did not give in to the impulse to fire off a cannonade of inquiries.

Let this winter world reveal what it will in its own time, he thought to himself.

Without being asked, he got up and washed the dishes in a tub. The priests observed him silently, no doubt trying to make sense of this odd tourist from the West.

"I am going back to the poustinia, Aleksandr", Father Sergius said. "Would you like to accompany me?"

"Very much, Father." Then, because he could repress himself no longer, he added, "There is so much I would like to ask you."

"The poustinia is a place of silence, but we can talk on the way."

Bidding Father Serafim good-bye, Father Sergius slung a knapsack over his shoulder and went out, Alex following. They made their way down to the river on the footpath and turned north. The wind had blown much of the river clear of snow during the night, and the surface had become a hard, fast highway, rippled sufficiently to increase the traction underfoot, making their journey easier. "Six months of the year we walk on water", said the priest with a smile.

"How far is the poustinia?" Alex asked.

"As close as your heart. But in terms of footsteps, it is about three kilometers."

Alex began to ply him with questions. Several subjects were covered during their walk, and among them he learned the following:

The people who had attacked the train the previous day were a Siberian branch of a group of Russians who had established communities near the major cities in European Russia. It was fairly certain that no agitators or cultists from the West were involved. They were, for the most part, young people trying to imitate whatever cultural patterns they had gleaned from television and films. Their encampments squatted on unused state land. They tried to survive by hunting and fishing and by begging in the streets of Moscow and Saint Petersburg during the annual influx of summer tourists. The media had devoted some attention to them, and their publicity events were well attended by tours from Germany, France, and America. Most of the members had once been atheists and now threw themselves wholeheartedly into a belief system that offered spiritual vision, community, and cultural identity. They were considered to be harmless fanatics. A mystical religious sect, they worshipped the spirits of the earth, combining diverse elements of ancient pagan ritual with the traditional Russian love of the Motherland. They were often to be seen at public protests against ecology abuse. The synchronized attack upon the Trans-Siberian Railroad was their first act of overt violence.

"I noticed that you found it amusing, Father", Alex said.

"The violence is not amusing, nor the confusion that it represents. But you must admit, Aleksandr, it was a surprise."

Alex asked more about Father Sergius' life. Was he attached to one of the Catholic dioceses in the Russian Federation? What was his work exactly?

To both of these questions the priest responded with a certain vagueness, as if he were still functioning in an underground Church.

"I am under proper ecclesial authority", he said after a considerable pause. "My presence in this country is legal, but I am involved in a labor that is hidden. I am known to the bishops of this land and work with their permission. But it is not ordinary work."

"A special mission", Alex prompted.

"Nothing so dramatic, if you mean an important clandestine project. No, my labors are small in the scale of things.

I am under obedience to travel through the land praying in reparation for the sins that have been committed against her people—all her people. If a soul comes to our Lord through my work, I send him to the ordinary parishes, where he will find a spiritual home."

"Then you are a pilgrim."

"Yes, in a sense."

Alex's questions now returned to the subject of Father Serafim.

"After he was released from the Gulag, did Father Serafim return to his monastery?"

Father Sergius nodded. "After he was set free, he was unwelcomed by the hierarchy and went homeless. He wandered on foot for many months. He worked at manual labor and saved money for train fare. He still had some strength, but he was much older by then. He was no longer able to walk thousands of kilometers. Finally, when it became legal to travel wherever one wished, he made the journey back to his monastery. Upon arrival there, he found that not a trace of it existed. Not a stick, not a stone remained. After all those years, the taiga had reclaimed the land, and a forest of saplings was growing on the spot. He remained there for three days, praying and fasting. He felt the great darkness of the place. Do you know what I mean by this?"

"No."

"In the places where great evil has occurred, a presence of evil lingers. One feels it in eastern Siberia, especially the Kolyma, where the worst atrocities took place. But it can be felt anywhere. Thus did Serafim understand that his brothers had been destroyed. He alone had been spared—and through an act of holy foolishness. Because he had obeyed the call of God, because he had been willing to lose his life, he had gained his life."

"Not without suffering."

"Not without unimaginable suffering. Life always has a cost, you see. For him it cost not only the years of imprisonment, the loss of the monastery, and all he had worked for as a young monk, but the destruction of his brethren as well. This was the most terrible suffering of all. It cast him into the test that had afflicted the bishops and metropolitans. Should they have compromised in order to save the lives of the flock? Or should they not have compromised, thus condemning the flock to more severe persecution and possibly extinction? Now he asked these questions of himself. Was the blood of his brothers upon his head? Had his pilgrimage to speak the truth in Moscow been an act of disguised spiritual pride? Had others been forced to pay for his heroic gesture? With many such questions did the devil torment him."

"Surely, Father, he must have known the truth of this. With all his prayer, his sacrifices, and the years in the Gulag, God must have given him some certainty about his mission."

"Ah, but certainties have a way of crumbling when every human strength has been battered down or stripped away to nothing. When he knew for certain what the cost had been, he was devastated. He was greatly reduced in strength and had traveled long and hard roads to reach his beloved sanctuary only to find that Satan had obliterated it. Do you think even the greatest saints are invulnerable to temptation? Would you or I have resisted it? I do not know if I could have endured such a trial. He was weakened, and in that weakness the adversary struck again and again, seeking to tear his faith from him. He later told me that it was the worst struggle of his life."

"It is plain to see that he has recovered from the experience."

"Recovered? It depends on what you mean by the word. Did the devil overcome him during that terrible wrestling match? No. Serafim has faith such as is refined only in the darkest of fires. But he is not unchanged by his sufferings. He is a poor man, not only theoretically or symbolically or mystically. He has become a little one. He is God's humiliated. He is *urodivi*. Thus, he wins many souls to our Savior."

"This word, *urodivi*—a fool."

"*Urodivi Khrista radi*—he was, and is, a kind of Christ-fool. Did you know, Aleksandr, that in this land there is a long tradition of holy fools, similar to ours in the West? Think of Saint Francis of Assisi. Think of Benedict Labre the beggar of Rome, or Philip Neri. These are our *urodivoi*. In Russia such men were numerous, and whenever the official Church was silenced, they increased in number. They were despised and rejected, possessing nothing, not even their own lives. They would go anywhere and do anything to spread the Gospel. They were signs of contradiction, drawing many souls to Christ."

"And Father Serafim continues the tradition."

Father Sergius nodded. "Yes, but not as a pious form of life that one puts on like an overcoat. Rather, he lives this mystery without thinking about it. It is not something he *does*; it is something he *is*."

"Because of your regard for each other, it seems you have bridged the division that exists between the Churches of East and West."

"What do you mean by *bridged*?" the priest asked, furrowing his brow. "Do you think we have dispelled the effects of the Great Schism in one stroke? No, of course we have not. In the camps, we heard each other's confessions and strengthened each other through prayer. That was a situation *in extremis*. Charity to souls overrides ecclesiastical law when death is near."

"But—"

"Ah, you begin to feel the frustration and pain of our division, do you not, Aleksandr? Of course you do, because you love the Bride. Yes, you love her; this I can plainly see. Why else did Serafim and I recognize you on the train—know you not so much in the mind as in the heart?"

Alex was flattered by this, but his curiosity was still not satisfied.

"Do you attend his Divine Liturgy and receive the Eucharist from him?"

"No. I stand at the back of this little church and I pray. We bear the pain of division as part of the cost of healing it. Both he and I are in complete obedience to the positions of our Churches. I respect the laws of his Church because that is what charity demands at this time. Charity does not batter down the gates of a wall in the name of love or in the name of a unity that does not yet exist."

"And what does he feel about our Mass?"

"This is not a matter of what he feels or I feel. He believes that the Body and Blood of our Savior are present on my altar just as I believe in the Real Presence on his. Yet he does not partake of mine, nor I of his. He prays as I offer the Holy Mass. I pray as he offers the Divine Liturgy. Our union is of the heart and spirit. He and I yearn for the time when we will be a single reunited Body. Some day it will come. It *will* come. But we do not pretend it has already arrived."

"How do you live with such a contradiction?"

"By understanding it. We rarely discuss it, and we never argue about the theological difficulties involved. I am embarrassed to admit to you that I am a doctor of theology. Serafim has less education, but his spiritual wisdom is vast and deep. He is great in the Kingdom. Even so, 'greater' and 'lesser' are not our concern. We pray and love."

During all this conversation the Little-Little Ob had wound circuitously through the flatland, the forest of leafless trees on both banks thickening as the two men went. A single crow flew low above them beating its way upriver, turning its head left and right as if searching for a desert prophet. The sun climbed higher, and the air warmed a few degrees. There was no wind.

Presently they came to a bend where a footpath on the right cut down through the snowbanks to the edge of the ice. Father Sergius began to climb. Alex went up behind, slowly, for the bank was fairly steep at this point, and lacking Siberian footgear, he kept slipping and sliding backward. The priest offered a hand and pulled him up. When they reached the top, Alex saw a small log cabin nestled among the trees. Its roof was heavily laden with snow, a snowdrift sweeping up to it from the northern side. On the south side stood a few cords of stacked firewood. Smoke rose in a thin line from the metal chimney pipe.

"Petropavlovskaya Poustyn", said the priest. "It is not the Peter and Paul Fortress, as you can see. It is a trapper's cabin. The fur harvest has been poor for several years, and the trapper, a member of Serafim's parish, has no use for it. He permits us to use it whenever we have need."

Father Sergius went in first through the unlocked entrance, and Alex followed, ducking his head under the low door beam. Inside, he saw that the little desert lived up to its name. It was a single room, roughly ten feet square. On the wall opposite the door was a small window. To the left was a sleeping bench covered with a fur rug; to the right, a cast-iron stove. Beside it, nailed to the wall, was an unornamented Byzantine cross painted bright red. Beneath this was a shelf on which stood a copy of the Scriptures and two little icons, one of Saint Peter and the other of Saint Paul. A paraffin lamp hung suspended on a chain from a rafter. The only other furniture was a three-legged stool and a wooden box that served as a table. On the side of the box, stamped in Cyrillic letters, were the words "Winter Ermine, Third Class". The floor was unvarnished birch planks.

Father Sergius sat down on the stool and gestured that Alex should sit on the sleeping bench. The priest took a loaf of bread and a water bottle from his pack and put them on the wooden box. After that, he seemed to withdraw into himself, peacefully, saying nothing. The silence grew. Without effecting any obvious change in the atmosphere, the silence began to stretch into a seamless flow of eternity, and so unobtrusive was this that it did not immediately register on Alex. The only evidence that some sort of special law was at work lay in the fact that both men were content to remain motionless and without comment for a good deal longer than was customary in either of their cultures.

A crow flew over the cabin, leaving a trace of caws in the air. Shaking himself, Alex cleared his throat and said, "Well, I should leave you now. I can find my way back to the village."

Father Sergius merely smiled in acknowledgment.

Alex stood.

"Aleksandr, stay for a while. Sit down."

Though there was no tone of command in this, Alex instinctively obeyed.

"Speak with me a little", said the priest.

"Speak with you in the poustinia? Father, I have been doing nothing but speaking. I am ashamed of my verbosity."

"Ashamed? Why is this?"

Alex shook his head. "I do not know."

Once again Father Sergius fixed him with a probing look.

"Speak to me about your mission, if you will."

"My mission? I am a father. I am looking for my son. It's not going very well. That's all there is to it."

"Why do you think it is not going well?"

Feeling some gratitude that the priest was interested in his tale of woes, Alex began to recount all that had happened, beginning with the fall through the ice at the Halcyon dam almost three months before. Listening throughout with an expression of concern, Father Sergius said nothing as Alex went on, never taking his eyes from him. It came to Alex that he had been carrying the great load of his troubles in a state of solitude, or more precisely a state of isolation. He had not given this much thought because his habitual state had been one of isolation. Throughout his life he had preferred it to be so. Now, however, he saw how impossible it was for any man to prevail in such a condition. Moreover, he saw that it had taken its toll.

"I regret some of it", said Alex, rubbing a hand over his canary hair. "Lying, deceiving, ridiculous disguises."

"The deception was only for the purpose of arranging a meeting with your son?"

"Yes, it was."

"For getting past unjust barriers."

Alex nodded.

Father Sergius gazed for a few moments at the cross nailed to the wall. When he looked back at Alex, his eyes contained something that had not so far been evident during their conversations. What Alex had taken for a humming of intellectual engines, he now saw was a different process. In the priest's glance was some distillate of spirit—a spirit purified in long, hard experience. To call it a light or an inspiration would have crudely approximated the phenomenon. It seemed to him that what he now saw in the man's eyes was a window opening onto the infinite; they were, in fact, nearly iconographic in their stillness and presence.

"Russia is a land where truth has been crucified", Father Sergius said at last.

"My land also", Alex replied.

"In my land, the truth is betrayed not in the name of affluence but for the purpose of survival. Few are the souls who do not maintain two sets of standards, two sets of accounts, two moral systems. This in modern form is what we call *Aziatchina*, 'Asianness'. Under the Tartar domination, we first learned to survive by cheating and manipulation, cruelty and slaughter. *Stalintchina* drove us deeper into it. And now the new *Kapitaltchina* rewards it. The power of money has become absolute. To a degree all men are deceived into this way of thinking."

"All?"

"I am not speaking of the exterior form, as if the problem could be reduced to questions of socialism versus capitalism. I am speaking of the division within all hearts, East and West."

"Isn't it in the mind?"

"The fracture lines in the mind run in every direction, but they have their roots in the heart. Do you see what Satan has done to all of us? Whenever he cannot entice us into direct evil, he will try to allure us into passive evil. No, that is not the exact word—I should say that he always seeks to deceive men of good will by offering them what appears to be a *lesser* evil."

"You mean he offers them a terrible evil on one hand and an apparently small evil on the other?"

"Yes. This is his great subtlety with us. He has observed us for millennia. The devil is an outstanding psychologist."

"So we choose the lesser evil, thinking we have been saved from the great evil, when all the while his real purpose was to bring about the evil we have chosen."

Father Sergius nodded. "He wishes to infect everything, every particle of creation, with compromise. If he cannot entice a man into participating directly in his Great Revolt, he will work to infect him with its lesser attributes."

"And does so by presenting us with false choices."

"Yes. Let me give you an example. Let us say that you are a prisoner in a camp. It is the middle of Siberian winter. Each year many men in your barracks die of exposure to the weather or from brutality, sickness, and hunger. There is never enough food. Men are worked to death—death by physical exhaustion, death by exhaustion of the spirit, death by absolute demoralization. Despair kills as effectively as the bullet and the virus, and more dreadfully, for it corrupts the soul as well.

"Let us say that in your camp, the camp where Aleksandr Graham is a zek, there has been a theft of bread. One of the zeks steals a quarter kilo from the kitchen. You see him do it. You know who he is. You say nothing to him, but the knowledge is now lodged permanently in your memory. The guards measure everything to the smallest gram. They know that the bread is missing. Such theft is punishable by death. They conduct an investigation. Now comes the first level of temptation: they offer a double ration of bread to whoever informs on the thief. Although you are starving, this is not so difficult to resist. It is not even a question because you know you cannot kill a man unjustly, and certainly not for an extra bit of food in your stomach.

"Then comes the second level of temptation: the guards declare that unless the thief is turned over to them, one of the zeks will be chosen at random and executed. Ah, now the moral problem becomes more complex. Your silence will condemn a man to death, almost certainly an innocent man. You wrestle with this more than you did with the first temptation. You hear the arguments rage in your thoughts—remember that when you are hungry and exhausted, it is very difficult to think clearly. Even so, it does not take long for you to see that the authorities want to trick you into preserving life by taking life. They want you to participate in their evil. But you realize that you cannot let the system turn you into an extension of their apparatus.

"No one comes forward. Now they pull a man from the huddled group of prisoners and throw him to the ground. You know he is not the thief. You stand paralyzed as they shoot him in the head. Blood spills out onto the snow. A pool of it spreads toward you. The loud report of the gun, your own terror, your agony of mind—it all combines, and suddenly you are no longer sure of anything so finely tuned as a moral nuance. You say to yourself, *Surely his blood is on my head. Did my silence kill him?*

"Now they pull a second man from the crowd and throw him to his knees. A guard puts a gun to the man's temple. The man's eyes are open wide, staring at the ground, staring at the end of everything, at the annihilation of hope. He is an animal searching desperately inside himself for a scrap of manhood. His eyes—oh, his eyes are the most terrible thing you have ever seen.

"You know who the thief is. You know he is standing only a few paces away from you, hiding in anonymity. He too has become no more than an animal in a herd of frightened animals. You plead with him silently to be a man again, to give himself up. He does not move. He does not speak.

"The commandant spots you in the crowd. He knows you are a Christian. He knows you do not sin. He despises your little code of ethics that he believes to be founded only on superstition, but he thinks those superstitions might be useful to him. He comes to you and asks if you know who took the bread.

"Now the temptation becomes immediate, personal, proposing new subtleties. Of course, you cannot say who the guilty one is, for that would kill him. Now the wrestling of conscience grows intense, and very confused. It is not a matter of careful thought; it is a struggle of spirits, forms, wordless meanings screaming in your confused mind. Only a little scrap of will holds firm.

"You wonder if you should give him the only thing you can give. Should you say, 'Yes, I know who took the bread'? That would be the truth, would it not? Would there be a lie in it?

"Now all eyes are turned to you. The commandant bellows at you. He demands to know the thief's identity. You are silent. They can break you—they can make you tell, if they decide to torture you—but for the moment you have the power of silence. 'Speak!' he shouts, and slaps you hard in the face. Now you are shaking in every limb; fear is a fire scorching you from within. You try to pray, but it is almost impossible to pray, for every element of your humanity is overwhelmed by fright.

"'If you will not speak,' says the commandant, 'then at least point out the thief to me.'

"Still you are silent. What to do? They could easily kill you for your silence. Why should you, you who are innocent, pay for the sin of the thief? You shake; you do not know what to do; you are about to open your mouth.

"Suddenly, a man steps forward from the crowd. Not the thief. Another man. He comes before the commandant. He points to his own heart.

"'So, *you* are the thief!' screams the commandant.

"Once again the man points to his own heart.

"Everyone is stunned. Who would have believed it of him, for he is the best, the strongest, and the humblest of the zeks. It is unthinkable that such a man would steal. Even in the camps, where starving men have a moral right to steal bread without guilt, this is one who is scrupulously honest. Never would he let a fellow zek be shot for his crime! And yet one has just been shot. Only you and the real thief know he is innocent.

"Everyone is confounded. The zeks are perplexed. The commandant is uncertain. The guards are confused. You can see the doubt on every face: Not him? Surely not this one? The silence becomes unbearable. No one is able to break it. At this moment, which for prisoners and jailers alike is the very axis of history, anything said would have completely exposed their souls. All eyes drop to the ground.

"Finally, because he is a man of power and burdened with responsibility, the commandant looks up. He gestures to a guard; then he gives the word of command, and the guard drives the butt of his gun into the face of the prisoner. He collapses to the ground. He is struck again and again. Blows from the rifle, kicks, punches. Other guards join in the beating. When the man is a heap of pulp, they drag him away, leaving a bloody trail. This trail crosses the river of blood spilled by the first man. A cross is now written in the snow."

Seeing the whole scene with his mind's eye as if he had personally witnessed it, Alex sat upright.

"This really happened! It was Serafim!"

Father Sergius nodded. "Yes, it was Serafim. When he stepped forward, he was offering his life."

"Why did they not kill him?"

"I do not know why. Was it because the hand of God restrained them for a purpose that even now we do not know? For five months we had no word of him, and then he was returned to us. As you see, he bears the marks of the beating, yet his soul has only grown stronger because of it."

Alex shook his head. "But...but what does it mean?"

"Is that not obvious?"

"I see that he saved the innocent man who was about to be executed and also the guilty one. But—"

"Serafim did not speak a single false word. He spoke with his life. He spoke with his silence. He merely pointed to his heart. Do you know what he meant by that?"

"I suppose he was trying to tell the commandant that he was the thief. But that was a lie, was it not?"

"When he pointed to his heart, he was saying, 'Take me, if you must have a victim. Sin dwells in me, and without the grace of God I am capable of all sin. I too am a thief.' Those were his thoughts, and that was his meaning."

"You were the man who saw the thief, weren't you? You were the man the commandant questioned. So in the end Father Serafim also saved your life."

"No, Aleksandr. I was the man on the snow with the gun at his head, the man staring at the annihilation of all hope."

"And the thief...?"

500

"One of the nameless. He never confessed. He watched the sacrifice being made for him, and even then he clung to his own life. Did the sacrifice change him? I do not know. What became of him I cannot say, but I am certain that if he is still alive he has not forgotten it. He remembers it every day of his life."

Daylight was now waning in the window. Beyond the small square of glass, the forest colors shifted imperceptibly, shadows deepening, the hillocks of snow turning from pale rose to red as the sun dipped into the western horizon. Father Sergius got up and lit the paraffin lamp. He put more wood into the firebox of the stove.

Alex asked the priest to hear his confession. Father Sergius removed an old purple stole from his pocket and placed it about his neck. Alex knelt before him, and the priest draped one end of the stole over the penitent's shoulder. Alex spoke to him about his moment of rage in Moscow when anger had erupted into hatred, the desire to smash, the desire to kill. Digging deeper, he examined his heart with new awareness and told the priest what he saw.

"At the core of my being", Alex said in a voice full of sadness, "is a fear that God really is not my Father. I have believed with my mind that he is all he says he is. But in my heart I have lived as if it were not so."

The priest replied:

"You describe the human heart. In the innermost being of each man is a universe. There are stars and empty spaces, spiral galaxies and supernovas, solar systems and terrifying black holes. Why are we so surprised when we discover the darkness alongside the splendid beauty of light?"

"But the darkness should not be there!"

"No, it should not be there, but it is. He who begins to recognize this is able to open the gates to the light that Christ wishes to pour into the dark places."

The rite of confession was concluded in formal fashion. Afterward, Father Sergius asked if Alex would like him to celebrate Mass. Alex wanted this very much. The priest explained that he was permitted to offer the Ukrainian Catholic liturgy as well as that of the Latin Church. However, he had come prepared only for the Roman Mass.

And so Mass was said on a wooden crate in a tiny log cabin in the heart of Siberia as the sky turned black and the universe slowly manifested its glory. The Scriptures for the day commemorated an early Roman martyr, Saint Polycarp. Alex was moved by the first reading, a passage from the book of Revelation. It was the Lord speaking to one of the seven churches, exhorting her to stand firm, not to be afraid during the coming trials.

As he read it aloud from Father Sergius' lectionary, he felt as never before the universality of the Church, for today this Scripture was being proclaimed in every language across the face of the earth. Yet the Russian text contained its own music, with its flavor and its solemn character heightened by the stark surroundings—a little island of light within while all around the cabin night was falling on the ice void.

Throughout the remainder of the Mass, he asked for the grace to overcome fear. For the first time since his fall through the ice at the Halcyon dam three months before, he repeated a prayer he had made to God shortly before that event.

Do whatever you want with me.

At the Consecration and after receiving Communion, he repeated it with earnestness, and with it came peace.

As Father Sergius packed his vestments and Mass articles into his knapsack, he asked Alex if he wished to remain in the poustinia. After consideration, Alex said that he would like to stay; indeed, he needed a time of solitude.

"Good", replied the priest. "He who would know the bounty of the Lord must dwell in an uninhabitable land."

Alex smiled at the paradox.

"Let those who would become citizens of heaven become guests of the desert", Father Sergius added.

"What should I do here?" Alex asked.

"Do nothing."

"Nothing?"

"Wait upon the Lord. Listen. Pray. Read sacred Scripture. Perhaps you need only sleep. For each person, it is a different experience. Sometimes the Lord merely wishes you to rest. At other times he will speak quietly; at times, not at all. Sometimes there is consolation; at other times there is struggle. Whatever occurs is his gift."

Father Sergius made his departure, promising to return the following day around noon. After watching him walk upriver on the highway of ice under a canopy of stars, Alex went back into the cabin and shut the door. Relishing the peace that lingered in his heart and saturated the room, he stoked the fire, trimmed the lamp, and sat on the stool by the box table. He ate a third of the loaf of bread and drank from the bottle of water. Then he lay down on the sleeping bench and closed his eyes.

When he awoke, he squinted at the dial on his watch. It had stopped. He rewound it, listened to the soft ticking, then stood up, wondering what time it was. It was difficult to say with certainty, but a glance out the window at the position of the stars indicated that several hours had passed.

Why do I need to know the time? he asked himself. *I don't need to know.*

Removing the watch, he put it away in a pocket of his greatcoat, then sat down again on the bench, his back leaning against the log wall.

"I will not *do* anything", he said. "I will be still. I will be inactive."

With that, his mind churned into action, launching a convoluted process of sorting ideas and information.

"Enough thinking! Be quiet, now!"

But his mind would not remain quiet for more than a few
minutes at a time.

He knelt on the floor before the cross and turned his attention away from a thousand avenues of thought and the images
that sprang up in his imagination. The images were the most
intrusive, pleasant but very strong: the hills of the Clementine,
the woman recumbent on the winter fields with the jewel
of Halcyon on her breast. Carol dancing in his arms—I'm
nobody, who are you?—three prancing deer. Andrew holding
up a sports trophy, his face beaming. The girl from Smolensk
glowing with restored innocence. Alyosha clean and happy,
his wounds healed. A kingfisher plunging, seizing an underwater fish and flashing with it into the sky.

The images changed: a leap from a bridge under a beating sun, his body falling, shattering on the ice of the frozen
Clementine. Neva, Moskva, Little-Little Ob. Kolya skimming
away; screaming children swept over the lip of a dam; kingfishers bursting into flame, reduced to ashes. Plunging aircraft,
blizzards, an iron man-trap clamping his body in its jaws; a
cemetery below a grocery store where a plastic pony shattered
into pieces. Angus Graham swigging his whiskey, Alex swigging from that same bottle decades later, Andrew swigging
from a bottle of occult spirits. Jacob erecting a Meccano tower
of Babel, the tower falling. Andrew tossing his Swiss knife
into the air, watching with hypnotized wonder as it reaches
the height of its upward flight, turns in slow motion and
begins its descent like a spent missile, the boy's eyes wide and
glistening with vital exultation as he watches the blade fall,
fall, fall and pierce the temple of his skull. Blood spurting.
Dad! Dad, Andy's cut himself! Furious Jacob. Anxious-furious
Alex. Stone Giant brooding over a captive son.

His fist ramming into the faceless face of Gustav Bloch; a rifle butt smashing the face of Father Serafim.

"What?" said Alex, aloud, in the silent cabin. "What is happening to me?"

An arrow bolted straight toward him, so vividly that his eyes flew open and he jerked away before it pierced his skull.

He laughed nervously. How real it had seemed! Where did this cinematic barrage come from? His tired brain, of course! He supposed it was like a waking dream, an eruption of the subconscious demanding resolution.

Now his mind moved into action again, trying to assert reason over random imagination. But reason sputtered and failed.

Random—a man pulled at random from a huddle of zeks, a bullet fired through his skull, spattering a bloody cross over the snow.

Tiny flecks of red paint in the eyes of the father in Rembrandt's *Prodigal Son*. The red sinew in the eyes of the youth who had stood beside Alex gazing upward at the painting. Private weeping. Good weeping and bad weeping. The killer bite of anguish when you understand at last that the great love, the only love of your life, has been taken away. When you knew: All is weakness, all is loss. All is sucked down into death. Beloved spouses down into death, fathers and sons down into death. Down, down, down.

Alyosha of the underground, Alyosha Karamazov, Alyosha Graham, all the Alyoshas swirling down the drain hole of the universe.

Alex jerked his imagination away from this last image, which threatened to suck everything into a lightless vortex in his mind.

"Be quiet", he said to his mind.

"But what is my mind?" his mind replied. "What is it, really? Intellect? Imagination? Feeling? Intuition?"

"Shut up! Shut up!"

Breathing heavily, he got to his feet and stood in the center of the cabin, the images fading slowly.

"Is this what happens in a poustinia?" he whispered to the cross. "Is this what you wanted to show me?"

Glancing at the wood stove, he saw that the vent was open, sucking up the cabin air; it was possible that too little outside air was replacing it. He went to the cabin door and opened it a crack. Cold drafts rushed in. He put on his greatcoat, opened the door wide, and stepped into the snow of the yard. Taking several deep breaths, he remained outside for a few minutes, clearing his head.

"Oxygen", he said to himself. "That's all it was—not enough oxygen."

Out of nowhere, Oleg of Viborg appeared.

"We provided you with a form of primitive theater, did we not, Mr. Kingfisher?" he accused. "You liked the exotic settings, did you not? The drama of purely vicarious radical fear? The literary romance? Even the spiritual romance?"

"No, Oleg! What was crushed by brutal force in your land is dying quietly, discreetly, in my land, suffocating from lack of oxygen!"

"Is it really?" Oleg replied with cold irony.

"Which one is the more dangerous, Oleg? The unmasked enemy or the masked?"

"Is the spilling of blood less sinister to you than the spilling of unread ink? That is self-pity, the whining of the privileged! How dare you speak to me about violence and nonviolence? Pick up your pen and write. No one will steal your child, smash your hands, or obliterate your face."

"They would nullify my words. Is that not violence? Can you not see that masked evil always leads to unmasked evil? Do you not know that unread ink, if given enough time, will translate into spilled blood?"

Fuming, Alex stomped around the yard until, without warning, he found himself stopping in his tracks and looking up at an astonishing outpouring in the heavens. Shooting stars fell among the constellations. He saw that he was fighting an old battle in his mind—his resentment against the artificial culture of the West, the hedonistic commercialized pop culture with the deadly intoxicant in it—a perfect match for the mind-numbing socialist realism of the East. Realizing how ridiculous this monologue-dialogue was, he laughed ruefully. All vehemence drained from him, and his thoughts grew calmer. The night sky was too beautiful for anger. The air was so pure that filling his lungs with it induced an unexpected sensation of well-being. Beyond the cabin, meadows of radiant blue snow beckoned to him through gaps in the trees, where lunar harmonies flooded the woods in every direction. A breath of wind set the frost-covered branches tinkling.

He felt invigorated, his cheeks flushed with the cold, his feet crunching in the snow, sinking only an inch into the surface. A delicious sound: a memory of youth's ignited fire braving the winter night, evoking in him an uncanny sense of home. All about him was stark and dangerous Siberia, yet so familiar was this sensation that he could not help but feel himself a child again. He was now without thoughts, and his eyes were wholly involved in the pleasure of seeing. Walking deeper into the woods, he paid no attention to where he was going. Pausing at one point, he gathered snow in his mitts and tossed it in the direction of the moon. Chimeras of blue crystals fell slowly through the air. The million bells of ice-covered branches resumed their chiming as if all the void were covered with chapels and cathedrals, their campaniles manned by tiny figures thrashing the pull-ropes and waving to him, transforming the bright realm of the taiga into an empire of enchantment.

He now broke into a slow run, zigging and zagging between the trees for some minutes until the forest abruptly ended at a clearing. He entered it and jogged around the outer rim, circling it three times, round and round in the dance of holy harts, and Carol was with him again as a form of light dancing in his arms, in his poor aging idiot body, while the spray of immortal diamonds flew up in his wake.

He tripped and fell into the snow. Stunned, panting, he lay without movement as his breathing returned to normal. The chill swiftly invaded his limbs. He was on the verge of getting to his feet when a shadow moved across the trees on the opposite side of the clearing. Slowly, slowly it went, neither approaching him nor hurrying away. When it stopped, its form blended into the background and became invisible. Was it a wholly immaterial being, or was it a mirage, a shadow trick played by the moon?

It snorted, and a puff of frost appeared in the air. It moved again, and he saw that it was a white stag. Suddenly the rack of antlers tossed, and it heaved forward, leaping, leaping, leaping across the expanse of open ground, and melted away into the forest.

Upon his return to the poustinia, he found it so warm inside that he left the door slightly ajar and stripped down to his trousers and undershirt. His torso was sweating, but his fingers and toes began to shriek with pain as the frozen flesh thawed. He ate more bread and took a long draught from the bottle of water. After that, he stoked the fire and closed the door. When the pain declined, leaving only a pulsating in his extremities, he blew out the lamp, lay down under the fur rug, and fell asleep.

Father Sergius woke Alex, looked into his eyes, nodded as if he was satisfied by what he saw, and went outside to gather firewood. He was soon back with an armload of birch. As the priest fed the stove, Alex sat up like a child rising from pleasant dreams, unwilling to leave them, drifting back into them for moments at a time, then slowly reawakening.

"The desert has blessed you, Aleksandr", the priest said, cutting the last of the bread into two slices.

"Yes", Alex whispered.

Father Sergius gave Alex both pieces of bread, taking nothing for himself. Conversation seemed unnecessary. The priest swept the crumbs into his hand, opened the door, and flung them out onto the yard. The day was overcast, with heavy snow falling softly. A large crow swooped down and pecked at the bits of bread. The bird was identical in every respect to the North American crow except for its gray head and a wedge of gray feathers falling down its back like a babushka's kerchief.

"Eat, Voronushka", said Father Sergius to the bird. "That is all we have to spare today."

Closing the door, he returned to his seat by the table and opened his breviary. Alex sat on the sleeping bench and gazed out the window. The timelessness that he had experienced the night before was still with him. The dance of the snowflakes preoccupied him until the priest closed the book and removed vestments and altar vessels from his knapsack. He set the box table with an embroidered cloth and various instruments, then robed himself in the sacred garments. For the next two and a half hours he celebrated the Divine Liturgy of the Eastern rite. Communion was a small cube of transubstantiated bread dipped into the sacred Blood in the chalice and spooned onto Alex's tongue. Its consolation filled him as it had the day before, though he now received it in a more recollected state.

When the liturgy was over, he looked up to find the light fading in the window and was surprised that so much of the afternoon had gone without him taking note of the passage of time. As Father Sergius was unvesting, he asked if Alex would like to spend another night in the poustinia. Alex said that he would like that, but perhaps he should go to Novosibirsk. Had the priest heard any information about the trains?

"Our friend has returned from Barabinsk with news", Father Sergius replied. "Army engineers and workers from the Railway Ministry are here in great numbers. They say that two smaller bridges between Obsk and Novosibirsk will be repaired by tomorrow. Unfortunately, the bridge over the Little-Little Ob will take more time—perhaps a week."

"Then I must remain until then."

"There is another way. Tomorrow we can arrange for someone to take you to Barabinsk, if you wish. From there you may be able to get a ticket for a local train into the city. If you are hoping to meet with your son—"

"Yes, I should make haste", said Alex with a surge of anxiety.

"If you remain in God's will, Aleksandr, you will find him." Father Sergius paused. "We will pray it is so. You too must pray for this."

"Yes, but maybe I should go tonight."

"Tonight it would be difficult, if not impossible, to find our friend, the one who is to take you. Also, we do not know for certain if there will be any trains out of Barabinsk tomorrow."

"I see", Alex said with a torn feeling—wanting to go, wanting to stay.

"There may be more trials ahead for you. Perhaps these delays are God's way of preparing you. He sees your son. He sees your path. Perhaps all he asks of you now is to stand still. To pray a while longer."

After some hesitation, Alex said, "You're probably right. I could use another night here."

Father Sergius blessed him and put a loaf of bread and a jar of water on the box. After a few friendly words, he departed into the dusk.

Alex remained in the cabin, prayed a rosary, read Psalms and the Beatitudes, then lay down to rest. It puzzled him a little that he was experiencing simultaneously a sense of timelessness and so swift a passage of time that he felt it as acceleration. The seeming contradiction was reconciled by the peace that had returned with the priest's blessing. He felt no need to understand it.

He thought of his sons. He began to miss them very much, to feel his love for them, to ponder their fine characteristics with gratitude and their faults with mercy. His anguish over Andrew's bondage had diminished, and he now realized that a certain detachment had entered the emotional equation since his confession and Communion. He understood that the intensity of his anxiety had come from an imperfect trust in the providence of God. His mind had proclaimed its faith, but his heart had screamed its doubt.

"Is God my Father?" he whispered to the cross. "Yes, I believe this with my intellect, but I have acted as if it might not be true. Fear has ruled me."

He mused on the power of fear, saw its insidious and corrosive qualities, saw as well how extensive had been its control over him. He began to pray. The prayer took the form of stillness, of *attention* before the presence that was everywhere, that had created it all and loved it all. He did not feel the slightest desire to assess this new awareness, to articulate and categorize it, to store it in the architecture of his mind. Nor was there any need to manufacture words to say to God. By the same token, he did not think that God should deliver a message to him. If God was silent, he had good reason to be. If God did not speak, maybe it was because he, Alex, was not yet ready to hear, and premature speech would have made him more incapable of hearing.

As he listened to the silence, he could almost hear the snow falling on the roof; words drifted into his mind, random phrases out of his past, the name of Christ or a saint, or his own name whispered as if by a benevolent breeze. He recalled the hallucination of the previous night, the arrow shot into his skull, and the more real stag, but the disorienting barrage was not repeated. Snowflakes fell slowly past the window, their radial arms spinning out of the galaxy above. Alex watched them for a time. Hungry, he got up and ate more of the bread, and lay down again under the fur rug. He closed his eyes, listening to the fire softly consuming embers.

Alexander, you are not dying; you are being born.

Snow blanketing the earth. Snow sifting through the birches and pines. Snow covering the marked and unmarked graves.

He who would save his life will lose it.

Carol's face bending over the candle in their bedroom, blowing it out.

He who loses his life for my sake will save it.

Jacob sliding into his wet, blood-covered hands, pulling the blue coil of umbilicus after him.

"It's a boy, Carol, a boy!"

Laughter-tears, joy-tears, the exultation of life triumphing over death, the world beginning all over again.

"A boy!" she laughed, haggard and radiant.

And when Andrew made his entry into the world two years later, she cried again the laughter-tears, joy-tears, the exultation-of-life-tears.

Everything! I give you everything! he had said to each of his sons on the days of their births. Then slowly retracted it, inch by inch, over the ensuing years.

"Who are you, child?" Carol asked, pressing her nose to the tiny brown nub of Andrew's nose, laughing as the baby's toes curled reflexively around her finger, smiling to herself as her lips touched the downy top of his skull, helping his miniature lips find her breast. "Who will you be?"

Memory, the soul's deposit, the private trove, the casket with two keys—hers and his.

Alexander, her breath in his ear, in the night.

Beloved. My beloved. My forever-spouse.

Her eyes during the death agony. His eyes became hers, and hers became his. One body—one body, staring together at the threat of finality. Almost mesmerized by the annihilation of hope, a gun to the temple of the Holy Spirit, they knew that they must pray. And, yes, both of them prayed the words that pushed away the cold muzzle of the gun, hers feeble, his broken. And they held each other as the demon fled and the angel took her quietly.

Alexander.

Because time continued to play with him, Alex awoke uncertain whether the dawn was near or far. He sat up, staring blindly. The stove spat, and a spark appeared in a crack of the iron top. He got up and felt his way across the room toward the place where the hanging lamp must be. When it thumped his forehead, he grabbed it to keep it from swinging dangerously. Shaking the brass reservoir, he heard no sound of oil sloshing within. It had used up all its fuel because he had forgotten to lower the wick.

No light came in through the window. Blindly retracing his steps to the stove, he fumbled for the latch of the fire door in its side and opened it. The remnant of coals glowed red-orange, throwing just enough light for him dimly to make out other details in the room. He located the pile of birch by the cabin door, brought some of it to the stove, and pushed a solid chunk into the firebox. The bark ignited, crackling loudly, churning out a fragrant smoke, shooting beams of light through the cabin. He left the fire door open an inch so that the heavy piece of wood would burn strongly for ten or fifteen minutes. He returned to bed.

"Don't forget to close the door, Alex. Don't fall asleep", he admonished himself. "Too much air, and the fire will rage out of control."

To keep himself awake, he sat up, knees under his chin, a blanket around his shoulders and legs. Staring into the flames, his mind wandered, and he fell into half sleep. Images began to course through his imagination again, fragmentary and unobtrusive at first, then growing in power. Words of love, memories of love. Followed by a wave of loneliness. Followed by images of Carol's grave under a blanket of hard snow. Jamie and Hannah Colley swept over the lip of a dam. A bullet fired through a man's skull. A stab of fear. Then, surprisingly, a jolt of lust. The red-taloned Valkyries of the Helsinki sauna opened the cabin door and walked into the room, talking loudly, stark naked.

Alex's heart suddenly pounded, his head snapped back, and he struggled to push the thoughts away. "Stop!" he murmured blearily, trying to bring himself fully awake. But the hot drone of carnal desire would not go away. So vivid were the images now cavorting in his mind's eye, and so different were they from the sacramental love he had known, that he felt sickened. He wondered where the thoughts had come from and why they had appeared at this moment. Like all men, he was no stranger to this particular battle. In the past he had always been able to defeat the temptation by a stern effort of the will, by increased prayer, and by marathon walks along the heights of the cold and utterly sobering Clementine hills. He rarely drank coffee, and then only in the morning, sparing himself the insomniac struggle at night, when such images were most likely to appear. He usually slipped into sleep either praying or reading dry tomes, the most notable quality of which was their soporific effect. No such books were now at hand.

He found his rosary and prayed it. This helped, but within moments of completing it the Valkyries returned. Ignoring them as much as he could, he thought he should read Scripture but realized there was no light. He got up, paced back and forth in the dark, repeated his wife's name lovingly, prayed for her soul, remembered, remembered...but the remembering ignited residual passion-memories that shifted his imagination back to the more immediate passions now leaping about the room.

It was ridiculous! At his age! Why were the images so powerful, and why was he having such difficulty ignoring them? It was all in his mind, of course, fueled by the imagination. Fueled also, he supposed, by the increased loneliness of his journey through this strange land and by his long absence from his home, where passion was never permitted to enter except in the refined and licit form of poetry or symphonies. He told himself that whatever the cause, its power over him was augmented by his fatigue. Long past was the virility of youth; safely constrained were the surges of hormones that once had threatened to reduce him to the level of a beast. Grace, sublimation, physical exercise, and the equally determined exercise of the mind's authority—these had always succeeded in keeping lust at bay. Where had all that moral strength gone? Was it gone?

No, it was not gone, he told himself. Tearing the socks from his feet, he strode to the door, threw it open, and stepped outside. Coatless, barefoot, he took three paces forward into a snowdrift, inhaling the frigid air in great angry gusts. With gratifying speed, lust and its maidservants disappeared. Shivering with chill, he shook his head and grimaced, "You're not an old man yet, Alex." Glancing up at the sky to reestablish his equilibrium, he saw that it was black with thick overcast. The snow had ceased falling, and there was no wind.

In that preternatural stillness, he heard a sound that froze him with terror. From behind and above there came a low growl. Turning slowly, he tried to see what had made the sound, but the feeble light from the open cabin door revealed nothing. When the growl came a second time, Alex yelled and sprinted for the door. Within two seconds he was inside, slamming the door shut, gasping for breath.

What was it? A bear? No, bears hibernated. A mountain lion? Were there lions in Russia? A dog? Maybe. A wolf? Maybe. A trick of the mind? Maybe. A demon? Didn't demons attack pilgrims in solitary places? No, that was only in the lives of the saints or in fairy stories. He was not a saint, and this was no fairy story. Was it a teenager or some other unpredictable creature of that sort? Quite possibly. Yes, yes, of course! He would wager that some of the village youths had heard about the foreigner who was staying alone in the cabin, and they had hiked along the Little-Little Ob in the middle of the night to have a bit of fun. What a fine tale they would have to tell their friends on the morrow.

Crunch-crunch-crunch—footsteps on the roof.

Whatever it was, it was real. Delete one possibility: it was not a demon. Hopefully not a demon. Could demons make sounds?

Crunch-crunch-crunch. It crossed the roof back and forth.

Choking back his fear, he decided that bravado was the best policy.

"You up there", he called in Russian. "Little jokers, I want to sleep. Go home. Or come inside for a slice of bread before you go."

The footsteps stopped. Once again the growl vibrated through the cabin, softened by the snowcap but no less sinister. Alex glanced at the door. Did it have a lock? No lock! He raced to it and piled three birch blocks against the planks. Glancing at the window, he wondered if the growler could smash it and leap inside. Of this he was not sure. Was there anything in the room he could use as a weapon? The large cross? No, it was nailed to the wall, and he had no tools to free it. The hanging lamp? No, it was too small. The iron fire poker? Realizing that this offered some defense, he grabbed it from the nail where it hung behind the stove and, gripping its hilt with both hands, stood in the center of the room waiting for the attack. He strained to hear where the footsteps might lead—to the door? to the window?—but the pounding of blood in his ears and the sharp inhalations of his breathing became deafening. Painfully long minutes passed. He stood without moving, his legs shaking, hands cold and sweating. At the risk of letting down his guard, he stepped slowly backward to the door and leaned against it, facing the window on the far side of the room. This cut in half the number of points from which the—the *thing*—could attack him. He hoped his body weight was sufficient to resist any strike on the door.

No more sounds came from above. It seemed to Alex that hours went by. Adrenaline pumped constantly through his system; his eyes were wide, staring at nothing. Little by little his breathing eased, but he did not relax his vigilance. He tried to pray but could not produce anything other than half-hearted utterances. The fire in the stove slowly died. Did he dare leave his post and his weapon in order to throw more wood on it? He decided to let it go out. The room gradually cooled, then grew steadily colder. The stove began to clank as its iron plates contracted. He wriggled into his greatcoat, slipped on his socks and shoes, and pulled his boots over them. Despite the added clothing, he began to shiver as the Arctic temperature relentlessly invaded the interior of the cabin.

Blackness. As black as a tomb, and as eternal. The stove ceased its clanking. Silence spread. Only the sound of his heart remained, running faster than it should after the passage of hours, rapid rabbit thumps, sometimes skipping a beat, sometimes palpitating, adding scare to scare, for he remembered that his was not a mighty heart and that it bore the scars of an old frailty. It was his personal self-destruct time bomb.

Now anger swelled in him—anger at his physical weakness, anger at the absurdly tangled series of errors that had brought him to this place, anger at his enemies, anger at his friends who were enjoying their safe and orderly world back home in a land that was fast becoming a myth. Anger at abandonment. And beneath anger, he remembered with a pang of remorse, was the core of unbelief. Only hours ago he had prayed with confidence to God. Immersed in that wondrous peace, he had seen the exact contours of his soul, had declared that God was his Father and that he was his child, resting like a newborn baby in the hands that held him.

Now he saw that the umbilical cord of fear had not yet been cut. In his own hands was a poker that he would, without hesitation, smash down on the head of any man or beast that attacked him.

Blackness, blackness.

Where was God? Where was his Father?

Maybe he was not really here. There. Anywhere.

Blackness and again blackness.

"Is this what I am?" he asked in a moment of astonished illumination. "Yes, this is what I am."

Then he threw the poker to the floor, listening to its thump-clang as if it were the hinge of a door opening into hell.

Was death hell? Did he really think so, or did he just fear that it was so? His mind told him it was not so, but his heart screamed otherwise—again this damnable, this unreliable, this unruly heart! Cavorting Valkyries and ravenous beast alike had access to it. Was he completely defenseless? Was his character without armor of any kind? Must he always be reduced to cowardice?

Was he really a coward? No, he had thrown away the weapon, hadn't he? Hadn't he?

He looked at the poker, thinking that maybe he should pick it up again. Then he realized that pale gray light was filtering in through the window and that his eyes were now able to make out features in the room. It was dawn. At the very moment when this realization came to him, a knock sounded on the door.

Alex shouted a loud roar and bounded to the other side of the room.

The door slowly opened. Father Sergius stepped inside and looked at him, puzzled. Alex breathed a great sigh of relief, sank onto the sleeping bench, and put his face in his hands.

22. *The Well in the Desert*

The walk back to Obsk was a dismal affair. Alex was exhausted and dispirited. The low overcast darkening the morning was a perfect match for his gloom. Plainly, Father Sergius sympathized with Alex's difficult night but would not offer an opinion about its causes. As for the growling beast, the priest pointed out that a trail of canine prints circled the cabin, climbed the snowdrift onto the roof, criss-crossed back down, and ambled off into the taiga on a disorderly course.

"It was a wolf", he said. "A small one. And sick, I think, or starving, for its paws did not press deeply into the snow."

"Well, so much for my spiritual experience, Father", Alex mumbled as the river bent and the village came into view.

"Not what you expected, perhaps," said Father Sergius, "but it was a gift."

"A gift? It seems a total failure."

"What is failure? The only failure is to reject what God wishes to show us. You experienced many things, did you not?"

Alex nodded glumly.

"Joy and sorrow—and especially the areas of your life where there is weakness?"

Again he nodded.

"But that is wonderful! See how he loves you!"

Alex cast a sidelong glance at the priest, unable to produce another nod of agreement.

They now arrived at the rectory and, after brushing snow off their boots with a twig broom, entered to find Father

Serafim busy at the stove. Looking up at the arrivals, he continued to stir a simmering pot but offered no word of greeting. He merely regarded Alex's face with a look so penetrating that nothing could be hidden from it.

"Ah", he said.

Alex sat down on the coffin—it now looked more like a coffin than a sofa.

"Soup?" said Father Serafim.

"No thank you", said Alex.

"A man must eat", the priest countered. "To cross the desert you must have food in your belly."

"No, I must fast. I have been a fool. I found out last night that I am not a spiritual person at all. It is time I began to take the spiritual life seriously."

Father Sergius smiled affectionately at Alex. Father Serafim also smiled. Ignoring Alex's refusal, he poured ladles of borsch into three tin bowls and set them on the table. Beside each place he put a cup of tea. The priests bowed their heads and prayed grace, blessed the meal with signs of the cross, and bade Alex sit down with them. Alex did so with reluctance. As he nibbled at chunks of dark brown bread flavored with sunflower seed and anise, he stared at the contents of the bowl, lost in his own nonthoughts, aware that compared to these two priests he was a rather poor example of a Christian and that they had not failed to grasp this fact. It bothered him greatly.

After the meal, Father Serafim cleared away the dishes and brought a little wooden platter of gingerbread and three pieces of poppy seed candy. The priests did not scruple over this. Alex reached for his portion with hesitation.

The dessert was accompanied by more cups of tea. The priests sipped theirs slowly. As Alex drank his, he sensed anew how different he was from these men and wondered if culture could ever be merely a matter of arbitrary surface details. No, their customs and habits were deep-rooted, connected to a vision that integrated heaven and earth. He, Alex Graham, was a water skimmer. A dabbler. A citizen of Flatland. No matter how he tried to break out, he was forever a soul-zek. He told himself that he did not really care, that it was no longer important for him to obtain a deeper understanding of the Russian spirit, or the Russian genius, or whatever the mystique really was. His only need was to get to Novosibirsk as quickly as possible, grab his son, and get out as fast as he could, leaving this pain-wracked, scrambled country behind him forever. It crossed his mind, also, that as soon as he arrived home he would sell the Russian collection at a bargain price to the first buyer who happened along.

"Another cup of tea, Aleksandr?" Father Sergius said.

"No thank you."

Alex looked up into Father Serafim's eyes. The eyes were as deep as a well. The priest said nothing, merely looked. Alex resented it a little.

"How will I go to Barabinsk?" he asked.

"Later in the morning our friend will take you in his snowmobile", said Father Sergius. "There you can see if the trains are running. Afterward he will bring you back if you need to remain with us a while longer."

Alex murmured uncomfortably that it was really time for him to be moving on. Not that he wasn't grateful for all they had done for him, he added.

"Aleksandr," Father Serafim said after a considerable pause, "the desert is not a place but a world. When one enters that world, all securities are left behind. It is where one will lose everything. It is also where one is given everything."

Alex nodded, as if to acknowledge that he understood the point, that yes, he had read a good deal about Russian spirituality.

"To become a poor man is the greatest thing that can be given to us", Father Sergius said. "It is the foundation.

Unless one throws away all weapons, all armor, he cannot learn meekness."

Meekness? What was meekness? Gentleness, absence of violence, kindness? Of course it was all of these and more. But was it also a consoling self-deception that victims must desperately cling to, lest they sink into despair? He did not voice this argument.

Father Serafim went on: "A man leaves the safe haven of his familiar world. And even if his home be a difficult place, even though it be a place of slavery, he experiences it as his own. It is knowable, the dangers identifiable. In the desert all certainties fall away. He feels his weakness as never before. There are joys and consolations, but during the periods when these withdraw and desolations take their place, he feels more helpless than ever. He asks himself, 'Is there truly a Promised Land? And if there is a Promised Land, will I ever find it? And if I do find it, am I fit to live in such a glorious country? No, I am not fit in any way', he says to himself."

Father Sergius took over: "Then comes the dark temptation. Not lust, though lust presents itself. Not murderous emotions, though they also arise. Not fear, though it too seeks to overwhelm. Now comes the subtlest and most dangerous temptation of all, the archenemy—pride. Because he has made the amazing discovery that he is unworthy of the Promised Land, because he has not lived up to his own expectations of what a spiritual man should be, he is angry or he is discouraged. Disguised beneath his anger or despair is a presumption—a belief that he, surely, should be capable of doing what is needed to inherit the Promised Land! But because he has seen how incapable he really is, he rejects the promise itself. Now he wishes to go back to Egypt, to the land of bondage, where at least there is enough to eat, where there is some reassuring order to his life. After all, when he was in chains, he was not lost. He knew his place in the world. If he obeyed his master and asked no questions, he was always safe. He did not have to face the dark places."

Alex made no reply.

"Do you know when the trains will run again?" he asked abruptly, inferring in as polite a way as possible that he could stand no more of their holy wisdom.

"At Barabinsk, they will tell you", said Father Sergius.

"Freedom of the heart has a price, Aleksandr", Father Serafim continued in an unhurried tone. "To face the darkness within oneself is part of it."

Alex stared into his empty cup, his mood of wretchedness increasing. He thought to himself: *Not only am I unfit for the Promised Land, but I cannot bear the realization that I am unfit. Pride! How can you uproot it from your heart? The moment you spot it, it mutates and pops up in another un-uprooted corner of your heart. They're telling me that all I have to do is keep plodding across the desert and let the storms and the lions tear it out of me, leaving nothing behind. Nothing.*

Sensing that poor Alex was being devoured by private metaphors, Father Sergius stood and said, "Serafim, I am going for a walk. Aleksandr, you come too."

Alex stood, put on his greatcoat, and followed him outside. Father Sergius led him into the woods behind the church, in the direction of the road to the burned bridge. A few hundred yards into the trees, the route turned east again and drew near to a small hill, about a quarter mile upstream from the village. In that part of Siberia, the hill stood out as a singularity. Though it was no more than a few hundred feet higher than the surrounding taiga, and about as wide in circumference, it seemed much higher; in fact, it looked like a little mountain. It was densely covered with pine trees, with a spray of naked birches near the crest. As the two men climbed, they were forced to bend from time to time, pushing back overhanging branches from which benign avalanches fell on their necks and shoulders. As the slope leveled out at the top, the footpath entered a clearing that was a bare expanse of pure snow, broken only by three birch trees. The birches were extraordinarily large; indeed, they were the tallest and thickest of their kind that Alex had ever seen.

Near them, almost in their shadows, stood a church, or what Alex took at first to be a church. In this region of primitive buildings it was incongruously beautiful; even in European Russia it would have been a marvel of Byzantine architecture. It was a square white tower, bricked and stuccoed, flanked by four attached apses, each of them capped with royal blue hemispherical cupolas. The whole was surmounted by a magnificent onion dome of shining new gold. Contrary to Alex's expectations, this cathedral-like building did not grow in size as they approached. When they arrived at its gate, he saw that it was no more than seven feet in height. The three mighty birches were, in fact, small.

Momentarily distracted from his dark mood, Alex exclaimed, "But what is this, Father?"

"It is a well."

"A well? How did it come to be here? Who made it?"

"Serafim and I."

Father Sergius went forward, knelt on the front step, opened the blue door, and, bending his head, went in. Alex followed. There was just enough room inside for both men. The interior was a replica of a cathedral, complete with windows, small icons, a miniature iconostasis screen, hand-carved "royal doors" leading into a sanctuary, and a dome on which had been painted a mural of Christ reigning over the cosmos. In the center of the floor, there was a circular stone wall about two feet in height, covered by a wooden lid. Beside it was a tin ladle, and a bucket tied to a rope. Father Sergius lifted the lid and bade Alex to look inside, where he saw a pool of water several feet below at the bottom of a dug shaft.

The priest dropped the bucket into it, let it settle and fill, then pulled it back up. Using the ladle, he dipped some from the bucket and offered it to Alex. Alex sipped. The water was cold, but not painfully so. It tasted clean and sweet. He handed the ladle back to Father Sergius, who also drank from it.

"The desert is a place of desolation", the priest said. "But there are hidden springs in it. In the desert one must learn to stand still, to wait for God in emptiness. Standing still in this way is a purifying fire. One must not run from it, for it is a great gift."

"A gift?"

"Is it difficult for you to grasp, Aleksandr? I suppose it must be. May I tell you a story?"

"If you wish."

"In the early 1990s, when word reached me that Serafim was still alive and functioning as a pastor in western Siberia, I went in search of him. When I found him here in Obsk, we had a great reunion, such as only former zeks can know. What prayers of praise and thanksgiving poured from us as we rejoiced that the reign of darkness had been broken and we had been spared to work for a new springtime. He asked me to stay with him. But this was not for selfish purposes. No, it was his gift of discernment. He was wise in a way that I was not, for he saw the pain that was still in me from the days of imprisonment. With my intellect, you know, there is always a more complicated process of..."

He paused for a moment, then continued.

"...of becoming a desert dweller. Like Serafim, I had suffered on the cross with Christ, but unlike him, I had not yet given everything. You see, Aleksandr, in each heart three trees grow. Life cuts them down, trims them, crafts them into crosses. Then they are lifted high on a hill—a hill like a skull. One is the cross of Jesus, the second the cross of the repentant thief, and the third the cross of the unrepentant thief."

"In each heart?"

"Yes. We like to think that in times of trial, we will suffer like Jesus. If we are a little bit realistic, we will say to ourselves, 'No, I am not much like him. Therefore I will be like the repentant thief, and go straight to Paradise.' But so often when the trial arrives, we find to our dismay that in fact we are the unrepentant thief. We grow angry at our suffering; we resent and complain and make others pay for our unhappiness."

"Yes", Alex said morosely, nodding. "That is true."

"This is not a cause for sadness", the priest said with a smile and outstretched arms. "This is a great victory. To see ourselves as we are is the precondition for repentance. When we understand that we *are* the unrepentant thief, then and only then are the wellsprings of conversion opened to us. We can turn to Jesus hanging in agony on his cross and beg forgiveness from him. And on *that* day, we enter Paradise."

Alex made no comment. He was more interested in the well's origin.

"Why did you build this so high above the river?"

"I will tell you how it came to be here. After release from the camps, and long after my arrival here, I was still haunted by what I had witnessed and endured. I struggled to forgive my enemies, but again and again those memories came to me, growing stronger as time went on. Often I prayed to the Lord to heal me of this, but he did not grant my request. One afternoon, seven years ago, during the time when the leaves had just appeared on the trees and all the world seemed born again, I fled from the poustinia in despair. I walked along the river, intending to reach the railway bridge. I had decided that I could remain here no longer. I would go west, maybe to Ukraine, maybe to France or Germany—anywhere but here. Moreover, I was certain I could no longer labor as a priest. Although I had survived many tribulations for the sake of

God's Kingdom, I felt I had become unfit for that Kingdom. I still hated. I could not forgive. I wanted the guilty ones brought to justice—as if such a thing could be obtained in this world. And in my darkest moments, I desired that they should fall under the ax of vengeance. Not by my hand, of course, but at the hand of some other former victim. You see, Aleksandr, I wanted the oppressors' deaths, but I did not want their blood on my head.

"Are you shocked by this? No? Well, I am shocked. It did not cross my mind that such vengeance would have in all likelihood condemned them to hell, and me along with them. Many more temptations came to me as I fled from the desert, terrible thoughts, thoughts that nearly drove me insane. So dark was my mood, and so obsessed was I by this inner conflict, that I walked past Obsk, too ashamed to say farewell to Serafim. Farther on, I passed this little mountain. Who can explain what then happened? At the base of the hill I stopped and could go no further. My eyes were drawn to the height, and I knew—do not ask me how I knew—that I must go there. When I reached the top, I found only this meadow, full of weeds, scattered stones, and sterile soil. I threw myself down on the ground and wept. It seemed to me then that I had no place to go, that even if I were to flee across the whole world, I could not escape my burdened mind and deformed heart. I was lost. Perhaps I was insane.

"The wind rustled in the trees—a sighing sound that grew steadily into something like the voice of a gently singing woman. I looked up, and there in the arms of a birch, the sun appeared to have been caught in the branches. The leaves burst into flame, a holy golden flame, shot with all the colors of the rainbow. My eyes were blinded by the wonder. A hush fell on everything; even the leaves slipped into slow motion. Then to my astonishment I saw a woman's shape in the burning tree, holding a child in her arms. She floated to the earth and alighted on a stone at the base of the trunk. The child was wrapped in a cloth, as if he had just come from a bath. In one of the woman's hands was a basin, and over her arm was draped a long towel of the kind we use for washing feet.

"I knew who she was. Of course, I knew her. I pressed my face into the earth, not daring to look at her.

"She spoke—in my ears, my heart, my mind, I do not know. She asked me to make a little shrine here, a place of pilgrimage for the time when darkness would be completely banished from the land. In the years to come, she said, many men would build dwellings on this mountain and live here devoting their lives to prayer. She asked me to make a well within the shrine. In my heart I said yes. Then, when I looked up, she was gone.

"I ran forward to the tree. At first I saw no evidence that she had been real. I fell to my knees, doubting, thinking that I had imagined everything—after all, had there not been a similar apparition at the great monastery of Pochaiv in Ukraine and the shrine at Lichen in Poland? Was this not just something that my madness was producing, tangling it with the memory of childhood tales? Then I looked at the stone on which she had stood. The shape of a foot, the foot of a small woman, was impressed in it.

"I ran down the mountain, ran all the way to the village, shouting for Serafim. All ababble, I told him what had happened. Without hesitation he believed me, and together we went back to the top of the mountain. Reaching the place where she had stood, we knelt and kissed the imprint of the foot.

"'But a well!' I said, having doubts again. 'To make a well would be impossible, for it is very dry here, and we would have to dig through a hundred meters of rock.'

"'If that is so, we must begin', Serafim said.

"With our hands we scooped the gravel away from the front of the stone. The soil was damp there. We scooped some more, and now droplets of water appeared. The more we dug, the more the water seeped. It quickly filled the hole, a few inches deep. We scooped more and more, and the more we did, the more the water flowed, as if man and God were laboring together to accomplish the impossible. And that is how it came to be."

"Seven years ago", Alex breathed, shaking his head.

"Many people have worked to build what you see today, hundreds of souls coming from all the surrounding region, and even the first pilgrims from beyond. More arrive each year."

"Then it is becoming famous."

"Only among the small of the earth."

"Does it have a name?"

"Serafim and I call it Mother of the Tree of Life. Some call it Mother of the Unexpected Water. Others say it should be called Mother of the Reconciliation. While the darkness lasts, we are not certain of the name. She will give the name when the time is ripe. For now, we pray."

"Is it an Orthodox shrine?"

"It is a shrine belonging to the whole Body of Christ."

"And you, Father, do you not want to live here? When we first met, you told me that you have no home."

"I pray that I will live on this mountain as a *poustinik* some-day, but my task now is to live as a *strannik*. I travel throughout the land bearing the word of promise—the great promise that there will come a time when we shall all be one."

They drank more water. Then Father Sergius opened the child-size doors into the sanctuary and showed Alex a stone lying on the bare wooden floor. The shape of a small foot was imprinted in it, as if pressed in warm wax. Alex stared at it and said nothing. Father Sergius made the sign of the cross over him. They got up off their knees and went out, closing the door behind them.

Arriving back at the village, Alex realized that his wretched mood had entirely lifted, though when precisely it had gone he could not recall. As he and Father Sergius stood quietly talking beside the church, they heard a low rumble coming from the general direction of the south. The noise increased steadily, then became a roar, then became a deafening series of explosions. Instinctively Alex ducked. He was utterly astonished when an apparition came around a bend in the river and headed straight toward the village. A machine of some kind, it plowed into the riverbank, tilted its bullet nose upward, and climbed with screaming engine to the flat ground in front of the church, where it came to a stop and fell silent with one last explosion and a puff of black smoke.

It looked for all the world like a hybrid of an old-style Volkswagen car and a Bombardier snowmobile. The machine was a hump of green tin riveted and bolted together, mounted on two great skis under the front chassis and propelled by ovoid treads that looked as if they had been cannibalized from a small army tank. Two smokestacks jutted from the hood in front of a cracked windscreen. The metal body was punctured with what looked like bullet holes. Painted on the door were the words "I. N. Putkov, Prime Sable".

It was perhaps I. N. Putkov himself who now kicked open the driver's door and scrambled out. When he had succeeded in standing himself upright, he greeted the priest with a laugh and a warm embrace. His merry face was as mixed in breed as his vehicle, for it bore traces of both Tartar and Slavic origins. He was about fifty years old, black haired and black eyed, dark skinned with bright red cheeks. He was smoking a cigarette and was somewhat drunk.

"Taxi! Taxi!" he roared, brandishing a bottle in one hand, grinning at Alex as if he knew him.

Father Serafim came out through the door of his rectory, strode over with a smile, and embraced the newcomer.

With a sure touch the two priests appropriated the swaying man—whom they addressed as Innokenty Nikolayevich—and ushered him inside. There they sat him down at the table, where they proceeded to joke with him and serve him bread, soup, and a continuous stream of tea. Alex sat down on the coffin and watched them sober up his taxi driver with great tenderness and respect. Father Serafim removed the man's felt boots, exposing very dirty wiggling toes (causing jocularity all around) and set the footgear to thaw by the stove. Father Sergius poured steaming water from a kettle into a metal bowl. Then he washed the man's feet and dried them with a long, narrow towel. Putkov squinted and smoked another cigarette, teasing all the while, singing bits of songs, and making crude jokes. Under the influence of the priests' ministrations, he gradually quieted down.

By one o'clock in the afternoon, his conversation had become more or less normal, and a certain innocence had returned to his jokes. Standing suddenly, he announced that it was now time to take the *burshui* to Barabinsk. *Burshui*—the Russian word for bourgeois—was apparently his term for any wealthy person, regardless of nationality.

They all went outside and stood in a ring by the driver's side of the machine. Putkov called it a *motóski*. Declaiming to Alex the various fine qualities of this invention, which he had apparently constructed himself, he made as if to lean over and give the roof of the cab a great kiss. Both priests leaped forward and grabbed his arms, holding him back with reminders that it would hurt him badly if his lips froze to the skin of his beloved "Motushka". Deftly, Father Serafim relieved the man of his quarter-full bottle of vodka, while Father Sergius got him another drink of tea, which was downed in a gulp.

After more banter and negotiations, Alex gave Putkov a hundred rubles. They got into the cab, Alex contracting his body painfully in order to fit. His seat was a pile of wadded burlap reeking of oil and animal musk. There were no safety belts, and his head brushed the roof. He anticipated a dreadful ride to Barabinsk and back again. The priests made signs of the cross over the vehicle, and Alex waved good-bye. The driver ignited the engine and pulled an iron bar that served as a gearshift, and the machine jerked forward. It made a single teetering pass around the church, then plunged precipitously down the riverbank and onto the ice.

From the moment the journey began, Innokenty Putkov talked continuously. Not a word of it did Alex understand, for the deafening roar of the engine obliterated all other sounds, and he was preoccupied with keeping his head from bashing the roof and his bone structure from being shaken to pieces. They drove south on the river as far as the destroyed bridge over the Little-Little Ob, which was now at the halfway stage of reconstruction. Laborers and armed soldiers paused to watch as the *motóski* swerved up the east bank onto higher ground and began to race along beside the track bed. The surface was rough and the machine rougher. Alex hoped in vain that the town was a short distance away. As it turned out, it was at least an hour's journey at breakneck speed. Within forty minutes his feet went numb with the cold. His jaw vibrated in perfect unison with a motor that combined the characteristics of a rocket about to explode and the rattle of an old set of dentures.

The machine slid into the yard of the train station at Barabinsk, coughed, and died. Alex wished he could do the same. Kicking open the door, he crawled out, banging his elbow on the metal frame, grabbed the exhaust stack in order to pull himself upright (burning his hand), screamed, and tumbled onto dirty snow beside the tracks.

"Ha ha ha, Burshui", laughed Innokenty with his hands on his hips. "That's the way to do it! No more *turisti-chitski* for you. You're a real Siberian now."

Grumbling, Alex got to his feet and stomped up the steps of the Stalinesque station, and went inside to search for a public telephone. There was a lineup of eight people waiting to use it. He went to the end of the line and during the next hour inched ever closer. When it was his turn, he began the laborious search for the number of the Hotel Ob in Novosibirsk. It was fairly noisy inside the station, as several people whose schedules had been disrupted by the destruction of the bridges were now loudly renegotiating their rail passage.

As Alex talked with operators and information people, Innokenty sidled in and stood leaning against the wall beside the phone, sipping from a bottle. At one point the man grabbed his own nose with his thumb and forefinger and blew hard to clear it, flinging the results onto the slushy floor. No one seemed to notice.

Finally, Alex connected with the lobby desk of the Hotel Ob. Clerks in Siberia, it seemed, were not quite as secretive as their counterparts in Moscow and Saint Petersburg. He learned that the Bloch party had left the city three days before, bound for a resort in the east. It was somewhere—the clerk did not know where exactly—on Lake Baikal. They had flown to Irkutsk, intending to make their way from there to Listvyanka, a jumping-off point on the lake. Perhaps the caller should contact someone in Listvyanka. Maybe they could tell him the location of such a resort. Alex asked the clerk if he could suggest the name of a person or travel organization that could be contacted for the information. The clerk could think of none.

"It's called the Dacha", Alex told him.

"Dacha? There are a million dachas in that part of the world—everywhere, in fact."

Alex hung up the receiver and stared blindly at the floor.

"What's the matter, Burshui? Trouble?" Innokenty said with feigned sympathy.

"Yes, trouble."

Alex stepped aside to let others use the phone and walked to a corner of the room, where he turned his face to the wall, trying to think. Filtering toward him through the uproar around the ticket window, he heard a piece of news: "Yes, yes, the train for Novosibirsk has places for you all. It will be here before the sun sets!"

Returning to Innokenty, Alex asked him if he could deliver a message to the priests at Obsk. With the aid of a few more rubles, this was no problem. Alex wrote a note explaining that he must move on, because there was no time to be lost. Chasing his son farther into the east might well prove to be a hopeless venture, but it was the only thing he could do. He thanked them for their hospitality and begged their prayers.

Innokenty stuffed the letter into his parka pocket and left without a parting word. A minute later the rocket engine started up in the train yard and disappeared into the west.

23. *Clerks and Ballerinas*

Thus it was that one evening in late February, Alexander Graham of Halcyon, Ontario, found himself seated on a wooden bench in an overcrowded train car, going deeper into the *terra incognita* of Siberia. He was shaken in body, rattled in thought, and utterly dispirited. Although the events of the previous three days had encouraged him to some degree, the cumulative effect, all told, had been to drive him ever closer to the end of his resources. He could no longer muster the energy to tell himself optimistic things. He had lost confidence in himself and was fast losing confidence that the benevolent hand of God was upon this quixotic quest, if it ever had been. His left hand throbbed, his right elbow ached, and his emotions teetered back and forth along the borderline of despair. Miraculous wells seemed to be for other people—for him there were bruises and burns.

He was losing all affection for Russia. It was a crazy country, full of crazy people. At any moment, crazy things came out of nowhere and ran over the unsuspecting traveler, shot him with an arrow or shook him like a pea in a tin can. Moreover, he realized that he had left behind at Obsk the bag in which he had carried his clothing, and he was doubly disturbed that he had not noticed until now. He possessed only the clothes on his back and the shoulder bag containing his documents, money, and a few books. Once again, everything was going wrong.

He could have permitted himself some anger at the protesters who had interrupted his journey and delayed the meeting with his son, but he told himself it was petty to focus on such small foes. He admitted that their ridiculous media event had been the occasion of his meeting with the two priests, but he wondered if he had gained anything by that interlude. Too many intense conversations containing too much densely packed information had passed through his mind during his time with them. Indeed, he tried without success to recapture the contents of those discussions. Most of what he had heard seemed to have been erased, leaving random images—a stag, a wolf, a well, a stone with a footprint, a bullet hole in a skull.

As he peered out into the moonlit infinity of the winter taiga, he thought of Napoleon standing on a rise overlooking Moscow, the conqueror of the West feasting his eyes on the East, listening to the city's bells with skeptical interest.

"Is it true that Moscow is called the holy city?" Napoleon had asked. "How many churches are there in Moscow?"

When he was told there were more than two hundred, he said:

"Why are there such a great number?"

A general replied, "The Russians are very religious."

"A great number of monasteries and churches are always a sign of the backwardness of a people", Napoleon sneered, looking about at his marshals for appreciation of this remark. And because none dared to offer a different interpretation, within months he was scurrying back across the frontier, leaving hundreds of thousands of his troops to fertilize the soil with their bodies.

Well, Alex thought to himself, *the Russians are no longer a very religious people. But the frozen void is the same.*

He longed for a bottle of Baltika beer. He wanted to go home.

The train crept slowly across the land, its engineer cautious about the danger of sabotage by ecoterrorists. A small track car puttered ahead of the engine, scouting for missing rails and burned bridges. They encountered none. From time to time the train stopped at villages, where conductors jumped off the carriage steps for hurried conversations with railway officials and soldiers, then jumped back on whenever the go-ahead signal was given. The journey to Novosibirsk was about three hundred kilometers, a stretch that ordinarily would have been crossed in four hours. Now, however, it took eight hours, and at one o'clock in the morning the train passed into a massive low-hanging cloud covering the capital of Siberia. Few details of the city could be seen from the carriage window. A lurid acid-yellow light glowed all around it, the result of an atmospheric inversion that pressed the illuminated exhaust of industrial smokestacks close to the ground. The train slowed to an agonizing crawl.

Around two in the morning it halted in a smog-shrouded station, and the passengers were told to disembark. On the platform, Alex learned that another train was waiting to take all eastbound passengers on the Trans-Siberian route. Following directions, he made his way to track number 1 and found train number 3, bound for Irkutsk and points beyond. It was a diesel, larger and longer than the electric train that had brought him from Obsk. Despite his ticket, there were no first-class berths available. A surly conductor could only suggest that he find himself a place in car 11.

Entering the carriage, he saw that it was nearly full of people, many of them grumbling or gazing out the windows in a state of morose indifference. For the most part, his fellow passengers were humbly dressed women, middle-aged or older, carrying (or sitting upon) mammoth clear plastic bags containing brightly colored clothing. He found a seat on a bench on the right side at the rear. Throughout the carriage a few benches had been reversed so that some of the passengers could face each other in groups of four. Alex's was one of these. Across from him an old peasant couple leaned against each other, head to head, shoulder to shoulder, sound asleep. Beside him, a dozing babushka held on her lap a fitfully sleeping girl with fevered cheeks and a dribbling nose.

His back was beginning to hurt from the long hours spent on hard benches, and this, added to his other pains, provoked a mood of such frustration that he was on the verge of barking something irrational. He sensed that if he was to let this mood go on, he might erupt into loud, unstoppable ranting that would get him ejected from the train. He had not once in his life ranted vocally, but in the present circumstances he felt himself capable of anything. He told himself to keep quiet and forced a return of perspective by training his mind on a mental image of Father Serafim beaten to a bloody pulp in a prison camp. That was real suffering, he admonished himself.

The train began to roll, dispelling the looming claustrophobia. It took an hour to cross the other half of the city, which seemed to be an endless graveyard of concrete apartment blocks frozen in time, relieved only by occasional orange trolleys covered in rust and frost, idling empty at crossings. When at last the train gathered speed and left the great cloud behind, he saw that the taiga was now visible, white under the moon and stars. He watched it pass for a time, and when the lights of the carriage were dimmed, he closed his eyes and tried to sleep. The train rocked sideways frequently, and the knee of the sleeping child bumped his bruised elbow more than once. The grandmother awoke, scowled at Alex, shifted her body, thrusting an ample hip against his hip, and mumbled irritably.

Irritated himself, eyes and mouth slits of frustration, Alex thought:

Where are you, Andrew? Are you enjoying your ride on the eagle? Do you ever think about your family? Does it cross your mind that you may be destroying your life? Destroying my life too?

Like an angel of mercy, an elderly lady wearing a floral kerchief on her white hair made her way down the aisle carrying
a wicker basket, calling out that she had pickled eggs, bread,
fish, and drinks for sale. Most people ignored her. When she
came to Alex, she opened a paper bag on which a dancing
bear had been printed. Obeying her command to look inside,
he saw three bottles of Baltika. He bought two, and these
were to him like a reprieve from hell. He immediately opened
one and began to sip from it. It was cold with a slush of ice
particles floating on the top. It tasted wonderful, and a glow
began to spread through his chest, easing his anguish.

One of the passengers across the aisle bought the third
bottle. Alex glanced over and saw that this person was an
attractive woman in her late thirties, though her features were
marred by a furrowed brow and a set of ugly reading glasses.
Set on the floor between her feet was a scarred leather briefcase splitting at the seams, the sort of bag that functionaries
of all kinds were in the habit of carrying. Her brown coat
was thread-worn, but on her dark hair sat a jaunty beret of
maroon velvet. She did not seem to notice Alex's scrutiny,
which was entirely a product of his loss of all social discretion. He merely stared because her image was a relief from
the surrounding drabness. She had been writing in a notebook
when the old lady interrupted in order to sell her wares. She
now resumed writing with her right hand, from time to time
lifting the bottle of Baltika to her lips with the left. In another
country this might have appeared crude and unwomanly, but
she drank with such reserve, even delicacy, that no observer
would have mistaken her for anything other than a person
worthy of deference.

What was she? An official of the Railway Ministry? Perhaps, but not very likely. Her clothing indicated a person of
modest means. A student? No, she was too old. A teacher?
If so, it meant she was dedicated and capable of some degree

of learning. And yes, the eyes were intelligent enough, flickering across her tablet, glancing out at the passing moonlit scene, back to the paperwork again, writing once more, then pausing to reflect.

Because his seat faced the front of the carriage and hers the rear, Alex was able to look at her surreptitiously without being obvious about it. He noted with undue interest that she was relaxing. She had a finely shaped forehead, thin black brows, and long eyelashes. The eyes were dark—brown or black, it was hard to tell. The cheeks wide, Slavic. The lips naturally red, accustomed to frowning but capable of a smile, pressed firmly together now in concentration. A small dimple in the cheek and another in the chin. She wore no makeup.

His heart beat a little faster. He told himself it was because of the alcohol in his bloodstream, and he looked away, trying to ignore the lingering afterimage of her face. With some effort he invoked Carol's image. This was not so much a memory recalled to the mind as it was a sense of her presence, though in what way she was present it was hard to say. He closed his eyes and felt her in his arms as they danced the mystical leaf-dance in a land far away and long ago, when the world had been sacramental with summer, before the great disenchantment.

But this was an acute reminder of her material absence, and though he clung more tightly to her, it only increased his feeling of desolation—which he defined to himself in the mundane term *loneliness*.

Why was he feeling so lonely? Loneliness was pathetic, childish, was it not? By contrast, solitude was noble. He had always loved solitude, even within the small and undemanding community of his family. Then, in later years, when his bereavement had left him more alone than ever, the passage of time had transformed the dreadful loss into a quiet background ache. Solitude had been the effect and the healing of that loss. Now, however, in his depleted condition, he felt the old wound opening afresh. A wave of grief rushed up from within, threatening to break out in sobs. If such a humiliating thing were to have occurred, it would not have been so much an emotional protest against the loss of his beloved wife as it would have been an outcry against the radical poverty of his present condition, his insufficiency in the face of all that life now seemed to demand of him. That his quest was in some sense heroic was, he knew, only a superficial thing, for he had been growing steadily more disheartened for many weeks. Although there had been momentary reassurances of the supernatural kind, and human help had come from unexpected quarters, his situation was relentlessly plunging downward.

Bit by bit everything was being taken away, including the resources of character that he had once assumed were the summation of himself. His worldly resources also. No doubt the Kingfisher would soon be foreclosed on by the bank. He regretted it—indeed, he hated the thought of it—yet he could not abandon a son in order to prove himself a good borrower. But why was it happening? Why did God permit it? Why was his fate (Was it fate? Was it providence? Was it merely random disorder?) now set on a course that seemed inescapable? He could not say, did not know. It was a fact, and he was being swept along in the trajectory of this fact like a makeshift rattletrap vehicle plunging across an ice void, its driver careening without caution, drunk and obsessed, the engine about to explode at any moment.

So, in the end, all romance, even the romance of a heroic search, was reduced to craven desperation.

"What next, Alex?" he asked himself. "Will you despair? And then, in order to escape your despair, will you lean across the aisle and ask that woman, that stranger, to speak with you? Will you use her presence to salve the wound of your losses, to replace all those who are absent, those whom you would prefer to be here? Will you indulge in a scenario borrowed from a penny romance, complete with the transparent plot, the predictably exotic setting: balalaikas begin to strum, and the beautiful mysterious Russian lady looks deep into your eyes and engages you in a dialogue that enflames you, sinking your mind in a pool of delicious consolations, complete with arabesque backdrops, the stroke of fox fur, the blood-hum of vodka, and the perfume of delirious passion? Is that the drug you want?"

His thoughts grew sterner against himself, because he sensed how very close he was to the dissolution of the self, how easily his loneliness would succumb to the merest hint of human warmth. Angrily he sat straighter on the bench and glared out the window. Then, gathering the last scraps of intellectual force, he tried to give himself a lecture on the follies of romanticism.

"Listen to me, Alex, listen! You cannot waste energy on phantasms. Even if she had a moment to spare for you, which is unlikely, and even if she would consider the innocent dalliance of a conversation, which is also unlikely, it would be unfair to her and unfair to you.

"Yet how beautiful she is! Those dark, intelligent eyes and sensitive lips. Oh, the fine head and slender neck, her beauty seasoned but not old. She emanates warmth. Warmth, warmth—O long-forgotten warmth!

"Carol! Carol, why am I here? Why are you not here beside me? Why did you die? God, why did you let her die?

"Be still! Be still! Think! Think!

"Why are you feeling these things for a stranger? Is it desire? No, it's not, though doubtless it's lurking here and could be set afire in an instant. This is no more than feelings. It has nothing to do with that woman reading over there, oblivious to my mad musings."

He cast a swift glance across the aisle. The woman was asleep, the writing pad open on her lap, hands folded on it, the pen drooping between her fingers.

Relieved at his narrow escape, he closed his eyes and drifted away, first into half sleep, then at last into the full sleep of blessed oblivion.

Morning came. Alex stirred and glanced out the window to see low hills on the right of the track and flatter land unchanged to the north. The dawn was only beginning, but the sky promised a cloudless day. A few stars could still be observed. The babushka and her grandchild were no longer with him, and he supposed that sometime during the night the train had stopped and let them off. Across from him the old couple were still asleep, the woman's cheek resting on her husband's chest, his chin on the top of her head, her right arm wrapped around his waist. His left hand on her shoulder was set in a mold of unselfconscious tenderness. On their hands they wore wedding bands of cheap metal. Young lovers grown old. Alex looked away.

Across the aisle the beautiful, mysterious Russian lady was awake and had resumed her concentration on the notebook. She had been transformed by the wan light of day into an ordinary woman with pale skin and troubled eyes. Much experience was written in her expression.

"A teacher", Alex decided. "Definitely a teacher."

He dozed for another half hour, until the conductor came through the carriage calling out that Krasnoyarsk was the next station, ten minutes to Krasnoyarsk. Passengers stirred and stretched. Murmurs of quiet conversation rose above the steady clickety-clack of the tracks. The old couple awoke, eyed Alex cautiously, and began to straighten their clothing and baggage. They communicated to each other without words, the expressiveness of their faces sufficient for the tasks at hand.

When the train slowed and eased into the station at Krasnoyarsk, Alex looked out to see rows of women standing on the platform in front of rusty baby buggies and collapsible wooden tables, all of which contained baked goods and various other foods. Many of the passengers left the coach with their baggage, and almost all detrained for a short respite of solid ground and relatively fresh air. Alex got out as well, stepping down onto the cement platform, where a wall of frigid air brought him fully awake. For several minutes he strode back and forth along the platform, breathing the mixture of diesel fumes and the sweeter scents of hot bread, smoked fish, and steaming tea urns. He bought a cup of tea, which he drank on the spot, and a bag of sweet buns and another of smoked fish, which he saved for the next stage of the journey.

The engine thrummed loudly and beeped its horn, and all passengers hastened on board. Alex waited until the last moment of freedom before leaping onto the steps of the coach as the wheels began to inch forward. Making his way to the rear, he noticed that half the benches were now empty. Arriving at his seat, he saw that a new passenger was sitting alone on the spot the old couple had vacated. He sat down opposite and tried to ignore her. This was impossible.

She was the most beautiful woman he had ever seen in his life. She was beyond beautiful. To look at her was to be lost. She was in her early twenties and of medium height, wearing a slender greatcoat of fine magenta cloth, brown leather boots, a pink silk scarf around her neck, and a cap of sable fur on her blond hair. She did not acknowledge Alex's arrival but continued to read from a book that she held open in her hands. Squinting his eyes, he deciphered the title on the cover: Mikhail Lermontov's *Mtsyri*. Alex had read it long ago. It was a dramatic poem about a young slave who dies of a broken heart, exiled from his beloved Georgia. It was pure romanticism.

A sudden movement outside the window alerted him to the sight of a young man running along the platform beside the coach, his eyes wild with anxiety, waving his arms at the girl. She did not look out. Her eyes were red rimmed. They were blue eyes. The young man—boyfriend, fiancé, husband—came to the precipitous end of the platform and stopped, dropped his arms in a gesture of despair, and disappeared into the past.

Alex knew just how the boy felt. He wondered how he could possibly travel as far as Irkutsk without becoming completely demolished by unrequited love. Involuntarily, his eyes flicked to her hands and noted the absence of rings on her fingers.

Move to another seat, Alex! he thought. *Now!*

But he was unable to move.

You're tired. Your defenses are down; you're lonely and capable of all sorts of foolishness. Move to another seat.

But it was useless. The intoxication of beauty was busily igniting his heart, and he knew that the other passions might not be far behind. The firebird of adulation was already flashing in the trees, rising into leaves that burst into golden flames, and all about were swirling turquoise, incandescent red, and velvet black—inviting him into a classic fairy tale painted on enameled *palekh* boxes or varnished eggs, pulling him irresistibly into the phantasm. He was Prince Alyosha the Wise and she the princess whom fate had ordained for him, if he could defeat the seven manifestations of Baba Yaga the witch.

Please don't eat me, Puny cried!

Alex laughed.

I'll make a meal for you one day
If I could only wed
Your fairest daughter over there,
Who's weeping in the shed.

Again Alex laughed, oblivious to the fact that this self-mockery might be overheard and misinterpreted.

She's lonely, Baba, can't you see?
I'd make a lovely mate!

The situation was absurd, he told himself, completely absurd! *He* was absurd!

Alex stood and was about to find another seat when the girl suddenly burst into tears and covered her face with the little book of poetry.

He sat down on the edge of his bench.

She turned sideways, facing the window, her eyes closed tightly, tears spilling from them against her will, shuddering now and then with the effort to contain the noise of crying. Finally she closed the book in her lap and stared out the window in an attitude of total misery.

All the while Alex sat without moving, torn between leaving and staying, certain that he should let the poor girl grieve in private, and at the same time detained by a haunting sense that another human presence—his—might be of help. That his motivation was perhaps a little mixed was not unknown to him, but he could do nothing about it. His awe before her beauty did not disappear, but there now accompanied it a sense of sincere human sympathy. She rummaged in her pocket searching for a handkerchief but found none. Alex opened his carry bag, found a package of paper tissues, and offered her one. She nodded and whispered, "*Spasiba.*"

She dried her face, sniffed, and wiped her nose, trying to recompose herself. Alex sat back and said nothing. He extracted his book of Hopkins poetry and opened it at random. In this delicate moment, he planned no strategy of familiarity, not even an innocent conversation. Strangely, he felt an upsurge of the paternal instinct he had felt so often in the face of suffering Russians, the young and the elderly, on the streets, in the underground, as if they were a nation of abandoned children, trapped beneath the wreckage of a dark century. She too was a child—as much a child as little Ksenia in Saint Petersburg who had kissed the icon, or the gypsy boys singing their triumph over the witch, or Alyosha wallowing in a latrine, or the peasant youth in pain before Rembrandt's painting—yes, even those whose material forms had expanded into adulthood.

Thus the firebird tipped forward into its downward parabola, falling from the bridge that spanned heaven and earth, splitting the surface of the nameless northern river, plunging deep into pools of love, the red fire-feathers falling away in its rapid descent. Touching the riverbed, reversing direction into the upward surge, blue feathers sprouting, crest arching, the father-kingfisher rose to the surface and burst into the clear summer's air.

He read quietly to himself, aware that he must not intrude on her sorrows, for intrusion, if it was merely a way of feeding attraction (even under the name of compassion), would have been a lie. The kingfisher might catch fire again, reducing everything to ashes.

Hills swelled on the right, bristling with snowy birches and firs. Alex laid a slice of fish on a bun and offered one to the girl. She shook her head. He returned to his book.

Sometime later he looked up to see that she was regarding him with a steady gaze that combined both sadness and curiosity.

"Why did you laugh at me?" she said with only a faint tone of reproach.

"I was not laughing at you", he replied.

"It seemed to me that you were."

"No", he shook his head somberly. "I was laughing at myself."

"Why were you laughing at yourself?"

He held up the book as if in explanation—or as a shield. "A private joke. A literary joke."

"It is not our language. Are you a foreigner?"

He nodded.

"You do not look like one."

He remembered that he was still wearing his disguise—the shabby greatcoat, the dyed hair. It struck him suddenly that he must be a wretched sight, and this increased the sense of absurdity that he felt about himself. He laughed again.

A little smile flickered at the corner of her lips.

"It is the poetry", he said. "Poetry sometimes makes me laugh."

"I too like poetry", she said, holding up Lermontov for him to see.

Although he knew that she was conversing with a bedraggled, unshaven, poorly dressed middle-age man solely for the purpose of distracting herself from her pain, he could not resist pleasing her. A few little red feathers sprouted among the cobalt. He recited from memory a beloved passage from *Mtsyri*:

> "Lured by earth's bright
> Beauty I was, and longed to see
> If born for dark captivity
> We mortals were, or freedom."

Her eyebrows raising, she said with something close to reverence, "You know Lermontov?"

"A little."

"My favorite line is similar to the ones you just spoke. Maybe you know it: 'A slave in alien parts, unloved have I lived, and a slave am meant to die.'"

"I know the passage well", he said.

"But we are not slaves", she said in a hushed voice. "No longer", she added.

"The poet gives to the slave a remembrance of his future", Alex said.

"What do you mean?" she said with a puzzled look.

"He gives a dream of liberty to those who do not yet know that they can dream."

"It may be so", she sighed.

"A poet sees his father in his son and his son in his father."

She gave this some thought before replying, "And himself in both?"

"Yes."

"And mothers and daughters?"

"The same."

She smiled and leaned forward a little, her glance passing over the bag of food on the seat beside him.

He opened it and invited her to take something from it. She took a bun and a slice of fish. He took some for himself, and they ate in silence. He opened his book and resumed reading. She did the same with hers.

By now he was hopelessly in love. His blue feathers were emitting wisps of smoke and had begun to glow with combustible colors. He knew that he should make some excuse, go for a stroll from one end of the train to the other, stand in the connecting passageway for a while, freeze the irrepressible courtier within, try to recapture the paternal instinct. Instead, he worked hard at keeping his eyes away from her, and stared at the passing scenery until the forest became a blur.

Dancing deer and rustling leaves. Sacred marriage beds and fertile holiness.

She fell asleep, but he refused to let his eyes linger on her face. He looked down at his book and forced himself to read. The afternoon wore on.

Later, Alex looked up to see that she was awake again, gazing at him with interest.

"It is not German or French, I think", the girl said. "Is it English? You are English?"

"*Kanadits*", Alex said.

She asked him about his country, and he told her a few things—about the climate mostly. There seemed little else to tell. He would have liked to discuss the subject of love ("Excuse me, miss, what is your understanding of the genuine apotheosis of love?") but decided against it.

She asked about the poems he was reading. What were they about? Who had written them? Could he translate one for her? He explained that this particular poet was very difficult to translate because the sounds of the words were a vital part of the poems. She replied that this was true of all poetry.

He agreed but said that this was truer of Hopkins than of any other poet he could name. She asked him to try anyway. It would have been next to impossible to translate from the book in front of him, but he recalled the short passage he had laboriously translated for Oleg months ago when the Russian visited his shop in Halcyon. Closing his eyes to shut out the image of the enchanting girl, he recited the stanza from "That Nature Is a Heraclitean Fire".

Glancing over to see her response, he was surprised to find that she was looking out the window, her face a complete mask. He attempted a rough description of the remainder of the poem, but he began to falter as he wondered if she was really listening.

"Everything in life is a being", he explained, summarizing. "No one thing is entirely like another. Everything has fire in it, and if you know how to unlock it, the fire is released."

"What kind of fire?" she asked tonelessly, still staring out the window.

"Good fire. Sweet fire that does not destroy its fuel but frees it to become what it truly is."

"And what is that?"

"Love."

Soundless tears spilled from her eyes. Alex was at a loss for what to do or say. Presently, she dried her eyes on her coat sleeve, reached into her pocket, and with trembling fingers extracted a package of cigarettes. Its cover was a soaring rocket, a brand called Kosmos. Alex attached no cosmic significance to this, did not try to read symbols in what was really nothing more than decoration. But what next occurred did, perhaps, have some significance.

She put the cigarette to her lips and raised her eyebrows to inquire if he had a light. Alex remembered that he had a box of wooden matches he had saved from the table of his room in the express train. Jumping to his feet, he fumbled in his pants pocket, his fingers touching a variety of tangled items—handkerchief, rosary, kopecks, comb, and a jumble of spilled matches. Intending to pull out the entire mess, he yanked too hastily, jamming it on a ripped seam. He pulled harder, which had the disastrous result of rubbing a match head against something rough. The sulfur flared and burned the tip of his index finger. In one reflex motion, he pulled his hand out, forgetting that the match was still alight. A stab of pain hit him in the thigh. Then his pocket exploded as all the other matches burst into flame and his trousers caught fire.

With a howl he leaped into the aisle and jumped about, beating at his thigh. This, as well as the puffs of smoke and sulfur fumes, created a little disturbance in the vicinity. Passengers turned their heads to watch in amazement. An enterprising old man threw a cup of water at the general area, and the fire went out.

Utterly humiliated, Alex sat down, rocking forward and backward, his face contorted in agony. What to do? He could hardly drop his pants to inspect the degree of the burn, nor was he yet able to walk to the far end of the carriage to the toilet cubicle, where he could nurse in private his wounded leg and his wounded dignity.

The clerkish woman whom he had admired so much the night before leaned across the aisle and handed him a half-full bottle of beer. Her eyes were sardonic, peering at him over the top of her glasses.

"Pour it on the burn", she commanded. "You must cool the flesh quickly. That will reduce the damage."

Alex did as he was told, ignoring the people who had crowded around to watch. Emptying the bottle onto the blackened blast hole, he felt some relief but noted that the patch of exposed skin beneath was livid red. Again the clerkish woman intervened, offering him a small tube of ointment. He took it from her, squeezed a blob onto his index finger, thrust it inside the hole, and smeared it around.

When he handed it back, she said, "At the next stop, get out and find some ice. Put it on the burn."

He nodded, still unable to speak.

Various fellows, young and old, vied for the privilege of lighting the girl's cigarette with their butane lighters. She accepted one and sat back, inhaling deeply, watching Alex. Tears were still in her eyes, but she was shaking with suppressed mirth. When he caught her eye, she burst out laughing. Covering her face, she gave full vent, a high, uncontrollable giggling that set off others nearby. Soon the entire rear of the carriage was in an uproar of hilarity, and among the comments, Alex was chagrined to hear the words *foreigner*, *fool*, and *idiot*. The clerkish woman alone did not join in the fun but did indulge in a cool smile before returning to writing in her notebook.

When he was able to stand the pain, he limped to the toilet, where he found a line. News had already reached that end of the carriage, and people kindly pushed him forward to the front. When he was safely inside, he dropped his pants and inspected the wound, which was halfway up his outer thigh. It was about six inches in diameter, blistering, ugly as a burnt bird. He did not want to splash tap water onto it because a sign over the sink said that the water was not drinkable. Desperate, he pressed his flank against the wall and lifted his bare leg against the window, hoping that the cold glass would relieve his suffering and reduce the damage caused to the skin. It was unfortunate that in this particular carriage the original window had apparently been broken and its customary opaque glass replaced with clear glass. So preoccupied was he that he failed to notice the train slowing, and he looked out the window only when he heard a babble of voices and giggling coming from outside. To his horror he realized that the train had arrived at a station and that a group of women with buggies full of food were standing no more than a few feet away, pointing and laughing at him. He hurriedly covered himself and slinked out of their line of sight.

Deciding that the ice could wait, he stumbled into the passageway between the carriages and waited there until the train pulled away from the station. Fuming, hurting, ready to fly into a rage at this latest blow from fate, he added it to the growing list of his grievances. When he had calmed down, he returned to his seat.

The girl was reading her Lermontov and did not look up. That was fine by Alex. He would be quite happy never to talk with her again.

Now as the train rolled at top speed into the late afternoon, a dusky-rose light settled on the taiga, the forest thickened, and the hills climbed steadily higher against the sky. A star appeared in the deepening blue. Hands pressed between his knees, Alex stared at his feet and brooded. If he met the metaphysicians, he decided, he would physically manhandle them. Andrew would get a tongue-lashing he would never forget. Maybe the boy should get some manhandling as well.

The girl laughed again, her eyes fixed on a page of her book.

"Why are you laughing?" Alex growled.

"It is the poetry", she said. "Poetry sometimes makes me laugh."

"Lermontov makes you laugh?"

She collapsed once more into uncontrollable giggles. He stared at her, feeling a great dislike for this former beauty.

"I am sorry, sir", she said when she got control of herself. "Does it hurt?"

"Yes, it hurts", he snapped. "Did you enjoy your cigarette?"

"Y-yes!" she hooted.

The brainless laughter infuriated him. He turned his head and fixed his gaze at the passing landscape. Try as he might, he could not help but notice that she was still looking at him. From the corner of his eye he saw that a certain sympathy was mixed with her amusement. She reached into her purse and withdrew a small bottle.

"Would you like a sip of vodka?" she asked in a voice dripping with kindness.

"No thank you", he said coldly.

"It will ease the pain a little. Come, try it."

He accepted the bottle, unscrewed the lid, and put it to his lips. Throwing back his head, he took a good swallow. Now he was becoming a water skimmer, he thought bitterly. Well, so what! Fire spread down his throat and into his chest. It helped. She watched him as he took sip after sip.

"Not too fast or you will get drunk", she cautioned.

"Thank you for your advice", he said.

"Are you angry?"

"Not at all. I am having a lovely time."

She laughed again and closed the book. He hated her laugh. But he could not deny that, well, her beauty really was quite astonishing. It was a shame about her personality.

By the time he finished the bottle, night had fallen. His tension and rage had been reduced to almost nothing. The pain in his leg (and his left hand, and his elbow, and his back, and his heart) had also declined.

"I am sorry", she said in a conciliatory voice, leaning forward. "It was not proper of me to laugh."

"That's all right", he said with a wave of his hand. "I suppose it was a ridiculous sight."

Her eyes were really quite lovely. And thoughtful. She liked poetry. She had cried—over that frantic boy at the station, no doubt.

"I would have laughed too", he admitted.

"Would you have? No, sir, I do not think so. You are a person who does not enjoy another's misfortune. This I have already seen in you."

"Me?" he muttered. "I'm just a foreigner, an idiot, and a fool."

"A fool? No, I do not think you are a fool. You are a nice man. Why are you in Russia? You do not look like a tourist."

He described the reason for his journey in a single sentence.

"That is a worry for you", she said. "Then I have made your travel more difficult."

She smiled at him. His mouth twitched into a return smile. She looked away shyly.

For a time, Alex slipped into a vodka-induced doze, but his leg began to throb again and woke him. He sat up straighter, trying to guard his leg. The girl was gone. *Well, so much for that*, he said to himself.

But within a few minutes she was back, carrying a paper bag. "Mister, I have been through the train and found people willing to sell me some medicine for you. Everyone is sympathetic, but you must admit that it was like the circus—a little."

She pulled a bottle of Baltika from the bag and handed it to him.

"Here, drink this medicine. It will cheer you up."

He opened the bottle and drank. The beer was warm but very comforting. There was another bottle for her and two more in reserve.

"Thank you. It was thoughtful of you", he said.

"It was the least I could do."

As the evening wore on, Alex began to regard her more kindly. Sometimes a hint of the firebird returned and sometimes the kingfisher. Gradually it all seemed to dissolve into an atmosphere of congenial warmth. He scolded himself for his judgment of the Russian people. They were not crazy, and neither was their country crazy, though it certainly operated according to standards different from his own. Yes, he liked the Russians very much. If you could make them smile, make them laugh, they dropped the mask, and underneath you always found the basic human material. Was it the beer that was making him so magnanimous? He knew he was becoming tipsy, but his thoughts were still coherent, and surely tipsiness was preferable to fury or despondency.

She finished her bottle, opened the Lermontov, and returned to a serious study of the lines. He wished she would speak with him again. What a fine young woman, so considerate, and so beautiful—breathtakingly so.

Looking up suddenly, she caught him staring at her. She smiled and closed the book.

"Are you hurting still?"

"Not much."

"Would you like to hear some poetry, sir?"

"My name is Alexander", he said.

"I am Valentina."

"Valentina. A beautiful name."

She opened her book and began to read to him from Lermontov's *Mtsyri*. At first he did not so much listen to the meaning of the poem as to the cadence of melodious words filling up a void. As she read on in her soft, modulated voice, so different from her ordinary conversational tone, he was entranced.

O Valentina, he thought, *I would fall in love with you forever. I would remain a perpetual stranger to my homeland for the sake of you. A slave in alien lands, I would live for you. And as the days and years wore on, accustomed to my chains I would grow. Yet lured by earth's bright beauty, I would learn if we are born for dark captivity or freedom.*

"Love *is* freedom", Alex said out loud.

"What did you say?" she asked, pausing in her recitation.

Realizing that he had spoken without intending to, he motioned for her to go on.

As she did so, the pain in his leg began to clamor for attention again. He reached for the second bottle of beer and opened it. As he drank, the pain receded, but in its wake it left a melancholic sense of the unreality of this transient romance. He knew that his love was undeclared, and would remain so because it had no hope of resolution. She was probably in love with that boy, and he, Alex, was no more than a useful stranger who had patched her broken heart, which on the morrow would doubtless break again.

Nevertheless, he told himself that even if a man were in chains, to contemplate beauty was to remember freedom. In this little island of light, in the midst of the great Siberian void, which would freeze him to death in minutes if he were abandoned in it, the presence of such beauty and the inference of love did not fail to do its work. It thawed the numb limbs, warmed the frostbitten heart.

The words of Lermontov dissolved in the air as she spoke them, replaced by his own silent declarations: *You are as beautiful as a ballerina! You are a dancer! You are a swan upon the lake!*

As the beer flowed through his system, currents of pity and passion blended, astringent with the tragedy of her land and rich in affection.

"O ballerina!" he breathed.

"What did you say?" she asked, looking up from her book again.

"Nothing. It was nothing."

She closed the book. "Would you read to me more of your poems?"

"But you understand no English."

"It would not matter. I would listen to the music in it."

Alex pondered her request for a moment, then closed his book. Feeling the massing pressure of his heart's enchantment, he leaned forward and said to her in great earnestness, "I know a poem."

"Yes? It seems you know many."

"This one is different. May I tell it to you?"

"Of course", she said with a look of curiosity.

Alex returned her look with an expression so warm, so profound, that she was arrested by the fervor of his emotion. Inhaling deeply, he put both of his hands to his heart and slowly opened his arms wide. It was a gesture so instinctive that he was barely conscious of it and fully oblivious to its lack of originality. If it happened to be the very stance taken by many a famous lover in the operas of Puccini, Glinka, Gounod, and Tchaikovsky, that was not really his fault. In the surge of his love, which of course was like no other in the world, all signs, words, and gestures became wholly fresh and unprecedented. For Valentina it was not, perhaps, a unique experience. But she was intrigued nonetheless and looked forward with interest to whatever pronouncements might be made by this totally sincere and eccentric foreigner.

Alex decided to address her in English, not so much because he wished to cover his feelings with deceit, but because if he were to have spoken the words in Russian she might have misunderstood his intention and drifted away into studied indifference or abruptly left and found a safer seat. In fact, he wished to unburden his heart without consequences in a fashion that would neither captivate nor alienate. In this sense it was an exercise for himself alone—or at least the literal content of the message was for his ears only. It was not entirely self-serving. The act of dramatic recitation, which involved elements of entertainment and the release of indecipherable music into the atmosphere, would serve her needs by distracting her from her own wound. There was no desire for conquest in his motivation, nor even a schoolboy infatuation. He felt his admiration was of the most noble and purified sort. If he resembled any other lover in the long history of love, he was sure that he was most like Dante.

Of course, there were flickers of fiery plumage beneath the dominant cobalt—this could not be helped—and he was not indifferent to the feelings of pleasure these gave him as he spoke to her. If the root of it was sexual, it was only partly so, for what was pouring from the fracture in his chest was of such great strength that he knew it was more than simple carnality or even romanticized, idealized carnality. If he had met her in other circumstances, free of his loneliness and natural attraction, he would still have loved her. So he told himself.

As the current now fountained up from the flesh, it did not remain fixed there, for it continued to rise and fall, and rise again, soaring through the aesthetics of creation toward some inaccessible realm of the spirit. All of this transpired before a single word had left his mouth, though he was under the impression that his heart had already begun to speak.

"The poem?" Valentina prompted uncomfortably, for he had been staring at her with open arms for longer than was considered normal in her society.

"Oh, yes," he blinked, "the poem."

Then, in English, he began to speak in a low voice full of emotion. The words rolled from his tongue slowly, composing themselves of their own volition:

"O beautiful woman..." He cleared his throat and continued. "O beautiful woman, we are the braided wake of firebirds dancing in the air; we are the story that was written from the beginning; you are Halcyone, O daughter of Aeneas, and I am Ceyx your spouse. You grieved at our parting, for always partings great and small did make you weep. Far from you upon my voyage, I shouted as I was pitched from the vessel of my quest. 'I am drowning, Halcyone!' I cried. 'I am facedown upon the sea.'

"You flew to me, and when you saw my body floating on the waves, you knew the final parting was complete before you reached my side, for I was fully drowned. Yet Love the King saw our grief and pitied us. Your tears covered me; I rolled with the sea swell, then rose as the four-cycled Aeolian winds filled my breast, and I lived again. The bird of dawning, of crested head and bluer wing, *kolibri* we became, fisher-king and fisher-queen, laughing as we flexed our wings and rose to thank the Daystar for his gift.

"Upon the shore, the poppies drooped with seed, the harvest bear and cub roamed fat among the stands of grain, but we unshored desired a water nest in which to raise our young. Many were the young that we would have; unruly was the sea that tossed them. 'Come, Aeolus,' we sang, 'servant of the overarching love, blow, and blow again till all four quadrants of the turbulence are stilled; push it back unto tranquility; let your peace fall upon the waters of the abyss! Calm the upper waves and many deeps, and give us seven placid days, or twenty-one in generosity, that we might fledge our young and train them in the praise of flight!'

"Love did as we asked and sent his servant Aeolus. Now did love burn hotter upon that coldest sea, all ice dispersed by his breath, his hand stroking the tidal race until it fell asleep. We too fell asleep and, dropping into deeper passion, forged our young within our flesh. Sweet was their birth, and sweeter still their cries and flexing wings. Sweetest of all was the knowledge that came to us in that winter world, for we had learned that love is stronger than death. And more, we learned that only in the dying did we find the victory."

Alex fell silent. The sounds of the carriage wheels and its occupants rushed in, filling his ears. Looking at the girl, he saw that she was listening, her face quietly absorbed, though she could not have understood a word. He went on in a subdued voice:

"What is love, Valentina-Halcyone? What is love to you and me? Why have we forgotten it? If I greet you now, as stranger to stranger, and am entranced by you, it is no more than a wakened dream. I will not cling to you that two may drown and never rise, but I will detain you for a while in search of memory, for I remember what I could have been. Do you hear my soul amidst the tides and waves? Do you also hear the singing of our children who will never be?"

Alex sat back and turned his head away. He did not want to look at her, for though he loved her, he knew that she could not comprehend the language he had tried to speak, and thus she would be constrained to talk as if he had not poured out everything. And so it was.

"That was very nice", she said in the tone of a serious student striving for gravity. "There was a bird in it—I heard you say *kolibri*."

"Yes."

"And you spoke my name. Why did you speak my name?"

"I was addressing the poem to you."

"Why did you?"

"Because a poem cannot exist floating in nothingness. It is a bridge that stretches across the oceanic spaces that exist between soul and soul."

"Oh, that is a beautiful thought."

"Thank you", he said, smiling politely.

Without warning, Valentina got up, stepped along the aisle, and asked a passenger for a lighter. She put a Kosmos to her lips, lit it, and returned the lighter to its owner. Then she sat down across from Alex, crossed her legs, opened the little book of Lermontov, and resumed reading to herself. From time to time she took a puff from the cigarette, and when it had burned low, she threw it onto the floor and stamped it out with her heel.

Alex closed his eyes. As he sank, his pounding heart slowed to its normal pace, and before drifting into a half sleep, he felt a moment of gratitude that he had spoken his poem in his native tongue.

When he awoke, he saw that she was gone. The carriage lights had been turned low for sleep. The train vibrated and clattered normally. Looking out the window, he could discern nothing of the passing landscape and guessed that a thick overcast was hiding the moon and stars. Frost had crept up the inside of the panes, and he knew by this that the temperature outside was colder than before.

His leg throbbed again, but now he had no beer or vodka with which to ease it. The carriage was almost deserted. Sometime during his sleep many of the passengers had detrained, Valentina-Halcyone among them, and there were now no more than a dozen people scattered throughout the sixty seats.

In the aftermath of his outburst of passionate creativity or creative passion, Alex felt very depressed. He sat bent over, elbow on knee, forehead in his right hand, left hand cradled across his lap. There was nothing he could do about the ache in his thigh, so he let it throb and throb and throb, mesmerized by the extraordinary precision with which it kept time to the rhythmic clatter of the tracks. Added to his depression were other feelings: a guilty sense that he had somehow betrayed Carol. He told himself it was not so, reminded himself that he was a widower and free to court another woman. After all, he argued, he had not actually crossed the frontier into the territory of sin. But his heart showed him that he had been a fool on every level, forgetting the past, hoping for a future that could never be, limping up and precipitating down the mountains of reason and unreason with such instability that he was now a stranger to himself. He was not Dante addressing Beatrice; he was Angus Graham drunk—drunk and spewing cathartic verse.

He let the train rock him, let his several wounds keep contrapuntal time. It would have been a relief to weep, but he could not. Seeing again the chain of events that had taken place since his departure from Halcyon, he felt himself descending into a nightmare like a man fleeing from a monster that is chasing him, his feet mired in invisible mud, running slower and slower until he can barely lift one foot after the other. Panic stabs him, and he wakes up panting, thankful that it was only a dream. In Alex's case, however, there was no waking up. Moreover, he was chasing the monster, the *thing* that held his son by the throat. As it fled on swift heels, his pursuing feet went slower and slower, falling farther and farther behind.

"O God," he whispered, "where are you? And where am I?"

"You need more of this", a woman's voice said. Startled, Alex looked up and saw that the clerkish woman across the aisle was offering him her tube of ointment.

"Thank you", he murmured and took it. Turning away in shame, he squeezed a coil of translucent grease onto his finger and applied it to the burn through the gaping hole in his pants. He also put a little onto the burn on his left hand. After recapping the tube, he handed it back to her, thanking her again.

She returned to her book. He returned to his solitary brooding, head in hand. For a time he nursed the agony and

564

confusion that he felt, trying valiantly not to slip further into depression. But waves of panic rippled up from inside, withdrew again, then returned with greater frequency. He tried to dispel the muscular pain this caused in his chest by sitting back and breathing deeply. It helped to a degree. He realized also that he had not been praying as he ought since Obsk and that he had let himself become completely entangled in fantasies and grievances. He saw that he had been building a case against—well, against God. Or more accurately, against the concept of God's goodness. But the realization changed nothing. He felt incapable of dispelling the resentment with prayer.

He thought of Father Serafim and all that the priest had suffered, and of Father Sergius as well. He wondered how they had kept faith. He also remembered Alyosha of the underground, a degraded prince who had lost faith, or perhaps had never had it, yet survived on scraps of hope. For Alyosha, hope had come through the syringe and the bottle. Alex remembered also the prostitute whom he had helped in Moscow, a degraded princess, a woman without a name. *Interdevushka*, she had called herself, "international girl", servicer of foreign needs—identifying herself as a function. Where had she found hope? In a fugitive devotion to a reformed harlot of the desert? He saw that these people had experienced depths of suffering he could not begin to understand. And there were depths of human endurance in them as well. This thought cast him down still further, for he saw that his readiness to plunge into despair over his minor afflictions revealed a great deal about his own character. Now, added to his other burdens, Alex began to suffer from an acute dislike for himself.

He tried to pray but could only mouth silent words, hoping as he sank that they escaped the pull of planetary gravity, hoping that somewhere this last shout was being heard above the wail of Aeolian winds.

"Please, God, please," he whispered, "I don't have much strength left. If you want me to go on, I need more help."

The man's body was substantial, his mind and will also. But at this darkest moment he understood the uselessness of all former strengths. There was nothing of the hero cry of drowning Ceyx in his prayer. It was a child's plea.

He had only just completed the prayer when once again a voice from across the aisle broke into his solitude. He looked up to see the woman seated sideways on her bench, legs covered by a fleece rug. She had removed her glasses. She was staring at him with an inquiring look, as if waiting for an answer.

"Did you not know the word for it?" she asked with raised eyebrows. The eyes were latent with some peculiar Russian irony.

"Pardon me", he replied. "I did not hear what you said."

Switching to perfectly enunciated English with a faint Slavic flavor, she said, "*Kolibri* is our word for hummingbird. You should have said *zimorodok*—the bird you call kingfisher."

With a jolt, Alex realized that she had overheard his poetic outpouring to Valentina. How much had she understood of it? A great deal, he guessed, because she could not have made the leap from *kolibri* to the concept of a kingfisher without a knowledge of mythology, and a lot more besides.

"You speak English", he said, turning red in the face.

"Obviously."

"*Zimorodok*", he mumbled.

"Do you have much pain in your leg?"

"Not so much. The ointment helped."

"It is antibacterial and should also hasten healing. Did you get off at a station and find some ice as I suggested?"

"No."

"Why not?"

"I was distracted."

"I noticed."

"You overheard everything?"

She shrugged, as if it was not a matter of any consequence. The whiff of irony in her eyes edged toward amusement.

"Bad to worse", he groaned. "Bad to worse."

"Come, it's not so bad."

"Really? That's reassuring."

"You are far from home?"

"Obviously."

That made her smile briefly.

"You are angry."

"What reason could I possibly have for anger?" he said with heavy sarcasm.

"Why are you in Russia if you don't like it here?"

"I'm here against my will. If you're so good at listening to other people's conversations, surely you heard me explain to that girl."

"No, I heard only your poem. You were hard to ignore at that point."

"I was quoting. I was acting."

She gave this lie the response it deserved—silence.

"You speak good Russian", she said after a pause. "Most people would think you're a cultured man from Saint Petersburg. But the accent is faintly provincial, mixed a little with the style of nineteenth-century novels."

He nodded coldly.

"That is an admirable achievement. Tell me, are you a Russophile?"

"I used to be."

"Good. I'm a Russophobe myself."

This little joke, offered with a wry half smile, was difficult to resist. But resist it he did.

She let him stew for a while, observing him without expression as he adjusted his body, his clothing, and his pathetic male ego. He faced forward abruptly, scowled, opened the Hopkins book, and forced his eyes to move back and forth across the page.

This made her laugh. He was getting rather tired of Russians laughing at him.

"Would you like some tea?" she asked in a kinder voice.

"No thank you."

"Someone has a samovar three carriages ahead, I'm told. Would you like to go forward with me?"

"No."

"The leg needs circulation. It would hurt, but it would be better if you walked a little."

"I can do without the tea."

"All right, suit yourself."

She got up and walked unsteadily down the aisle of the rocking carriage, holding onto the backs of the seats as she went. She had removed her coat, and he saw that she was a fine-looking woman, trailing a colored scarf about her neck. The beret was still perched at an angle on her dark hair.

Ten minutes later she was back with two paper cups. She handed him one.

"Some of it spilled, but most has arrived safely."

He took it gratefully, and she sat down in the seat facing him.

"Drink. It will improve your outlook on life."

Again the wry smile.

He drank. It was strong and very sweet.

"How much do I owe you?" he asked.

"Nothing. It was a few rubles. I had some to spare. Do you still hate Russians?"

"I have never hated Russians. Why do you say you're a Russophobe?"

She shrugged.

"You didn't mean it. You're a Russian yourself."

"True. But that doesn't mean I like everything about us. So, tell me, why are you here?"

"Are you with the KGB?"

She laughed and nearly spilled her drink.

"You mean the FSB. The KGB has gone out of business. But I am neither."

"Let me guess. You're a teacher."

"Wrong."

"A writer."

"Also wrong."

"You're a former Communist apparatchik who has become a minor capitalist", he said sourly.

"Wrong again."

"What are you, then?"

She offered her hand and said, "I am a physician. My name is Irina Filippovna."

Humbled, he shook her hand. "Alexander Graham."

"Hello, Aleksandr. May I call you that? You may call me Irina, after the custom of Americans, who are always on a first-name basis within seconds of meeting each other."

He explained that he was not an American. He sipped more tea.

"So...why are you here?" she asked again.

"I have two sons", he said, staring out the window. "My youngest has disappeared in Russia, and I'm trying to find him."

"That is a burden", she said with genuine concern. "I am sorry."

He did not feel capable of telling her any more. She let him be. Quietly sipping from her cup, she seemed preoccupied by her own thoughts. When at last their eyes met, she frowned.

"I also have two sons."

"And a husband?"

A flicker of pain crossed her face, but she hid it immediately.

"My husband is dead."

She paused only a moment before glancing at the wedding ring on his hand. "And you? Your wife must be worried about you."

"My wife is dead."

The symmetry of their situations was so perverse that both Alex and the woman raised their eyebrows simultaneously as it hit them. They both shook their heads. Then, seeing these almost-perfect reflections as strange and a little disturbing, they both shook their heads again.

"Maybe we should get up and run around the carriage", said Irina Filippovna. "Do not look at me and I will not look at you, and we will see what happens."

"Maybe we're mirror images of each other", Alex suggested.

"That is surreal. I hate surreal."

"So do I."

"Oy, oy! Stop it."

"It *is* strange, isn't it?"

"Perhaps not so strange. But we must stop imitating each other. Let's change the subject. Do you like literature? It seems to me that you do. Poetry, obviously."

"Obviously."

"How about Pasternak?"

"Yes."

"And fiction? How about Solzhenitsyn?"

"I like him very much."

"So do I. All right, what is your favorite of his novels?"

"*Cancer Ward.*"

"Good. I prefer *First Circle.* Things are improving. Maybe we are real after all."

"I think we are."

"Why do you like *Cancer Ward? First Circle* is richer in politics."

"Yes, but in *Cancer Ward* the politics is embedded in the metaphor", Alex countered. "It strikes deeper that way."

"Does it?"

"The regime destroys normal human relationships—for example, the way Kostoglotov's and Vera's love for each other never connects."

"Vera Gangart is a great character—a dedicated doctor—but let's not call it love. That was loneliness."

"Don't you remember at the end of the story, when Kostoglotov becomes a free man at last, liberated from the Gulag, and his cancer is in remission? He lies down in a train carriage and is suddenly seized with anguish. He buries his face in his coat, which is his only home."

"Yes, I know that scene very well."

"It's a simple moment, yet it says everything. The greatest cancer is unseen and is within the soul, waiting to be faced. Implicit in Kostoglotov's willingness to feel again is the promise of hope."

"Hope?" she said with a doubtful look. "How do you think his hopes were answered? In those lines I saw his despair."

"You are interpreting in a limited way."

"Are you not interpreting?"

"I suppose so. Yes, we all do it. But why choose despair?"

She did not reply to the question directly. Instead, she said:

"Do you know Pushkin's famous lines about prisoners? No? He said, 'In our vile times, man was, whatever his element, either tyrant or traitor or prisoner!'"

"In our vile times, are we not all prisoners?"

"Are you a prisoner, Aleksandr Graham?"

"Yes", he said glumly, and stared at the floor.

She checked her wristwatch. "It is time for another change of subject. Let us go find more tea. It will be morning soon. No use sleeping now. We arrive in Irkutsk about nine. The schedules are all off." She glanced at the burn hole on his leg. "Do you think you are able to walk?"

"I'll try."

So he hobbled along behind her toward the front of the train, feeling a growing gratitude that she had interrupted his downward plunge, feeling also a certain sanity returning. Three cars ahead, they came to the seat of two sly-looking women presiding over a portable samovar. These ladies immediately recognized Alex as a foreigner. Although he did not at the moment resemble one, there was no doubt that his reputation had spread from carriage to carriage. They ogled the blast hole in his pants. They demanded fifty rubles for a cup of tea. Irina Filippovna squabbled and scolded and got them to accept ten. For her own cup she paid five. When the money and cups had been exchanged, everyone reverted to cordiality. Alex and Irina returned to their seats and sat together chatting and watching for the dawn.

PART THREE

24. *A Bad Day at Listvyanka*

A ghostly mountain range appeared in the south, its upper levels pink with alpenglow. In the east the serrated edge of higher peaks was dark against the floodlight of the rising sun. The train sped through the forested basin of a wide valley.

"The Angara River", Irina said, pointing to a winding ribbon of white in the distance. "It is very big. It drains Baikal."

"Where do you live?" Alex asked.

"A village on the west shore of the lake, a half day's journey from Irkutsk. Where are you going?"

"I have to get to a place called Listvyanka."

"Why Listvyanka?"

"The people who have my son are somewhere on the lake—where, exactly, I do not know. Have you heard of a place called the Dacha?"

"The dacha? That could be one of a thousand places. Even the poorest people like to have a shack or cardboard shelter they call the dacha."

"It's the only lead I have. A hotel clerk in Novosibirsk said that someone in Listvyanka might be able to help me find this resort or retreat center."

"Did he say who?"

"He meant no one in particular. Just that I should try asking there."

"It won't hurt to ask, but Baikal is hundreds of kilometers long, and seventy to a hundred kilometers wide over much of its length. Numerous villages dot the shore, and some larger towns. There may also be special resorts that are not well known."

"Then the chance is small."

"It seems. But I will introduce you to someone at Listvyanka."

"Are you going there?" he said, surprised.

"I must. My village is on a road accessible only through Listvyanka."

"Does the road go all the way along the lake?"

"No—about forty kilometers through the forest along the west shore. It is for horse and sleigh only. There is an ice road as well. Motor vehicles travel up and down the lake on it, but we seldom use it."

"I wonder if my son traveled on it."

"Possibly. Visitors use many means of travel in these parts—snow vehicles, trucks, ski-planes, all sorts of things. But they stay far out on the ice. Because the shape of Baikal bends, the journey is shorter if they head north in a straight line. We rarely see them. We go through the trees."

"Wouldn't it be faster for you to travel on the ice?"

"Faster, but very cold in an open sleigh. The forest provides shelter from the wind. There are no vehicles where I live."

"Your village sounds remote."

"Not really. It's just very small and uninteresting."

"Why do you live there?"

"It's my home."

Her facial expression told him she was not enthusiastic about answering more questions. He wondered why.

The engine hooted and slowed as it entered the city of Irkutsk. Divided by the Angara into uneven sections, the larger and older part was on the east bank, looped by the river. The train stopped at a station on the left bank, and here Alex and Irina disembarked. As they made their way through the terminal,

Alex offered to carry her heavy briefcase, but she declined. Going out onto the street, they spotted a city bus by the curb and climbed onto it. It took them across the river on a large concrete bridge and dropped them a few blocks from the bus station that served the outlying regions.

"Behold, the Paris of Siberia", Irina said with the wave of an arm as they walked in haste across Kirov Square, Alex hobbling behind because of his leg. He stopped to rest it for a moment and gazed at an old church, but his guide prodded him to keep moving.

"No time for sight-seeing. There is only one bus a day, and we have to hurry if we want to catch it."

They reached the station, bought their tickets, scurried to the platform, and found their bus just minutes before the driver closed the door and pulled away.

South of Irkutsk, the road hugged the bank of the frozen Angara, running through pine forest, crossing small rivers that drained the hills on the left and fed the great river to the right. An hour and a half later, the bus came to the outflow of Baikal at Listvyanka.

This was an unassuming little town strung along the lakefront. Irina told him that in summer it was a busy place with buses parked at the quay and ships of different kinds going in and out of the bay, including tourist cruisers, tugs used for towing logs to the mills, smaller boats belonging to fishermen, and research vessels carrying scientific survey teams. The ice-locked harbor was deserted now. The sun was bright, but a haze hung low over Baikal, and little could be seen of it aside from a few hundred meters of snow stretching away from the shore. In the southwest the white tips of the Sayan Mountains lifted high above the layer of yellowish haze, which Irina said was produced by the pulp and paper industry farther south on the lake.

The bus dropped them on the road next to a wharf, and from there they walked uphill to a hotel. This was a humble two-story affair of wood construction containing a few rental rooms and a modest restaurant. There they ordered tea, which arrived at their table in cups and saucers imprinted with the image of a whiskered seal balancing a red star on its nose.

"Old cups", Irina said, pointing at the star. "Pre-perestroika. A collector's item."

Alex pointed at the seal. "A strange symbol. Aren't we a thousand miles from the ocean?"

"One of Baikal's mysteries", Irina said, smiling. "There are seals in the lake. The *nerpa*. They are the only land-locked species of seal in the world. They live in fresh water year round. No one knows how they got here."

"I'm not sure how I got here either. But I *am* here."

"Another mystery."

"I want to thank you for your kindness to me. Your ointment helped my burn, and the conversation helped my poor addled brain. I think I was going a bit crazy back there on the train."

"Yes, you were. But a bit crazy is not the same thing as insane. You recovered quickly, which speaks well for your poor addled brain."

"It will do even better when I am returned to my natural environment."

"Where is that?"

He gave her a brief sketch—Halcyon, the Clementine, the bookshop—a world admirably devoid of mystery.

"A bookseller?" she chuckled. "I should have guessed."

"What do you mean by that?"

"Your appearance is misleading. Forgive me, but you do resemble a tramp. However, the words that flowed from your mouth were not those of an ordinary tramp. They were rather overloaded with classical references. The young lady would not have understood it even if you had spoken in Russian."

Embarrassed again, Alex colored and exhaled loudly. "*You* understood all too well. You are an educated person, I see."

She shrugged indifferently. Looking out the window at the bay, she said, "My son will arrive soon. We should try to speak with someone who might be able to help you. Semyon, I think. He would know anything there is to know."

They paid their bills and left the hotel, walking side by side on the unplowed lane going down into the town. On the main street close to the wharf, Irina led Alex to the front door of a clapboard building, with a sign by the door: "Semyon P. Timonin, Registered Captain, Baikal Tours".

Entering the building, they penetrated an atmospheric pollution of cigarette smoke that seemed to fill the cramped office entirely as if with a cloud. The walls were covered with maps and lewd calendars. A black-and-white television set was playing in a corner, and watching it was a sixty-year-old man seated in a wooden chair. When he finally noticed the visitors, he pulled his eyes from the television with reluctance and swung his legs off the desk.

"Ah, Irina Filippovna", he said, without standing. He squinted at Alex but did not bother to inquire about the visitor's identity or to introduce himself. The man was short and squat, smelling of cheap shaving lotion, tobacco, and diesel fuel. He wore a fleece-lined vest, and perched on his greasy head was a naval cap.

"Semyon Petrovich, I bring a visitor from the West. He is searching for a family member who arrived here sometime last week with a party of visitors from Europe. He does not know where they went on the lake."

Spitting his cigarette butt into an ashtray that looked to Alex like the skull of a large mammal, the captain peered at him suspiciously and said nothing.

Turning to Alex, Irina said, "Can you tell him anything about the other people in the party?"

"There were a few Russians, some people from England, maybe others from Finland, and at least one German."

"Scientists?" the captain asked.

"No. Their leader is a man named Bloch—the German."

Scratching his chin, Semyon said, "A German. Yes, I remember him. I had nothing to do with them. They came by private vehicles from Irkutsk a week ago—nice Japanese vans. A plane met them out there on the ice." He pointed to the window.

"Do you know where they went?"

"No."

"Are you sure it was the people I am looking for? There was probably a dark-skinned man from India or Pakistan among them."

"Yes, that's them. Hard to miss that lot. They were rich looking and having lots of fun."

"Do you recall seeing a young man among them, a tall, blond-haired Westerner?"

"They all looked Western to me. There were young people among them, but I could not see if there was a blond man. They were all wearing fur hats. I did not speak with them."

"Who flew them out, Semyon?" Irina asked.

"A charter from Ulan-Ude. That big yellow thing that lands on skis. Slava would know where they went."

Semyon Petrovich reached for a black telephone on his desk, dialed a four-digit number, and, when someone answered on the other end, talked into it in a language that was not Russian.

"He speaks in Buryat", Irina explained to Alex. "Slava is a Buryat who sells aircraft fuel."

Semyon hung up. "I told you, Slava knows everything. He says the plane went north to a place on the Brown Bear Coast. A new resort that the state built for government officials and high-class guests from abroad."

"Is it called the Dacha?"

"He called it the dacha. Is that its name?"

Growing excited, Alex stammered, "How can I get in contact with the people at the Dacha?"

Irina broke in: "If they are important people, Semyon, they will have a telephone. Can you find out for us?"

"Maybe."

Irina turned to Alex and said in English, "He will need a few rubles to cover his expenses."

Alex offered the man twenty. Semyon stared at the bills in his open palm, grunted in disgust as if to say, "What a paltry sum this is", and closed his fist.

"*Spasiba bolshoye*, great thanks", said Irina Filippovna with undisguised sarcasm.

Semyon picked up the phone and once again talked into it. When he hung up, he squinted at Alex and said, "Slava is calling back in a few minutes."

When the phone rang, the captain picked it up, barked "*Da!*" into it, and listened.

"*Da, da, da!*"

He hung up and said, "They have a phone, but it won't help you."

"Why not?" Alex asked.

"They flew out yesterday morning."

"Everyone?"

"Everyone. Slava talked to the housekeeper up there, a cousin of his. He says they went to Kiev and won't be back until next year."

"Kiev, in Ukraine?"

"The same. From there they plan to go to Italy—a place called Milano. That's all he knows."

Alex rubbed his forehead distractedly. He thanked the man and went out into the street. Irina followed.

"Not very good news", she said.

"Very bad news. That's it. It's over."

"I am sorry. What will you do now?"

"I will go home."

They stood together in silence while Alex collected his thoughts.

"What a mess. What a disaster", he said, staring at the ground, shaking his head repeatedly.

"The bus to Irkutsk has already left", Irina said. "You had better get a room for the night. I'll walk you to the hotel."

And so they trudged in silence back up the hill. In the lobby, Alex registered and paid for a single room. When this was done, Irina asked him to join her for lunch in the restaurant. They chose a table by the large window overlooking the bay. The pollution haze was blowing away, and a magnificent view of Baikal had appeared. Mountain ranges were now visible in the arc of space from the northeast to the southwest. Far out on the lake, a vehicle of some kind was speeding along, leaving a slow-motion spume in its wake.

They ordered tea, soup, and buttered bread, and when it arrived, they ate in silence. Alex did not look at Irina. He was completely engrossed in his private struggle, and bitterness was pushing for total possession. She did not intrude. Over a second cup of tea, she ventured an interruption.

"If you have enough money, you should take the jet from Irkutsk to Moscow. Then from there to Canada."

"I think I have enough", Alex mumbled, fingering the wad of rubles in his shoulder bag.

"Good. It will save you time...and much anxiety. You don't do well on our trains."

Irina glanced out the window. A horse was nosing up the hill, drawing a sleigh behind it.

"There is my son", she said, getting to her feet.

Alex stood also and walked her to the lobby entrance, where they shook hands.

"I don't ordinarily strike up acquaintance with strangers on trains", she said. "But—"

"But in my case you made an exception. Fools, generally speaking, are harmless."

She appraised this remark with a firming of lips. "Your mind is quick and articulate. But so often wrong."

"Are you saying that you decided to speak with me because you were impressed by my dignity?"

"I was impressed by your poetry." She smiled. "The hummingbird-kingfisher. The Pushkinesque quality."

"Your mind also, Irina Filippovna, is quick and articulate. And wrong."

"In your case I was right. In any event, it's over. If I've offended you, I'm sorry. I wish you well."

"Thank you."

"You'll recover. Humiliation usually doesn't inflict mortal wounds."

The horse halted before the entrance and shook its bells. More accurately, it was a pony covered in shaggy gray hair. Arching high above its neck was a wooden yoke decorated with painted flowers. Behind it was a two-passenger open sleigh on fiddlehead runners, its back end a flat platform for carrying cargo. A lanky adolescent in a fleece cap with long earflaps, a dirty canvas coat, and fur boots jumped out and busied himself tying the reins to a pine tree. His leather mitts extended halfway to his elbow. Lumps of frost stuck to the scarf at his neck and on the forelocks over his brow. He looked disgruntled, or perhaps the scowl on his face was his ordinary expression—a variation of the national mask.

"I must go. He does not like to be kept waiting", said Irina Filippovna. "Good-bye, Aleksandr. It was diverting to have made your acquaintance. I hope you find your son."

As she went out through the door, she did not look back. Alex turned away and went to the lobby desk to speak with the employee on duty. From her he learned that the bus for Irkutsk would leave the following morning just before noon, arriving in the city by 2:00 P.M. There was more than one flight a day to Moscow, she told him, and there were usually seats available. He could purchase his ticket at the airport.

His room was a cubicle lined with varnished pine boards. There was a television set (not working), a telephone, and a cot with a down pillow. The single picture was a photograph of a white ship steaming along a shoreline in calm water under towering mountains. Printed across the bottom was "Science Ship *Albatross* at Barguzin Bay".

The Russians, it seemed, had not read Coleridge. Feeling very much like the Ancient Mariner himself, Alex locked the door and stripped off his clothing. Tenderly he probed the wound on his leg. Guarding the angry blister on his hand, he held up his trousers to inspect the gaping burn hole. In the bathroom, he found a shower stall, sink, and toilet. He turned on the taps in the shower, expecting to see a rusty hemorrhage but gratified when steaming clear water gushed from the nozzle. He stepped under it, heaving great sighs of relief. There was a little bar of gray soap in the dish, and with this he lathered and rinsed his hands, which were greasy with fish oil, and his hair, which was lank with a week of neglect, not to mention the smoke cure it had undergone at the hands of Captain Semyon. Then he proceeded to the business of thoroughly cleaning his leg wound, despite the pain this caused.

Stepping out of the shower, he dried himself, arched his back until it made clicks along the vertebrae, then bent forward and touched his toes. Wrapping a dry towel around his waist, he washed his socks and underwear in the sink and draped them over the electric radiator. There was nothing much he could do to improve his dirty shirt and trousers, so he let them be, resolving to buy new ones in Irkutsk. After that, Alex went to the cot and lay down.

"It's over", he said to himself.

The bitterness he had felt upon hearing the news was gone. He had entered that curious state which a runner sometimes reaches after a marathon—exhausted beyond all capacity for emotion, relieved of the need for decisions or further exertion of energy, floating in a state of preternatural calm. The path was now clearly defined: reverse direction, go straight home. With a hop, skip, and a jump he would soon be unlocking the door of his shop on Oak Avenue in a land where things did not break down and people behaved as they should. Two days from now, three at the most, and he would be crawling into his own bed, dragging a mind-numbing book along with him. Of course, he would still have to deal with the problem of Andrew, but for the moment there was nothing more he could do.

"Later", he said. "Later."

He fell asleep. So deep was this sleep, and so long overdue, that he awoke several hours later feeling largely restored to his former self. His thoughts were clearer, and he was able to see his situation objectively. Still feeling the undertow of grief over his son, he also had an uncanny sense that other forces would work toward his liberation. Chasing the boy across half the world had produced no good results. It was now very clear that God alone had the power necessary for storming those kremlin ramparts.

The socks and underwear were dry. Alex dressed, got into his boots and greatcoat, and went down to the lobby, hoping that the restaurant was still open, intending to take a stroll outside after his meal. The restaurant was closed, however, and the desk clerk told him that it would not be open until six in the morning, when breakfast would be served. She suggested that if he was very hungry, he could go into the town, where one café remained open until midnight and a bar until 2:00 A.M. Alex reset his wristwatch to the local hour, eleven fifteen, realizing that he had slept ten hours. He went outside. The temperature was brutally cold, but there was no wind.

He estimated that the walk to the main street would take only a few minutes, not enough time for frostbite to set in.

Searching along the waterfront, he could not locate the café but soon was in no doubt as to the location of the bar, which was producing a great deal of noise. Arriving there, he found that it was the ground floor of a house that leaned at a slight angle, pushing its wooden eaves against the cement block wall of a neighboring warehouse. A sign nailed above the door of the bar read "Doshkin-noyon". Below the words was a crudely painted cartoon of a sailing ship tossed on stormy waves. The music blasting through the half-open doorway was Russian pop rock of a particularly whiny variety, dominated by thunderous bumpa-bumpa-bumpas from guitars and drums. Pushing his way inside, Alex entered an atmosphere saturated with the stench of beer and body sweat, thick with unidentifiable smoke, reeling with flashing colors projected by some kind of hallucinogenic light machine, and latent with the more subtle element of danger. The twenty or more customers crammed into the small space contributed to this sense. As Alex approached the bar, every eye in the house followed him. The electronic music did not cease its roar, but an incongruous silence seemed to fall.

"Good evening", Alex shouted to the bartender, a gnomish man with puckered face, slitted eyes, and gold rings in both ears. The man did not return his greeting.

"Do you serve food here? They told me at the hotel I could buy a meal."

As if the request was an insult, the man snarled, "What kind of food do you want?"

"Anything."

"How about some dead sailor?"

"Dead sailor? Is that the name of a dish?"

Unfortunately, the "song" had ended a second before Alex opened his mouth to say the foregoing, and thus he heard himself shouting the question into the silent room.

The bartender wiped his hands on his apron and winked at the crowd. They erupted with jeering laughter.

"Sure. Boiled sailor is fine eating. Why waste good meat? We net them sometimes, after Burkhan has done with them and Doshkin takes his pick. We get the leftovers."

"Burkhan? Doshkin?"

"The gods of Baikal. Don't you know about them? They're dangerous. If you don't give them a bribe, Mister, you won't make it back alive to Moscow or wherever you're from."

More laughter.

"Less exotic food for me, please", Alex said with a smile, trying to tame the man.

"You hear that, Fox?" the bartender called to someone at the back of the room. "*Exotic*, he said. Sounds like intelligentsia! Burshui from Moscow or Petersburg, eh?"

By this point, Alex had lost his appetite. He was about to make his way to the exit when the bartender grinned at him and slammed a glass down on the countertop. He filled it with a slug of vodka and slid it toward Alex.

"I'll get you bliny, and there's borsch too. Bread and cheese? Eggs?"

"Anything, as long as it isn't a dead sailor."

This earned him a grudging laugh, and the other customers promptly lost interest.

Alex took the glass of vodka to a small round table in the corner nearest the bar and sipped from it while his meal was being prepared. The music began to blast again. It was physically painful, but Alex chose to endure it for the sake of food.

A little man with a wrinkled brown face and outrageously red hair sidled up and squatted beside him. The Fox, Alex guessed.

"Eh, Burshui, don't be stupid, eh? You have to give Burkhan and Doshkin-noyon their due. Here, let me show you."

He took Alex's glass, tipped a few drops into his cupped palm, which was missing a thumb and two fingers, and sprinkled it on the floor. "There, now you're safe."

The Fox went away, dancing, both arms in the air. Alex stared down at his glass, wondering if it fell into the category of food sacrificed to idols. He pushed it away.

Finally, the bartender brought a loaded tray and with faked elegance performed a ritual of setting the various plates and bowls onto Alex's table. He concluded with a mock bow, towel over his arm, making the crowd roar again.

Alex ate his meal hurriedly. When it came time to pay, he stood and removed the wad of money from his shoulder bag, tore off a fifty-ruble note, and handed it to the bartender. "Is it enough?"

"It's enough. I owe you change."

"That's all right. Keep the change."

Alex left the bar with the sounds of *burshui, exotic,* and *turist* ringing in his ears.

The overcast hung low above the streets, and few lights were visible in the vicinity. Alex turned right and, going more by sense than by sight, headed in the general direction of the hotel. He had just turned onto a side street, thinking that it was a shortcut to the lane that led up the hill, when he realized he had made a mistake. The street was no more than an unlighted alley between two warehouses. He was about to retrace his steps back to the main thoroughfare when he heard feet drumming on the snow, approaching him swiftly. The sound came from two directions, ahead and behind.

A shadow blacker than the shadows of the alley rose up in front of him and grabbed the lapels of his greatcoat.

"What? Whoa!" Alex yelled.

Other hands grabbed him from behind, and then his head exploded in white light and he felt himself falling.

He hit the ground and lost consciousness.

"Kiril, did you give Kolo her oats?" said a woman's voice.

"I did, Mama. She's off her feed. She's caught a cold. Ilya didn't blanket her last night."

"Ilya, Ilya," the woman said, "you will be the death of us!"

"Kiril was supposed to do that", argued an irritable male voice, a man-child voice. "You always spoil him, and you always scold me even though I lost half a day because of you."

"You know very well that whoever brings her in must look after her. Poor thing. Go now and apologize."

"Apologize to that dumb brute? Why should I?"

"At least take her a sugar lump."

"All right", said the resentful voice.

A door slammed.

The explosions in the back of Alex's head continued to detonate.

"Mama, what if he wakes up? What will we do with him?"

"I don't know, Kiril."

"Why did Semyon bring him to us?"

"Because he thought we knew him. The hospital at Irkutsk will not take him."

"Why not?"

"He is a foreigner, without papers, without money."

"How did he get here, if he has no papers or money?"

"Everything was stolen from him."

"Why did Semyon think we know him?"

"Because I traveled with him, and we spoke together with Semyon."

"Do you know him, then?"

"Not really. He is a stranger I met on the train."

"Is he dangerous?"

"I don't think so...no, he isn't. I'm sure he isn't."

A door slammed.

A rooster crowed.

Music. "Turn off the radio, Kiryusha." A strumming guitar stopped abruptly.

"Look, it's bleeding again."

"I know. I'm sorry. We'll wash your blanket. And I'll buy you a new pillow in the spring. Later we'll put him in the clinic."

"He's too big for us to carry."

"We'll get Volodya and Grig to help."

"Aglaya says we should pray."

"Aglaya can pray if she likes. We will give him real help."

"What was the language that came from his mouth?"

"English."

"What did he say?"

"Nothing. It was gibberish."

"He's not crazy, is he?"

"No. He's had a bad blow on the head. If you want to study medicine, Kiril, here is a chance to begin. Look, this is a primary symptom."

His eyelid pulled up. Light stabbed into his brain.

"See the dilation. That means concussion. By the looks of it, no grave damage was done, but one can never be sure in such cases. There is the possibility of internal bleeding in the brain. Damn, if only they would let me have an x-ray!"

"Mama, when he wakes up he'll have a sore head, won't he?"

"A very sore head. He must lie still for a few days, and then we will see. He should be in the hospital. Stupid Semyon!"

Horses whinnying.

Reindeer snorting, tossing antlers.

Swords clashing soundlessly.

Detonations.

Napoleon strutting on horseback through the gate of the Kremlin right up to the doorsteps of the Cathedral of the Assumption, the hooves clattering on the cobblestones.

Arrogance, arrogance! cried the thousand bells of Moscow. *Kolokol-kolokol!*

Cannon fire through the back of the brain.

Father Zosima kneeling before Dmitri Karamazov.

"What are you doing? Why do you bow to me, a sinner, bearing in my flesh the sins of my father?"

"Because you are going to suffer."

The idiot Myshkin speaking of beauty even as he thrust out his arm, knocking a priceless vase from the mantle—smash!

Smashed brains sprayed across the snow of the Gulag.

Raskolnikov, the murderer-theorist kissing the feet of Sonia because she had given everything away—even herself—to save the children.

"But you, yourself, Rodion, have killed in the name of a good! Is that not also moral degradation?"

"That's different. I am above all laws."

"You are beneath all laws. If you do not allow me to love you, you cannot rise."

Then Sonia washed the feet of the murderer with her tears.

And Father Sergius washed the feet of Innokenty.

And the Mother of the Tree of Life washed the feet of the Child who would bear all sin to the mountain of immolation.

Foot pressed into stone.

Other stones, striking skulls, breaking ramparts, pressing a word of ultimate *nyet* into the warm wax of memory.

Alyosha of the degradation—Alexander of the degradation.

Alexander, father of Andrew—Andrei, father of Alexei.

"Lord Jesus, have mercy on me, a sinner!"

Towel and water.

Wash the degraded features, reveal the hidden face.

"I . . .", Alex groaned.

"Is he waking up, Mama?"

"Perhaps."

"Soup for the invalid, Irina Filippovna. I killed a chicken."

"That is too generous, Aglaya. But he cannot eat it. He is not yet with us."

"He sleeps?"

"Like sleep, yes. But deeper."

"I am praying for him. Who is he?"

"A man from a distant country. He has lost his way."

"In the eyes of God, no man is lost unless he chooses to be so."

"Aglaya, Aglaya, no more cawing. Do not speak superstition in front of my son."

"It is *not* superstition, Irina Filippovna."

"Kiril, give Aglaya an egg."

"I have enough eggs."

"A jar of kvass, then?"

"I wouldn't mind a sip of kvass. *Spasiba*."

Then one day he did awake, consciousness welding the bits together.

"Oh, oh, oh", he groaned, lifting his hand slowly to cradle his split skull.

"Shh, now, shh, you will be all right. Here, take this."

"What?"

"A pill. I'm putting it under your tongue. Don't fight. Don't fight me now, Aleksandr."

"How do you know my name?"

"*Zimorodok*, kingfisher", said the woman's voice. "*Kolibri*, hummingbird. Halcyone and Ceyx. Remember?"

"*Nyet, nyet, nyet*. Drain hole of the universe."

A puzzled laugh. "Small and ugly Ozero Baikal may be, but it is not the drain hole of the universe. Can you open your eyes?"

"I think—"

"No, don't think."

One day he sat up. Where? In a bed? Yes, a bed.

Across the room a boy of about ten or eleven years was seated at a table, pulling a string through a metal eyelet on a toy sailboat. Concentrating hard on this task, he did not notice that the stranger was awake.

Alex's head throbbed from the bright light streaming through a window. Four panes divided by a scabby crosspiece. Outside, a single element only—snow. A jar of water on the window ledge. Floating in it, an onion shooting a long green spear toward the sun and a lace of thread-roots down to the bottom. He squinted and glanced about the room. It was a kitchen. Chinked log walls, a low ceiling, a worn linoleum floor. A refrigerator, wood stove, electric hot plate. Cupboards, and a long countertop made of rough wood. On it a kerosene lamp and glass jars containing grain. Books and loose papers piled about the table. A ticking wall clock. Arms that said ten thirty-five. A pot simmering on the wood stove. A samovar emitting wisps of steam from its vent. Beside the stove, another window. Beside it, a door that would open to the outside world.

The boy was bathed in light, his flaxen hair glowing like an icon's nimbus. His patterned blue sweater reached white jeans tucked into fur boots halfway up his calves, tied at the top by braided red and yellow thongs.

"Tch", he said, struggling over the rigging of his toy.

Alex watched him, thinking, *It's Andrew! How young he is. I thought he was a man. When did I make that boat for him? I don't remember it. A long time ago, it must be.*

The boy looked over at him, and when he saw that Alex was awake and sitting up, he put down his ship without a word and got slowly to his feet. Motionless, staring at Alex, he called, "Mama!"

Expecting Carol to enter the room, Alex was greatly surprised to see the clerkish woman he had met on the train.

She came to the bed, her brow furrowed, and sat down on the edge of the mattress.

"Ah, improving, is he? Let me see." She reached over to touch Alex's eye with a forefinger. He jerked back.

"Now, now, let me look."

Gently lifting one eyelid, she put her face close and peered into his eye as if there were not a person looking at her through it. Taking a pen flashlight from her pocket, she pointed its tiny brilliant beam at his pupil. First one eye, then the other.

"Good, no sign of bleeding. How is your head?"

He reached to the back of his skull and felt a great pack of wadding taped to it. Part of the scalp around the bandage had been shaved. "It hurts", he murmured, looking at her suspiciously.

She smiled suddenly. "Kiril, make us some tea. I think our guest is going to recover."

"Where am I?" he asked.

"Ozero Baikal, my village. Do you remember me?"

"Yes. Why am I here?"

"Isn't that self-evident? No? Well, it seems you had an encounter with some ruffians who took your money and documents and left you to freeze to death in an alley."

"Who were they?"

"No one knows. Not locals. The police say it was probably lower-class criminals passing through town. This sort of thing does not happen in Listvyanka. They want to know who you are and what you were doing roaming around at that time of night."

"I was hungry."

"I told the police that's probably what it was. I also told them the little I knew about you. It wasn't much to go on."

"But how did I get here?"

"Semyon brought you by snowmobile."

"Why? Why here?"

"He thought I knew you. Also because I am a physician."

"Shouldn't I be in a hospital?"

"I tried to get them to take you to Irkutsk, but I am sorry to tell you that no one there really wants to deal with the problem. The hospital officials say you do not qualify for citizen's benefits because you have no proof that you are a citizen. Nor do you have the proper health insurance that foreign visitors must carry with their visa. I could have sent you away to the emergency ward in the city, where no doubt they might have kept you for a few days until they figured out what to do with you, but that would have meant another long trip with Semyon and a longer one after that in the back of a truck, and either the one or the other might have killed you, in your condition. All in all, we thought it best just to let you stay here until your status is sorted out."

"We can look after him, Mama", said the boy, moving closer to the bed and gazing at Alex with sober appraisal.

"Aleksandr, this is my son Kiril."

Kiril inclined his head in a slight bow and stuck out his hand. Alex shook it.

"Where are you from?" the boy asked.

"No more questions. It makes his head hurt, can't you see?"

Kiril continued to look on Alex with a gaze that seemed older than his years.

"We shaved the back of your head", he said. "Mama stitched it. Semyon and Volodya held you down."

"It didn't take much holding", Irina put in. "You were quite unconscious."

"Who found me?"

"A man named the Fox. You can thank him for your life."

"Maybe it was the Fox who hit me on the head."

"He is an unsavory sort but not really a criminal. If it was him, it was his first crime of violence that we know of. He is a maker of clandestine alcohol. The police questioned him, but he knows nothing about who robbed you. He said you ate at the bar and then left. He lives in a flat above the warehouse on the alley where he found you. I doubt your papers or money will be found."

Alex lay back and listened to the war drum in his skull.

Irina brought him another pill and made him swallow it with a glassful of water.

"I will try to pay you", he whispered with closing eyes. "I will. I promise. When I return. When I return...when I return to my..."

Drowsiness took him, and he could say no more.

25. *The Clinic at Ozero Baikal*

He awoke in the night. An electric lamp burned on the kitchen table. Irina was sitting by it, reading a book.

He blinked, and the room was empty, sun pouring through the windows. The clock on the wall said two forty-five. Below it on a shelf sat two model sailboats, one white-hulled with red trim, the other royal blue with yellow trim.

Night again. A strange old woman sat down on a chair beside the bed and told him to sit up. She was very short and bent, her eyes like two black beads. Her clothing was also black. Over her white hair, she wore a featureless gray kerchief.

"Baba Yaga?" he said, trying to clear his thoughts.

She looked slightly offended. "Baba Aglaya", she corrected, making a sign of the cross on her chest. "With a bowl of soup for you."

She spoon-fed him the entire bowlful, a salty broth with noodles and bits of chicken. After that, more water. After that, he badly needed to get up.

Irina and her sons were eating a meal at the table by the window, Kiril and an older boy whom Alex recognized as the driver of the sleigh in Listvyanka. The window was black, wind rattling its frame. The boys looked at Alex for a moment, then returned to their plates.

"*Tualyet*", he groaned.

"Do you think you can stand on your feet?" Irina asked.

He swung his legs over the side of the bed and tried to get himself upright. He felt very weak, and his head throbbed suddenly with blinding pain. He sat down again.

"Ilya, you help him", Irina said to her oldest son. The boy pushed back his chair and came to Alex reluctantly.

"Here", he said, handing Alex's greatcoat to him, then helping him get his arms into the sleeves.

"This way", said Ilya, taking Alex by the arm. Walking slowly on trembling legs, he let himself be guided across the room. They entered a small parlor stuffed with armchairs and bookshelves and headed to a door in the middle of the far wall. Ilya opened it, stepped through, and beckoned Alex to follow him into a corridor made of rough planks nailed to upright pine poles. It was outside the main building, and the air was severely cold. Icicles hung from cracks in the plank ceiling. A single dim light bulb swayed on a wire.

Holding the wall, Alex made his way along this passageway until it ended twenty feet from the building at an outdoor toilet similar to a Canadian outhouse. He went into it, shivering, and when he came out again he was shivering harder. He saw that Ilya was busy talking through a hole in a wall. The creature on the other side whinnied at him, and the boy pushed a lump of sugar onto a large pink tongue that poked through the opening.

Back inside the house, Alex returned to the bed, which he now recognized as a sleeping bench affixed to the wall at right angles to the wood stove. He lay down on it and pulled the greatcoat over himself. The boy returned to his meal without comment, a scowl permanently affixed to his face. After the dishes had been cleared away by all members of the family and placed into a large copper tub on the counter, they returned to their seats. Ilya brought out a chessboard and set up black and white pieces on it. Irina put on her glasses and read a journal of some kind, from which she extracted information that she occasionally wrote on her tablet. Kiril stood on a bench, got the white sailboat down from the ledge, and began to tinker with it. Aglaya sat on a chair by the foot of the bed knitting with skeins of raw wool on two overlarge wooden skewers, looking up from time to time to peer at Alex with an expression that he took to be one of ferocious disapproval.

In those few moments he felt the full weight of his predicament. He was a man without proper documents or means, thousands of miles away from his home, recovering from a fractured skull, at the end of a long and useless quest that had utterly ruined him. Moreover, he had been cast upon the mercy of decent people whose generosity was doubtless costing them more than they could afford. He was an imposition, a burden. He rolled over and faced the wall, burying his face in the lining of his coat.

As he drifted in and out of sleep, he heard snippets of family conversation. There were hints of a certain astringency in the style of their communication with each other, especially between the mother and her elder son, but he sensed also their bond of trust. Although he was the beneficiary of this familial goodness, he was outside it, and the strangeness of the situation contributed to his feeling of helplessness.

"Nine o'clock, Kiril", Irina said.

"All right, Mamasha."

"Ilya, you too."

"Can't I finish the game?"

"Who are you playing against?"

"Myself."

"Then who will be the winner?"

"I will."

Laughter.

"You'll also be the loser", piped Kiril.

More laughter.

"Should I stay tonight, Irina?" Aglaya croaked. "You need sleep. One more night won't hurt me."

"If you wish, Aglaya. But I think the worst is over. Tomorrow we'll move him to the clinic. In the morning, would you ask Volodya and Grig to help me? His legs are unsteady."

"Of course, of course", said the old woman. "Good thing you move him. Tongues will wag if you don't."

"I don't worry about tongues."

"You're foolish not to worry about tongues. The tongue can kill."

"Those days are over."

"Even so, the tongue can still kill a community. People here don't take kindly to foreigners. They're rich and arrogant."

"Not this one."

"Think of the tales that would scurry up and down the lake—Dr. Irina Filippovna has taken a man under her roof, they'll say."

"Such tales are told about many people—"

"And most of them true."

"True or untrue, no one is going to worry about a man under my roof."

"Maybe so. But God will worry. God sees everything and waits."

"*Please*, Aglaya!"

"Think of your soul, Irina."

"Now stop it. We'll move him to the clinic tomorrow, and that will rob the tattlers of anything to chew on. Say no more, or you'll wake him with your babble. And what a silly thought you're pecking at. You know there has never been anyone else for me but Yevgeny. And there will never be another."

Here the conversation abruptly ended.

The next morning, Alex lay facedown on the bed while Irina changed the dressing at the back of his head. She warned him it would hurt, and it did.

"It's healing", she said. "No infection. In a few days from now, I'll take out the sutures. In the meantime, you will continue to rest. No walking about unnecessarily. No reciting poetry."

"That's not funny", Alex mumbled.

"Sorry. Hold still; I'm putting a clean dressing on the wound."

When she finished, he sat up, letting his legs dangle over the edge of the bed. Though he must have seen them the day before, now he took notice of the fact that he was wearing long underwear and a sweater of knitted raw wool.

"Whose clothes are these?" he asked.

"They belonged to my husband."

"Who changed my clothing?"

"Poor man. Always worried about humiliation. Semyon and Ilya changed you. You were in no condition to do it yourself. How often do people bathe in North America?"

"As often as they like."

"Your clothes smelled like a fish market and an opium den when they brought you here."

He stared at a lump on his right thigh—bandages on the burn, he supposed.

"It's healing too", she said. "A fine holiday you've had."

"Intourist neglected to tell me about some of the details."

He looked at his left hand and saw that the blisters were gone and fresh skin was covering his palm.

"Why do you dye your hair?" Irina asked.

"My hair? I don't dye my hair."

"Yes you do. It looks absurd on a man your age."

Then he remembered his disguise and guessed that the gray-blond roots were now growing in beneath the canary yellow.

"Do you want to look like an American rock star?"

He laughed, then winced, because the laugh set off a kettle-drum in his skull.

"A disguise", he whispered, trying to reduce the head-cracking noise.

"Why a disguise? For what did you need such a thing?"

"To find my son."

"Your son", she said with a dubious smile. "Dyeing your hair helped you find your son?"

"It's a complicated story."

"It must be. Can you tell it?"

"Another time, please."

Shortly after, there was a knock on the door, and two old men entered. They bowed slightly to Irina and were introduced by her to Alex. They were Volodya and Grig. Peasants or fishermen, he supposed. Irina brought him his trousers, which were now washed and the hole in the thigh repaired by a patch of cotton. One of the men helped him slide his legs into the trousers and got him standing and into his greatcoat. The other old man had brought a pair of blue felt boots that slipped easily over his feet.

"Where are my boots?" Alex asked.

"On the feet of the man who took your money", Irina said.

That done, the four of them went outside through the door in the kitchen and down two steps onto hard-packed snow. The light was dazzling, the sun beating on the yard. Alex had only a moment to take in the surroundings. Ozero Baikal was a cluster of log cabins, with the exception of a few clapboard buildings. A bare white field sloped upward behind the village and ended at a forest of evergreens. The trees climbed at a steeper pitch toward rounded hills as high as mountains. The lake was nowhere in sight, and Alex deduced that he was facing north or northwest, away from Baikal.

Following Irina's directions, the two men put their shoulders under Alex's arms and walked him along a snow-covered lane to a frame structure that stood about thirty feet to the right of the doctor's home. It was smaller than the cabin where she lived and not as weather-beaten. Irina unlocked the door and went in, beckoning the men to follow. Inside, Alex saw that the clinic was a two-room shack about twelve feet wide by thirty feet long. The walls, ceiling, and floor were varnished plywood. In the front room was an examination table, a padlocked medicine cabinet, a shelf of books, a sink that drained into a bucket, and a wood stove that threw out visible waves of heat. A stainless steel cauldron steamed on top. Along one wall was a counter on which lay surgical instruments inside clear plastic bags.

She pointed to the back room, and the two men took Alex there and lowered him onto a bed. There were four metal beds in the room, their army-green enamel chipped and dented. Beside each was a washstand with an aluminum pitcher and basin. The only decoration was a circular copper basin about four feet across and a foot deep, hanging from a nail on the wall. A large window offered the view of a slope sweeping down to a vast expanse of white. In the distance, mountain peaks edged above the horizon.

"The lake", Irina said. "We're putting you here so you can have something pleasant to look at."

The old men bowed their way out, leaving Alex alone with Irina.

"Well, Aleksandr Graham, I'm still not sure what we're going to do with you. But I will go to Listvyanka in a few days from now and speak with the management of the hotel. They will have a record of your passport and visa numbers. That way I can telephone your embassy and try to obtain some help for you. They may be able to send documentation swiftly, and then we will return you to your home."

"Can't you phone the hotel?"

"There are no telephones in our village. We had one, but I'm sorry to say it was disconnected for lack of payment."

"Surely a doctor needs a phone."

"Yes, I need a phone. But I do not have the money for it."

"Aren't you paid by the state?"

"A token. I am not a city doctor, and my practice, if you could call it that, is small. The people of the region have little

money and none to spare. I deliver babies at the nearby villages, and people bring me cuts to sew up. If there is serious
illness, they usually go to Irkutsk, and then the state takes
over very nicely."

"But how do you live?"

"As others live. The boys fish in the summer and earn a
few rubles. Ilya has a trapline. Now and then he gets a black
Barguzin sable, and through secret dealings that he will not
tell me about, he is able to get a pretty sum for the pelt. But
that is a rare event. For the most part people give us barter
goods—eggs and butter, milk in the summer. We always
have lots of potatoes and dried fish. Each spring I give a
few weeks of lectures at the medical college in Irkutsk, and
the wages from that pay for most of our needs throughout
the year."

"What do you teach?"

"Immunology."

"Are you from Irkutsk? Is that where you studied
medicine?"

The mask instantly covered her face. "No."

"Where did you study?"

"Moscow Second Medical Institute."

Turning away from him with some abruptness, she said,
"No more talk. You need to rest. I should go back to the
house and make lunch. Kiril will be home from school in an
hour, and he eats like a bear."

"There's a school here? The village is larger than I thought."

"Not a proper school. We have no hired teacher. There
are fourteen children all told, ranging from ages five to sixteen. Ilya is the oldest. A few people in the village can read
well enough to help the children though their texts. We take
turns at it. The state sends us a box of books each year, and
an inspector now and then."

"Do you teach there as well?"

604

"Yes, I teach history."

"A dangerous subject."

"Indeed. Go to sleep, Aleksandr. That will get you home faster than anything else."

"Thank you, Irina Filippovna. I'm very grateful for your help. When I'm able, I'm going to return your kindness. I'll help you and your village."

She cocked her head and smiled wryly. "*Turist, turist*, go to sleep."

He did not sleep. He removed his coat and felt boots and stretched out on the bed facing the window. He could see a part of the lake and the notched rim of the horizon. There were mountains everywhere in this land of vast spaces. Siberia had as many people as Canada, but they were spread out over unthinkable distances. Canada had five time zones, Russia eleven, most of which were in Siberia.

For a while he was content to watch icicles drip from the eaves above the window, impressed by the power of the winter sun. But the drops were few, and when a cloud layer passed across the southern sky, the icicles ceased dripping.

Around noon the door in the other room banged open and closed again. Into the "ward" came Kiril, teetering on the toes of his fur boots, carrying a cloth-covered plate in one hand and a wicker basket in the other.

"*Zdrastviytye!* Hello!" he said to Alex in a cheery voice.

"*Dobry dyen*, good afternoon."

"Mama sends you lunch. She says I'm not to bother you."

"Please, bother me."

A swift grin lit up the boy's face.

"Mister—"

"Aleksandr."

"Aleksandr, I heard you speaking to Mama in English. I would like to learn English. But first you must eat."

Alex sat up and took the bowl onto his lap. The deep container was full of chicken stew. He made the sign of the cross and prayed a silent grace. The boy watched him.

"Aglaya does that too", Kiril said. "But you do it backward."

"Yes, we do it this way where I come from."

"So, now I'm ready to learn English."

"I should swallow a few bites first."

"Yes. I'm sorry." Kiril bounced slightly on the end of the bed.

Alex ate most of the stew with a spoon; then toward the bottom he simply put the bowl to his lips and gulped the rest down. He took some rolls of white bread from the basket and ate them. After that he rapidly consumed three slices of thick black bread smeared with butter that tasted like sour cream. In the basket was a jar of clear tea. He unscrewed the cap and drank the contents. It was sweet and oddly smoke flavored.

"Now you will teach me English", the boy said.

"It can't be done all at once."

"Why not a few words to begin?"

"All right. What would you like to know?"

"What's your word for Mama?"

"The same as yours."

"And Papa?"

"Also the same."

Raising his eyebrows, the boy said, "That's very interesting. And what's the word for me?"

"It's like your word, *syn*. We say *son*. You are the *son* of Irina Filippovna."

"I meant my name. Are there any boys named Kiril where you come from?"

"Yes, but we say Cyril."

"See-rill. Very strange."

"Few people now give this name to their children."

"Here it's popular. Do you have a son?"

"I have two sons."

"Oh yes, Mama told me. She says you're looking for one of them."

"That's right."

Kiril whipped out a book from under his sweater and flipped it open on his lap.

"Show me where you live, please."

The boy handed it to Alex and slid himself closer. It was a small atlas of the elementary school variety, rather outdated. The configuration of European states had changed a great deal since its publication. He found the page for North America.

"Here is Canada. Here is the city of Toronto. And here is where I live, in the woodlands north of the city."

Halcyon was not on the map. Neither was the next-largest town, nor the small city beyond it. Only the largest metropolises were represented.

"I see you live near this place", Kiril said, bending over the book, putting his forefinger on a black dot that represented Boston.

"Boe-stone", the boy enunciated slowly.

"It's far from where I live, though it seems close on the map. I'm near this lake."

"Ozero On-tay-ro", Kiril laughed. "A poem!"

"Lake On-teh-ree-oh, we say."

The boy repeated it clumsily.

"It's almost as big as Baikal", Alex said. "It's one of the great lakes of North America. There are larger lakes beside it, as you can see, and they're bigger than Baikal."

Kiril's face grew serious as he studied the map.

"I thought *we* had the biggest lake in the world. Mama says Baikal has more water in it than any other lake in the world. One-fifth of the world's freshwater, she says. It's sixteen hundred meters deep."

"That's very deep. Our lakes are shallow by comparison."

"Ah, interesting", Kiril said, digesting the information with a faraway look. And in that look, Alex saw that he resembled boys everywhere. Indeed, Alex recalled how Andrew had sat by his side just like this, ten years ago, poring over the large atlas that had belonged to his grandfather Graham.

"What's this country, Dad?" Andrew had asked.

"It's called Siberia. A very big and very cold place."

"Do people live there?"

"Yes, they do."

"I wonder what they're like."

"Probably a lot like us, but their language and customs are different."

"Oh."

Swinging his feet, lost in concentration, Andrew's face had grown serious as he studied the map.

Kiril slammed the book shut and jumped off the bed.

"I have to go", he said. "Thank you for teaching me English."

"There's more to English than that", Alex said, smiling.

"Then you have to teach me more", Kiril declared, as if this roundly concluded the matter. "Good-bye. I'll see you after supper."

The boy went out the door carrying the empty dishes, light on his feet, flax hair spoking in all directions from static electricity.

Alex got off the bed and walked unsteadily to the window. He stared out at Baikal for a time, then returned to the bed and lay down. He slept throughout the afternoon.

It was dark when the door opened again. Irina came into the ward, took a look into his eyes with her penlight, asked him how he felt, and said that supper would be delivered shortly. A different courier, she added.

"I enjoyed the last one."

"Did he drive you crazy with his chatter?"

"Not at all. He reminded me of my own son, many years ago."

"Your missing son?"

"Yes."

"Kiril likes you. He says we should adopt you and turn you into a Russian."

"Thank you for the offer, but I doubt I would adjust—much as I enjoy your culture and climate."

"You're getting better. You're making fun—a good sign. Your poor addled brain hasn't suffered permanent damage."

"*Matto-pazzo*", he said, then wondered why he had.

She gave him a puzzled look and decided not to pursue it.

"I go to Listvyanka tomorrow. I'll get the information about your documents at the hotel and make telephone inquiries."

"Will you have to pay for the calls?"

"I'll call from Semyon's place. He owes me a favor. Last year I performed a surgical operation on his beloved cat, who had been run over by a motor scooter."

"You do a lot of medical work for free."

"Credit is sometimes more useful than cash."

She checked the bandage on his head and told him there was no bleeding—another good sign—but warned him to stay quiet, to get as much rest as he could. She said she had some tablets for killing pain, if he needed one. He declined, wondering how she got her supply of medications, feeling certain that she had little to spare.

"Tomorrow, if you wish, you can recite poetry", she said with a sardonic smile.

"Ouch! I'll take that painkiller now."

"You can recite to the boys or to Aglaya. There are no unattached maidens in Ozero Baikal."

"None? What about you?"

She got to her feet, sighing with weariness. "I have already heard your poem. It was an interesting experience, but once is enough. Do you want company after supper?"

"Yes, I would like that."

"I'll send Kiril to you. He is desperate to learn English. He told me the words you taught him today." She turned to go. "I'm grateful. He hasn't had a father."

"When did his father die?"

"When he was six months old."

She said it without emotion but turned and left without another word.

Not long after, the door opened and closed, and seconds later Aglaya entered the room bearing a tray. She set it on the bed and gave Alex a hostile nod, indicating that he should commence eating.

"Thank you", he said.

She stood back a pace and watched. He made the sign of the cross and prayed his grace, then whisked the cloth from the top of the tray. Looking up, he saw that the old woman's face had thawed a degree or two, though its fundamental suspicion was still intact.

"You pray?" she asked.

Alex nodded. "*Khristos voskrese!*" he said.

"*Voistinu voskrese!*" she instinctively replied. Then her face brightened. "Ah!" she breathed. "Ah!" Suddenly transformed from a carrion bird into a sweet little old lady, she scurried out to the surgery and returned with a wooden chair. She thumped it down beside his knees and sat on it. Gazing at him fondly, rocking back and forth in a series of full-body nods, she observed the progress of his meal.

It was more of the chicken stew accompanied by a plate of fried dumplings, boiled beets in sour cream, a single onion shoot, and slices of black bread spread with the sour butter. He was hungrier than he had been earlier in the day and ate it all hurriedly, finishing off the meal with the jar of hot tea.

"Don't gulp!" Aglaya scolded. "Don't burn your throat!"

This was so doting, so motherly, that it made him laugh. He held his cranium to keep it from shaking into fragments.

"What's wrong? You hurt?"

"It just hurts when I laugh. What is your patronymic, may I ask?"

"Pavlovna."

"Are you a relative of Irina Filippovna's?"

"I'm no relation. I'm a neighbor."

"It seems you're like a grandmother to them."

She shrugged. "Yes, it's so. Those poor boys. That Ilya—so rude, so unhappy. He needs a spanking."

"They have suffered from the death of their father."

"Who can live without a father, I ask you! Well, many do these days. No one respects the holy bond. Men come; men go. It's a bad world. Why the good die young is a mystery to me. It's not my business. God alone knows his business."

"Did you know Yevgeny?"

"Know him? Yes, I knew him. The best of men. Those bastards in Moscow killed him as sure as if they shot him."

"How did he die?"

"Cancer. The cancer from wormwood."

"Chernobyl?"

"Yes. They made him go in to help the people with atom burn. To convince people to leave their villages. That was in Ukraine, where he comes from. But he would have gone anyway. He would have gone to help even if they hadn't forced him."

"Siberia is a long way from Ukraine."

"No matter. They scraped up the politicals from here and there and threw them into the atom fire."

"Yevgeny was a political?"

"Yes. Didn't Irina tell you?"

Alex shook his head.

The suspicious look returned to the old woman's face. She peered into his eyes without blinking, then looked down at her gnarled hands folded on her lap.

"It's not my business to say such things. Forget what I said."

"It's forgotten."

"Tomorrow I'll bring you a little cake."

"Thank you. You're very kind. Cake is good for healing the brain. I need it badly, for it seems to me that I cannot now remember a thing you've told me this evening."

She shot a swift look at him, a cagey peasant look, half-amused, half-scolding.

"You're a good fellow, it's plain to see. Had enough to eat?"

"Yes, thank you."

"Stop thanking me all the time. It's not dignified."

He laughed again.

"And stop that laughing. People will think you're silly in the head."

"I am."

"Well, no matter." She got to her feet. "Give me those dishes. I have to go. The doctor will kill me if she thinks I've been bothering you. And watch out for that little squirrel Kiril. He charms everybody, and he'll get you to do his will no matter what."

"Does he get you to do his will, Aglaya Pavlovna?"

"Every day of his life", the old woman sighed.

The boy returned bearing a chess set in his arms and a hungry-for-conquest look in his eyes.

"Do you play, Aleksandr?"

"It has been a while since I last played. But I can try."

"Don't worry. I'm easy to beat. Ilya wins every time."

Kiril put the board on the blanket between them, and together they set up the chess pieces.

"You move first, Aleksandr", said the boy, rotating the board so that Alex had the white.

"No, you, Kiril."

"It would be improper. You're our guest."

Alex took the first move, pushing a pawn forward two squares. The boy countered with an innocuous riposte. Alex moved another pawn forward. Frowning and indecisive, as if he was not very good at this sort of thing, Kiril moved his knight to the front. Alex did the same.

Twelve moves later, the boy checkmated him.

"Well done, Kiril. I didn't see it coming."

The boy glowed with pleasure. "Another game, Aleksandr? Just one more game?"

"All right."

Alex was checkmated in seven moves. He had never seen a subtler ambush. He was accustomed to playing against himself, and less frequently against Jacob whenever his son was home from university, and had considered himself moderately accomplished in the game. He now wondered if his skills had been undermined by the events of recent months.

"You're good", he said.

"Not very, Aleksandr. Another game?"

"Hmmmm."

"Please."

They played five games that evening, and Kiril won them all. The boy was fiendishly clever. Alex resolved not even to bother playing with the older brother. He enjoyed the match of wits, but the mental energy required to defend himself against so prodigious an opponent cost him a lot. His head pounded. He lay back on the pillow and closed his eyes. Kiril tiptoed out, pockets bulging with chess pieces, the board under his arm.

The next day, Aglaya brought him barley porridge, yogurt, and tea for breakfast.

"Irina Filippovna has gone with Volodya to Listvyanka", she announced, "and will return by nightfall."

At lunchtime Aglaya brought a tray of soup and bread, tea, and a small cake. The cake was an unglazed brown lump that in appearance was most unappetizing. However, when Alex bit into it, feigning dramatic pleasure, the pleasure became real enough, for the old woman had made it with honey and currants.

"This is a marvel, Aglaya Pavlovna. Already my head is better because of it."

"Don't tell lies. It's not good to play tricks with truth. But you do like the cake, don't you?"

"I like it very much. Would you eat some of it with me?"

"No, I'm fasting today. It's Friday."

"Do you fast every Friday?"

She shrugged and nodded.

From under the flap of her black coat she withdrew a hard-bound book and threw it on the end of the bed. Its corners were frayed and bent, and it lacked a dust jacket.

"The doctor told me to give you this. She said to tell you it's medicine."

After Aglaya had taken away the dishes, thrown wood into the firebox in the other room, and departed from the clinic, Alex opened the book.

It was Dostoyevsky's *The Humiliated*. He was familiar with it, had read it many years before under its English title, *The Insulted and Injured*.

Opening the flyleaf, he noticed an inscription penned in purple ink:

Yevgeny Dmitrievich Pimonenko

Below the name was a handwritten quotation:

Suffering is the origin of consciousness.
F. M. Dostoyevsky

It was a poorly printed edition, the pages yellowing and brittle, the font so small it strained the eye. He spotted several typos. It would take an effort to read it. In obedience to Aglaya (a personage whom it would be unwise to cross), and in deference to the wishes of his personal physician (to whom he could not lie), he decided to read the story. Tonight he would be able to tell her, in all honesty, that he had taken his medicine like a man.

His eyes were aching by the time he had gotten a third of the way through the book. He slept for a time, and when he awoke, he saw that the snow on the lake had turned blue with dusk. The book was sprawled open on the blanket beside his legs. When he picked it up, a slip of paper fluttered out. On it was written the following:

Ira,

A hundred years ago Dostoyevsky wrote that the intelligentsia were in the grip of some madness of negation. Now, the madness has become institutionalized, and Marx's dictum that negative Communism was a necessary first step toward positive and absolutely human Communism has been radically disproved. Good cannot build upon evil's foundation without the whole inevitably becoming infected by the part, no matter the corrective forces applied. Why? Because man is not a builder's brick. He is a work of art.

Nowhere else in this world has the meaning of the word *equality* been so radically inverted as in our land. The Revolution has demolished hierarchy in the name of equality and replaced it with a horizontal hierarchy of its own. Everything is reduced to the realm of objects. None of us are equal, for all have been robbed of transcendent value.

Do not hate me for seeing these things. I will not endanger you. I will not ask you to marry me though everything in me yearns for your assent. I love you.

Burn this.

Y.D.P.

Alex inserted the note carefully between two pages, closed the book, and put it on the bedside table. For an hour he looked out at the lake, watching the colors change on the vast canvas until it grew dark and stars pricked the lower regions of the sky.

Kiril brought supper and with it the news that his mother had not yet returned from Listvyanka. As before, he observed Alex's every movement. After the meal, Alex taught him the English words *art, eternal,* and *soul.*

"Aglaya is always talking about that", the boy said. "I don't understand it. Does a fish have a soul?"

"It has life but not an eternal life."

"We have life, Aleksandr. How do we know that we aren't just like fish?"

"We are capable of thinking."

"Dogs think. Horses think."

"Not the same kind of thinking as ours."

"Tell me the difference."

"Another time I'll be glad to answer you. Tonight I'm very tired."

"All right. How about some chess?"

"Another time."

"Please, just one game?" the boy beamed with an inviting smile. "You're *very* good at it."

"You're *very* good at flattery, Kiril, but the answer is no."

The boy seemed in no way cast down by this series of blockades, and indeed he smiled to himself when he realized he had been checkmated.

After Kiril left, Alex took up the book again, read until his eyes could stand no more, then closed it. He shut off the lamp on the headboard, prayed, and drifted into sleep.

Rising slowly from unremembered dreams, he heard crows calling and felt a beak pecking at the back of his head. Was he carrion on a battlefield?

"Tsk, the shaved part is growing. The tape will pull the hair", said one crow to another.

The beak-stab and the rip of flesh brought him fully awake.

"*Nyet!*" he gasped.

"Quiet! Lie still! Give me the swab, Aglaya. No, no, the one in the alcohol jar. That's right."

"Why don't you take the stitches out, Irina Filippovna? It's a fine job you did on him. Clean as a candy dish. That seam will hold for sure."

"The wound needs another day or two."

"When will he be going?"

Irina did not answer. She tapped Alex's shoulder. "Sit up", she said.

Alex rolled over onto his back and sat up, gingerly fingering the fresh dressing.

"Thank you", he said.

Irina did not reply and merely examined his eyes with a cold demeanor. She turned to the old woman, who was standing at the end of the bed with elbows resting on the foot bar.

"Aglaya, I need to speak with the patient alone."

"Yes, yes, I know when I'm not wanted", said Aglaya, shuffling out of the room. When the clinic door slammed, Irina sat down on the chair, folded her arms, and stared at Alex.

"Is something wrong?" he asked.

"Who are you?" she said in a low voice.

"Who am I?"

"You're not a bookseller, are you? You're not a poor man who has lost his way in a foreign country. That was an act, wasn't it? It was all an act."

Totally baffled, Alex shook his head. "I don't know what you mean. What has happened?"

She regarded him for some moments with an expression of suspicion and hostility.

"How clever of you", she said. "What an extraordinary story. To think you could have kept it going for so long—"

"Kept what going? What on earth are you talking about?"

"Don't lie to me. You take our hospitality, you invade our home, you let me doctor you when all the while..."

He stared at her, unable to make any sense of what was happening.

"What is it you really do? Smuggling opium from Mongolia? Eh? Be honest. I can read you like a book now. I won't be fooled any longer."

Stunned by the unreality of her accusation, he could only shake his head again.

"Close your mouth. It's hanging open", she said in disgust.

"Irina..."

She snorted and looked down at the floor.

"Tell me what has happened", Alex demanded.

Her scowl deepened.

"Tell me now or I'm going. I'll walk to Listvyanka, if I have to."

"Ha! You don't mean that. You don't mean anything you say."

Alex shook his head in amazement. "I just never know when the bottom will fall out of things in this country. One minute everything's fine, the next I'm falling down a manhole. Why are you so upset? What do you think I've done? Tell me."

"Why should I speak with you at all?"

Stung, Alex flared, "Tell me, or I'm leaving this instant!"

She continued to stare, her eyes black with bitterness.

He threw back the covers and got his legs over the side of the bed. Furious, he struggled to put on his trousers.

"Holy Russia", he murmured bitterly. "Another little surprise from Holy Mother Russia! Unmitigated disaster from the moment I arrived in this country. Nothing works properly. You're all crazy. Nobody escapes. Bullets in the brain or bullets in the thinking—take your choice. I've had enough of this insane country! They smash your skull if you don't pour libations to their idols. Maybe an insult or two, if you get off lucky."

"Nothing you say can be trusted", Irina snapped.

"Nothing I say can be trusted? It's a country of lies, right, so why should I presume you'd believe me? Stupid me. In the country of liars, an honest man is the biggest liar of all, right? Thank you for a very interesting tour, thank you for the bed, thank you for the painkiller, thank you for the food, the concern, the lack of faith in human nature. I'll be going now."

He stumbled and fell onto the floor, breaking the fall with his arm. So angry was he that he continued to rage from that position, buttoning the trousers and turning red in the face. Then he struggled to his feet and stomped around the room, holding his head to keep it from cracking.

"Where's my coat? Where are my boots? Oh yes, they stole my boots. Well, it's a long walk, so I'll need to borrow a pair. Don't worry; I'll pay you for them. I'll send you money once I get home. Money! That's the real issue here, isn't it? Well, it's the same where I come from. Nobody's worth a buck, a ruble, a penny, a kopeck. Life's cheap. We're all fish to you, aren't we? It's the same where I come from. Life's cheap, and truth's cheaper still."

She watched this amazing performance without moving, arms tighter than ever, face twisted cynically.

"Where *do* you come from?" she said in a hard voice.

"I told you where I come from, and I don't need to tell you again. If you don't believe me, that's your problem."

He found his greatcoat and got his shaking arms into the sleeves.

"Where are you going?" she said.

"Canada. If anyone wants me, that's where I'll be found. I'm going home."

He sat down on the edge of the bed and made some unsuccessful attempts to get a foot into a felt boot.

"I hate your country", he growled. "It kills people. Lots of people. *Huge* amounts of people."

With a reflective tilt of her head, Irina Filippovna said, "More than ninety million killed."

"Well, that's honest of you. I can see *you're* not a liar. Good for you! And by the way, thanks for the book. Dostoyevsky's great. He got it right. I don't need to take it with me because I've got a copy of my own, right there at home in my *bookshop!*" He barked the final word.

She looked away.

Boots on, he buttoned his coat with trembling fingers.

"Thank you for everything. I'll send money when I get home. I promise. You'll get a telephone, I guarantee it."

"I...", she said, unable to meet his eye.

Just as he was about to leave the room, he hesitated, reached for the book, and opened it. He removed the slip of paper from it and handed it to her.

"Doesn't this mean anything to you? Why did you give it to me?"

She took it from him and read it swiftly. She froze and did not look up.

"Your husband wrote it, didn't he?"

She nodded woodenly.

"He was an honest man", said Alex. "It's nice to know there was at least one. Good-bye."

He had reached the outside door when he heard footsteps hurrying after him. She grabbed his arm.

"You would die out there. Within an hour you would die." Tears welled out of her eyes. "I offended you, and I'm sorry for it. I was angry. Come back inside."

He glared at his wristwatch—which was no longer ticking. "Sorry. Got to go. It's a long way home."

She began to cry in earnest—which of course was a force so monumental that few men have ever been able to resist it.

"Please", she said, pulling him back inside and shutting the door.

He reached for the handle.

"Please go back to bed. You're in no condition to walk anywhere. Look, your wound is bleeding again. We must talk. Maybe I've misunderstood."

"*Maybe* you have?"

"Lie down before you do any more damage to yourself."

He lay down on the bed without removing his coat or boots. He crossed his arms and glared at her, waiting for an explanation.

She sat down on the chair and dried her eyes.

"I'm confused", she said.

"*You're* confused?"

"If what you told me about yourself was the truth—"

"It *is* the truth."

"I don't understand this."

"What, exactly, do you not understand?"

"Today at Listvyanka I went to the hotel. I explained your situation to the girl at the desk and asked her to let me see the register. She said that I couldn't see it. She wouldn't budge. She told me the police had come from Irkutsk and they said no records can be divulged until the investigation of the robbery has been completed.

"Then I talked with the manager. I told him it was ridiculous not to let me copy the numbers, because I had to telephone Moscow to speak with your embassy. He refused.

"Later, when we were alone, he told me more. I've done medical service for his family in the past, you see, and though he's not a friend, he is a person I can trust. He said that the *militsiya*, the regular police, had come and gone and were still investigating the assault, but another branch of criminal investigation had come out to Listvyanka to ask questions. He didn't say who they were. He didn't know for sure, only that they threw their weight around and had an official permit of some kind. They asked him for his register, defaced the lines where your numbers were written, and stamped it with an official emboss. It's a genuine one, the state's, but the name of the particular bureau is not defined on it. This is most unusual. They wanted to see the list of telephone calls you had made from your room. He told them you hadn't made any. Before they went away, they instructed him not to tell anyone about their visit."

"But why would they do that?"

"I don't know. I went to Semyon and begged him to let me phone Moscow. It took some bargaining because the call is expensive. I reached your embassy and spoke to a secretary. I gave your name and a description of what has happened. She said she would talk with a person higher up and promised to call back. I waited at Semyon's for an hour before they phoned. They said there was no record of a Canadian citizen by the name of Alexander Graham traveling in Russia."

"What!"

"They checked their computer, and it told them no one by that name had entered Russia during the previous year, nor was there a Canadian named Alexander Graham presently in Russia. I spelled it correctly."

"You spoke English?"

"She spoke Russian. I gave the information in Russian, then repeated it in English to make sure nothing was lost in the translation. I asked if there was a possibility of an oversight. I suggested that perhaps you hadn't registered with them directly. She said there could be no mistake, because Intourist automatically informs each embassy about its foreign

622

nationals on a daily basis. The moment you cross the border, everything is known.

"Then I recalled that you told me your son's name is Andrew. She promised to check that name as well."

"And?"

"That took longer. When she called back, she said there was no record of an Andrew Graham entering the Federation territories."

"But that's impossible!"

Irina sighed. "This was your own embassy, your own people, who told me this. What was I to think?"

Alex shook his head. "It doesn't make sense. My embassy should have all the facts. It was the Russian embassy in Helsinki that told me about Andrew's entrance into the country and exactly where he was staying in Saint Petersburg. Intourist approved my own entry."

"Do you have enemies?"

"It seems I do."

"Who?"

"The people who have my son. They're the only ones. And they know I'm on their trail."

"Well, you didn't make *them* up", she admitted. "Semyon saw them too."

"I haven't made anything up."

"But if what you say is true, how could they have interfered with your government and my government? And why are the police involved—the other police, I mean?"

"And why would a branch of your government know about me while my own government doesn't? Something's wrong here. Very wrong."

"The hotel manager thinks it was the FSB who came to investigate. They wouldn't tell him why they effaced the record. Of course, he didn't ask. It's always a bad idea to ask such men for explanations."

"The FSB—that's the new version of the KGB, isn't it?"

"Yes and no. Who can tell what their new role is? Some say they fight organized crime, but no one knows if they really do."

"Why would the FSB be interested in my movements?"

"That's what I asked myself. So you see, I had reason to be upset."

"Irina Filippovna," Alex said with all the sincerity he could muster, "I understand why it's hard for you to believe me. I would probably react in the same way if I were in your place. But I ask you to believe me. What I told you about myself is simply the truth. I don't understand what is happening, not a single shred of it."

"What are you going to do?"

"I . . . well, I don't know what to do. I just don't know."

They sat in silence for several minutes, each of them glumly considering his own private thoughts. Looking up suddenly, Irina said, "Well, one thing is for certain: I will not allow you to walk across the Bering Sea, even if it is frozen." She pulled the boots from his feet and stuck them under her arm.

"I was being hasty", he said.

"We both were."

She dried her eyes on the sleeve of her sweater. In her left hand she still held the letter from Yevgeny Pimonenko. She glanced at it and bit her lower lip.

"Where did you find this?" she asked.

"In the Dostoyevsky book. Surely you knew it was there?"

"No. I've never seen it before. I hadn't read it—not ever."

Irina covered her eyes with her hand and remained without moving for a time. When at last she looked up, Alex saw that she had been weeping silently.

"He never gave it to me. It was written twenty years ago. Even after our marriage, he didn't show it to me. Why?"

"Maybe because he decided to ask you to marry him, and the note no longer applied to your situation."

She gave him a sad, grateful smile. "Perhaps you're right. It was certainly not because he was afraid to show it to me."

"In those days wouldn't a letter like this have gotten him into trouble? That was why he told you to burn it, wasn't it?"

"I would have burned it. He took a terrible risk keeping it. As a Ukrainian he was under more surveillance than ordinary students. In Moscow they kept an eye on all of us, even at the institute, and especially on those from the lands where nationalism was a problem."

"Was Yevgeny a nationalist?"

"Not at first. He was never an active political. But his sympathies...his sympathies just grew and grew until it got him—us—into trouble."

"Can you tell me about it?"

She shook her head and stood. In a choked voice she said, "Not tonight. We'll see each other tomorrow. Too much has happened. Everything at once. It's like the old days. It's as if the darkness is returning. Why now? Why here?"

"And my presence is making it worse. I'm sorry I brought trouble into your life."

"It's not your fault. It was an accident of fate that brought you here. A series of ridiculous accidents. The train. Your burn. The robbery. But now it's becoming complicated— Yevgeny too returns from the past. What does it all mean? In any event, we can do nothing about it for the moment. Turn over, please; I must check the dressing."

She brought the bleeding to a halt and cleaned the wound with stinging alcohol.

"Well, Mr. Aleksandr Graham, you have delayed the removal of your stitches several days. That is the cost of emotional vehemence."

"There has been a great deal of emotion here tonight, Doctor."

"Do all your countrymen allow themselves the luxury of such emotionally satisfying outbursts?"

"Rarely. We are a placid people. Sheeplike and easily manipulated."

"Except when you're humiliated."

"Even then, it takes a great deal to animate us."

"That is pathetic."

"You prefer tantrums?"

His face in the pillow, he heard her utter a short, melancholic laugh.

"For tonight we should call a truce", she said, taping the packing over the back of his head. "There, it's done. I must leave now. The boys, no doubt, are into mischief. You must go to sleep. You will stay here. You will not walk to Listvyanka."

"Nor across the Bering Sea."

"We will sort out this mess in the morning. Good night."

"Good night."

26. A Voice from the Past

Nothing was sortable. Nothing explainable. So they waited.

Four days later, after a great deal of tedium broken inter-mittently by games of chess with a merciless competitor, Alex's stitches were removed. This occurred one evening as a blizzard howled down from the north end of Baikal. The clinic walls shook from time to time under the ferocious assault of high-velocity winds. The stove in the other room roared with increased consumption of wood; its pipe glowed red and moaned like a dying man.

"Hold still", said Irina sharply.

"I am holding still", Alex mumbled. "It's the room that's moving."

"One more and then you're fixed."

"Eighteen. I counted seventeen so far, and one more makes eighteen."

"Absolutely correct. Your higher brain functions are still operating, I see. You can be grateful nothing worse happened to you."

"Ouch!"

"There, it's done. You're a free man at last."

She swabbed the damaged area with alcohol, and Alex could feel by the line of fire the antiseptic traced along the back of his skull just how extensive the wound had been.

When he was permitted to sit up, he thanked her. She gave him a studious look and began to gather her instruments into a tray. Stacked on the bedside table were books in Russian, literature mostly, as well as a tablet of letter paper, a pen, and the chessboard.

"Where is Kiril tonight?"

"He cannot see you this evening. He has been neglecting his studies since you came."

"Once again I see the extent of my status. An intruder on every level."

"I brought you pen and paper. It seems your only recourse is to write to your government. I've tried to beg money to pay for a telephone call. But no one has that kind of money."

"Won't Semyon let you make another free call?"

"Not to North America, which would destroy in one blow a week's wages for him. Your embassy in Moscow is obviously not willing to help, so you must write to your home and to your capital."

"But...but...", Alex sputtered. "This is an impossible situation. It could take months to get an answer. I can't just stay here."

"Think of it as a holiday."

"A holiday!"

"Look, Aleksandr Graham, you are not in the West. People here would like to help you, but they can't. And it seems your own people can't or won't. Maybe I'm wrong about that. We could always try again. If you wish, we can go to Listvyanka soon, and then you can talk with the embassy yourself."

"How soon?"

"Tomorrow, if the storm ends."

Alex got up and walked to the window, where he stood for a while staring out at a torrent of snow blowing horizontally, reducing visibility to zero. Despite the triple-pane glass, the ward was colder than usual, and he now wore two sweaters and kept the felt boots on his feet at all times.

He shook his head. "It's crazy."

"Crazy? No, it's just the sort of idiotic thing that happens all the time in this country. Bureaucracy is slow here. It's faster when rubles warm palms, but without the rubles it's as slow as birch sap in March."

"Drip, drip, drip—just like maple trees in my country."

Irina smiled ironically. "Ah yes, but when you have a pan full of drips and boil it down, you get sugar syrup. Bureaucracy is necessary. It keeps the world sweet."

"Sweet", he mumbled irritably.

Irina sat down on the wooden chair and crossed her legs. Her fur boots, calf-length dress of brown wool, and heavy gray sweater made her look frumpish, but in the subdued light of the bed lamp Alex realized anew that her face was lovely. He looked away. Irina watched him make short paces back and forth in front of the window, his eyes focused on the floor.

"What are you thinking?" she asked.

"I'm thinking I have to get out of here. I'll go mad waiting for an answer to a letter that might take weeks to reach Canada. Then more weeks waiting for a response."

"Waiting is the primary recreation of Russia. You could try getting used to it."

"I would rather not, thank you."

Rising suddenly to her feet, she said, "We should celebrate your recovery. I have some things to show you. Will you wait here?"

He laughed shortly. "I'm not going anywhere."

A few minutes later she was back, cheeks flushed and snow-flakes melting in her hair. In one hand she bore a glass jar with brown liquid swirling in it, and in the other a large book.

"It's kvass. A gift from Aglaya the Crow."

"Aglaya the *Crow*? Why do you call her that?"

"It's a term of fondness. Does she not resemble the *voron*?"

"Yes, I suppose she does. The black clothes and the gray kerchief."

"And she will peck you if you're not polite to her, and peck you very hard if she takes it into her head that you're not a good person."

"Have I passed her test?"

"Yes, with excellent marks, though you did not score as high as you might because of the Romanism, and, well, because you're a man."

"Does she not like men?"

"She likes men well enough but on principle retains a certain mistrust of the gender."

Irina poured the kvass into two medicine beakers and handed one to Alex. Switching to English, she said, "You should probably sit down when you drink this, Mr. Aleksandr Graham. In your present condition your head might not be able to cope with it."

"Oh yes, my head. I imagine I must look quite a sight."

Most of the back of his skull was shaved and scarred. Doubtless his appearance was worsened by the darker roots growing beneath the yellow hair. His face too was itching with stubble.

He sipped the kvass, which tasted like yeasty bread. The alcohol content was low but began to take effect. He sat down on the edge of the bed.

"Thank you", he said, raising his glass to Irina. "And great thanks to Aglaya the Crow."

"Do you feel better now?"

"I do. This is wondrous stuff."

"The primary fuel of Siberia. It drives away the cold—and anxiety."

"Aglaya is a good woman."

"What is your definition of a good woman?"

After another sip, Alex said, "A generous person."

"Upright, moral, and true?"

"Yes."

"And what is your definition of a good man?"

"The same."

"What a simple world you come from. What nice people you must be."

"Not all of us."

"Most of you, I think. A fine *idealistic* people."

"But we understand so little about reality—is that what you're implying?"

Irina shrugged.

Opening the book that she had brought with her, she showed him the inside cover.

"What is it? Something for me to read?" Alex asked.

"If you are interested in intestinal parasites of the Trans-Caucasus region, you are welcome to read it. But it contains a surprise. After you showed me the note from my husband, it struck me that there might be other memories hidden among his belongings. For two days I have gone through his books with great care. As you can see, this volume is old and is bound with wood and leather. The inside back cover is sealed with a heavy paper endsheet. But the glue was of poor quality, and now, years later, the paper has pulled away from the wood. See?"

She leaned forward and put it on the bed. Gently she lifted the endpaper from the cover, revealing a rectangular compartment no more than two millimeters deep. Fitted into this space were folded pieces of tissue-thin paper. She took them out and held them in her hands.

"It was reckless of him, very reckless. These are extracts from his private journal written when we were students in Moscow. Why he thought this could escape detection by the KGB is a puzzle to me. Perhaps he underestimated their cleverness, their thoroughness. In those days he was more of an optimist. But now it seems his optimism was not unfounded because these have survived after all." Her voice faltered as she struggled to keep from choking on her words.

"May I read them?" he asked.

She handed the sheets of paper to him and took a sip of her kvass.

"Your husband was a doctor?"

She nodded. "We met in Moscow and married there. Ilya was born there also."

Suddenly the lights went out.

"Oy, *foo!*" she said. Alex listened to her moving about the room in the dark, then heard a scratch-scratch sound, followed by a flare of sulfur light. He saw her by the door putting a wooden match to the wick of a candle in a metal holder.

"The storm has torn down a power line. Well, it's not the first time, or the last. Here, take this. See if you can read by it."

Alex put the candle on the bedside table and opened the sheets of paper that she had given him. In the dim amber glow, he made out the words at the top of the first page:

The Slavic soul will never be satisfied by materialism—

Alex looked up. "Your husband was a thinker."

"He was an academician for a short while before our life fell apart, but that was in a medical institute."

Irina folded her arms and stared at the floor for a moment before raising her eyes.

"Read my husband's papers. There you will meet a true man of our land."

With no more said, she departed from the clinic, leaving him alone with the papers—alone, it seemed, with Yevgeny Pimonenko.

Alex turned onto his side, put the papers close to the candle, and read through them slowly. The contents were not a single unified work, for they were short fragments, somewhat disconnected. It was possible that they had originated in other writings by the author and that he had saved these few extracts because they were of great importance to him. Some were dated, others were not, but Alex presumed that the entries on the first pages were from an earlier period of the doctor's life and the passages at the end from a later one.

8 December 1979

Yesterday, Academician Z approached me after class and invited me for a walk in the Lenin Hills, which he pointedly referred to as the "Sparrow Hills". I agreed to go with him, much intrigued, because he is a reserved man and usually quite cold with students. We strolled along making pleasant conversation until, in the middle of the park, after carefully looking over his shoulders to make sure there were no listeners, he said, "Pimonenko, I have been asked about your political affiliations." He held up his hand as if warning me to say nothing. "I know you are not a political sort, but your origins draw eyes to you. Curious eyes. Beware of any taint on your reputation. Ahead of you is a promising career in medicine."

I thanked him. There was no need to articulate the name of the bureau that is suddenly curious about me. I assured him I had no interest in antisocial elements, that I would remain "apolitical", as he calls it. However, in a rash moment I did say, "All truth is inherently political." He did not answer this remark. Today he reverted to his customary distance, as if our conversation had never taken place.

*

1 May 1980

Irina refused to come to the theater with me today. It is not for lack of enjoyment of my company, she hastens to reassure me. She declares it is simply a case of her mind being overstuffed with examination data and needing a radical change of scene. "Real theater!" she said, by which she meant that she would be going with friends to Red Square.

The music, the parades, the pageantry all enthrall her, though only in an aesthetic sense. Like me, she is "apolitical". Unlike me, she has no justification for this. She tells me that "all that business" is so boring, so dark and burdened with the tragedies of the past.

I think I am falling madly, irredeemably, in love with her. So far, not a hint of this has escaped my lips, though perhaps she suspects. I cannot pretend much longer that our frequenting the theater together is no more than a shared appreciation of culture. Tonight, I remained in my room and wrote to Mama and Papa. Still no reply to my last three letters. I also read part of a manuscript K gave me, a copy of something by Soloviev—not an approved, butchered version of early Soloviev, but an edition of later writings published in France before the Revolution. It is astonishing work. V.S.S. is nothing like the image presented to us by state censors.

*

The West is an intellectual disaster zone. If we were more rational by nature, we would be just like them, or worse. After the Renaissance, one needed an intellectual machete to hack through the jungle of rationalism. Their philosophers remind me of overinflated balloons. When you let go of their tails, they go shooting in every direction making a lot of noise as they deflate. Our philosophers—if one can call them that—are no better.

I am sick of intellectuals. The impulse to explain and analyze, if it is not subsumed in the pursuit of wisdom, is usually nothing more than a means of control—knowledge and power as a method of self-elevation above the dreary lot of the masses. How long has it been since wisdom was honored in this land? No one took the trouble to teach us about that aspect of our history. We have learned only an ersatz history.

Now and then, scrawled on the walls of public toilets or inserted into textbooks by anonymous hands, are little messages about our true past—a kind of black-market history of Russia.

*

The moment one makes a fundamental choice for truth, the architecture of reality expands dramatically. One discovers new pieces of the puzzle wherever one looks. Here is a piece of black history:

V, a Ukrainian Christian whom I met in the lobby of the symphony after the Rachmaninoff concert, told me that I do not have any real understanding of my own homeland, which of course I have not seen since I was a boy. My self-justifications did not impress him. He is an angry fellow and quite dangerous. Still, I learned a lot. The state suppressed the Catholic Church in Ukraine and turned over its property to the Ukrainian Orthodox Church, which, he tells me, is merely a puppet in the hands of the state. He says that the majority of religious prisoners in Soviet prison camps are Ukrainian Catholics, including priests and bishops. I asked him how he knew this. He answered that he would rather not say. Where does this leave me? Nothing is verifiable.

V is the first Catholic I have met face-to-face. Papa once told me that before the Revolution, Grandmother Pimonenko was a believing Catholic. I never knew her. She died during the starvation.

*

28 May

The Slavic soul will never be satisfied by materialism. If by some unexpected magic of history, we are able to throw off the yoke of dialectical materialism during the decades to come (if the West does not burn us to ashes first), and if by that same magic our standard of life were to improve, the new materialism of capitalism would only sicken us still further. Even though we desire it with all our hearts, our hearts can never be satisfied by it. If Russia rediscovers humility, she will rehumanize the world. If she does not rediscover it, the world will continue to destroy itself. What is our mission in history? Are we predestined to be the destroyer of civilization? Or are we, as we long supposed, the bearers of a saving truth? The Russian Idea has been eclipsed for more than sixty years. Can it be relearned?

*

Afghanistan is humiliating Brezhnev. The propaganda in the press cannot dispel the rumors that are now everywhere. Our military are defeated again and again by small bands of guerrillas, reaffirming the power of conviction over ideology. What a dirty little foreign adventure this war is.

On all sides serious people ask if détente is a sham or an honest effort at dialogue with those on the other side of the wall. Can the Americans really be trusted? The British? The French? And who could ever trust the Germans? The real question is, can *we* be trusted? The answer is obvious. The West desperately wants to be deceived by our pantomime. It is all a show for the Americans. Since the war, they have lost their vision, their courage. Will they ever learn?

What a farce! Nothing will change internally. Z says the Helsinki Human Rights observers in Russia are being arrested one by one.

*

Tensions grow. If Russia finds herself unable to feed her people, or feed the millions of regular army troops, an invasion of Western Europe will soon follow.

*

16 September

A day of rain and moodiness. Irina admits she is attracted to me but cannot envisage life with a madman. She laughed as she said this and rewarded me with a kiss on the cheek. An extraordinary girl—moral—a rarity. Though I am demented with the very thought of her, I too resist the universal habit of promiscuity. Is there something wrong with me? No, I think not. I sense it is a kind of subconscious memory—an intuition about love. By grasping the sensations of love without commitment, even the best of lovers risks losing love altogether. In his desperation to escape despair by purchasing a ticket to the "theater" of the senses, modern man indulges his passions thoughtlessly, thus stunting them and redirecting them away from their fullest realization, which is to be found in the most sublime and elevated love. Irina says I am a romantic. So is she, but she won't admit it. As for me, I prefer reality. Perhaps I am a romantic realist. That kiss was worth a thousand fornications.

I am interning at the Second Medical Institute. The cases that come through the door are frightening. The prostitutes especially break one's heart. Some are hardly more than children. Behold the liberation of Soviet Woman!

Think of it! Imagine this analogy, if you will: An ideologically motivated woman rejects marriage in order to become a prostitute so that all men might have equal access to what rightly belongs only to a husband. She convinces herself that in doing so, she is a democrat and generous to a fault, but in truth she only furthers the communal ownership of women

637

that is the reduction of the eternal to the dimension of material-social property. The same holds true for the state. Russia is a bride who rejected her bridegroom in the interests of becoming a free woman and became instead the worst of prostitutes—she now kills her customers and her children indiscriminately.

*

Anniversary of the October Revolution, 1980

Needless to say, I busied myself with other matters. Met with Academician Z today for another walk. He tells me the good news that I am to become an assistant professor at the institute. He hinted that he knew something about my situation, and I asked him point-blank if he had picked up anything regarding the KGB's interest in me. He said he thought that all danger was now past. It was routine surveillance. My proletarian background was of some help. But I must not grow lax, he emphasized, or lose vigilance in any matter whatsoever. He warned me to be extremely careful about whom I talk to—especially strangers. Does he know about my meetings with K and V? What it all means, I cannot say. Perhaps it is nothing. Still, I am grateful for Z. He took a great risk.

*

30 October

Today I lost a prostitute who hemorrhaged from a botched abortion at a state clinic and was brought in to the hospital by her "co-workers". Also lost were three people dragged in off the street by police. They died of toxicity and exposure—alcohol related. One was very young. Tragedy in every direction. A grand total of fifteen suicides were wheeled past my eyes today—mostly old people and youths. Colleagues tell me this is growing more frequent, though they are at a loss to explain it. Things are better now than in the "good old days", so why is this happening?

Out of thin air, V appeared beside me on Gorky Street as I was walking home from the library. He pretended he did not know me. But under the guise of asking directions to the metro, he slipped me a copy of the Bible and whispered that it had been smuggled into the country from abroad. It is in Ukrainian, which I know less well than Russian. But quite readable.

*

4 November

The Scriptures are apocalyptic from start to finish, with brief interludes for rest and instruction. Well, I suppose it is all instruction. Both the Old and New Testaments are concerned with the End. Although the definitive climax of history is not peculiar to Judeo-Christian literature, no other religion has articulated it with such astounding complexity (and sustained it for four thousand years). This is absolutely unique in the history of mankind. Moreover, no other Christian people has been as preoccupied with the concept of the End as we have been.

Supposedly, we are no longer a Christian people. At best the Christian consciousness has been driven underground, or, alternatively, neutralized as cultural artifact. I looked at the Kremlin cathedrals today and seemed to see them for the first time. I was overwhelmed by the sense that no purely aesthetic interest could have produced these marvelous entities. Only a dynamic conviction about living realities could have done so.

The Revolution was a catastrophe for mankind, as dire as the Black Death of the Middle Ages. If the tyrant state does not soon destroy itself, the situation will degenerate steadily, will become worse than the Great Flood. Then will come the Flood of Fire, leaving nothing but ashes.

*

The Revolution was a struggle over the definition of the meaning of human life. It was about power, of course, and about progress, but at the root it was a war between two opposed concepts. On one side was the monarchy and its aristocracy, ostensibly based on the Gospels, a social order that supposedly reflected the divine hierarchy in creation. On the other side was socialist democracy, ostensibly based on concern for the common good, a social order that supposedly reflected the divinely ordained value of each human life. Because both failed at a fundamental level to live both the divine and human aspects of love, a host of aberrations were flung like poisoned seed throughout subsequent history. Czarist repression was succeeded by Bolshevik repression, followed by the Hydra-like monsters it spawned. All was done in the name of mankind. And in the end, all found themselves killing the poor in the name of the poor.

*

"For he has made known to us in all wisdom and insight the mystery of his will, according to his purpose which he set out in Christ as a plan for the fullness of time, to unite all things in him, things in heaven and things on earth" (Ephesians 1:9–10).

"He has put all things under his feet and has made him the head over all things for the Church, which is his body, the fullness of him who fills all in all" (Ephesians 1:22–23).

What is the fullness of time?

What does the passage mean when it says the Church contains the fullness of Him? What constitutes His Body?

*

Easter! *Khristos voskrese!*

Today I told Irina I have become a Christian. She is frightened and wants to know why I am endangering myself. What of the future? she asks. By this I understand that she has already begun to think of a future by my side. Another kiss! I am ecstatic. I told V about my love for Irina. He rejoices— a genuine, spontaneous eruption of delight—over the gift of faith and the gift of love. How rare are such emotions among my colleagues, whose high spirits are engendered only by vodka.

V urges me to become a Christian in more ways than the heart. I tell him I wish to be an autonomous Christian. He replies, "Zhenya, is this not merely a variation on the atheist's refusal to submit to anything outside his own sphere of control, his own knowledge?" V warns me against Descartes and Kant. Suggests Soloviev. His eyes grow wide with wonder when I tell him I have a manuscript from S's late Christian period. V begs to make a handwritten copy. Of course I agree.

*

5 December 1981

Three copies completed and scattered in the underground. Soloviev now circulating as samizdat. Like yeast in the dough. V asks me to consider Baptism. Is this necessary? The Gospel says it is.

I like him very much. The Gospel is a living thing for him, and he readily quotes from it without a book in hand. He has begun to take a cup of tea with me now and then. It is reckless, of course. I know little about his past or his activities. But he prays—that is obvious—and there is something in his eyes. What is it? Sincerity? Honesty? Suffering?

Yes, but suffering overcome by some strength of soul that is a complete mystery to me.

*

Jesus is alive and with us! Yes, even here in this place where Satan has made his foothold on earth. But I am mystified. I ask V why the demon has had so much success in a land where God was once so loved and honored.

His reply was interesting. He believes that Satan's attack on civilization struck at Russia *precisely* because God was so honored here. But we had become complacent and hypocritical in our practice of the faith. We failed to live the Gospel as we should, leaving the door wide open to the thief. When the good are corrupted, he said, it is always a more dreadful corruption than that of those who have never seen the light. It is like the corruption of Lucifer himself. Thus the evil stemming from this sort of betrayal is the worst.

Two fundamental gifts of God have been corrupted: the light of reason in the West, the fire of authentic spirituality in the East.

He believes that the assault upon Christianity in the West took the form that best suited its reigning characteristic (the rational), its dominant cultural model (its concept of the universe and its way of interacting with the universe)—which is the mind. Thus the materialist revolution of the West was caused by philosophies and ideologies that affected everything gradually, and with relatively little bloodshed. This revolution took several centuries to accomplish and has not yet arrived at the point when it will act out the most horrible aspects of its perverse logic. A violent revolution would never have succeeded for long—it would always have reverted to the dominant model. Thus the revolt against God in the West was painstakingly slow, incremental, and seemingly benign.

642

Satan's assault upon Christianity in the East took the form that best suited our dominant characteristic (the passionate, the irrational). He assaulted us according to our cultural model—which is the heart. An intellectual revolution would not have succeeded in the East—it would always have reverted to the dominant model. Thus the revolt against God in our land was swift and brutal.

*

31 December

Swift and brutal! And it remains so. V has been arrested. I went to his flat and found it stripped. The landlady says "the police" have taken him away. "A common criminal", she said. "I always knew there was something sinister about that man."

*

January—Epiphany

There is a little church outside the city where one may worship in relative privacy. It is a child of the "catacomb Church" that survived underground during the Stalin era and is now poking its head above the melting snow. At any moment it can become invisible again. It is Orthodox, but one hears (in prudent and charitable conversations between priest and believers) the agony they (we) feel over the hierarchy. The office is holy, but the men who occupy it at this moment are compromised. How do we resist the compromise without damaging the office, which will one day be filled by true apostles? An abiding theme, an abiding dilemma.

The official Orthodox Church in Russia that functions aboveground was a child of Stalin—a "Stalinist church". Is this my Church? One may choose to worship in such approved churches, but even if one does, a black mark is entered against one's name. So, underground we go. I was received. The sacraments—oh, why did no one ever tell me? Why have we been robbed of this treasure!

Still no word of V, though I have inquired about him among the contacts in various official and unofficial church circles. This is a risk, of course. But one cannot abandon a brother. Are not all men our brothers?

*

2 February 1982

Ira and I are married by Father F. She agreed to the clandestine ceremony for the sake of my conscience. Afterward, we made the usual state formality. The former was glorious, the latter a dead letter.

Joy! She lives the mystery also, though she does not yet believe in it.

*

19 May

Today she said a thing that moved me greatly. "Zhenya, though I do not understand, I believe in you. And that is good enough for me. And for our child!"

Yes! A child is on the way!

Joy leaps unto joy, as deer upon the mountains. I am reading to her from the Song of Songs at night. Never have we been so happy.

Life always conquers. I shall never again doubt this.

Jesus, restore our beloved land, our people, our Church! Come swiftly!

*

More and more I see the connection between the love of spouses and the love of God for mankind. Abandonment in the darkness of radical trust is nakedness. It is the unveiling between lover and beloved at the moment of conjugal love. When God is the lover, and His creature the beloved, the unveiling takes a form that the creature will not at first understand. The bride cannot know all that is in the heart of her groom. She must trust in His love to the point of rashness.

*

We call our land the Motherland because the Slavic spirit is mystical, assuming an essentially "feminine" stance before God, influenced by the Greek Byzantine spirit.

Germans call their land the Fatherland, because the Germanic spirit is imbued with a concept of the "masculine" derived from pagan worship. It seems to me that they do not understand what real fatherhood is. Nor do we.

*

Communist life is ritualized—building upon the Russian psychology of a world radiant with signs, existence as word incarnate, expressed in its rites. The corruption of our symbols, our psychological cosmos, is a diabolical strategy!

*

Winter 1983

Many visitors, new friends. Kitchen conversations of an edifying and enjoyable sort. Irina likes the visitors but is wary. "They hope for too much", she says.

*

Despite all the propaganda, violation, and suffering, God has not been banished from the Russian heart. New ideas (actually old ideas) are being excavated from unmarked graves.

*

Theology is a typically Western discipline. Religious philosophy is typically Russian.

*

Russian guilt—how readily a Russian slips into dreadful sins, yet unlike the men of the West, he cannot jettison his guilt or paper it over with new philosophies. The duality in us is not the fault of the Byzantine vision of existence (in all its fullness). It is the fault of corrupting our form of it.

Yet our suffering and our isolation forged a unique character, a spiritual culture that still endures beneath the smothering cloud of "socialist realism". Music, which is inherently spiritual, is our primary art, our only art untainted by ideology. In the nineteenth century, when Western thought began to influence the intelligentsia, some of our greatest saints lived and our great music and literature grew. As Western intellectual revolutions seeped into our life, God raised up these saints and artists as signs of a larger universe. We did not hear them, or if we heard them, it was only to appreciate the style and the ethos, so charmingly Russian, so amusingly eccentric! We smiled indulgently at our excesses, then turned to the West, so cool, so rational, so imbued with the bracing atmosphere of intellectual genius. We were tired of being Europe's ignorant peasant. We became proud, and this pride was our downfall. Hegel and Kant helped to enlarge us—and to ruin us. The exaltation of intellect without a grounding in the hierarchical cosmos, without humility, will end (and did end) in a hyperassault upon the Fatherhood of God. This is patricide on a catastrophic scale. The child who attempts to kill his father—Karamazov was right—creates for himself a living hell.

We were called to be God-bearers, but such a high calling was latent with the most terrible temptations, and we succumbed to them.

I am confused, still picking my way through the debris of our shattered history. What is true? What is false? One can hardly trust anything in the libraries. Who are we?

*

Our culture was always deeply religious, even when it was wrong. The Russian understanding of hesychasm and kenosis was a genuine inspiration, a knowledge of our place in the divine order before the hidden face of God. However, between the hammer and anvil of historical forces, the original gift was damaged. Two paths emerged from this catastrophe: One, negative, led to dualism and the Revolution—the realm of hatred. The second led in the direction of poverty of spirit—the realm of Love.

*

Today Z says to me, "We are forced to live with a kind of double vision: to love Russia—the Russia that might have been and still may become—while at the same time seeing the reality of what she is now."

"The system is evil", I say to him. If he is a duplicitous man, I have sealed my fate.

"The Soviet system is evil", he replies, sealing his own fate (if I am a duplicitous man). "But our compromises began long before 1917, before 1905. They go perhaps all the way back to the eleventh century."

Feeling that this casts unfair aspersions on what we had before the Revolution, I say nothing in reply.

"You do not believe me", he says with typical calm. "You are loyal to our meta-identity. I admire your fervor, Zhenya, but you must understand that we all have lost our consciousness of time."

"Historically, you mean?" I ask.

"I mean the breaking of continuity. When you lose your place in the stream of time, you become a person who is completely dependent on the social."

*

For every Z or V there are ten thousand apathetic or greedy people. Indifference to the real issues is a way of blocking out fear. Cynicism is another. To live fully as a human being, one must face his own fear.

*

Father F gave me a hard word today. It stung, but it had the good effect of making me see something about myself. During my confession, he said, "Yevgeny, your greatest fault is that you do not believe in the Fatherhood of God."

"But I do!" I protested.

"You believe with your mind but not with your heart."

*

Mind and heart. "The dialectic of the Holy Spirit", Father F calls it. He is not overly fond of Romans, especially "Jesuiticals", as he calls them, but he knows of "passion sufferers" who are Catholic.

Here is his intuition about the future of Christianity:

Satan split and resplit the body of believers in order to weaken its effectiveness in the social-historical context. Yet God is always bringing a greater good out of the evil designs of the adversary, always overcoming him. In the case of the

Schism and Reformation, it is possible that God permitted them in order to save the multiplicity of culture and all the riches of diversity. Russia has been kept isolated for the purpose of radical impoverishment and protection from the diabolical errors of the Enlightenment. Her role is reserved for the End.

Just as the Western Church cannot return to the medieval ideal, Russian Orthodoxy cannot return to the prerevolutionary church-state theocracy even if the grip of Marxism-Leninism should loosen. Nostalgia is the idealization of the past. Neither the West nor the East can afford nostalgia. What is needed is a revolution of the Holy Spirit in which an outpouring of unprecedented grace would reveal to both East and West their distinct roles in a single, organic whole.

There is only one antidote—to find again the Bridegroom and beg His forgiveness. He will forgive. He is love, and He is truth. He will forgive everything.

.   *

18 January 1983

Snow is falling heavily outside. Our love grows and grows. Ilya is born! A beautiful child. Irina sings to him constantly and calls him *zimorodochka*—the little winter-born. Baptized by Father F on the eve of my hearing before the hospital committee. The political officer informed me that I risk trial and imprisonment if I do not appear. A patently KGB "laborer" shovels and reshovels the snow of the lane in front of our building, keeping a constant eye on the door and the window of our flat. We now have the cleanest lane in Moscow.

*

1 August

The hearings have lagged for lack of evidence, and because of the fine summer weather, which of course draws all officials away "on important business" at their dachas. Still, they warn me that the investigation is not yet complete. I expect the institute has obtained a delay so that I can finish teaching the autumn courses.

*

It struck me recently that God wrote a large story in the lives of the people we read about in Scripture, and it was usually for reasons beyond their understanding. He did so for several purposes, but one of them was to teach and illumine others who would not be born until thousands of years after the events. Is it possible that He is "writing" our lives as well, for purposes we cannot begin to understand, and perhaps may never understand in our lifetimes? Our inexplicable sufferings, especially the blows of injustice, may be far more valuable to other souls than we can now guess. Thus the necessity of thanking Him for all our trials, adversity, unjust sufferings, because the fruit of these may be of incalculable worth, though hidden from our eyes.

*

25 November

Hearings resumed. Today Academician Z appeared on my behalf. He argued that, as my professor and "friend" (this astonished me greatly), he knew me very well and assured the committee that I was completely unpolitical, that my contact with the Orthodox Church was not strictly illegal, and that it was primarily a cultural interest.

I was grilled extensively by the committee. I was able to navigate without lies but feel certain I have destroyed any future I might have given to my family. What does Christ our Savior think of me today? Did I bear witness for Him as boldly as I should have? I do not know. If it was a question of martyrdom alone, I would have been more outspoken, but what then would have happened to Irina and Ilya? Do I have a right to martyr them?

*

30 November 1983

A meeting with the political committee to learn my fate. They were not satisfied by my testimony and told me they were close to a decision. Some members thought a complete investigation of all my affairs by the KGB was in order. A minority dissented. Why on earth they were telling me this was perplexing because they always do whatever they want. And as for the KGB, they do not need committees to tell them what to do. Was this a show trial of some kind? If so, a rather paltry one it was.

Z stepped forward and, with truly admirable style, performed as I have never seen him perform. Witty, chuckling like a grand old bear, the quintessence of reasonableness, saying comrade this and comrade that, emphasizing his own record in the Great Patriotic War (he had taken care to wear his medals), Z told the committee that they were making a grave error. Dr. Pimonenko was one of the country's most brilliant physicians, was destined for advanced work in medical research that would benefit the Party and the People. Why should a man like this be cut off at the very beginning of a productive career for the crime of—the crime of—naïveté! Z grinned and waved his arms quite melodramatically when he said *naïveté*, evoking smiles from committee members and—I am ashamed to admit—from me also.

"Intemperate he may be; lacking in judgment in a wholly innocuous manner he may be", Z went on. "But does not this very lack of guile prove the opposite of the accusation? This is not the behavior of a *dangerous man*" (more dramatics and more laughter). "The poor fellow was simply entranced by art and architecture and music."

How Z could have pulled off such an act when the stakes were so high is still a mystery to me. The KGB apparatchik, seeing that he was about to lose his prey, stepped in and said that regardless of what the committee decided, Pimonenko would be investigated. There was ample evidence for a criminal charge.

"Ridiculous, preposterous!" grumbled a number of learned doctors seated about the table.

"Perhaps *you* are overdue for an investigation, gentlemen", the agent replied. Of course, absolute silence fell, and there were no more objections.

In the end a compromise was worked out. They will call off a criminal investigation if I agree to accept a post at a hospital in Siberia. I agreed. They can do anything they like with me, so why should I not agree?

"Siberia is a land of many facets", Z said to me during the tea break. "Do not lose heart. Exile is difficult but not impossible. You are in great company—the best of Russia has always gone into internal exile."

"Where do you think they will send me?" I asked, thinking of Novosibirsk and Irkutsk. In such large cities it is still possible, after all, to find music and theater and like-minded people.

"They are going to send you to a place a little farther East, Yevgeny. You are going to Magadan."

"Magadan!" I protested.

"I'm sorry. It is the best I can do", he said with a look of embarrassment and pity.

We go by military cargo plane at the end of the week. We must leave all possessions behind except what we can carry in our hands and a single trunk. A few of our books, paintings, mementos, photographs are packed in it. Z has given me as a parting gift a copy of Dostoyevsky's *Humiliated*. Strangely, he did not use the word *podarok* (a material gift) when handing it to me but used the word *dar* (spiritual gift).

Perhaps I will at last begin to read some of our literature.

Irina is extremely upset, but she tells me that she is determined to be happy no matter what. If we three are together, nothing can take away our happiness, she says, and I agree. Still, it is bitter.

*

Magadan. January. Winter rules.

The spiritual battle that you feel everywhere in Russia is particularly intense in the camps and in this city built by zeks—built upon the bones of hundreds of thousands of nameless zeks. Gogol could not have envisaged this even in his worst nightmares. We are stuffed into the pocket of Akakii's overcoat. The pocket is so dark that one wonders if the coat has been cast into a bottomless pit. Without Irina and Ilya I would surely succumb to...

*

Here Yevgeny's notes ended. Alex folded the papers, replaced them in their hiding place, and turned out the light. For several hours he did not sleep. He stared at the darkness and listened to the howling wind.

27. I Give You Everything

Three days later the storm ended and the sun rose in a sky of purest blue. The lake and all its environs were blasted with a splendid light. Faces appeared at every window, soaking it up. Soon people were outside their front doors shoveling paths, shouting greetings to each other across the half-buried tops of willow-web fences. The still air was aromatic with some absolute purity.

Kiril came bounding into the clinic and told Alex he must get dressed because Mama wanted him to come to the house for breakfast and to talk over the possibility of a trip to Listvyanka. Alex complied, glad for a chance to exchange the little medical institution for the sights and sounds of a home. He also wanted to discuss Yevgeny's notes with Irina, which had stimulated in him a number of questions. He had not yet had an opportunity to do so because she had been away for two days at a village farther north along the shore, attending a difficult birth.

Irina greeted him and asked about his health. Kiril plunked himself down at the table and began to gobble a dish of kasha. The older boy, Ilya, got up and went outside without saying hello. When Alex asked Irina about her trip, which had occurred during the height of the storm, she remarked that it had been arduous, but the mother and newborn were in excellent condition. She set a bowl of kasha in front of him and the welcome treat of a cup of strong coffee.

"A gift from the baby's family", she said, smiling triumphantly.

After breakfast she sat down opposite him, poured herself a cup, and drank it black. She told Alex that Ilya was willing to take him to Listvyanka, where he could call Moscow from Semyon's phone. She gave him a note for the captain, which would smooth the way.

Shortly after nine o'clock, Ilya came in from the stable to announce that Kolo was harnessed to the sleigh and that they could leave whenever the visitor was ready. Irina and Kiril walked them to the stable. Irina cautioned Alex to keep the sheepskins and rugs over himself for the duration of the journey and warned Ilya to go slowly to save the guest's poor head from any unnecessary jostling.

Ilya tossed his head and said he knew very well how to drive the sleigh. Alex climbed on board beside him, Ilya flicked the reins, and the shaggy pony lurched against the traces. As they left the village and entered the trees, the fiddlehead runners cut through the new-fallen snow and skimmed over drifts hard packed by the wind during the previous three days. The air was calm, the sun slowly warming it. Birds were making noises in the trees, a dog barked somewhere behind in the village, and the sleigh bells jingled merrily. Kolo's frosty breath gusted in steady puffs, and she nickered whenever the driver gave her backside little flicks of the rein. Ilya stood for the first mile or so, controlling the direction of the sleigh with confidence and pleasure.

"I am the man of my house", his manner seemed to say.

The track through the woods was a narrow one; the hills pressed close to the shore at this point, and the forest of evergreens was thick. In the shadows of the trees, the deeper snow made the going slow.

"How long will it take us to reach the town?" Alex asked.

"Three hours", the boy answered.

Alex sat back, bundled and warm, his face flushed with the cold and his lungs filling with invigorating air. From time to time he glanced at the driver, recalling to himself a passage in the journal of the boys' father.

Ilya is born! A beautiful child. Irina sings to him constantly and calls him zimorodochka—*the little winter-born. Baptized by Father F on the eve of my hearing.*

He was born in January of 1983, Alex thought to himself. He's sixteen, and like many a boy of that age, he strains to appear older. *Zimorodochka*—the little winter-born.

Zimorodok was also the Russian word for kingfisher. He now realized that the word was a remote derivative of the Greek myth of Halcyon. Born at sea—born in winter—born in adversity.

Ilya was baptized, but is he a believer? Alex wondered. *It doesn't seem so. Such anger in him, such unhappiness. Does he ask, as his father once asked, who are we?*

"This is too slow", Ilya said abruptly, sitting down on the driver's plank. "We'll take the ice route."

The boy's mouth was set in a firm line, the eyes hard with determination, the chin tilted up arrogantly as if defying Alex to raise objections. Tugging the reins to the left, he directed Kolo toward a break in the trees. The arch of the yoke swayed as the pony turned and increased speed along a sloping path through the woods. The runners creaked more loudly, and wakes of granular snow flew up on both sides. The sleigh rose and fell like a boat on tossing waves and plunged over an embankment down onto the flat of the lake.

A few inches of snow covered the ice, offering a perfect surface for a hard run south to Listvyanka. Kolo's hooves began to clop audibly, and her snorts blew gusts of hay-scented breath. When Ilya stood and flicked her rump with the reins, she began to trot. Though there was no wind, the passage through the air felt like a penetration of invisible water. It was cold but not harsh. Ilya thrust the reins at Alex, who took them while the boy buttoned down his earflaps. Frost was collecting on his hair and on the downy adolescent mustache.

Taking the reins again, Ilya flicked them harder. The horse trotted more rapidly now, clippety-clippety-clippety, its head bobbing up and down, its flanks heaving, foam-frost speckling its mouth and whiskers. Occasionally the runners hit uneven ridges in the ice, and the sleigh jumped or swerved violently, but Alex did not mind. If his skull hurt a little, it was no more than the discomfort of a mild headache. He was enjoying himself, though he kept a firm grip on the wood sidebar of the passenger box.

Ilya continued to stand, bracing his legs, alternately smiling and frowning—though none of this was directed at Alex.

"I am no longer a child", said his eyes and his body. "No longer am I in submission. I choose my own course. I am in control of a strong beast and a vehicle that takes me beyond my too-small world. Out into the great world I go, there where my destiny, my name, and my own true self await me. Who am I? I will know, soon I will know, and I am racing toward that knowledge, learning it even as I go! Let no one hold me back!"

Alex thought that in his own homeland, young men were speeding up and down streets in sports cars with the same expression on their faces. He could not recall a similar moment from his own youth, for he had never owned a car, never wanted one. There had been the greater challenge of mastering his defective heart, driving his body (poor beast) by sheer force of will against the pull of gravity. To stride up and down the escarpment of the Clementine had always been enough for him, roving the hills, gathering metaphysical impressions that by inference and atmosphere defined the shape of the man he would become. And at the apex of all testing had been the topmost span of a bridge where he had climbed the scaffolding of fear and leaped out into the great world. Rising in the time-suspended arc, then falling slowly through the line of the parabola, falling, falling—controlling the fall as this boy controlled the horizontal pitch of his pony. He had plunged to the bottom, somersaulted, driven upward, and broken the surface of the underworld, tested, a victor. A man.

The ride to Listvyanka was shorter by the ice route, and thus Alex spotted the first of its cabins an hour and a half after leaving Ozero Baikal. Ilya drove up a slope onto the unplowed main street and guided the sleigh more slowly to the building that housed Baikal Tours. When they slid to a halt by the front door, Ilya jumped out and began to pound the frost from Kolo's back. The pony was winded, head down with exhaustion, sweating and dribbling from her lips. The boy threw a blanket over her back and said to Alex without looking at him, "I will wait outside."

Semyon P. Timonin was positioned exactly as Alex had last seen him. This time he did not bother to remove his feet from the desk. Alex handed him Irina's note and stood by, impatiently eyeing the television screen while the captain read it. Oddly, the program was a drama set in Texas. Its title was *Dallas*, which seemed to be some kind of drama about a family of very spoiled, rich, degenerate Americans. The dialogue was spoken in Russian—a badly patched voice-over.

Semyon threw the note onto his desk and jerked his head in the direction of the telephone.

"Ten minutes, no more", he grumbled. "Tell Irina Filippovna it's the last time. Ask her why she's trying to ruin me."

Alex soon found himself talking to a trilingual secretary (French, Russian, and English) at the Canadian embassy in Moscow. He described his predicament. She recorded the particulars and promised to pass on the information to someone higher up. He told her where he was staying—she wrote that down also but could not find Ozero Baikal on the map in front of her.

"You must mean the lake", she said.

"No, it's a village with the same name as the lake."

Speaking in English, he gave her the phone number of Baikal Tours and said that a message could be left with the captain. Failing that, a letter could be sent in care of the post office in Listvyanka.

"It's south of Irkutsk", he suggested.

"Yes, here it is."

"Miss, please move on this as soon as possible, if you can. I'm desperate."

Her tone chilled noticeably. "We receive numerous inquiries here, sir, and many people consider their difficulties fairly serious. They forget this isn't North America. All I can suggest is that you try to be patient, and we'll get new documents to you as soon as possible—after we do some checking, of course. You are a Canadian citizen, aren't you? I mean, if you aren't, there's no way you can fool us. Also, I should mention that, if your application passes the certification process, you're going to have to forward the necessary fees."

"I *am* a Canadian citizen, miss. I am also out of money. Is there any possibility the embassy could lend me some funds temporarily? That way I can get back to Moscow and speed up the process."

"Funds are a matter of a traveler's personal responsibility, sir. We really can't be giving money to just anyone who calls. You don't have a passport number to give us, you don't have a visa number, you don't have any credit card numbers, and—"

"Miss, I told you—I've been robbed."

"Please consider our position. You're a voice calling out of the blue asking for money. You speak English, but who are you, really?"

"Are you saying that if a Canadian citizen is robbed while traveling in Siberia, you just wash your hands of him? 'You're on your own, buddy! Tough luck, pal.'"

"Of course not. I'm just saying that it's going to take a bit longer until we can verify what you've told us. Now, I suggest that if you've been robbed—"

"I *have* been robbed. And hit over the head too."

"If you've been robbed, you'll have to get a copy of the police report of the incident and send it to us."

"The police are forty miles away in Irkutsk."

"Then you'll just have to go there and talk to them."

"I don't have any money for the bus!"

"Then I suggest you write us a letter describing what has happened. Make sure you sign it legibly, and then fax it to us. That way we can fax it on to the passport bureau in Ottawa for verification."

Alex turned to Semyon. "Is there a fax machine in Listvyanka?"

"A fax? No, nothing like that here. Maybe there's one in Irkutsk."

"There's no fax here", Alex said to the secretary.

"Surely there's one in Irkutsk", she replied. "You'll just have to send it from there."

He raised his voice in frustration. "I told you, I don't have any money to get myself there!"

"Don't shout at me. If you want the Canadian embassy to be of service to you, you will have to observe the ordinary standards of courtesy."

Her snippy tone was so rankling that Alex turned red and counted to ten before answering.

"I'm sorry", he apologized. "I'm a bit distressed. I'm recovering from a skull fracture and a lot of other troubles besides. I'm caught in a situation I had no way of foreseeing or avoiding. And I just don't know what I'm supposed to do to get out of it. Could you possibly contact friends of mine in Canada?"

"Can't you do that yourself, sir?"

"I have no money to pay for a call. Please, I'm sure they'll be willing to forward money to get me out of here. I'll reimburse you, the embassy, the government of Canada, whomever, for whatever it costs."

After some hesitation, she agreed to try. Because his address book had been taken in the robbery, he could give her only the names of Father Toby and Charles Findley in Halcyon and Jacob in Toronto. He suggested that she try to obtain their numbers through Canadian telephone information.

"Can you please let me know as soon as you make contact?" he said. "I'll wait right here by this phone. Ask my friend and my son to call me here—right away, if possible."

"It's the middle of the night there, sir."

"They won't mind being woken up", Alex replied in a voice of supreme patience. "Thank you for your assistance", he added, trying to make it sound as sincere as possible.

"Not at all", she said, and the line went dead. Alex replaced the receiver on its cradle.

Semyon tore his eyes away from *Dallas* and lit a cigarette.

"So? Anybody going to help?" he drawled.

"I have to wait. May I wait here until they call back? It won't cost you a kopeck."

"Be my guest. Have a seat."

Alex sat for two hours. During that time he inhaled a great deal of smoke and alcohol fumes, mentally composed a series of angry letters to his government and its embassy in Moscow, and tried not to watch the television. Texas ended. "Space—the final frontier" began. It was disconcerting to hear the great, the noble, the mighty Russian tongue pouring from the mouths of humanoid aliens.

Alex, who was feeling very much a humanoid alien himself, became obsessed by the strangeness of it all. He was lost in space. His reality was becoming stranger than fantasy. He was relieved when the captain of the starship *Predpriyatie*

661

(Enterprise) was beamed up to safety after blasting into molecular dust the alien invaders of a helpless planet. He wished he had one of those atomizer guns. He kept hoping the phone would ring. It did not make a sound. Semyon filled a glass with a drink that looked like gasoline and shoved it across the desk. Alex sipped it and gagged. The captain poured another glass for himself and downed it in a gulp.

Alex got up and went outside to see what had become of Ilya and found that the boy and his pony had gone off someplace, leaving the sleigh parked by the front door. He went back inside and waited another half hour before deciding to place a call to the police in Irkutsk.

Semyon found the number for him and made the connections, but the result was more disturbing than ever. A detective informed Alex, after checking his books and asking around the office, that there was no record of any assault or robbery in Listvyanka during the past few months. Nothing.

"Then who were the police who investigated?" Alex cried.

"I don't know", the policeman replied, and hung up.

"That's two calls", said Semyon P. Timonin, taking the attitude of an astute businessman who is not easily fooled by down-and-out scroungers. "Irina Filippovna owes me plenty."

By then it was midafternoon, and Alex was running out of ideas. "I'm going to look for Ilya Pimonenko", he said. "If anyone calls for me, I'll be back within half an hour. Ask them to ring again."

Storming out of the building, he trudged along the street through foot-deep snow, following the trail of a man and a pony. It led directly around a corner to the bar called Doshkin-noyon, where he found Kolo tied to an iron ring in the wall beside the door. Alex went inside and saw that the establishment was almost deserted. Ilya was seated on a stool at the bar, skulking head-to-head with the bartender. The boy had a bottle of beer in his hand, and a cigarette dangled from his lower lip. He squinted at Alex.

"Hey, Exotic! Burshui! Want a sip?" said the bartender, lifting a bottle. Ilya smirked.

"No thank you", Alex said. "Ilya, we have to go."

Giving Alex a slow, cold look, the boy said haughtily, "What's the rush? I'll finish my drink first."

Speaking in a low voice, without betraying any of the emotion he felt, Alex said, "Get moving or you'll regret it."

The boy's face flamed, his eyes snapped, but he swallowed the dregs from the bottle and slid from the stool. Stomping out the door ahead of Alex, he untied Kolo and made off down the street in the direction of Semyon's. Alex arrived there a minute behind and found Ilya cursing under his breath, strapping the pony into the harness.

"Wait here", Alex said and went inside.

Semyon was talking into the phone. "*Da, da, da!*" When he saw Alex, he handed the receiver to him.

"Graham here", Alex barked.

"This is the Canadian embassy calling from Moscow", said the snippy-sweet voice. "I talked with a Mr. Charles Findley in Halcyon, Ontario. He says he's unable to forward any more funds to you because you've exceeded your credit limit. I haven't been able to reach the other parties."

"Will you try the other parties again, please. If you're able to reach them within the next hour, get them to phone me immediately. Any time after that, please ask them to wire as much money as they can spare to the largest bank in Irkutsk. I'm not even sure what that is. Just a moment..."

He asked Semyon for the name of a bank.

"Sibirbanc is the best", said the captain.

Alex spelled it out for the secretary. "S-i-b-i-r-b-a-n-c. It should be wired to my name, in care of the main branch in Irkutsk—please."

Then he restated his situation with a certain intensity and urged her to do whatever she could to speed the process.

"The embassy is doing its best, sir", she said, switching from snippy-sweet to snippy-defensive.

"I'm sure you are. Thank you for your help."

He went outside and told Ilya there would be an hour's delay before they could depart for Ozero Baikal. The boy could come inside and get warm or stay outside and freeze in the sleigh, but in either case he had better wipe that sneer off his face.

"What will you do if I don't?" Ilya said with a toss of his head. "Old man."

Alex suppressed an urge to strike the surly face now before him. Instead, he merely stared at the boy without blinking, seeing beneath the veneer a pathetic rebellion that would almost surely drag the youth into a life of rash acts. Alex saw, as well, that the mask was just that, the armor of a fatherless boy who felt he had to convince the world how tough he was.

Alex shook his head sadly.

"Why do you look at me like that!" Ilya shouted.

"I know your father", Alex said.

"You don't know my father!" Ilya shouted again, his hands curling into fists.

"I know him quite well. Ask your mother if this is not true. If Yevgeny Dmitrievich were here today, he would be ashamed of you."

With that, all juvenile braggadocio melted away from Ilya's face. His mouth quivered and he turned away, jerking furiously at Kolo's traces.

Alex went inside and sat down. He gave it an hour and a half, but the phone did not ring. Standing, he tried to catch Semyon's attention. On the television screen, a team of live bears was skating around an ice rink, sweeping hockey sticks back and forth.

"The circus!" Semyon cried with glee. "Those are real bears. Look at them go!"

"Captain Timonin," Alex said with a no-nonsense air, "I am returning to Ozero Baikal. I ask you to be patient a while longer. There will be telephone calls, possibly today or tomorrow. The callers will speak English. Do you speak some English?"

"Sure, I hear it all the time on the television."

Alex looked at him dubiously. "I will return in a few days to see if there have been any messages. Will you take the messages for me?"

"Sure, sure, that's no problem."

"Just write down the words they say, even if you don't understand them."

"You're asking a lot."

"I will repay you for your trouble."

Alex went out and saw Ilya sitting in the sleigh, head down, hands between his knees, brooding. The reins were wrapped around his arms. Alex got into the passenger side and said, "Ozero Baikal."

Staring straight ahead, the boy clicked his tongue and flicked the reins on Kolo's back. The pony jerked forward and sideways, pulling the sleigh in a wide arc toward the lake.

When they hit the ice, Alex said, "Slow. No racing."

"We must go quickly", Ilya murmured. "It will be dark soon. Storms sometimes arise."

"We will go slowly. If a storm comes, take the forest path."

Ilya guided the sleigh into the north, making Kolo move at a moderate trot. There were no more wild bumps, there was no careening, just the sound of steady hoofbeats, the whisper of the runners and the jingling of harness bells.

The sun touched the rim of the west, and dusk washed the lake with rosy tints. The air grew steadily colder.

An hour passed, during which neither the man nor the boy made an attempt at conversation. Alex could not tell whether

Ilya was enraged, humiliated, or simply depressed. In any event, he told himself that he was beyond caring about this surly brat's moods; he had real problems to face, and he was not going to let himself be upset again.

The sky darkened from deep blue into charcoal. There was not a wisp of cloud to be seen anywhere. Stars appeared above the vast expanse of frozen void. The panorama was so beautiful that it comforted Alex, recalling him to countless night walks that he had taken in the distant past when he had lived in a place called the Clementine Valley.

The moon rose, almost full. It flooded everything with a silver light that cast shadows of a sleigh and two riders on the snow behind them.

Another hour passed.

In the north, pinpricks of cabin lights appeared along the black shore. The electric power had been restored. Ilya pulled the reins to the left and eased Kolo in the direction of Ozero Baikal.

"Please", he said, after clearing his throat. "You will not tell my mother."

"About what?"

"About Doshkin-noyon. And the beer and cigarette."

Alex said nothing.

"About..." The boy paused. Several seconds passed. "About my rudeness."

Alex pondered the request long enough to let Ilya know that he was asking a great favor.

"I will say nothing to her about it", he said at last. "Do you know why I will say nothing?"

From the corner of his eye, he saw the boy whip his head toward him for a quick look.

"No."

"Today you behaved without sense. You were like a fox. Is that what you wish to make of your life?"

"No."

"I will say nothing to your mother because I see the man you will one day become, Ilya Yevgenyevich. I know that you are not a fox. I know that inside you is a man as brave and as strong as your father. But you do not yet know it."

Now the village drew nearer, and individual houses could be discerned in the moonglow.

"Still, I warn you", Alex said in an even voice, a tone containing neither threat nor weakness. "If you ever again speak to me with disrespect—"

"You will tell my mother? Please do not—"

"I will not speak to your mother about what passed between us today. She is a great woman and does not deserve to be shamed by her son. No, I will do worse to you."

A long silence ensued.

"What will you do?" the boy asked in an anxious tone.

"I will feed you to Aglaya the Crow."

Again the head whipped sideways for a swift examination of Alex's face. Unable to decide whether the guest was joking or offering a legitimate threat, he said no more.

Alex went ahead into the house while Ilya took Kolo to the shed. Irina had a late supper waiting for them, and as she laid it on the table, Alex told her about the phone calls. The situation was a nest of confusion, he said. It would take some untangling, and that would demand a certain amount of time.

"You see, Aleksandr, waiting is our national pastime", she said dryly. "You are getting used to us, I think."

"It's my own countrymen who are now presenting problems. But I'm very disturbed by what the police told me."

"It was a stupid error", she said, lifting her shoulders and making a sour face. "It happens all the time. The *militsiya* on duty just didn't check properly. You can be sure the report is there somewhere in their files. When your money arrives in

Irkutsk, we'll go to the police and get a copy of the report. Then you can fly directly to Moscow and sort it out at the embassy. After that, you can go home and forget all about this unfortunate experience."

"*Mat'!*" Kiril piped up, using the formal term for mother. "What are you saying? He cannot forget about us! Aleksandr, we are not an unfortunate experience, are we?"

"No, you are a wonderful experience. This is an excellent hotel."

Kiril's laughter bubbled merrily. "See, Mama, he likes us. And someday we'll visit him in America."

"Not America, Kiril—" Irina was interrupted by the door banging open. Ilya entered, stamping snow from his boots.

"Cold", he said, meeting no one's eyes. "Very cold tonight."

Irina went to him and kissed him on both cheeks. "Oo-oo, Ilyushka, apple cheeks! Thank you for taking our guest to Listvyanka. It was a long day for you. I appreciate it very much."

Ilya eyed Alex. "A long day", he mumbled.

"What did you do?" Kiril asked Alex brightly.

"Many adventures, many telephone calls", he replied.

"Shh, Kiril, don't bother the men. They're starving. Sit down, Aleksandr; sit down, Ilya."

Alex had not had a meal since the morning and ate everything Irina set before him with indiscriminate gusto. Savoring the afterglow of fullness and warmth, he settled back in the chair and tried to forget that he was among strangers, ten thousand miles from home. Irina poured three cups of coffee, for herself, Alex, and Ilya, and a cup of tea from the samovar for Kiril. They made light conversation for a time. Ilya remained totally silent.

Casting curious glances at her oldest son, Irina said at one point, "Are you feeling all right? You didn't catch a chill, did you?"

Ilya shrugged.

There was a knock at the door, and Aglaya entered, looking more crowlike and predatory than ever. Her bead-black eyes glittered with excitement.

"Here I am, Irina Filippovna! Late as always. But it took longer than usual to thaw those frozen mulberries. And the sugar! Don't ask me about the trials I endured obtaining sugar. I had to give twelve eggs to that stingy Antonina Arkhipovna in exchange for a single cup. But the sugar did the trick, sure enough. Took the sour right out of the berries. What a pie I've made. Look!"

The old woman whisked a cloth from a metal pot missing a handle. Inside was a steaming deep-dish pudding, heavily crusted, filling the room with the scents of baked pastry and hot fruit.

Kiril bounced up to her, sniffing, pushing his face close to the pot. Aglaya slapped the back of his head but not too severely.

"Get your nose out of the feed bag, you runt. Let the voyagers be first."

"Here, let me cut it", Irina said. Aglaya handed over the pot and sat herself down beside Ilya. She pinched his cheek. He jerked his head back and averted his eyes.

Kiril brought the old woman a cup of coffee.

"Oh, how rich you are! Where did you get this?"

"My wages, Aglaya", Irina said with a smile as she cut the pie into big hunks that dribbled hot berry syrup. "Drink as much as you like."

"You may regret your offer."

Distributing the pieces evenly into cracked white bowls, Irina sat down and joined in dessert. Kiril finished his in a twinkling; Alex consumed his with nearly equal enthusiasm. Aglaya nibbled; Irina ate with her usual delicacy. Ilya played with the pie, moving bits of it around the bowl with his fork.

"Is the boy sick?" Aglaya said with a suspicious peer into Ilya's eyes.

Irina felt Ilya's forehead with the palm of her hand. "No, he's just tired, I think."

The boy stood and scraped back his chair.

"One moment", Alex said.

Ilya glanced at him nervously.

"Ilya Yevgenyevich, I have heard much about your chess skills. Would you consider playing a game with me?"

The boy's face flushed, and his eyes filled with confusion. He nodded and sat down.

Kiril brought the board and chess pieces and set them up, excited by the match that was about to take place.

"It won't be fair", he warned. "It will be like shooting a pig in a pen!"

"Kiril!" his mother cried in dismay. "That is rude!"

Alex was the first to laugh. This precipitated the others into a fit of giggling. Even Ilya allowed himself a small smile.

"You move first", he whispered, his eyes flickering briefly in Alex's direction.

"Please call me Aleksandr, Ilya."

"What do you call each other in your country?" Aglaya challenged. "I hear that you don't use names the way we do. No patronymics at all, they say. That's hardly proper. How does anyone know where anyone else comes from?"

"*Whom* they come from, Aglaya", Irina corrected.

"My father's name was Angus", Alex said.

Kiril and Aglaya coined the odd patronymic—Anguseyevich—trying out various stresses on the syllables. This set off another round of giggling.

"Your move, please", said Ilya in a deferential tone.

And so the game began. At first it seemed to proceed as expected. No one in the room had any doubts about who would win. The only controversy was how soon Ilya would be able to beat the guest. But the boy hesitated over each move, and by the fifteenth, it was plain that his strategy was not working well. Alex put him into check, eliciting gasps from the audience. Ilya deftly escaped and three moves later checkmated Alex.

"Another?" Alex asked.

Ilya nodded. He won in twenty moves.

"One more game?" Alex said.

The boy shrugged and set up the pieces. This time he won in twelve moves.

"Thank you", he said standing abruptly. "It was interesting."

Ilya left for the room that he shared with Kiril off the parlor. Aglaya departed for her home, and Kiril was told to get ready for bed. He returned from the bedroom dressed in pajamas and fur slippers, toothbrush in hand. While Irina and Alex drank another cup of coffee, the boy busied himself scrubbing his teeth over a bowl of water at the kitchen counter. He spat and dried his mouth on a sleeve.

He came to his mother and kissed her on both cheeks.

"Ilya is crying", he said in a whisper.

"Why?"

"I asked him but he won't answer."

"Let him be, Kiril. I think he's very tired and maybe a little ill."

"All right. Good night, Mama. Good night, Aleksandr."

"Good night, Kiril."

When the boy had gone, Irina sipped from her cup, glancing curiously at Alex.

"Did something happen to him in Listvyanka?"

Alex shrugged, Russian style.

"He's in love with a girl", said the mother. "He thinks of nothing else. Perhaps it was that."

"Perhaps."

"But I don't think so. Tell me what happened."

"It's nothing for you to concern yourself with."

"I know my son. Was he difficult?"

"We had a discussion."

"A discussion."

"It ended well. As you say, he's tired, and perhaps a little ill. Nothing more need be said."

"If you say so."

Their conversation now turned to Alex's situation. Once again he apologized for being a burden on their family and tried to assure her that he would send compensation as soon as he was home.

She waved this away.

"We haven't had an opportunity to speak about my husband's journal", she said. "Did you find it interesting?"

"I was moved by it, Irina. I'm grateful you let me read it. In a few pages much is revealed about the recent past. And about your husband. I wish I could have known him. Would we have been able to understand each other, I wonder? How superficial I would have seemed to him after all he had been through."

"I don't think so. Yevgeny was always one to find the hidden depths in people. Then, later, his faith gave him tools to see things that others fail to see."

"Yet you do not have faith."

"No", she said, shaking her head. "I do not."

"Did you wonder why the man you loved became a Christian?"

"Of course I wondered. I still wonder. But people believe all sorts of philosophies in order to make sense of the world. He chose to believe the philosophy that is most traditional for our people. That's all it was."

"You call it a philosophy. Is it only that to you?"

"What is a philosophy, in essence? Isn't it a search for what is true? A world of symbols can mean many things. For him, I think, the symbols of Christianity offered an identity for man. Without it he would have died of despair."

"You did not die of despair."

"Yes, but I had *him*."

Alex fell silent. This insight contained an unspoken inference: that she had not been enough for her husband. He did not touch the subject. He waited as her eyes grew moist, as she wrestled with the unspoken corollary, then put it away from her thoughts.

"Are we not all prisoners of circumstances?" she said with a sigh.

"What do you mean?"

"Are not our lives determined by our personal histories?"

"I don't think so."

"I know you don't think so", she said with an edge.

"Irina, do you remember when we first met, that night on the train? You quoted Pushkin. You said that in our times man was either tyrant or traitor or prisoner."

"I have not changed my opinion."

"But the Christian is a prisoner in Christ, and with Christ, and thus he is the only free man on the planet."

She rewarded this fine insight (of which he was perhaps a little too proud) with a dubious look. With a wave of shame he recalled that she had observed a good deal of his behavior on the train and could not have failed to note symptoms of a man with little faith.

"Do you dislike us?" he asked.

"Us? What is *us*? Are you asking if I dislike Christians? There are all kinds of people who call themselves Christians in this country, and abroad as well, I suppose. I take each person as he comes. But I think you're really asking me if I'm a bigot."

"I didn't say that."

"You didn't have to. No, I am not a bigot. There was Yevgeny, after all. If everyone were like him, the world..." She left the thought unfinished.

For a time they said no more on the subject.

"Irina, what happened after you arrived in Magadan? The journal ends at that point."

Her eyes looked back into the past as she told Alex the following:

Magadan, a city on the Sea of Okhotsk, was two thousand miles east of Irkutsk, five thousand miles from Moscow. In a setting of stark natural beauty, the human habitation seemed a blight. Cradled in the close arms of rugged mountains, the factories and bleak apartment blocks were of the crudest construction, built by slave labor. The numbers of former zeks and their families, upgraded to the level of citizen-inmates, peaked after the death of Stalin, though the stream flowing into the city from the Kolyma region of northeast Siberia never entirely ceased. Efforts were made to maintain a veneer of civilization; thus there were schools, hospitals, and some cultural life. But after Moscow it was, for Irina, the last outpost, a desolation.

Yevgeny was employed as a general practitioner and a surgeon specializing in cancer treatment. The treatments were, even in the 1980s, a scandal. The hospital where he worked was disorganized and filthy, smelled ghastly, and lost an inordinate number of its patients. Yevgeny persevered, saved lives, argued for better conditions in the wards, and begged for improved medical equipment. He, Irina, and Ilya lived in a one-room apartment near the hospital.

Irina did not work as a physician, restricting herself to tending the baby, who was now toddling about in a world that seemed perpetually given over to winter—a true winter-born child. Summer was simply a waiting-for-winter, the other seasons almost nonexistent. Because she had studied the field of immunology in Moscow, she distracted herself by cultivating relationships with certain people in the area, hoping to develop her knowledge of natural medicine. Not a few of them grew odd little plants in flower boxes, patches of garden, and pots on windowsills. She met many who used herbal recipes for a variety of ills ranging from baby colic to cancer. Intrigued by the remedies used for the latter, she asked questions, bartered tea for hoarded lore, probed and analyzed, and gathered a notebook full of untested data. Some of the remedies were clearly nonsense, but others were made from plants that had chemical properties known as stimulants of the immune system, a key factor in the body's struggle against cancer.

Irina's face saddened as she continued:

The people she knew in Magadan, the survivors of Kolyma, were great souls living humble lives, with memories so painful she did not understand how they bore it. She wanted to know more, but they were reluctant to tell her much. The shame of being criminals—even though unjustly arrested and condemned—was still with them. She thought it was terrible that they should feel that way after so many years. She tried to tell them this, and they were grateful, but she could not erase the feeling from their hearts. Yevgeny seemed to have more success at this. He was not afraid of them. He was drawn to them. He respected them very much, and they sensed it.

During the all-too-brief summer, Irina packed Ilya on her back and walked in the surrounding hills searching for the flowers, herbs, berries, and roots that her informants had described. This soon developed into a major research project. Yevgeny helped in his spare time.

In March of 1985, Mikhail Sergeyevich Gorbachev became general secretary of the Soviet Communist Party. "He may have a nice smile," said Andrei Gromyko to the Central

Committee, "but he has teeth of steel." Even so, perestroika and glasnost had begun.

Later that spring an article on natural immunology co-authored by Irina and Yevgeny appeared in a Siberian medical journal. In June of 1985, Yevgeny was transferred to a hospital and medical college in Irkutsk.

"This was release from hell", Irina told Alex. "Yevgeny called it release from *Purgatorio*, but for me it was liberation from a place of zero dimensions. Moving to Irkutsk was like going from Devil's Island to Paris. Music, opera, ballet, libraries, large numbers of happy people. Life was still hard in many ways, but everything was cleaner, healthier, warmer, sunnier. We now had a two-room apartment off Gagarin Boulevard, near the bridge. We could walk to the college in twenty minutes. I was very happy there. We had been pulled from the bottom of Gogol's overcoat."

Irina's eyes looked away from Alex for a moment, then returned to him:

"A great change had come over Yevgeny during our time in Magadan. His faith had taken on a new dimension, as if it were the diametric opposite of the zero dimensions that had been our environment in the Kolyma. He had grown—how shall I put it—more compassionate. He was reading the writings of the Russian saints whenever he could get his hands on copies. He had come to love the 'passion sufferers', as he called the former zeks, and missed their company. I didn't miss them—well, I admit I didn't get to know them as he did. They seemed a brutalized people, so many of them bearing psychological scars along with their physical scars and all too ready to inflict brutality on each other. The number of mentally ill people in Magadan was disproportionately high. I'm speaking not so much about depression but of overt and dangerous insanity. The quantity of such people in a single city was truly astounding. It had frightened me. I wanted to befriend them, but what did I have to offer? A little sympathy? But what good was that! Besides, I was depressed over my own situation, unable to look into the pits of hell they had survived. I was ashamed of my reaction, very relieved when we were transferred to Irkutsk. Now we had left it all behind."

Irina went on to describe the months that followed as a euphoric period of their lives. They grew close to one of the academician-physicians, a man who had rights to a dacha on Lake Baikal, in a small village on the west shore. The Pimonenkos spent two weeks with him that summer, glorying in the pristine beauty of the lake and the sensation of newfound freedom. He owned many books, which he kept at the cabin. The unique botanical species of the region was an added attraction. Yevgeny confided to Irina that, although he longed to return to Moscow, he would not be sorely disappointed if they remained in Irkutsk for the rest of their lives, because this would give them opportunities few Russians enjoyed. Baikal was a place where they might raise a family in conditions of health and sanity—and faith, he added. In Listvyanka there was a small Orthodox church consecrated to Saint Nikolai that had stood empty for decades. An old priest from the cathedral in Irkutsk was now coming to it each Sunday to celebrate the Divine Liturgy. Yevgeny attended the services twice during the vacation.

That autumn their friend learned that he was being promoted to a medical faculty in Novosibirsk. He bargained intensively and obtained permission for the transfer of dacha rights at Ozero Baikal to the Pimonenkos. They were ecstatic. Moreover, their friend was leaving his private library in their care.

At the end of April 1986, Yevgeny was called by certain officials and instructed to proceed immediately to the airport. He and two other Irkutsk doctors (both oncologists) were taken by military transport to a destination somewhere to the southwest. Irina was told only that a minor "nuclear incident" had occurred at a power plant and that physicians trained in the treatment of cancer were needed.

Three weeks later Yevgeny returned, utterly exhausted, appalled by all he had seen, and very worried.

"There are going to be casualties", he told her. "Many. For the moment we're facing perhaps fewer than a hundred immediate deaths. But a high measure of radionuclides was released by the accident—as many as fifty megacuries, millions of times greater than any other nuclear accident in history. A cloud of contaminants has spread to the north and the west. The cloud has divided and is also striking Asia. The worst is falling on Europe. Poor, poor people."

"How many casualties do you estimate, Zhenya?" she asked.

"It's a secret, Ira, but I can't withhold it from you. The Western press will soon be shouting it from the rooftops. In the next year or so, there will be a few hundred, even a few thousand, deaths from the immediate effects of radiation exposure. We can't tell for sure at this point. But it's the long-term effect that's truly disastrous. There will be horrible birth defects—who can guess the number? And between seventy-five thousand and two hundred thousand will die prematurely of cancer."

"Oh my God. Where is this place?"

"Near Kiev, in my homeland. A place called Chernobyl."

"Did you go close to it?"

He nodded. "I had to. I went into villages near reactor 4 on day 2. There were lives to be saved—"

"And what about *our* lives?" Irina cried, bursting into tears.

"I was fully protected with a suit and air filters. There's nothing to worry about."

Even so, clumps of hair dropped from Yevgeny's head during the following weeks, and he fell sick and took to his bed.

"It's like a bad flu", he told Irina, who was frantic with anxiety. "I'm recovering."

And he did recover. Within the month he was back at work, his hair grew in, and he was his usual robust self. They spent the summer of 1986 in the cabin at Ozero Baikal. The local people were taciturn but not hostile to the new tenants and thawed considerably when Yevgeny provided some minor medical services. Irina saved a cow with a bit of deft surgery. Ilya was coddled, showered with gifts, adored. It was a community of old people for the most part, and the little boy delighted all the hearts who had longed for grandchildren.

Yevgeny was asked by a woman to provide an abortion for her daughter. He refused. He told her that abortion was evil and that Russia had seen too much evil. She must welcome the baby, he said; God would provide. He reminded her of the old Russian proverb: "Every baby is born with a loaf of bread under his arm." The woman was angry, but her anger dissolved when he offered to help financially with the raising of the child. He was true to his word, and the baby was born, a girl whom the parents named Tatyana.

"Does she live here?" Alex interjected.

"She lives in Listvyanka. She's the one who served our table that day we had lunch at the hotel. Her father is the manager."

Irina went on to say that she too was approached by people up and down the lake who wanted abortions. She had never done one and refused to consider it.

"I told them to spread the news, to let the people know I don't do these things. I said that Russia is tainted with death and we must have no more of it, if we want to make a future for our children. If we want to have any future at all."

"Your decision wasn't based on religious convictions?"

"It was based on ethical considerations. On life. We need life in this land, and hope, in a way that no other nation can understand. Even now, death continues to stalk us. I refuse to listen to its arguments."

Irina and Yevgeny spent the following summer at the dacha, cautiously optimistic that Gorbachev meant what he said about perestroika and glasnost. Rumors abounded regarding the introduction of a private sector into the economy. Articles of daring honesty began to appear in various journals.

Most important to the Pimonenkos, Irina was expecting another child, conceived at Eastertime during a weekend at the dacha. A year had passed since Chernobyl, and Yevgeny appeared to be fully recovered from his exposure to radiation. They worried about genetic damage to the baby but grew hot with indignation when colleagues at the hospital encouraged them to have an abortion—"just in case".

Irina wanted to give birth at Ozero Baikal, in the log cottage surrounded by gentle light and the heat of the wood stove. Yevgeny obtained a leave of absence in January of 1988. They went as usual by bus to Listvyanka and hired a horse and sleigh to bring them over the winter road to the village. The journey took long hours because Yevgeny insisted that they go slower and slower. Bundled in furs, four-year-old Ilya stood with his mitts clamped on the front board, singing and laughing and chatting to the driver, an old man named Grigory—Grig for short.

That night, while the boy lay sleeping on a cot beside the stove, Irina and Yevgeny read by the light of an oil lamp, luxuriating in the silence and peace. Day after day Yevgeny grilled the fish villagers brought to them, made tea in the samovar, talked about the past and the future, and read Scripture. Irina read medical journals and poetry.

A week later Yevgeny delivered Kiril on the bed in the kitchen, the very bed where twelve years later Alex would recover from his head wound.

"I can see his face", Irina said to Alex, speaking in a whisper, "as if it were happening this very moment. So clear is it to me that even now I hear the baby's first cry, smell the boiled cotton sheets, see the look in Yevgeny's eyes. Right there in that spot he stood, a fine man, a handsome good man, pressing the bloody cheek of his little son to his lips. The blood smearing them both—my blood. Yevgeny wept—something I had never seen him do before. Then he cut the cord and brought Kiril to me, and we held each other, we three, bound together forever."

Irina fell silent and wiped her eyes.

"I'm sorry", she said.

"Don't be sorry."

"And you, Aleksandr Graham. Do you have happy memories?"

"Many."

"What was your wife's name?"

"Carol."

"Do you remember when you first held your child in your arms?"

"Never will I forget that moment, Irina Filippovna. Never. I too was present at the birth of my sons. Only the other day I was thinking about it, surprised that time had passed so swiftly, surprised also that I remembered it as if it had happened only moments before."

"Perhaps that's true for all the great moments of our lives."

"My wife and I felt it together—as one person we felt it."

Irina nodded. "Yevgeny and I also."

"I remember my wife's face, so full of love and suffering", Alex said. "In birth, in death, she was always beautiful. She wept, just as your husband did. 'A boy!' she cried."

"That's what Yevgeny cried also. In all places on the earth this same cry is uttered, in all the tongues of man—A boy! A girl! A new human life!"

"I said to my son, '*I give you everything!*'"

Irina smiled. "My husband had these same thoughts in his mind. Later, when he became sick with cancer, he told me that his greatest suffering was that he could give so little to his sons."

"Yes, that is mine as well. I wanted to give everything, you see, but in the end I wasn't enough for them."

"Are we supposed to be everything for our children, Aleksandr? I think not. We cannot be, for no person is the whole world. All of us are incomplete. Still, we must cling to the moments of great love, for they are more real than our failures. I recall so clearly now the wonder in Yevgeny's eyes as he pressed his nose to Kiril's. He laughed and said, 'Who are you, child?'"

"Who will you become?"

"This too he asked."

They fell silent, thinking about their children, their lost spouses, their memories.

Alex stood and put on his coat. "It has been a long day."

"Yes", she said, shaking herself as if waking from a dream. "You're tired. Good night."

"Good night."

28. *The Enchantress*

The next morning Alex woke to the sound of running water. Strong sunlight poured through the ward window, and long icicles curtained the outer glass, dripping steadily.

Is the winter ending? he wondered. *How long have I been here? Two weeks?*

He dressed and walked across the yard to the Pimonenko house. The snow was soft underfoot, and though the air was not warm, it had lost its sharp bite. Small birds pecked for seeds in the dung heap beside Kolo's shed.

Irina greeted him like a family member, as if his arrival was now so ordinary that it needed no special protocol. She put a bowl of kasha in front of him and brought a cup of tea for him as well. The coffee had been used up.

"Volodya has gone in his sleigh to Listvyanka", she said. "Last night after you went to bed, he popped in to say he was going to town for supplies and the village mail. I thought of waking you to go with him, but he was leaving at five in the morning. I asked him to check with Semyon for messages."

"I should have gone", Alex said, realizing that if there was a message from Father Toby or Jacob, he wanted to have it immediately because it would speed his departure.

"With that head of yours, you need as much rest as you can get", Irina said in the appraising voice of a physician. "You really should have been examined in a hospital before we turned you loose. Yesterday was perhaps a mistake. Too much shaking in the sleigh. How do you feel?"

"As if my head has been kicked by a horse."

"Any dizziness, any inability to cope with the light?"

"It was a very small horse", Alex said. "A pinto pony."

"The bone is healing", she said. "The surface wound also. But you mustn't take risks."

"What day is this? How long have I been here?" he asked, wondering at the same time how he had lost the habit of monitoring the clock and the calendar.

"Four weeks."

"You're not serious."

"Yes. Today is the twenty-fourth of March."

Speechless, Alex could only stare into the bottom of his cup. Irina took it from him and filled it from the samovar.

"I don't understand", he said. "Maybe something's wrong with my mind."

"You were unconscious for part of it, Aleksandr. Then you were semiconscious for some time after that."

"It can't be, it can't be", he repeated, shaking his head.

"Well, it's true. Don't look so distressed. Doubtless, Volodya will return this evening with good news for you. Your money is probably sitting in the bank in Irkutsk at this very moment. By tomorrow you will be flying away from us forever."

This was said with a cheery tone, but there was an almost imperceptible drop in her voice at the last word.

Alex realized suddenly that his sojourn was drawing to an end. This could very well be his last full day in Ozero Baikal and also the termination of his relationship with the family Pimonenko. He felt a sadness over this. They had been generous to him, and he had given little in return. His fondness for them had grown with every passing day. He would miss them. And not only them, but the handful of villagers he had met, Aglaya, Volodya, Grig—even Kolo.

"It's strange", he said. "I have been here so long and I really haven't had a good look at Ozero Baikal, except the interior of this house and the clinic, and what can be seen from the windows. Will you show me around?"

"If you like."

As she put on her coat, Alex went to the window and looked out at the radiant snow in the front yard. "I want to remember it", he said. "Every detail."

"You will forget", Irina said. "We are creatures of habit. Only what is in front of our eyes is real. Other things fade away."

"I suppose you're right, Irina. I have the strangest feeling I've always lived here. This kitchen, your faces, Kolo the pony—it's all so ordinary, so comforting and normal, as if this is my real life. But when I think of my own home, my town, and the people I love—well, they're blurred. I can't remember some of their faces. Is that a result of the blow on the head, do you think?"

"It could be, depending on the nature of the blur. But I expect it's simply a matter of the tyranny of the immediate. Let's go for a walk."

As they stepped outside, Alex looked at the surroundings with new attention, fixing them in his mind. Everything was curiously familiar, as if he had only just returned to it after a long journey abroad. His past seemed to be no more than a sojourn in an alien land. The present did not tyrannize him, but neither was he entirely at home in it. The convergence of these two contradictory impressions contributed to his feeling of dissociation, of belonging nowhere. He put it from his mind and tried to focus on what was before his eyes.

Irina led him on a melting footpath around to the front of the house. The yard on that side inclined down toward the lake's edge, which was about a hundred feet away. A fence of woven willow pickets surrounded it.

"Your garden?" he asked.

"That's right. Under four feet of snow you'll find black soil."

"Do you grow vegetables?"

"Salad greens mostly, and medicinal herbs. We grow potatoes at Aglaya's place."

They walked down to the lake and out onto the snowpack
covering the ice. The surface gave way a little under their
steps, but it was not nearly as soft as the snow in the village.

"The wind is so strong out here, it blows much of the
snow away", Irina said, guessing his thoughts. "What remains
is beaten down as hard as a city street."

"When does the ice melt?"

"Usually it begins to thaw by the end of April. It's at least a
meter deep. At the north end of the lake, it can sometimes last
into June. We have open water for about five months of the year."

"That is a short summer."

"This is Siberia but nothing like the true north. This far
south, and especially around Baikal, everything explodes with
life and color during the warm months. Winter or summer,
it's the most beautiful place in the world."

Side by side they walked farther out from shore before
turning around to look at the village and the mountains rising behind it.

"The Primorski range." Irina laughed gently to herself.

"What is amusing?" Alex asked.

"Kiril calls it the sleeping giant." She pointed to the bulging head, shoulder, and hip of a reclining human, formed by
the heave and dip of the mountains. Its legs receded south
into a blue haze, and its outflung arm stretched north to the
vanishing point.

They were now about a quarter of a mile from shore, and
the village had shrunk to the size of a finger held at arm's
length. Above the rooftops, a white patch of cleared land was
visible. The sum total of the settlement was no more than a
nick on the massive flanks of the giant. In all directions there
was no other human habitation.

"How is your head?" Irina asked.

"It doesn't hurt much. The fresh air is wonderful. And the view is...is..."

"Yes", she said, smiling. "There are no words for it."

Elemental, monumental, haunting—all of these terms came to mind, but Alex did not give voice to them.

The mountains of the western shore were round topped, high but not so high that they rose to an altitude where trees no longer grew. A forest of firs covered them entirely. There were no sharp crests. To the east, on the far side of the lake, snowy peaks were visible, gold and pink in the morning sun. They looked very distant, solemn, and mystical.

"What are those?" he asked.

"That is the Khamar-Daban range", Irina said. "It's eighty kilometers away—very high. It goes into Mongolia."

They had just turned around to begin the walk back to shore when Irina spotted a puff of snow rising on the ice to the north. The air shimmered with mirages as they watched, a horse floating in the air, a rider floating above it, the layered forms severing and congealing intermittently.

"Sonia", Irina said.

Presently the layers melted together and approached at a gallop, slowing to a trot when the rider, a woman astride a full-size sorrel horse, spotted Alex and Irina.

"Irina Filippovna", the rider called as she reined to a halt a few paces away.

Sonia was about sixteen or seventeen years old, and quite tall, judging by the long legs clad in bristling reindeer hide. She patted the neck of the horse, which was frosted about the mouth and huffing mightily. The girl had ridden hard.

"Sonia, cover your ears; you'll get infection!" Irina scolded.

"Don't worry about me", she replied with an insolent toss of the head. "Is Ilya at home?"

"He's at school", Irina said with a neutral look. "Better not to interrupt the class."

"He won't mind", said the girl. Kicking the ribs of her mount, she drove him from a stationary position into a gallop within seconds, making for the shore at top speed.

"I will mind", Irina murmured to herself.

"Who is she?" Alex asked.

"She's the daughter of trappers who live on the shore about twenty kilometers from here. She has come a long way and at great speed. I wonder why."

"To see her friend, no doubt. Is that the girl Ilya is fond of?"

"That is indeed the girl he is fond of. Mesmerized, hypnotized, spellbound would be better terms for it. She is wild. She plays games with boys along the lake."

"Games?"

"She likes to stir up trouble between them. They're all in love with her, poor fools. She's bored and lonely, and it gives her pleasure to get them fighting over her."

"Youth", Alex said with a shake of his head. "It's the same everywhere."

"Really? What a pity. We weren't like that, Yevgeny and I."

"Nor Carol and I."

As they walked back to the village, Alex puzzled once again over Irina's moralism. On what was it based? She had used the word *ethics* the day before, but he now asked himself where she had found her ethics. Perhaps by osmosis, through her believing husband? But he recalled what Yevgeny had written in his journal, that he too had wondered over her principled nature when as a young man he had begun to court her. It seemed that Irina Filippovna had listened from an early age to the truth embedded in her own heart, had instinctively obeyed the natural laws that led to life. If so, how had she arrived at such maturity in a land that had been given over to the antihuman for so many years?

Irina led Alex through the haphazard maze of lanes that were the streets of Ozero Baikal. All of the thirty or more houses were log or plank cabins, many of them banked with snow for the purpose of insulation. Wood smoke rose from every chimney. A few slender birch trees leaned at angles here and there, competing with the ugly trapeze of electrical wires strung along tipsy poles that receded into the bush at the southern end of the settlement. A pony whinnied, a goat bleated, invisible hens clucked and squawked.

A crow flew low over the rooftop of the clinic and landed with a mighty swoop on the top of Kolo's dung heap, scattering a flock of tiny brown birds. The crow's gray kerchief reminded Alex of Aglaya. He asked Irina where the old woman lived.

"Up in the trees at the base of the mountain."

She pointed to the forest, but he could discern no sign of habitation, only the thread of a snow path disappearing into a wall of black pines.

"If I'm leaving tomorrow, I would like to see her one more time, to thank her and say good-bye."

"If you wish. She will be glad for the company. For my part I think I will go have a few words with my son the idiot and his enchantress."

Irina went off, looking none too happy, in the direction of the frame schoolhouse at the north end of the village.

Alex walked up the snow path through the clearing and followed where it led into the trees. The slope was steep, the path icy. His head had begun to throb, and he was short of breath by the time the ground leveled. Tucked inside the forest was a plot of open space about half an acre in size, so irregular in shape that if seen from the air it would have been dismissed as a natural formation. He wondered if he had taken a wrong turn somewhere along the way and was about to go back to the village when he noticed at the far end of the clearing, huddled in the shadow of a vertical cliff of rock, a little wooden structure. A wisp of smoke drifted from a pipe on its snow-covered roof.

Viewed from the outside, Aglaya's home was a small barn. No more than seven feet high and about twelve feet square, its logs were very old, black with age, chinked with mud and moss. Unlike many buildings in the village, which was built on low, wet ground, this structure did not lean at an odd angle. It sat square on its foundation—Alex supposed it was stone, an outcropping of the cliff. The door was a low rectangle of planks, its hinges made of thick leather straps, its hardware an iron ring attached to a latch bar of ancient make.

When he knocked, a faint voice said from within, "May God keep all evil from this house and bless the one who enters."

Alex turned the ring and lifted the bar, pushed the door inward, and bent to enter. It was so bright outside and the interior so dark that at first he could see nothing. The smell of baking bread rushed out to greet him.

"Ah, it's you!" said the voice of Aglaya the Crow. Her short body came forward from the shadows. The kerchief was gone from her head, and her hair loomed like a nimbus of white wool above her black eyes. She smiled at him and bowed slightly.

"So, you've come to say hello. Or is it good-bye? Of course it's good-bye. Just as I thought! Nobody gets the better of me. I can sniff a parting in the wind before the traveler knows he's going. Well, it can't be helped. But you have time for a cup of tea and a crust of bread, don't you?"

"Aglaya Pavlovna, your eyes see far ahead of the rest of us. Your guess is correct. I'll be going soon. Tomorrow, I think. I didn't want to miss the chance of thanking you for your kindness."

"What kindness? A little pie, a little soup, wash a bandage or two! Sit down, sit down here on this chair. It's my only chair, but you're the guest, and who can fault you for it? I'll take the bench, and no argument about it. Why are you squinting at me like that? Can't you see properly?"

There was only one window in the building, and it did not permit much light to enter. The glass was smoky, the panes cracked and flyspecked as well. The old woman scratched a match and put it to the wick of a hanging oil lamp. As Alex's eyes adjusted to the gloom, he saw that the room contained few earthly possessions, merely a sleeping bench similar to Father Serafim's, a "beautiful corner" where an icon and a candle flickered with their respective fires, and a wood stove made out of a ten-gallon barrel with a smokestack as thin as a sapling.

Aglaya fussed with a samovar on a table under the window, cranking a squeaking spigot that dribbled tea into two glass jars. Six tin cans sat in a row on the windowsill. The bread aroma came from them. Mushroom-shaped crusts spilled over the tops. Aglaya upended one and cut the roll into slices, spread butter over a piece, and handed it to Alex.

"Eat!" she commanded as she thrust into his free hand a jar of tea. "Sugar?"

"No thank you."

"Milk? I heard foreigners drink milk with their tea—a very bad habit that is, but who am I to criticize."

The back quarter of the room was divided off by a heavy canvas curtain, much stained and mended. From behind this partition Aglaya dragged a clay pot and tipped it so that a stream of yellow liquid ran into a small jug she had set on the floor in front of it.

"Only the best for our visitors", she said.

She made the sign of the cross three times and poured a dollop of lumpy cream into his tea.

"There!" she sighed and sat back on the bench. Her short legs dangled over the edge like a child's. She adjusted the black dress so that its hem covered her shin bones to the top of her woolly socks. Wrapped around one of her wrists was a cord of knotted blue string with a cross dangling from the end of its loop. Coddling her jar of tea in both hands, she peered at him inquisitively.

"This is a wonder", she said, rocking slightly forward and backward. "A lovely gift from her."

"From who?" Alex asked.

"Why, the Bogoroditsa, of course. Here I was groaning and complaining to her, praying the chotki for you—yes, you, your very self—and who comes knocking at my door!" Aglaya smiled with great satisfaction. "Yes, yes, very nice. A lovely touch. The Mother of God knows all hearts, to be sure, but she puts her ear to my mouth, she does."

"Were you complaining to her about me, Aglaya Pavlovna?"

"Not exactly, Aleksandr Anguseyevich."

Alex laughed.

"Don't laugh, young man. You never know what's going to happen in life."

"I agree with you, Aglaya. Since coming to this land, I have experienced many surprises."

"Specially the bump on your head, eh? Feeling better now?"

"A little better each day. Irina Filippovna warns me to be careful. She says I really need six or eight weeks to recover. It is only four weeks since the...the incident."

"Well, she's a smart woman, to be sure, and if she says you can go hopping around like a sparrow in a bush, she must think you're all right. It's a shame."

"What is a shame?"

"It's a shame you're going."

"I will miss you all. Yes, very much. I won't forget you."

"Nor will we forget you. But what can a person do, eh? Home's the best place for a potato seed to make a little family of potatoes, right? Your own soil, right?"

"That is true", Alex replied in a tone of philosophical complicity.

"Usually it's true. But I always say that the best proverbs are made to be broken now and then. Sometimes you need to change the soil, go to a new field. Other times you just need to put a new seed into the old field. It depends on the seed and the soil, of course. Now, you take a little patch of dirt like I've got out my front door. If every year I grow potatoes there, soon the earth gets tired of it. It needs a break. It says, 'Stop! Enough, Aglaya! Give me something different for a change, won't you!' So I do. This year I plant squash and turnips. I walk around the garden, talk to the soil in a manner of speaking, thank it for its generosity, thank the good Lord at the same time. Kiss a handful, say a prayer, throw it back on. Oh, I give it a treat too—chicken and horse and cow manure, and mulch. You shouldn't forget the mulch. It needs to eat green now and then. Then, lo and behold, once it's had a vacation, it's pushing up fine fat potatoes the year after. It's never failed me yet."

"How many years have you lived here?"

"Since 1930."

"Were you born here?"

Aglaya's face momentarily assumed the Russian mask.

"I was born over there." She nodded in the direction of the door.

"In the village?"

"No. Beyond the Sacred Sea."

"Beyond Baikal?"

"That's right."

"What was the name of the place where you were born?" Alex asked.

"It doesn't matter", the old woman shrugged.

"Did your parents bring you here when you were a child?"

"Tch—foreigners! Never stingy with their questions! Well, it won't hurt to tell you: my mother brought me here when I was six years old. I don't remember much about the before-time."

"You said you were complaining", Alex prompted, sipping his tea, looking at her over the jar's rim.

"Yes, yes. My grumpy old heart. I'm ashamed of it. You'd think I'd learn! After all these years, I never seem to learn."

"Learn what, may I ask?"

"How well they tend the garden."

Alex began to think the old woman's rambling conversation was not quite rational.

"The potato garden, you mean?"

"I mean the garden of life. The people. Their hearts."

Dropping the mask, she looked at Alex closely.

"How is your heart, young man?" she said, thumping her chest.

Oddly, she did not say *serdtse* for heart, a term used by Russians to mean the heart organ and sometimes used to mean the center of the emotions. She had said *glubina dushy*—the heart of the soul, the depth of the soul. A distinctly spiritual expression.

"In the *glubina dushy*, Aglaya, I need to go home and find my family."

She gave him a dubious look. "You need to pray again as you ought to."

Alex wondered how she had guessed that his fervor had been whittled away by the events of recent months. He did not want to admit that her intuition was correct, for she was too much like an Old Testament prophetess, and he was not ready for more guilt.

"I pray", he said glumly.

"Of course you pray. But do you pray from the *glubina dushy*?"

He shook his head.

"Too full of troubles, it is, that heart of yours." This time she said *serdtse*. "Too full of sadness. Listen, Aleksandr, you're wallowing like a pig in mud. Never let yourself get depressed like this. It's so stupid. It's a hangman that will kill your heart. You need the Holy Spirit, and how can he come in if you've got your heart choked by a rope? If you stop praying, you're dead. Are you listening?"

"I'm listening."

"Then why are your eyes wandering like that? Pay attention to what I'm saying. Now make the sign of the cross."

"What?" he said, uncertain of her meaning.

"Make the sign of the cross. Many times a day make this sign. If you do as I say, the ranks of the spirits of the air will fall. Do it now."

Alex made a Roman sign of the cross on his forehead, chest, and shoulders.

"Not perfect but good enough", Aglaya said with some satisfaction. "Every time you do that, the devils fall back in fear."

"Thank you for your advice, Aglaya. I will do it more often."

"Don't forget."

With that she got off the bench, took the jar from his hand, and poured him more tea.

"Now," she said, returning to her bench, "down to business. We haven't yet discussed Irina Filippovna."

"What is there to discuss?"

"You and her."

Alex laughed. "There is nothing to discuss."

Aglaya raised her eyebrows. "Ah, don't say that. You can't fool an old woman like me."

"Truly, Aglaya Pavlovna, there is no need to fool you or not fool you. There is no question. There is no possibility—"

"Possibility of what? Aha! See how the thoughts are already in your mind!"

"No, really, there is nothing to discuss—"

"Yes, there is. I know that poor girl very well. She has suffered. That wretch Ilya needs a firm hand on the back of his neck—a *man's* hand. He's going to make her suffer more, unless..."

"Unless what?"

"Unless she finds a husband. A good Christian husband."

Now Alex began to laugh in earnest.

"Why do you laugh so much? Have you no wits about you?"

Still chuckling, Alex looked down at his hands, trying to quell his amusement. "The world is full of matchmakers, Aglaya Pavlovna. None of them can stand to see a person live a solitary life."

"It is not good for man to be alone. The holy Scriptures tell us that."

"God has called many to live alone."

"A few, not many. Are you a hermit? Eh? Eh? Of course you aren't. You're a flesh-and-blood fellow, that's plain to see. You're so lonely, it's seeping out of you like a cracked pot."

Slightly offended, Alex sat straighter. "Please", he murmured.

"Oh, I know, I know. You're thinking about your dear wife. She must have been a fine woman. And if she were here today, she'd be scolding you for not taking Irina Filippovna into consideration."

This nonsequitur made Alex chuckle once more, but there was an undercurrent of pain in it.

Aglaya pressed her case: "And don't you think Yevgeny's up there looking down on this?" She pointed dramatically to the rafters above her head. "He's watching too, I guarantee it, just pleading with you to consider Irina."

"I rather doubt it, Aglaya."

"Men! Blind as bats. Listen, you got a knock on the head and it's fermented your brains. I see the way she looks at you."

"Aglaya Pavlovna," Alex said with sudden coolness, "that is entirely in your imagination. Irina is a very fine woman—she has helped a stranger who had no other choices, she is a doctor, she is self-sacrificing and noble. She thinks of no one but her husband. Yevgeny was a great man. No one can replace him. I sincerely doubt the thought has crossed her mind to replace him. And if it were to cross her mind, I expect I would be the last person on her list of suitors. Believe me, I'm not worth considering."

"It has crossed *your* mind, obviously."

"Not at all. You brought the subject up."

"What ready answers you had for me when I brought it up."

"I have a fast mind."

"Fast minds make hasty mistakes."

She smiled at him wryly.

He sipped his tea.

"We're making progress", Aglaya said. Perhaps she was speaking to the Bogoroditsa.

Alex was convinced they were making no progress whatsoever and that the conversation had been an exercise in regression. He stood and was about to take his leave when Aglaya said, "Yes, yes, it's always the case. Never try to teach a fool! If you call him to church, he says, 'No, the path is too icy.' Call him to the tavern, he says, 'I'll walk very carefully.'"

Alex smiled. "A good proverb, Aglaya Pavlovna. But it proves my point."

"What point? I haven't heard you make a point so far."

"My point is, the heart is unreliable. It tells lies to us all the time."

"That is true of the *serdtse* but not true of the *glubina dushy*."

"I'm not sure I know the difference."

"Yes, and that is your *real* problem", she said, stabbing the air with her forefinger.

"I suppose it is", Alex said, buttoning his greatcoat. "But what can I do about it? I am what I am."

"Nonsense", Aglaya said as she limped toward him. "None of us are what we think we are. Listen, I'll tell you something my old mother told me years ago. Many a time she said to me—and again on her deathbed she said it—'Agladusha,' she said, 'the only whole heart is a broken one.'"

"A broken one", said Alex uneasily, heading for the door. "Thank you again for all you have done. Good-bye."

As he went down the path, he looked back once and saw the old woman stooping in her open doorway, staring after him, shaking her head. It was disconcertingly like his meeting with the beggar woman in Mammon Mall near the Moscow Kremlin. At the time, Alex had smiled over the quaintness of the beggar's appearance, her words, her persona—as if she were no more than a parody of a literary type. Now, however, he did not smile.

I tell you, your heart will *be broken, and then only will you find your true heart.*

The memory irritated him. Russia was infested with self-appointed prophets, he told himself, and always had been. Where did they get their cryptic sayings? How did they come by their confidence? Who had bestowed on them the right to speak with such certainty?

On the path down to the village, he slipped on the ice and fell. Grumbling, he got up and continued on his way.

Where the path joined the large field, it forked toward the north and south ends of the village. Not thinking about his intended goal, Alex turned north and walked along absorbed by the thoughts Aglaya's conversation had prompted. Oblivious to where he was going, he arrived at the school yard, and there he found himself in the middle of a situation that was at first indecipherable.

Several children were standing by the porch of the school, giggling and whispering. Among them was Kiril, hands in pockets, an anxious look on his face. He was watching his mother stalk away in the direction of her house, her face contorted with anger.

The girl Sonia was seated on her horse, fixing her eyes on Ilya Pimonenko with a mocking expression. The boy stood a few paces away, red-faced, his neck thrust forward, hands in fists by his sides. Apparently the girl had just said something that infuriated him.

Ilya yelled at her. She laughed and kicked her horse, spurting past him toward the lake. Spatters from the hooves hit him in the face, which made him angrier than ever. Strangest of all, there was a fish lying in the snow at his feet. He picked it up and hurled it after the girl, spun on his heels, and ran toward home. Alex followed.

Arriving a minute behind, he went into the kitchen to find Irina and Ilya struggling over a long sword of the sort once used by Russian cavalry. They were screaming at each other.

"Don't!" Irina cried. "It's insane!"

"I will! They can't get away with it", Ilya seethed, yanking the sword by its hilt.

"She's goading you. Don't let her trick you."

The scabbard lay on the floor, and the sword blade flashed this way and that as the boy and his mother wrestled over it. Irina held her son's wrists and tried to gain control. Alex leaped forward and wrapped his arms around Ilya's chest.

"Drop it!" he roared.

Irina was so surprised by this that she let go of her grip. Ilya seized the opportunity, jabbed an elbow into Alex's stomach, and broke free. He bolted to the door and was gone.

"Stop him!" Irina cried. "He's going to kill someone! He's going to get himself killed!"

Alex ran out to find Ilya emerging from the shed, leading Kolo by her halter. Quickly Ilya began to harness her to the sleigh. He had thrust the sword through a leather belt binding his coat waist.

"Give me the sword, Ilya."

Cursing under his breath, the boy ignored him and climbed onto the driver's seat, grabbed the reigns, and slapped them on the pony's back. She jumped against the traces, and the sleigh jerked forward.

Alex sprinted and grabbed the back end of the cargo platform. Gasping for breath, he tumbled onto it as the sleigh banked around the corner of the shed and made toward the lake. He scrambled forward, shouting, "Don't do it, don't do it!"

Now the sleigh tilted over the edge of the slope and pitched onto the lake, where it leveled and increased speed. Whinnying in protest, Kolo broke into a trot as the boy lashed her again and again. The runners hit a patch of ice and skidded sideways, throwing Alex off the sleigh. He slammed onto the surface and rolled. Stunned, he pushed himself up on his hands and knees and saw that the sleigh was slowing as Ilya realized what had happened. The boy pulled hard on the reins and came to a halt about thirty feet ahead.

Alex struggled to his feet and ran toward him. Though hurting from his fall, he was charged with adrenaline, the tamp-tamp-tamp of his boots drumming the glass surface, his head pounding brutally. As the gap closed, Ilya turned away and yelled at Kolo. The sleigh jerked forward again and began to accelerate. The flaps of Ilya's hat fluttered, and his unbuttoned coat billowed behind him. Standing with legs braced, sword brandished in his right hand, reins clutched in his left, he lashed the pony onward with a fury that seemed the outer limit of desperation.

Turbulent stormclouds closed over the blackening sky. As he raced away, Ilya looked back at Alex. The face of the boy flickered in the weird light. It was Andrew!

Lightning stabbed the earth on the eastern shore. Another spear was hurled, this time to the west, onto the mountains of the Primorski range. Thunder cracked a second later. The cloud bank roiled south with incredible speed, and cold rain began to drop out of it, spattering the ice.

Alex tripped and fell to his knees.

"Come back!" he cried as Ilya drove on into the north.

Irina asked Grigory to go off and search for her son. By the time the old man had harnessed his pony to his sleigh, the boy had a long head start.

"How could he do this to us!" she cried. "And with a sword! Why is he so completely without sense!"

"He is young", said Grig soothingly. "Don't worry; I'll find him."

That evening, Irina, Kiril, and Alex sat around the kitchen table in a state of gloom. Irina's eyes were red and her mouth down-turned with bitter anxiety. She explained that the girl on the horse had provoked Ilya by delivering a taunt from a boy who lived in a village farther along the coast. The boy, one of Sonia's many suitors, had sent word that he was going to destroy Ilya's trapline. As proof of this, Sonia herself had delivered one of Ilya's traps with a fish clamped in its jaws.

Irina got up from the table and opened the door into the yard. For a minute she stared out into the darkness; then she sat down again, despondent.

After supper, for which Kiril alone had an appetite, they remained at table with little conversation passing between them, until there came a knock at the door.

It was Grig, looking very wet.

"I'm sorry, Irina Filippovna; I couldn't find him. The rain has washed away all tracks. I can try looking again in the morning."

"Thank you, Grig", she said.

After he had gone, she sat down again, and the three remained without speaking, listening to the ticking clock. Kiril for the first time in memory was absolutely silent. He took his sailboat from the shelf and began to tinker with it at the table.

"That is a fine boat", Alex said, trying to break the paralysis.

"Not very", the boy replied, licking the end of a string before pushing it through a metal eyelet. The white hull was elegantly carved. The cotton sail was laced carefully to a whittled mast and boom, the rigging cords correct.

"But it's beautiful, Kiril."

"It doesn't work properly. It falls over."

"In the water, you mean?"

The boy nodded.

"Yevgeny made it for him", Irina said in a muted voice, and glanced at the other sailboat. "He made one for Ilya also."

"It doesn't float either", Kiril said with a sigh. "Papa was very smart, but he didn't know how to make boats."

"Still, it's fine to look at", said his mother. "It's good for remembering."

After Kiril had been sent off to bed, Irina and Alex shared a final cup of tea.

"He made the boats in the spring, shortly before his death. For weeks the kitchen was a mess, wood shavings everywhere, bits of metal and canvas. It was difficult then to believe he was dying. I was so certain we would beat the cancer. But he knew. Yevgeny knew very well that he was going to die, though he never said a word to me about his certainty. He made these toys as a message to his sons, a memory for them to hold on to. So they wouldn't forget him."

She sighed heavily, and tears were not far away.

"Each spring Kiril tries again to make his float. Long ago Ilya gave up. I don't know what's wrong with the boats because they look fine to me."

Hoping to distract her from her anxiety, Alex said:

"I've always loved boats. When I was a boy I used to make them with bits of castoff wood. None of mine worked properly either. Once my father bought me a model of a three-masted schooner. Solid wood, made to scale. All the fittings were brass. It even had a captain's wheel on the deck and rigging that worked. It was very expensive."

"Did it fall over?"

"No, it sailed beautifully."

"A great treasure", Irina said, eyeing him unhappily. "Do you still have it?"

"I gave it to a friend during my youth, at a time when I was very ill. I was supposed to die. No one told me directly, but the atmosphere was thick with it. I overheard conversations between the doctor and my parents. There was no hope, they said; I wouldn't live long enough to become a man. I decided to give the ship to my friend, so he would remember me."

"You didn't die, obviously. Did you ask for it back when you recovered?"

"He offered to return it, but I refused. He still has it, and I'm glad he does. You know, Irina, I never really liked that boat."

"Why not?"

"It was too perfect. It had been made in a factory. Someone else had done all the work for me, you see. What pleasure my own little boats gave me. They were incredibly ugly. They were disasters. Most of them sank or were swept away by the river where I lived."

"The Clemintinya?" she said.

"That's right, the Clementine. You remembered."

She nodded.

"One thing I learned about model boats is, you have to weight the hull or they'll tip sideways."

"A detail Yevgeny didn't have time to learn", she sighed. "Ah well, what counts is that he wanted to give his sons something of himself. Later they will…"

She stopped and did not finish her thought.

"When they are older they will read his journal", Alex said in a quiet voice. "Then he will give them a greater gift. Something of himself, something from the *glubina dushy*."

She looked at Alex curiously. "How do you come by such good Russian? It's more than reading Tolstoy or studying a Berlitz course."

"I knew a Russian man when I was a boy, during the time of my illness. He helped me look beyond the little valley where I was born. I dreamed of sailing away, far, far away, to a land where everything was different and life was always an adventure."

"And now you have your adventure."

"My first."

"I too dreamed of sailing away when I was young. Far, far away to a land where everything was different and life was always an adventure."

"Is that why you learned English?"

"Part of the reason. When I studied in Moscow, I became friends with an East German girl who was married to an Englishman. He was a socialist and very crazy, but he put me onto some excellent books. I had studied English in high school, as many do, but when I discovered your literature I soared. After medicine it was my consuming passion. It was foolish, and I now regret it."

"Why do you?"

"Because I was being unrealistic. Aside from the fact that in those days there was no hope, *absolutely* no hope, that I would ever see the West, it gave me false dreams about life; it made me waste too much time. I know now that I could never live anyplace but here."

"Because of Yevgeny?"

"That, certainly. And for another reason: it's very difficult to live in Russia, even for me, a person with many privileges; but it's impossible to live elsewhere."

"Have you ever visited outside Russia?"

"Never."

"And you have no desire to?"

"No. Many Russians yearn to leave, but not I. You have to understand, Aleksandr, that for a true Russian, there can be no other place. We're connected to our land in a way that's unique. Life is *here*."

Her face fell again, and she stared morosely at the floor.

"You're connected to your homeland in the heart."

"Yes, in both the *serdtse* and the *glubina dushy*."

"Do you believe in the existence of the soul?"

"What is the soul? Who can define it?" she said, with a glance toward the window.

Alex heard nothing outside, but a moment later there was a knock on the door and Volodya entered.

"Very wet out, Irina Filippovna", he said in a loud voice, shaking his body like a dog. "But the temperature's dropping and the rain's turning to snow."

"You came by the ice road, Volodya?"

"I did. Very swift it was, but the sleigh swam half the way, and I'm soaked through and through. Brrr! No worry; it will all freeze tonight, to be sure. Here's your mail."

Volodya threw a packet of envelopes and journals onto the table. Looking at Alex, he put a finger to his forehead and shook his head.

"Gaspadin, I asked about messages for you at Semyon Petrovich's. There was nothing. He said to tell you no phone calls have come for you."

After Volodya left to deliver mail throughout the village, Irina leaned forward and clasped her hands on the table.

"Perhaps the embassy is still trying to reach your friend. Or, if they did reach him, the money may already be at Sibirbanc."

"If so, why didn't my friend call Listvyanka to say it had been sent?"

"Maybe they tried and Semyon was asleep or drunk. A little more patience is required, it seems. You can stay with us as long as you need."

"You are very kind", Alex said gloomily. "I guess my only choice now is to go to Listvyanka and try to phone the bank from there. They'll tell me if the money has arrived."

"Volodya won't be going to town for another two weeks. And with this unstable weather, I don't know if anyone else will be willing to try. The snow on the forest route will be too soft now, unless we get a deep freeze. But the ice route on the lake will probably be solid by tomorrow. I'll ask Ilya to take you." Her eyes grew dark again. "Ilya…"

The unspoken questions: Where was he? What was happening to him? Though she had distracted herself for a time, anxiety now returned with greater force than ever. She got up and paced back and forth, wringing her hands, sighing heavily. Abruptly she covered her face with a hand and strode into the parlor. A moment later Alex heard the door to her bedroom close.

He sat alone in the kitchen, listening to the ticking of the clock and the whisper of the wood stove. At half past eleven he got up and put more chunks of pine into the fire. Not long after, he heard feet shuffling on the porch.

Ilya pushed the door open and entered. He was soaking wet; his cap was gone and his coat torn. His face was bruised in more than one place, and he had a black eye. His nose had bled, and a red crust clung to his swollen upper lip.

He stopped short when he saw Alex, and the look in his eyes was unreadable. He went into the other room. This was followed by muffled conversation, muted and conciliatory in tone, salted with a few sobs—the woman's or the boy's, Alex could not tell.

Some time after, Irina returned to the kitchen with Ilya in tow. He was dressed in dry long underwear, his shoulders covered by a blanket. She sat him down on a chair by the stove and proceeded to doctor his battered face. The boy sat with his back bent over, hands between his knees, his whole body exuding shame and exhaustion. His mother spoke quietly to him as she wiped his face and applied a cold cloth to his eye. From time to time he murmured, "*Da, da*", in a tone of deep repentance. She gave him tea, then sent him off to bed.

Irina removed the empty scabbard from the table and put it on a high shelf beside the two sailboats.

"It was a trap", she said. "She hurt his pride, made him lose his temper. She knew what she was doing. She knew right from the beginning that he couldn't resist a fight with the boy who had threatened to destroy his trapline. When he got there, they were waiting for him. Six of them, boys from other villages. They beat him badly. He left a few marks on them too, I imagine. But that girl! What is the matter with her! Why are these young people so miserable with each other?"

Irina began to cry.

"What is going to become of him? How can I raise my children in such a situation? I'm at my wit's end. Is this what will happen to Kiril? If only Yevgeny..."

She stared at the floor, her face dark with the undertow of discouragement. When the hand of the clock reached one in the morning, she dried her eyes and stood.

"We had better get some sleep. It has been an unpleasant day for you, Aleksandr. I'm sorry. We're not always like this."

"I know that, Irina. In the morning things will appear in a better light."

"Yes. Thank you. Sleep, if you can."

29. Snake and Crocodile

Ilya remained in bed for three days, and during that time Alex did not see him at all; he kept to his own bed in the clinic, nursing the bruises he had obtained while chasing the boy across the ice. His skull hurt with renewed intensity. He did not feel like eating.

He filled the hours with napping and prayer. In obedience to the wisdom of Aglaya the Crow, he practiced making the sign of the cross more often and with less than his usual absentmindedness. Because his rosary had been taken in the robbery, he prayed it on his fingers. Aglaya came into the ward on the second morning, bearing tea, a bowl of kasha, and a chunk of her cake. Bent like a prophetess sagging under the weight of secret foreknowledge, she said, "You see! Man asks, God gives the answer!"

"I don't understand that statement, Aglaya", Alex said. "You'll have to explain."

Cackling to herself, nodding with satisfaction, she said, "He's got plans for you, Aleksandr Anguseyevich."

"Please, Aglaya, please drop that patronymic. You have no idea how weird it sounds to the Western ear."

"All right. Mind if I call you Alik?"

"That will be fine."

"Big plans", the old woman chuckled, looking for all the world like the fox who swallowed the duck. "Yes, yes, it can be arranged. The Church of Saint Nikolai in Listvyanka would be perfect. A summer wedding, I think. After the purple primroses come out. Irina Filippovna is so beautiful in purple. With the pink earrings from Ulaanbaatar. But what will we do about you! Tsk, tsk, you're a sorry sight, I must say. Where will we find a proper suit and tie for a fellow as big as you?"

Appalled, though somewhat amused, Alex could only shake his head. "Your imagination, Aglaya Pavlovna, gets confused with your spiritual insights."

"I don't understand that statement", Aglaya said, unconsciously mimicking him. "You'll have to explain."

Alex pondered her question and arrived at an answer he thought might suit her understanding.

"The voice of your *serdtse* sometimes speaks too loudly, and you mistake it for the voice of the *glubina dushy*."

Peering at Alex with her carrion bird look, Aglaya replied in the tone of a prosecutor, "How do you know it isn't the *glubina dushy* speaking loudly?"

"I don't know, and that's precisely my point. We do not know. That's why we have to be very careful not to confuse the two, because if we make a mistake in this, Aglaya Pavlovna, we go running around telling people that our imaginings are commands from God."

Aglaya's eyes narrowed, and she sat back, folding her arms.

"What would you know about it?" she cawed.

"Nothing at all", Alex said. "Why should I have anything to say about it? I'm just the groom, after all."

"Ha!" said the old woman, and she went out grumbling over the blindness of men.

From time to time Irina brought him books and news about the condition of the ice. The weather was still vacillating between shallow freezes and unseasonable rains. No sleighs were departing for Listvyanka.

When she brought him supper one day, she handed him a package sent by Aglaya, a handkerchief tied by a piece of twine. Inside was a chotki made of purple cord, and a note penciled on a slip of paper.

Pray this.
The mercy prayer is powerful.
God's will is found when praying it.
God is love, and he who abides in love abides in God.
I am speaking *glubina dushy.*
A. P.

Alex read it to Irina.

"She's very religious", Irina said. "Slightly eccentric but well intentioned. She means no harm."

"I know. She intends only the best for my future." He paused and looked at Irina uncomfortably. "I suppose she has had a discussion with you about your own future."

"That is an unceasing habit of hers. I don't pay any attention to her prattle. Well, good evening, Aleksandr. I'll leave you to your meal and your books. Should I send Kiril to you?"

"If you like. The day seems less bright when he doesn't appear."

"Yes, everyone feels the same about him. A little sunrise, he is. But don't be misled, Aleksandr. Kiril has his faults. Ilya's are all out in the open. Kiril's are quietly lurking beneath the charm."

"I expect he's made of basic human material like everyone else."

"Definitely. Now, try to be patient with your situation. In a few days the weather will return to normal, and the sleighs can run again. Then you'll speed on your way."

Alex did not reply, and she went out.

He was, of course, frustrated by the delay but also saw it as a chance to experience a few last moments of Russian village life. The time passed slowly, yet in another sense too swiftly, for he knew that when he returned to Canada he would want to remember the place as it was. He would never return here, to the land that had captivated his imagination for so many years. The reality of post-Soviet Russia had proved to be lacking in any of the fanciful intoxications he had anticipated during his romantic period, but there was, nevertheless, something to be learned from it.

That afternoon, while reading on his bed in the clinic, it struck him that his recent experiences had revealed the nature of his own habits of perception and the assumptions that so often derived from them. He closed the book (a badly typed manuscript of outdated samizdat), and thought about what he had just read. Published during the 1970s, it was a long essay by someone named Vadim Borisov, called *Personality and National Awareness*. Alex had found it in the parlor, where most of Yevgeny's book collection was housed. When and how the doctor had obtained this particular item, and others like it, was something of a puzzle because before the fall of the Soviets it would have been a dangerous possession. The author left no doubt as to whom he blamed for Russia's current troubles: the Godless state. Borisov contended that a people could die without actually being physically annihilated. In other words, its true genius and its providential role in history could be lost by removal of its memory. Into the resulting vacuum, he warned, would pour catastrophic aberrations. Alex was stalled at a passage that echoed a comment of Father Sergius', one that he had paid little attention to at the time. *What you fail to realize is that our situation in Russia can go either way—to God or to Satan, to Holy Russia or to Gog and Magog.*

Now in front of him was the same thought expressed by a Russian intellectual:

> Hope and faith are locked in a struggle with despair and blind ill will. In the present debate on Russia, notes of truly apocalyptic alarm are increasingly in evidence.

Are we an accursed and corrupt race or a great people? Are we destined to have a future, or was Russia only created, in the words of Konstantin Leontyev's crazed prophecy, to bring forth from its vitals the Antichrist? What lies ahead—a yawning abyss or a steep laborious ascent?

Both warnings underlined in Alex's mind his newfound understanding (helped along by blows and bruises) of the complexity of any cultural context. It also reinforced his awareness of the layered perceptions he had brought to bear upon Russia. The first layer had been sensory: snow and cloud, the sea of faces, the conversations, the cultural norms of manners and lack of manners, the paintings, the music, images of grand hotels and log hermitages, luxury cars, sleighs and "motushkas", the taste of beer and smoked fish, the touch of grime and silky fur, the smells of incense and horse dung. This level informed him that the Russians, despite all their suffering, were an irrepressibly vital people, full of energy and endurance, ingenuity and passion, declaring in millions of forms, "This is who we are!"

The second and less obvious layer was just below the surface impressions. This was a combination of mood and intuition, a sense of the psychological atmosphere that registered on the subconscious or semiconscious organs of perception. It took a good deal longer for this layer to make itself evident, but it was there like a haunting presence that would not go away. Its effect had grown steadily since Alex's arrival in Russia, and his thoughts turned to it more and more. Much of it was a reading between the lines of the more conspicuous elements of the new Russia. His mind could not decipher the undercurrent with any precision, but he thought that its meaning was this: the Russians were anxious and depressed, still afflicted by their grief over the past and their uncertainty about the future, declaring to themselves: "This is who we are—but really, who are we?"

The third layer was spiritual. If the voices of Christian prophecy were correct (and many of those voices had been extraordinary saints and men of giant intellect), Russia had been given a role for the end of history. The crushing weight of materialism had come close to annihilating that national consciousness, the thing Borisov called the national personality. But it had not been eradicated altogether. Indeed, it was experiencing a kind of rebirth, though the springtime was, like the weather itself, still unstable. If what Yevgeny Pimonenko said was true, Russia had been blessed with a unique gift of insight into the Kingdom of God. If she had lived it badly, at least she had tried to live it, in season and out of season, and in conditions of extreme adversity.

The West, by contrast, was abandoning its own spiritual birthright without a whiff of pressure from tyrants. Alex's homeland was among the most pleasant countries on earth. On the whole, its citizens were an idealistic people, a well-mannered people, a nice people. Why, then, had he always felt so isolated among his own? And by the same token, why did he feel so close to these people into whose lives providence or accident now cast him? Pain had shattered their assumptions and put them to a test that few in the West had ever faced. Suffering had been the origin of a kind of a consciousness relatively unknown to his own people. Sunk in a miasma of materialism, his countrymen did not recognize their condition. They lived in a psychological cosmos every bit as flat as the brutally flattened cosmos of Soviet Russia. Their inability to recognize this condition was due to the fact that they had abandoned the scale of absolutes by which their world could be measured. No visible signs of a tyrant state could be discerned, and the near-zero dimensions were packed full of endless entertainments, comforts, and drugs of various sorts.

Yevgeny had believed that it was still possible for Russia to find her soul. And if she did, she could offer to Western man a way to rediscover the sacredness of existence. East and West might then understand, in a way that neither had yet understood, the beauty and holiness of human life. And in doing so, man would also find his own lost identity. But if Russia did not find her soul, then the West would continue to degenerate, and both East and West would be locked together in a double helix that would spiral them both into the drain hole of the universe. Their last cry, the eternal *nyet, nyet, nyet.*

Alex stared for a long time out the window. It was an overcast day, and the lake was invisible under a heavy mist.

And what about Andrew? Where was he?

A bolt of anguish hit him, and he cried out: "Come, Christ our Savior! Come quickly!"

With the piece of twine, he knotted a single-decade rosary. He prayed five decades, begging God to melt the stone giant of the West and to give it a heart of flesh. He also begged God to awaken the sleeping giant of the East and to heal its broken heart. Then he prayed the chotki, begging mercy on both. And finally he just pleaded wordlessly for the rescue of his son.

Kiril danced into the room at about eight o'clock that evening, chessboard under his arm. They chatted for a while, and Alex taught him three more English words: *heart, truth,* and *boat.* Kiril's sharp little mind forgot nothing. Quivering with suppressed energy, bouncing on the end of the bed, he pleaded for three more. Alex gave him *universe, time,* and *sword.*

"Mama is very angry at Ilya", the boy said. "He lost Grandfather's sword."

"Did the sword belong to your mother's father or your father's father?"

"My father's father. Now it's Mama's. But stupid Ilya has gone and lost it. For two days Mama babied him, but now he's getting better and she's telling him off. She sent me out of the house so I wouldn't hear it."

"Would you like a game of chess or more English words?"

"More words. I would like at least ten new ones each day. That way I'll know thousands by the end of summer."

"Unfortunately, I won't be here until summer. I'm leaving within a day or so."

"Aglaya says you're staying. I overheard her tell Mama."

"And what did your mother say?"

"She just laughed. She said—" Kiril turned red and clamped his mouth with both hands.

"Come on, what did she say?"

"Teach me ten more words, and I'll tell you."

"It's a deal."

"She said a beaver cannot turn itself into a bear."

Alex laughed. Then he taught Kiril ten more words. After that, he played three games of chess and, despite his best efforts, lost them all.

When the boy accepted that Alex had had enough for one night, he got up and went to the front door of the clinic. A squeal from that direction propelled Alex off the bed and into the surgery, where he found Kiril standing in the open doorway with his arms lifted high and a look of joy on his face.

"Snow!" the boy cried.

A fall of heavy, wet flakes was tumbling down. Two inches had already collected on the step. Kiril leaped out into it, as if parting a curtain, and disappeared.

"See you tomorrow, Aleksandr!" his high voice called through the thickening air.

The next morning, the ward window offered a complete blank, snow still falling soft and windless on the world, visibility reduced to a few feet. When Irina came in with a tray of kasha and tea, her coat was white.

"No one goes anywhere today", she said. "But when the sun comes out again, the ground will be excellent for travel, either by the lake ice or by forest path."

Over breakfast, Alex asked her how she had come by the Borisov manuscript and a few other titles that not so long ago might have earned her a trip to prison.

"Even ten years ago some of these were dangerous to own, were they not?" he said.

"Yes, of course. But we had ways of keeping them from the eyes of the sniffers. We endured five separate searches during the period between Yevgeny's hearing in Moscow and his death. The KGB confiscated several things—nothing very damning—but they never found out the full extent of material in our keeping. Some belonged to the doctor who gave us the dacha. He has now passed away. The religious books were Yevgeny's, collected with great effort and risk and kept hidden in a buried container beyond Aglaya's house. I dug it up a few years ago. The Solzhenitsyn books reached me when we lived in Irkutsk. They were smuggled in by my East German friend. I suppose because her mad socialist husband was such an admirer of the Soviet Union, he was able to bring things across the border more easily. Why he risked it is still a puzzle to me. After Yeltsin came to power, they separated. He returned to England, where perhaps he is still a mad socialist. I don't know. His wife is now a very successful physician in Frankfurt and extremely antisocialist. She has often invited me to move to Germany, but—"

"But, as you say, it's harder to live outside Russia. I was intrigued to see Orwell and Huxley in your collection."

"Yevgeny was very interested in them, especially the essays written after Orwell rejected his youthful infatuation with Communism. I translated from the English. Yevgeny never learned English."

"What did he think of Huxley?"

"He thought Huxley was wrong about many things. But he felt that in one of his novels Huxley had been right. Yevgeny said that we were suffering under a regime like Orwell's *1984* and the West under a system like Huxley's *Brave New World*." She paused and gave Alex a curious look. "Why do you stare at me like that?"

"Yevgeny's insight is one that hit me several years ago, Irina. The same."

"Tell me, Aleksandr, now that you have spent a little time in the rubble of 1984, how does it compare to your own brave new world?"

"I'm not sure. Each condition has its weakness. Each violates something in the human person. The question is: Which of the two will do the more damage in the long run?"

"Damage is damage. That's like asking if you prefer the fast bite of a crocodile, or a snake to hypnotize you before swallowing you."

"That's an oversimplification."

"I would say it's definitely an oversimplification. When you swim in a river of crocodiles, as I have all my life, you tend not to focus on the subtler distinctions. But let me at least make a little objection: you ask if the soft tyranny of the West is as bad or worse than ours. From my perspective it's nowhere near as bad as ours. You have always enjoyed the right to earn money, speak the truth, do good whenever and however you wished, without fear of unjust punishment."

"From a strictly material viewpoint you're right, Irina, and I'm wrong. It's definitely better to live with choices. But capitalism has its faults, especially when it turns people into consumers without conscience or into objects to be consumed. These faults need to be examined objectively. Few are willing to do so because it's difficult for people to criticize the faults of their own system as long as it provides them with the comforts and freedoms they value, and when at the same time they see the horrifying alternatives."

"Aleksandr, let's say for the sake of argument that you and Yevgeny are right. Let's conjecture that there is something inherently wrong with the West. How do you explain that you enjoy the right to protest the things you dislike about your system?"

"A good point. But let's consider the man being swallowed by the snake. He is going in feet first, eyes closed. As yet he feels no pain, only a certain psychological discomfort (he has been hypnotized, after all). He says to himself, 'Not everything is quite right about my situation here, but if I wish I can simply wiggle out and walk away. I'm a free man. And look at that poor fellow over there who has just been bitten in half by a crocodile!'"

"Now *you're* being simplistic. That's not a good analogy."

"Why not?"

"Because the moment you kill the snake (if you can—which I doubt), the crocodile will notice the commotion, come crawling swiftly to you, and bite your head off."

"So, Irina Filippovna, are you trying to say that capitalism is the only form of economics that can preserve human rights?"

"The only one I know of. Even when the citizens of a capitalist democracy waste or abuse those rights, at least the *potential* for good is still there. But in the mouth of the crocodile, the opportunities for good are severely reduced—in fact, terminated."

"Well, how can I argue with that? I suppose you're right."

"You say one thing with your words but another with your eyes. Come, Aleksandr, speak plainly."

"I believe the danger the West faces is ultimately spiritual."

"That's an abstraction."

"An abstraction your husband staked his life on."

She fell silent.

"*Khamstvo*", Alex said.

"Why do you use that word? What do you mean?"

"Shamelessness takes many forms, Irina. You have suffered under a regime that was shameless in a blatant way. The capitalism of the West is not evil in itself. But when *khamstvo* poisons the souls of more and more capitalists, freedom gradually becomes a veneer, a friendly mask hiding a deep cynicism about the meaning of human life. Pleasure, security, and profit become everything. All other considerations are pushed to the side, and this is justified as a defense of freedom and avoidance of the crocodile."

"Do you prefer crocodiles?"

"No, I prefer freedom with conscience. Freedom with responsibility. And that's impossible without a moral vision, without knowledge of the purpose of man's existence."

"You call it knowledge; I call it a theory."

"Theories about man rarely bear the weight of testing. Truth always stands the test. Even here it has withstood a great many tests."

Irina's eyes grew troubled, not so much because of the intensity of their discussion, Alex supposed, but because some private thought seemed suddenly to preoccupy her, and elude her. They sat in silence, Irina staring at the floor with her arms folded and knees crossed, Alex gazing out at the curtain of snowfall. Finally, she looked up.

"I had a strange dream last night, Aleksandr. You were in it, but I can't remember much of your part. You were a good presence. The scenes were all tangled up, as dreams usually go. I was wandering aimlessly across the lake, in spring. The ice was clear of snow but still thick. Ilya and Kiril were with me, and you were there also. You had a sword in your hand. Suddenly, a hole opened up under Ilya's feet, and he plunged through the ice. You jumped in and caught hold of him as he sank. When your heads emerged, Kiril and I dragged you both out, but as we did, Kiril changed into a man.

"In a deep voice he said, 'Mama, Ilya is crying, but he has forgotten the song.' What sense does that make? A cry is not a song, is it? Anyway, it seems the dream was a mixture of things that have happened this week. But why had Kiril become a man?

"Then he said, 'Papa wants us to receive the visitor. He is covered with light!' At first I thought he meant you. But no, Kiril was pointing not at you but to the south, in the direction of Listvyanka. I saw a tiny man-shape approaching from that direction. You were trying to revive Ilya, and I could see no light covering you.

"Ilya's face was coated with ice. He was alive, but barely. Then his face just shattered. His face broke into many pieces and fell onto the ice all around us. It was terrifying. I woke up at that point."

"A disturbing dream", said Alex. "Perhaps it's no more than an expression of your worry over Ilya. How is he? Has he recovered?"

"He's up and about, doing his chores. He'll be nursing his bruises for a time. But I think he has learned a good lesson."

"About infatuation?"

"Exactly. Infatuations come in all shapes and sizes, and usually we don't recognize them until they've bitten us in half or swallowed us whole."

Having come full circle, they smiled at each other.

Irina suddenly jumped to her feet. "It's my day to teach. I must go and meet the children at the school. The snow is even heavier than yesterday, so I think I'll call off classes until it's over. There will be much rejoicing when they hear the news."

At lunchtime Alex ventured to the house, almost missing it in the whiteout. He saw how easy it would be to lose one's way in a storm and supposed that was the reason Irina had closed the school for the day. The kitchen was wonderfully bright and warm. As Alex entered, Irina and Kiril gave a smile of welcome and brought him something to eat. Ilya got up from the table and went to his bedroom. Kiril asked for more English words. Within a half hour the boy learned ten new ones and did not forget.

Irina suggested that if Alex wanted a change of scene, he might like to read in the parlor for the afternoon. Alex accepted, glad for the opportunity to investigate the books that lined the walls. She said that she needed to prepare the clinic for a minor surgery scheduled for the following morning and needed to catch up on her medical records. She would return to the house around suppertime.

"But who will make supper, Mama?" Kiril asked with eyebrows raised high.

"I would be happy to make it", Alex suggested.

"I don't think there are any ingredients in the house that you would know what to do with, Aleksandr", Irina said. "Besides, I arranged with Aglaya days ago that she eat with us tonight. She insisted on making the supper. A special one, she said, a treat to make sure the visitor stays a while longer. The way to a man's heart is through the stomach, she says."

"Interesting. We have the same proverb in my country."

"It's a universal truth, then."

"A universal myth, I would say."

"When I think of mulberry pie," Kiril exclaimed, rubbing his belly, "I fall totally in love with Aglaya Pavlovna!"

Before departing for the clinic, Irina put an oilcloth packet on the kitchen counter and said with hesitation that she had something to lend Alex for the remainder of his stay. She apologized for not thinking of it sooner. Opening the packet, she removed a bone-handled stainless steel razor, eight inches long, and a disk of brown soap that smelled of lemon and tallow. It was Yevgeny's shaving equipment, she explained in a subdued voice.

"I suppose I do look rather unkempt", Alex admitted, rubbing his chin. There was no mirror in the clinic, and the few times he had chanced to glance into the little mirror nailed to a cupboard door in the kitchen, the sight had not been appealing. The face was bristling with several weeks' growth of beard. The hair on his head was ash blond from the scalp to the two-inch mark. The older growth was still canary yellow.

After Irina left, Alex took off his shirt and rolled up the sleeves of his undershirt. Kiril brought a steaming bowl of hot water to the counter and set out the shaving gear beside it. Soaping his face, Alex stared at the pathetic fellow in the mirror. He grimaced and began to scrape at his beard. Beside him Kiril propped his elbows on the counter, chin in hands, and watched the procedure with interest.

At one point the boy ran off to his room and returned a moment later with a framed photograph in his hands. Holding it up, he glanced back and forth between the image and Alex.

"What are you doing, Kiril?"

"I wanted to see if—but no, you're too different."

"Different from whom? Who is that in the picture?"

"Papa."

Alex glanced at the photograph. Yevgeny Pimonenko's face was not what he expected. He had supposed Irina's husband had been a typical blond Slav, but the features were swarthy, his hair black, his eyes vaguely Mongolian, revealing a little Tartar influence. Somewhere in the remote past an ancestor had succumbed to Aziatchina or to love.

Alex put more soap on his face and resumed his valiant efforts to improve his own image. The blade was not very sharp, and he was unused to the antiquated method of shaving, but as he scraped and scraped he saw in the mirror that he was becoming more or less recognizable. In fact, he looked somewhat better than he had in years. Despite the mishaps of recent months, simple food and fresh air had brought a luster to his eyes and a sheen of blood to his cheeks. He was leaner and, he thought, younger.

Irina's lovely face came to mind unbidden. He realized that this was Aglaya's fault, for she had planted her insinuations with too much conviction. But he was determined not to let them sprout and succeeded in uprooting them quickly. What a manipulator she was, he said to himself, and worse, for she did it in the name of God. A terrible old creature she was.

Alex washed his face, cleaned up the counter, and went into the parlor, where he threw himself onto the mangled upholstery of an armchair. He took a book at random from the shelf beside him—it was something about the building of the Baikal-Amur railway, mostly photographs—and began to leaf through it. Kiril took the only other chair in the room and studied his atlas with quiet absorption. Just after three o'clock, the terrible old woman entered the house, cawing loudly to all within that it had nearly cost her life to bring them a mulberry pie!

Kiril bounded into the kitchen and leaped all around her, earning himself another friendly slap. Aglaya was covered with snow, and her sharp nose had turned blue at its point. After shaking herself dry and stamping her boots clean, she exposed the pie and set it triumphantly on the heating shelf of the wood stove.

When she spotted Alex she said, "Oy, oy, how fine he looks! Good thing you got yourself fancy. Soon they'll be holding the crown above your head."

Alex assumed she meant he looked regal but was later to learn (much to his chagrin) that she was referring to a groom's crown, part of the Orthodox wedding ritual.

"The face is nice," she said, "but that hair makes you look like a sick dog. How about I clip it for you?"

"No thank you, Aglaya."

"Why not? Do you *like* looking that way? Do men look like *that* where you come from?"

"Actually, only teenage boys."

"And very silly teenage boys they must be! Well, if you need to look that way, who am I to say a word about it? When have you ever listened to anything I told you?"

"Due to the fact that the term of our acquaintance has been rather short, Aglaya, I don't think you've given me much of a chance to do what you told me."

"Don't talk fancy. Say it simple."

"I mean, we haven't known each other very long."

"Ha! We're going to know each other a long, long time, Alik, unless the Savior takes me to my eternal reward before the..." She winked and grinned broadly. "Before the purple primroses bloom."

"What are you talking about, Aglaya?" Kiril asked curiously.

"Nothing", the old woman replied, distracting him with a piece of syrupy crust that she tore off the pie and pushed into his mouth.

"Mmgh-mghm-mgm."

"Don't talk with food in your mouth!" she scolded. "Now, where are your mother's scissors?"

Kiril ran and got them, along with a comb, and handed them over. She rewarded him with more crust.

Clacking the scissors menacingly, she eyed Alex. "Come on, it won't hurt, and you'll feel better for looking like a *real* man."

"A real man!" Alex laughed. "The way to a man's heart is through an insult, is it? Oh well, Aglaya, you might as well do what you want. You'll get your way in the end, no matter what."

Gloating with pleasure, she sat him down on a kitchen chair and snipped merrily away, standing on tiptoes from time to time to reach the high spots.

"Peel potatoes, Kiryusha", she said with an inimitable combination of command and tenderness. "Then get a sausage boiling in the pot. I've brought cabbage too. Oh, what a feast we'll have. Won't Irina Filippovna be surprised when she sees it." Humming to herself, she sang a little ditty in a low voice that only Alex could hear. "And won't she be pleased when she sees this great big lout all cleaned up and ready for the crown."

"Enough", Alex warned. "No more of that nonsense."

"Be still or I'll make a mess of it."

When she had finished, she brushed off his neck and shoulders with slaps of a towel, thrust her little brown hands into his scalp and massaged some kind of balsam oil into it, then rubbed it all off again. After that, she parted his hair and combed it. Coming around to view her handiwork from the front, she glowed with pride.

"*Da, da*, a good job! How fine he looks, don't you think, Kiryusha?"

"He looks better, Aglaya, that's for sure."

"As long as he keeps the back of his head away from other people, no one will notice that horrible great scar. Hideous it is, to be sure."

"And the chunks of hair you cut by accident, Aglaya. Very ugly."

"Be silent, you squirrel. He looks just fine except where the pipe hit him."

"Maybe it was a hammer", the boy offered.

"No, a hammer would have smashed a hole for sure, and knocked his brains all over Listvyanka. They just cracked the nut for him, and now it's healing. Thank God your mother is a smart woman."

"I'd be a dead sailor if she weren't", Alex said.

"Don't you forget it", Aglaya scolded.

By late afternoon a mood of bustling cheer filled the house. Aglaya cut the boiled potatoes into slices and fried them in butter, dashing them with vinegar, herbs, and tiny pieces of chopped chicken. In a separate pot she made a sauce of sour cream, spices, and melted cheese. Sliced sausage sizzled in a pan until it reached a uniform red-brown, then was tossed onto the potatoes.

Kiril went to the door from time to time to check the weather. At close to five o'clock the snow stopped falling and the light increased. The whole world was blanketed in a thick white quilt, softening all contours. Shortly after, Irina returned to the house and was enthusiastic over the lovely smells and the great gift of a meal cooked entirely by another woman. She glanced indifferently at Alex and gave Kiril a hug. After washing her hands in the bowl on the counter, she went off to see Ilya in his bedroom.

"You see how she couldn't take her eyes off you, Alik", Aglaya whispered, pressing her conspiratorial little mouth close to his ear.

"Quite the opposite." Alex shook his head in disgust at the old woman's persistence. "Quite the opposite. And now, will you please never again bring up the subject. It's all in your imagination, and I won't hear any more of it."

"We'll see, we'll see", Aglaya smirked, then scurried over to the stove to scold Kiril about the careless way he was transferring the food from pots to serving bowls.

When everyone was seated around the table, Aglaya made an ostentatious sign of the cross. Alex followed suit, doing it "backward". None of the Pimonenkos took exception to the Christians' behavior, and then they all dug in with enthusiasm.

After it was over, Aglaya announced that she was going home to bed. She had worked like a slave making the pie and nearly died getting it to them and deserved a good night's sleep! Irina asked Ilya to walk the old woman up the hill to her cabin, and he obeyed without argument, though his face had slipped back into its customary scowl. Alex took his leave as well and returned to the clinic.

Feeling fuller, cleaner, and more groomed than he had in weeks, and anticipating that in the morning he would be on his way home, he was in good spirits. He regretted leaving this family and their village and knew that he would miss them at first, but he entertained no false notions that either he or they had made deep impacts on each other's lives. He would, of course, send Irina money when he returned home—or would try to. In the unlikely event the bankruptcy of the Kingfisher left any books in his hands, he could send her some of those as well. He read more of Borisov and drifted into a dreamless sleep.

Morning dawned sunny and cold. Alex dressed hastily and made his way through the drifts to the house. There Irina informed him that she had arranged with old Grig to take him by the ice route to Listvyanka. He would be knocking at the door shortly, she said, so Alex should sit down and eat while he could.

Over breakfast the boys said their good-byes, each according to his temperament, Kiril effusive and Ilya guarded. The older son approached Alex, nodded his head in a jerk, and offered a stiff hand for a shake.

"Good-bye", he said curtly.

Having completed his duty, he disappeared back into his bedroom.

Kiril copied down Alex's postal address and also wrote out the address of the family Pimonenko, which he handed over with a sad face.

"Will you write to us, Aleksandr?"

"I will write, Kiril."

"But I ask myself, will the man from a distant land forget us?"

"I will not forget you."

"But if you do forget, I won't learn any more English words."

"I'll send you books, including a very big Russian-English dictionary. Also, there's a boy in my town who may be interested in writing to you."

"Really?" Kiril piped, stretching up on the toes of his boots, his face brightening. "Is his name See-rill?"

"No, his name's Jamie. His life is a lot like yours. He has lost his father."

"Oh, that's unfortunate for him. Does he play chess?"

"Actually, yes, he does. Maybe you can play chess by mail."

This novel idea so intrigued Kiril that he was momentarily distracted and began to plan how it would be done.

Turning to Irina, Alex said, "Well, Doctor, this may be good-bye at last. You have probably saved my life. I won't forget it, or your kindness and many sacrifices. When I return home, I'm going to do whatever I can to help you."

"No need", she said in a small voice. "We have enjoyed your company, but now it's time for everyone to get back to normal."

"What is normal?" Alex sighed.

She did not respond to this, and then a knock was heard at the door.

"Grig is here!" Kiril said with a mournful look.

The old man stood at the door, hat in hand, and pointed to his pony and sleigh waiting in the lane. Alex took one last look around the kitchen, then went outside. Irina and Kiril followed in shirtsleeves. The boy danced up and down, hung onto Alex's arm for a moment, then let him go.

Alex shook Irina's hand. Her face remained masked, her arms instinctively retreating into a tight fold across her chest. She nodded once and went back into the house. The cold, Alex supposed.

He boarded the sleigh, and as it pulled away, Kiril piped, "Don't forget us!" as he continued to dance and wave.

When they had passed between the last cabins of the village, Grig slapped the pony with the reins and pulled left, heading down toward the lake. The snow was deep; the runners skimmed through it softly. Alex did not allow himself to look back. The journey to Listvyanka was swift and unbroken by conversation.

Semyon Petrovich did not seem overexcited to see him, but he did remove his feet from his desk and shut off the television.

"No messages for you", he said. While Alex digested this bit of information, the captain read the note Irina had sent him. Finished, he pushed the telephone in Alex's direction.

Half an hour later, after two disturbing phone calls, one to Moscow and the other to Irkutsk, he had learned that no progress had been made. The embassy informed him that messages had been left on the answering machines of the two parties whose names he had given and that no more could be done. Any further communication to Canada was his personal responsibility. Sibirbanc told him that no money had arrived for him, neither at the main office nor in branches throughout the country.

Grasping at the only straw left to him, Alex decided to walk up to the hotel on the hill while Grig went shopping for supplies. Arriving in the lobby, he asked to see the manager, who turned out to be a man of about forty years of age. He treated Alex courteously and invited him into his office. There Alex explained that unless the numbers of his passport and visa could be recovered, there was no way of obtaining duplicates.

The manager was plainly embarrassed and ordered tea for them both but insisted there was nothing he could do. He had not memorized the numbers—why would he do such a thing!—nor had a copy been made of them. The numbers had been effaced from the records and were beyond recall. Glancing at Alex with a mixture of curiosity and thinly veiled suspicion, he said that such a thing had never happened before, not in Listvyanka, not to him.

"That is the question, isn't it", Alex said. "Why has it happened? Do you know who these people were? Were they really police?"

"I didn't recognize the men, but that means nothing. There are many police in the city, all sorts of police. As for the question of which agency they worked for, I cannot say. Their permit and stamp looked real enough. I'm risking trouble by even discussing this matter with you. To speak plainly, Mr. Graham, I'm doing it for the sake of Irina Filippovna, to whom I owe a great favor. But in the end, there's nothing I can do or say that would solve your problem. Please believe me."

"Were they FSB?"

The man shrugged uneasily.

"Another of Baikal's mysteries", said Alex.

The manager stood and offered his hand, delivering the clear message that the interview was over. Alex shook the hand and left. Going down the trail into town, his confusion gradually turned to fear.

Why had the numbers been effaced? Had someone wanted to eradicate any record of his presence in Russia? If so, what was their purpose? Surely only state agents of a certain class had that kind of authority.

Had someone wanted to kill him and leave no trace? Had the attack in the alley been a botched attempt? Would they try again?

And why didn't his own embassy have a record of his or Andrew's presence in Russia? The embassy would not lie about such a matter. It was no lackey of any other government than his own. Surely it had forwarded his SOS to Canada. The secretary had told him so.

With a note of alarm Alex remembered the unreliability of Jacob's answering machine. And the message to Father Toby had been left on the parish office machine in Halcyon. What if Monsignor Penney or the secretary had dismissed it as a misdirected or a nuisance call? What message, exactly, had the embassy left on those two machines?

On the other hand, what if the messages *had* reached them? Maybe Father Toby or Jacob were trying to pull together a decent amount of money to send, which would take some time. Or maybe money was already on the way to Sibirbanc but had been sent by mail instead of electronic transfer. Perhaps they had tried to relay this information to Alex but had failed to reach Semyon's phone number. Or if they had, they had bumped into the solid wall of the language barrier. Realizing that this was the most likely cause of the delay, Alex felt a portion of confidence return. His panic was groundless. Semyon spoke broken English, the problem doubtless compounded by the amount of alcohol in his system. The confusion was nothing more than a chain reaction of incompetence, inevitable when trying to bridge the gap between nations, times, and cultures.

Arriving back at Semyon's, he asked the captain if he had received any calls from foreigners speaking a language that he could not understand. Semyon shook his head. Alex told him there was a possibility that such a call might be coming, and if it did, he was to tell the foreigners the English words "Call tomorrow. Same time. Alex will be here then. Try again each day, same time, until he answers."

Alex wrote the words on a piece of paper in Cyrillic letters, spelling it out phonetically. With a chuckle and a glug of vodka, Semyon practiced making the sounds. Alex asked him to repeat it until he got it as right as a Slavic tongue could manage. The captain treated it as a good game, and when he had more or less mastered it, Alex asked him for another favor. It was urgent, very urgent, he emphasized, that the moment such a call arrived Semyon must send a messenger to Ozero Baikal.

"It's a long way to Ozero Baikal", said the captain with a significant look.

"When the message reaches me, I'll come right away to you and be here to take the call next day. Then I'll go at once to Irkutsk, obtain my money, and give some to everyone who has helped me."

"How much?"

"More than the labor is worth", Alex said as he went out the door.

Grig, fortunately, was still loading sacks of grain onto the back of his sleigh.

"So!" the old man said, doffing his cap. "Godspeed you, then. Nice to have met you."

"Grig, it's not yet over. Nothing is ready for my departure, and I must return to the village. May I ride with you?"

"No need to ask! Hop in."

The afternoon was cloudless, and only a little wind beat on their backs as they proceeded north along the lake at a fair clip. Winter was definitely in its final stages; the day was cold enough, but the westering sun warmed the air. When at last Alex spotted the cluster of dwellings at the base of the range, he realized that once again he was to be the unexpected guest. He wondered how Irina would take the return of this burden. Kiril would not mind, but Ilya would no doubt register his disapproval.

When the sleigh pulled up to the house, Alex thanked Grig and trudged slowly to the door. When it opened, three surprised faces greeted him—Kiril's grinning, Irina's puzzled and half-smiling, Ilya's simply blank, neither happy nor hostile.

"Can you receive a visitor?" Alex murmured.

Kiril, at his most squirrelish, jumped on Alex and dragged him inside. Irina sat him down at the table and brought tea and bread. Ilya leaned against the doorframe of the parlor, observing, listening as Alex explained all that he had learned in Listvyanka.

Spreading his arms wide in exasperation, he said in conclusion, "I have no place else to go. I must beg you for shelter once again."

"You don't need to beg", Irina said quietly. "It's a delay. We didn't expect it, but no matter. You must wait a little longer, that's all."

"Really, Irina, I dread saying to you, 'Another day, another two days.' How tired you must be of hearing this."

"Not at all, Aleksandr. If it will make you feel any better, you can have a new status. We'll call you the working guest."

"Ah, you mean I can pay for my keep with labor?"

"Exactly."

"I'll be happy to do that. Yes, very happy. Then I won't feel so guilty about eating your food. What can I do that would be of help to you? Chop firewood? Shovel out Kolo's barn? Would that be a good place to start?"

"No. Nothing too physically demanding until your cranium is completely healed", Irina said in her doctor voice. "But what *will* we do with you? Hmmm. Kiril, any suggestions?"

"We will make him the English teacher, Mama."

Everyone laughed. Surprisingly, even Ilya smiled.

"Then it's done!" Irina said. "You are now officially the English teacher. You will teach the children of Ozero Baikal to recite Shakespeare."

"*All* the children?"

"Of course *all* the children. There are not enough educated people here to do a proper job at the school. So, if you're willing, it would be a help to us if you could teach them a few words. It would bring variety into their lives."

"There's not much I can give them in a day or two."

"True, but a little goes a long way here. Please? Will you?"

"Of course I will."

"Do you know what they call you in the village, Aleksandr?" Kiril tossed his head, laughing.

"Maybe I shouldn't ask."

"They call you the man who fell from the sky!"

"And why do they call me that? It seems to me I'm the man who was dragged in here half-dead."

"They call you that because Aglaya Pavlovna has told everyone that she prayed for a smart teacher to come to us—" His eyes danced sideways at his mother. "Mama is very smart, but she's the only *really* smart one. Anyway, Aglaya says she prayed that another smart one would come, and that he would be a man, and that he wouldn't be too old, and that he would be a Christian. When you came she said, 'You see, God never ignores my prayers. He has dropped an answer right into our laps. Right out of the sky!' she said."

"Well, I'm honored. I must say that being picked up out of my home and carried across the sea and dropped from the sky was a bit of a surprise for me. The fall to the ground left me somewhat stunned. But I suppose you think it's worth it for a day or two of English lessons."

"Don't be so sure it's only a day or two", Irina said, smiling. "Already your visit has been extended far beyond your original plans."

"I know", he said ruefully. "It just keeps stretching on and on. But the end is near, I'm sure, and if in the meantime I can do a little for the children, I would be delighted."

"Good, then it's settled."

The remainder of the day proceeded as usual. *As usual*, Alex thought. Yes, this alien family and its strange ways were becoming so very much the fabric of normality that he was forced to remind himself more than once that he had another life. This was not home, he had not always lived here, he would be leaving very soon, a day or two at the most—probably. Maybe. Hopefully.

After supper, Alex insisted on doing the dishes in the big copper tub on the counter.

"The slave labor is overjoyed at your return", Irina said to Alex. Spotting her youngest son sidling out of the kitchen into the parlor, she called, "Kiril, get back here this instant. Where do you think you're going?"

"To get a book, Mama."

"You can't escape that easily. Come back and dry the dishes for Aleksandr."

"Oh, all right", the boy said, dragging his feet into the room.

"If you don't mind, Irina, I would feel better if you'd let me do this alone and give the slave a holiday."

"If you insist. But really, he's getting so spoiled. You hear that, Kiryusha—go read your book."

When the boy had disappeared, Alex began to wipe the dishes with a clean cloth. With his head lost in a cloud of thoughts, he did not at first notice Irina taking up a second cloth and working beside him.

"The man who fell from the sky", she said. "It was quite a thump you had when you hit the ground. Actually, more than one thump. I wonder sometimes what you must think of this country, Aleksandr. How difficult it must be for you; how strange we must seem to you."

"Not anymore, Irina. The thumps hurt, as you know. But they're mending, and in their place has come a..."

"A...?"

"A happiness. A small happiness that grows and grows. Your kindness moves me. You have given me so much from the little you had to spare."

Irina said nothing in reply to this. She busied herself putting plates onto the cupboard shelf.

"I won't forget you", said Alex. "No matter what you think, I will never forget you."

He meant the family as a whole. But for the first time he understood that his mood of gratitude contained a more specific feeling. Without giving voice to it, he realized that he would especially remember this woman.

"We won't forget you either, Aleksandr", she said in a quiet voice, without emotion.

Remembering Aglaya's heavy-handed plans for his life, Alex decided to divert the conversation.

"Do you remember the bottle of Baltika you told me to pour on my burn?"

"How can I forget that memorable event?" she said wryly.

"Never would I have guessed that the lady across the aisle was a doctor, and one equipped with such unusual remedies."

"As for me," she said lightly, setting to work drying the knives and forks, "never would I have believed that the gentleman across the aisle was a poet, and one so capable of composing on the spot."

"Please don't remind me. Erase that memory from your mind."

"Memory isn't so easy to erase. In fact, the important memories mustn't be lost."

"That one should definitely be lost."

"No, you're wrong", she said abruptly. "I..."

She frowned and turned away to wipe off the table.

There was a knock on the door. Irina opened it to Aglaya the Crow, who was standing on the doorstep peering inside with a look of intense interest.

"Well, well, well", she chattered as she entered. "There he is, just like in the fairy tale, just like the orphan who wouldn't get lost. And how come he didn't say good-bye to me, eh? Eh?" Aglaya pointed to the ceiling like a prophetess about to denounce an apostasy. "Maybe because he *knew* he was coming back!"

"Honestly, I didn't, Aglaya."

"Even worse. Now I'm hurt. Now I'm insulted. And when I think of the cakes I made for you when you were on the bed of affliction! Ungrateful you are! Ah, but that's always the way with men."

"A cup of tea, Aglaya?"

"Yes, please, Irina Filippovna. I could use a drop or two. It would do my old bones good. What are you going to do with him, this poor fellow who doesn't know when to go home?"

"I thought you wanted me to stay, Aglaya", Alex defended himself. "Well, now I'm staying."

"Is that so? Until the purple primroses bloom?"

"Only for a day or two. Help has not yet arrived, and I must wait a while longer."

"In the meantime, he's going to teach the children a few words of English", Irina said.

Aglaya sat down and sipped her tea, grinning wickedly, saying no more. Emptying her cup in record time, she slapped her knees and pushed herself upright.

"Well, I'm going."

"So soon?" Irina said.

"I just came to see if the rumor is true. Sure enough, it's true. He's back."

"Not for long", Alex said.

"Aleksandr Anguseyevich," Aglaya said in a commanding voice, "tomorrow you will visit me in my home. I will tell you a story."

"A story? I would like to hear a story, Aglaya. If there's no message from Listvyanka, I'll come after school."

"Good. Don't forget."

Alex and Irina returned to the dishes. Irina seemed preoccupied, and Alex did not intrude on her thoughts. When they had finished putting everything away in the cupboard, Irina threw wood into the stove and stood for a few moments staring at the flames before closing the firebox door.

As if speaking to herself, she said, "What did you mean by the *zimorodok?*"

"The kingfisher?" Alex replied with some hesitation. "It's the name of my bookstore. Actually, it's a play on words. The name of my town is Halcyon, which is from the Greek myth of the kingfisher."

"I have read the myths", she said. "I'm asking what its deeper significance is for you."

"I suppose it's a symbol of something. The whole thing is blurred in my mind—symbols, images, thoughts. I'm afraid I'm not quite right in the head. Don't ask me to explain anything you heard me say since we met."

Turning to him, she searched his eyes.

"Aleksandr, I don't understand."

"Nor do I."

"I don't understand why you're here."

"It's an accident. You said so yourself."

"Yes, it's an accident, *if* life is nothing more than a series of accidents. But is it, I wonder? Is it?"

The question did not seem to be rhetorical. She waited for his answer.

"If you're asking me, Irina, I'll tell you what I think. In life there are indeed many accidents. But the accidents are part of something much bigger. I believe in providence—the will of God acting together with human will. But he respects our will absolutely. He does not force. Love never forces. It only invites."

"How can I believe such a thing, Aleksandr? Many things are forced on us."

"Not by God. There is a war between good and—"

"Ah yes. Aglaya too has much to say about 'the war'. She thinks devils are the cause of all troubles."

"Some of our troubles but not all. I think Aglaya understands the world very well. She enjoys her reputation as a crow, but in her heart there's something warm and kind."

Irina smiled. "She cawed something about you the other day: 'There's a fire in that poor fool's heart', she said. Of course, I told her about the incident on the train when you set fire to yourself."

Chuckling ruefully, Alex said, "A poet once wrote that kingfishers catch fire. It was a manner of speaking. Kingfishers don't really catch fire."

"I assumed as much. Do you know, Aleksandr, you have a little fault that makes discussion difficult?"

"Oh? What fault is that?"

"Always you try to explain the obvious. You think other people are not bright enough to understand you."

"That's not true. I think most people are just bored by me. If I have a fault, it's that I babble too much. It's the result of too much solitude, I guess."

She shook her head in amazement. "You think you're a babbler? How strange! You are one of the quietest persons I have ever encountered. You say little unless you're provoked. Yevgeny was like that too. He was frequently accused of 'antisocial' behavior. You should have met. You should have known each other."

"I like him more and more, Irina. But what would we have talked about, two antisocial men staring at each other uncomfortably?"

"Perhaps you're right. He too was a kingfisher. Very noble, full of dignity and idealism. But also full of light, shining and enthusiastic for the things he loved."

"Ah, like Kiril."

"Kiril shines, but Ilya is the one more like his father." Here Irina's voice faltered and her eyes clouded. "But my son did not have a chance to learn from him. I used to call Ilya my little *zimorodochka*."

"The winter-born."

She nodded. "Kiril also was born in winter."

Irina went to the kitchen window overlooking the lake and stared out into the night.

"The world is growing colder", she said. "There are times when I think to myself that it will become warm again. At other times I look across Baikal and I know that a billion people on the other side of the Sayan Mountains resent us, fear us. I can see millions of their troops swarming through the passes into Russia, destroying everything in their path." She shuddered. "I see their tanks, their bombs, their hatred, and I see poor Russia with her dying population, her few children.... All the children of this age are born in winter, for the cold numbs every heart."

"Every?"

"Perhaps not every heart. For us—you with your Carol and me with my Yevgeny—there was a fire in winter." She turned from the window and faced him. "But why was the fire taken away? Why was it snuffed out? Death is cold. The cold tells us that everything is accident. How can I argue with its logic?"

"You gave the answer to that when you told me about your first summer here in Ozero Baikal. You said that Russia had seen too much death and that now was the time to create new life."

"Yevgeny was with me when I said it. With him by my side, it was easy to say. It's harder to believe it now. I haven't taken it back because the people of the lake need words of confidence. Yet my heart feels the cold as never before."

"Are you afraid of the future?"

"No, not for myself."

"For your children?"

"Yes. You said something on the train, to that girl, even though she couldn't understand it. I think you were actually trying to tell it to yourself. You said, 'Sweetest of all was the knowledge that came to us in that winter world, for we had learned that love is stronger than death.'"

Silenced by the realization that she had remembered so much, Alex was at a loss for what to say. For some moments they looked into each other's eyes, reading many things there, wondering if their translations were exact, each pondering the other's experience, so similar that it appeared to be a mirror image. In the subdued light of the kitchen, in the ethos of sanctuary, an intimacy was established that was neither passion nor simple friendship. Because it hovered in the field between the two, latent with possibilities, and equally latent with the threat of loss, they said nothing. Irina dropped her eyes.

"And more we learned", she whispered.

"What did we learn?"

"We learned that only in the dying did we find the victory."

Looking up suddenly, she crossed her arms and said with a calm voice, "It's late. I should go to the boys. You know your way to the clinic. Good night."

"Good night."

30. *The Snowhouse*

Irina walked Alex to the school around ten the next morning.

"They've all been told", she said. "They're very excited by the news because they've all heard about the man who fell from the sky. Though some have seen you passing through the village once or twice, most of them think you're a kind of mythological creature who lurks inside the clinic."

"Maybe I am."

"I want none of your surrealism, Aleksandr. Try to be objective. Pretend you're a teacher."

"Now *that* is surreal, Irina."

"Shh!"

Stopping in the empty play yard, she told him that the school was dedicated to the memory of Aleksandr Pushkin and had been built by the villagers at their own expense only eight years before. The building looked much older. Its tin roof was rusted, and the single-story clapboard structure leaned at a slight angle toward the north. Although it sat on a foundation of piled stones, the deep frost of Siberia had not been impressed.

"There were only three children in the village when Yevgeny and I first came. Little by little, things have changed. These days people have more hope. There are fourteen children now."

"How many people, all told, live here?"

"About two hundred. Fewer in the summer when many go out to live in the bush or fishing camps."

"Fourteen is a small number of children for a community this large."

"Compared to the past, it's a big crowd. Sadly, the crowd is shrinking again. No child has been born to our people during the past six years."

"Are the people losing hope?"

"No, they have discovered contraceptives, imported from the West."

"The crocodile went away, and the snake arrived to take its place."

Irina shot Alex an uneasy glance. "No politics today, Aleksandr. Just enjoy the children. They are beautiful. They are our future."

The interior of the school was a single open space lined with plain pine planks and furnished like a pioneer one-room schoolhouse. Twelve long tables and benches faced the front, six to a side. In the middle of the aisle, a wood heater crackled as it burned birch logs. Standing in front of a blackboard, a heavy matronly woman in a flowered dress and high rubber boots was waving her arm up and down.

"Six times six equals thirty-six!"

"Six times six equals thirty-six", the children echoed.

"Seven times seven equals forty-nine!"

"Seven times seven equals forty-nine."

The mathematics drill was for the younger ones. At the back of the room, Ilya and two other adolescents hunched over their notepads, copying from textbooks.

"Ah, Irina Filippovna!" the teacher said. "You're here at last. We are so happy to see you. Please introduce the English teacher to the class."

"Thank you, Dusya Lukasheva."

All eyes swiveled to the rear. Many little mouths dropped open; shining faces stared in fascination. Kiril bounced in his seat. Ilya put down his pencil and stretched his legs into the aisle.

"This is Gaspadin Aleksandr Graham", Irina said, enunciating the foreign part of his name with care. "Stand up, children, stand up! What do you say to him?"

Everyone got to his feet, with a scraping of benches and a few giggles.

The teacher gave her fat hands a loud clap. "What do you say? What do you say?"

"Good morning, Gaspadin Aleksandr Khrim!" the children chanted in unison.

The teacher extended an arm at right angles to her ample body, indicating that Alex should come forward and take over the class. He walked to the front of the room, shook hands with her, and waited while she took a seat beside Irina at the back of the room. The children too sat down, folded their hands on their desktops, and looked up at him expectantly.

At first Alex was unsure of himself. What would he say to them? The myth had descended to earth, but even a myth could not hold anyone's attention for long if it said nothing. This minor terror passed quickly because self-consciousness was impossible in such company. They were, as Irina had promised, beautiful. Bright as new kopecks, their eyes sparkled with intelligence and humor, their faces stretched up like spring shoots seeking the sun on necks as thin as flower stems. The shine was completely infectious.

"Irina Filippovna called me *Gaspadin*", he began. "The English word is *Mister*. Can you say *Mister*?"

"Myee-strrr!" cried a dozen voices.

"Very close. But not quite right. Say *mih*."

"Myih."

"Now say *stir*."

"Strrr."

"Now put them together and say *Mister*."

"Myih-strrr."

Alex laughed. The class erupted in giggles. The teacher's belly shook, and her face turned red. Irina smiled and crossed her arms, her face sending signals to him: So, what are you going to do next, Myihstrrr?

"Good", Alex said. "Soon you will be able to speak English with Kiril, who knows a great many English words. How many do you know, Kiril?"

"Forty-seven", the boy answered, bouncing with aggravated pride, goggling his eyes and pushing his eyebrows impossibly high. Apparently Kiril Pimonenko was a bit of a clown, and his theatrics caused another outburst of giggles.

"You will have to study hard, Kiril, if you hope to stay ahead of your friends. They learn very quickly. Now, class, I have a riddle for you. If you can guess the answer, I will tell you the English for it."

Every face looked at him with anticipation.

"What is white and falls out of the sky?" Alex asked.

Hands shot up all over the classroom. A small girl in the front row looked so eager that Alex could not resist her.

"You!" she said with grave sincerity. The older ones guffawed. The girl turned red and hid her face in her hands.

"Yes, I did fall out of the sky. But that is not the answer. Is there anything else that is white and falls out of the sky?"

Again hands shot up.

"The winter bird!" cried a boy.

"A blossom in a storm!" ventured a girl.

"Ashes!"

"Paper!"

"Dead leaves!"

Alex was surprised that none of them had hit upon the most obvious, the one item that dominated their environment for six months of the year.

"Very close but not the answer", he said, glancing out the window at the white field.

Brows furrowed throughout the room as intense guesswork got under way.

"I know, I know!" Kiril called out, throwing his arm up again and again, as if he were trying to rid it of the hand.

"All right, Kiril, tell me what it is."

Kiril jumped to his feet with arms at his sides and recited in mock solemnity: "A clever white fox climbs up a tree. He wants to see what he can see. He holds on tight as tight can be. Along comes the wind and blows him free."

Kiril's rhyme achieved its intended effect—general applause. Alex, Irina, and the teacher joined in. Kiril bowed at the waist and sat down. As he clapped, it suddenly struck Alex that he had told them beforehand he would present them with a riddle—in other words, a trick question. Their fast young minds had automatically discarded the most obvious answer: snow.

"Excellent, Kiril, but that's not it."

Sighs of disappointment greeted this, heads were put together, whispered consultations began, mouths screwed up in concentration as they strained to think of an answer. Crossing his arms and slowly pacing back and forth in front of the class, Alex strained to think of an answer as well.

One by one the children gave up, folded their hands, and stared at the English teacher.

"All right, I'll give you another hint", he said. "What is white and falls out of the sky and you can live inside it?"

Groans of dismay arose from all quarters. Glancing to the back of the room, Alex saw Irina smiling, her eyes telling him: Very good, you've caught them now.

A hand shot up at the back of the class.

"Yes, Ilya?"

"Gaspadin—Myistrrr—I think I know."

"All right, what is it?"

"A house of snow!"

Alex nodded emphatically with a wide grin. "You got it!"

A storm of applause broke out. A blush spread beneath Ilya's bruises as he tried to make himself look indifferent. Irina leaned forward and patted her eldest son on the shoulder.

"But what is a house of snow?" said the little girl in the front row. "I never heard of that."

"And what is your word for it?" asked another.

"Snowhouse", Alex said slowly in English.

"Snoh-kha-oos!" the children chanted.

"In my country the people who live in the far north dwelled in such houses at one time", Alex said.

"Didn't the houses of snow fall down on them?" someone asked.

"No, they didn't, because the people of the Arctic built them cleverly."

"Igloos", said Ilya.

"That's right—igloos. Very good, Ilya. Where did you learn that word?"

"I read about it. Our Chukchi people are similar to your Eskimo."

"We now use the Eskimo's own name for themselves. They say *Inuit*, which in their language means 'the people'."

"Communists say that", an older girl offered.

"They mean something different", Ilya said in a bitter tone.

"But we are the people too", said a big, rawboned boy sitting beside Ilya. "We are the people of Ozero Baikal."

"Do you mean the village or the lake?" Ilya asked.

"Both."

Ilya nodded sagely.

An animated discussion now broke out among the older students, a spreading overflow of subject matter and participants. Younger ones turned in their seats, put chins in hands, and listened intently. Alex stood back and enjoyed the flexing of minds.

747

Around noon the teacher stepped in and clapped for attention. It was lunchtime, she said. Tomorrow, perhaps, Myistrrr Khrim would return to teach them more English words—*if* they behaved for the rest of the day.

"But we only learned two new words!" a boy protested.

"And one of them wasn't English!" cried another.

As Alex headed for the door, he was surrounded by children clamoring for answers to their many questions. Making his way into the school yard, he responded to their queries as best he could. Irina stood off to the side, smiling and watching his reactions.

"What does an igloo look like?" asked the little girl from the front row. "Is it square like a shed or pointed like a house?"

"It's neither square nor pointed", Alex replied, dropping to his knees. "It's round, like this."

Scooping handfuls of snow, he packed it into a dome shape on the ground.

Fourteen faces gathered around and stared down at the creation.

"It doesn't look like a place you could live in. Do they dig a hole in it?" Kiril asked.

"No, they build a shell of snow bricks."

"How?"

Standing, brushing the snow from his hands, Alex thought for a moment; then his face lit up with an inspiration.

"Let's build one!" he said, and the children burst into cheers.

And so it came to pass that after hastily gobbled meals, everyone followed Alex down onto the lake. Older boys ran to fetch digging tools, and when they returned, the English teacher asked for a long, machete-like knife that one of them had brought. Bending, he cut a square in the compacted lake snow.

"You see how the wind has pressed it into a hard layer?"

"The *sarma* did it!" one of the children told Alex. "The sarma wind is mighty. It's so strong it turns ships upside down."

"Ah, that's something I didn't know. Well, we can thank the sarma for making excellent material for us."

"The mountain hides our homes from the sarma", said another.

Alex nodded with interest. "And that's why we can't use the snow in the village; it's too soft and would collapse. We need the kind of snow that can stand up."

For the next hour Alex and the children busied themselves cutting square and rectangular blocks of various sizes, larger ones that would be used for the base of the igloo, and smaller ones for the upper section. He taught them words as they went along: *knife, square, white, cold*. They were insatiable.

A trail of porters carried the blocks to the field beside the school, losing only a few pieces along the way. Ilya stayed at the construction site in the field beside the school and supervised laying the blocks out in lines according to size: small, medium, and large.

Irina had begged off the monumental project and returned to the house, but Dusya Lukasheva threw herself into the task with gusto, shouting orders left and right (all of which were ignored) and having a good deal of fun. At one point, bending to lift a small block of snow, she was hit on her hind end by a snowball. Shouting with outrage, she gave as good as she got, scooping up a mittful of loose snow, packing it hard, and hurling it at the miscreant, who was none other than Kiril Pimonenko.

"Ooo, I will tan your hide when I catch you, you pepper pot!" she cried, and took off after him. Squealing, Kiril ran circles around her. Despite her portliness, Dusya was fast on her legs and went hopping through the snow close on his heels, casting dire threats that only spurred the boy on to another fusillade. Alex fired a snowball that splattered on the side of Kiril's face.

"Good shot!" Dusya cheered gleefully.

"Not fair! Not fair!" Kiril wailed. From all sides his schoolmates pelted him. He fought back, dancing around, calling friends to his side. Some rallied beside him; some didn't. A furious snowball fight now broke out in every direction, noisy and hilarious and not terribly dangerous. Only the youngest ones scurried to the sidelines, where they continued to throw their little missiles from a safe distance.

At one point Kiril tripped and fell. Dusya was on him in seconds.

"She's squashing me, she's squashing me!" he screamed.

"Take that, you imp", the teacher giggled, washing his face with snow.

"Mama! Mama!"

"Kiril is a baby!" the cry went up from many voices.

Wriggling out from under the weight of his teacher, he bounded to his feet, scooped up more snow, and ran straight for Alex with every ounce of Tartar blood flashing in his eyes.

Alex ducked, stepped to the side, and stuck out a foot. Kiril tripped over it and went tumbling. By then everyone was convulsing with laughter. Children and adults fell in the snow, rolled onto their backs, and stared at the sky. A truce was called, and no one broke it. After catching their breath, they headed back to shore carrying the last small blocks of snow. Dusya was still bossing, but only by force of habit, because no one bothered to obey. Kiril skipped along with his arm linked in Alex's.

"It's good you came back", he said with a grin and a dance of the eyes.

The building of the igloo took several hours. Alex showed the children how to make a ring of standing blocks about ten feet in diameter. By design, the lowest level was not horizontal; the upper edge angled gradually like a ramp, and as it completed the circle it began to form the second level. Alex showed his helpers how to lean the blocks carefully a few degrees toward the center. Each successive layer increased the incline until a dome began to take shape before their eyes.

"Why doesn't it fall down?" one of the children asked.

"It's like an arch in a kremlin gate", explained Ilya. "Each piece holds up the others, and the others hold it—everything supports everything else. That way it becomes strong."

"Like the people", Kiril said, hands on hips, cheeks flaming red, breathing deep from exertion.

"What is the English word for kremlin?" one of the children asked.

"*Fortress* or *castle*", Alex said.

They repeated the words with some effort, trying to get them right.

From time to time children ran off to get drinks of water, but they always quickly returned. Adult villagers stopped to watch, commented, applauded or criticized in a friendly fashion, then drifted away on more serious errands. It was getting dark by the time the last cap pieces were ready to be laid in place. Being the tallest, Alex stretched as far as possible, but could not reach the center. Ilya and the other teenage boy held him by his coat so that he could lean at a sharp angle over the outer wall without toppling onto the structure, but even the added inches were not enough. The boys pulled him back.

"Of course!" Alex said to the children as they crowded around, curious to see how he would solve the problem. "I completely forgot. We will do it the way the Inuit do it."

Taking the long knife, he cut a hole in the base of the igloo and pushed the white square inside.

"The gate of the kremlin!" he said, earning some laughter from the onlookers.

On hands and knees, he crawled through the hole. Several bodies crawled in after him. They all stood up oohing and aahing. Above their heads the open hole let in enough light for them to see. The sky was deep blue, and a star shone in it. More snow blocks were pushed in through the entrance. Alex cut them and lifted them to the ceiling, a foot above his head. One by one they shrank the sky until a single hole at the top of the dome remained, awaiting its cap.

Alex cut the final block about ten inches square, its edges sharply beveled so that they would fit snugly with the surrounding blocks. Using both hands and going more by touch than by sight, he pushed it through the hole at an angle, felt it fall onto the roof, then pulled it back toward the hole. Lifting with fingertips, maneuvering carefully, he positioned it above the hole and let it drop gently into place.

"It fits! It fits!" the children cried excitedly. Cheering could be heard from outside.

"It's too dark in here", a small voice trembled.

Everyone crawled outside again and stood around admiring their creation.

"We're not finished yet", Alex said. "Ilya, do we have some big, strong blocks left?"

"Several."

"In the Arctic of my land, the wind is sometimes as strong as your sarma, and the Inuit make a snow porch to keep it out."

The older boys brought thick rectangular chunks, and within minutes, following Alex's directions, they had constructed a simple tunnel, walled and roofed, extending about four feet out from the entrance. After that, Alex got the younger children busy packing soft snow into the cracks.

By then most of them were beginning to think about food. Alex said that it was time for supper, but if anyone wanted to return after the meal, he had something interesting to show them about the igloo. They all scurried off, and it was clear from their eagerness that meals would be consumed hurriedly and that they would all be back in short order.

Irina fed Alex and her sons a meal of boiled potatoes and fish that they ate heartily. From time to time Alex glanced up to see her looking at him with a thoughtful expression. Each time, she looked down at her plate and continued eating. Once she smiled and said, "Well, Mr. Graham, no doubt you have affected the cultural life of Siberia in a way unequaled since the railroad was put in during the nineteenth century."

"I hope I have affected it to the good."

"Mghm-ghm-mghm", said Kiril, stretching his neck high and bouncing.

"Swallow first, Kiril", said his mother.

"He has affected it *very good*!" Kiril declared when his mouth was clear.

"Irina, I have a favor to ask of you", Alex said. "Would it be possible to borrow an oil lamp or candles for the igloo?"

"Of course."

Ilya jumped up and said, "The lanterns in Kolo's shed. I'll get them."

Kiril also leaped into action. "The candle stubs, Mama. Can we have them?"

His mother nodded. When the boys returned—Ilya with two wire-handle barn lanterns, and Kiril with a bag of candles—they all got on their coats and headed for the school yard. The boys ran ahead, and Irina walked slowly beside Alex.

"You haven't exhausted yourself, I hope", she said. "How is your poor skull today?"

"A bit sore, but I haven't noticed it much. Really, Irina, it has been a long time since I've felt so well. As you promised, the children are beautiful."

"Aren't children everywhere beautiful?"

"Yes, they are. The world is born again with each new life."

"You've given them a fine gift today, Aleksandr. It has been a long time since I've seen such happiness among them. Let's hope it ends well."

"What do you mean?"

She sighed. "In this land hope so often arises only to be dashed to the ground."

"Don't let yourself be a pessimist, Irina."

"Am I a pessimist or a realist? You're naïve about human nature, I think. In the prettiest of places, yes, even here in Baikal, human nature is ever the same. Every village has its poets and its bullies, its Pushkins and its Stalins."

"Stalinism is dead and its memory hated. Pushkin's work remains and is loved. Pushkin is teaching your children, not Stalin."

"Perhaps you're right, Aleksandr. I will hope for this."

Arriving at the school yard, they came upon a small crowd. All the children and several parents had returned.

"The man who fell from the sky! The man who fell from the sky!" shouted the youngest.

"The Inuit is here, the Inuit is here!" called the oldest, laughing.

"*Inuit* is plural, *Inuk* is singular", Alex said, slipping into instructor mode.

"Myihstrrr Khrim," said Dusya, pushing forward, "these bold imps wanted to light the lamps, but I wouldn't let them. Please, it must be you who enter first."

"Thank you, Dusya Lukasheva."

Alex crawled into the tunnel. Ilya and Kiril crawled in after him, carrying the lamps and candles. The interior of the igloo was black, the air still and soundless. Alex stood upright and fumbled in his coat pocket. Extracting the box of matches Irina had given him for the occasion, he opened it carefully (this action stirred bad memories), removed a match, and struck it on the side of the box. Never had a spark of light dazzled the human eye as brightly as this one.

The boys pressed close, Ilya lifting the glass chimney of the oil lamp. The light grew. When the second lamp was lit, a muffled cheer erupted outside. Kiril busied himself lighting candles and sticking them around the circumference of the snow floor. The interior was now glowing with soft radiance.

"It's warm in here", Ilya said. "It's really warm!"

"That's the genius of the igloo", Alex explained. "No matter how cold it is outside, the interior hovers near the freezing mark—zero degrees Celsius. Body heat warms it enough for comfort."

"The freezing mark is not comfortable, Aleksandr", Kiril argued.

"If the temperature outside is thirty degrees below zero and inside it's zero degrees, what is the difference?"

"Thirty degrees."

"Correct. Now combine that with the absence of wind, and you begin to feel very comfortable indeed."

"But why doesn't the igloo melt?"

"That's part of its genius too, and a mystery, but it has preserved the Inuit in the coldest regions of the earth for thousands of years. After many weeks a little coating of ice forms on the inside walls, and then the insulation is weaker. Whenever that happens, the people simply move to a new house."

"They build a new one?"

"That's right. Half a day's work, and they have a whole new castle."

"It's getting stuffy in here", Ilya said.

"I forgot the breather hole", said Alex. He poked a little hole in the ceiling near the top, and a trickle of draft began to flow.

"Come out, come out!" several voices shouted through the tunnel.

Crawling back outside, Alex and the boys exited into the cold air.

"Look, look! How beautiful it is!" cried children and adults.

The night was moonless, and there were few lights on in the houses at this end of the village. The igloo glowed like a blue coal. From every joint of the snow blocks, lines of radiance showed.

Silence fell on the crowd as they gazed at it. Instinctively, people stepped back, withdrawing farther and farther in order to have a better view of the whole. Doors opened in the nearby houses, and more people came out to see what was happening. Soon the entire igloo was ringed by admirers. As each new person approached, he fell silent. Within fifteen minutes it seemed as if the entire village had arrived, for the igloo was now surrounded by a ring of people three and four deep.

"It's a diamond", said one old man.

"It's a comet that fell from the cosmos", said a woman.

"It's blue fire", said another.

"Burning snow!"

"A jewel in an icon!" a small voice rasped, for Aglaya the Crow was among them as well. Standing at the bottom of the trail, leaning on a cane as she inspected the new creation, she nodded her approval. Without warning, she lifted her head in the silence and began to sing. Her voice was thin and tremulous, an old woman's voice, yet rich in emotion. Alex did not know the song, and what it meant he could not guess, for Aglaya's words were unclear. People on all sides began to hum, for it seemed they knew it, or if they did not, they were able to enter into its spirit without difficulty. The tune was in a minor key, melancholic and evocative.

A man's voice rose above the chorus of humming.

"In the night of winter", he sang in a tenor that wavered, steadied, then rose again.

"*Mm-mmm-mmmm*", hummed the crowd.

> "The light came to us—"
> *Mm-mmm-mmmm*—
> "Unexpected it came, in the dark and the cold—"

Now a woman's voice took over, as soulful as the man's: "It seemed to us like a dream", she sang.

> *Mm-mmm-mmmm*—
> "Just when we thought that the dawn would not come,
> A light burst forth in the gloom."

Other voices, young and old, strong and weak, contributed lines.

> "Then we awoke to see
> The dream among us at last—"
> *Mm-mmm-mmmm*—
> "The waking dream—"
> *Mm-mmm-mmmm*—

The lyrics were overlapping and repetitive; they were variations on each other, inflections, each one adding to the meaning and to the symphonic effect. Alex understood—though he did not know how—that this was neither an unveiling of a collective soul nor a manifestation of the group's psychology, nor anything other than what it was. The people of Ozero Baikal, many of whom had survived a diabolic century by ingenuity or miracle or a combination of both, were living in the new era as if awakening from a dark dream. Now, as they sang, they listened to themselves singing.

Some of them joined hands, old and young. Bodies began to sway forward and backward in a gentle current like seaweed in the flow of tides. Irina between her two sons, Ilya hand in hand with Grig, Kiril with Dusya. Aglaya too joined the ring, grabbing the hands of two old women.

Standing back a few paces, Alex kept his bare hands thrust into his pockets. He did not join in the phenomenon, though he desired to be part of it. There was no great discomfort in his feeling of separation, for throughout his life he had always observed from the sidelines. He had always been a foreigner. Even so, as he glanced up from the glowing diamond to the spiraling cosmos above, he felt the first stirrings of that moment of seeing that he had experienced in the Moscow underground when glory had appeared in a vault of degradation.

"Aleksandr?" said a woman's voice.

Irina stood before him, arm extended.

"Join us", she said.

He stepped forward and entered the ring. Irina had removed her own mittens, and her hand was warm in his, so warm that it took his breath away and hammered his heart, though the song restrained all igniting feathers in the polyphony of *zimorodochka* blue. Another hand took his. It was Ilya, his bruised face glancing swiftly to see if this was permitted, if the man he had so recently insulted would accept his hand. Without words the consent was given. Alex grasped the boy's large hand, now firm, now trembling, fingernails bitten to the quick, knuckles raw from fighting, skin chapped and scabbed. Between woman and man, and man and youth, there passed an understanding, and the song continued, each taking his part. As this understanding grew, it seemed to change into a covenant, its bonds a mutual gift.

Mm-mmm-mmmm—

"Alik, you too must sing!" cried the voice of Aglaya the Crow in her most demanding tone.

Laughter came from all sides, for Aglaya was famous for her lack of tact. The laughter fell away, and the humming resumed.

Mm-mmm-mmmm—

"Alik, Alik! Sing, sing!" pleaded the voices of several small children.

"What will I sing?" asked the man who fell from the sky.

"Anything!" the children cried.

Mm-mmm-mmmm—

Now the rhythmic hum softened as the people waited for his answer.

Irina's hand pressed his. *Continue,* it said. *Do not fear.*

Mm-mmm-mmmm—

It had been a long while since Alex had sung in public. In the past he had done so only in crowds of churchgoers, his voice hidden among theirs. He now saw that true humility was to permit exposure. It was to become a child. A singing child.

And so he sang:

"O children of Baikal—"

Mm-mmm-mmmm—

"O children of Baikal, you whom I do not know,
You who know me not,
In beauty did Love make us, but we have lost,
Oh, we have lost—"

Mm-mmm-mmmm—

"Our hidden face, our name, our way.
But Love, a genius, takes us by the hand this night
And guides us through the mountains and the ice.
Love knows us better than we know ourselves,
Though we in our disbelief could not keep faith with him,
Or with each other."

Mm-mmm-mmmm—

"Blinded we were, and blind we are,
To trees bursting into flame all about,
And the hand of Love pressing into the cold stone
A memory of heat."

Mm-mmm-mmmm—

"O *serdtse,* O *dusha!*

From the west I came like sarma wind,
Out of emptiness the storm-tossed came;
I did not fall from the sky, but I fell."
Mm-mmm-mmmm—
"In the east you dwell, which is another's west,
And gather here beside the waters of abyss
To forge your young within your flesh
And sing together of the unremembered dream."
Mm-mmm-mmmm—
"I was drowning, I was drowning, children of Baikal,
As you would drown upon *my* sea.
Yet Love the King has seen our grief and pitied us,
And drawn us to this house
To give a place where all might live."
Mm-mmm-mmmm—
"I must go into the west and never more be seen,
Yet ever will I carry you, as you must carry me.
The hearing heart forgets no word that love has sung this night;
Remember it and light the heart-lamp of the soul
To push back all this northern void—"

At the word *void*, Alex's voice failed him. The palpable reality of both *void* and *heart* were in such stark contrast to each other that he was suddenly overwhelmed.

Other voices, other lyrics arose, and the song went on. When at last the spirit of the event had waned, people ceased humming, turned to each other, and chatted quietly in a neighborly fashion. Hands were dropped; kisses were exchanged here and there. The children began to run about, and parents called them toward home. Conversation swelled and faded; the crowd thinned. Ilya crawled into the igloo to check the lamps. Irina held onto Alex's hand. Or was it that he would not let hers go?

"Irina."

"Say nothing, Aleksandr", she whispered. "No words are needed."

Without warning, Aglaya broke in, limping forward, supported by her cane.

"Alik Anguseyevich", she cawed. "Such a night! Such a song! I didn't know you had it in you!"

"Thank you, Aglaya Pavlovna. Do such events happen often?"

The two women looked at him solemnly.

"Actually, never", said Irina, letting go of Alex's hand. "It was as great a surprise for us as it was for you."

"Never would I have suspected such spirit in the village. Never", Aglaya said. "It does my heart good, I must say. Though sometimes there's a dance in the school, and of course, some of the people go to Saint Nikolai for Christmas and Easter, nothing like this has ever happened."

Aglaya walked to within a foot of Alex and said in her commanding tone: "Bow."

"Bow? You mean I should bow to you? All right, if you wish. I suppose you deserve it."

"Ha! I'm not the czarina. I just want to tell you something."

"It's because you're too tall, Aleksandr", said Irina. "She can't whisper her secrets unless you put your ear to her level."

Alex bowed. The old woman dropped her cane. He bent lower to pick it up for her. She stepped on it with the toe of her boot.

"*Nyet!* Leave it!" she said. Then, taking him by the shoulders, she kissed him on one cheek, then the other. Putting her wizened lips to his ear, she whispered, "Progress."

"Progress?" he repeated.

Putting her lips to his other ear, she whispered, "Fool."

"Fool?"

"That's right, young man. There are good fools and bad fools. Tonight you were a good fool. That is progress. Now pick up my cane for me, if you please."

And so he did.

"Thank you. Now I won't scold that you forgot our date. You got sidetracked with the snowhouse, and that's a good enough excuse. But don't let it happen again. You can come tomorrow to hear the story."

"I'll come after the English lesson."

"No, come before. That way I'll be certain you'll keep your promise. Since you got that bump on the head, you're late for everything."

Aglaya turned and climbed the path toward her cabin.

The boys, who had come up behind their mother, asked if the lights could be left on in the igloo throughout the night. Alex thought that was an excellent idea and asked Irina if she minded the waste of fuel. She said it would not be a waste.

After taking a last look at the glowing dome, Alex, Irina, and her two sons made their way back along the path to the clinic. They stopped by the porch and looked up at the stars.

Ilya and Kiril told their mother they were going out onto the lake to see if the igloo was visible from there. She watched them run down the slope through the dark.

"Irina…" Alex whispered, turning to face her.

"It's late", she said. "It's not necessary to speak."

"You helped me to sing."

"Your song was from the *glubina dushy*. It was similar to the poem on the train. But that was half-*serdtse*, half-*dusha*. This was entirely from the depth of the soul."

"You opened my soul", he said, touching her arm.

"Please, don't", she said. "It's foolish to begin what can never be completed."

"But tonight I found something I've been seeking all my life—and didn't know I was seeking."

"What you seek is already within you."

"Is it? Where within me?"

She did not answer.

762

"Irina, I—"

"Please, do not say it."

"I don't understand why you refuse to hear what's in my heart."

"The heart? You don't know what you mean by that word."

"You refuse to hear what I want to say because you're afraid."

"Afraid? No, I am not afraid."

"Yes, you are", he said gently. "Is it because a man such as I might depart as swiftly as he arrived, might take everything you have to give, then disappear?"

"What makes you think I would want to give everything?"

This reduced Alex to silence.

"A word once spoken cannot be taken back", she went on with quiet intensity. "It goes out into the world. It changes the world. You must take greater care with your words."

Hands thrust in the pockets of his greatcoat, the coat that had once belonged to a nameless dead man, he stared up at the stars.

"Of course. What right do I have to say anything? Who am I to you?"

"You feel lost, and you're trying to anchor yourself by connecting to someone."

Although he did not like what she said, it struck him that it could very well be true.

"Maybe you're right, Irina. I'm somewhere on this planet, but I no longer know which is east and which is west. Am I to become a man without a home, without a country?"

"Why do you ask such a thing?"

"I've lost my home and my business. When I return to my country, what will await me there? I will be as lost and without resources as I am here. Even the name of my town seems strange to me now—fading, fading like a half-remembered fable."

"You have been through difficult experiences, Aleksandr. When you return to your family and friends, *we* will become the faded dream."

"Never. Never will I forget you."

"You will return to your land, and then you will have everything back again."

"Everything? No, it's gone now. I have only this coat, this moment, and..."

And you. But he did not say it.

Ilya and Kiril came running up the hill, shouting.

"Mama! Mama!" Kiril cried. "It's *very* beautiful. For a thousand kilometers it can be seen! All travelers on the lake will look at it and say how lucky are the people of Ozero Baikal!"

Irina opened her arms to her sons and embraced them. They bid Alex good-night and walked slowly to their home.

No messages came from Listvyanka the next day. In the morning, Alex climbed the hill to Aglaya's cabin to fulfill his promise. She welcomed him as before and plied him with her cake and tea.

"Where do you get all this cream?" Alex asked. "I haven't seen a single cow in the village, and only a few goats." He sipped from the jar. "And this is definitely cow's cream."

"It's a secret", the old woman said with artfully slitted eyes.

"You have many secrets, Aglaya Pavlovna, it seems to me."

"Can you be trusted, Alik? That's the question."

"That's for you to decide."

"Oh, I know that every good fellow thinks he's reliable. Never would he divulge a secret—oh no, he would die rather than break a confidence, wouldn't he? Then along comes a trusted pal of his, and before you know it, he says to him, 'Look, I'm not supposed to tell you this. It's a secret. I'll tell you if you promise to keep it totally, strictly, no exceptions, a secret just between you and me.' So of course the pal agrees, and the secret slips into another head. Then that one goes running off to *his* best friend, and before you know it—"

"Before you know it, the whole village knows."

"The whole *world* knows, and in a twisted way, you can be sure."

"I think I get your point, Aglaya. You would rather keep the secret of the cream to yourself."

"Oh well, I might as well tell you", she grumbled, as if she had been argued into bestowing a great favor.

"It's not necessary to tell me. I respect your right to privacy."

At that moment a long, low *mooo* came from behind the back wall of the cabin.

"There she is now, asking for more. Never satisfied, she is. But then she's an honest beggar, gives for what she gets. Not like some I could mention."

"Your cow lives behind your house! But it seems to me there's only a cliff wall there, and your house is built against it."

"Seems, seems! People always judge by what *seems* and not by what *is*. Well, if you're going to become one of us, you might as well have an eyeful."

Aglaya got off her bench and flipped back the canvas that hid the end of her room. In the wall of the cabin was a low doorway, covered by a second piece of canvas. Barnyard smells wafted in.

"Take a look, take a look. But first promise not to tell anyone who doesn't belong to Ozero Baikal."

"I promise."

"He promises", she muttered, raising her eyes to heaven, whether in witness or mockery, it was not clear.

Alex lifted the canvas and, bending low, went through into what he took at first to be a cave. Inside was an irregularly shaped cavern, half-filled by a stack of hay retained behind a barricade of sapling logs. A cow lay on a bedding of straw this side of the barricade. She was white with irregular black spots. She stared at him and chewed her cud as if to say his presence was mildly interesting but not especially notable. Half a dozen red pullets clucked at the intruder, fluttered their wings, and hopped through gaps in the saplings into the safety of the hay mow.

As he looked more closely, Alex saw that the "barn" was not so much a cave as it was a recess beneath an overhang at the base of the cliff. It was hidden from view by the back wall of the cabin. Two other sides were stone, and through the fourth side light streamed. Beyond it was a paddock fenced by woven willow pickets. Stepping out into the frozen mud of this yard, he saw that it was a narrow ravine, completely hidden by evergreens.

He went back into the cabin and sat down.

"It's wonderful, Aglaya. A very private place. And you say it's a secret. The state doesn't know about it."

"Why should they know about it? What good would it do them if they knew? You can't pay taxes with butter."

"The villagers must know, surely. And they all keep your secret?"

"They all like butter."

"Even during the dark years they kept your secret?"

"Those were hungry years. Then they were even better at holding their tongues."

"That is amazing. Rare is the place on this earth where there isn't a traitor or two."

"True. But Ozero Baikal is unusual in this regard. We all know each other so well—too well, I might say. If one suffers, all suffer. If one is blessed, all are blessed."

"That is indeed rare."

"We have worked hard to make it this way. The alternative was death."

"Still, it's a mystery to me how you've made it work."

"The secret is prayer and fasting. Two days a week on bread and water for sixty years."

"Now that the Soviets have fallen, surely it's safe for you to live openly?"

"Now is the most dangerous time of all."

Alex did not respond. He did not like to contradict a woman who had fasted for sixty years, no matter how mistaken she was.

"No, don't look at me like that, Alik. I can hear your thoughts. You think I'm a hen of habit, can't change my ways, can't believe it's all over. Listen to me, Alik Anguseyevich—this is the most dangerous time of all because now he has become invisible."

"Who has become invisible?"

"The dragon. Just when you think he's getting smaller and smaller, no bigger than a lapdog, he opens his little mouth and swallows the whole world in one gulp."

Alex said nothing for a time.

"So, Aglaya," he said at last, "the state doesn't bother you with taxes and documents and all those matters?"

"The state doesn't know about me. Never has it known about me." She grinned, exposing crooked little brown teeth. "I am a nonperson."

"Did they know about your mother and father?"

Aglaya cast her eyes down and nodded.

"You told me the other day that your mother brought you here in 1930, when you were six years old."

Aglaya nodded again but said nothing more. Finally, breathing a deep sigh, she looked up and said, "Now I will tell you a story."

31. *The Icon in the Fire*

Though Aglaya had been born after the Revolution, she had
nursed at the breast of a mother raised in the old days, who
had tried to live as if the Revolution had not really occurred.
In the remoter regions of Siberia, this was still possible in
the 1920s.

"Our troubles began with collectivization", Aglaya said.
"In 1930 we were living just outside a city on the other side
of the Sea of Baikal, near the mountains of Khamar-Daban.
My father was a cobbler. Pavel was his name. He was very
religious, as was my mother. Marfa was her name. In our village, a stone's throw from the city, was a holy priest. From far
and wide pilgrims came to see him and listen to his spiritual
counsel. He was a great faster and a passion sufferer. The white
passion all his life, and the red passion of blood at the end.

"One day in January, the political police and GPU soldiers
came to our village—I would rather not tell you its name.
They came to 'clean house', as they called it. In those days
Stalin was trying to force collectivization on the peasants. My
father was a kulak but a poor one. He had a little plot of land,
not much—he was not a *barin*, you can be sure! He grew some
grain. The grain was a big problem during that period. The
state was confiscating whatever people grew. Many kulaks
were sent to the camps; many were killed. Stalin decided to
break our spirit by destroying our churches. Thousands of
holy places were burned or turned over to the local Communists. The one in our village was burned too. They shot
my father and other church elders because the men tried to

stop them from pouring cans of gasoline all over the floor. I did not see his death, and for this I am grateful. But I saw things just as evil. They tortured the priest, cut off his hands and feet in the square in front of the church. The church was dedicated to Saints Boris and Gleb the Passion Sufferers, and the priest cried out to them by name as he died. I still remember the sound of his voice, for though I was only six years old, the entire village was forced to watch the execution. My mother held her hand over my mouth so I would not scream. The scream did not come out, so it went deeper inside. I am still screaming. But the scream has become tears and supplications. Do you know what that priest cried as he bled to death? No? Well, I'll tell you.

"He pleaded with the brother saints to pray for the ones who were taking his life. With each blow, he begged God to have mercy on Russia and her people. He begged that a remnant of the flock would remain and that it would one day rebuild the Church. I watched as his lifeblood was spilled on the snow. In the end he took so long to die that they just put a gun to his head and shot him."

Aglaya winced. "I still hear that shot whenever I have a bad dream."

"What did your mother do then?"

"My mother? My holy and beautiful mother, a saint she was, no doubt about it. Before they torched the church, as a special insult they stripped it of all the icons. Even the big ones in the iconostasis they ripped out. A huge heap was made in the church square. Soldiers went all through the village, breaking into many houses, taking the holy images from the walls. These too were thrown onto the pile. By then the soldiers were drinking. You could see that some of the young ones, even though they were Communists, felt guilty about what they were doing, and one or two (God have mercy on them) even crossed themselves secretly as they threw the icons onto the pile. So, you see, they needed the vodka to kill their pain. But most did not feel any guilt—oh no, they were prancing with glee. Like devils they were. They got drunk too, but for pleasure.

"One by one the people drifted away to their homes, where they wept bitterly and prayed. My mother brought me home and buried her face in a pillow. She wept as I had never heard her weep before or since. My father's body was lying frozen in the square. There was no way to bury him, or the others; the ground was like iron. The soldiers would not let us collect the bodies.

"That night, the soldiers threw burning rags into the church, and the wooden floor caught fire from the gasoline. My mother put me to bed, said prayers with me, and left me in the care of my grandmother—my mother's mother she was. She went out, taking with her the pull sled. This was a thing my father had made for hauling firewood. It had good runners and a long rope. You could carry a lot of weight on it. Grandmother told me that Mother was going to beg the soldiers to give her my father's body and the body of the priest, so that they might be buried. She hoped that when the soldiers left, in a day, a week, or a month, the villagers would be able to dig a hole and mark the spot. Then pilgrims might come one day and pray at the tomb of the priest-martyr. But when she arrived at the church, she saw that it was burning up. The priest's body was being thrown onto the back of a truck, then his severed limbs, along with the bodies of the other men they had shot. My father's body, she thought, was among them, though it was impossible to know for certain. It seemed like the end of the world to her.

"The truck took the dead away; I do not know where. To this day no one knows. It was late at night by then, and the church was roaring with flames. The soldiers were very drunk, racing around screaming, singing, and laughing. One of them poured a bit of gasoline onto the heap of icons and threw a match at it. It burst into flames.

"My mother crawled on hands and knees across the square. No one noticed her. She pulled an icon from the fire. Its metal cover was hot. It burned her, but she did not drop it. She stuffed it inside her coat. Then another and another. Most of the flames were at the top of the pile, but even as she pulled the icons from the bottom, the flames crept downward. She took what she could and crawled away into an alley. There she made a little pile of icons.

"Back she went to the fire. One, two, three, she took. Four, five, six, she took. Her dress front was scorched away, and now the icons touched her skin. Each one burned her more badly than the others. For the most part these were small icons, though just at the end she was able to pull out a few larger ones. Back she crawled to the alley, cooling the images in the snow, adding them to the pile of the saved.

"Snow began to fall, as if heaven were weeping over the sacrilege, over the dead, over the blindness of the soldiers. This dampened the flames a little, giving her more time. The soldiers patrolled around the square, if patrolling you could call it, for they were all staggering. If they had once spotted my mother, she would have been shot on the spot. Back she went through the staggerers, back and forth, for hours. Oh, my mother! Oh, my mother, what a *velikaya dusha*, a great soul, she was!

"By then her hands were a mess, bleeding and skinless on the palms; raw meat they were. One more time she went back. Just as she was reaching in, a boy with a rifle came around from the other side of the pile. He was drunk but not as drunk as the others. And what did he see? He saw a woman on her knees, her hand reaching into the fire to pull out her last icon, her hand enveloped in flames. He pointed his gun at her.

" 'I forgive you', she said, and closed her eyes. But he did not shoot. When she opened her eyes to see why he had not killed her, she saw that his eyes were filled with horror and shame. He lowered his gun and walked away. He said nothing to the others. He went to the far side of the square and stared at a stone wall.

"Mother pulled the last icon from the fire—a Bogoroditsa, the Vladimirskaya. It was already burning. She threw snow on it to put out the flames, stuffed it inside her coat, and crawled away into the alley. Then she loaded all the icons onto the sleigh and dragged it home.

"The place where we lived was on the Selenga River, which flows into Baikal from the east. My grandmother bandaged Mother's hands. Terrible were the cries of her pain, and more terrible the sound of their weeping as they held each other, trying not to let me hear. My grandmother said we must flee to our ancestral village in the high Khamar-Daban, where she still had some family who might take us in. My mother was not sure. She thought it was too dangerous, that the GPU would go everywhere; we might arrive at the place of refuge only to suffer again what we had just barely survived. She had heard rumors that not a stone would be left unturned in the Khamar-Daban.

"My grandmother said that in Listvyanka on the west shore of Baikal, she had a sister married to a man of that region. Perhaps in the summer they could try to go there by boat, if they could find someone to take them down the Selenga River to the Sacred Sea. It would be a hundred and twenty kilometers on the river, and two hundred more on the lake. A long journey. If they could survive until spring, they would surely go.

"Just as they were saying this, they heard gunshots in the village, many gunshots. The soldiers were running through the streets shooting people, setting fire to homes. A voice shouted in the street, 'Death to the kulaks! Onto the garbage heap of history with you!'

"Oh, how we prayed! The soldiers passed by, running this way and that. At any moment they might return and break into the house. The sled was in the shed at our back door, still loaded with icons. While Grandmother dressed me in my winter clothes, Mother put bread and blankets onto the sled. Then we all went out through the back door, Mother, Grandmother, and me. It was the middle of the night. They put me on the sled and covered me. They wrapped the icons in canvas and tied the bundle to the crossbars. My head rested on the pile. The two women pulled the sled down an alleyway and out onto the dark fields, the snow still falling, covering our tracks. The angels hid us from all eyes.

"Passing the end of the field, we followed the slope down to the frozen river, turned west, and went along the ice throughout that night. I did not understand what was happening. I was still screaming inside from the sights I had seen in the church square, but even so, I could not keep my eyes open. I cried, and then I fell asleep.

"In the morning I woke up to see that we were far from any place where men lived. Along the banks of the Selenga, trees and bushes were covered in thick frost. The sun was rising on a world of great beauty; all white and crystal it was. The women sat on the end of the sled and ate bread. They gave me a portion as large as their own.

"'This little one is growing', my grandmother said, stroking my cheek. 'She needs food more than I do.' From then on she would eat no more and gave me her portions.

"For two days and a night we walked, sleeping once in a hay barn near the river. We took the left channel, and on the afternoon of the third day we reached the shore of Baikal. Mother and Grandmother fell to their knees, crossed themselves, and gave thanks to God.

"My grandmother was very tired, and she constantly beat at her breast, for her heart had been weakened by the journey. Mother made her lie down on the sled, and we set off across the lake. For a time I walked, helping to pull. What a blessing it was that the wind had blown the lake so clean. A light blanket of snow covered the ice, just enough to make it easier to go fast without slipping.

"The sun set, and a bad wind arose, the sarma—very wild and fierce. Even so, the stars were out, and the moon came up and made the lake shine like a looking glass in a fairy tale. I expected at any moment to see troikas come galloping out of the north, driven by princes who would stop and pick us up and take us to Listvyanka.

"In the night, Mother fell to her knees and wailed. That sound was more terrible than the sound of a gunshot. She rocked her body, for her hands were in agony. Not a word, not a whimper had I heard from her until then, but now she could go no farther. Grandmother was very weak also, and she said that we must rest or all of us would die. We made a wind block with the big icon of Vladimirskaya, and another of Boris and Gleb, also big, which had been torn from the iconostasis. Then the three of us lay down together, holding each other tight, covered with blankets and protected by the Bogoroditsa and the Two Brothers. It was cold beyond imagining, so cold that even now my bones retain the memory of it. Mother and Grandmother held me between them, and though I was chilled and shivering, I was in no danger of freezing. But when we woke up in the morning, Grandmother was dead.

"To this day, I see her blue face, her open mouth, her eyes open also, with a stream of frozen tears on her cheeks.

"I will not tell you about the rest because it is too hard. I will say only that we left Grandmother's body on the ice, and I think for my mother there was no more terrible moment than this. It was equaled only by the death of my father. But he had been torn from her by force. Now she was abandoning the one who had carried her in the womb, the one who had given her life.

"On the evening of the next day, we reached the west shore of Baikal. Mother would not let me walk much, only long enough to warm my body from time to time; then back onto the sled she sent me. We had eaten the last of the bread. We turned south and walked along beside the Primorski Mountains, a few feet from shore, the blessed mountains blocking out the wind. It was warmer. We were exhausted. Not long after, we came to a fishing village. It was Ozero Baikal.

"We went to the first house—in fact, the one in which Irina Filippovna now lives. An old couple lived there at the time and took us in. Like most people in those days, they were Christians. Though you could see they were suffering from the hard times like everyone else, they had fish and plenty of firewood. Ozero was such a nothing place that the powerful rarely noticed its existence.

"To make a long story shorter, Alik, I will tell you that we never made it to Listvyanka. Years later we found out that Mother's aunt had died of illness and that her husband had been taken away to a prison camp. He was a kulak also, one of the millions who perished.

"Pity moved in the hearts of the old couple. They told us of a shelter above the village where they had a little barn. They were infirm and their children gone. One of their sons had died in the White Army fighting Bolsheviks. When they told Mother this, she knew they could be trusted because the information was something that would have ended their lives if the state were to hear of it. One of the many secrets of Baikal. These old people needed a servant badly. The man was lame and the woman suffering from lung sickness. They had no money. Truly they didn't. But they could offer shelter and food in exchange for labor. Mother and I moved into this very cabin, which at the time was a pig shed. The first year, we shared it with a pig, though later we moved the creature into the cave. He snored too much and ate our clothing if we didn't keep an eye on him.

"It took six months for the burns to heal. There was infection. The old woman nursed Mother back to health. Once I saw Mother's body when the bandages were changed. Her chest was wrinkled, clawed by terrible scars, seeping bloody fluid. Her hands were worse. For the rest of her life it was not easy for her to use them; like mitts they were, and frightening to look at. She taught me how to work. Always I have loved to work with my hands."

Aglaya peered anxiously at her guest.

"More tea?"

Alex cleared his throat and nodded. She filled his jar from the samovar, added cream, handed it to him, and returned to her bench. He said nothing and sipped from the jar. Aglaya observed this, rocking gently.

She continued her story: "So many times my mother said to me—'Agladusha,' she said to me, 'the only whole heart is a broken one.'"

Aglaya had said this to Alex days before, but in the light of the story, he now seemed to hear it for the first time. It was no longer a folk insight or a gem of piety but a truth refined in fire.

"She died in her fifties", Aglaya went on, "and is buried in the cemetery beyond the schoolhouse. It's covered in snow now, but I'll show you her grave in the spring. It's just by the edge of the forest where the footpath goes north to the other villages."

"You never married, Aglaya?" Alex asked in a quiet voice.

"Never. Oh, I had my eye on a few lads, but one drowned in the lake during a storm. Two others were killed by the

Germans in the Great Patriotic War, one at the siege of Stalingrad. Never a lover's kiss have I had in all my years, and now I am too old to desire one. But many fine kisses of another sort have I had, much love have I had—all my life. A saint for a mother, good friends, and in later years fine people like the Pimonenkos, especially that Zhenya, whom you never knew. Like a son to me he was. Though he could be rude at times—called me a crow whenever he kissed my cheeks. Knew how to charm an old woman's heart, he did. But a good man to the core. Tsk, what a loss to us all when he died. Some wonderful memories he left behind, good words and good medicine, all for free. Memories cannot be taken from you. I am a blessed soul, and don't you doubt it."

"What an excellent grandmother you might have been."

"I am a grandmother to all the village. Many children have I. Many."

"Tell me about the rest of your life, Aglaya."

"Oo, that is a long and boring story. But since you ask me, I'll tell you the really important parts. In the late thirties the old couple died, and their house was given over to a big family of fisher people who had little use for the barn and the cave. They were Christians as well and offered to continue the agreement. The barn and cave became ours in exchange for potatoes and a little labor during the fishing season. In the fifties a priest came through during the wintertime. He was a logger. No one reported him to the police. All believers in the village confessed, and even some unbelievers came to faith. Then we received the Holy Gifts. Not since my childhood had I taken the Body and Blood. Oh, it was wonderful. Peace reigned among us for a long time after that.

"In the sixties I obtained a calf, and that was the great-great-great-grandmother of the cow you see in the cave. We've had trouble from time to time with the lack of a bull. But if you like butter, you must have a cow with calf, and if you want a cow with calf, you must have a bull, eh? No one wants to be the one to keep the bull. Sad to say, the only bull in the village died last year, and where we'll find another is a big worry. It's always the same—from mice to humans, the males are always a problem, no offense to you.

"People still help me by harvesting hay along the lake, bring it to me in boatloads every summer. For years I was the cow woman of the village—that's better than being the *crow* woman, I must say. My energy is failing me a little in these later years. How, I ask you, can an old woman keep a whole village in butter and cream? Others have brought in cows and goats, so they don't need me as much as they used to. Even so, people never forget things, especially the good you do for them. Of course, they never forget the other things too, the things that should be forgotten. But that's life.

"Let's see, what else is there to tell you? Not much. Oh yes, once in the seventies I went to Listvyanka to attend the Easter liturgy. It was in a house. That was a miracle, I can tell you. After that, priests came now and then to Listvyanka, increased in number during the eighties. Then the cathedral opened again in Irkutsk, and a priest was sent down regularly to Saint Nikolai's Church. It had been a storage shed and a fire hall for decades, but the state finally gave it back to us. Now we go in to church a few times a year. But that Listvyanka—oy, it's too big and rotten for me! I'm always so happy to get home to my own fire and a strong cup of tea."

"Your health seems good, Aglaya."

"Never been better. I hope to die in my tracks. I don't want to linger in a hospital up there in Irkutsk among strange people. No, let me drop dead among my potatoes, that's all I ask. Or maybe a day or two in Irina's clinic with everyone waiting on me hand and foot—that would be a nice way to go. Then, plunk! Into the soil beside my mama."

"God willing, may that not be for many more years."

Aglaya shrugged. "More tea?"

"No."

"Why are you crying?"

"I'm not crying."

"What's that on your face—rain?"

Alex wiped his eyes.

"What happened to the icons?"

"What icons?"

"The ones your mother brought across the lake when you fled."

"They're safe."

Her guarded look had returned, and Alex did not want to intrude on whatever she was hiding. She eyed him for a minute or two, trying to decide how much he could be trusted.

At last she said, "Oh well, I've told you this much, I might as well tell all my secrets."

Slipping off the bench, Aglaya pulled back the canvas partition. Behind this, to the right of the door leading into the cave, a curtain hung in front of the log wall. She drew it back. The wall was completely covered in icons. Aglaya lifted high her oil lamp.

In the center was a large image of the Mother of God of Vladimir. It was a good copy of the prototype, though it had suffered from its journey and long exposure to smoke and humidity. The upper third of the image was charred, the blackened area scarring the lambent gold leaf and just touching the top of the Mother's head. Like the Vladimirskaya that he had seen in Moscow's Tretyakov Gallery, the faces of Mother and Child seemed to float above the plane of the surface, the eyes deep and sorrowing yet radiant with love.

Alex bent and kissed the foot of the Child. He dropped his arms to his sides. As he did so, a peace beyond anything generated by the *serdtse* filled him. As before, the eyes in the icon seemed to penetrate without overwhelming. They were grieving one moment, full of tenderness the next, then full of yearning, desiring that he understand the necessity of all that was happening.

Alex dropped to his knees and put his forehead to the floor.

"Oy, oy!" exclaimed Aglaya Pavlovna.

"O God", he breathed. "Save Russia!"

He sobbed inwardly, and all the while the old woman stood by his side, gazing at him with furrowed brow. Now his prayers became silent pleading, yearning, yet filled with the strangest peace:

O Russia, poor Russia! O mankind, poor mankind! O Andrew, my son, my son, my son! O save him, Savior of the world! Save us all, for we are blind and poor and lost, and know not what we are doing!

Aglaya tugged on his arm.

"Get up now, Alik. That's very nice what you're doing, and I don't say it's unappreciated, but you don't really understand. Get up now, get up."

He did not hear her.

"Oy, oy!"

She went away and left him for a time.

Later—he did not know how much later—he lifted his head. The samovar clinked, the cow mooed, Aglaya coughed, time accelerated, and all things contracted from radiant blur into placid normality.

"Oy, oy, Alik. Well, come and have another jar."

He got up off his knees, kissed the burned icon, and returned to the chair in the front part of the cabin. Aglaya handed him more tea. He drank it. She sat on her bench watching him, her fingers moving on the knots of the chotki.

He stood and put on his coat.

"Wait!" said Aglaya.

She went behind the curtain and returned a moment later.

"You are a bigger fool than I thought", she said. "And that is good. That is what you must be. Here is a gift for you from the Bogoroditsa."

The old woman handed Alex a square of wood the size of his hand. The back was scorched. He turned it over and saw that it was an icon of the face of the suffering Christ. Battered, thorn crowned, weeping blood. The face, like the face of the Mother of God, was nearly three-dimensional: it floated; it looked back.

The image was badly stained with small black holes and spatters of wax; the gold leaf was dark with a patina of smoke—ages of incense and the fumes of a brief wrath. Fingerprints were visible in the gilt—the impress of Aglaya's mother, her burned hand grasping the heat-softened glue beneath the gold as she pulled it from the fire.

"I can't accept this", Alex said. "It's too great a gift."

"The proud man refuses a gift; the humble man accepts it."

"I'm not humble, Aglaya, but I will accept it after all, for perhaps it will help me to learn humility."

"You will learn, you will learn", she said with uncommon gentleness.

She bowed to him. He bowed to her. And because there was no more to be said, he left, bearing the gift close to his heart, beneath his coat, beneath his shirt, next to his skin.

As he made his way down the hill, he saw that Ilya and Kiril were at work in the yard of their home. They were rolling logs into a pile, levering them skillfully with long poles, loggers' pikes tipped with iron barbs. Volodya was leading Kolo along the lane toward the house, the pony leaning into the traces, pulling a log on a chain. Arriving at the Pimonenkos', Volodya brought Kolo to a halt and unchained the log.

The boys rolled it into the yard and added it to their pile. With that, Volodya turned around and led the pony back into the forest.

Filled with the peace that had come to him while praying before the icons, Alex did not want to engage in conversation, and for that reason he bypassed the house, heading straight for the clinic. Kiril waved. Alex waved back and went inside. There he removed his outdoor clothing and lay down on the bed. Opening his shirt front, he pulled out the icon and held it in both hands, and gazed at it until he fell asleep.

At about three o'clock, he awoke from his nap and made his way to the school, worried that he was late for the English lesson. But Dusya told him that schedules were always flexible at Pushkin School. She also explained that several of the older ones were missing, including Ilya and Kiril, because people sensed winter was drawing to a close and wanted to get their logs cut for firewood. The wood needed to dry during the hot months in order to be ready for next winter's burning, and it was best to cut it now, before the sap began to run.

Alex spent an hour teaching English words to the children. Afterward, he checked on the igloo, which had suffered no mishaps during the night. Hundreds of fresh footprints were visible in the snow all about it, revealing that it had been the object of much interest during the day. On his way back to the clinic, he stopped in the yard to chat with the boys and saw that they were now beginning to cut the logs into blocks on a sawhorse. The brothers, one on each end of a long bow saw, were sweating hard, their coats off despite the cold. Kiril informed Alex that no message had come from Listvyanka. He said it with a grin that expressed what he thought about this. Alex thanked him for the news (or lack of it) and asked him to tell his mother that he would not be needing supper tonight. He preferred to rest in the clinic.

"No chess?" Kiril wailed with dismay.

"What about the snowhouse?" Ilya asked in his gruff adolescent voice.

"If you can find more candles and fuel, Ilya, call me after dark, and we'll go together and light the snow lamp for all Baikal to see."

"If you wish", the boy said with a somber bob of his head.

"And after that—a game of *chess!*" Kiril pressed.

"I think not, Kiril. Another night."

The boy accepted it with good humor, pointing out to Alex that "another night" meant he was staying another day and perhaps longer.

"Will you stay even if a message comes from Semyon tomorrow?"

Alex paused. "Yes. I'll stay one more day after a message arrives. But *only* because I want a final chance to beat you at your own game."

This was greeted by dancing eyes.

Alex read more of Dostoyevsky's *The Humiliated* until seven o'clock, when Ilya rapped on the doorframe and entered the ward.

"We're ready. Do you want to come and light the lamps with us?"

Alex and the boys went up to the school yard, where a small crowd had already gathered. As on the night before, the lamps were lit, and the enchantment of the glowing igloo spread among them. There was no singing, but a hush settled on everyone, expressions of awe and pleasure evident on many faces. There was little conversation, and this was subdued, as if the people were experiencing an instinctive reverence, believer and nonbeliever alike, in the presence of such beauty.

Many went down onto the lake to see the igloo from a distance and returned with enthusiastic reports. People did not stay as long as on the previous evening. Alex, Ilya, and Kiril were the last to leave.

"We'll leave the lights on again, won't we?" Kiril asked.

"Of course", Alex said.

As the boys strode on ahead for home, Alex noticed a solitary figure standing at the base of the trail leading to Aglaya's hill. It was the Crow herself.

"A fine house you've given to Ozero Baikal", the old woman said. "A great gift."

"Your gift to me is far greater, Aglaya. Its value is beyond measure. I will always treasure it and remember you whenever I pray before it."

"Thank you. The enemy of light can burn the icons, but he cannot banish the light. Do you know, Alik, what this house is to the people?"

He shook his head.

"Many of them have no faith. You've built for them a little house of light. Fragile it is but strong in their eyes. They have few words for such things and even now cannot understand what it means."

"What does it mean, Aglaya?"

"This house teaches them. It tells them that a house of light *is* possible, and more than that, it shows them that other houses of light are possible, perhaps very great houses of light. They don't think this with their minds but with their hearts. As they go back to their homes and lie down to sleep, they gaze into the darkness, and the darkness is no longer burdensome, for the house glows in their minds. It shows them that they love the light and that they love its beauty. They see no more than this. In time they will come to hunger for the House of Light that is in the heavens and can never be destroyed."

"The snowhouse is a sign, then?"

"Yes. It's half-*serdtse*, half-*glubina dushy*. But the half can lead to the whole, if the heart listens. If the heart learns."

Alex took the old woman's arm and walked with her up the slope to her cabin. They said good-night on her doorstep, and he returned to the clinic. There he read for a while, prayed the rosary and the chotki, and fell asleep with the string in his fingers.

During the night he dreamed of horses.

32. The War of the Winter-Born

The morning dawned so mild and cloudless that a happy day seemed assured. No one was prepared for the sight that greeted their eyes when they arrived at the school yard. The igloo was demolished. Horse and pony hoofprints covered the area all about the igloo and were thick in the debris.

"Sonia", said Irina with a bitter look.

Dusya scolded loudly with no definite object for her outrage, shaking her fist in the air. The children stood around mutely, the youngest ones crying. A few parents arrived, paced about the site, shaking their heads, muttering. Then a look of resignation settled on their faces, and they walked away.

During the minutes when the village was absorbing the news, Ilya had stood with hands in fists by his side, his face working with anger. He now turned and strode deliberately in the direction of home. Irina and Alex followed him, after shooing Kiril into the schoolhouse with the other children. They arrived at the Pimonenko yard just in time to see Ilya emerging from Kolo's shed leading the pony by the halter and carrying a pike pole in his other hand.

Stopping short, Irina said, "Where are you going with that?"

"They can't get away with it!" Ilya said in a tone of cold fury, devoid of any visible passion. His mother rushed over to him and grabbed the shaft of the pole.

"No, you're not."

"I am."

"No."

"Stand aside, Mother."

Irina raised her voice and launched into a tirade. Though he did not let go of the pike, Ilya listened to her, staring all the while at the ground.

When she had finished, he said in a low voice, "They steal my traps, they steal Grandfather's sword, they destroy the snowhouse. They must pay."

"If you go after them, they'll make *you* pay. If you take their bait, they'll add insult to insult, and you alone will suffer."

"I am *sick* of cowardice!" he shouted.

"Your courage is foolishness!" his mother cried.

"Maybe so, but they're going to wish they had not done this."

Ilya wrenched the pike from his mother's hands and threw his leg over Kolo's back. Irina burst into tears and fled head down into the house.

Alex stepped forward and grabbed Kolo's bridle.

"It's a trap, Ilya, just like the last time."

"This time I'll be more careful", the boy snarled, drawing a long fish knife from a sheath on his belt. He pushed it back into its leather holder and jerked Kolo's head up with the reins. Alex jumped and caught the bridle again.

"Ilya Yevgenyevich, if your father were here, he would not let you go."

"My father is not here!" the boy yelled.

"Wait, wait a moment and think. What would your father do if he were here?"

"I don't know! I don't care!"

"Yes, you care. Your problem is you think he's not here. But he is here."

"He is *not* here!" Ilya shrieked, and pushed away Alex's chest with the sole of his boot.

Alex wrestled with the bridle. Kolo's tossing head made him lose his footing, but he did not let go of the leather straps.

"There is another way!" Alex shouted.

"There's no other way! There's only cowardice or courage!"

"The coward grasps at hasty revenge. The courageous man seeks wisdom!"

"Wisdom, wisdom! You're an old woman like Aglaya the Crow!"

"Aglaya the Crow has more courage than all the boys of Lake Baikal!"

This captured Ilya's attention for a few seconds, enough for Alex to grab the pike from his hand and fling it away. In a flash Alex grasped the hilt of the fish knife and hurled it onto the roof of the shed.

Infuriated, Ilya jumped from the pony and grabbed Alex by his coat lapels. Alex grabbed the front of Ilya's coat. The boy tried to throw him to the ground. He was wiry and very strong, but Alex was a head taller and had not lost all the strength he had gained during years of walking and swimming. He braced his legs, twisted Ilya's body around his hip, and flung him onto the manure pile, which under the late winter sun was thawing. Splattered with wet dung and filthy slush, Ilya leaped to his feet, cursing, flying into a complete rage, pummeling Alex with his fists. Alex stiff-armed him, pushing him back onto the manure pile. The boy jumped up again and resumed his attack with renewed fury. Alex was shocked but equally surprised by his own ability to deflect the blows. One, however, glanced off the bridge of his nose, making it bleed. Ilya's rage was astonishing in quantity and quality, but so intense was it that it quickly exhausted itself. He suddenly sagged, let go of Alex, and staggered back a few steps. The sight of the man's blood reduced him to silence. Wheezing, fists curling and uncurling, Ilya stared at him with hatred and shame alternating in his eyes.

"You are not my father!" the boy screamed.

"No, I am not your father. But if he were here, he would do exactly what I am doing."

Ilya sat down on the manure pile and covered his face with his arms.

"Ilya Yevgenyevich—"

"No...I..."

"There is another way", Alex said, wiping blood from his nose with his sleeve.

"There's no way, there's no way", Ilya sobbed.

"There is another way. And we will do it."

Returning to the scene of the disaster, Alex met with the group of adults who were still standing there discussing what had happened. Although they regretted the destruction of the igloo, they dismissed it as "hooliganism" and did not see any cause for response. Nothing of value had been lost, they told each other, so why get upset about it? Alex agreed that there was no need for retaliation. That was how feuds got started, he said, and feuds writ large were wars.

Even so, he worried about the way the children observed their parents' reactions, the way they were learning to accept defeat in a mode that was not altogether healthy. Of course, it was good that none except Ilya were drawn to seek revenge. At the same time, he noted the speed with which a spirit of dark resignation settled upon the other young people. Their tears spoke of some convulsion of their hearts deeper than anger, deeper than apathy. It was as if they were saying, *You see, beautiful things always get destroyed; our efforts come to nothing in the end, so why did we waste our time?*

This was a grievous thing to see on the face of childhood, and something in Alex revolted against it. He set to work immediately in an effort to offer a third alternative. The political negotiations and the psychology involved in marshaling the village, and especially in restoring the children's confidence, demanded considerable ingenuity. But his sheer doggedness convinced many to help him build a second and larger igloo higher up on the field. Throughout the remainder of the day, children and adults labored diligently but with none of the excitement that had been evident during the first project. Ilya arrived after the work had begun and threw himself into the task with fierce determination. Kiril worked with his usual cheer but was quieter than usual. Aglaya the Crow stood at the edge of the forest, leaning on her cane, fingering her chotki, watching them.

During all this period Irina remained in her room and did not come out, not even to make meals. Alex supposed that she was wrestling with her own alternatives: swinging between anger and discouragement. During breaks, Alex, Ilya, and Kiril rummaged in the kitchen for bits of bread and dried fish. Mostly they lived on tea. The sun had set by the time the new igloo was completed.

After supper, the people of Ozero Baikal gathered around with mixed emotions. They had worked long hours to re-create what had been so quickly destroyed. In every mind was the question: Will this also be destroyed?

The Pimonenkos had no more barn lanterns, and Irina refused to lend the house lanterns for the project. Volodya and Grig each brought pressure lanterns, which they said would cast much brighter light than the wick lamps. Several villagers brought candles as well.

Once again Dusya declared that Alex should light the lamps. He declined, explaining that he was just a visitor, and insisted that Ilya Pimonenko be the one. Ilya crawled into the tunnel. Lamps, candles, and matches were pushed in after him, and minutes later the igloo bloomed like soft stellar fire.

People cheered and clapped. The outburst was not as strong as on the previous two nights, nor did it stimulate hand holding or singing. But they stood for a long time admiring what they had done. Many arms were dropped beside thighs in the subconscious gesture of reverence. As the evening wore on, one by one the villagers drifted away.

"Ilya," Alex said, "let's go to the lake and see what our new snowhouse looks like from there."

"I'll come too, Aleksandr", Kiril piped.

"No, Kiril", Alex said firmly. "It's late. Go home and put yourself to bed."

The boy began to argue, but Ilya silenced him with a gesture. Huffing and pouting, Kiril stomped away in the direction of home.

Alex and Ilya walked side by side down onto the lake and struck directly east across the ice. Neither man nor boy said a word. About a hundred yards from shore, they turned around. Above was a vast field of stars, uncommonly sharp in the moonless sky. Below it was the black hulk of the Primorski range, and nestled at its bottom was the jewelry of Ozero Baikal crowned by a luminous blue sapphire burning in the upper field.

"Will it be destroyed?" Ilya asked.

"Tonight we will defend it."

"How?"

"Not with weapons, Ilya."

"How then?"

"We'll find a way."

This was greeted by silence.

After a time, Ilya mumbled, "I'm sorry."

"*Nichivo*", Alex replied evenly. "Let's just enjoy what we've made."

"Your nose." The boy's voice was low and shaken. "Is it all right now?"

"It's fine. That's a strong punch you have."

"You're strong also. I didn't know you were so strong."

"Thank you."

"I didn't mean what I said to you when I was fighting you. You're not an old woman."

791

"Thank you again", Alex laughed.

"You shouldn't laugh. I was wrong. I struck a guest, and you were only trying to help me."

"But some of what you said was true. I'm not your father. I can never replace him. I don't wish to replace him."

"Today you stood in his place and acted for him. That was good. I was stupid."

"Yet you recovered and did the right thing. Only a true man does this."

Ilya looked at him out of the corner of his eye.

"Your father would have been proud of you", Alex added.

"What do you mean?"

"Everyone makes mistakes in life. It takes courage to learn from our mistakes and to begin again. Today I saw you learning. It was hard for you, but you did it."

No more was said, and a few minutes later they walked back to the village.

That night Alex drifted off toward sleep with an ear cocked for sounds of attack. From time to time he heard men talking as they passed the clinic, and realized that villagers were taking turns standing guard over the igloo. Why they should do so for the sake of such a useless structure was inexplicable to Alex and perhaps was inexplicable to them as well. In the morning they reported that no incidents had occurred. No messages arrived from Listvyanka that day, nor during the following three days. Neither were there any further assaults on the igloo. Irina had emerged from her room on the morning after the fight with Ilya and made breakfast. From then on she made no reference to the conflict, and Alex assumed that she and her oldest son had worked out a reconciliation. Both of them acted as if nothing had happened.

He taught English vocabulary at the school for an hour each day and greatly enjoyed the children. Their distinctive personalities began to emerge, and thus he learned that the spectrum of human personality was universal, regardless of race and culture.

Following Irina's instructions, Alex spent two days shoveling manure into a long wooden barrow and rolling it on its iron wheel to the bare patch below the house. There he made heaps of "brown gold", as Volodya called it, and tried to spread it as evenly as possible over the snow-covered garden. In the afternoons he slept and read. Occasionally he succumbed to the irrational impulse to peer in the direction of the road to Listvyanka, along which no sleigh had yet come.

On the evening of the third day, Irina asked him to share a private cup of tea with her in the parlor.

"Aleksandr," she began on a serious note, "I want to reassure you that you're welcome here as long as you need us. But you should consider that there may be no response from your home. Communications in Russia are sometimes confused. It's possible your telephone messages didn't reach your friends. However, the postal system is usually reliable, and I suggest you try to contact them that way."

"It may take months to get a reply by that method."

"Yes, but if your telephone messages didn't reach your people, you would wait far longer to hear from them—forever, in fact. If such is the case, you're sitting here without purpose."

"Without purpose? Yes, it's true. I don't want to fool myself into thinking I'm anything but a drain on your resources. I feel very badly about it."

"Aleksandr, I expressed my suggestion poorly. Your presence has done us good. I mean to say that for your own good, for your own life to return to its proper place and purpose, you need to get the machinery moving that will return you there."

Alex sighed. "I suppose you're right, Irina. Until now I've kept hoping that just around the corner, the next hour, the next day, the next week, the money will come, the documents will turn up, the embassy will do what it's supposed to do. But nothing—I mean *nothing*—is happening. It's bizarre, as if I've become a nonperson like Aglaya the Crow."

She smiled with her old irony. "Perhaps you will never go home. If so, we will call you Aleksandr the Zimorodok."

"I would be honored by the title, Irina. But that would be an unsatisfying situation for all concerned."

"Why do you think so?" she said guardedly.

He hesitated before replying. "Because it's not easy for you to have me here."

She shrugged. "It's not a great difficulty."

"It's not easy for me either—to be here with you."

He used the intimate form of *you*, which conveyed his unmistakable meaning. She looked intently at him, betraying nothing, then dropped her eyes.

"You don't understand your motives", she said in a hushed voice, still not meeting his eyes.

"That's probably true", he answered in the same tone. "Can't we speak openly?"

"Speak openly? What do you want to speak openly about? A feeling? Feelings come and go."

"This feeling grows and grows—against my will. I didn't choose it. I didn't feed it. At every turn I seek to remove myself from your life, for I dread to think what I am to you."

She looked up curiously. "What do you think you are to me?"

"At worst a burden. At best a representative. You lost the real thing; nothing and no one will ever replace it."

"You don't understand me."

"I don't pretend to understand you. I'm saying only that I know I'm not Yevgeny and never can be."

"Then why speak of it at all?"

"Because..."

794

Because I love you, he thought, *and because I don't know how it happened that I have come to love you. And because I long for you to greet this word that rises in my heart and dare not hope for it. But if there is no hope for it, at least you will settle the question for me.*

"Aleksandr, what do you want me to say?" She stood and walked uneasily to the end of the parlor, where she pulled distractedly at the spines of books. "So you feel some interest. You feel some affection, maybe some attraction. Perhaps you tell yourself it's love. That's not unusual. But you don't know what you love. The girl on the train—did you love her also?"

"How can I deny it? You heard the outpouring of my infatuation."

"And now another feeling has come to you. How do you expect me to take it seriously?"

"I expect nothing from you."

Glancing at him, then looking away just as quickly, she returned to her seat. Folding her hands on her knees, she leaned forward and looked him earnestly in the eyes. She was about to say something, something important, when Ilya barged into the parlor. He nodded to his mother and went into his room. The house was so small that anything further Irina and Alex might say would be overheard.

"This is not Dr. Zhivago and Lara we're discussing", Alex whispered.

"I know", she replied sarcastically. "Neither are we Dr. Vera Gangart and poor Kostoglotov. Nor Prince Andrei and Natasha, nor Prince Myshkin and Nastasya, or any other of the fictional characters who populate the Russia of your imagination." She paused and looked briefly at the door to the boys' bedroom. "Ilyushka, are you there?"

"Of course I'm here, Mama."

"What are you doing?"

"Reading."

"Are you listening to us?"

"No."

No, but the boy closed the door to the bedroom with a thud.

Irina looked back at Alex. Switching to English, she said, "You're a fine man. And it would be a lie if I were to say I didn't like you. But you don't understand—"

"Irina, it's true I don't understand what has come upon me, but—"

"You fail to realize that the heart is unreliable."

"No one knows this better than I."

"Many a lover doesn't recognize that his beloved is a mirror in which he beholds himself."

"What do you mean?"

"You look at me and see someone who might love you, as once you were loved by your Carol. You don't seek *me*; you seek love itself."

"How can you speak with such certainty?"

She sat back, her face strained. "We shouldn't have begun to discuss this subject. It's useless. We're unintelligible to each other. We have no common language."

"Here we are, speaking together, and between us we have not one but two languages."

"You don't know my language."

Taken aback, Alex shook his head in perplexity.

"What I mean to say, Aleksandr, is that you don't know the language of a woman's heart."

"Perhaps you don't know the language of a man's heart. Shouldn't we try to establish what we mean by our vocabularies?"

"Poor Alik, you live in your head too much."

"Irina, you continually confuse me. I thought the problem at the moment is my living too much in my heart."

"But what do you *mean* by the heart? Can't you see that it's futile to attempt a common understanding of our vocabularies? We can arrive at no such agreement, you and I."

Alex threw up his hands in frustration. "Why not?"

"Because, if we were to arrive at an understanding of sorts, even then the words would mean two different things."

"Are the different meanings in opposition? A man's interpretation, a woman's interpretation—perhaps they complement each other."

"Such a thing is possible only when their love is more than the feelings of the *serdtse*."

"What if the feelings arise from the *glubina dushy*?"

"How would you know that's where they come from?"

"I don't know. And that's why speaking with you about it would help."

"Would it? And what of my heart? Do you think I am a lake of ice? The clinician, the technician?"

"No, of course not."

"And let me ask you, Aleksandr Graham, do you know what it would do to me if I were to confess that I am drawn to you, and like poor little creatures in a Pavlovian experiment we were to rush into each other's arms on signal, only to have you disappear from my life the moment you get a call from Listvyanka? Good-bye, Irina, you would say, it has been very nice knowing you, good-bye, good-bye, and thank you for the wonderful experience in an interesting and strange land; I especially enjoyed the exotic flavor of Russian love, but I have to go home now!"

"Irina, I—"

"No, don't come near me. Don't touch my hand like that. Please, do not be a Pavlovian, Aleksandr."

"Then what am I to do? You lock me in the Pavlovian maze of my heart with no escape—me in a male maze and you in a female maze!"

"For now my own maze is all I have. Don't make it more complicated."

"All right", Alex said in a hushed tone. "I won't make your life complicated."

They regarded each other for several seconds without speaking. Alex stood up.

"Where are you going?" Irina asked.

"I'm not sure."

"Don't walk to the Bering Sea."

"I won't. Where is Kiril? Probably guarding the snow-house. I'll go see if I can keep him company."

She followed him to the door. "Aleksandr, please try to understand me. I'm sorry for this conversation. I listened badly, and I spoke even more badly. What I want to say is that I am grateful for what you're doing for my sons and for the village. But we can't afford illusions. For almost a century my people have drunk deeply from a cup of illusions. We are a people of the broken heart, and I've had my share of it. I couldn't bear any more."

"Irina," he said, "the only whole heart is a broken one."

Her face fell and she turned away. He went outside and walked through the village under the stars, aching with confusion and grief.

Kiril was patrolling the igloo, chatting with his friends and a few of the village men. A dog was tied to a stake beside the tunnel, sitting on its haunches, salivating. Alex made small talk with the boy, taught him a few more English words, then retired to the clinic for the night. There he wrote letters to Jacob, Father Toby, and Owen Whitfield. Because he did not know their precise addresses, he addressed the envelopes with the names of their respective institutions and hoped that the post offices would have sense enough to find them.

Mixed into his other emotions was a degree of frustration. The smallest details of living here presented difficulties he had never given a second thought to in his native land: where to find postage stamps, what value they should be, how to repay Irina for them—and for the food, the shelter, the medicine, for everything. But he understood that his frustration was not really about the inconveniences of life. He was angry at himself, doubly angry, because he knew he should not be so upset by what were really only human reactions. He realized also that Irina was correct in her assessment of his "love" for her. She had every right to question it. On what was it based? What psychological, spiritual, social, or familial foundation was there for it? Why had it so suddenly appeared out of nowhere? By what stages of development had it arrived, full-blown, presumptuous, threatening to complicate her life? He had no answer to these questions, and thus he went to bed feeling hurt and did not sleep well.

The morning seemed to dawn earlier than it had throughout his stay in Ozero Baikal, but that was only another illusion. He had lived here for more than a month, and winter was nearing its end. The huge icicles on the ward window began to drip steadily in the early sun. Alex dressed and walked up to the field to inspect the igloo. There he found Volodya crawling out of the tunnel carrying his pressure lamp. The dog was scratching its ear with a hind leg.

"A pretty sight while it lasted", Volodya said. "Today will be warm, and the snowhouse will soon melt. Good thing we built it in the nick of time. But it's good to see spring too."

"It is, Volodya. Do you think it will melt today?"

"A thaw is overdue. Within a few weeks the lake will begin to break up. Then I can go fishing again."

"Is that your work?"

"Yes, I'm one of Baikal's fisher folk and a blessed man because of it. Though I lost my papa in a storm when I was young, and a son as well"—he crossed himself—"God has preserved me to a ripe old age."

"I'm sorry about your father and son. That is a grief."

"Oy, indeed a grief, and another grief. But one gets over things. Life goes on. And who can judge the hand of God? He gives; he takes away. Blessed be his name forever."

"Blessed be his name", Alex murmured, "forever."

Over breakfast Alex and the boys discussed the coming thaw. Irina was pleasant but neutral, as if the conversation of the night before had not occurred. Alex told her that he had written letters. She replied that this was good. If she heard of anyone going to the post office at Listvyanka, she would be sure to send his letters along. It was likely that someone would be going to town either today or tomorrow because the weather threatened to make the lake and bush impassable during the coming weeks.

Alex thanked her.

In Kolo's shed he found a hammer, a can of bent nails, and coils of rusty wire. With these he worked throughout the morning repairing the picket fence around the garden. In the yard by the shed Ilya and Kiril continued to cut logs into firewood. Irina was busy at the clinic, seeing to a mother and baby who had come to the village by sleigh, seeking a cure for the child's rash. Just before lunch Alex heard shouts coming from the clinic and hurried there to find out what was happening. He saw Dusya on the steps with a little girl in her arms, crying out that a dreadful accident had occurred. Irina stood in the open doorway listening to the barely coherent account. The girl was the child from the front row of the schoolroom, the one who had believed Alex fell from the sky. Her eyes were frightened, but not a sound came from her mouth. Blood dripped from a rip in the ankle of her boot.

"She was jumping around in the old snowhouse", Dusya wailed. "She stepped on the broken lamp chimney."

"Come inside", Irina said with professional calm.

Alex returned to the garden. At lunchtime he went into the kitchen and ate bread and soup with the boys. Irina arrived during the middle of the meal and sat down with a frown. "Five stitches", she said. "A brave girl, that little Lena. Not a cry from her. Dusya did all the crying. Now we see what these dreams, these hopes, do to us."

Though she resolutely stared out the window as she said this, Alex knew she was addressing him.

"Without dreams man would die", he said with a severity for which he was embarrassed the moment it was out of his mouth. "Dreams always have a cost."

"That is easy to say, Aleksandr Graham. Too easy. It is easiest to say when someone else pays the price for one's dream."

Ilya and Kiril cast nervous looks at their mother as they continued to spoon down the soup.

"You are right about that, Irina Filippovna", said Alex. "But is it sufficient reason to banish all dreams, all hopes?"

He stood abruptly, put on his coat, and went outside. In the shed he found a wooden hay fork, a battered iron shovel, and a tin bucket. Then he proceeded to the site of the old igloo. For half an hour he sifted through the debris and collected broken glass and stubs of candles. He put the bucketful of garbage in the shed and replaced the tools. After that he went to the school, where he taught the children more words. He also told them a story he made up on the spot. From what inner storage chamber it was drawn, he did not know, for the tale grew of its own accord. Ilya and Kiril came in and took their places just as he was beginning. And this is the story he told:

A long time ago, in the barren lands of the north, there was a village by the name of Zimorodok, for it seemed to the people that there was no other season than winter. From time out of mind it had been called that, and none living had ever seen a true summer, or spring or autumn. They were the

Winter-Born. They had no word for summer, which was only a few weeks long. They called it the "lesser winter". Nor did they any longer recall the meaning of the word *born*, for no people had been born to them for seventy-five years. But they were hardy and very long-lived, and the oldest remembered the songs and dancing of children, for they had once been children themselves. The memory was now so dim that they believed it was a dream that time had proved to be unreal.

Only the animals gave birth, and the people believed that was because the poor creatures were ignorant and did not understand that life was cruel and always winter. Chief among the animals known to that people were the reindeer. Their hides were red and their antlers silver. The people of Zimorodok herded them and milked them, and used their skins for clothing, and their long antlers for the ribs of their shelters, which they covered with the red fur.

Save for a few weeks a year, when the sun circled in the heavens and did not set, snow was always upon the surface of the land. During the lesser winter, however, the snow melted away, revealing rocks and thin soil and a bitterly cold river. Sometimes they pulled fish from it. Both man and beast scratched at the lichen that continued to grow on the rocks, and at the little shrubs and berries that grew on the low hills, where the sun beat longest each day. From the lichen the people made a bitter tea that they called *luna chay*—moon tea. From the berries they made a sour mash that tasted very sweet to them. They called it *svezda krem*—star cream. The reindeer grazed on the blue moss of the mountain glens. Leaf and berry were white or silver, and no other color was known among the people save the red of blood, which was the color of life, the life of the warm-blooded.

Always the sun dipped again below the line of the earth; lower and lower it went until the night fell and the light did not rise for many months. During that time the people remained in their shelters eating meat and burning the fat of the deer in stone lamps. They told tales about small people who came out of the flesh of their ancestors. The small people (children, they were called) danced and sang, though no one recalled what a dance or a song really was—it was a legend, very old. But the people preserved the legend, though they did not understand why they must keep it from being lost. It was a custom of theirs that they did not question. Nor did they ask themselves why they existed. It was enough to live; they assumed they had always lived this way.

There were some among the Winter-Born who believed that the times of the people were drawing to a close. They asked themselves and each other what purpose they had.

"The End is near", said many. "One by one we are dying, and none replace us."

But the eldest among them asked, timidly at first, then with growing boldness, if perhaps the legend was more than a legend. Was it not possible that one day they would discover other people on the earth? If the Winter-Born were to conquer new lands and peoples—peoples with strength and fertility in their marrow—new life might return. The blood of some would be spilled in battle, but afterward the blood of two peoples would be mingled into one and strengthened. Then small people might come out of their flesh again. But this was greeted by scorn. It was an imagining, because as everyone knew, no other people lived on the earth.

The oldest among them recalled an ancient legend that told of a race living beyond the mountains to the east, which none of the Winter-Born had ever seen. There, by a sea of ice in a land that was forever dark, there dwelled a tribe who lived, as did the people of Zimorodok, by herding reindeer, though both they and their herds were less in number, for the moss was not as thick in that region. Their reindeer were blue with brass antlers, which was very strange—unthinkable, really—for deer, as everyone knew, were red with silver antlers. No one took the legend seriously, though it was pleasant to think of it from time to time.

Then came a year more bitterly cold than any in living memory. The lesser winter did not come, and the river of the taiga froze down to its stony bed. No fish could be pulled from it, for the fish had frozen solid in their prison of ice. The snow fell so deep that reindeer could not forage; they grew thin and died in great numbers. The wind ripped across the land, uprooting the dead tumble bushes that the Winter-Born called "steppe witches". Night and day the witches rolled across the snow whispering their curses and lies.

"Die, die", they hissed. "You will die, you will die; there is no hope for you."

The people grew thin. Though they ate the corpses of the fallen deer, there was no fat upon the flesh; it was tough and poor in nourishment. One by one, the people sickened. Some died.

Then they remembered the old legend about a land on the far side of the mountains.

"It is nothing but a dream", they said at first. Later, they began to mutter among themselves, "Perhaps we are wrong. Maybe the dream is more than a dream. We should go there and see for ourselves."

"No," cried many voices, "it is a false hope, and if we should arrive there only to find that our hope is illusion, then we shall be worse for it. We will have exhausted ourselves for nothing and cast our hearts into a deeper darkness."

But one of them objected: "Is it not better to seek a hopeless dream than to lie down and die without struggle? For surely we are now bound to die unless we seek for what is not among us."

Thus did the Winter-Born sharpen their spears of silver antler bone, and make bows and arrows for themselves of ivory and sinew, and dress themselves in their red furs. When they were ready, they set out as one body into the east.

Night and day they traveled across the snowfields. The pinwheel of the stars revolved upon its allotted path until the people became dizzy with its motion. Yet they kept to their course, drawing ever closer to a shadow climbing over the horizon. And when the silver ball of the moon soared up over the rim of the world, they saw that the shadow was not a shadow but a great formation in the earth, a wall of stone robed in white, stretching from north to south. It was the Mountains of the Moon. Closer and closer they came, until the mountains loomed high above them.

They craned their necks in order to see its crests, and suddenly they noticed far above, among the stars, two mighty creatures locked in mortal combat, their swords flashing back and forth. One of the creatures was tall, bright, and brave; the other was dark, subtle, and cunning. No sound did the warriors make, though their weapons swung in great arcs through the heavens, clashed, and swung again and again, knocking the night planets this way and that, sparking them, shooting flaming comets across the sky. Some fell to the earth, where they sizzled out in the snow.

The people continued to walk, the land sloping upward under their feet as they entered the foothills. So intent were they upon the battle above their heads that they gave no thought to where they were going. Higher and higher they went, until at last they came to an alpine glen ringed by peaks. To their surprise, they saw that on the far side of this bowl a pass opened to the eastern slopes of the range. And there they saw another group of people heading toward the west, on a course that would bring both parties into direct contact in the center of the glen.

Cries of alarm arose from the Winter-Born. Cries also arose from the people in the eastern pass. Then all cries fell silent as both races faced each other at a distance—equally amazed and equally frightened they were.

"There *are* other people on the earth!" the Winter-Born exclaimed, trying to gather their courage. "They are the East-Born, and very fierce they look. See their blue armor and their weapons of brass! How terrible they are; how our hearts fail within us at the sight of them! We must build a fortress!" they cried.

Thus, in great haste, the people, hundreds strong, built for themselves a snow kremlin and huddled inside it, peering over the battlements to see what the East-Born would do.

To their surprise, they saw that the East-Born had also made a kremlin. At the head of the pass it stood, so that the Winter-Born could not proceed into the east, nor the East-Born proceed into the west. Day after day they watched each other. From time to time the fiercest among both parties sortied forth from the walls of their kremlins and roared and shook their weapons in the face of the enemy. Terrible were those cries, fearful to the ear and the heart. On both sides terror of the other increased without respite. The moon bathed the red garments and the blue garments, making them appear magical and sinister. The weapons on both sides glinted with menace.

Unbeknownst to each other, the peoples had come to the same decision: upon the next rising of the moon, they would attack. The East-Born intended to sweep all aside in their journey to the west, which they believed to be warm and rich in food, and the Winter-Born determined to break through the pass into the east, which they believed to be warm and rich in food.

There came at last a night when the moon rose in full. Both armies poured out of their kremlins and rushed toward each other. But because both were equally frightened and equally hungry and fatigued, they stopped in two great tides, facing each other a hundred paces apart.

Then occurred what neither side expected. A trumpet blast echoed from the heavens, and so terrible was it that both armies fell to their knees and covered their faces with their hands. The trumpet blew once, and only once. Then a silence filled the cold air of the mountains, so that both sides heard only the sound of each other's breath.

"The East-Born are breathing", came the thought to the minds of the Winter-Born. "They are men like us and are frightened too. Hear their hearts pounding hard."

The same was in the thoughts of the East-Born: "Listen to those people from the west", they thought. "Their breath and their heartbeats are like ours. They are as frightened as we are."

Into that stillness a greater sound now came. All recognized it as the steps of a reindeer. So loud was it that all knew it must be the father of all deer upon the earth. Looking about in search of it, neither Winter-Born nor East-Born could see a thing.

Then a shape appeared on the highest peak. It was a stag of immense proportions, noble and fierce upon the height. Its antlers were neither silver nor brass, its hide neither red nor blue. It was of purest white, so dazzling that it outshone the moon. It leaped from crag to crag, descending to the glen in mighty bounds until it stood in the midst of them.

On both sides the thought was in every heart, "See this terrible creature, greater than both peoples. Surely it will destroy us! We must strike it, lest it leave no man alive."

The great stag stood motionless, waiting, and starlight was in its eyes. It looked neither to the left nor to the right. It braced its legs and lifted its long neck and rack of antlers, and a trumpet blast bellowed from its throat.

Overcome with frenzied terror, the people of east and west leaped to their feet and hurled their spears and shot the bolts from their bows, and the creature took it all into its flesh.

Blood spurted from its many wounds, and it fell to its knees, then crashed onto its side and lay still.

The peoples of east and west came running forward to see the creature they had killed. As they gathered about it, they gasped in amazement at its great beauty and strength, yet dismay filled them, for they wondered why it had stood between them and taken such wounds upon itself when it could have defeated them without effort.

One by one the people came forward to touch its sides, to put fingers into the wounds that were running with rivulets of crimson blood. They gazed at each other also, their eyes meeting across the hill of the creature's body and through the branches of antlers as thick as mighty birch trees.

Then they saw that the eyes of their enemy were like their own, their faces no different from theirs. The pity and indignation welling from their hearts was the same. Shame filled them. They fell to their knees, all, without exception—east and west they grieved.

With that, another trumpet sounded. A shiver ran across the hide of the stag. The white trees on his noble head shook and lifted, and the creature lived. He stood up on his four great legs and looked slowly to the east and to the west. None could meet his eyes. Then he turned and walked to the north. When he had parted the sea of men, he stopped and looked back at them, and they understood that they must follow him.

And this they did. Red and blue flowed together behind him, silver and brass dropped into the snow, all hands were empty, all hearts full of wondrous fear. Higher and higher they went to the rim of the glen, and came to another pass that they had not seen until then. The stag entered into a cleft in the rock, and went on, drawing the people after him.

On he went through a ravine as wide as a river, flanked on both sides by canyons that soared up from the earth as far as the heavens. The air grew warmer. The darkness seemed to lessen a little, though the stars did not dim. As they followed the great creature, the people blended, the colors of their garments mingled and were no longer strange to each other. And they whispered among themselves.

"Is the west warm and full of food?" asked the East-Born.

"No, it is cold, and we are starving", came the reply. "And what of the east? Is it warm there, and do you have enough to eat?"

"No, it is always night, and we have no food", the East-Born replied.

And none doubted that this was true.

On and on they went, until at last the sky above was flushed with mother-of-pearl, and the stars grew dim and winked out. The canyon widened, and its floor began to descend. The air grew warmer still, until the people were forced to drop their fur garments, red and blue, beside the trail. Underfoot there was no longer any snow, only thick moss.

At last they came to an opening where the canyons drew apart as if they were gates, and the people entered a valley unlike any they had ever seen. It was bathed in a golden light and filled with luminous mists, and the sounds of running water could be heard on every side. Silver fish leaped in the streams, and beside the path were plants of many kinds, all of a color never before seen by the eyes of men—it was the blending of sunlight and skylight, and its name was "green". And upon all those myriad green things, there appeared flowers of many other new colors, and the stag spoke into the minds of men the names of those colors.

Then a warm wind blew and the mists dissolved, and before the eyes of everyone there appeared a wondrous sea. Beside the sea there were fields and houses of wood and stone. And along its shore were slender boats and fishing nets. And all about was a forest of mulberry trees, and limes and larches and pines perfuming the air.

At the edge of the water, the stag halted and turned to face the peoples. He lifted his head and trumpeted a blast that shimmered through all blood and stone and waters and set the forest swaying as if in a dance.

"This is your home", cried the stag. "Here you will learn to sing and dance and love one another. And if you learn what I would have you learn, many are the peoples and nations that will flow from you; born from your flesh, they will push back all the northern void, rebuke the darkness, and cover the earth with rejoicing."

With that, the stag turned and walked into the water, and as it departed from the people, they wept and stretched out their arms toward it, pleading with it to come back to them, but it did not. Then the golden light filled their eyes, and the sounds of brooks and wind filled their ears. Their tears turned to laughter and their cries to songs. The stag disappeared into the light of the sun, and his going from them was no longer a death but a promise of return.

Alex stepped back into the winter world. The younger children's eyes were staring into space, their thoughts focused inward, trying to absorb the meaning of the tale. The older ones observed him somberly.

Dusya Lukasheva heaved a deep sigh and got to her feet. She gave a single clap with her hands. The students startled and blinked.

"Thank you, Aleksandr Khrim", she said, and wiped a tear from her eye.

When the children emerged from the school, they jumped from the porch and ran in every direction, shouting and laughing. Games spontaneously erupted, undirected, disorderly, and great fun. A version of the snowball fights universal in all northern regions of the world now broke out, and everyone joined in. As on the day when they had built the first igloo, the battle raged with a certain ferocity but without malice. Alex was pelted by everyone, which he interpreted as their highest gesture of friendship.

Patches of brown grass had appeared in the field. The lanes were showing signs of turning to mud. The new igloo still stood in the sun, but even as the fight raged about it, the dome whispered and sagged. Voices called children home to supper by the time the play had run its course. As Alex waved good-bye to them, the top of the igloo collapsed, and seconds later half of its wall fell inward.

"No matter", said Ilya, coming up beside him. "It was good we made it."

"Was it worth it?"

"Yes", the boy said, nodding, then turned for home.

33. *A Cadre of One*

After supper, with Ilya and Kiril deep in concentration over their chess game at the kitchen table, Irina asked Alex if he would join her in the parlor. They brought their cups of tea along and sat for a few moments in silence.

"Aleksandr, while you were at school today, a sleigh left for Listvyanka. It may be the last journey for weeks to come. I sent your letters with the driver. If this warm weather continues, the bush will be impassable until the snow is gone, and the lake treacherous until the ice recedes."

"More waiting", said Alex. "An answer will be a long time in coming. I'll try to make myself useful until then, but you must think of more tasks for me to do."

"There's no lack of tasks in this house and always something to repair. But you should be careful with your skull a while longer."

She asked him for details about his health, and his answers reassured her that he was healing well.

After the passage of a few more minutes, she said, "I regret our conversation the other night."

"So do I", he answered.

"I was tired and worried. And so were you. Things were said—"

"True things were said. There's no need to retract them. It may have saved us both a good deal of unnecessary pain."

"How objective you are this evening", she said with a faint show of humor.

"You also, Irina Filippovna."

"Then there are no hard feelings?"

"None. It's all for the best."

She laughed, and he could not resist joining her.

"Why are we laughing?" she said.

"I don't know. Maybe because we're ridiculous. We're children one day and wise old people the next; then it's back to childhood the day after."

"Always changing. Tell me, Aleksandr Graham, what were you like as a youth?"

"What do you think I was like?"

"Are you asking for a diagnosis? Well, as a *scientist* I would not know how to collate the data I have observed into a theorem, but as a *person* I would say you were a boy who wandered alone on the mystical heights of your land, reading Shakespeare—that's right, isn't it? Shakespeare is your Pushkin?"

"No, they're very different, and I didn't read much Shakespeare when I was young. However, I did read our Romantic poets. As for the heights, you're correct. How did you know?"

"It was easy. Romantics are the same everywhere."

"Was Yevgeny a romantic?"

Her face grew solemn. "In a way. He loved science, medicine, knowledge. But there was another side of him, the part you saw in his journal. The part of him that didn't want to leave Baikal."

"Did he climb the mystical heights of your land?"

"Yes, in fact, he did. He liked to hike in the summer to the crest of the Primorskis, but always alone. In this regard he was like you—a solitary person. Yet he dreamed of taking his sons with him one day. He talked of climbing with them to the peaks of Khamar-Daban when they were older. He dreamed of this to the end, even as he was dying, even when he knew for certain that he would never go there with them."

"The mountains meant a great deal to him."

"I think they were a symbol. He said a strange thing before he died. He told me I must pass it on to Ilya and Kiril when they became men." Irina rubbed a hand across her forehead. "I had forgotten that", she said abstractly. "How easily we forget our promises. Now it comes back to me."

"What did he want you to pass on to his sons?"

"He said, 'Tell my sons that they must always keep a distant mountain in their hearts. Always they must lift their eyes to it, especially when it is impossible to go there.' I understand the sentiment, of course. But why did he want to pass *this* on to them? Why especially this, when so many other things were left unsaid?"

"They're the words of a psalm—from the Scriptures."

She shook her head. "I didn't know. That's interesting."

"Psalm 121", Alex said.

"Oh", she replied.

Shaking off a looming sadness, she leaned forward and said, "Aleksandr, I have a favor to ask of you."

"Ask it. Ask anything."

"When the water is open sometime around the beginning of May, I go by boat to teach my spring classes at the medical college in Irkutsk. I'll be gone three weeks. If you still have not heard back from your homeland, would you be willing to remain here during that time and keep an eye on the boys? Usually it's Aglaya who moves in and feeds them and scolds them, but this year for some reason she refuses. She claims she's getting too old for it and they too unruly."

He hesitated, torn between his desire to help her and his longing for home.

"Of course I can stay", he said at last. "It's a small thing compared to what you've done for me. But will the boys be willing to submit, I wonder?"

"I think so. Kiril will offer no resistance, though he'll try to manipulate the situation with his charm. Ilya may be rude and willful, but there's no guile in him. Which of the two approaches do you find more difficult?"

"Ilya's, actually. He's so much bigger than Kiril, and stronger. I don't think I could survive another fistfight."

"Fistfight?" she said with a note of alarm. "Did you and Ilya have a fight?"

"Uh, that was a poor choice of terms. We had a disagreement. It was a good experience for us both. The worst that happened was Ilya fell into the manure pile."

She peered at Alex suspiciously. "He can be stubborn."

"So can I."

"Well, if you think you can put up with his moods and get along together, I'll go to Irkutsk in peace. But it won't be smooth waters, I warn you. My oldest hasn't been himself lately. "

"Is it the presence of the guest that makes him difficult?"

"No, this has been coming on for a long time, since he was fourteen or fifteen. Anger is growing in him, frustration, insecurity. I really don't know what's going to become of him."

"Irina, have you considered moving to the city? Ilya and Kiril are both intelligent and would do well there. Forgive me for intruding in your private family matters, but it seems to me that their futures are somewhat limited here in Baikal."

"Yes and no. In one way, they're deprived of Irkutsk cultural life and education. But in another way, they're protected here. Drugs, vodka, gangs, the rootlessness of youth in modern Russia—these are widespread. One day we hope to save enough money to make a trip back west, perhaps even to find a place for ourselves in Moscow. Until then—"

"Until then, poverty keeps you here. But are you really as trapped as you think? You teach at a medical college, and that must mean you're respected in your field. Couldn't you open a medical practice in Irkutsk or Novosibirsk, where you could make a better living?"

"That would be true in North America, but here doctors are underpaid when they are paid at all. Openings in hospitals are few. In Baikal we have benefits that money cannot buy: we have a community that cares about us, fresh air and food, a house of our own, a little garden, books, and friendship. And we have the lake. I realize that before too long these won't be enough for my sons, and they'll leave, but our remaining years together will be well spent. I want to keep them here as long as possible, so that when they go out to find their place in the new Russia, they'll have a foundation that's strong and healthy. They'll remember the beautiful sea, the mountains, and the faces of honest people."

"When the time comes for them to leave, how will they do it?"

"We'll find a way. For the moment we're hemmed in by circumstances. But don't pity us, Aleksandr, for we're among the most fortunate in Siberia."

"If I may be so bold, Irina, I think there's another reason you remain here. You've made a decision to serve the people. If you were to leave, they would have little access to medical services. Some would even die."

"Yes, some would die. But there is no need to be dramatic. Wherever people live, people also die."

"You project indifference. Yet you've chosen to stand firm as a bulwark between life and death."

"Life costs", she said. "Life always costs. Surely you know this."

"I think I'm learning it. Now it's my turn to ask a question: What were you like as a young woman?"

"What there is to know is in Yevgeny's notes. He saw me accurately. We met when I was in my early twenties. My parents, all my family, are now dead. I was an only child. My grandmother taught me many things. She was a believer, but didn't advertise it, for reasons you can well imagine. She gave me a sense of moral order in the universe. As a child I accepted what she told me because all around me I saw what happens when people do not accept it. By the time I finished high school, half of my friends had committed suicide. Others killed themselves slowly, with alcohol, drugs, frenzied love affairs. Is the universe a Christian universe? I don't know. But I saw a lot as I was growing up. I learned that whenever a person refuses to live according to moral laws, love cannot survive."

"But surely the existence of those laws points to God."

"Does it? How can I know that? I cannot know it. There is no empirical evidence for a primary cause, only the existence of the natural laws. For all we know, they've come into existence as a purely biological mechanism."

"If it's just biology, why does love exist? Love isn't necessary for survival of the species."

"Perhaps human love is an advanced mechanism for the perpetuation of a more complex organism."

"Was Yevgeny nothing more than a complex organism?"

She did not answer.

Pressing his case, Alex went on: "If we're only organisms, why not rush into each other's arms like Pavlovian test animals?"

"Don't be absurd. Here we go again, Aleksandr. Straining our eyes to see beyond the range of human vision. If you peer at the moon long enough, you'll see cities on the mountains of the moon and whales swimming in its seas, but if you were to go there, you'd find a handful of dust."

"So, you're saying we should just be content with our world and not raise our eyes to the heavens."

"Raise your eyes if you wish, but do not hallucinate, do not project a country in the sky that's not really there, for then you'll become unable to function in the country that does exist."

"There's a half-truth in what you say, Irina. Of course, man must care for the soil in which his feet have been planted. But if it's *only* the soil, without a higher vision of the meaning of his life, what then?"

"He finds some reason to live."

"But how can he escape the myth that he is nothing but a product of the soil, destined to fertilize it with his own flesh? And if he's only fertilizer, what stands in the way of killing him, if the garden needs enrichment by some blood? Isn't the history of your country an illustration of what can happen when this lie rules?"

"You asked what I was like when I was young", she said, abruptly changing the subject. "Well, I'll tell you. I wasn't always like the fine young lady in Yevgeny's notes, the dedicated academic. Before I went to university, I was every bit as charming and guileful as Kiril and every bit as ferocious as Ilya."

"That's hard to imagine. You seem such an even-tempered person."

"Of all the Russians you've met so far, none resembles me more than Sonia."

"Sonia on the horse?"

"The very one."

"Sonia the destroyer and temptress?"

Irina laughed. "I didn't destroy igloos. Nor did I break the hearts of young men—well, not so many. Nor did I seduce or let myself be seduced."

"So far you haven't described anything like wildness."

"No? How can I tell you what I was like? When I think of the way I was, I seem like another person."

"I'm sorry, Irina; you'll have to be more descriptive."

She smiled. "If I were to describe my adolescence, you would interpret it according to your Western eyes."

"My apologies, but they're the only eyes I've got."

"If I were to tell you that I was a rebellious youth, you would think one of two things: either that I was immoral or that I was a heroic dissident, or perhaps a combination of both. But I was neither. If I were to tell you what I was, I wonder if you would believe me."

"Please, continue."

"In Moscow I lived with my family on a street just off Dzerzhinsky, near the Lubyanka prison. As a child I used to pass by that big yellow stone building and look at the barred windows, heedless of what was going on inside. Big men in leather coats were always going in and out of it. I thought I had nothing to fear from them. When I was fifteen and was pressured to join the Communist youth organization, my father begged me not to join. I insisted that I would join because the Komsomol was the way to get ahead in the world. It was then that he told me the story of our family.

"My father was an electrician. We lived in a two-room apartment on the fifth floor of a tenement. He was a little man in the eyes of the world, and I'm ashamed to say that as I grew from childhood into early adolescence I didn't respect him. When I compared him to the strong, handsome men who hung around the entrances of the Lubyanka, he seemed to shrivel in my eyes. I thought he was a coward.

"When I told my parents that I would be joining the Komsomol, their faces went white with terror. I was baffled by their reaction. Why terror? I asked myself. My grandmother threw herself on the bed and wept for hours. This infuriated me. Their behavior was idiotic, irrational. Then my father told me that his father had died in the Lubyanka and that I was proposing to join the party that had killed him. My grandfather had been an artist. He was not a great painter but a competent one. I've never been able to find his work in the galleries of Moscow. Perhaps there's something of his in the museums of Saint Petersburg; I don't know.

"I shouted in my father's face, 'Why would the state kill an artist? He must have done something terribly wrong!'

"My father looked into my eyes as if I were an alien creature. Then he told me the whole story. In the 1930s, my grandfather was a teacher at the Moscow Art Institute. In private he painted canvases that would have gotten him into trouble with the secret police, but he hid them well. How he survived those years, I cannot begin to guess. He had always succeeded in avoiding scrutiny, perhaps because he was a very insignificant man, a man of gentle temperament who kept his head down and his mouth closed.

"In 1935 he and many other artists were commissioned to paint portraits of Stalin. These weren't very good pictures; they were just for hanging in the offices of bureaucrats in the ministries. He merely copied from photographs. One day, however, he made the mistake of crossing Dzerzhinsky Square carrying an unfinished portrait of Stalin under his arm. He had fallen behind in his painting schedule and was bringing it home to work on at night. He was tired and distracted, and thoughtlessly he carried it upside down. As he passed the Lubyanka, an NKVD agent noticed this and stopped him. He demanded an explanation. He wanted to know if Grandfather was trying to insult the General Secretary. Was he using his art as a veiled attempt to call for the downfall of Stalin?

"My poor grandfather was a man of nervous disposition. He stuttered as a habit, and under the cold eye of the police it grew worse. So suspicious did he appear that he was hauled inside the prison and put through an interrogation. They let him go three days later, unharmed but badly shaken. Really, only the vilest and most paranoid of people would read into a little man's absentmindedness a sinister counterrevolutionary act. But from then on they kept an eye on him. Every Saturday for the next four years, my grandfather was forced to return to the Lubyanka and undergo another 'interview'.

Each time, he had to write out a statement explaining why he had been carrying a portrait of Stalin turned upside down through the streets of Moscow.

"Then in 1938 Beria became head of the secret police and launched another wave of the Great Purge. Historians now say more than seven million were killed during those purges. In 1939 it swept into its net fresh catches, famous Communists and countless small people who, regardless of guilt or innocence, had somehow gotten their names on a list. My grandfather was arrested and executed—his body disposed of, we don't know where.

"This was the story my father told me in the autumn of 1970, when I was fifteen years old. Not a word of this had he shared with me during my childhood. I hadn't known who I was, you see. I had suspected nothing. Now my world was turned upside down. Some of my friends at school had learned similar revelations about the pasts of their families and despised them for it. Strangely, the revelation of my own past had the opposite effect on me.

"I began to think. I began to look at the world with new eyes. Anger grew in me. Of course, I was every bit as ideologically conditioned as my classmates, but from then on my doubts about our government and our way of life in Russia just grew and grew. It seemed to me that there was something not right about killing an artist. It was like killing a summer bird because it dared to sing in winter without the permission of the state. If the state did those things, then the state might be wrong about many things.

"What finally broke the chains that encompassed my mind was not so much the story as it was something my father gave to me that year, shortly after I learned about our past. When I had made a final decision not to join the Communists, he gave me a painting. He took a terrible risk in giving it to me, because I was, to tell the truth, rather unreliable. One evening, while my mother and grandmother looked on, he pulled my grandmother's bed away from the wall and cut into the wallpaper with a knife. Behind it was a well-plastered hole. He cut through the plaster and pulled out a section of wall board, revealing a narrow, dusty space. My father said it hadn't been opened since the day Grandfather was first arrested. There were three paintings inside. One was an old icon of Christ; the second was a painting of the Monastery of the Holy Trinity at Zagorsk, north of Moscow. Grandfather was born in a village near the *lavra*. He had wanted to be a monk when he was young, but the Revolution had swept all that away. He was no longer a believer, but he had painted the memory so that he wouldn't forget its beauty. Beauty was his religion, and painting was its liturgy.

"The third image was very small, a tiny masterpiece, and it was this my father gave to me. Would you like to see it?"

"Very much", Alex said, leaning forward.

Irina went into her bedroom and returned a moment later with the painting. It was unframed, about eight inches square. She put it into Alex's hands and sat down, watching his reaction.

Deceptively simple, it was a bird rising out of a fire. The bird's tail was singed by the flames, its upper parts illumined by a golden sun that hung suspended in a deep blue sky. The tail feathers were black, the body indigo, shimmering into turquoise at the head. Every element in the composition surged upward—the devouring flames, the beating wings, the fearful yearning in the bird's posture. The meaning was obvious: *Will it escape?*

Irina reached over and turned the canvas so that Alex could see the back. Inscribed on the stretcher frame in tiny Cyrillic letters were the words "*Svoboda*. Moskva 1932." It was unsigned.

"What kind of bird is this, Irina?"

"Not a bird that I know of. Do you suspect it's a kingfisher?"

"I did wonder."

"That would be consistent with your symbolic tendencies. No, it's merely a beautiful bird. I've often wondered why it wasn't a specific species. I think my grandfather wished to make an embodiment of all winged creatures that seek freedom in the skies. Tell me what you see in it. Does it escape the flames?"

"That is what I hope."

Again she nodded. Alex continued holding it in his hands, lost in a confusion of meanings and chronologies.

"What happened after your father gave it to you?" he said at last.

"He put the other two paintings inside the hole, replastered the joints, covered it with the old paper, and pushed the bed against the wall. Then he scraped the title from the back of the painting and said to me, 'If you're ever questioned about this, you're to say it's a phoenix. It's nothing more than a phoenix, a bird in an old story the Greeks made up. Its title is *Phoenix*. There's nothing political about a phoenix.' When Yevgeny and I first came to Baikal, I repainted the words exactly as I had seen them that day in Moscow. I hadn't forgotten them."

"Its true title is *Svoboda*—Freedom. A very political title."

"Very."

"This still doesn't explain how you became a wild girl."

"Oh, but it does. From then on, I decided that the world was a web of deception. Only science, I believed, escaped the flames of falsehood. So I began to concentrate on sciences, and as a result my studies soared. I was obsessed with learning, and I earned the highest marks in my school. But in secret I was also obsessed by a desperate search to escape the confinements of my world. Little by little I pieced together hidden facts. I figured out that Russia was held captive by the most catastrophic lie in history and that this lie had corrupted practically everything within her borders, and now she sought to spread the lie to every corner of the world.

"By then I was fifteen, almost sixteen, and mad with rage, horror, fear. My friends, to whom I confided little of this transformation, began to disappear from my life. Suicide, as I said before, was epidemic. None of it was reported in the papers or on television. It was just a fixture of everyday life, a continuous, growing trend. One week a friend would cut her wrists; the next month, another would jump into the Moskva; the following year, another would throw herself on the tracks of the metro. And to tell you the truth, Aleksandr, I don't think any of them really understood why they were doing it. Life had simply become meaningless, and the pain of existence unbearable.

"I was determined not to end like them. I fought everything. I thwarted my parents at every turn. I humiliated them often. I was awful, Aleksandr. Their only consolation was that I hadn't become a Communist. I was especially good at attracting young Communist boys and breaking their hearts. This gave me much pleasure. I tore posters from walls, threw bundles of *Pravda* and *Izvestia* into the river. I set fire to buildings. I—"

"You set fire to buildings?" Alex interrupted.

"Yes, me, the person you now see before you."

"Astounding", Alex shook his head. "Were you never caught?"

"Never. I am very clever."

"I noticed."

"I don't want you to get the impression that I burned down apartment buildings or anything like that. I chose carefully. I set fire to the offices of various small Communist organizations. I always made sure they were places that were empty at night, where no one lived. I didn't want people to get hurt. I wanted to hurt the organization—as a sign that the Russian people could still make their voice heard."

"Do you think your activities had any effect?"

"Articles appeared in the newspapers about arsonist hooligans. But I suppose fire was more of a private symbol. Horribly naïve, of course. I fell into the old trap of thinking destruction was regeneration. I failed to understand that this was precisely the thinking that had ruined Russia. I was merely substituting one form of tyranny for another." She sighed. "The list of my clandestine crimes is long. I needn't bore you with them."

"You won't bore me."

"I considered myself a revolutionary, though of course if I had been caught, I would have been classified as a counterrevolutionary. I gave myself a secret name—*Svoboda*, head of the revolutionary cadre Phoenix. A cadre with one member! I lived a double life for several years. I was slightly insane, a cross between Rosa Luxemburg, Anna Akhmatova, and an Amazon woman. By day I was a model Soviet student, sitting primly in class taking notes. By night I became an amateur anarchist. No, don't look at me that way, Aleksandr. I know how utterly ridiculous and improbable it sounds, but that's the way it was. Much of it I regret, because it was really just an adolescent tantrum."

"A highly dangerous tantrum."

"Yes, but worse than the danger of prison was what it did to my personality. If I hadn't gotten over it, I might have become genuinely unbalanced."

"You think you weren't?"

Irina laughed. "I mean *severely*, permanently unbalanced. The degree of my madness can be measured by how readily I dropped it all when I first saw Yevgeny."

"How readily?"

"Instantly. When I first encountered him at the university, I fell in love. Not that we spoke, not that he even noticed me—it was a year before we were introduced. But I seemed to know him in my heart the moment I saw him. I knew that there would never be another. And when that happened, I wanted to live, to live by his side forever. And as soon as I realized this, I understood a second thing: that I had been trying to kill myself. I was a bird trying to escape the flames, but because I was convinced I could never escape, I had tried to destroy as much as possible. I knew that I couldn't destroy the entire system, but I had thought that if there were a thousand crazy girls like me, we would make a difference. But when I saw him, that ended. I discovered another path out of the flames."

"Love."

"Yes. Even in prison love is freedom—and our nation was one gigantic prison at the time."

"His journal indicates that you treated him rather distantly."

"Yes, that's true. You see, I realized I didn't know how to love. I couldn't have endured the typical thing that goes on among the young, the attracting and seducing, possessing and discarding. I let him be the one to make the first move. For a year after I first saw him, he didn't know I existed. Then we were introduced by the man he calls Academician Z in his journal. From then on we became friends. Though both of us were soon in love, neither of us would tell the other. We waited. We couldn't bear to use the usual methods of securing an object of affection. I doubt he knew how. I knew very well how, but I knew also that to use these methods would kill the freedom that love needs. Though we saw each other infrequently at first, he was a presence that steadily expanded until he seemed to fill my whole world. Everything that was horrible about our country faded into the background. He was on this earth with me, and even if I were to lose him, I would at least have the joy of knowing of his existence. And as a result, our love deepened. There were moments of despair when we misread the signals, but in the end love conquered."

"Was it the same process for him, do you think?"

"Similar, as similar as the differences between male and female hearts will allow. But always he valued freedom—my freedom. So much so that we very nearly did not speak of our love and might even have lost each other altogether. Of course, in the end this made it so much more wonderful. I hadn't suspected such happiness was possible."

Still gazing down at the painting in his hands, Alex wondered why she was telling him about so intimate a matter. Was she trying to reinforce what he already knew, that no one could ever replace her husband? Or was the reason less oblique than that? Perhaps she merely desired to speak about what had been the greatest treasure of her life, in order to relive some of its consolation.

Suddenly, as if reading his thoughts, Irina shook herself and sat up straighter.

"Forgive me; I didn't mean to go on about it. It was a long time ago."

Alex handed back the painting, and she took it to her bedroom. Shortly after, he said good-night, declined the boys' offers of chess games, and returned to the clinic.

Deeply moved, disturbed, wrestling with his own memories of courtship and spousal love, he sat in the dark and gazed out the window through the bars of dripping icicles. The moon was rising, and the lake ice, now covered with inches of water, reflected it back in ripples of miniature fractured moons. As he pondered what Irina had told him, the bleakness of her childhood and youth materialized in front of him like a morbid painting or a defaced icon. The moon floated slowly across the black canvas. At one point he thought he saw a horse and rider crossing the lake parallel to the shore, water spraying out behind the silently pounding hooves. It probably was an optical illusion, the product of moonlight and imagination.

In his mind's eye he saw a young girl of fifteen or sixteen, leaping onto the back of a white horse and galloping through the streets of Moscow, her teeth bared and her dark hair flying as she pressed the mount forward seeking to escape the past, the confinement of the present, and the hopeless future that stretched out before her into an infinitely receding illusion of freedom. She was too full of life for suicide, too shocked by the evil around her for apathy. She had seized the only route open to her—violent gestures of a private revolt, an insurrection of minor proportions. She had galloped blindly through the winter world, little realizing that a few short years ahead, a light was waiting. Love would unlock the prison gate, a certain kind of love—selfless, heroic, sacrificial. That neither she nor Yevgeny had known its identity in the beginning had not prevented them from discovering it. If God had been banished from the mind of young Russia, he had not been banished from the heart.

By mid-April, days of hard rain alternating with radiant sunlight had emptied the bush of snow. The muddy lane that stretched eighteen miles to the south was beginning to dry. The lake at first glance appeared to be open water, though this was an illusion, for beneath the waves were treacherous slabs of ice, cracking and groaning. Then a windstorm blew up during the last week of the month, and for three days Baikal became a writhing mass of tossing ice floes. A few more days of squalls opened the water entirely, and the ice pack receded into the north.

On April 30 a scout plane flew low along the lake, waggled its wings over the village, then proceeded northward on its inspection tour of the surface. On May 2 a radio announcement proclaimed Baikal open for shipping. The following day, Irina packed a bag and briefcase in readiness for her annual lectures at Irkutsk. As he did each year,

Volodya would take her by boat to Listvyanka, and from there she would proceed by bus to the city. Over breakfast, Alex noticed Ilya and Kiril counting out coins and crumpled paper rubles, which they had retrieved from secret troves in their room. With an air of loving pride, they handed their mother what cash they had found. Irina promised that one day she would be able to return the money to them. They told her that she must not.

"We are a family", Ilya said, thumping his chest with a fist. This made Irina's eyes fill with tears. She embraced him and kissed his cheeks. He blushed and returned the kiss with a feint of manly indifference. Kiril simply kissed and hugged and received the same back as if it were his due.

Alex walked down with them to the curving beach of pebbles. He stood with Volodya by the bow of his white open-top fishing boat, not wanting to interfere with the family's last moments together. Finally, after more hugs, kisses, and admonitions, Irina was ready to go. She shook hands with Alex and said in a voice low enough that her sons could not hear, "Firm hand on the reins. Be calm. They like you but will test your strength."

Alex was loath to release her hand. She withdrew it, turned away, and was about to climb into the bow of the boat when on an impulse, she turned back to him, stood on tiptoes, and kissed his cheeks.

"Good-bye, Aleksandr Graham. Thank you for staying with my family. *Dasvidanya.*"

Speechless, overcome with emotions that he wanted no bystanders to observe, Alex leaned his shoulder into the bow of the boat. Ilya and Kiril took the other side, and together they pushed the craft out into the water. Ten feet from shore, Volodya yanked on a rip cord and ignited the inboard motor. His hand on the tiller, he guided the boat in a wide arc and, gathering speed, headed for the south. Seated primly in the bow, the former Soviet maiden, the former anarchist, waved to all onshore.

Alex and the two boys stood by the water's edge waving back until the boat had disappeared around the curve of the headland. Looking up, Alex noticed Ilya staring at him with a cool, analytical gaze.

34. *Strength and Weakness*

Alex observed the spaces Kiril left empty in the air beside him as the boy leaped too quickly into energetic gestures, reaching out for the ends of logs, carrying sacks of cabbage or the rope of smoked *omul* fish that Volodya dropped off a few days after Irina's departure. Though Alex felt younger than he had in years, his minor ordeals had left him with smaller reserves of strength, and he could not always keep pace. Yet he worked beside the boys with his sleeves rolled to the elbows, the muscles of his forearms turning copper in the growing light of spring, accomplishing much through perseverance. Streaks of gray now spilled from under the cloth cap he wore to shade his forehead.

"That was my papa's hat", Kiril informed him with a smile that said, *I'm glad it's on your head; it's a fine thing to see it in use; that's what hats are for.* And so Alex felt the pain of his new role, a transient father filling in the gap left by the real father. A token hat. Could a child survive on symbols alone?

Alex felt at such moments the strangeness of his situation, as if his life's meaning was taking a form that had been chosen for him by someone else, leaving him only small freedoms. Within that limited zone he could choose to love or not love, to speak truth or not speak it. But it was undeniable that he was locked within a prison of circumstances.

He reminded himself that he was not in solitary confinement. This was some comfort, but it did not answer the fundamental question: Why was he here? If life was neither purely accident nor purely determined, what was going on?

Was it a mixture of accidental and determined? And why was the world perceived so differently by two souls standing side by side? For Alex, the world threatened at every moment to become a neo-Pavlovian maze. For Kiril, it was always a vast playing field. Which of the two was the correct view of existence? Neither? Both?

Absorbed by such questions, his brows were often knitted as he turned away from the boy toward some misplaced hammer or thought, rusty nails tucked between his teeth, whistling in a distraction of borne weight, a sweat of victory over decay. He moved slowly, with a careful eye to the way certain leaves would twirl in the wind as they crossed over the village, or to the soil in Irina's garden as it dried. The Russian love for the earth was infectious. He and Kiril turned over the black loam with spades, mixing in the manure he had spread on it weeks before. They varied their labors by stacking the split firewood in the shed. Alex taught the boy how to build North American cords, bracing the ends with interlocking squares so that the wall would not tumble down. At other times they shoveled sawdust and harvested wild straw along the shore for Kolo's bedding. In the forest they filled burlap bags with pinecones to be used as kindling during the coming winter. Picking among the needle-covered forest floor, listening to the zinging of birds flying up from invisible flames, they grew dizzy with symphonies and the incense of hot, bursting sap.

The lesser-winter, I called it, he thought. *But that is not correct. Though summer is short here, it is very warm. Yes, warm and fertile, a blessed land, a land of great silence and great beauty. And now it seems it is always summer.*

One afternoon in the second week after Irina's departure, the weather was so hot that Alex removed his shirt and split birch blocks with a chest bare to the sun and the little benevolent showers. The grass that grew in the lanes of the village pushed up a variety of wildflowers unknown to him, and the upper field shifted hue and tone as one species after another bloomed, folded, curled into seedpods. On the lake distant ships plied the waters, going north and south, suspended on heat mirages.

A few days later, cool winds blew down from the north, and Alex was forced to keep a sheepskin vest on his back, a castoff from Aglaya the Crow, or perhaps a precious thing—it was not always easy to know.

When the wind shifted and the sun began to beat again, Alex, Ilya, and Kiril planted the old woman's secret field with squash and turnip seed—it was the year to let the potatoes have a Sabbath rest, she reminded them. Afterward, she rewarded them with cakes and jars of tea so thick with cream that it was more pudding than drink. They sat in the grass of her dooryard while she reigned over all from a bench on her rotting porch, waving her cane, making pronouncements, telling stories. She made them laugh, and then scolded them for laughing. It was her game, and they all knew it.

Aglaya ate supper with them from time to time, always a welcome intrusion now that the feminine presence was missed.

"It won't be long, Alik, it won't be long", she grinned one evening with a wink, sending her devious code to him above the heads of the boys. "Purple primroses bloom in August."

"We'll plant our garden this week", Ilya said. "Mama left a paper showing where everything should go."

"Little seeds will be planted, sure enough", Aglaya said. "Oh yes, and what a fine crop we'll have, won't we, Alik?" Wink-wink. "Before you know it, psst! Potatoes aplenty!"

"Aglaya," Alex said with a look of severe disapproval, "what would the Bogoroditsa say about someone who meddles in another's garden?"

"She would say, 'What a good neighbor!' She would say, 'Nice to see you helping things along.'"

"I think she would say, 'Be careful; do not presume God's will.'"

"Why would she say such a thing? Isn't God's will obvious? A garden must be fruitful!"

"The garden may need to lie fallow for a time. Or it may need flowers. Or it may need vegetables different from the ones you think it needs."

"What's needed here is plain enough!"

"Nonsense."

"Ha! Men!"

"Alik," Kiril said, screwing up his face in perplexity, "what are you and Aglaya talking about? I never understand you. Is it something Christians know that we don't know?"

"Yes!" Aglaya pronounced with smug satisfaction.

"No! Absolutely not, Kiril", Alex said, shooting a look of grim reprimand in the direction of the Crow. "Aglaya is joking."

"Ah", Kiril said, his mouth working on a boiled potato. "Can you explain it to me? I'm sure I would find it amusing."

"I'm sure you wouldn't", Ilya muttered, standing abruptly and leaving the room.

The next morning Ilya went north with Volodya by boat to Olkhon Island, where he would spend the day helping the old man net omul fish. Alex did not miss the older boy's presence, for in his mother's absence he had reverted once again to his perennial scowl.

Alex and Kiril resumed their attack on the mountain of firewood.

"Why do you stop so often?" Kiril asked as he chopped and split like a dynamo.

"It's the slowing down of a man's fires", Alex explained.

Kiril laughed and hurled his ax at the woodshed door, where it lodged with a *clunk* in the battered gray doorpost. They sat down on the log pile with arms hanging sore between their knees, facing each other. One big and wearing out, and foreign, and rich—no amount of explanation would change Kiril's mind on this matter. The other, Kiril, poor and lean in the wealth of his youth. Kiril seeing in Alex what he hoped to become, tall and fabulous and Western. Alex seeing what he had partly been, small and full of life, with everything important about to begin.

"Alik, do you promise to send me English books when you go back to your home?"

Home? Did he still have a home?

"I promise, Kiril."

"And one day may I visit you there?"

"Yes, one day you may visit me there. You and your whole family must come. We'll drink lots of tea. We'll make toy boats together and sail them on my lake."

"Ozero Ontéro?"

"Yes, and the other lakes also. And we'll walk in the high hills. You must come in autumn, when the trees turn bright red and orange. There's no sight like it."

"That's something I *must* see! Here the leaves only turn yellow—foo!"

"Yellow is nothing to scoff at. Baikal is a beautiful place. The beauty of my land isn't better, merely different."

"You must teach me many English words before you go. When will you leave us?"

"I promised your mother I would stay until she returns from Irkutsk."

"That's not much time. I wish I could go with you."

"Tell me, Kiril, what would you do if you could leave Russia?"

The boy looked into the distance, giving the question serious thought. With great soberness he said, "I would go to America. I would become a doctor. I would become very, *very* rich."

Alex laughed.

"Why do you laugh, Alik?"

"Because when a person gets older, he finds that wealth isn't as important as it seems. When it comes into your hands, it's so often empty."

"I don't believe that."

"Don't you? Listen, Kiril, money is a tool, but it can be a dangerous one. Is a golden ax better than a steel ax? They're both tools, aren't they? But which would you choose for splitting a block of hard birch?"

"The gold one."

"Gold is too soft."

"Of course. But I would sell the gold ax and buy a chainsaw and a mechanical splitter, with plenty of money left over to buy Mama an x-ray machine!"

"What a fine capitalist you are, Kiril."

"Thank you."

Kiril retrieved his ax from the doorpost and resumed his attack on the firewood. Alex sat down on a stump and watched him.

"Does your head hurt, Alik?"

"No. A little rest, and then I'll work again."

"That's good. Mama said we have to keep an eye on you, keep you out of trouble."

"Trouble?"

"You're not supposed to work too hard. She says we must obey you and not wear you out. How are we doing so far?"

"Outstanding. Superb. Obedience and tolerance at every turn."

The boy's childish laughter pealed through the yard and echoed on the surrounding hills. Cheerily impatient, huffing and puffing, the inimitable Kiril. He was capable of swinging the broad blade of the ax into the hardest block of wood with finality, delighting in his powers, trembling with an excess of energy, stretching like a golden bow in a land that was dying—a bow that might never shoot its bolt. If Alex sometimes looked long at him, it was not from dissatisfaction with his own impossible situation but in wonder at the mystery of another life unconsciously taking forms of free choice. The freedom was in his gestures, his enthusiasm, the imperfectly enunciated English words (Kiril knew 170 now), and his native joyousness.

And what of the real father? Surely Yevgeny had longed for the day he would see his son so vital, so strong, and had felt the agony of knowing he would not see it. Had he ever regretted the creation of this boy, this new being he and his wife had made? Had he foreseen those altars where Kiril and Ilya might be offered up, in a land where the angels seemed to have departed, especially those angels who stop a hand from plunging the sacrificial knife?

These things moved behind Alex's eyes, but Kiril did not know of them, seeing from the corner of his eye only a tired man resting on the woodpile.

"Do you want tea, Alik? I'll bring you some, just like Mama makes it. With sugar? I know you like it with sugar."

"No, *without* sugar, Kiril. With a drop or two of milk."

"Tea is not tea with milk! Tea is only tea with sugar."

"All right, we'll do it the Russian way."

"That's the *only* way!"

How different this was from the mood of the older boy, who stood in front of the kitchen mirror each morning, daring Alex to interrupt him as he scraped the bristle from his chin with his father's razor, his inscrutable eyes staring at himself and at Alex simultaneously. Now he was young, now he was old, now his eyes betrayed the sadness of experience, now they were irritated in their youthful rancor. Now he was an ally; next he lapsed into suspicion.

Why are you here? the eyes challenged. *What do you want from my mother?*

How greatly Alex desired to speak to him, to be at least an uncle if not a surrogate father. To tell him that life is change and that everything insufferable in life will eventually pass, and that many things which are taken at first for intrusion are in fact a gift. Of course, this would have been interpreted by the boy as an intruder's self-justification.

Listen, Ilya, listen to me. Change is the permanent state of affairs; your mother can tell you that and perhaps already has.

Or might not have, for she clung to stability with a dedication that permitted no questioning. Alex, who had been conceived, born, and raised in a small place and had clung to his own version of permanence, could not fail to understand her motives in this. Nor did he misread the older boy's hostility. For one personality, intrusion was adventure; for another, it was destabilization. Where Kiril admired and pressed close for the pleasure of feeding his insatiable curiosity, Ilya withdrew, cautious and resentful. Alex remembered his own youth, its brooding uncertainties, and saw that for the time being he must accept his untenable position.

Every evening he read to Kiril from Russian stories, making him translate simple passages into English. The boy was a little lazy in this regard, but he always made a greater effort when Alex reminded him that knowledge of English would be necessary if he desired to live in America. And some nights he merely told stories that he composed on the spot. First a Russian version, then in English. The boy liked this practice best of all, for it both entertained and offered a puzzle for him to decipher.

"The white stag is freedom, isn't it, Alik? I'm certain of it. That's what you meant by it, didn't you?"

"Not exactly, Kiril, though freedom is certainly part of it."

"Part of what? What is *it*, really?"

"Love. Truth."

The architecture could be laid out only in blueprint form, through the medium of invented tales. Ilya would listen sometimes, leaning against the doorframe of his bedroom, arms folded, resembling no one more on this planet than Jamie Colley. Two fatherless, angry boys, refusing a substitution. And in a strange parallelism, Kiril and Hannah Colley, both of them less complicated or perhaps more hungry for affection.

Alex composed his tales on evenings when summer winds blew in straight courses through the woods, haunting him with memories of his past, so similar were they to the sounds of his homeland. On such nights he would put down his book and go to look through the window. He would see the secret shapes of the wind and imagine them crossing the arc of the globe, carving messages in the swaying forests of the Clementine valley, a mythical place that he had known in a dream a long time ago.

Then back to his reading or his storytelling as the ticking of the clock measured the soft collapse of time, as the world itself drowsed in the soothing mother-sounds of the whispering samovar. He did not speak to Kiril of the wind, nor of the people he had known—the memories of his lost wife and his lost sons.

Throughout one long day, they planted the kitchen garden. The mosquitoes were now out in force—large, hungry mosquitoes that seemed to know that Alex possessed a supply of exotic blood. Clouds swarmed him. They whined like North American mosquitoes, but their skill in evading swats was uncanny. Ilya and Kiril stood by, watching with delighted expressions Alex's "mosquito ballet" (as Kiril called it). Finally, moved by pity, Ilya made a paste of mud and smeared it on the exposed parts of Alex's skin, covering every centimeter of his head and neck and hands.

"*Spasiba bolshoye*, great thanks", Alex grumbled as he submitted to this primitive rite. When the anointing was completed, Kiril and Ilya stepped back and belly-laughed. Alex laughed with them, relieved to find that the mud was an effective deterrent. They resumed planting.

He was impressed by the way the boys worked. Ilya's pace was measured, thoughtful, totally focused. Though capable of dangerous eruptions of temper in his relationships with human beings, he was serene in physical tasks, exercising an instinctive Slavic connection to the soil. He worked for long hours without a break. By contrast, Kiril, whose human relationships were lighthearted and peaceful, worked at an impulsive pace, half-focused, capable of great bursts of energy interspersed with daydreams and distraction. He was always the first to quit. The pattern was so much like that of Jacob and Andrew that Alex found himself relating to the Russian boys automatically in the way he had done with his own sons. Whenever he forgot who they were, he experienced a disturbing shift of perception. Disoriented for a moment, he would stand up straight, wipe the black dirt off his hands, and say to himself, *This is not my home. I am an alien. These are not my sons.* Remembering that Andrew was still missing and in danger, he felt the disorientation dissolve, and he was simply a man separated from his real life, to which he needed to return as soon as possible.

On a drizzly Sunday morning, finding themselves with nothing to do, Alex and the boys decided to take a walk. They meandered through the village and made their way along a wet path leading north beside the lakeshore. A short way beyond the last house, they came upon the village cemetery, a sloping square of weeds and wildflowers surrounded on three sides by forest. A few hundred graves crowded close together, each enclosed by picket fences of iron or willow. The majority were marked by weathered wooden crosses, leaning at angles. The boys fell silent.

Alex turned off the path and ambled among the memorials, reading names. At the top of the slope, he came upon a hump of sod crowned by a two-foot-high wooden cross that had been freshly painted powder blue. Nailed to the crossbeam was a tin pie plate on which was etched:

Marfa
Great Soul
Hidden in the Heart of God
1902–1953

A fine mist saturated the green shadows, and the trees dripped as Alex went from grave to grave. Behind him, Ilya and Kiril did likewise. They said nothing, moving as if in slow motion. Ilya's face was masked, chin up, displaying no emotion. His arms were crossed tightly across his chest. Kiril was also masked, but his eyes were hooded, mouth frowning, arms dangling by his sides. Presently they came together at a heap of stones topped by a simple cross of unpainted iron. Welded to the joint of its bars was a square of metal on which was engraved:

Dr. Yevgeny Dmitrievich Pimonenko
1954–1988
"Seek the things that are above."

"Papa", Kiril whispered.

They remained in silence for some time, until the boys, Ilya first, then Kiril, turned and went back to the path. The walk continued without comment.

In the days that followed, Alex found that Irina's absence amplified her presence in his thoughts. Though his affection for her had been subdued by the tangible evidence of her husband's life, this mood—dominated by the feeling that he was an interloper—soon passed. She occupied his mind especially late at night, whenever he sat by himself in the clinic. At such times his loneliness burst into flames—yes, it felt exactly like a fire in his breast, sometimes sweet, sometimes bitter. Whenever he prayed, it lost its obsessive quality, but it never entirely ceased.

There were times when, with a pang of remorse, he saw Carol's face and wondered why his love for her had receded into the background. He made an effort to recall memories of her eyes, her smile, her voice, their most intimate words and experiences, but again and again these were replaced by Irina's face, then by other faces, including Valentina of the Trans-Siberian Railroad. Once, when the face of Theresa Colley appeared suddenly in his mind's eye, he was startled and walked about the room shaking his head. He now saw with merciless clarity that, regardless of the intensity of his feeling for Irina Filippovna, it was an emotion as undependable as passing weather. In an instant anything or anyone could displace it. He concluded that at worst, his heart was still rooted in selfish desire; at best, he was seeking not so much a specific person as love itself.

One morning, he and Ilya climbed onto the roof to pound nails into sheets of tin that the winter wind had lifted. The sun beat on their bare backs. Sweating profusely, they paused to take a rest. As they sat side by side on the peak, gazing out at the lake, they spotted a small boat come around the headland from the north and angle toward the village. It approached at high speed, driven by a powerful outboard motor. The pilot, a girl, killed the engine not far from shore and let the bow drive a wedge into the beach. She jumped out and stood on the shore with her hands on her hips, glaring up at the Pimonenko house.

Ilya grabbed a crowbar and rose to his feet, his face writhing with hatred.

"Sonia", he snarled.

Seeing that the boy was about to scramble down the ladder, Alex reached for him and grabbed him by his belt.

"Wait!"

"Let me go! I will kill her!"

"That's what she wants", Alex said in a calm voice. "She wants you to race to her like a mad dog, and then she will subdue you. She will control you. And when she insults you for it, she will laugh and get into her boat and go away. She knows exactly what you will do and why you are doing it." Alex yanked hard on the belt, and the boy collapsed onto the tin. "Sit still. Don't move."

Ilya obeyed, though his eyes flashed and his lips worked with loathing.

"There is another way", Alex said.

"There is no other way! I hate her!"

"No, you love her."

"What!"

"Yes, you love her, but you hate the falseness that she's flaunting at you. She is not yet the woman she may someday become."

Turning his unhappy eyes on Alex, Ilya said, "What are you talking about?"

"See that wretched girl. She looks so beautiful and strong, doesn't she? But she's miserable and full of confusion. In her heart of hearts"—Alex said *glubina dushy*—"she wants you to resist her. She wants you to be stronger than her control. If you resist with anger, that's not true resistance, because it means she still has you under her power. You must be stronger than that."

"I *am* stronger. I'll make her pay."

"How? With a weapon in your hand? You know very well you won't hurt her."

"I'll scare her!"

"The best thing you can do is ignore her. That will demand great strength. Do you have that kind of strength?"

Flushing, Ilya bowed his head and nodded.

"Good. Let's continue our work."

"Ilyushka!" the girl called in a sneering tone.

Alex and Ilya turned their backs to her and began to hammer nails into the sheets of tin.

"Don't bang your thumb, Gaspadin", said Ilya.

"That's the way, Ilya. There's nothing more powerful than humor. Show that we're not disturbed by her presence, or interested."

Alex laughed loudly. Then he made a feeble joke, and Ilya produced a fake guffaw. As they eased into a meaningless conversation, the frenzy left the boy's eyes and a smile flickered across his face.

"Ilyushka! Ilyushka!" the girl mocked as she climbed the slope to the house.

Alex murmured and laughed. Ilya did the same.

"Don't pretend you can't see me!" Sonia shouted. "Are you afraid of me?"

The frenzy returned to Ilya's eyes.

"Don't give in to it", said Alex. "Laugh."

Ilya produced an artificial laugh.

"Excellent. You've got her attention. She's going to get mad as hell now, but underneath all that, she'll begin to respect you."

Ilya stood up, put his hands on his hips and stared down at the smirking face below.

"What do you want, Sonia? Why do you bother us?"

"I came to deliver a message!"

"I'm not interested in your messages."

He turned and dropped to his knees and began to bang nails.

The girl shrieked something at him, but it was drowned out by the racket of hammer on tin. Alex and Ilya continued to work for several minutes. Then they paused.

"We're making a gang", Sonia shouted. "We're going to beat the weaklings of Ozero Baikal into meat."

"Laugh, Ilya, laugh", Alex whispered.

Ilya laughed but did not look at the girl.

"We're going to beat you, I said. We're the Wolves. The Tartar gang in Listvyanka is going to meet us here and help."

Marshaling a little wisdom of his own, perhaps liking the flavor of resistance, Ilya stood and faced the girl.

"You're a child, Sonia", he said with a broad smile. "I'm not interested in your games. Go away."

She spat on the ground, huffed, and spewed invective in Ilya's direction.

"What a baby", he scoffed. "Go away. If you come here again, I'll throw you in the lake."

"You threaten me! I'll tell my father!"

"Tell your father to give you a spanking."

She screamed more abuse. Alex shuddered at the vile language. To his credit, Ilya did not respond. He merely produced a wider grin, which perhaps appeared authentic at the distance separating him from the girl.

He turned his back to her, knelt, and continued hammering. During another pause, Sonia shouted a final taunt: "We smashed your traps. What are you going to do about it?"

Bang-bang, bang-bang.

"We broke your sword!"

Bang-bang, bang-bang.

"Coward!" she screamed.

Every muscle in Ilya's body flinched. His eyes bulged, his face flushed, but all this was hidden from the girl. He did not turn around. She wheeled and stomped back to her boat, jumped in, and tore at the rip cord. Within a minute she was speeding away into the north.

"Well done, Ilya", Alex said.

"Coward, she said", Ilya muttered, wiping sweat from his brow. "Maybe I am a coward."

"Only a truly brave man could resist an attack like that. I congratulate you. You are a brave man."

"Am I? Well, I wonder what will happen next."

"Maybe nothing. Don't worry about it."

"You don't know her. Sonia's a she-wolf. She'll get her Tartar hordes after me."

"No she won't. You're stronger than all of them."

"No, I'm not."

"Yes, you are. You just proved it."

Suddenly tears filled his eyes and he hung his head. "My grandfather's sword. It's gone forever. It's my fault. It's all my fault."

"The sword may be gone, Ilya, but you now have a more powerful sword in your hands. And you'll pass this sword on to your own children one day and to your children's children. It's greater than all the swords on earth."

"I don't believe you. I don't believe you", the boy groaned, shaking his head.

The sun soared higher day by day. One evening not long after Sonia's visit, Alex, Ilya, and Kiril sat on the shore eating lumps of Aglaya's cake. Hearing a rumble to the north, they noticed a boat rounding the headland and moving slowly through the water in the direction of the village.

Sonia cut the motor near to shore and let the boat drift onto the beach, where the bow rustled against the pebbles and stopped not ten feet from where they were sitting. Her face was brooding, but on it there was none of her previous arrogance. Neither Alex nor the boys stood to greet her. They continued to eat their cake. She got out and lifted three burlap sacks from the boat. Head down, she walked toward Ilya and dropped the sacks at his feet.

"Your traps", she murmured. "They're not broken."

Opening one of the bags, she pulled the long cavalry sword from it and handed it to Ilya.

"It's not broken either", she said.

Turning abruptly, she went back to the boat and made herself busy coiling a rope. Ilya's face was a study in concentration. Suddenly he jumped to his feet. For a moment he hesitated; then, arriving at some decision, he strolled casually to the boat. Sonia looked up, then down at her feet. Ilya made a gesture with his head, and they walked away along the beach, side by side, separated by a foot or more, both of them with hands in pockets.

"Girls", Kiril said with disgust.

"And boys", Alex said, smiling.

"I do not understand people", Kiril declared with a note of indignation. "Ilya is an idiot."

Alex let this observation stand. Kiril would learn soon enough that certain forms of idiocy were unavoidable.

After Sonia left, Ilya returned to the house carrying the sword. He brought it into the kitchen and laid it on the table, where Alex was busy teaching the younger brother more English words. The blade was nicked in spots and rusty from its exposure to the elements. Ilya told Alex and Kiril that yesterday Sonia had returned to the place where he had been beaten by her friends months before. The sword had been dropped during the scuffle, and no one had paid any attention to it at the time. Lost in the snow, and later rained upon, it had remained there until the morning of her most recent visit.

The boys were not sure how to clean it. They had no sandpaper or any other abrasive that might remove rust, and wiping it with rags did little to restore its former glory. Alex showed them how to scrub the steel by alternating treatments of wood ash and kerosene. Kiril ran off to beg a little gasoline from Grig or Volodya and returned with a tinful in one hand and a small sharpening stone in the other. Out on the back porch, they took turns working on the blade, and gradually it began to shine in the light from the open doorway. When the moon rose above the Primorskis, the steel turned blue. Alex honed the cutting edge with the stone.

"This is a noble sword", he said, lifting it high, the hilt to his forehead. "It is more than a weapon. It is a symbol of the great sword that you wield within your hearts."

The boys smiled, admiring the drama of Alex's performance.

"The sword that you carry in your hearts is not for killing or wounding, neither is it for threatening or cowing the weak. It is the sword of the guardian, the reminder, the overcomer when all seems lost!"

Ilya and Kiril rushed forward and reached for the sword at the same time. The older brother seized it first, but Kiril held onto it, jerking it, whining, pleading, and demanding. "Let me, let me! Let me have it!"

Alex caught Ilya's eye, and Ilya quickly took his meaning. He released his grip and let his brother have the sword. Kiril ran off with it into the dark, heading straight up to the big field, where he cavorted around, slashing at the air. The moon glint on the polished steel revealed his position.

"Once again you've proved yourself the stronger, Ilya", Alex said. The boy did not reply, but by his measured silence it was plain to see that he understood.

If Ilya had leaped forward to a new level of maturity, Kiril seemed to have taken a step backward. That night he slept with the sword and would not relinquish it. Around lunchtime the next day, however, its weight was becoming a burden, and he inserted it into its scabbard on the high shelf. Spying the sailboat his father had made for him, he took it in his hands and left the house. A few minutes later, glancing out the kitchen window facing the lake, Alex noticed Kiril down at the shore trying to get the boat to sail.

He pushed it into the water again and again. Each time, it knifed across the surface a foot or two, then toppled onto its side and sank. Kiril repeatedly waded into the ice-cold lake, soaking himself to the knees, retrieved the boat, retreated to shore, and tried again.

Peering out the window beside Alex, Ilya said, "He's crazy about that boat. Every year he tries, and every year it won't work."

"Does your boat work?" Alex asked.

"No, mine's the same. My father made it to look nice, but he got something wrong in the design."

"Did you once do as Kiril now does?"

Ilya shrugged. "I don't bother anymore."

An hour later Kiril trudged into the kitchen, shivering, soaked to the neck, carrying the boat in his arms. His lips blue, his eyes filled with mute sadness, he climbed onto a stool and replaced the boat on the shelf. Alex told him to go change his clothes. Kiril obeyed without a word but did not emerge from his room for several hours. When Alex went in to see what had become of him, he found the boy sprawled on his bed asleep, his mouth open, his face streaked with tears. He covered Kiril with a blanket and went out, closing the door behind him.

35. *The Bell Tower*

The next day dawned without a cloud in the sky. By seven in the morning, the air was already warm. There was not a breath of wind, and for the first time Alex saw the lake without a ripple or a wave. As he sat by the window of the ward trying to come fully awake, he realized that it was Sunday. Not since Father Sergius' Mass in the poustinia on the Little-Little Ob had he received the Eucharist, and he asked himself if the unruliness of his emotions was due to the absence of sacramental grace. Though he had made every effort to maintain a regular routine of prayer, his world had been so disrupted that time no longer plodded along with the reassuring pace of a workhorse following a straight trail into eternity. Instead, it bucked and bolted, scattering the past, present, and future in every direction.

As he did each morning, he read a little from Yevgeny's Ukrainian Bible and prayed a rosary and a chotki for the accomplishment of God's will, for his permanent family, and for his temporary family. He had developed the habit of carrying the icon of Christ's face with him during the day. It was small enough to fit into the breast pocket of his shirt, and it rested there like a quiet presence to which he could turn his thoughts from time to time. Now he gazed at it, holding it in his hands, merely looking. The eyes of the painted face were sometimes in agony, sometimes at peace, but always suffering. They seemed to ask a question of Alex, but what the question was, he could not guess.

Over a breakfast of kasha and boiled eggs that he made for himself and the boys, Alex thought about how little there was in post-Soviet Russia to distinguish one day from another. Three generations of Communism had come close to obliterating the concept of Sabbath rest. Though it lingered in other forms, stripped of the sacred, its role as a major signpost pounded into the ground of history had largely disappeared. It no longer pointed to the transience of man's estate, nor to the Resurrection, nor to eternal destinations. Thus, the days rolled into one another without much difference.

How could he hope to undo what generations of suppression had accomplished? How could he convey to Ilya and Kiril an awareness of sacred time?

A good place to start might be in nature itself, he thought.

Yes, he must get the boys out of the village for a change of scene, a break from the ordinary. Then their eyes might be opened to the extraordinary.

Kiril's eyes lit up when Alex proposed a hike along the coast to see more of the wilderness on the west shore. Not so easily excited was Ilya, who on principle maintained a judicious reserve about any new proposals. Even so, Alex could see that he was mulling it over.

"The bush path is open now", Alex said. "It goes north for many kilometers. Why don't we see what we can find?"

"It's still muddy and very slowgoing", Ilya replied. "Besides, you can't see much that way. The best places are reached only by water."

"I wish we had a boat of our own", Kiril said despondently.

"Volodya is planning to go to Olkhon sometime this week", Ilya said. "Maybe he'll go today if we ask him. Do you want me to ask?"

"Please", Alex said.

Ilya barged out the kitchen door and before long was back with the news that Volodya would not mind taking them in his boat and could go this morning. He had business in the village of Tutai on the mainland, across the narrow channel from Olkhon Island. It would be a long journey, at least two or three days round trip.

"He wants to make an early start", said Ilya. "I'll get Kolo into the shed. Kiril, give her enough hay and water for a few days."

When that was done, Alex and the boys packed sleeping gear, bags of food, and various other items they thought they would need. They hoped to camp on the island or in the Primorskis somewhere along the northwest coast. An air of excitement gripped all three; it seemed that the promise of new sights and challenges was a potent antidote to the stresses of the past few weeks. Volodya knocked on the door about nine o'clock and said he was ready to go, if the Gaspadin and the two squirrels were ready.

Down at the beach, Volodya's fishing boat floated on the still water. This open-topped vessel was about thirty feet long, wide waled, and much battered by years of service. White with red trim, it was powered by an inboard diesel motor. Trailing behind on a length of rope was a smaller skiff twelve feet in length, shaped like a spear and with a flat stern, to which an outboard motor was bolted. It was black with a gray *nerpa* seal painted on the bow.

In the bow of the larger boat was a triangular seat, which Kiril immediately appropriated for himself. Volodya went to the tiller at the stern, and Alex and Ilya took the only remaining seat, a plank a third of the way back. The center section of the hull was a wooden tank for holding fish, and it smelled like it. The day was growing hotter.

Volodya told Alex that Olkhon Island was a hundred and thirty kilometers to the north, and if they made good time, they would reach their destination in five or six hours.

The diesel engine chug-chugged, then fired, belched black smoke, and rumbled steadily. Ilya poled the boat away from shore, and Volodya steered it around to face north. Pulling on the throttle, he made the engine roar, and the boat accelerated, cutting a silver swallowtail in the water. Glancing over the side, Alex looked down and saw that the lake deepened without losing any of its clarity. It was difficult to gauge the depth, which might have been ten feet or a hundred.

To their left, the rolling, tree-covered heights of the Primorski Mountains towered. To their right, snowcapped ranges rose along the horizon in the east. The air was so fresh and bracing that they all breathed deeply with raw pleasure. Kiril sat with his knees drawn up and his arms resting on the bow plate, staring straight ahead like a ship's figurehead. Throughout the next hour, they traveled without speaking. The noise of the engine inhibited conversation, but when there appeared a scattering of cabins on the shore, every head turned to watch it pass.

"What is that place?" Alex shouted to no one in particular.

"Sonia lives there", Ilya shouted back, his face inscrutable.

Later, the boat passed a headland and entered the crescent of a sweeping bay that did not eat far into the escarpment. Volodya pointed to an outcropping of stone that resembled a ruined castle. It was a natural formation, towering over two small coves on each side.

Volodya cut the engine and let the boat drift parallel to the shore.

"The Bell Tower", Ilya said to Alex.

"Kolokol-kolokol-kolokol!" Kiril sang, cupping hands to his mouth, making echoes.

"Yevgeny Dmitrievich gave it that name", said Volodya. "Here, you boys, listen to me! Did you know I brought your father here a long time ago? Fourteen years ago it was; I took him fishing. With a string and hook he caught a big fat omul. We cooked it on that beach right over there. That was before he got sick in the atom fire. A fine man the doctor was—never a finer."

Ilya and Kiril absorbed this information soberly, then stared back at the little beach with new interest.

"We climbed that tower together, we did, he and I. Stood on the top, side by side. I thought he'd get himself killed, and me with him. It was a day just like today. Little did we know he'd soon be under the earth."

The boys glanced at Volodya nervously.

"Just like you did, Kiryusha, your papa put his hands to his lips and sang out over the waters—'Kolokol-kolokol'. He made a big announcement, told it to the birds and the *nerpa*, he did. Claimed the rock as a bell tower of the Lord. Said he would someday bring his children here with him to pray and watch the sun come up. Ah well, such is life. Man has one idea, God another."

Volodya seemed oblivious to the effect his meditations might have on his two young passengers.

"Can we stop here?" Kiril asked in a small voice.

"Not today", Volodya said. "I need to get to Tutai by suppertime. But I'll tell you what. After you've had a look around Olkhon tomorrow, why don't you take the skiff and come back this far by yourselves? You can climb the Bell Tower, sleep in the bush, catch fish. I'll pick you up the day after. Or you can just come along home by yourselves, whatever you like. It's a free country."

The boys' faces broke into big smiles. Alex nodded his assent, and Volodya fired the engine.

Into the afternoon they traveled, plying the serene waters at a steady pace, until at around three o'clock a low mound appeared out of the heat haze.

"Olkhon!" Volodya shouted.

They beached in a sandy cove on the east side of the island, beneath a hill covered by brown grass and bent pine trees.

"Olkhon is the Buryat word for dry", Volodya said to Alex. "Be careful about fires. The island is a tinderbox. The mountains to the west guard it from the snow and rain, but the sarma can kick up quickly from the east. One false spark and your souls will be sailing to the heavens."

Volodya fixed a stern look at the boys and wagged an index finger at them. "This is a shaman island. Pagan spirits are here in plenty. You listen to what the Gaspadin tells you. He's a Christian, he is, and knows more about these things than you two pups, so don't be scoffing at his prayers. He's going to keep you safe from Burkhan and Doshkin-noyon!"

Ilya's face slid into sarcasm, but he made no retort. Kiril's eyes grew large, and he also remained silent.

Having delivered his last warnings, Volodya resumed his customary cheeriness, grabbed the towrope, and pulled the skiff alongside. Ilya and Kiril waded into the water, yelping involuntarily from the cold, hopping up and down as they pulled the skiff's bow onto the shore. Kiril tied it to a bush. In the meantime, Volodya tossed Alex the bundles of blankets, packs of food, and other camping items. When all the baggage was ashore, the boys put their shoulders to the prow of the big boat and pushed it off. When it had drifted out a sufficient distance, Volodya started the motor. With a wave he gunned it and roared away, heading for the channel between the island and the mainland.

Alex told the boys that their first objective was to find a camping site that would be safe from the wind and the danger of fire. Ilya wanted the hilltop, which he said had a better view. Kiril wanted to be by the shore, close to fishing. They spent an hour exploring the area and found a spot that was a good compromise. It was a shelf of fine gravel about forty feet from the lake, partway up the hill, backed and flanked by rocks scabby with lichen. Firewood was in abundance: dead pine branches and a carpet of brittle black cones that had fallen down from the trees on the ridge above. They busied themselves clearing the area of debris and stacking the larger branches in a heap near the place where Alex intended to make the fire. While the boys unrolled their bedding and unpacked supplies, he built a stone fire pit in the shelter of a large rock on the east side of the shelf. In the event that a sarma arose, it was unlikely that sparks would go anywhere where they could do damage. A light breeze was now blowing, keeping down the mosquitoes. The lake rippled like silver foil. The boys brought handfuls of twigs and cones and dumped them into the fire pit. When Alex put a match to the fuel, it flared, wrapping them with the incense of burning pine gum. The snapping and bubbling and the subdued roar of the flames was so pleasurable that Alex and the boys began to smile. Ilya broke larger branches into short lengths, and Kiril fed them one by one into the pit. They agreed that it was best to keep the fire small until it was time to cook.

"Hmmm, but what will we cook?" Alex asked. "We have bread and cheese, and smoked fish."

"Tea!" said Ilya. "We cannot live without tea!"

The older boy laid a metal grate across two stones and pushed some of the embers beneath it. He placed a full billy-can full of water on it and threw in a handful of tea leaves.

"*Luna chay!*" Kiril exclaimed, remembering the moon tea of the Winter-Born. After more banter, Ilya announced that he was going up to the top of the hill. Kiril pulled a roll of string and a fishing hook from his pocket and said that he was heading down to the lake to catch supper. Alex remained by the fire to keep it from getting out of hand and stood gazing at the small figure of the boy on the shore, tossing his string out into the lake. When the water had boiled, he lifted the can from the grill and gingerly poured tea into one of the tin cups they had brought along. He sweetened it with sugar, the proper way.

The sun continued to beat down. Alex sat and rested his back against the warm stones, inhaling the fragrant wood smoke, listening to the hum of insects and the little conversations of Asian jays and spotted brown nutcrackers that had flown in to investigate. In the crevices of the rocks tiny flowers grew, yellow and pink and orange. The breeze stiffened but did not whip the fire dangerously. The dry wood burned quickly and needed replenishing from time to time. The sun rolled on toward the southwest. Above and to the north, the sky became a deeper blue.

Later, he got up to check on Kiril and stood watching him cast his string into the water again and again, the boy's optimism in no way dampened by lack of success. He was now barefoot and in shirt sleeves, his pants rolled up to his knees. Alex touched the icon in his breast pocket and pressed it to his chest. Then he sat down again and drowsed for a while.

At around six o'clock, a shout from below brought Alex to his feet. Kiril had his legs planted in the water, wide apart, and was leaning back, hauling in the string hand over hand. Whatever was hooked on it was strong, zigging and zagging underwater not twenty feet from shore. Alex went down to help.

"Let him run for a bit, Kiril", he said. "You don't want to break the string."

Following Alex's directions, Kiril hauled in no more line, and let it slip slowly through his fingers, extending the arc of the attempted escape. He played the fish for a while until the frantic movement beneath the surface slowed. When it was plain to see that the fish was tiring, the circles of its struggle declining in size, it was time to pull it in.

Slowly, man and boy worked together to draw the catch ever closer. Now and then the fish renewed its fight, but its strength was nearly at an end. Finally, a flash of white appeared five feet from shore. The fish, sensing the shallows, began to lash in a last bid for escape. Alex leaped into the water, shouting when his feet hit the numbing cold, "Bring it in, Kiril!"

The boy walked backward out of the water, pulling steadily, and Alex herded the fish onto the stones, where it gasped and flapped furiously, trying to flip itself back into the water. Kiril ran forward and hit it over the head with a rock until it lay still. It was an omul, silver white, long and fat. Though not as big as its resistance had implied, it was at least six or seven pounds.

Kiril cut the hook out of its mouth, stuck a finger through a gill, and heaved it over his shoulder. Grinning in triumph, he and Alex walked up the hill to the campfire, where they proudly showed their prize to Ilya, who had just returned from the heights.

"*Spasiba*, Kiryusha!" Ilya cried with admiration. "Now we will really eat!"

Ilya offered to gut the fish, and while he was doing this, Kiril jumped up on the rock above the fire and faced the lake. Bracing his legs and thumping his chest like a little primate, he bellowed in a man-child voice:

"See Kiril the Conqueror! See Kiril the Great, the mighty fisherman!"

Alex laughed, and Ilya threw a pinecone at his brother's head, knocking him off his throne. A pinecone war broke out in which all three participants gave no quarter.

"Why are you picking on me?" Kiril cried in a fake whine. "Are we going to fight or eat?"

They grilled the omul over a fresh brace of pine, seasoned with the tiny green leaves of a bush Ilya called *Bogorodskaya trava*—God's grass. He told Alex that his mother used the herb for curing sick babies of stomach cramps but that it was not yet ripe enough to be used as medicine. He threw bunches of it onto the flames, making a sweet-acrid smoke similar to that of burning maple leaves, which Alex vaguely remembered from the autumns of his former life.

When the meal was cooked, they gorged themselves on the oily flesh that tasted something like salmon. Great amounts of tea followed, and a dessert of crumbling "Crow cake".

After that, they lay down on their backs, sighing with contentment, gazing up at the sky without a thought in their heads.

The longest day of the year was only weeks away, and though the evening was getting on, the sun was only now touching the bronze haze of the horizon. The wind increased a little, and far out on the lake, spiral gusts and whitecaps could be seen. In the lee of Olkhon, however, the air was still warm enough that no jackets were needed.

When all the southwest began to bleed with sunset, they sat up and watched it for a while. Ilya suggested that Alex and Kiril come with him to the top of the hill because there was something he wanted to show them. They climbed among the rocks and dunes to a high rolling plateau of grass stretching away into the north. Olkhon was a big island, forty miles long and three to five miles wide. Stands of small pine trees with broad arms swayed and whispered in the wind.

Ilya led them across a hundred yards of steppe-like open space toward a stony knoll. The sky was now violet. The wind dropped, and an unnatural stillness seemed to spread about the scene. On the top of the knoll, they came to a ring of ancient stumps, burned down to their roots, still black but weatherworn for untold years. In the center of the ring, poking out of gravel and chunks of charcoal, were white bones. Sitting among the debris was a human skull.

Kiril gave a cry and stepped back. Ilya laughed, squatted on his haunches, and poked at the skull with a twig.

"What is this?" Alex asked in a low voice.

"Volodya took me here once", Ilya said. "He told me the Buryats used to burn their shamans when they died. They believed that if you buried them, they would never get to see the sun. They burned them so their souls would fly up to the spirit world." Ilya snorted, his face clearly showing what he thought about this. "Volodya said it might also be a zek. There used to be a prison camp on the island. They killed lots of people here. But he wasn't sure if they burned them or not."

"Let's go back to the fire", Kiril said nervously.

"Scared?" Ilya said.

"No, I'm cold."

The wind had picked up again, moaning across the grassland and wailing in the pines. They shivered and went back down the hill to their campsite. By then it was growing dark. They fed the fire and rolled themselves in their blankets.

For a time they watched the sky and listened to the lapping waves and the fire collapsing into embers. Although Alex and the boys were tired, sunburned, and full from the day's adventures, they were not yet ready for sleep. They chatted about inconsequential things—boats, fish lore, the behavior of the lake in its changing seasons, the life of the village. Alex told them about his homeland, the town of Halcyon, and a little of his background. Then, as the stars came down close to the world, he felt moved to tell them about the death of Roger Colley. He described the canoe trip the man had taken with his son Jamie, and the drowning.

"He's the boy you told me about", Kiril said. "The one who plays chess."

"That's right", Alex said.

"Do you really think he'll play chess by mail with me?"

"He might. I'll ask him when I return home."

"Is he sad?"

"Yes, he's still sad. His father died only a short while ago."

"Alik, do you really think souls go up to heaven when they die?"

"Yes, I do, Kiril."

"Are you sure? Maybe it's just a story—like the Winter-Born and the East-Born."

"I'm not sure in the way that a man may be sure that he has eaten a fish for supper", Alex slowly replied. "But I believe it's true."

"There's a big difference between believe and know", Ilya said sleepily from under his blanket.

"Yes, that's true, Ilya. Let me ask you a question: Do you believe that far to the west of here there's a city called Moscow?"

"Of course."

"But how do you *know*?"

"I've seen pictures of it. My mother once lived there."

"But what if the pictures were of someplace else? What if your mother was just telling you a story to make your life more interesting, using a fairy-tale city to express an idea?"

"My mother doesn't tell fairy stories. She speaks the truth. Always."

"Suppose, then, that a person whom you know to be very honest tells you that he has been to heaven."

"That's different."

"How is it different?"

Silence reigned for a long time after that. Alex thought that the boys had dropped off to sleep with the question lingering in their minds, seeping into their dreams. He got up and doused the last of the fire with water from the billycan, and lay down again.

"Alik?" Kiril whispered. "Do you think my papa went up to heaven?"

"I believe he did, Kiril. He was a good man. He believed in heaven."

"Why didn't he come back to tell us about it?"

"He wants something better for you."

"What is it?"

"He wants you to journey where he has gone. He wants you to come to him, because he's in a better place."

"Better than Baikal?"

"As hard as it is to imagine, yes, it's much better than Baikal."

"I don't understand. If what you say is true, why hasn't he sent a message to us, telling us to come to him, showing us the way?"

"He has sent you a message."

"No, he hasn't."

"The messages from heaven are spoken gently. Heaven never forces us. It always makes an invitation, and we are free to listen or not listen."

"Alik, I still don't understand. I haven't heard a thing. I never got an invitation from my papa."

"He speaks in a language you haven't yet learned, Kiril. One day you'll learn it. And one day you'll see him."

"Will I?"

"You will see him. You will see him face-to-face."

No reply was made to this. Kiril rolled over and sighed. Not long after, sleep took them all away into dreams.

The morning dawned with a chill in the air, yet the clear sky promised another fine day. After breakfast Alex suggested that they explore the island, but for some reason neither of the boys were interested in this. United for once, both Ilya and Kiril agitated for a return to the Bell Tower. And so they broke camp, boarded the skiff, and made ready for departure. Ilya, who was more familiar with the craft, took the stern seat and eased the outboard motor downward until the propeller was in position beneath the water. He bolted it tight and hooked up the fuel line to the jerry can of gas.

Kneeling in the prow, Alex used an oar to push the boat from shore. It glided backward into deep water just as Ilya pulled the cord. The motor began to whine as he turned the throttle, banking sharply toward the south. Unlike Volodya's large boat, the skiff skimmed the water like a spear. It threw up a lot of spray, and the force of the onrushing air struck its passengers as if it were wind. The boat bounced alarmingly a few times when it crossed eddies of actual wind that had begun to rip up the surface of Baikal. After that, Ilya eased nearer to shore, into a band of calmer water in the lee of the mountains. The sun rose higher and hotter.

The journey southward along the coast was completed in less than three hours. It was not yet noon when the skiff slowed for its entry into one of the little coves flanking the Bell Tower. Ilya drove it hard onto the sand, then killed the motor. Alex and the boys jumped out and stretched their cramped muscles. Onshore, out of reach of the lake wind but fully exposed to the sun, they now felt the summer heat and removed their jackets.

They ate a lunch of bread and the last of the omul fish, which still retained its smoky flavor, then flung themselves down on the sand and put their faces into the lake, sucking deeply, their heads aching from the cold water. Refreshed, they got to their feet and gazed up at the tower of rock. Its walls soared upward hundreds of feet, surrounded on three sides by water, approachable only by a steep wooded incline that sloped halfway to the top like an outthrust leg of the Primorski range. From this perspective, it looked more like a jagged Gothic spire than a castle.

"Ready?" Alex asked.

"Ready, ready", chimed Ilya and Kiril.

For twenty minutes they climbed through a forest of slender pines intermixed with larch and birch. The route was pathless with a lot of stone rubble underfoot. Arriving at the rounded top of the "leg", they turned to the left and went blindly along its ridge in the direction of the spire, which soon became visible beyond the line of treetops. Coming to its base, they made a halt in order to catch their breath and muster their courage. Fortunately, on the landward side, the formation of stone had split and crumbled in many places so that the climb could be made more easily. At first they followed wherever their feet led, Alex in the forefront, Kiril in the middle, and Ilya taking the rear.

"I'll catch Kiryushnik when he falls from the nest!" Ilya said.

As they ascended, it became clear that many of the paths opening before them were cul-de-sacs. Taking more care, they slowly advanced from precipice to precipice, stopping now and then to steady their nerves and to reconnoiter the heights above. By two in the afternoon, they were near the top, gripping at handholds, their boots clinging to footings with the tenacity of mountain goats but without any of those animals' confidence. They kept reminding each other not to look down, for the suction of fear might drag them off the rock to their deaths. They were spurred on by the knowledge that Yevgeny and Volodya had reached the top without mishap.

At last Alex pulled himself over the uppermost ridge and onto the pinnacle of the tower. It was irregular in shape, roughly six feet by eight feet across, angled slightly toward the mountain side. The surface was covered in pebbles, lichen, and fish bones.

Pushed by his brother and pulled by Alex, Kiril was next to scramble up over the edge. He rolled onto his back and lay on the stones panting for breath.

"Kolokol", he whispered.

Ilya followed shortly and stood himself upright, motionless for a few moments. As if on signal, he and Alex sat down to regain their balance. For a long time all three looked out over the immensity of the lake. An eagle soared past, rising on an updraft without a single beat of its wings. It gave a piercing cry, then circled to the west, where its dark feathers turned invisible against the black forest of the Primorskis.

Ilya had brought along a knapsack, and from this he now removed a bottle of water and offered it around. They drank, taking care to divide it equally. Then the boys stretched out on their backs, flung arms across their eyes, and dozed.

Alex stood and gazed at the lake. The sun was high and beating it into silver. Far out, the wind stirred the low heat haze that hung suspended over the surface, churning up gold and saffron so that Baikal appeared to be in flames. He recalled that villagers had sometimes referred to it as the Sacred Sea and sometimes as the Lake of Fire. Where had the names come from? Their origins might be pagan or Christian, but in any event, they pointed to some long-forgotten mystery that this immense inland sea represented. And why *fire* for so cold a body of water?

In the book of the Apocalypse, a lake of fire was mentioned as the place of destruction into which the Antichrist and the False Prophet would be cast when Christ returned. But these waters spoke more of regeneration than destruction, of rebirth rather than condemnation. Of course, there were many kinds of fire, including the fire on Mount Horeb, which had burned in a bush without consuming it. The voice of God had spoken to Moses from that bush, calling him to go to the Hebrews captive in Egypt, to lead them from bondage into the freedom of the Promised Land. Similarly, love was a fire. So too the passion for freedom. *Svoboda.*

Alex stood by the sleeping boys and prayed silently, thanking God for the privilege of spiritual ascent, for love, and for fatherhood. He begged God to send light upon Russia, a fire of zealous love that would rekindle the faith that had once been her soul.

Removing the icon of Christ from his shirt pocket, he lifted it high over the water and spoke in a quiet voice:

"Christ humiliated, Christ rejected, Christ crucified! Bless and protect this land and this people. You have called us out of darkness into your own wonderful light! Nourish us unto eternal life!"

"Alik?"

He looked down and saw that Kiril had half-risen and was leaning on his elbow, watching him curiously. Ilya too was awake, staring at him, his face guarded.

Alex lifted the icon over them and prayed.

"Father, bless these sons! Bless them greatly, for they are without a father in this world. Bless their father, Yevgeny, who once stood in this place and lifted his eyes to you and called unto you. Hear my prayer—hear his prayer. Out of the depths we cry unto you, O Lord, for you are the Father of all!"

Kiril's eyes were wide, and tears started in them. Ilya looked away. Neither said a word. The moment over, Alex sat down beside them, and all three resumed gazing out over the sea.

Silence was the natural climate of the Bell Tower. During the next hour while they remained there, they were content merely to soak in their surroundings. At about four in the afternoon, speaking with their eyes only, they agreed that it was time to begin the descent. After casting long looks in every direction, one by one they slipped over the edge and carefully picked their way back down to the forest canopy below.

That night they camped in a clearing near the beach. Kiril caught a small omul, and this, combined with their rations, made for a plentiful evening meal. After that, their extreme fatigue sent them all to their blankets in search of an early sleep. As they drifted off, Ilya told a few hair-raising stories about bears, emphasizing how they liked to visit beaches at night to drink from the lake and to eat whatever could be found. But everyone was too tired to worry, and they were all asleep before the first stars had appeared.

The next morning was as fine as the previous two days, and Alex proposed that they take advantage of the good weather by climbing up into the Primorskis. To this the boys readily agreed. Knapsacks over shoulders, they set off at a slow but steady pace, bushwhacking straight up the side of the hill through heavy timber. In time they crossed a stream that tumbled down in a series of little waterfalls, and on its other side (no more than a single leap from bank to bank) they found a rough path through the undergrowth. They guessed that it had not been made by human effort, for in the few sections where mud or gravel appeared between the rocks, they found the paw prints of various small mammals. After two hours of climbing, the angle of ascent increased sharply, and though the contours of the range were hidden by the forest, they realized they were nearing the top. The stream was now no more than a trickle fed by small springs or water oozing from underneath rocks and carpets of moss. The tree trunks were thinner and their leaves or needles less abundant. Ahead, a line of ridge appeared through the branches.

Alex and the boys were now at a higher altitude, where they had expected to find cooler air, but the sun seemed to beat down on their backs with greater force. They kept to the shadows as much as they were able. Without warning, the path ended on a dome of speckled rock. They were only a few dozen yards from the crest at this point, and though they wanted to sprint forward to reach it, each of the three stopped to catch his breath. Hands on hips, jackets tied about their waists, shirt sleeves rolled up to their elbows, they broke into grins. Their chests heaved in the thinner air, and they did not waste energy in conversation. Nodding to each other, they began the final climb. The smooth rock ended, and they passed through a thicket of knee-high juniper bushes on which shriveled white berries hung, a remnant of the previous autumn. Beyond it they entered a moss-covered open space that rose gently to the very height of the range. Stopping to take in the view, which opened up in every direction, they panted and sweated, waving away small golden bees that tried to fly into their mouths. A light breeze was blowing from the north, winnowing along the ridge. Glancing in that direction, Kiril gasped and pointed.

"*Izhuber, izhuber!*" he whispered.

At the end of the clearing, thirty feet away, stood a red deer, whose rack of antlers shone like gold in the sun. The deer was poised on an outcrop, looking back over its shoulder at the intruders.

Paralyzed with wonder, hearts thrumming, Alex and the boys watched for a minute. Then Kiril, openmouthed, eyes shining, walked toward the creature with his arms outstretched.

"Wait, Kiril; don't startle it", Alex said in a low voice. But the boy did not heed and continued to move forward as if in a trance.

Without warning, Ilya shouted, "Oy!" and clapped his hands loudly.

The deer sprang, leaping over the crest of stone in a single bound. With a cry of dismay Kiril ran to the spot where it had been standing. Ilya strolled up beside him and laughed. Alex slowly followed. At the edge of the outcropping, they peered into the forested saddleback below and watched a flash of red disappear into the trees.

Kiril gave his brother a long look and walked away.

They remained on the top for hours. The boys headed off in different directions to explore the ridge while Alex napped in the shadow of a low rock. The breeze held off the bees for a time, but when it dropped, they returned and began to swarm. He stood up, batting them away, and called for the boys to return. Their voices answered from some distance. While he waited for them, he walked to the eastern side of the ridge and looked out over a limitless space filled with corrugated ranges of dark green taiga, spreading away in fading layers of gray-violet until, near the horizon, it was hard to tell what was mountain and what was sky. Immediately below, the Primorski range swept down into a wide, uninhabited valley. On its far side another range ran parallel to the mountains on which he stood. He saw a silver ribbon many miles away at the mouth of the valley and supposed that it was part of the Angara River, perhaps the wide basin above Irkutsk.

Eagles circled below him, spiraling upward, then soaring at slow angles across his line of vision. At one point they crossed the path of a white bird that was flying up the valley from the west. Alex's eyes followed its path, and he was intrigued when it performed a feat of aerial acrobatics that he had not known birds were capable of. It stopped in midair near the height of the opposite range and descended vertically into the trees. Then he realized it could not possibly be a bird, for the other range was miles away. He concluded that it was a helicopter.

Giving it no more thought, he turned to greet the boys, who came crashing out of the bush. They had both found "treasure" that they wanted to show him: Ilya, a set of three-pronged antlers, and Kiril, a little cross. The latter was a single piece of wood, rather primitively carved and so old that it was bleached white by the weather. Its surface was soft as silk, lined with thin cracks.

"Where did you get it?" Alex asked.

"It was sitting on a pile of stones in the trees. There are words scratched on the stones too."

"What do they say?"

"It was hard to read. Some of the letters are missing. Do you want to see it?"

Alex followed Kiril and Ilya along the ridge. A hundred yards into the trees, they came upon a rectangular heap of stones that evidently had been piled there by human hands. The rocks were covered in white lichen and capped by rough granite slabs.

Kiril held up the cross. "I found this in a crack between two of those stones when I lay down on them. See, here are the letters. I couldn't read all of them."

Alex knelt and bent over the foot of the slab. Scraping away bits of lichen, he uncovered words cut crudely into the stone. Several of the Slavonic letters had been obliterated beyond recall.

"*Muchenik*", Kiril said, tracing the surviving runes with a finger. "The tormented one. Why would anyone write that here?"

Surprised that a Russian boy did not know the meaning of the term, Alex said, "The *muchenik* is one who is put to death for his faith in God. In English we say *martyr*."

Kiril read on, mouthing slowly whatever he could decipher:

Porf [missing] eyevich
Martyr
His blood [missing]
[missing] 1934 [missing]
to God [missing]

"It's a grave", Alex said. "The grave of a holy person who suffered under persecution."

"In 1934", Kiril said.

"Stalin's time", said Ilya with a scowl.

Alex crossed himself and prayed for the soul of the one whose remains were buried here.

"There are more letters, here at the top", said Kiril, pointing to the other end of the heap.

Svyashchennik

"Beneath these stones lies the body of a priest", Alex said. The boys glanced at him, then at the grave. Kiril seemed lost in thought for a moment, then stuck the wooden cross into a crevice in the stones.

"It belongs to him", he said, and stepped back with his hands by his sides.

The descent to the shore of Baikal took less time than the climb, and they arrived at the beach by midafternoon. Hungry and thirsty, they drank from the lake and ate the last of their food, then took a final look at the Bell Tower before launching the boat. As before, Ilya commanded the stern and got the motor firing smoothly.

Kiril cupped his hands to his mouth and bellowed, "Kolokol-kolokol-kolokol!"

The journey south was uneventful. An hour later they beached the skiff below the Pimonenko house at Ozero Baikal.

Weary and sunburned, Alex and the boys foraged for a meal in the kitchen, drank all the milk that Aglaya had left for them in a crock by the back porch, and sat around for a few hours, reading, thinking, or staring out of the window. Between them there was no conversation.

Around seven that evening, when Alex bid the boys goodnight, they looked up from their chess game and responded with friendly smiles. Back in the clinic, he washed with basin and jug, lay down on the bed, and gazed out the window at the lake, which was stained red with the falling sun. He tried to read for a while but could not concentrate. Instead, he prayed a rosary and chotki for the conversion of Russia, for his own deeper conversion, for the conversion of the West, and for his sons.

As he drifted into sleep, he murmured, "Father Porfiry, pray for us all."

36. *A Message in the Ark*

The next morning was overcast and not as hot as it had been during the past several days. The air was heavy with humidity, but as yet no rain had fallen. The upper field was thirsty, and the house garden was also in need, for its dry soil was dull brown though pushing up rows of green shoots. After breakfast, Alex and the boys watered the plants from big wooden rain barrels that stood at the four corners of the house, dipping into the lukewarm reservoirs with metal cans that had been punctured with nail holes. Walking slowly up and down the rows, they made an artificial rain on the herbs and vegetables, and the soil turned black. Small birds fluttered down to play in the puddles, and swallows darted here and there, swooping low over the boys' heads, making them duck and laugh.

Ilya was in unusually high spirits, joking with passersby in the village lanes, whistling to himself, a bounce in every movement. Later, he took Kolo up into the field that was used by the community to pasture its animals. He pounded a metal stake into the ground, tied a long rope to it, then attached the other end to the pony's halter. While he was doing this, Aglaya tottered down the hill on the footpath and whiled away a few minutes chatting with him about the boat journey to Olkhon. She was interested in what he told her about the grave on the mountain and went to the house to find Alex and dig more details out of him.

Over cups of tea, he told her everything. She was impressed by the story, even moved.

"'Porf' was all we could read of the name", Alex said "It seems to imply Porfiry. Did you ever hear of a priest by that name?"

"Hmmm. You say it was 1934 he died? I would have been about ten years old at the time. We hadn't seen a priest in all the years since we left the Selenga. And it was many more years before we saw another. No, no, I can't say I know the name, but this means little. Those who perished under the red star are numbered in the millions, and countless were the saints among them. More than the bright white stars in the heavens. Well, we know his name now, and that gives us some pull with him. Say a prayer, Alik; say a prayer to him, and he'll pray for you before the throne of the Most High."

"I already have, Aglaya."

"What did you pray for, may I ask?"

"For the conversion of Russia, the conversion of the Western world, and my own conversion."

"A good prayer. The last he will answer swiftly."

"You're sure about that, are you?" Alex said with a smile.

Leaning forward to peer at him with her most penetrating carrion bird expression, she said, "Ask and you will receive; knock and it will be opened. Things hidden will be revealed. Things in the open will shrink to nothing. The poor and the humiliated will be crowned. Do you want a crown, Alik?"

"No."

"I don't mean the wedding crown—I mean the crown of a true son of God."

"I wish to be a true son of God. But I don't need a crown."

"Are you too proud to accept a crown if the Lord himself places it on your head?"

"If you put it that way, Aglaya, I would be quite a cad if I refused."

"Indeed you would, indeed you would—playing at humility and knocking a gift from the hands of the Lord himself! What sort of ninny would do a thing like that, I ask you?"

"You have a point."

"And an excellent point it is. Don't you forget it."

"I'll try not to."

Sitting back with an air of pontification, Aglaya inspected Alex with unsentimental eyes. Presently, a look of profound sadness settled on her old face.

"What now?" he asked, sipping his tea. "Why are you scolding me?"

"I'm not scolding; I'm mute."

"Mute indeed. You were giving me a tongue-lashing without opening your mouth."

"Was I?" she said in an uncharacteristic tone of apology. "Forgive me, but I don't think you understand me at all, Alik. I was only seeing what's to become of you."

"*Only* seeing what's to become of me? What on earth do you mean by that?"

"I don't know. It's strange. I saw you falling into water. Your head pushed under by a hand. A cruel hand. I saw you suffering."

A little disconcerted, Alex said, "Perhaps you imagined it."

"I must have", she said, and changed the subject. Not long after, she took her leave and went back up the hill to her home.

After lunch, Kiril moped about the house aimlessly. His thoughts were somewhere else, his mood melancholic. It seemed that, like Ilya and Aglaya, he was not quite himself. Alex supposed that the change of weather was the cause. For a while Kiril stood on the bench in the kitchen and fingered his grandfather's sword, sliding it in and out of its scabbard. Finally he took down his sailboat and went outside with it.

Happening to glance out the window some time later, Alex saw that the boy was down at the shore trying to make the boat float. Sensing that Kiril was lonely and dissatisfied, perhaps missing his mother, he decided to keep him company.

Coming up behind without a sound, Alex sat on the grass above the pebble beach and observed Kiril pushing the boat out into the water again and again. As he watched the boy go through these futile motions, he wondered at his determination. Eventually Alex understood that this was not really about a young lad's desire to make a toy function properly. It was about the need to connect to his father through a word the father had left for him, and only for him. For most of Kiril's life, Yevgeny had been little more than a face in a photograph.

"Poor is man from his mother's womb unto his grave", Alex whispered. "Born with a cry, he lives tossed up and down as a ship on the sea, and dies with tears."

There came a moment when Kiril gave up. Once again the boat had sunk. Unaware of Alex's presence, he sobbed, his chest heaved, and his hands curled and uncurled by his sides in frustration. With a cry of anger he leaped into the water, grabbed the boat, and hurled it at the shore. It struck a rock not far from Alex's feet, snapping the mast and scattering chips of paint. Kiril waded out of the water, covering his face with his hands.

"Come here, Kiril", Alex said.

The boy dragged his feet slowly toward the wreckage of his boat and stood gazing down at it with an expression of abject misery.

"Sit down; sit down here by me."

Kiril flung himself onto the ground and buried his face in his arms. Alex picked up the boat and inspected the damage.

"We can fix it", he said.

"I don't want to fix it. It's no good", Kiril cried.

"It's a good boat. It's a beautiful boat. There's something not quite right with it, that's all. We'll find out what it is, and then we'll change it."

"It doesn't matter."

"We'll do it together, you and I. Here, look at this. See what I've found."

Kiril squinted at the stern of the boat, to which Alex was pointing with his index finger.

"What? I don't see anything."

"Some paint fell off when you tried to make the boat fly. And look what was hidden beneath it. Do you see this screw? My guess is there's a weight inside, probably an iron bar."

"Why would Papa put an iron bar inside?"

"To make the hull heavier, to make it sit in the water properly."

"But it doesn't."

"That's because it's just a little off to the side. If you look closely, you can see that it's to the right of the rudder. Not much, hardly noticeable to the eye."

"Yes, I see now. But what can we do about it?"

"We'll pull out the bar, drill a better hole, and put the weight back inside. Then we'll cut a new mast and put up the rigging. You'll be sailing by the end of the day."

"No, it's useless."

"Do you have a drill and screwdriver?"

"They're in the shed."

"Let's go find them."

Expecting to spend a prosaic day repairing a toy boat, Alex and Kiril sat side by side on the back porch with a collection of screwdrivers, a hand brace, and a box of rusty drill bits. After looking carefully at the damage, they decided first to remove the weight in the hull that seemed to be the source of the trouble. Alex unscrewed the brass bolt and drew it out.

As he did so, a circular crack appeared in the paint around the hole. Using an awl, he scraped away the paint, revealing what appeared to be a cork plug. It was brittle, and it disintegrated under the point of the awl. When the fragments had been cleared out, Alex looked into the shadowed hole and saw the butt end of a metal object—an iron bar, he supposed. He turned the hull stern down, and the metal slid out. It was not in fact a bar but a shiny tube of some kind, about nine inches long, with two sections that fitted together snugly at the middle. The joint was sealed by resin.

"What is it?" Kiril asked, taking it from Alex. He shook it in his hands, and it rattled with a dull clicking sound.

"It's hollow", Alex said. "I wonder what's inside."

Stamped on the metal's outer surface was the universal symbol for the medical profession, the caduceus, a winged rod with two entwined snakes, representing the staff of life overcoming the symbol of death.

Kiril tried to pull apart the sections, but the seal resisted his every effort. Taking it back, Alex pressed the point of the awl into the resin and inscribed a line around the circumference. Bits of yellow fiber cracked off, and the two halves slid apart. Inside was a roll of paper. Kiril pulled it out carefully, a look of intense curiosity in his eyes. He unrolled it and read aloud, "My dear son, my Kiril..."

There he stopped and fell silent. He swallowed.

"Papa?" he breathed.

His face paled. He got slowly to his feet and went inside the house, carrying the paper with him.

Alex followed a minute later and found that the boy had gone into his bedroom and closed the door. He was about to go in to talk with Kiril but paused with his hand on the doorknob, then withdrew and went into the kitchen. He took Ilya's boat down from the shelf and brought it to the table. Scratching at the stern of the hull with the awl, he exposed a screw similar to the one on Kiril's boat. It too was slightly off-center. He unscrewed it, removed the cork, and tilted the boat. A metal tube identical to the first slid out into his open palm. He pushed it back into the hole and reinserted the pieces of cork. He went out the kitchen door and called up the field to Ilya, who was feeding handfuls of oats to Kolo.

Ilya said nothing when Alex showed him what his boat contained. Betraying no hint of excitement—in fact, showing no emotion whatsoever—he took the metal tube and walked slowly around the corner of the house and out of sight. Half an hour later, Alex went to look for him. He spotted him on the roof, lying on his back, head on the peak and legs stretched down toward the garden. His arms covered his face, and a roll of paper was held in one hand.

Alex went back inside to make supper. As he was peeling potatoes to throw into the pot of boiling water on the stove, the bedroom door scraped open and Kiril came out. Red-eyed, he came up beside Alex, standing close, not quite touching, and watched him cut potatoes into quarters. Alex put an arm around his shoulders.

"It's a letter", Kiril said. "Would you like to read it?"

"Yes, I would", Alex replied, wiping his hands on a cloth.

Kiril gave him the roll of papers and returned to his bedroom. Alex walked up the hill and sat in the field. Kolo swished her tail back and forth and tore up clumps of grass that she chewed contentedly. Swallows darted low among the wildflowers.

Alex unrolled the letter and read the following:

13 May 1988

My dear son, my Kiril,

You are only four months old as I write these words. You are asleep in my arms as I sit with you. You and I together, we are by the window, watching the swallows soaring and diving above the garden. Spring is here at last, and the Angara is running out of the lake. Soon Baikal will be thawed.

I am very ill. I will not be much longer on this earth. With all my heart I desire to remain here so that I could be with you as you speak your first word and take your first step. How often I have dreamed of taking you into the mountains with me, to the highest peaks, where we would look out over the world and see its hugeness, its immense beauty. We would climb to the heights of Maloye Kolokolnik and pretend it is a cathedral whose bells awaken Baikal each morning. We would sleep on the shore beneath the Bell Tower. I would fry an omul fish for you for breakfast, the fish that we caught before dawn. In summer we would pick berries on Olkhon Island and make our mouths purple. We would gather the wild rhododendron blossoms for your mother. We would swim in a pebble cove at Pribaikalsky, so cold it would make our teeth chatter. We would warm ourselves by our campfire and tell stories under the stars. So many things would I do with you, my son, but I cannot.

Now that you are a young man, it may be that you will do these things for yourself. It is my hope that you will. Perhaps your brother Ilya will take you. If he does, or if another man takes you there, please remember me, and know that I thought of you in those places and that I thought of you and me going there together. I pray to our Father in heaven that you will know I am with you.

"How strange", you will think. "How strange that my father, who was a scientist, speaks to me of God. Is not God an old man with a white beard in the tales told by the babushkas?" Oh no, He is not that. He is so much more; even scientists cannot measure Him. He is so far above us that our thoughts cannot comprehend Him, yet

He is near. He is as close as your heartbeat. He fills the space that I will soon leave empty. I offer my death for my sons, and I ask God to send you both a good father—a father to your souls.

These are dark times in which I write, Kiril. Everywhere there is talk about a new openness and a new restructuring in our country. I would like to believe this is true, but our entire history is one of not-openness and not-changing. Is it true that dawn is coming for us? Do the shadows recede just a little? It may be so, yet easily they can return, and then the situation may be worse than before. By now your mother will have explained to you that our government considers me a danger to our land and our people. This is not because I have done any wrong but because there is a great darkness in the places of power, and this darkness does not comprehend the light. I have spoken of our need for freedom, and for this I have been banned from my native land, and your mother with me. Though it is not as hard now as it once was, and though I have learned to love Baikal in its ever-returning beauty, even so, it is a place of exile. Still, all men are in exile. We are not yet in Paradise. I go ahead of you, my son, and it is my prayer that we will meet again in Paradise, there where our Savior reigns, there where no tears fall and no fear enters. From that far country, if God grants it, I will watch over you and pray for you, as I will for Mama and Ilya.

Perhaps you will ask yourself why your father has done so strange a thing as hiding his letter inside a toy. It is because my words are considered dangerous by our government, and especially my words about the living God, who is our Father, and His Son Jesus Christ, who is our Savior, and the Holy Spirit, who is the fire of love. The darkness hates the light and seeks to snuff it out.

So many times have the KGB come to our house and searched my papers and my books, and they have taken many things from us. Thus, this letter must remain hidden, awaiting the time when you will be able to understand it. Even Mama does not know of it. It is a surprise for you. It is a message that you will find only when you become a young man.

Yes, I can see you now, Kiril. I see you sitting in the kitchen one fine morning in spring, when the ice is gone, and you will hold the boat in your hands. You will want to take it to the lake and sail it, as you have tried to do many times, never succeeding in making it behave as a boat should. You will think to yourself, "Why did my father give me a boat that does not float properly? Why does it do such strange things?"

Then, because you will have grown into a clever young fellow, you will think about the little screw beneath the rudder. Perhaps you will unscrew it. When it has been removed, a crack will appear in the paint, and because you are a curious boy—I am sure you will be such—you will wonder what is behind it. You will scrape a little, and you will see that behind the paint is a cork. You will remove the cork because you wish to know and understand many things that are a puzzle to you. Behind the cork you will find this metal pipe and, sealed within it, my last words to you.

Perhaps you will think it is an odd thing to do, to hide a message inside a little boat, in such a way that it is very difficult to find. Why not bury it in the garden? Why not hide it in the rafters of the outhouse? The answer is, because hiding it from the men of darkness is the least of my reasons. The real reason is that this letter is not my only word to you. The boat also is my word. The game of hiding and seeking also is my word, for I would greatly have loved to play with you in the evening light, and to see you laugh.

Are you laughing, Kiril? I hope so, for I am laughing with the fun of it. Is this not a clever trick? Is this not a good joke? Come on, laugh with me. Do not be sad. Though I do not want to die, though I do not want to leave you without a father, I know a great secret. It is this: You have a Father who sees you and is never apart from you. I laugh, my son. I laugh with pleasure because I know that you will be a shining boy, for I see that you have your grandfather's gold hair and his rosy face and his sweet disposition. It is many years since I have seen him, and now I will not see him again. But I remember him. I remember so many things, and it is right to remember. Above all, we must try to remember the good things of life, for these are the truest and most eternal. So too we must forgive the failures of the past, for in forgiving we become free. Then we are like a heavy boat that steadies itself and grows light before the wind as the sails fill with joy.

I am dying because of the negligence and sins of others. I forgive them, and you too must forgive them. They took away your father, but that is not a good reason to let hatred into your heart. For if you do let it in, they will have taken your soul as well.

You will see me again.

I hold you always in my arms, my Kiril,
as I do now, at this moment,
Papa

PART FOUR

37. *To Another Country*

After Alex read Yevgeny's letter, he returned to the house and found Kiril in the kitchen. The boy was standing in the middle of the room and staring into space, holding the boat in his hands. Alex gave him the letter.

"Your father has sent a message to you. He sees you. He is with you."

Kiril nodded curtly with full-blown Russian formality and disappeared into his room. Ilya was totally unreachable and made no reference to his own letter. Throughout the remainder of the evening, Alex and the boys ate and puttered about in silence. Alex knew they were absorbing the messages from their father and that neither of them wished to talk about it.

Just before bedtime, Volodya popped in to say that a note from Irina Filippovna had come to him through the hand of one of the villagers who had been to Listvyanka that day. She would arrive there by bus in two days and wanted Volodya to pick her up in the boat.

The next morning, Alex rose at dawn, prayed, and sat down on a chair by the ward window in order to do some serious thinking. He told himself that his feeling for Irina was a product of natural attraction combined with loneliness. Before his trip to Russia, he had not given loneliness much thought. He had always been more or less a solitary man; he had worked hard to construct a life shielded from the demands of unpredictable human personality; he had resisted their every infringement on his interests and equilibrium.

And he now saw that ever since Carol's death, he had been steadily withdrawing from other people.

He was not so simpleminded as to think that a migration to another country would solve his problem. He knew that if he lived long enough in Ozero Baikal, it would prove itself every bit as irrational as his own community. He had, he believed, abandoned forever the lure of romanticism. If he had become attached to Irina and her sons, it was only because of his dependency on them. They had opened their home and their hearts to him with little recompense. A few English lessons, after all, could have been derived from a book. He had dug up the garden and helped to plant it. He had repaired a few things, but all of that could just as easily have been accomplished by the boys or by neighbors. It was obvious that he was the sole beneficiary of their extraordinary generosity.

Irina had mentioned more than once that she was grateful for his presence, that he was a help to her growing sons. He did not dispute this, but he also saw that a transient father was only a stop-gap measure. Perhaps he was more to them than that, but of this he was not sure. In any event, it was unrealistic to consider such a radical change of life. He had no roots here, and he had no skills that would be of service to their family. Could he open a bookshop in a remote village where the majority of its people valued a book less than a new fishhook? The notion of making a home among these people was simply ridiculous, out of the question.

Even if it could be a viable option, what about Irina herself? Why would she be interested in a second husband? Although the thought of marrying again had a few times presented itself since Carol's death, he had always dismissed it. He knew that to marry for the purpose of relieving loneliness was not love. To make a marriage of two groundless optimisms was a recipe for suffering, and neither he nor Irina needed any more of that. No, it was better to remain a cracked pot.

Aglaya the Crow might or might not be the village prophetess, but it would be foolish to base so grave a decision on her cryptic sayings. Purple primroses, crowns, and wedding bells! What a fine party the village would have on the day Irina and Alex made their vows—but who would be there to help when the optimism turned to disappointment, when the newlyweds discovered that number-two spouse was not number one and never could be?

Alex stood up and paced the floor back and forth.

"What am I talking about?" he muttered. "I'm leaving Ozero Baikal. Soon. Forever. If they want to write to me, I'll answer. I'll be their pen pal in the West, the 'man who fell from the sky'. I'll keep contact with them, but I won't be fooled. I won't succumb to Aglaya's insinuations. Oh, that manipulative woman! She's utterly predictable, dreaming of a nice match just so she can indulge in a few happy tears! Playing with us the way little girls play with dolls. That woman would say anything to make her fantasy more delectable. Well, she's not going to get away with it. I'm not going to trot through the script she's plotted for me. I'm not going to court Irina Filippovna, and I'm not going to teach her sons to play baseball and eat hot dogs. I'm not. I'm simply not. I refuse to spend whatever remains of my life trying to build a new family when the situation has disaster written all over it!"

This cataract of rhetoric was an unusually long one for Alex. Stopping in midstride, realizing that he had been declaiming aloud, he groaned and sat down again, staring out the window.

"But what can be done about this country, these people? They set your heart on fire one moment and hit you over the head the next. They understand nothing about what matters in my world, and I understand even less about theirs.

"The only thing we have in common is that we all believe in love. Everyone swears by it, stakes his life on it, and just about everyone disproves it in the end. What a sham. East and West, in every direction, marriages fail in droves, in flocks, blasted out of the sky by shotguns of unfulfilled desires and false expectations.

"The only way it could work is if both of us were to expect nothing and vow to give everything. Am I ready for that? Have I ever been capable of that? Would grace be enough to overcome temperament? Two temperaments? Four, if you count her boys? Six, if you add my own sons into the mix?

"Would there be some transcontinental visiting? Maybe. But how? Neither Irina nor I have any money. How would I earn a living? Pulling up omul from the lake? Trapping? Teaching English to a dying race of winter-born?

"Would Jacob lend me some money in order to survive? Could I bear to beg money from my middle-class son? A fine legacy to leave one's family: downwardly mobile Dad! Deadbeat Dad, the dreamer who finally ran off into the mysterious East to check out his fantasy and never came back. Like little Puny in the fairy tale, he spent the rest of his life in a brightly colored fable."

Coming to the end of his rather limited store of vehemence and his box of mixed metaphors, Alex slumped and shook his head.

"I don't know. I just don't know. What does God want from me? Did he bring me here for a reason? Am I an answer to Yevgeny's prayers? Am I to be a father to his sons? But what of my own sons? What about Andrew? Where is *he*?"

By now Alex had worked himself into a stew of emotion. Realizing that he was getting nowhere, he jumped up and left the clinic. Striding down to the shore of the lake, he turned left and paced along the beach fighting a growing despondency. He hoped that Irina would bring back a message for him—money, reassurances from friends, the promise of an imminent return to his safe and orderly world. Of course, he would also have to face her. A kiss now hung suspended between them. It could not be ignored. Neither could it be acted upon. He could not bear to confirm her bitter comment about the fickleness of alien lovers:

Good-bye, Irina. It has been very nice knowing you! I especially enjoyed the exotic flavor of Russian love, but I have to go home now!

She protected herself with cynicism, hid her broken heart beneath a veneer of hard realism. He had no right to offer a token refutation, to invite her to expose her heart only to turn his back on her the moment a plane ticket was in his hands. That would be callousness of the worst sort. That would be to reduce her to the realm of objects—a walking, talking, distraction from his pain. In short, a lie.

Alex dropped to his knees and plunged his face into the lapping waves. The sun had warmed the shallows, and thus he was surprised to find that the lake was not uniformly Arctic in temperature. He got up and wandered along the shore, passing beyond the north end of the village. On the far side of a copse of bushes, he came upon a little stretch of sand. Checking to see that there were no observers, he stripped down to his shorts and waded in. In the shallows the water was cool, not unbearable, but the moment the bottom dropped away, Baikal's illusion was dispelled. The shock of perpetually cold water hit him at once. For a moment he wanted to retreat, but the memory of his old battles with the limitations of the flesh rose up, and he drove himself farther out into the open lake. Gasping, forcing his arms and legs to do their work, he swam fifty meters, then turned and headed back to shore. By the time he reached the shallows again, he was utterly exhausted, his skin shivering and red, his breath coming in great gulps. He crawled out and fell onto the sand.

"Gaspadin," said the voice of Volodya, "what are you doing? You trying to catch a *nerpa*?"

Alex looked up to see the old man standing at the top of the bank, staring down at him with a humorous look.

"I'm trying to clear my thoughts."

"You'll *freeze* your thoughts that way."

"You call it the Lake of Fire. It should be called Lake of Ice!"

"To be sure, but sometimes when the sun dances on it, it's like a fire."

Dressing himself, Alex felt curiously refreshed, his dilemmas reduced to manageable proportions.

"Do people do such things where you come from?" Volodya asked in a wondering tone. "Here, we sometimes jump in after a big sweat in the *banya* house. But we jump right out again."

"I needed a shock, Volodya, to help me see things more clearly."

"Need a change of scene? I'm going up lake for the day. Want to come with me?"

After a moment's pause, Alex nodded. He went back to the house to tell the boys where he was going. They were nowhere in sight, so he left a note on the kitchen table. In the clinic he toweled his hair dry, put on his fleece vest, and as a final thought put the icon of Christ into his shirt pocket. Returning to the beach, he found Volodya loading jerry cans into the skiff.

"Not using the big boat?" he asked the old man.

"I won't be fishing today. I'm going to see my brother in Tutai. This is faster. Gas costs a bit more than diesel but saves money in the long run."

As they boarded the skiff and pushed away from shore, Volodya made other remarks of a practical sort, for which Alex was grateful. He was thoroughly sick of his mental ruminations, dissecting the imponderable, trying to solve the unsolvable. He decided that good old-fashioned escape was a much neglected and underappreciated art.

As they roared north, the wind was fresh in their faces, and the lake somewhat unruly, but this only added to Alex's feeling of expectancy. As they rounded the headland of a long bay, he spotted the Bell Tower in the distance and signaled to Volodya to slow down.

"Would you take me ashore?" he shouted above the rumble of the motor. "I'd like to climb the Primorskis today."

"Are you sure you want to do that? I don't have time to wait for you."

"Why don't you go on to Tutai and pick me up on the way back?"

"All right. But I won't return till nightfall."

"That would work out well. I'll wait for you in the cove around sunset."

"As you like."

When the boat angled into the cove on the south side of the tower, Alex stood on the bow plate and leaped onto the sand. He waved, and Volodya gunned the motor, spinning the boat in a tight half circle, pointing the bow to the north. Within a minute he was out of sight, and Alex was left alone on the shore, breathing forest air and listening to the twittering birds.

Retracing the route that he and the boys had taken days before, he reached the creek and crossed it, then followed the animal trail, climbing at a leisurely pace. He was certain now that he would be returning home within days and that this was his last chance to fix the natural iconography of the land in his memory. Despite his affection for Kiril and Ilya, he was glad for the solitude and savored the sweet melancholy of the moment. He was ascending to a high perspective from which he could meditate on the Sacred Sea and the vast panorama of the taiga.

Reaching the mossy clearing on the crown of the mountain, he stood for a time gazing into the northwest, straining his eyes toward the ultimate reaches of Siberia. Then he turned left and walked along the ridge to the grave of the martyred priest.

As on his previous visit, he sensed that he was penetrating a zone of sacred silence. He knelt and closed his eyes, laying his arms on the foot of the flat capstone. The peace he felt might have been caused by the beauty of the mountain or the presence of a passion sufferer's remains, or it could be simply that he had exhausted all adrenaline in reaching the top. He remained without moving for some time, then he got up and found the little wooden cross that Kiril had stuck into the crack in the rocks. He sat down, holding it in both hands, his back against the tomb, facing west. He kissed the cross.

He saw that Russia had been bathed in blood. Many had drowned in this blood, and no Aeolian wind had come to their rescue. Countless martyrs were lying within her soil.

He sighed, and a wave of sorrow overwhelmed him—grief for Russia. He also saw the plague that was afflicting the Western world, where freedom seemed to reign. All peoples and nations and races were falling in the great and terrible falling of the present age. Halcyon was Baikal, and Baikal was Halcyon. Each soul was endangered, and each strove to hold its ground upon the earth.

The birds swooped and sang. The golden bees hummed and probed.

Was God saying to him, "Will you come with me into this place of powerlessness? Will you accept to be poorer than you have ever been before?"

"Must I go the way of all exiles?" he asked in a subdued voice. "Must I be to this place what Oleg is to my homeland?"

There could be a role for him in this land, if he chose to accept it. It would be hard, and he would have to die still further to the things that he had clung to for most of his life. He did not know for certain if this meant he was to remain on the shores of Baikal. In a sense it did not matter, for love was needed everywhere.

"But I have nothing to give you", he said. "There is so much darkness in the world—everywhere. It spreads, shifts its methods, its masks, its words. How can we defeat it when there is no weapon in our hands?

"Is that what you brought me here to show me? That there must be no weapon in our hands? Are you asking me to make a stand in the realm of broken hearts? And if I plant my feet in the soil of Russia, is there another whom you will send to my own sons, to be for them what I cannot be?"

Then, without any rational cause, he whispered the prayer he had offered to Christ so many months ago: "Do whatever you want with me."

Alex lay down on the moss beside the tomb and fell asleep holding the cross in his hands. Dreams came to him, and in them he saw, beyond the outermost end of human strength, the abyss of abandonment. And he understood that he must leap from a span overarching the river of time and that he must trust as the force of gravity took him—trust that the falling was a descent into the waters of life.

Then other images followed: stars falling from the heavens, cities in flames and oceans in tumult, and above these, a great multitude of people from every race and nation and tongue, standing before a throne and a Lamb, wearing robes soaked in blood that turned to dazzling white as they cried out in loud voices, *How long will it be until the inhabitants of the earth are brought to justice!*

Be patient a while longer, replied a voice like thunder, *until the number is fulfilled.*

Alex woke suddenly, startled by the cry of a raven that swooped low over his head.

Groggy, disoriented, he saw through the trees a line of little lights winking in the dusk. Had he slept this long? Getting slowly to his feet, he stretched his limbs and walked to the edge of the escarpment. As the sun fell below the horizon, the mountain all about him was bathed in a fading glow, now rose, now silver, now violet.

He strode back to the eastern brink and looked out over Baikal. It had become blood red. Realizing that Volodya would soon be waiting below, he walked north along the ridge in search of the pathway down. At last he found it and began to pick his way through the underbrush until he reached the stream. For twenty minutes or so he descended beside it, tripping again and again in the deepening gloom. Stars were now visible in the sky above him. At one point a large stone loomed suddenly in his path and he swerved to avoid it, but as he did so, he tripped and fell onto soft moss, rolled, and continued rolling, for the terrain pitched steeply downward. His body smashed into a tree trunk, breaking his fall—and cracking something in his rib cage. He cried out in pain and gasped for breath.

The forest was now completely dark. Only a patch of charcoal showed in an open space among the blacker branches above. He lay on the ground panting, hand on the invisible knife pressing into his side. Sitting up with great difficulty, groaning, he leaned against the tree. He cocked his ears in the hope of catching the sound of the stream tumbling down its little waterfalls, but he heard only a breeze. In this way he realized that he had come downhill some distance and that the hill was blocking the noise of the stream. In any event, down was down, and thus he believed he could find his way back to the cove by any number of routes, as long as he continued descending to the east.

Now he proceeded slowly, putting one foot after another, from stone to stone, holding out his right hand to catch onto the trunks of trees, resisting the pull of gravity. With his left arm he cradled his ribs. The pain screamed at him, dividing his attention. Trying to ignore it, he continued on for some time until it seemed that the ground beneath his feet began to level off. This was not so, for immediately after, he stepped into space and fell three or four feet onto a tangle of brush, and continued rolling downward until he came to a stop against a rock.

It took several minutes to regain his senses, and when he did he was completely lost, unsure of which direction the lake would be. The night sky was still moonless, but there were enough stars to see that he had tumbled into a narrow ravine between two humps of the Primorskis. Judging by the surrounding shadows, he thought his route lay in a descent to the right. If he continued in that way, he would eventually arrive at the shore of Baikal. Even if he missed the cove, he could light a small fire and attract Volodya's attention. Failing that, he would try to hail any other boats passing near to shore.

For the next hour he inched through the bushes that covered the floor of the ravine, the ground tipping steadily downward. The contours of the two walls were irregular, and thus at no point was he afforded a view of a star-filled lake. Another hour passed, during which his ribs began to completely dominate his mind. He groaned loudly and regularly and once or twice called out Volodya's name, only to be answered by echoes on the flanking stone ramparts.

Finally the ravine leveled off, and Alex stumbled out into an open stretch of earth that was soft underfoot. Easing his body onto what he thought was a beach, he found that the surface was moss, not sand. Straining his eyes for signs of open water, he saw ahead of him a long shadow, its silhouette stretching from one end of the compass to another, blocking out the stars close to the horizon. They were mountains. But this did not make sense, for the mountains to the east of Baikal could not have loomed so close. Indeed, the Khamar-Daban was high and white, its crests sharper than those of the

Primorskis. The mountains now facing Alex were rounded and black. At their base a line of red lights winked on and off.

With a sinking feeling he realized that he had descended the western slope of the range by mistake and was now standing in the wide valley he had seen two days before. He thought for a moment that he should try to go back up the heights of the Primorskis but realized this would be a dangerous and futile exercise. Utterly exhausted and in a great deal of pain, he was now afflicted with a terrible thirst.

It came to him that the lights indicated some kind of man-made establishment, perhaps a bush airport or a village. Either of these meant that a road would not be far off. A faint glow in the southwestern sky confirmed his position. The glow was Irkutsk, about forty miles away at the mouth of the valley. His only recourse was to make straight for the red lights, which appeared to be no more than a few miles distant.

He knew it would be foolish to try to stumble through unknown territory in the dark. There might be marshes or any number of other perils lying between him and his destination. It was difficult to know how far he would have to travel, for even on the mountaintop he had been unable to estimate the distance between the two ranges.

Retracing his steps to the mouth of the ravine, he groped about and found a cluster of boulders, lay down beside one, and tried to sleep. But the pain in his ribs would not let him escape. It was so severe that he could not bear to probe with his fingers to find out whether the bones were fractured or only badly bruised. Each breath cost a great deal.

The short summer night of Siberia was a blessing, however, for the sky soon paled and a wide lowland appeared before him. He got up and walked across what now was revealed as a meadow of wild grass, damp underfoot. On the far side a brooding pine forest rose up like a palisade. He entered it and wove his way through a maze of ghostly forms. Here the ground was devoid of underbrush, thanks to the thick carpet of needles, but branches repeatedly tore at his face and hands. At one point, just after the sun rose, a creek crossed his path, and he fell to his knees beside it, putting his lips into the shallows. He rested for a while, waded to the other side, then continued his journey.

The sun was high over his left shoulder when he came to the edge of the trees and stood before what he took to be a gravel road. As he stepped onto it, he realized that it was too narrow to be a road, and no tire tracks were visible on its surface. On the opposite side was a chain link fence, twelve feet high, topped by barbed wire. The fence stretched into infinity, north and south. At distances of a hundred yards or so, red lights on the top of metal poles winked on and off at regular intervals. Beyond the fence was an inner wall of fencing, separated from the first by a space of about ten yards. It hummed.

"Electric", Alex thought.

He wondered for a moment what was contained within such an elaborate defense work. There was nothing to indicate why it was there. Beyond it was the lower slope of the second range, merely a continuation of forested hills and mountains.

Realizing that no help would be found in that direction, he turned left, to the southwest, and began to walk along the gravel path beside the outer fence. At no point along the perimeter were there signs warning of high voltage, neither were there any gates. From time to time he noticed small black objects mounted on the poles that were topped by flashing lights. These were pointed at an angle along the wire. He had passed three of them before he was struck by the possibility that they were surveillance cameras. This was an encouraging thought, because it meant that somewhere eyes were watching monitor screens fed by the cameras and that he would eventually be noticed. Someone would come out to rescue him.

He had passed two more black boxes before he heard low throbbing in the southern sky, the whump-whump-whump of a helicopter increasing steadily in volume. He stopped and waited, preparing to wave it down. A few seconds later it appeared around a bend in the forest, flying low and swift. It was a white helicopter of unfamiliar design. He stood motionless and stared at it. It banked sharply and hovered for a few seconds, staring back like an enormous wasp, leveled off, and sank onto the ground about thirty feet away. A door in its side slid open. Five military men bearing machine guns jumped out and ran toward him.

"Good morning", Alex said in Russian.

Their grim faces did not return the greeting. A black sack was thrown over his head; someone grabbed him, lifted him, and carried him. The agony in his ribs forced violent shouts from his mouth; he thrashed his body and tried to tell them they were making a mistake. They threw him onto a hard surface while all around he heard the whining of motors. Hands pinned his arms, his legs, his head. Something sharp was jabbed into the base of his neck, and a bolt of light entered his skull. He fell through space and lost consciousness.

38. *We Know Everything*

He lifted his head and opened his eyes. He was seated on a metal chair in a bare room. The walls were high and white. There were no windows. The floor swayed, then steadied.

"Give him a few minutes", said a voice. "The dosage was low; he'll surface slowly."

"Bring coffee."

"Yes, Lieutenant."

Then someone shoved a plastic mug into Alex's hands and said, "Drink."

He drank the coffee in three gulps. His eyes began to focus.

Across from him, seated behind a metal desk, was a man of about forty years, lean, swarthy, rocking back and forth on a swivel chair. He wore a leather jacket opened to the waist, revealing a checked sport shirt. He was smoking a cigarette and gazing at the tip of it with some interest. Two younger men, dressed in green military uniforms, stood nearby.

Alex looked down at his own clothing. He wore a gray jump suit, and on his feet were cloth slippers. His chest ached. Something was binding his ribs tightly.

"Good morning", said the man behind the desk, in English. "Do you speak Russian?"

Alex nodded.

"I thought you might."

"Thank you for...", Alex began, then stopped in midsentence when he remembered their rescue methods.

"You are thanking us?" said the lieutenant, leaning forward with a look of sour amusement.

"I was lost", Alex said. "I was climbing in the mountains. I came down the wrong side."

"The wrong side", the man repeated.

Alex offered his right hand. "I'm Alex Graham", he said. The man stared at the hand.

"If you wish", he said, ignoring the hand. "I am Lieutenant Arbat."

The soldiers chuckled, though why they should do so was inexplicable.

"Where am I?" Alex asked.

"A shopping mall", said Arbat. "We are store security. We do not like shoplifters."

The soldiers tried unsuccessfully to hide their mirth. Arbat fired a round of Russian at them, and they sobered.

"I'm not a shoplifter", Alex said weakly, his face twitching involuntarily.

"You are not a shoplifter. But what kind of thief are you? No, do not answer. There's no need to bore us with that tale. Have another cup of coffee." He snapped a look at the guard. "Give him more coffee."

"Yes, sir."

The soldier brought a metal carafe and filled Alex's cup. He drank it.

"How long has Langley had an eye on our establishment?" Arbat asked.

"Pardon me?" Alex stammered. "Who is Langley?"

"Who?" Arbat said with a smile. "*Who*, he asks."

Alex blinked rapidly and shook his head. "I'm sorry; I don't know what you're talking about."

"Was it satellite photos only, or was it on-site human intel?"

Alex shook his head again.

Arbat rolled his eyes and sat back, lacing his fingers on his belly. For a minute or two he regarded Alex with a cold, analytical look, exhaling through his nostrils, his mouth twisting in irritation.

"All right, we'll do it the slow way. Tell us your little story."

"My story?"

"Your cover story. Why not? It's a quiet afternoon. Waste our time, why don't you?"

Alex was not sure what the man wanted exactly. His mind blurred, and the pain in his ribs clamored for attention.

"Tell us who you are and why you are here", Arbat prompted.

So Alex did. He rambled and stammered throughout his explanation, and the men followed the account without interruption, staring at him as if they were listening to a not-very-interesting child. When Alex had finished, Arbat dropped his chin to his chest and made some brief notes on a pad of paper. Then he removed the icon of Christ from his jacket pocket and threw it on the desk.

"This is part of the cover, no doubt. Where did you get it? Saint Petersburg? Moscow? Did Langley give it to you?"

"A friend gave it to me", Alex said, realizing only after he had spoken that he must not betray Aglaya's secret.

"A friend. Tell us about your friend."

"There's nothing to tell. I was robbed in Listvyanka and taken to the closest doctor. I've been recuperating at a clinic on Lake Baikal."

"Recuperating from a skull fracture, you say."

"That's right."

"In this detail he is telling the truth", said a voice directly behind Alex. A fourth man stepped forward, wearing a lab coat. "Both scar and x-ray confirm a healed fracture, quite recent."

"Who hit you?" Arbat asked.

"I don't know. Thieves, I think. The police in Irkutsk investigated."

Arbat nodded at someone behind Alex, and a fifth man came forward. Like the lieutenant, he was dressed in civilian clothing.

"Check with *militsiya* in Irkutsk about an assault in Listvyanka", Arbat said. "Also contact the Canadian embassy. We'll see very quickly if he is who he says he is. Of course, we know that you aren't who you say you are, Mr.—well, let's stick with *Graham* for the time being."

"Yes, please contact my embassy and tell them what has happened."

Arbat shot a look at the other civilian. "Use maximum discretion. Mr. Graham wants us to inform the Canadian embassy for a reason not entirely clear at the moment. But it has a great deal to do with the Americans, I believe. Doesn't it, Mr. Graham?"

"Americans?"

"And you're hoping very much that Canadian intelligence will immediately alert American intelligence in your embassy, aren't you?"

"In my embassy?"

"Excellent acting, Mr. Graham. A superb performance. You look so very much the part of the bewildered tourist. But really, you people shouldn't go so far as to hurt yourselves when you put together the act. The crack on the head was unnecessary. Where are you from?"

"I told you. I'm from Canada. Your embassy in Ottawa can check it out."

"Oh, I'm sure they will. And I'm sure they'll find ample evidence to prove that your story is reliable. Langley leaves no detail hanging in the wind. Our only difficulty, however, is that your story is not true."

"But it is true!"

Arbat stood and nodded to the soldiers. "Please show Mr. Graham to his room."

A black bag was thrown over his head, and hands grabbed his arms. He was walked along a hallway and pushed through a door. A guard removed the bag, went out, and locked the door behind him.

His cell was exactly like the interrogation room: clean, white, stark, windowless. The only furniture was a lidless toilet and a cot. Alex lay down and tried not to worry. The embassy would confirm what he had told these officials.

He wondered why they were treating him this way. Possibly because he had come too close to a government compound of some kind, and they were probing to find out if foreign intelligence had been snooping around it. What was this establishment? Perhaps a scientific center of some kind, or a secret military project?

No one bothered him for three days. He spent a lot of time pacing in his cell when he was not tossing and turning on the cot. The doctor entered each morning and again in the evening, always accompanied by a guard.

"Three ribs have been fractured", he said on the first day. When Alex asked him where, precisely, he was, and what was the nature of this institution, the doctor fell silent, changed the bands around Alex's chest, and departed without giving any answers.

On the fourth day, Alex was brought again to the interrogation room. Now there were four civilians and three guards. The guards were young, slightly cynical, but in no way sinister. This could not be said of the civilians.

The latter group sat on chairs beside Arbat, who took the central place facing Alex. Their expressions bespoke some indifference regarding his fate. They all smoked heavily. Arbat offered a cigarette to Alex. It was a Marlboro. The American cowboy gave Alex a look of confidence, congratulating him on his boundless adventure.

"No thank you, I don't smoke", Alex replied.

"Very admirable", said Arbat.

The Russians smoked and stared at him, smoked and stared, smoked and stared.

"When are you going to let me go home?" Alex asked.

"Actually, never, Bell", said Arbat with a friendly smile.

"Bell?"

"That's right, Mr. Bell. Never. You will not be returning to Virginia. Our only question is, do we permit you to exist a while longer, or do we wring everything out of you at once and drop you into a hole?"

This was said so amicably that Alex did not at first react. In fact, he laughed nervously.

"Really, Mr. Arbat, there's been a mistake. My name isn't Bell. I'm Alex Graham, and I'm from Halcyon, Ontario."

"Moscow has done its homework, Mr. Bell. And just as you anticipated, we found that a certain Alexander Graham, a bookseller from Halcyon, Ontario, is in fact a resident of that town. However, he is not currently at home."

"He's sitting right in front of you, Mr. Arbat."

"I expect he is now enjoying an all-expenses-paid holiday in the Caribbean, in exchange for the use of his name."

"No, he's enjoying an all-expenses-paid holiday in a Russian institution, or whatever this place is."

Arbat smiled. "A nice touch. But no one is convinced. We know who you are, so you might as well drop the charade."

"I—"

"The name. It's so obvious. The people at the Company surely have more imagination than that. Or did you choose it yourself? No, don't answer; I can't stand to hear any more of your lies. The point is, you must think we're very stupid."

"No, I don't. You're just mistaken", Alex said a little desperately. "Please, can't I make a telephone call to my embassy?"

"Which one? Which is your embassy today?"

"The Canadian!" Alex shouted.

The civilians in the room leaned forward with interest. The soldiers straightened themselves. But otherwise no one moved.

Arbat lit another cigarette. "Give it up, Mr. Bell, give it up. Do you think we're children? The alias. Think about it."

"What alias?"

"The Alexander Graham alias. Your real name is Averell James Bell. You were born in Kansas City, Missouri, in 1952. You are a graduate of West Point, were educated at Georgetown University in political science, studied at the Russian Institute at Columbia, taught linguistics at Princeton, and were recruited by Langley in 1981. You arrived in Saint Petersburg by train in February of this year and spread a rather interesting cover—the tale of the missing son, a sad little papa traipsing from one dashed hope to another, telling anyone and everyone his woes. Pathetic. And very clever."

Dumbfounded, Alex could only shake his head.

"You still deny it?"

"Yes."

"Who invented the telephone?" Arbat asked.

"I forget. Uh—Alexander Graham Bell, wasn't it?"

Arbat raised his eyebrows and smiled encouragingly.

"Oh," Alex said, "I see what you mean."

"Not very creative, was it? I mean, it's one of the oldest, and might I say more *reckless*, tricks of the trade. To use an alias close to one's own name, so that one is not taken by surprise. Correct? Really, the choice was too obvious even for the lamentable FSB to ignore."

"Is that who you are?"

"No."

"Who are you, then?"

"We're something special."

"Do you work for the government of Russia?"

"Absolutely. But we aren't here to talk about us, Bell; we're here to talk about you. Tell me about the stopover in England. Is MI6 involved in this?"

"No, they aren't—nobody's involved in anything."

"My, my—what innocents! All Western hands are clean! Obviously Canadian intelligence is cooperating. Are the Finns involved? No, let me guess. They don't even know you were in Helsinki. The Finland detour was just part of the cover, so you could slip into Russia quietly. The poor man's transport. So much easier than Sheremetyevo or Pulkovo. But we had our eye on you from the beginning."

Arbat put a disk into a machine on the desk and pressed a button. For some minutes Alex listened to his own voice conversing with a Russian voice on the train from Helsinki to Saint Petersburg, months ago:

"Listen, listen, Vasilinka, I am bringing you a prize.... This is Sony, Panasonic, Nokia we're talking about. Not that garbage from Minsk."

Then the rattle of railroad tracks.

"You are, I think, in telecommunications. Many foreign companies come to Russia now."

"I am traveling for personal reasons", said Alex's voice.

"Ah, personal", said the other.

Arbat pushed the off button.

"You see, Bell, we know everything", he said in a sympathetic tone.

"Not everything", said Alex heatedly. "The one thing you don't know is that I am who I say I am."

Arbat waved this away.

"I admit there are a few missing details. If you would prefer us to be lenient, you will have to fill in the blanks. First, we want to know where you went when you left the Trans-Siberian."

A chill struck Alex's heart. They knew about his journey. They had traced him from Moscow. Then with a second jolt, he saw the panorama of events that would unfold if he was to tell them about Sergius and Serafim. It could mean interrogations for the two priests, possibly prison and the destruction of their shrine.

"The train was attacked by protesters", Alex said.

"Yes, we're well aware of that farce. But you haven't answered my question."

"I hired a man to take me by snowmobile to the next station, where I caught a train."

"The original train was halted on the west side of the bridge. How could you have gone on to the next station?"

"It was easy. I crossed the river on foot, over the ice."

"And on the other side you hired someone. What was his name?"

"He was a local man."

"One of your contract agents?"

"Hardly. He was a drunk."

"So are many agents. You caught a train from where?" Arbat looked down at a map open on the desk. "Barabinsk is the next station after the burned bridge. But no trains were running from there for days after the attack. What did you do in the meantime?"

"I stayed in a cabin, a trapper's cabin, until the rail line was open again."

"Where?"

"A place where there was lots of snow and a river."

"There are hundreds of rivers in that region. What river?"

"It was called Ob."

"Which one? There are several Obs. Was it big or little?"

"A small one."

"All right, after you got on the train at Barabinsk, you traveled east. Where in the east?"

"The train arrived in Novosibirsk. I changed trains there and got off at Irkutsk."

"Why Irkutsk?"

None of the civilians in the room showed any change of attitude, but a subtle tension was now active in every set of eyes. Alex supposed it was because the trail he described was approaching their own facility, and like schoolboys, they were following the story as if they were inside of it.

"I needed to catch a bus at Irkutsk in order to get to Listvyanka. My son had been there, and I hoped to catch up to him."

"Please, we can dispense with the cover story. Why Listvyanka?"

"I'm telling you the truth. That's the only reason I had for going there."

"We know that you stayed in the hotel on the lake for one night, then disappeared. Where did you go?"

"I was taken by local people to a doctor near there."

"Why didn't they take you to the hospital at Irkutsk?"

"I'm not sure. Probably because I had no papers. Everything had been stolen. It was a long way to Irkutsk and a short drive to the local doctor."

"What is the name of the doctor?"

Alex paused. Thinking as fast as he could, he felt another bolt of fear as he realized that Irina was endangered. If he told them her name, they would surely investigate her. Then he realized they could obtain her name without much effort simply by questioning the hotel manager at Listvyanka. He decided to delay this as long as possible.

He shrugged. "It was a woman doctor. She has a clinic somewhere on the lake."

"Her name, Bell, her name."

"You could ask at the hotel. They know her name."

"You've been recuperating, as you put it, for months?"

"Yes."

"You spent all that time at this clinic under the care of a physician, and you can't tell us her name? Very odd."

"I forget a lot of things. Since the blow on my head, I don't always think right."

"A pity. Did you make any more trips to Irkutsk?"

"No, I didn't have any money for that. Everything had been stolen."

"The police in Irkutsk say they have no record of a theft or assault in Listvyanka. Why do you persist in lying to us?"

"Because there *was* a theft and an assault. Look at the back of my skull."

"Yes, but who did it? That's the question."

"I have no idea who did it. Maybe a petty criminal. In any event, I haven't been back to Irkutsk."

"Not even to see your friend—"

Arbat mentioned a name that Alex did not recognize.

"I don't have any idea who that is", Alex said.

"Really? He's now in the Lubyanka in Moscow. He has confessed to being a contract agent for the CIA. You were his case officer, weren't you?"

"No! I am not an intelligence agent. I'm a bookseller!" Alex cried in exasperation. "Ask me anything about literature. Anything! I'll quote Lermontov for you, if you like. Or Pushkin. Turgenev. Take your pick."

"Don't be insolent, Mr. Bell. You've made your point. We are now thoroughly convinced that you are an *educated* intelligence officer, a *cultured* intelligence officer. But then we already knew that, didn't we?"

"This is insane", Alex said. "This is a big mistake."

"Yes, a very big mistake", Arbat snapped. "You should have thought about that when you decided to spy on a sovereign nation." Turning abruptly to one of the guards, he said, "Take him back to his cell."

Two more days passed, during which time Alex became increasingly frightened. He prayed constantly, begging God to extricate him from this impossible situation. He asked that, if he could not be saved, then at least Irina and her family be spared any scrutiny by the state.

A third interrogation on the following morning (he thought it was morning—there were no clocks) was a repeat of the previous meeting. By then Alex was slipping into various aftershocks of radical fear. He was angry. And as he faced Arbat across the desk, he saw that the lieutenant was also running out of patience.

"Did you call my embassy—the Canadian embassy?"

"Of course we have made certain inquiries there. We have learned that there is no record of a Canadian named Aleksandr Graham traveling in the Russian Federation. Nor is there a record of his theoretical son, by the name of Andrew Graham. That is very bad news for you, Mr. Bell. Very bad. It's the end of your game. It may well be the end of your life, because, to tell you the truth, your embassy—the American embassy—simply does not know of your existence. Even the CIA station chief has never heard of you—a piece of information he does not realize he divulged to us; I will spare you the sordid details. So it seems you are a man who does not exist."

"I don't exist?" Alex said in a tone so perplexed that even the hardest of the interrogators could not resist a smile. There was no human sympathy in this; it was a reflex, the sort of thing one might feel while observing the antics in a zoo cage.

"But I do exist", Alex insisted. "There must be a thousand ways of verifying that I am who I say I am. Why won't you believe me?"

This was met by a wall of silence.

Arbat went on: "We are ninety-nine percent convinced that you were operating direct from Langley, on a special project that bypassed even the station chief in Moscow. The preparation was extraordinarily elaborate, but in the end it has failed. Whatever Siberian lowlife banged you on the head has done a great service to his country without knowing it. That doctor in Ozero Baikal verifies what you tell us, but we haven't quite ruled out the possibility of her complicity in the matter."

"Don't you dare touch her!" Alex erupted, lurching out of his seat. The soldiers leaped forward and pushed him back into the chair.

"Ah, he fell in love!" sighed Arbat. "Not very professional, Bell."

"She saved my life!"

"Yes, it sounds like love to me. No doubt about it."

With that, Alex began to rant, shouting his innocence and the innocence of everyone connected to him. While the prisoner was being forcibly restrained, Arbat sat back with his hands behind his head, smiling to himself.

"Relax, relax. Captain Semyon confirmed things as well. Also the bartender and a slimy character named Fox. So we know that part of the story is true. It seems you were sidetracked from your mission by an unfortunate incident. We will grant you that much. The question is, what precisely is your mission?"

"To find my son!"

"Tsk, tsk, Bell. Do you never weary of it?"

"Why are you playing with me? If you don't believe me, just drop me down a hole, if you want. But stop this. I'm not answering any more questions. You're wrong. You're so wrong about me you'd kick yourselves if you could see it."

"As I said before, we are ninety-nine percent convinced you're a very talented actor. That leaves one percent for doubt. And in this regard you have one thing in your favor."

"What?"

"Your professionally manufactured story should include all the correct steps for a tourist. Not a hair would be out of place. It is somewhat of a puzzle, then, why the Canadian embassy disavows your existence. Can you explain that to us?"

"No! I'm as astonished as you are."

"Now, it might be explainable—*might*, I say, not *is*—if Langley was simply using America's neighbor to the north without the neighbor's knowledge, pulling the wool over its eyes, so to speak, for reasons unknown to us. That would be strange, because in your club everyone's quite chummy right now, aren't they?"

"I wouldn't know."

"You're sure there aren't some nasty little tensions we haven't heard about?"

"I don't keep track of that sort of thing. It's all garbage and lies, whether it's West or East, North or South."

"Garbage and lies, is it? So you're once again the lowly bookman, apathetic about all things political. Let us say for the sake of argument that you're being honest with us. How do you explain that this son who is supposed to be missing in Russia has not entered the country?"

"But he has! He was registered at the Hotel Peterhof in Saint Petersburg and the Troika Kiel in Moscow."

"The Troika Kiel is a well-known haunt of the CIA. Is that where you met your station chief?"

"Damn it, Arbat, you just told me yourself that the station chief in Moscow never heard of me."

"Oh yes, I did, didn't I? Very good. You have a fine eye for detail. Still, that doesn't answer my question. You see, not a single hotel in Russia has a record of your son's existence."

"That's ridiculous. I have no idea why Andrew's name isn't on the records, but he was there. I know he was there. Maybe someone effaced the records in Saint Petersburg and Moscow. They did the same thing to me at the hotel in Listvyanka, so why not there?"

"We know they did it in Listvyanka, whoever *they* are. Of course, someone on your own team might have done it for the sake of the cover story—erasing your trail, so to speak."

"I don't have a team. Maybe it was the metaphysicians who arranged it."

"The who?"

"These cult people from Germany and England who brainwashed my son."

"Brainwashed your son?" Arbat said with mock sympathy. "The story grows more and more ominous. What monsters these people must be!"

"I'm telling you the truth. I've met them. The police in England know about them. Why don't you check with the detective in Oxford who was on the case? Check with the college where my son studies. Check everything before you drop an innocent man down a hole."

"We will. I assure you we will. But even if all those delicate touches of the brush add up to a lovely theater set, it is still theater; it is still a fabricated tale."

"Haven't you considered another possibility? Why don't you check with Intourist? They would know that I and my son are in Russia. Intourist is a state agency, isn't it? And that means it keeps accurate records. I can understand someone getting into the records of a private hotel and tampering with them, but surely they couldn't tamper with government files?"

For some reason Arbat made no reply. He firmed his lips and gazed at the ceiling.

"Unless—" Alex began.

"Yes, unless...", Arbat mused.

"Unless someone in your government is part of the group that has my son."

"The metaphysicians, you call them. Do you know their names? Is one of them, by any chance, Dr. Bloch? And is one Dr. Cunningham? And is there an odd assortment of other doctors clustering about them, these monsters?" Arbat laughed.

"That's them", said Alex, astonished. "How did you know?"

"Oh, we know them very well, though of course they do not know us. We follow their extremely complicated activities quite closely. The pertinent question here is, was the CIA piggybacking on their presence in Russia? Can you enlighten us?"

"No, no. Well, I just don't know about the CIA. These people had my son, and I was trying to get to him."

"The son whose existence seems to be somewhat problematic. Or was your desperate attempt to get to him a phantasmagoric dimension of your cover? A little extra snow dust in the eyes of state security? Tell me, Bell, which of the two was it, really?"

"My son is *real*. What I was doing was *real!*"

"Real? What, *really*, is real? I warn you, do not waste our time, Bell. Delaying tactics will not help you. You're mistaken if you think we will make a slip and alert your people to the fact that we have you in custody."

"I...I don't have any people."

So pathetic did Alex's plea strike all those in the room that no one said a word for some minutes. Arbat continued to stare into Alex's eyes, his expression skeptical, pondering.

"It won't help you", he said in a low voice. "Even if everything you tell us proves to be true, it won't help you."

"Why not?"

"Because, Mr. Bell or Mr. Graham or whoever you are, because you have stumbled upon a work of the Russian state that must remain obscure. And for that reason, I'm afraid I must tell you that you will not be returning to your homeland—wherever it may be."

"You intend to kill me", Alex whispered.

Arbat shrugged. "We do not want to end your existence. But our problem is, what did you see? What did you see before we picked you up? How many times did you come for a look at our activities before you were spotted?"

"Never. I still don't know who you are. I haven't a clue about what you're doing inside those fences."

"Ah," said Arbat, "regrettably, you have seen the fences. That in itself—"

"But surely Western satellites see those fences."

"Do they? Does Langley see those fences and wonder what is beneath the mountain? Didn't the satellite scan indicate a game preserve? A hundred thousand reindeer is nothing to scoff at, you know. And the mine should have satisfied your curiosity."

"Reindeer? A mine?"

"Were the herds insufficient? Was the machinery unconvincing?"

Alex fell silent.

"Remove this thief from my presence", Arbat said wearily.

"Where am I?" Alex asked Arbat during their next meeting.

"A city in Siberia."

"Are you the secret police?"

"That would be revealing a secret, wouldn't it?"

"Why do we go over the same questions again and again? I won't change my story, because it's really what happened. I am who—"

"You are who you say you are", Arbat said, lighting a cigarette. "Oy, boredom, boredom—the curse of the security business. Why can't life be like a spy novel?"

"I'm not a spy!"

"Maybe you are; maybe you aren't. It doesn't matter."

"If it doesn't matter, why are we continuing this discussion?"

"Because I am a merciful man. I am not like others of my agency, people who are never bored, who *enjoy* their work, who positively *delight* in resistance. It offers them a challenge, you see. And no challenge has ever been insurmountable for such men. I am the lowest grade of interrogation. If I fail by more humane methods, they will simply remove you from my custody. You will be transferred to another level and a different methodology. I promise you, Mr. Bell, if that were to happen, you would long for the days of Lieutenant Arbat. You would plead for the privilege of returning to me, so you could *tell all*. I love that expression. To *tell all*—so poetic, so cultured."

"There's nothing to tell", Alex mumbled, chin on chest, staring at the floor.

Arbat swung his chair sideways and watched Alex out of the corner of his eyes.

"There is always something to tell. Always."

"Then I'll be a first for you, Lieutenant. Why don't you give me a truth drug. I'll tell you everything. Or a lie detector test. I won't hold a thing back; I promise."

"We don't do those things because chemicals and graphs are subject to inaccuracies and the vagaries of human personality. They may open a closet here and there; they may even expose whole suites in the house, but not everything. The human will is another matter. It's a mechanism that never fails us. Apply sufficient pain, or the terror of pain, and the will makes a choice. It does all the work for us. It unlocks every door."

"In my case you're going to be very surprised to find an empty house."

"So you say *now*. Later you will change your story."

"No, I won't. Or, if you make me change the story, you'll just be squeezing lies out of me."

"Bell, Bell, it's no use anymore. The game is over, as they say in American films. The cat is out of the bag. The jig is up. We have arranged a reunion with an old acquaintance of yours."

"Who?" Alex cried, afraid that Irina would be brought into the room in manacles.

Arbat signaled, and a guard opened the door of the interrogation room. In walked a man who looked rather like Arbat himself, though younger by a few years. He seemed vaguely familiar.

"I don't know this man", said Alex, shaking his head.

"No, but he knows you. Don't you, Tver?"

The new arrival sat on the edge of Arbat's desk and swung a leg back and forth, staring into Alex's eyes. His eyes looked yellow, like a cat's. He mumbled something in Russian. Arbat threw him a cigarette, then lit it for him.

"It's him", said Tver. "Thinner. Different haircut. But he's our man."

"What are you talking about?" Alex said with a note of outrage.

Tver slid off the desk, stepped forward, and slapped Alex hard in the face. His yellow eyes had become slits, and his mouth twitched in rage. Then, for good measure, he slapped him again.

"Tver, Tver, no unpleasantness, please", Arbat said without conviction.

Blood began to trickle from Alex's nose. Badly frightened now, he felt himself slipping down into a world where everything was permitted, where an entire subculture existed below the surface of civilization.

Tver put his face close to Alex's and continued to emanate hatred.

"I have to waste three days on this kind of scum", he said. "I fly all the way from Petersburg to step on a bug."

"More than a bug, I think", Arbat corrected.

"So, Bell," Tver went on as if he had not heard, "not content with selling drugs to our youth, you want to sell secrets to the West."

"Drugs?" Alex stammered.

"We have Serov. He told us everything. He says you're the contact man for Germany and Turkey. What we want to know is, why the espionage? Weren't you making enough money with drugs? There's no real money in intelligence work. Or were you just doing it for the thrill of it?"

"Maybe Langley offered a very pretty purse for this project", Arbat suggested.

"I don't know what you're talking about", Alex said. "Who is Serov?"

"Who is Serov?" Tver spat on the floor. "You know very well who he is."

"Mr. Bell tells lies like an eyewitness", said Arbat.

With a sinking feeling, Alex recalled the rare book dealer on Kanal Griboedova in Saint Petersburg.

"Do you mean Viktor Serov?" he asked lamely. "He sells books. That's all I know about him."

At that moment he recognized Tver. He was the man whose car he had bumped into outside Serov's office, months before. During the few seconds when they had regarded each other's faces, Alex's mind had registered no more than an irritable stranger waiting at the wheel, reading a newspaper. He had called him the doppelgänger, half-humorously, because for a few days after his visit to Serov he seemed to see that face everywhere, as if it were haunting him, as if the man had a number of ghostly doubles. At the time he had dismissed it as a figment of his imagination.

Tver said to Arbat, "Serov covered his real work—Mafia connections, drug smuggling, prostitution—with books."

"A cultured man", Arbat said dryly.

"Are you a freelancer in that department, Bell?" Tver snapped at Alex. "Or is the government of the United States now interested in turning us into a race of addicts?"

Arbat sat up straighter and laced his fingers together on the desk. "The question is, what is he really? Is he an intelligence

918

officer making some drug money on the side, or is he a drug dealer making some extra cash in intelligence?"

"This is an important issue", Tver said to Arbat. "Two big issues. Drugs and the penetration of a security site—"

"It's doubtful he penetrated the perimeter."

"Doubtful? Absolute *certainty* is needed here."

"Regardless of whether or not he did, he will be passing no more information to anyone."

"In any event, he works for the Company. I think we will find that Mr. Bell is first and foremost a case officer and that he was making side profits for himself by collusion with our own underworld."

"That is the obvious picture. But we must not underestimate—"

"True, we must not underestimate. Which leaves us no option. Moscow said that if nothing conclusive can be obtained at this level, we should send him to Kochetov."

"Kochetov will be delighted", said Arbat.

"Actually, I don't think he will be. He's broken a ring on the coast. It's very big. So big that—"

"Not in front of the prisoner", Arbat scowled, flicking his eyes toward Alex.

Tver snorted. "He won't be talking to anyone from now on. As I said, this thing is so big, it extends from Petropavlovsk to Vladivostok. Information on Pacific Fleet logistics has been fed to NATO by this group, funneling it through the Japanese. Interrogations are now under way. It could take weeks." Tver gestured in Alex's direction. "He won't have time for this bug."

"Moscow wants the problem of the bookseller resolved quickly", Arbat said with a frown.

"Kochetov needs time to do his work properly. He's an artist."

"A genius", Arbat said, smiling crookedly.

Tver glanced at Alex as if the prisoner were already no more than meat. "So, what do we do?"

"Contact Moscow and advise them of the situation. Also talk with Kochetov to see if he can fit our tourist into his schedule. In the meantime, I'll put the bug in a holding tank."

"Kochetov may want him tonight. Can we get a flight on such short notice?"

Arbat shrugged. "Maybe. If not, we'll send him by another route."

"It's a long drive to Vladivostok. We don't have time to waste."

Squeaking his swivel chair, Arbat leaned forward and smiled at Alex. "A new hotel room for you, Mr. Graham. A room with a view."

39. The Realm of the Dispossessed

The black bag went over his head, and strong hands gripped his arms. He was walked through a confusing series of halls, taken up one elevator and down another. Trying to ascertain where he was by the senses left to him, Alex learned that he was in a warm, freshly painted place with echoing floors. The only sounds were footsteps, the hum of machinery, and the few muffled words of his escorts. He was pushed forward, the bag was removed from his head, and he opened his eyes on a cell just as the door clanged shut behind him.

The white metal room was windowless. A single light bulb burned behind a mesh screen in the ceiling, about fifteen feet above his head. It was four times larger than his previous cell and contained six cots. It was, he supposed, the holding tank. He sat down on one of the beds, his face in his hands, and tried to pray, but he could not produce anything other than fragmentary words of half-remembered prayers.

"Porfiry", he whispered. "Vladimirskaya. Bogoroditsa. Holy Trinity."

The name of Jesus surfaced in his mind, and he forced it to his lips, where it escaped as a whisper. He repeated it over and over. A small portion of peace returned.

He saw Father Sergius kneeling before a stone, and a small footprint pressed into the stone. After that a series of random images passed though his imagination: Carol, Andrew, Jacob, Irina, Kiril, Ilya, Aglaya, Father Toby—people from another universe.

Other faces, other voices, Kolya the Water Skimmer, the storyteller with an ax in his mind. The priest whose hands and feet had been chopped off. The zek with a bullet through his skull. The hands of Aglaya's mother, her scarred chest, her death cry: *The only whole heart is a broken one.*

Or was it *The only broken heart is a whole one?* No, that did not make sense. But nothing now made sense. Would terror dismantle his mind? Yes, his mind would disintegrate first. Then his body. He hoped his soul would not betray itself. He would disappear. People disappeared all the time, and most of them were never found. Where did they go? Down the drain hole of the universe? Into the *nyet, nyet, nyet?*

He encouraged himself by thinking about the black bag they persisted in putting over his head. If they were really going to kill him, why did they keep blindfolding him? Surely this was an indication that they had not ruled out the possibility of releasing him. Then he thought that even now these people clung to their petty procedures—the rituals of hell's antiliturgy. The bag went on his head regardless of whether or not he was doomed to extermination.

He had been given no food that day, and nothing was brought to the cell during the torturous long hours that followed. Was it day? Was it night? Had eternal night begun? Groaning, shaking with fear, he tried to weep in order to relieve the intolerable anguish, but no tears would come. Prayer alone was left to him—fractured prayers, small bleats greeted by silence.

He woke from a troubled half sleep to find his body jackknifed, fists clenched between his knees. The cell door squealed. Opening his eyes, Alex saw a man stumble across the room. A guard came in after him, pushed him onto one of the other cots, then left. The door clanged shut.

The new arrival was about the same age as Alex. He was also dressed in a gray jump suit and cloth slippers. He sat with his head in his hands, sighing.

"Hello", Alex said in Russian.

The man looked up with a jerk of his head. The expression in his eyes was that of a frightened animal. Though no marks of physical abuse were evident on his body, there was ample evidence of some kind of psychological torment.

"Who are you?" the man asked in badly accented Russian.

"My name is Alex Graham."

With a look of surprise, the newcomer said in English, "Graham? You're Graham?"

"Yes, that's right. Who are you?"

The newcomer looked at the walls and the ceiling and put a finger to his lips.

"They're listening", he whispered.

"Yes, I suppose they are. But that doesn't matter—at least not in my case. I've told them everything about myself. They just won't believe me."

"About Graham, you mean?"

"What's your name?" Alex asked.

"I might as well tell you. I'm never getting out of here, that's for sure. I'm Carl Lesley."

They shook hands.

"So they caught you too, Graham."

"Yes. They think I'm a spy or something."

Lesley smiled sadly. "Yeah, they think I'm a spy or something too. Problem is, they've got my whole portfolio in some nice little file in Moscow Center. They knew everything. These guys are sharper than we thought." Lesley lowered his voice and mouthed, "Did they crack your cover too?"

Alex shook his head. "I don't have a cover", he said morosely.

"It's no use, Graham. They're going to send us to some guy in Vladivostok. Some leftover from the KGB days named

Kochetov. Even the interrogators got nervous when his name was mentioned. He must be some Frankenstein."

"Do you think he's going to torture us?"

"Sounds like it. Whoever he is, this guy is definitely not an ad man for Intourist."

"But why? What do they think we've done?"

"Call me Carl. And you're Alex, for the time being. Should I call you that?"

"Please. What sort of place are we in, Carl?"

"I think it's an interrogation center somewhere in Siberia."

"But what did I stumble on? I still don't know a thing except that there are a lot of fences east of Irkutsk."

"Yeah, they're quite miffed that we got an eyeful of the fence. It's some secret installation that's very, very important to them. But I never got past the fence. Did you?"

"No. I wasn't interested in the fence or whatever's inside it. I was hiking and got lost. I found it by accident."

Lesley winked and nodded.

"Really, Carl, I'm not part of whatever you were doing."

Beckoning Alex over to his cot. Lesley slid close to him and whispered into his ear. "Need-to-know basis."

"What?"

"It's all right. We can talk."

"Talk about what?"

"They can't pick up this level on their mikes."

"I've nothing to hide", Alex said aloud.

"Look, didn't they tell you about me? When I was sent out, they told me about you. I was to contact you at Irkutsk; then a second meeting was scheduled for Listvyanka after the operations."

"Meeting? What meeting?"

"I was told you were in the dark on some details, because it was on a need-to-know basis only. I was to fill you in when we met in Irkutsk. Didn't they tell you anything?"

Alex shook his head.

"Well, the question is, was it a duplicate mission, or a two-part operation? They told me it was going to be two-prong—you in the east, me in the west. But what did they tell you?"

"Nothing."

"Idiots! There are too many Ivy League bureaucrats at the Company these days. Someone messed up, but good! When you disappeared off the radar screen and missed our contact date in Irkutsk, I just went frantic thinking you'd been picked up. I decided to go on alone to the western perimeter. I figured there was a chance you'd already seen the eastern fence and maybe even gotten inside. Did you?"

"Did I what?"

"Get inside the compound?"

"No."

"Tell me about the accident—the head thing."

"How did you hear about that?"

"They told me during my interrogation, I guess because they were sure we were together during the months you went missing. Where the hell were you, anyway?"

"I was attacked and robbed in Listvyanka, and then I recuperated at a clinic on Lake Baikal."

"One of our contacts?"

"What do you mean?"

"I mean the clinic. She's one of ours, isn't she?"

"She?" Alex repeated dumbly.

"They said a woman looked after you. They thought I knew her too. I just put two and two together."

"The doctor's nothing more than that—a local doctor. The people who picked me up off the street after the robbery took me to her because she was the closest one. I had no money, no documents, so she just looked after me for the sake of charity."

"But we have *someone* on Baikal. Langley told me. I wondered if she's the one."

Alex stared at Lesley.

"Again, it was on a need-to-know basis, Alex. My contact was in Irkutsk; yours was on Baikal. I suppose she was your backup in case the web failed."

"Web? I don't know anything about a web, or about a Langley either."

It was becoming more and more difficult for Alex to use the man's first name. His suspicion increased steadily. He decided to continue the dialogue in order to do what he could to protect Irina.

"The doctor was just a local woman, Carl. A widow with two sons. Very nice people but completely nonpolitical. They're not with us."

Us?

"Whoever they think *us* is", he added. He then went on to restate his identity. Lesley listened closely, betraying nothing on his face, though his eyes now seemed to have lost every trace of the haunted prisoner. Behind his neutral expression was the silently whirring machinery of an analytical mind.

"This whole thing's a big mistake", Alex said. "They think I'm someone named Bell. An American."

Lesley leaned over and put his lips to Alex's ear. "I need to talk with you overtly", he whispered. "Let's drop the act. I'm too tired for it, and besides, they've got me. The cover's useless now. Looks like they've got you too. There's no going home for either of us. It's all over. The jig is up."

"The jig is up?" Alex repeated, peering intently into Lesley's eyes. A true professional, Lesley did not waver.

"Yeah, the jig's up, Bell. They know everything."

"I'm not Bell", Alex said, standing abruptly and returning to his cot. He lay down on it and rolled over, facing the wall.

A minute later Lesley walked to the door and shouted something in perfectly accented Russian. The door opened, and Lesley walked out.

Not long after, the door squealed open again, and four guards came inside. The black bag went over Alex's head, and he was taken out into what he supposed was the corridor. He was walked along in the usual fashion, but the destination was different. A downward-dropping elevator. More walking.

His heart racing like a rabbit in talons, Alex's terror grew. He wondered if the monster Kochetov had arrived and if he was now to be turned over to him.

He was pushed into a room and told to stand still. The hands that had gripped him let go, and Alex swayed a little on his feet. Other hands stripped off his clothing, everything except the black bag. His wrists were bound behind his back, and he was thrown to his knees. His head was forced underwater, bag and all. When he could hold his breath no longer, his lungs sucked in water. The hands let him drown for a few seconds, then pulled him out.

"What did you see?" a voice demanded.

He coughed water. They pounded his chest until his lungs worked.

"What did you see?"

They drowned him again. Revived him again. Drowned, revived. Drowned, revived. Rising and plunging. It was all black; it was all death.

Whenever they let him have a little air, he yelled, a wild animal yell.

The hand pushed his head under again.

He was ready to tell them everything, nothing, anything, reindeer, missiles, trees, germs, horses, bombs, chemicals, angels, swords—

Then a battery of fists beat every part of his body. And after that, electricity was used, and he heard for the first time in his life the sound of his own scream. It went on so long that he became nothing more than screaming inside a sack of pulverized meat. Then they let him drop to the floor, senseless.

When consciousness returned, he was alone. The bag was gone from his head. There was no noise, no light, but his senses told him he was alive. His flesh was one single wound, with blood running from his nostrils and ears. A floor beneath his body. It was ice, and blood was crystallizing on it. He was naked. He was deathly cold. His body contracted into the fetal position, shaking violently.

His groans slid into weeping, and the weeping slid back into groans until it was all the same. Time was the skewer on which he turned, burning, burning.

Iisus!

He felt that he was dying and that he had only a few moments left in which to pray. He tried to speak to God, but his mind was incapable of thoughts. His lungs breathed the name of Jesus over and over, though at the root of this utterance was no thought, no fervor. The name was in his breath, and his breath was becoming the name. As long as he did not move, the breathing remained. And the name.

Iisus!

Slowly, slowly his heart beat—a drum, a pause, and a drum.

Then his mind rose still further, and he sensed a presence with him. The darkness was total, but it was broken by breathing that was not his own. He now realized that someone was lying close beside him. From time to time low groans came from the other's throat. Using the dregs of his strength, Alex moved an arm. It screamed in protest. He moved it still farther, and his fingers brushed against something. It was a hand. A hand covered with blood.

It cost everything to roll onto his side. He gasped, cried out, then put his own hand on the arm of the other prisoner.

For a time he rested. It was strange comfort to know that another human being was with him in that place of absolute dark. A flicker of life stirred within him, a moment of pity for the suffering of the other. He felt that he might try to encourage him somehow, to offer solace—the fraternity of the absolutely dispossessed.

The arm of the other man moved. The man's hand reached for his. The grip that held Alex was mangled flesh, horrible to touch. With his other hand, Alex touched the face of the prisoner. It too was covered with blood. The man's chin and cheeks were bearded, his nose large, his eyes deep-set, pools of blood collecting in the sockets. His face was lacerated with many small cuts, and his lips were split, dry, parted. Blood ran from the corners of his mouth.

"Who are you?" Alex breathed.

"Alyosha", the lips whispered in reply.

"We are suffering, Alyosha", Alex sobbed, placing the palm of his hand on the man's forehead. "But we are not alone."

The flesh of the forehead was riddled with holes.

"You", said the prisoner, "are Alyosha."

"I?" Alex breathed.

The prisoner reached up and took Alex's right hand in both of his. He drew Alex's hand downward across his face, over the collarbone, over the chest that was sliced in every direction, the flesh slippery with blood. He pulled Alex's hand around the side of his chest and pressed the tips of his fingers to a large gash between two ribs.

Alex flinched and tried to draw back, but the other's hands gently held him.

"My son", said the prisoner, and drew the fingers deep into the wound beneath his heart.

Then Alex saw a flash of light and fell into oblivion.

Light sifted in. Noise also. Rumbling and rattling, muffled voices, a burst of song, as if crows had suddenly been given the gift of melody or leaping deer the power of speech.

"I?" he said with a mouth that somehow belonged to him. Then he became aware that his body was shaking.

"Make sure the bonds are secure", said a voice.

"They are, sir."

"Go forward; see when that tea is coming."

"Can we smoke?"

"In the passageway. One at a time. Four of you stay on duty; the rest can take a break."

"He's not going anywhere."

"When will he awake?"

"Sometime this afternoon. Then they'll give him another shot."

"Vladivostok wants him alive."

"What is he, a spy?"

"Don't know. Keep your mouth shut and don't ask questions, if you want to stay out of trouble."

"There's no one to hear. The ice-head from Moscow is getting drunk in the bar car."

"Shut up."

"Yes, Lieutenant. Sorry."

"They really beat him."

"Maybe he fell down."

"Sure, sure, everyone who comes out of that place has had an accident. They all fall down and never get up."

"Why can't they send him in one of their planes?"

"None available. Express is faster than car."

"Why do they drag us regulars into their dirty business?"

"Give me a light, Konstantin. And stop your complaining or you'll end up like this one."

"Shouldn't I turn him over? Maybe the cuffs are cutting off circulation."

"Go ahead."

"Look, his eyes are open."

"Is he dead?"

"No, he's waking up."

Alex focused his eyes and saw a long, dimly lit room that seemed to vibrate to the rhythm of clattering sounds. Four soldiers stood around him, all dressed in green. They were young, staring down at him with serious expressions.

"He's thirsty, sir. Look at his mouth."

"Give him water, then. Don't tell the ice-head."

"I hate those guys."

"Me too. Those bastards."

"Why can't they do their own dirty work?"

"I told you, shut up about that. Who has water?"

"I do. Here, take it."

"Poor dog."

Two of them sat Alex upright, and the pain this inflicted made him gasp. A third put the neck of a plastic bottle to his lips. He gulped the water, then coughed it back up.

"Oy! Foo!" said the soldiers, wiping their uniforms with disgust.

Feeding him the water more carefully, one of them said, "Slowly, now. Drink slowly."

Alex sucked at the bottle, swallowed.

"That damn medic's gone with the ice-head, drinking. He should give a painkiller to this one."

"Who is he?"

"Don't ask."

The shaking went on and on. He now knew that he was in a train carriage. Everything had been stripped out of it except benches running down both sides. Windowless, hot, stuffy. A soldier with an automatic weapon guarded a doorway at the end of the carriage.

Alex was bound hand and foot by metal cuffs and was dressed in a gray jump suit similar to the one he had worn in Arbat's prison. His feet were bare.

They helped him lie down again.

One of the soldiers rolled a jacket and put it under Alex's head.

"*Spas—*", he said. It came out as a croak. "*—siba.*"

The soldier sat down beside him.

The others scattered to places along the benches. Three of them began to play cards. The lieutenant went out the door at the end of the carriage, and presently two young soldiers entered. Two of the others left for their break.

The one sitting by Alex took a package from his breast pocket and shook a cigarette out of it. He lit it furtively and sucked deeply. Then he put it to Alex's lips.

Alex shook his head.

"Criminal?" the soldier asked in a whisper, after looking around at his fellows to make sure no one was listening.

Alex stared back at him, uncomprehending.

"Political?"

This too was without meaning.

"Hey, Konstantin!" someone shouted. "Kapitan says no talking to the prisoner. You want to go to the hellhole?"

The young soldier exhaled smoke, grinned, and said, "Aren't we in one?"

Laughter.

"Siberia's not so bad. Wait till you see the bright lights of Vladivostok. And those Arctic girls! Ooo!"

More laughter.

"Where is Kapitan?"

"Gone to drink vodka with the ice-head and the medic."

"Lieutenant will bring them back."

"In an hour, I hope, with antifreeze in their blood."

"Gimme a smoke, Konstantin!"

"Me too!"

"Dmitri, you pig! Don't grab!"

As the banter continued, Alex tried to sink back into that moment when he had placed his hand into a wound. No matter what happened to him at the end of the journey, he would have this to cling to. He would go down into death with a hand gripping his.

Laughter burst out from the direction of the card game.

"Keep quiet, you idiots! You're going to get us all in trouble!"

"So what! Hey, Anton, keep an eye on the door, will you?"

"I'll give you plenty of warning. Just cut me a piece of the winnings."

Alex closed his eyes and tried to sleep, though pain would not let him. He opened them again to see the soldier beside him gazing at him with an unreadable expression. The eyes conveyed no emotion but did not look away. This communication seemed connected somehow to the chain of mysteries that had enveloped Alex from the moment he had stepped across the borderland into the unknown country.

The soldier pointed to the center of his chest and said, "Konstantin."

Then he pointed to Alex and raised his eyebrows.

"Alyo—", Alex whispered, "—sha."

"Alyosha", the soldier mouthed silently.

Moments later, the train jerked and swayed. Some of the soldiers staggered and slammed into the bulkhead at the rear of the carriage. The cards fluttered about; cursing broke out.

"What's going on?"

"Why are we stopping?"

"The engineer's an idiot!"

The train ground to a halt, and Alex thought he heard a sound like corks popping.

To a man, the soldiers crouched down and grabbed their weapons.

"Something's wrong!"

"What could be wrong?"

"Problems on the track!"

"No, that was weapons fire."

More popping corks.

Cachunk-cachunk-cachunk-cachunk—

A line of puncture holes spread down the right side of the carriage, the metal peeling inward like opening flower petals, followed by loud bangs. The soldiers flattened on the floor. Anton hunkered down and pointed the muzzle of his gun at the doorway. Konstantin pulled Alex onto the floor beside him.

A tattoo of bullets sprayed along the carriage wall again, this time close above their heads.

Cachunk-cachunk-ping-ping-zip-zip-ping—

"Who is it? Who's doing that? It's crazy!"

"This is Russia! They can't do that!"

"We're near the Amur! Do you think—?"

"They wouldn't dare!"

"They've done it before."

Cachunk-cachunk-ping-ping-zip-zip-ping—

A howl. "I'm hit! My leg, my leg!"

The door burst open, revealing an empty passage. Two green-clad bodies lay there without moving. The soldiers aimed a volley of fire at the empty space, hitting nothing but the end of the next car. Suddenly a hand flung something into the room, and it burst in blinding light.

"Aaaagh! My eyes, my eyes! I can't see! I can't see!"

More gunfire, close at hand. Many voices shouting. Russian voices. Other voices.

As Alex was the only one who had not been looking at the doorway when the hand flung in the deadly light, he was the only one capable of seeing the attackers. At least a dozen shadows (he couldn't see their faces for the smoke) leaped inside the carriage and danced nimbly down the aisle, firing at the Russians, one by one.

Konstantin crawled under the bench, rubbing his eyes, his gun dangling useless on its shoulder strap. A shape materialized out of the smoke, spotted Konstantin, and slowly put the muzzle of its gun to the youth's head.

The detonation was deafening, for it was inches away from Alex's ears.

He knew then that it was time to die. He lay on his back with his manacled hands on his chest. It was over. It was all over, and now at last he would drown. He wept for Konstantin, for his lost youth, for his kindness, for the blood spurting across his arms and chest.

Then the shadow pointed its gun at Alex.

I give you everything.

Another shadow came up and spoke—a high, clipped sound, very rapid, like a volley of bullets. One of the shadows stuck the tip of his gun under the cuff chain and rattled it. A discussion between shadows ensued. Then hands lifted him and dragged him through the smoke and out of the train.

Dazed, Alex fell at the bottom of the carriage steps and from there was half-dragged, half-lifted to the edge of the gravel shoulder. He was thrown down onto the grass. Insects buzzed and leaped all around him, making zinging noises. He stared at the sky above. Gunshots continued. The sky was purest blue, filled with clashing swords striking one against the other without a sound.

The air was scented with wildflowers. Wind blew away the smoke. The sun beat down, and flies swarmed on his wounds. Shadows gathered around him. There was an argument. Then two shadows arrived, dragging a third between them. The tall shadow in the middle took a key from his pocket and unlocked Alex's manacles. The smaller shadows dragged the tall shadow to the side and pointed their guns at him. A volley of shots felled the tall shadow, and then everything grew silent.

A field bird warbled, and in the overarching dome above, a swallow sliced a curve in space.

40. *The Silence*

The incessant motion of armored vehicles and men in changing costumes gave way to the simplicity of space. Because suspension was no place, it was also every place. He watched, or felt, all that was happening around him but had no need to understand it. First the roaring half-track, into which he was squeezed with a dozen nervously chattering men, their hands covered with blood. His body, a single ache, was propped in the seated position between two of the bloodiest. The red star affixed to their metal helmets was redder than the streaks and spatters on their faces. Their faces were brown and clear, flushed with red beneath wide cheekbones.

He knew they were something there was a name for; both their race and their power had a character that he had once known but now seemed unable to identify.

Konstantin's blood soaked his prison clothing. Organic gravel of bone bits and brain matter were drying on the backs of his hands.

"I killed him", he said. "It was my fault, because I fell asleep and didn't think of the time. Then I stumbled. No, the rock killed him because it shouldn't have been there in the path. In the dark. And the blood of the tormented one. But I didn't know it would end this way. I had to go back to Porfiry. There was something calling me to him. I had to go. To see. To pray. Wasn't I listening? Did I kill them by my deafness, Konstantin and the others? They gave me water for my thirst. They asked me my name."

What was his name, really? *Alyosha?* Yes, it was Alyosha.

The half-track stopped by a wide, flowing waterway. The soldiers dragged him out into the bright light and laid him on a hummock of reeds by the shore. Over and over he heard the word *Heilongjiang*, as they pointed this way and that, mostly toward the river. One spoke into a radio. It answered him. One with binoculars watched the far shore. The sun was on that side. The volume of chatter increased when a boat was spotted, heading toward them at top speed.

When it arrived, they took him to the opposite bank of the river. There a military truck was waiting. They carried him into it and sat him up beside the soldiers. It bounced and roared, and the young men laughed as they lurched. His ears began to bleed. His nose also. One of the soldiers noticed it and wiped it with an oily rag.

Then they put him into a train. It was a very small train, but its engine puffed real smoke. It had four little carriages, and he was placed in the last, accompanied only by soldiers. They propped him on a bench between two men in green uniforms.

From time to time, others would come and stare at him, asking him things that he could not understand. The windows blurred, trees melting, pale green limbs on which flowers sang and waved, their petals scattering like burned mosaics in the wind that always blows after sacrilege.

They passed many country stations where people stood staring at the train, with chickens in their arms, or garden tools, or baskets of small golden fish. In a plowed field, beside a man and an ox, a little girl in a turquoise shirt raised her arms and smiled. *I greet, I greet you!*

On a station platform, a young man and woman, holding a baby in their arms, their clothing mere rags, cried out with their eyes, *We greet you, we greet you, we are with you, we are with you.*

Then the opera of yellow flags, and red flags and white flags, the prayer flags and the hate flags, all colors blending, fluttering, whirring, blurring into one. All diffusing into red, then fading to rust, to brown, to nothing.

"*Nyet, nyet, nyet*", Alex cried, shaking his body awake, blinking at the sun pouring through the carriage window.

The soldiers called an officer, a man with a red star above his forehead. They gathered around Alex, and the officer peered into his face and said, "Russki? Russki?"

But he had no right to answer this question. He did not know the answer. He had forgotten where he was from, where he had been, where he was going, because blood dissolves all frontiers. He knew his thoughts were not working properly. Rooms in the house were locked. Though the house was his own, he had lost the keys. Only the entrance hall was his, the front door open, his eyes looking out uncertainly. Beyond the porch was the land of flowering trees. Nothing was familiar to him, so he closed the door and slept.

The walls of his room were green, glossy paint applied over rough stucco. The weathered window frame was dark brown. The air was peach colored in the mornings, lemon at midday, plum at night. An ethereal sense of the nearby presence of multitudes was in the atmosphere, though to his eyes the land seemed deserted. Dry rolling hills were visible through a dusty window, above a high brick wall surrounding a courtyard. No living thing grew there.

He slept again, dimly aware that someone was dealing with his body, washing it, dressing it, pushing a needle into him, two needles, plastic tubes trailing down into his arms.

"I am not a bell", he whispered. "Not a bell, not a bell. Kolokol, kolokol. The telephone didn't ring. They didn't hear me on the answering machine. I didn't invent it. Langley did."

Because he sometimes wandered along the heights above a river where warm, weedy waters swirled over a dam and children ran playing in the red-gold leaves, he thought he might have found his home somewhere inside the locked rooms and could now live in it forever. But this was not so. Always he was pulled out into somewhere else. Faces came and went, men and women in white coats, men in green uniforms with red flashes on the lapels, or others with red shoulder boards.

"Epaulets", he said because the word rose to the surface. A real word—he was sure of it. This meant it was all inside; everything that he had been long ago was still stored away, and maybe it too would float to the surface. Or was he the shattered icon, the bits and pieces of colored stone reassembling? Maybe the hidden face would be revealed, because bits and pieces of skull had been blown into his eyes, and the solvent of brain fluid added to the artist's palette. His own face was partly himself, partly Konstantin, partly Alyosha of the underground.

Who? Who was Alyosha of the underground? Then he remembered a place where spigots spewed blood, water, fear, and namelessness. A man was slipping down the drain hole of the universe, though he was pulled out by the hands of a stranger.

Then a girl under a copper dome, making a sign of the cross on herself. Her heart full of darkness, her heart cast down. Was it her foot that pressed into the stone? No, that was someone else. Someone too beautiful to look at, her heart, her heart, her heart so full of light that he was ashamed to lift his eyes.

Then the bleeding body lying beside him on the ice-floor of the cell. The mangled hands, the wound in the heart. Putting fingers into the wound.

"Yes, I remember, I remember! I am ashamed, I am ashamed. No, I forget!"

The carol of the bells followed; it came in the night, when rain hammered the tin roof and made a curtain on the window beside his bed. The carol woke him because it was louder than the rain. The room was empty. He saw the tubes running into his arms and the high rails of the bed that kept him enclosed in a sea nest. And in the distance a voice chattering into a telephone. A woman in a white dress.

The word *carol* meant something important, but he could not find it.

"I fell through ice. Children fell too, sucked under. And there was a man lying on the ice with me, with holes in his brow, his hands, and his side."

He knew the man, yes, knew him in the deepest parts of the river, but could not find his name.

"What was his name? I can't remember. He was..."

The name would not float to the surface.

"Yes, he was...he was...!"

All language ceased in the Muchenik's presence.

"Muchenik!" he cried, later, to the man in white who removed one of the needles from his arm. "*Dusha...dusha ...dusha!*"

Now the window was open a crack, letting in the smell of hot dust and the distant rumor of thousands of pounding feet, and birds calling, and chickens and cattle making their sounds. The man in white took his pulse and listened to his heartbeat with a stethoscope. Then he removed the other needle.

"B-but who am I?" he said to the man in a language that faltered with disuse.

Konstantin?

"Is that me, or is it my son?"

Oh, my son, my son, my own lost son! Andrew!

Andrew?

"Another name", he said to himself, sitting up to drink from a bowl of soup, salty, filled with noodles and herbs. "Andrew was my son. But he was taken away." The man in white stared at him and shook his head, as if to say it was no use, they had no common language.

"But we have the *glubina dushy!*" he protested. This too the man in white failed to understand.

What was his own name? Really, what was the name below the suction of Alyosha, below the shattered skull of Konstantin, below the false names and good bells and bad bells that would not stop ringing in his ears? He slept again, and when he awoke it was morning, with roosters crowing and little yellow birds swooping and darting above the wall of the compound. A man in green carrying a gun strapped over his shoulder slowly paced around the yard.

"I fell down and froze to death", he explained to the guard, but the guard did not hear because words seldom rose as far as the surface of his lips. Words were too heavy. Words sank you.

So he understood that he was skimming the surface of the water.

"My name", he said whenever words did rise to the level of his lips. Heavy words dragging him back under, for the sky outside the window was full of stars.

"My name is not Konstantin", he said after a long struggle. "That was someone else. His memory is sprayed across the white canvas."

Now he understood that it was not his fault. The stolen loaf of bread was responsible. He wanted to help the condemned man, wanted to take his place, but when he opened his mouth to speak the words that would draw fury upon himself, the words were too heavy. There was no choice. At least it seemed there was no choice. How could a man discern between truth and falsehood when all points of the compass had dissolved? In what direction could he move—forward, backward, sideways? It was all a wall, a cement universe, without windows, without doors. This occurred on the bad days, when his body refused to let him remain suspended above the void.

On such days, and on the nights that followed, he had bad dreams: Drowning with a black bag over his head. Electric swords stabbing the vulnerable places of his body—his mind the most vulnerable of all. He woke screaming and panting, bleating animal cries. The people in white held him firmly to the bed and injected him with a needle. And from the needle there came blessed relief.

Cold. Cold.

Ice. Blood crystallizing on the ice.

The Muchenik took the kingfisher's hand and drew it gently to the wound in his side, beneath his heart. And the kingfisher's heart hammered with horror and worship, and the dissolving of every language save the language of love.

The Muchenik put his fingers into the wounds of the kingfisher—the heart wounds and the mind wounds—though he asked permission before doing so and did not use force. And the kingfisher replied *yes, yes, yes.* For both acts cleansed the degradation. And the *nyet, nyet, nyet* that had seized him during the torture withdrew for a time.

On other days, they made him get out of bed and try to learn to walk again—up and down a corridor with green guards flanking the white-robed medical people. Little words returned to him, one or two at a time.

"Doctors. Nurses. Soldiers." He practiced the words because they were not as heavy as other words, and because he wanted to skim away over the water and not sink again.

"But what is my name?" he said, standing by the window, staring out at a pale moon vibrating in the evening sky. "Does it matter? Does anything matter? Yes, it does matter, but I can't think why, really. Where am I? Why am I? He is dead because of me, Konstantin my son, and Anton, and the others. Andrew too is dead, because I was not enough for him. I walked alone, I did not climb the distant mountain with him, I did not show him the distant mountain that he must keep in his heart. The little boats I should have made for him and Jacob."

Jacob?

It was startling to possess this new word, to feel it as recognition and at the same time to have no knowledge of its meaning. A name that he sensed was more solid than the flowing-dissolving names. Jacob was real, as real as Andrew, but who were they, this Jacob, this Andrew?

"My name. I must find it again. I must."

In the dusk, fireworks exploded in the sky beyond the walls. The cheers of many people and the smell of gunpowder blew faintly through the open windows. He heard very distant and beautiful songs coming through the wall that surrounded his mind.

Pop—pop-pop-pop—Boom!—Bang!—pop-pop-pop—Wizzzz!

Colors bloomed in the night, fountains of flame and dazzling rockets. He wanted to jump up and down, to clap, to cry with delight, but his body was too weak. It would not obey the impulse; the flesh along his arms and legs was splotched purple and brown and screamed at him that he must let them rest. He returned to the bed and lay down, but fiery dragons came too, along with angels, pinwheels, ringing swords, and bullet holes flowering in the walls, and everywhere the young were struck from their course by a falling blade. And because splatters of brain matter terminated the dream, he touched the emptied mask with his fingers, closed the eyes of Konstantin, trying not to see the shattered skull. Then he closed his own eyes with his fingertips and stared within.

As before, he was stretched out on the ice, seeking the tormented one, reaching across the void.

"We are suffering, Muchenik," he groaned, "but we are not alone."

He touched the holes in the hands and feet of the prisoner. He lightly touched the face that a rifle butt had shattered. The hands of the prisoner drew his fingers to the wound in his heart, and his heart was a fountain.

"You", said the Muchenik, "are Alyosha."

Now most of his time was occupied on a chair or sitting up in bed looking out the window, waiting for what would be painted on the canvas. Birds mostly, occasionally a guard. The sky always changing shape and color. Rain. Sun pounding the mud back into dust. Then more rain. Night and day. Night and day, and night.

People came into the room and left again. They asked him questions.

"Russki?"

"Anglichanin?"

"Amirikanits?"

But of course there was nothing he could say to this. Nothing at all, because it did not really matter. The walls of the devastated city were too thick and high, and they encircled him totally. The unknown country was within. Always within. There were no gates to the exterior, no frontier posts, because inside and outside were both unknown country. Was out better than in? Was in better than out?

The people in white brought him green tea in which bits of wood and leaf floated. Sometimes they brought bowls of noodles. One day, a chicken claw in broth. Time was moving again, going steadily in a direction. Caught in its currents, he had only one choice, to float and go where it would take him, like a leaf in a flood, or to sink like saturated wood. Yet all things were swept forward with it, even the ramparts around the soul. There was one door only: silence.

What is this silence? he thought.

There came a time when they decided to take him to another place. He could walk now, unsteadily, with the help of the green men. There was little pain. The bruises were almost gone, islands of pale brown on the white of his arms and legs.

The islands were shrinking, fading. More and more words swirled in the pool of his mind.

They put him into a train carriage that contained only him and his guards. It took him closer to the sun. He slept through most of the journey. They put a glass bottle of sweet rice water to his lips. It fizzed in his mouth. And a bowl of bean curd flavored with black, salty sauce.

The train slowed as it entered a city, passing sidetracks where men in blue pajamas cut a rail with a hacksaw.

"*Hacksaw*", he said to himself. "That's a good word to know. Also, *blue*. Because blue is important to me, though I can't remember why."

Farther and farther into the city they went, past hundreds of young men standing to the side, leaning on pickaxes and shovels, all dressed in dirty blue.

"They are waiting to fly", he said. "They are like me."

Though some birds are crushed in an iron grip, a trickle of blood oozing between the fingers of a killer angel, these were alive.

"I know them. I know them. But their feathers are different; their eyes are...these people are..."

The word for their race came to him from inside, and he began to understand where he was, though of course even this meant little. It did not matter where he was.

The train halted at a station, as trains always do—all the trains he had ever ridden did this because it was their custom. The guards took him from the carriage and led him to an automobile parked by the end of the station platform. The air was thick with coal and sulfur fumes. A man in a black suit and tie greeted the guards. The guards bowed and handed the kingfisher to him. The man was shorter than they were and not much older. He wore spectacles and carried a leather valise under his arm. The kingfisher was put into the automobile along with new guards, and they drove away into the city.

They took him to an ancient stone mansion. The marble steps were foot worn and the banisters on the staircase rubbed bare by countless hands. They brought him into a yellow room with high ceilings and a cot, a wooden chair, and a barred window. Then they gestured that he should lie down on the bed and went out, locking the door behind them. He was alone.

He got up and was able to open the window, a very tall window, eight feet high. Through the bars he saw that the room was above a garden of trees and water pools enclosed within red brick walls. Nothing could be seen beyond the walls save numerous coils of smoke rising from the tips of chimneys. He left the window open despite the chemical smells that filled the air. Returning to the bed, he lay down and slept.

Night and day passed. The important work of remembering proceeded. He gathered words as others mined for gold, shaking pans of silt and gravel that were washed up by the nameless river, its headwaters in the unknown land. Little flecks appeared in the gravel as he sifted. None of it amounted to wealth, to knowledge. In a sense he did not want it to, because whenever he felt himself close to seeing the whole course of the river and the map of time, he felt the sharp pain of horror. He saw Konstantin's blood, and Serafim's, and Alyosha's, and Porfiry's, and the priest whose hands and feet had been chopped off. Whenever this happened, he threw the sifting pan into the river and turned his back to it.

At other times memory was a house. He slammed the doors and locked them before the images could burst out and shatter his mind. Only the prisoner remained, the man who had shared the cell with him after the beating, whose heart was a well of blood. This blood alone gave peace. It did not make him clutch his head with his hands and screw his eyes tightly in order to keep the images out, or in—he did not know which.

Night and day, and night again.

"Will you trust me?" asked the Muchenik.

"Who are you?" asked the kingfisher, though he knew.

Visitors came and went, asking him questions, mostly in Russian. *Russian*—another important word to remember. They were *Chinese*—also an important word.

"My name is Alyosha", he answered in Russian. More than this he could not tell them.

"Are you a criminal?" one asked.

"What is a criminal?" he replied.

They stared at him and did not answer, though they began to speak with each other in their language.

He strained to recall the meaning of *criminal*.

"Oh yes, a bad person", he said. "A person who hurts other people." He shook his head. "No, I don't think I'm that."

Then he remembered that Konstantin and Anton and the others were dead because of him. He burst into tears, and the visitors looked upon him with disdain, for they were strong men. They went away and left him alone for a time.

Another day the visitors asked him, "Are you an intelligence agent?"

He shook his head uncertainly. "I don't know what that is, but I don't think it's what I am."

"Why did you say *Langley*?"

"I did not say *Langley*", he replied.

"You did, when you were in hospital in the north."

"Where in the north?"

"Manchuria. After you were rescued. Do you remember the border incident?"

"What is a border incident?"

"The Russian provocation, to which our troops retaliated."

"All frontiers are dissolved by blood", he replied.

Once again they went away.

For an hour each day, a guard walked with him around the enclosed garden. It was soothing to be among the flowering trees. Green citrons hung from branches. Purple bushes grew heavy with white berries. In an ornamental pool surrounded by a low stone wall, a bronze heron stood forever poised to spear anything that moved in the water. Fish swirled their tails about its feet, gold and orange, white and spotted. One so black that when a beam of sunlight fell down through the pollen-laden air, it turned its scales to electric violet.

Then he remembered the flash behind his eyelids when they jolted his body with electricity, when he was drowning, when his mind was wrapped in a bag of blackest *nyet*. He cried out and began to shake violently. The guard took him back to his room and called a doctor. The doctor gave him a needle. He slept.

When he woke up, he said, "They beat me. They drowned me. They put electricity in my body."

"Why did they torture you?" asked the man in the suit.

"The drain hole of the universe", he replied.

"You are in intelligence. Whom do you work for?"

"For the..."

"For whom? Tell us."

"For the..."

"Say it."

"The *izhuber*."

"The deer? Is that a code name?"

"The mighty. The pierced heart. But no one understood. They killed him."

"Whom did they kill? His name, his name!"

"I forget."

He sat on the pool's stone wall and watched fish carve up the water as they nibbled the flecks of seed floating on the surface. For hours he observed them, letting words rise to the surface. The guard sat down under a tree and pulled a cap over his eyes.

Now the silence is no longer a prison, thought Alyosha to himself. *Now it is a pool. Sometimes it is still, and sometimes it is in motion with the life inside it, invisible beneath the surface.*

A man in a blue work suit slowly made his way down the walkway between the whispering trees, an old man, very bent, sweeping the path clean with a straw broom. When he came near the prisoner, he stopped and looked up. His eyes were ancient, veiled by ages of discretion. Yet within them, as in pools of clear water, many things were present. The old man bowed and continued sweeping.

Another day. In the garden two guards walked him around for an hour, lit cigarettes, then lost track of him. They were bored by the way he would sit or stand motionless, gazing at nothing for endless minutes. Side by side, they walked on around the circuit, talking quietly, leaving him by the fish pool. Escape was a thought that could not cross his mind.

The old gardener was in the compound also, and as before, he occupied himself sweeping the pathways, collecting pine-cones in a sack, or trimming bushes with clacking shears. Later, he came up beside the prisoner and threw bread crumbs into the pool. Fish swarmed and popped their mouths out of the water, swirling about each other like silken cloths.

The prisoner laughed.

The old man glanced at the guards, who were talking together on the far side of the garden. Then he glanced back at the prisoner. Touching his chest with a fingertip, he whispered, "Lin Jing."

The prisoner put the palm of his hand to his heart and said, "Alyosha."

"Alyosha", whispered Lin Jing. He bowed and went away.

There came a day when the air grew chilly and a dusting of frost coated the garden. Through his window Alyosha saw Lin Jing and other elderly servants gathering the last of the fruit. Were they prisoners, or were they hired laborers?

During his morning walk he tried to speak to the old man, but for some reason the guards stuck close to him, and there was no opportunity. He began to miss the old man whenever he was not present in the garden. This grew and grew until it became possible to see the shape of the world a little more clearly. "I'm not alone", he said to himself. "I'm not really suffering anymore, but I've been alone for a long time in the silence. The Muchenik has spoken no more to me, but he's with me here in this garden. I don't know how he is with me, but he is here."

Now the cold season began in earnest. The visitors brought him books to read, most in the Russian language, though some were in English. Alyosha could not concentrate on the printed lines. Each of the words meant something, but they did not connect to each other. They had no engine to pull the little black carriages along the tracks. When at last he answered questions regarding his name—Alyosha, he said— they stopped bringing English books.

They took him away to another part of the country, in a train heading south. The journey was comfortable because the train was electric. No steam and no coal smoke belched from the engine. The tracks were smoother. He rode in a deserted carriage, accompanied only by guards and a single civilian wearing a black suit and tie and a white shirt. This gentleman told Alyosha that his name was Mr. Zhang. He asked several questions during the long journey, but to these the prisoner could only respond with smiles and shrugs and sometimes with the bits of imagery that were returning to his mind. Whenever he was able to add a new word to his remembering, he would try to connect it to other words. Sometimes he made sentences that were about the landscape materializing in front of him.

He would say to Mr. Zhang, "The winter is lighter here."

And Mr. Zhang would reply in accented Russian, "Yes, it is a pleasant region."

As their habit of conversation grew, Alyosha would offer whatever came to mind, sometimes musing, always in the form of fragments, always obscure.

"I see that the world is a splendid sphere", he said at one point. "It revolves. A man might walk around it."

"A very long journey that would be", said Mr. Zhang in a philosophical tone.

"Not if he were to suspend himself above the ground. The planet would spin under his feet, and he would circle the world without effort."

"Your feet are rooted to the earth. Even the birds are pulled forward by the centrifugal force of the spin. They lift from the surface but only by a fraction of the circumference. They are deluded that they are free. Their prison is slightly larger than the prison of the earthbound."

"Am I a prisoner?" Alyosha asked.

Mr. Zhang hesitated.

"You are a guest."

"But why am I here?"

"That is the question. Why are you here? And why did your government have you in chains, and where were they taking you?"

"To Vladivostok", the prisoner said, astonishing himself, wondering where the answer had come from.

"Why to Vladivostok?"

"To see Kochetov."

"Ah, the infamous Mr. Kochetov. Is he still alive?"

"I think so. I never met him."

"That is evident. If you met him, you would not live to tell it. Why did they wish to introduce you to that man? It seems you are in intelligence after all."

"Intelligence..."

"Are you an agent for a foreign power?"

"No."

"But I think you are. You have merely forgotten that part of your past."

"Maybe..."

"Someday you must tell me your real name, Alyosha. And also who you were working for."

"I sell books", said Alyosha, astounding himself once again.

"Books?"

"Yes, the Zimorodok, the Kingfisher. That's part of it, somehow, but I don't know why. I see a house on a hill by a river, in a place far away."

"In Moscow or in Langley?"

"Where is Langley?"

"In Virginia, in the United States of America."

"I don't remember those names, not really, though it seems I knew them once, a long time ago. But when I left home, I was going someplace else. I wanted to circle the world and come home again with new eyes."

"With valuable information?"

"Yes. It would be necessary."

"Why would it be necessary?"

"For the seeing heart to see farther. Because the only whole heart is a broken heart."

"Is that a Russian proverb?"

"Maybe it is."

"You do not know for certain?"

"No, I forget many things."

"Do you like trains?"

"Oh, I love trains", the prisoner said with boyish enthusiasm, making even Mr. Zhang smile.

In the south it was warmer, plants were still blooming, and the countryside was full of shining mountains ridged by terraces of garden plots. Everything was green. There were large numbers of people wherever the train went, in the fields and villages and cities through which they passed. As the train climbed to higher altitudes, however, there were fewer and fewer people and more and more trees. In time they pulled slowly into a station on the side of a mountain in a narrow pass.

"Where are we?" Alyosha asked.

"Halfway between Kunming and Guilin", said Mr. Zhang with the air of a tourist guide. "Vietnam and Laos are below us, across the mountains."

A car was waiting for them at the station. It took Alyosha, Mr. Zhang, and two of the guards up a winding road into a high valley suspended between rounded crests. Stone canyons rose on every side, crowned by forests. Creeks spilled down from the heights and ran beneath the gravel road through culverts of hand-hewn stone. The sound of trickle water and the cries of forest birds soothed and gave pleasure. At the end of the road, the car passed through guarded gates and entered a compound dominated by a four-story building of ancient Chinese style, roofed with red clay tiles.

"Where are we now?" Alyosha asked.

"Paradise Mountain Retreat", said Mr. Zhang, stepping out onto a surface of white pebbles in the forecourt. "It was a resort for officials of the Kuomintang before the Revolution. You may think of it as a place of refuge for guests of the People."

"It's very kind of you to bring me here, Mr. Zhang."

"A small courtesy for an important visitor."

"I'm not important."

"Your government believes you are. And so do we."

As it turned out, the interior of the resort was luxurious, with rugs on the floors and art on the walls. Yet the windows were all barred, and his room was much like his previous one. The concierge locked the door behind him, and the guest soon discovered that there was no way to unlock it from the inside.

He remained there for months. He knew it was that long because several full moons, each preceded and followed by half moons and quarter moons, rolled across the sky. Most of the staff were medical professionals, and the remainder were political. There were no military uniforms in evidence. His meals were, for the most part, traditional Russian food. Much of each day was spent in physical and psychological rehabilitation, all conducted in the Russian tongue, though on occasion the political professionals tried to engage Alyosha in English dialogue. He found the Russian language easier.

At the end of the second month, he had become accustomed to spending several hours a day in discussion with his hosts. Uniformly courteous, they did not directly seek to extract any of the information they seemed to desire. Mr. Zhang was always present in the meeting room where such conversations were conducted. It was he who asked the most pointed questions, the less translucent, the least subtle. If he at times appeared to be frustrated by the inaccessibility of the guest's mind, he revealed little of it. The tightened lips and cool appraisal at the end of some of the later sessions were enough to convince Alyosha that he was the cause of displeasure.

"Why do you not disclose everything that is in your thoughts?" asked Mr. Zhang one day. "Truly, Alyosha, you would find peace in this."

"True speaking does not occur in noise."

"Is not speech a form of noise?"

"No, it is a form of silence."

"I disagree. It is a form of modulated noise, carefully chosen noise. Yet it remains noise."

"That is where you are wrong, Mr. Zhang. Did you not know that our loss of celestial language is the result of our loss of celestial silence?"

"Are you deliberately misleading us with such obscure phrases?"

Alex looked at him somberly and shook his head.

When hot weather returned, he was able to sleep only after lying awake for hours, panting in the heavy air. Dressed in cotton shorts, he listened in the dark to the night birds of the mountain, listened to the beating of his own heart, trying to remember.

He knew now that he was not Russian and that he had come from a place where English was spoken. He saw the whole panorama of the Clementine valley in his mind and thought that perhaps it was a place in America. As more and more pieces floated to the surface and coalesced, he remembered—and remembered remembering. Once he saw Oleg of Viborg sitting at the kitchen table in Halcyon, as both he and the bookseller reached across a void with the language of poetry. Language was the thread of connection. After Oleg came a vision of Kiril Pimonenko hovering over a book, translating Russian words into English, penciling with great effort the alien Roman alphabet into a notebook.

With that memory came a jolt of pain as he remembered Irina. And then a greater pain as he saw Carol's face in the many memories of their marriage. Then Jacob and Andrew. And with Andrew's face there poured in the entire history of his journey, its cause and its trajectory. And when he remembered that, he remembered everything. All rooms in the house were now unlocked. Though he could not yet face what was in some of them, he sensed what was behind the unopened doors and knew they were images of those who had died because of him. This was the greatest pain, the bullet in the skull, the brains of a youth splattered across his own face.

In the middle of the night in the darkened room, he contorted into a ball on the bed and rocked in agony, for it seemed undeniable that he had been responsible.

In the morning, after a fitful sleep, he was able to counterargue. He told himself that Chinese soldiers had shot Konstantin and the others, that a border violation had occurred for reasons that had nothing to do with himself, and that Konstantin might have been on the train that day regardless of whether or not he was on board. He wanted to believe this but in the end could not. He found a little relief in the thought that the attack would have occurred anyway and that someone else would have been killed in the place of the young soldier who had put a rolled jacket under his head, had given him water, had introduced himself and received Alex's name in return. But the fact remained that Konstantin had died. Who was that boy? Where had he come from? What might he have become?

Then it struck him that his hosts worked for the people who had destroyed him.

The next day, the regular morning meeting was electric with anger. Alex's face betrayed everything. He would answer none of their questions, would not respond to the mildest efforts to engage him in banal topics. He became absolutely silent and stared out through the bars of the conference room at the swaying trees. The officials ended the meeting abruptly.

For three days they left him alone. On the fourth day a new interrogator arrived—it was obvious that the word *host* was no longer valid. The new man introduced himself as Mr. Cui. He was about fifty, portly and balding, though his remaining hair was still black. He wore a brown suit, a white shirt, and a wide, dark tie. He looked like a businessman. He did not speak Russian and had brought an interpreter. This was a woman about forty years old, dressed in a Western pantsuit. In all other aspects she was indelibly a Party member. Her eyes utterly cold, her face immobile, only her lips moved. All Mr. Cui's questions were translated through her mouth.

"The time has come for openness", she said in faintly accented Russian.

Alex did not reply.

"Who are you?" she said. "What is your name, and what agency do you work for?"

Silence.

"Are you a native Russian?"

On and on the questions went:

"Are you FSB? CIA? SIS, MI6? The Mossad? What is your date of birth and country of origin? When and where were you arrested? Why did they torture you? What secrets did you know? Are you aware that we have the authority to give you refugee status if you are willing to assist us with the information?"

To all of the above, Alex made no reply. In the end, he decided to make a run for freedom. Speaking in English, he said, "They arrested me by mistake. They mistook me for a foreign intelligence agent. I know nothing."

A storm of conversation broke out among them, ending abruptly at a sharp word from Mr. Cui.

That evening he was taken back to the train station and put into a carriage with guards. Three days later he arrived at a northern city—he thought it was probably Beijing—and was returned to the prison where he had lived before. They gave him his old room with a view of the garden. Looking out the window the first morning after his arrival, he noticed the elderly servant named Lin Jing sweeping the walkways.

Alex had no meetings with interrogators that day, but the routine resumed as before, with the exception of meals, which were no longer Russian but simple Chinese fare. After lunch a guard took him for a period of exercise in the garden. There he encountered Lin Jing kneeling by one of the fish pools, scooping weeds from it with a net. Because the guard was by his side, Alex was careful not to greet the old man, though their eyes met in passing.

The pool of silence is still here, he thought. *And now I know that it is sometimes in men's eyes.*

The following day Alex was brought upstairs to the fifth floor and into a room that might have been a banquet hall or a library in times past, though it was now bare of any decoration or furniture other than a long metal table that ran almost the length of the room. Through a bank of tall windows on the right he saw the crowns of leafy trees. In the distance, visible above the wall of the compound, were the distinctive rooftops of ancient oriental buildings. Alex thought that they looked a lot like the photographs he had seen of the imperial palace complex, the Forbidden City.

He was told in Russian to sit down on one side of the table, near the middle. Opposite him on the other side was Mr. Cui (now in military garb of some kind) and another important-looking official (also in uniform). Flanking them left and right were men in civilian clothing and two others in dark uniforms with red shoulder boards and gold stars. Seated behind Cui was the cold-eyed interpreter from Paradise Mountain.

Cui gestured to the man beside him. This personage gazed a long time at Alex before speaking. The room became very still. Behind him sat a young woman, dressed in a simple black skirt and a white blouse. Her eyes were not cold, but they were expressionless. Another interpreter, the prisoner supposed.

"I am Dr. Xia", the personage said in heavily accented English. "You must now, in the interests of your own future and the interests of the People's Republic of China, speak candidly with us. First, you will tell us who you were."

The young woman behind him leaned forward and spoke softly in his ear.

"Correction", said Xia. "You will tell us who you *are*."

"My name is Alexander Graham", the prisoner slowly replied. "I am a Canadian."

The older woman interpreter relayed this information to Cui, who absorbed it without expression, though it caused a stir among the other officials. Cui stared at Alex as if probing the exact nature of a deception.

"I would like to speak with a representative of my embassy", Alex said.

"You are an American agent of the CIA", Cui said impassively. "Do not lie to us. It will not help you."

"I am not an agent of the CIA."

"The government of the Russian Federation assures us that you are. They want you back, Mr. Bell. Why do they want you back so badly?"

"They have mistaken me for someone else. My name is not Bell."

"A strange mistake, is it not? How could such a mistake be made? A person's face, his past, his trail—these can be erased only with great difficulty."

"I am Alexander Graham."

"Do you wish to speak with the American representative in the People's Republic?"

"I'm not an American."

"Why were you in custody? Why did they torture you?"

Alex briefly recounted the story of his journey. Their eyes told him he was not believable.

Through his interpreter, Cui demanded to know what he had seen near Irkutsk. Was it a military installation? Alex replied that he did not know what it was. He explained that he had come upon it by accident. He knew only that it was surrounded by miles of fences.

"But so are many innocuous things, in every country, surrounded by fences. Why were they so extremely disturbed that you found it?"

"I don't know why."

"I think you do know, Mr. Bell. We are sure that you know. And it is certain that you wish to relay to your own government what you saw. Of course, that is no longer possible."

Alex refrained from asking him why not.

"You see, the incident on the border of the Heilongjiang, the Amur River, was most unfortunate. It was not an approved action. The Russians are very upset, as are we. It was a renegade act. The Russian government is now willing to forget the incident, but only on condition of your safe return to their custody." Cui paused. "Perhaps by way of Mr. Kochetov", he concluded.

Alex shuddered.

"You would not like that, I presume?" said Cui.

"It would be a death sentence, doubtless", said Dr. Xia.

"There is another possibility", Cui went on. "If you tell us everything you saw at the installation, we would consider turning you over to the U.S. government. Then you would find yourself a free man and safely returned to your homeland. Would you like that, Mr. Bell?"

"I do not want to go back to Russia. I'm not an American. My name is not Bell. I've told you the truth. I saw nothing."

"You saw nothing at all? How do you expect us to believe this? Why would the Russian security police torture you and then send you to Kochetov for worse?"

"Because I told them what I'm telling you. Because they thought I knew something, and they wouldn't believe me when I told them I never got inside their fences."

"Were you trying to get inside? Is that what Langley wanted you to do?"

"I don't work for Langley."

"But when you first were brought into China, you spoke of Langley in your delirium. That is not the sort of thing that comes from the mouth of an unfortunate tourist."

"They put the thought into my head. They suspected me of seeing something. But I didn't."

"Was it a biological warfare plant?" Xia asked.

Alex shook his head.

"Chemical warfare?"

"I told you, I didn't see anything. Maybe it's a toy factory."

"Do not play with us, Mr. Bell."

"Graham. My name is Alex Graham. Please call my embassy. They will confirm it."

"The Russians tell us that is your assumed name. They have proof that you are a CIA agent operating under a false Canadian passport. The U.S. government has done it before, and they now have done it again."

"That's not true—at least not in my case."

"We are losing patience with you", said Cui.

"Would you please give me a lie detector test?"

"Such tests are inconclusive. Besides, even if you are the Mr. Graham you say you are, that could mean many things. Perhaps the bookseller from Canada is a contract agent, a tourist with a covert assignment. You see, we are in a difficulty. What shall we do with you? If you tell us everything, we will return you to whichever diplomatic station you prefer."

"You will return me to Russia", Alex said. "Because after you get what you want, you will then solve the border incident by throwing me to the Russian wolf."

"This is not so", said Cui. "When you tell us what we need to know, we can never return you to our friends to the north. They would try to find out what you told us, and that would create new difficulties. Be assured, if you are honest with us, we will not send you back to them. But if you refuse, what choice do we have? We can then solve only the lesser problem of the border incident. Our hands are tied, you see. It all rests on you."

Alex folded his arms and stared at his knees.

"Are you ready to answer?" Xia said.

"I've said everything I know. I've told you the truth. You won't believe me. There's nothing more I can do."

"Then we send you to Kochetov", said Cui with a voice as polite as death.

Instinctively, Alex bowed his head and made a small sign of the cross on his chest.

The officials stood up, scraped back their chairs, and launched into subdued conversations among themselves. Alex looked hopelessly across the table as his guard took his arm and pulled him to his feet. He noticed that Dr. Xia and the young woman interpreter were staring at him without expression.

"One moment", Xia said, turning to Cui. Switching to Chinese, he talked at length with his colleague. As Alex and the guard stood waiting, Cui glanced suspiciously at Alex, then gave an abrupt nod of his head. The officials left the room, and Alex was returned to his cell.

Throughout the night he prayed, expecting that the next day he would be sent back to Russia. He prayed every way that he could recall, including the rosary and the chotki, using his fingers as counters. But it was the memory of his fingers in the wound in the heart that gave him sufficient peace to slide into sleep.

41. *Upstairs and Downstairs*

In the morning, after breakfast, a guard took Alex to the garden. To his great surprise, he saw Dr. Xia and the young interpreter waiting for him beside the fish pool. Xia sent the guard to the far end of the garden.

"We will walk among the trees and pathways", he said, taking Alex by the arm.

"I have nothing more to tell you", Alex said coldly, staring at the small hand gripping his elbow.

"I believe you", Xia said.

Stopping in midstride, Alex looked at him incredulously.

"Why do you believe me?"

"I will answer you when we have had a chance to know each other better."

"What's the point, if you're going to send me back to Russia?"

"That may not come to pass. Do not be afraid."

Alex said nothing as they walked on. Three times they circuited the garden, Alex on one side of Xia, the interpreter on the other. He noted that the woman remained always a pace or two behind her boss. From time to time she would intervene to correct Xia's vocabulary or to express to him more precisely something Alex tried to say. He became more and more aware of her presence, adding up little details. She was a linguistic expert of some kind, for her pronunciation of English was perfect, though neutral, its origins indefinable. Her instantaneous grasp of whatever Alex said was equally impressive, for she conveyed it to Xia without hesitation, without a hint of straining for alien vocabulary. Though Xia was proficient in English, he faltered at times, and whenever this happened, she perceived the need immediately, filling in the gap with no intrusion of her personality. Once or twice Alex glanced curiously at her, wondering what sort of person she was, only to find her looking back shyly.

Their conversation was as follows:

"I have obtained a delay for you", Xia said. "I convinced Mr. Cui that we are being hasty. Why should the People's Republic let itself be bullied by the Russians? The prisoner has been psychologically and physically brutalized, I argued. He is not yet in his right mind. We should not discard a valuable resource so quickly. I have asked him to allow me a slower approach. A more fraternal approach. Cui is purely political. I am a psychiatrist as well as a political officer. I have obtained Cui's permission to try to win your confidence."

"It won't help if you do. I've told you everything I know. There's nothing more to tell."

"Yes, I believe you, Mr. . . . ."

"Graham. That is my name."

Xia looked into his eyes for several seconds, as did the woman standing quietly behind him.

"Then, Mr. Graham, I must ask you if the CIA was using a Canadian national to do its work in Russia."

"No. Not me."

Once again the two Chinese looked into his eyes with calm appraisal. The strangest feeling came over Alex, as if an inner barometer registered the fact that he was being scanned and read—accurately read.

Dr. Xia nodded and continued to walk.

For several minutes nothing more was said. Alex seized the opportunity to soak up what would probably be his last experiences of beauty. The garden simmered in golden light, in the smells of flowers and fruit, and in the sounds of birds.

At last they stopped in front of the fish pool. Xia sat down on its low wall, indicating that Alex should sit beside him to his right. The interpreter sat down on his left.

"Do you believe in God, Mr. Graham?" Xia asked tonelessly.

"Yes."

"Do you pray to him?"

"Yes."

"What do you think of the Chinese people?"

"You are human beings."

"Splendid. Thank you for the compliment. I would like to introduce you to my interpreter. Her name is—" Xia stopped. Glancing uneasily at the young woman, he did not go on. She said something to him in Chinese and lowered her eyes.

"Her name is Pin. That is part of her real name. You should not know our full names. In the future, when you turn your thoughts to us, you must remember us in a different way. I am John. This is Pin."

The two Chinese observed as Alex took in this information.

"John? Pin? I don't understand."

"In years to come, when you turn your thoughts to heaven, to the paradise mountain that is above, you will speak to our Lord on our behalf—this I hope."

Alex could only stare at them. He suspected a trick, a psychiatrist's ploy to win the confidence of a disturbed patient needing to unburden himself of tormenting delusions. They had seen him make the sign of the cross the night before, and now they were trying to unlock him with this key.

The woman leaned forward and said, "Alexander, we see. We see it all."

"What do you think you see?" he replied coldly.

"The fear in you. You mistrust us. Pray to him and he will show you."

Dr. Xia and Pin closed their eyes for a few moments. Pin folded her hands. Alex watched them as if they were performing a piece of Chinese theater. But when the woman opened her eyes, she looked deeply into him, as if she were able to walk through the front door of the house and glance all around, even into its locked rooms.

"What's going on here?" Alex said. "Who and what are you? You're intelligence people. That means you're liars. Don't waste your time. I won't tell you anything more because there's nothing more to tell."

After a moment of silent consideration, Xia said, "You should pray, Mr. Graham. He will show you."

"Who will show me?"

"Him. The One. Ye-su. Jesus."

Still mistrusting them, not knowing why he should do what they suggested, he stared at the pool.

Where is the silence? he thought. *How can I find it again? Is the pool full of weeds that will entangle me and pull me to the bottom?*

"Pray now", Pin said.

Alex closed his eyes. In the interior, below the surface currents of his fear and anger, he touched the depth of the soul and rested. But he heard no words from God, from *him*, from *Ye-su*.

"Yes?" said Xia. "Can you trust?"

"Not very much", Alex murmured.

"We put our lives into your hands, Mr. Graham."

"Your lives into my hands? Isn't that reversing things? I may be crazy, but I'm not that crazy."

"Mr. Graham, this conversation is very dangerous to me and Pin. And to hundreds of others who are her children." Xia nodded deferentially to the young woman.

"Her children?" Alex asked.

Pin said something to Xia in their language.

"She says you can be trusted", Xia said.

"How does she know I can be trusted?"

"She knows."

"Alexander," said Pin in a whisper, "we are Christians."

"If you are Christians," Alex said, with a certain hostility, "what are you doing in this devilish institution?"

Xia answered. "We will not remain here long. Recent developments, slow changes. In China we are more than a billion people; we are a millennia-old civilization. All things move slowly, or they do not move at all. Or if they move, as in the Mao cultural revolution, they are swift and brutal. But that is rare."

"What are you saying?"

"I am a recent convert. For several months I have been a Gospel disciple—Protestant, you say—and Pin is *Tsen-tu-tong*—Catholic."

"We are both *Di-zha-jo-hway*—downstairs Church, not upstairs", Pin said.

"Downstairs is underground believers—Catholic and Protestant. Upstairs is patriotic churches. There are believers there also, but not so many as downstairs."

Alex absorbed this, still wrestling with disbelief.

"How many are in the downstairs Church?" he asked.

"Even in the CPC, we estimate eighty to one hundred million", Xia said modestly.

"Are you serious? That's a lot of people."

"Less than one-tenth of our population", Pin said.

"You said *we*, Dr. Xia. Are you still a member of the Party?"

"I am a member in name but no longer in spirit. I am a political officer at my faculty in the university. But soon I will...retire. For reasons of health. Then I will become an evangelizer."

"Dr. Xia has risked everything", Pin said. "There are more and more like him. But the harvest is greatly in need of harvesters. He is learning wisdom swiftly."

"Before I leave the work of the devil, I will undermine it", Xia declared with quiet intensity.

Pin lowered her eyes.

Seeing this, sadness filled Xia's eyes. "Pin does not agree with me. She has asked me to leave immediately this work. But there are things to be finished, good work, setting captives free. Is this not in the Gospel, Pin?"

"Yes, but in another sense. We cannot work for the devil even for good purposes."

"I am leaving soon. Give me time, my mother."

This was an incongruous utterance, for Xia was in his sixties and Pin in her midtwenties.

"Why are you here, Pin, if it's the devil's work?" Alex asked.

Xia answered for her. "In the eyes of the state, she is nothing more than a worker. Her peasant background and lack of connections to the Party make it difficult for her to study. Yet she is a genius of languages, Mr. Graham. She has no academic future, and so I hire her as my translator from time to time, usually for ordinary work at the university. She is here with me because Cui thinks she is one of us. He does not suspect me. In a free country, she would be a professor. Now she works in a factory to earn her living, and at night she moves about the city and countryside tending the flock of the Lord."

"Doctor," Pin interjected, "you need not speak of my situation."

Ignoring her, Xia went on. "She has been responsible for the conversion of hundreds, including me, including other Party members. The Holy Spirit works through her, swift, far, deep. She prays with everyone who is willing to pray, Catholic and Protestant, upstairs and downstairs. She is mother to many, though, as you see, very young."

Alex pondered their faces soberly. "Why are you trusting me with this information? If I'm tortured, I might betray your secret."

Xia frowned. Pin said:

"In this world everything is risk. To trust is a choice."

"If what you're telling me is true, I still don't see how I can help you, or what you can do to help me", Alex said. "Your government will never let me return to my home. They'll send me back to the Russians to solve the border incident."

"It is possible. But that is a last choice. No one is certain what to do with you because the problem remains—what do you know? What did you see? They hold on to you because the knowledge of the secret installation is of utmost importance. Border incidents occur. They can be smoothed by blaming it on hothead soldiers. But this is a more serious incident because the train contained not only you but other sensitive items. Of this I cannot speak."

"Relations between Russia and the People's Republic are troubled", Pin said.

"They are at a dangerous stage", Xia continued. "On the surface we have new peace treaties, money flowing into the country, the end of the Cold War. But all is not as it seems. They were testing the perimeter."

"The Amur?" Alex asked.

"No, the psychological perimeter."

"What do you mean?"

"The Party needs to know what Russia will tolerate under the new government. Cui lied. The border violation was not a renegade act. It was tactical. You were an unexpected bonus. We are puzzled why the loss of you has made the Russians so very worried."

Pin said, "For both governments, what is known can be assessed, and corrective actions undertaken. It is the unknown that opens the door for misinterpretation and overreaction on both sides."

"And I am the unknown factor?" Alex asked.

The two Chinese nodded.

"There is an ancient proverb in my land," said Xia, "one that is still widely used. We say, 'A single ant can destroy a dam.'"

"And I'm the ant. But why can't I convince both sides that I know nothing? That would dispel the unknown."

"In the country of lies," Pin said, "nothing is believable."

"But *you* believe me!"

Again they nodded.

"Why?"

"Because the Holy Spirit has given gifts to our Church that are not, perhaps, well known elsewhere."

"What kind of gifts?"

"To see the heart. To hear the promptings of the guardian angels. To listen to the Spirit. To understand the position of a soul in the field of battle."

Like swords flashing in the sky, Alex thought to himself.

"Yes, like that", said Pin. "We are beneath the wings and the swords. We too make battle, though our weapons are prayer and love and truth."

At that point the metal door to the house opened on squealing hinges, and Cui strode into the garden. Xia and Pin sat straighter. Cui approached slowly along the walkway, tamping a cigarette on a silver case, staring at Alex.

Xia and Pin stood. Cui fired a question at Xia, and the doctor responded with cool professionalism. The two older men walked away, Pin following. The guard returned Alex to his room.

The next day they met again in the garden.

Xia began. "I have convinced Cui that we are making progress. I have told him it will take time to win your confidence. They watch from the windows. Perhaps there are microphones here, but I do not think so."

"Even so, we must take great care", Pin said. "We must pray first before speaking; then if we are heard, they will not understand."

So they prayed together, whispering the Lord's prayer in their respective languages.

"From now on we will speak simply", said Pin. "But beneath the surface of the water is the deep current. Listen carefully to it, Alexander. Water is important to you, is it not?"

"Yes, water has always meant something to me—something I could never really define."

"Why is it so?"

"Maybe because I lived beside a river all my life."

"It is a picture of *being*", said Pin.

"Also the water of Baptism", said Xia.

"And the dive from the high bridge", Pin gently added.

Startled, Alex stared at her. "How do you know this? Who are you, really?"

"I am your sister."

Later in the morning the old man Lin Jing came to them at the fish pool. He brought a little folding bamboo table and tray. As he set it on the flagstones before Xia and Pin, he smiled at Alex, bowed, and went away. The tray contained a clay pot of tea, three small cups, and a dish of cookies sprinkled with large sugar crystals. The cookies tasted of almonds and aniseed.

Yellow, spear-shaped leaves detached themselves from the trees and fluttered onto the walkways. Orange and purple fruit dropped onto little patches of blue grass. In the pool the bronze heron examined the unheeding fish, preparing to strike.

Who are these people, really, Alex wondered. *How have they become what they are? But are they really what they seem to be?*

Though he wanted to trust Xia and Pin, his fears rose up again and undermined everything they had told him. Surely they had created an elaborate deception.

"What is the agency you work for?" he asked.

"The Public Security Bureau", Xia replied.

"You're the secret police, aren't you? Well, you can just give up. I don't care how many psychology degrees you have, it won't work. I'm not going to tell you anything, because I don't know anything."

"Alexander," said Pin, leaning forward earnestly, speaking in a low voice, "do not lose the grace that was given to you. It is difficult to trust. We know how difficult it is. You must pray again, and let our Lord show you the truth."

There was a quality, an authority, in her words that could have come from nowhere else but the realm of Christ. Alex regretted his suspicion and bowed his head.

"I'm sorry", he said. "You're risking a lot, aren't you? You're doing it for me."

"And for the flock of the Lord", said Xia.

"Your brothers and sisters in China, they know of you", Pin said. "Many are pleading with heaven for you."

"Why for me? I'm not important. Not in any way."

"You are a brother", said Pin. "That is important enough. Does not Saint Thomas Aquinas teach that one human soul, any human soul, is worth more than the entire value of the material universe?"

Alex shook his head. "Does he say that?"

"Yes, he does", Pin said, nodding.

Xia said, "Our sister knows several languages, Mr. Graham. One of them is Latin."

Alex screwed his face into an expression that made the two Chinese smile.

"You think it is not credible?" Xia asked.

"It's, well, rather hard to..."

"Saint Thomas returns us to the greater universe", said Pin. "This universe has been hidden from my people. But the time of the Lord is at hand."

"The time of the Lord? Do you mean the end of the world?"

"Of that I am uncertain. But of this Jesus does speak to me: a time of ending approaches, and then comes a period of peace after much suffering. Until then, Jesus speaks to our shepherd, the Holy Father, and thus we listen to him."

"But how do you hear the Holy Father's teaching? Doesn't the government prevent any of his words from getting into China?"

"His words come; his teachings enter. The Lord opens doors that are locked. A fierce persecution is under way. The murder of children in great numbers continues. Shepherds are imprisoned, released after torture, then imprisoned again and again. News of it seldom reaches the West because the Party covers it with a red cloak. And the little that does reach the West is of no interest to them because they do not value Christians."

Xia said, "Recently eight leaders in the downstairs Church were executed publicly in a sports stadium. Forty thousand people cheered. This is our blindness. But you, the people of the West, also have your blindness."

Alex stared at the ground. Shortly after, a guard arrived and conducted him back to his room.

Following lunch, Alex was again brought to the garden, where Xia and Pin were waiting for him.

"Why are we meeting here?" he asked. "Why aren't we in a room where they can record everything?"

"Psychology, Mr. Graham. I have convinced them that the pleasant surroundings are helping you to relax. I assure them that you will soon trust us and tell us everything."

"But we're running out of time, aren't we?"

"Yes. Nevertheless, other currents are in motion. Downstairs channels. Efforts are being made to inform your embassy."

"The Canadian?"

"Yes, the Canadian."

"Thank God!"

"Yes, thank our God for his great mercy and power. Locked doors are opening, but of these it is better that you know nothing."

"Even so, Alexander," said Pin, "you must pray very much, for part of the problem is in your own embassy."

Xia explained: "Your country has been weak with us. It lacks courage. When it speaks against the human rights abuses, it always speaks with a little voice. The Party understands your country very well. It knows that your leaders make their protests as a formality, to reassure voters. But in reality your government is interested in something that is, to them, far more important."

"Only the humiliated and dispossessed have open eyes", Pin said with a note of sadness.

"For your country, money is everything", Xia said with a tone of exquisite disdain. "All Chinese employees of your embassy are—how do you say it—*vetted* by our PSB. Everything that is said and done within the walls of the embassy is known to us. Your own country has agreed to this, and why? Because of money, Mr. Graham. Money, that tainted thing."

Pin said, "Your country does not yet know you are in our hands. By tomorrow they will know. Then will be the most dangerous moment of all."

"Why?"

"Because it will be their moment of testing."

"Surely they'll make a diplomatic protest. I've broken no Chinese laws. They'll demand that I be returned to Canada."

974

"We must pray for this", Pin said.

"But—"

"You see, Mr. Graham," Xia said in his driest tone, "it is very much to the advantage of your nation to remain on happy terms with mine. The money, you see. The massive markets of China and the cheap labor are attractive."

Alex sputtered, "That's not possible. I'm from a democratic nation. They'd never sacrifice a citizen for a few dollars."

"Would they not? Are there no devils in your land? If not, a blessed land it must be. But I think you are naïve, Mr. Graham. Those who throw human lives into the jaws of death rarely understand what they are doing. The devils wrap thick blindfolds over their eyes. For most of my life I have been a blind man, and only when my eyes were finally opened did I see my own evil."

Xia's mouth worked bitterly for a few seconds, then returned to its customary calm.

"East and West—we have all lived in a flat universe. For us, it is the dragon universe; for the Russians, it is the wolf universe. For you, it is the money universe."

"You seem to think there's not much chance I'll get out", Alex murmured, feeling suddenly frightened.

"We will pray. You will pray. Many in this land are already praying for your liberation."

"But why? Why me?"

Pin answered. "Because you must bear a message to our brothers and sisters beyond the great wall. You must tell them about the persecution and beg their prayers for the Church in China."

"But they already know about it."

"They know it, but they forget it", said Xia.

"More voices bring more prayers", added Pin. She paused, then whispered, "And we pray for you because you are our brother."

His mind was exhausted by these meetings. Though they offered him hope, each encounter demanded more thought and more coherent response than he had been able to produce since his imprisonment began. His sleep was broken frequently by nightmares in which he was screaming in agony as fists rained on him and electric swords stabbed him without ceasing. Worst of all was the recurring image of Konstantin's exploded skull.

The next day was warm, misty with a drizzle so fine that it hung in the air. Alex was taken to the garden by a guard and left alone with Xia and Pin. As on the previous two days, they sat together on the wall of the fish pool.

"Is there any news?" Alex asked.

"Your country now knows", Xia said.

"Are they making a protest? Are they doing anything?"

"This is uncertain."

"If my embassy goes too slowly, or your government puts up roadblocks, what will Cui do with me?"

"His situation is now more complicated. Do not forget the massacre at Tiananmen Square. The Party gives some consideration to the reactions of foreign nations, but it is not a high consideration. State security is highest priority. In the face of a cowardly nation, it does not waver."

"A cowardly nation such as mine?"

"I regret to use the word, but it is accurate."

"Be honest with me. What will Cui do with me?"

Xia's face reverted to classic inscrutability.

"I will try to convince Cui that by every psychological method I have come to the conclusion that you are telling us the truth. However, you must prepare your soul, for it is unlikely he will accept my testimony on your behalf. The Party cannot risk that I am wrong. To take your life costs them nothing. They may seek to discover what you know by making you suffer. For that reason, you may die here. To let you go costs them a great risk."

"But I don't see how I'm a risk."

"You are a risk because there is positive information and negative information. If you were returned to the Russians, they would put you through more suffering in order to determine what you have told us or not told us. This information would be useful to them. If there is a threat to our country from the Irkutsk project, then the Russians would know we have learned nothing about it. On the other hand, if you remain here in China, the Russians cannot know exactly what we have discovered. If you are returned to your homeland, the knowledge goes with you, making the situation unstable for both Russia and China. This option cannot be chosen. There are gains and losses in each of the other two options. As you see, it is complex."

"But if my government demands my return—"

"China would ignore it. Officially, you would become ill and die, or you would be convicted of an imaginary crime and executed rather than be returned to Canada. As for the other two options, all factors will be weighed in the balance; what the final decision shall be is difficult to predict. One thing is certain: for you, all paths lead to the cross. I am sorry. I do not want to tell you this..."

Her eyes strained with pain, Pin said, "It is better to be prepared, Alexander, than to cling to false hopes. Still, we must hope and pray."

Shaken, Alex whispered, "You're right. It's better to know."

All three fell silent for several minutes. Alex tried to rejuvenate a scrap of hope that his government would behave honorably. Then, with a sinking feeling, he recalled an incident that had occurred in Canada a few years before. During the Asia-Pacific summit, many heads of state had gathered at a conference center in Vancouver, including the premier of the People's Republic of China. Just before his arrival, a large crowd had gathered in the streets to protest the human rights abuses in China and Indonesia. It had been a peaceful, legal protest. Without warning, the federal police had swooped down on the crowd, beating many demonstrators, blinding young and old alike with pepper spray. Agents had entered apartments up and down the street confiscating protest signs in the windows of private dwellings. Later, it was leaked to the press that the attack had been ordered by the prime minister. Citizens of a free nation had been treated with fascist tactics because the leader of Canada did not want to be embarrassed in front of the bloodiest dictators in the world. Did not want to risk the loss of a dollar.

Alex stared sightlessly into the pool.

Pin plucked some dry stems of pond flowers and braided them. When Alex looked up at her, she reached for his hand, timidly at first, because the gesture was entirely alien to her culture. She looked into his eyes with compassion and encouragement. Her face was so pure, he could hardly bear it. He glanced down at his own hands, which seemed to him naked, scarred, dirty. Sinner's hands.

"A gift for you", she said.

Overwhelmed, he could not speak.

"Will you open your hand, Alexander?" she said.

He opened his right hand but quickly clenched and withdrew it.

"It is for you to decide", she said gently. "You are free to open or not to open."

He opened his hand.

She cupped his hand in hers. Hers were warm, flawless ivory, a small temple.

"Who are you?" he said, unable to look at her.

"I am the smallest", she answered.

She placed into his hand a tiny fish woven from strips of dry weed.

Because there was nothing more to be said, Alex held onto the fish and hung his head. Xia, who had observed without comment, now made his presence felt.

"Mr. Graham, go and sit under the cherry tree, where the gardener is pruning bushes."

"I want to go back to my room", Alex said. "I need to be alone."

"No," said Pin, "you need to sit under the tree."

"You will speak with the gardener", Xia added.

Puzzled, Alex did as they said and sat down on the grass beneath the tree. Slung beneath its branches was a gauze sheet for catching the fruit. Though the time of the harvest was past, a few black cherries still clung to the branches, and in the net several had fallen and rolled together. Alex reached up and touched them from beneath. They tumbled around, then settled back into the depression caused by their weight. In the heat of the day, their smell was strong. Spices and herb smells were also present. Birds swooped through the garden while a pale sun began to glow through the mist.

Xia and Pin remained seated by the fish pool, their heads together in muted conversation, though he could hear none of their words.

The gardener—he remembered that the old man's name was Lin Jing—continued to clip the bushes three or four feet from Alex.

"Alyosha", the gardener whispered, without looking at him.

"Lin Jing", Alex said.

"Close eyes", said Lin Jing in badly accented English.

Alex stared at him.

"People look window", said Lin Jing. "People think you sleep."

Alex closed his eyes, wondering how a peasant in a prison had come to know English.

"Now, if you wish, confession", said Lin Jing.

Angrily Alex sat upright, thinking that the Party used everything and anything. To coerce an old man to participate in it meant that they considered Alex to be crazy or incredibly stupid.

"I have nothing to confess. I've already told you people what I know—which is nothing!"

"Confession of soul", said Lin Jing. "Sacrament."

He dropped to his knees and began to gather the clippings into a pile. Casting a swift glance about the garden, he surreptitiously made a small sign of the cross over Alex.

"You are Catholic", said Lin Jing. "I am priest."

"What?" Alex breathed.

"I am priest", he said again. "Ask that girl. She know."

"Pin?"

"Is it her name?" asked the old man.

"You don't know her name, but you say I should ask her to confirm your identity? This does not make sense. How can I believe you?"

"I do not know her name, but my soul see her soul. She is in the Communion. Do not be afraid. Our Savior want come to you. But you must choose. You must ask."

Alex glanced at Pin and Xia. The doctor was standing now, dabbling the surface of the pond with a dry stalk of bulrush. He was talking loudly in Chinese. Pin stood beside him, looking intently at Alex. When their eyes met, she nodded once, and glanced at Lin Jing.

"Close eyes", said the priest. "Guard think you sleep. Then speak to our Savior in sacrament."

Once again Lin Jing made a covert sign of the cross over Alex. Then he began to whisper Latin words. It was the old rite of confession, which Alex remembered from his childhood.

"Now, tell sins to Jesus", said Lin Jing.

So Alex did. He thought it was more than a year since his last confession, made to Father Sergius in the poustinia on the Little-Little Ob. As the Russian priest's face returned to his conscious mind, other memories flooded in, and along with it came anguish. He was acutely aware of his many failings and weaknesses, his lies, his rage, his fear, his lack of trust in God. When Alex had finished telling the priest what he could remember, Lin Jing said:

"Some is sin; some is wave of water, the heart pain, the mind pain. But Jesus takes it all into his heart. You touch him. You put finger in wound in his side, like Thomas. Thomas doubt. Thomas fear. Thomas want to be safe. Man here, man there, man all places want to be safe. Alyosha, it not safe in this war. Love him. Love him with much love. He love you. He love you. Take him with you into suffering place. You not alone, Alyosha. For penance, pray a rosary. Now you say *Confiteor*; then I absolve."

And so he did.

Like a man falling weightless, Alex lay back on the grass, gazing up through the veil that covered the sanctuary, watching droplets of blood dripping from branches.

Lin Jing gathered the last of the prunings and carried them to a corner of the garden, where he threw them into a stone catch basin. He set fire to it with matches and bundles of twigs and stood watching the smoke rise like incense. The guard sauntered over to him, and they chatted for a while; then the guard retreated to the steps of the building and sat down, took a little book from his pocket, and began to read with concentration.

Lin Jing returned to a spot a few feet from Alex and dug about in a flower bed with a hand tool.

"*Corpus Christi* now", said the priest. "He come to you."

Pausing for another glance, Lin Jing knelt, removed a cloth from his breast pocket, and tenderly opened it on the grass.

Enclosed in its center in a piece of metal foil was a small white particle. The old man closed his eyes and bowed before it. Taking it in his thumb and forefinger, he put it onto Alex's tongue. As Alex swallowed, Lin Jing picked up a broom, went to a far corner of the garden, and began to sweep the leaves.

Alex lay back and let the Presence radiate from the center of his chest to every cell of his body. As he was enveloped by the sweet burning in his heart, all fear departed. His thanksgiving was wordless and clear. Drifting deeper into a state of inner rest, closer to sleep than to wakefulness, he sensed that his prayer was rising into a chorus of praises from the countless martyrs of China and their angels and was joining the pleas of all the Communion of Saints. Pin's prayers were there too, with the singing of the smallest of the earth.

Among the saints was the greatest one, the Lady crowned with twelve stars. Standing on the moon, she gazed at him. It was his smallness that drew her eyes, his poverty and weakness, his foolishness, his broken heart. He had nothing to give her to assist with her work, nothing to help her Son. He had failed at everything, and others had suffered because of his arrival in the lands where he did not belong. But she showed him that he would come to understand the necessity of his journey. The words and the ways of his quest had been flawed, but his heart had persevered even unto the drowning, to the very edge of the drain hole. And because he had lost everything, had let go of all power, heaven had been freed to act in him. This he did not understand—no, not at all—yet there was peace in it.

As she gazed at him, it seemed that he heard the heart-words of the Woman, as if she were saying to him, "I am the Lady of the tides; I am the swift, bright water and the bay. I am with you; I am your Mother. Nothing need you fear."

Xia woke him. "It is time", said the doctor. "We leave you now."

Alex sat up and rubbed his eyes.

"There is still a chance. I will argue for delay."

"Will we see each other again?" Alex asked.

"Perhaps."

"But you don't think so, do you?"

Xia dropped his eyes and said nothing.

Pin stepped forward and said. "*Tsai-jien*, good-bye, Alexander. He is with you. He is in you. Fear nothing. If you are to suffer, the flock in China is with you. Word of you is now speeding along all the pathways; millions of prayers rise up for you. If you go to the cross, you are not alone. Never are you alone."

He nodded, then said in a trembling voice, "Pin?"

"Yes, Alexander."

"Pin, my hands have opened. You helped me open them. Pray that in the time left to me I will keep them open."

"Yes", she said. "We will pray."

The door to the building squealed, and Cui entered the garden. Xia and Pin inclined their heads to Alex and went away.

Back in his room he prayed his rosary. Later, throughout the night, he lay on his bed in the darkness and continued to pray. He felt that his allotted time on earth was coming to the end of its course, that it would spill over a dam and take him into the eternal sea. Beside him, swept along in the current, he saw the faces of Jamie and Hannah Colley rising from the waters of the Clementine, bobbing among the ice floes, pulled mercilessly toward the dam. A hand drew them to shore.

He supposed it was his imagination translating memory into symbols. Then he saw the face of Theresa Colley, a mother weeping in the night, a sword in her heart. He saw her loneliness and courage and felt that if he had been a different kind of man, a less solitary and self-protective man, he would have wanted to know her better, to help her family. After that came Irina and the sons he had adopted in his heart and the other children of Baikal. It seemed to him now that he was going to die and that what was begun with Irina could go no further. He prayed that his sufferings and his death would be united to the cross of Christ and that God would accept it as an offering for their salvation. He pleaded with heaven to send a good husband for Irina, a good father for Ilya and Kiril. He understood that their place in the great war was of a different order and that other souls would be brought into their lives to love and be loved. He would offer his death for this too.

Then came Jacob and Andrew. They were dying on the pagan altar of this world; they, more than any others, needed his sacrifice. And so he asked that whatever torment lay ahead would be joined to Christ's and that this would shift the balance of their lives.

Though the fear of what was coming returned to him a little, he looked upward to a presence and spoke with it and listened to the answering silence. He knew now that this silence was not absence or negation. It was the language transcending all language, and it crossed the void that man's will had made between himself and God.

Just before dawn it came to him that there was a single unresolved question that he had not yet faced. He saw his father, Angus Graham, standing at the crest of a hill playing the dirge of discouragement on his violin. The love and pity that Alex felt for him was subsumed for a moment in anger against him.

That Angus had been a good man, and even a great man, was not in question. But he had been marked by a compromise that was in the atmosphere of the age. He had compromised less than most, and he had to his credit that he had not lied to himself about his failures. Yet he had entered his office and locked it, shutting out his family, fearing weakness, hating it with a loathing so intense that he had mistaken his weakness for his very self. And in the end had hated himself.

The question of his father's death begged for resolution. Did Angus deliberately drive off the cliff above the Clementine that winter night so many years ago? Was it suicide? Was it half suicide—the subconscious suicide of self-neglect and indifference to safety? Was he drunk? The conspiracy of silence surrounding his memory—maintained by his wife, his cronies, his many admirers—had always prevented the question from being raised, let alone answered.

Now in the light of dawn, Alex saw his father as a boy. The magistrate, the judge, the aging scion of the Graham legacy, had once been a child as sensitive to metaphysical impressions as Alex had been. With all the passion of youth, he had desired to make a beautiful world, to add his portion of music to it, and when he had learned how difficult it would be, he had turned toward more obvious battles. He had charged into the field of justice, and when he learned that this was even more complex, he had persisted in it with a fatalism softened by alcohol and irony.

There had been pride, of course, and ignorance, but Angus Graham had been a man of faith, a public figure known for his courageous convictions. He had tried, like many a good man, to maintain the path of justice, but he had relied on his status, his money, and his ability to influence others. In the ensuing struggle, he had entered a private chamber where he could grieve without leaving any evidence that he was a man as small as any other.

"O my father", Alex cried into the dark. "We have all fallen. All of us, none excepted. I forgive you for what was left unsaid and undone. Pray with me now before the throne of mercy. Together, let us plead for your grandsons, that Jacob and Andrew might come through this dark age."

Alex now saw that his relationship with his father was the taproot of his own character and temperament. He understood that this root must be watered with grace if it was ever to grow up out of the dark soil and spread its branches and bear good fruit. There seemed little time left for such a resurrection, perhaps hours, days at the most. And the time remaining would be dominated by the effort to resist utter dehumanization.

When the sky over Beijing began to fill with yellow haze and birds filled the garden, Alex got out of bed and stood by the window. The world had never seemed as lovely as it was now. Blocked by walls, stained by industrial waste, the wakening city roaring all about, it was still beautiful. The sky always remained, as did the currents of air that brought the lexicon of many lives, cooking smells and motor smells, perfumes and the many other aromas of both earth and man.

To exist was the great miracle. Life was now to be taken away from him. For the moment, he had no great fear, though he supposed he would soon be afflicted by the worst kind of terror.

"O God, I thank you for my life", he said. "I thank you for what has been. Soon I will be unable to thank you with my thoughts or my lips. But now I do, so that these words may stand in my stead when the suffering begins. I thank you for all of it. And I offer it to you."

Cherries hit the net, the birds completed their trajectories, the breeze sighed, and the fish in the pool began to leap on the surface of the water.

42. *Integrated into a Mission*

He slept for an hour or so, until he was awakened by two guards. In the hallway, two more joined them and walked him down the corridor to a staircase. On the ground floor, they passed into the back wing of the building, then through an exit into an enclosed courtyard, where a car sat idling in front of an iron gate.

He was pushed into the rear seat; guards got in with him and squeezed close on both sides. They wore khaki uniforms, military caps with red stars, and side arms on black belts. In the front sat the driver and a man in civilian clothing who seemed to be in charge. He gave a signal with his finger, and the gate was opened. Driving out into a narrow street, they turned right. To his left, where the sun was rising, Alex saw a lake and beyond it the ornate compound of the Forbidden City.

No one spoke. Within half an hour the car entered the gates of a modern, non-descript building somewhere in another section of the city. It was, Alex supposed, a center where more advanced forms of interrogation took place. Three stories high, its ground floor was windowless. The windows on the upper floors were barred.

Cui and at least a dozen police and military of various kinds were waiting for him inside the entrance foyer. Cui made an angry gesture at two guards, who took Alex by the arms and escorted him to an elevator. Cui, Alex, and the others went up to the top floor. From there they proceeded into a conference room that was bare of furniture, save for metal chairs and a long desk of plastic material. The single decoration on the wall was a framed photograph, larger than life-size, of the current premier of China.

Alex was put into a seat facing Cui and his associates. Cui's hard-eyed interpreter was seated behind and to the right of her boss. Whenever Cui spoke, it came through her lips.

"This is your final chance, Bell", Cui said.

"I know nothing", Alex replied.

"If you refuse to answer as a civilized man, you force us to send you to other people who will obtain what we need to know. They have never failed. They know their work. The choice is yours."

"I know nothing."

"That is all you wish to say?"

"That is all I have to say."

"Then you bring torment upon your own head."

Cui stood, and the others all followed suit. The meeting had taken no more than five minutes. Cui made a combined gesture of contempt and dismissal. Two guards gripped Alex by the arms and drew him to his feet.

"You are making a mistake, Mr. Cui. I forgive you for it. I offer my suffering for your conversion."

"My conversion?" Cui sneered. "You are an insane person. If you survive what is coming to you, you will spend the rest of your life in an asylum." He went to the door, then paused. "Tell us what you know, and we will take you to your embassy."

"I know nothing."

Cui walked out, followed by the others. Alex's guards took him to the ground floor, then hurried him outside and down the front steps. The day was already warm, the sky clear, the sound of Beijing traffic deafening. He was certain now that this was his last view of the world. Only when he had reached the sidewalk did he see the long sedan car with tinted windows parked in the crescent driveway. Its front doors opened, and two Caucasians stepped out. One of them was dressed in military uniform, the other in civilian clothes. They stood by the vehicle, observing.

The Chinese walked Alex across the driveway and gave him a little shove toward the Westerners. Then they turned and went back into the building.

The civilian came forward and shook Alex's hand.

"Are you all right?"

"Who are you?" Alex mumbled.

"Please step into the car, sir, and we'll take you home."

"Home?"

"Yes, home. It's over."

Alex got into the backseat and sat beside a civilian who had remained inside the car. The military man got in and sat on Alex's right. Lying on the floor at his feet was a rifle. The man on Alex's left removed his sunglasses and gave him an appraising look. Then he turned and faced the front, saying, "Let's go."

The driver looked at him. "Straight to the fort, Av?"

"Yup. Quick time. Precious cargo. The natives are restless."

"What is happening here?" Alex asked, trembling. "I thought..."

The man with the sunglasses put them on again and said:

"We'll talk about it later. Right now you need to relax. Looks like you could do with a juicy red steak and a drink."

"But who are you?"

"I didn't say."

Stunned, totally perplexed, Alex stared at the little stars-and-stripes flag on the hood of the vehicle. As they turned east onto a wide avenue that ran between the Forbidden City and a large square, the military man said, "Think they'll ever get the bloodstains scrubbed off?"

"Sure. Bleach does it", said the driver. "Wish I'd been there."

"Bastards!" said the soldier.

"It's the bloodstains in the mind that'll never scrub out", said the man named Av. Turning to Alex, he said, "How about you, buddy? Did they rough you up?"

"Who?"

"The Chinese."

"No."

"You've been gone a long time. Spend all that time in China?"

"I can't remember. I know nothing."

"He knows nothing", Av said. Pushing the electric window button, he rolled down the glass and slung his elbow out.

"Warm day today."

"Warm for September", said the driver. "Close the window, wouldya, boss? The smog's killin' me."

"Okay. Put on the air conditioning."

Av closed the window, and the driver turned on the air conditioning.

"Is it September?" Alex asked.

His fellow passengers shot him a quick look.

"Yeah, it's September eighth", said Av.

"You said I'm going home?"

"That's right. You're flying out as soon as we can arrange it."

"But how did you know I was here?"

"Word gets around."

"Hey, Av, looks like we got vermin", said the driver.

"How many?"

"Four in a ricksha."

"That's no ricksha; that baby's a PSB eight cylinder", said the other civilian.

"Ah, pay 'em no mind", said Av. "They're just scouts. Want to see us safely to the fort. They wouldn't want us to lose Mr. Graham here."

"Thoughtful of them."

"Real thoughtful. Take us slowly around Ritan Park. Show them we haven't a worry in the world. I want Al to see the birdies and the flowers. The Temple of the Sun's so pretty this time of morning."

"Should we go by Dongdaqiao Lu?"

"Uh-huh, take the scenic route all the way."

The car turned several corners, passing children playing sidewalk games, then driving by tree-filled parks and stately homes. Finally it passed through gates guarded by soldiers carrying rifles. Their caps were white, their uniforms dark blue. The gates clanged shut behind them, and the car drove up a cobbled driveway between ornamental plum trees and beds of peony flowers.

"Welcome to Fort Apache", said Av. "Time to get out, Al. Time for a rest stop."

Alex got out and stood in the driveway. Confused, he merely turned this way and that, looking at the trees and flowers. The four Americans stood aside and watched him with amused or pitying expressions.

Inside the building he was led across thick carpets, past smiling secretaries, and into an elevator. Getting out on the third floor, they walked down a waxed hallway to a conference room that looked to Alex disturbingly like the one he had left less than an hour before. It was bare except for a desk that ran the length of the room and was surrounded by padded office chairs. The only decoration was a framed photograph of the current president of the United States. In a corner of the room stood an American flag.

"I don't understand", said Alex, shaking his head, as everyone settled into chairs.

"Oh, it's not all that complicated", Av replied. "They decided to give you to us as a goodwill gesture."

"Why didn't they give me to the Canadian embassy?"

"Not exactly airtight, that embassy of yours. Also, the People's Republic of China believes you're a Yank. Seems whatever you told them wasn't exactly convincing. We thought it would be better, all things considered, for you to have a little chat with us first."

"Why?"

"We'd like to ask you a few questions. Plus, it's more likely you'll get home this way. We play hardball with the Chinese. Your people play Mah-Jongg and always lose."

"There's not much to tell you. There's been a series of accidents. I don't know anything."

"The Russians and the Chinese think otherwise. You nearly fell through the cracks, buddy."

"Why did they let me go?"

"One of their techno-spies in our territory made a slip. We caught him. They want him back. We wanted you back. It was a fair trade."

"But I'm not worth anything to you. Why are you helping me?"

"I guess you could say, Al, that if Russia and China think you're a big deal, then we think you're a big deal too. Make sense?"

"Yes, except for the fact that I'm not a big deal."

"Ah, c'mon, don't be so modest. The Chinese are very, very unhappy about losing you, but they gave in because they want their own man back even more. We think—"

Av was interrupted by a cell phone vibrating in his breast pocket. Putting it to his ear, he listened and talked into it for a minute, then put it back into his pocket.

"He'll be delayed", Av said to the others. "Says we should go ahead and have breakfast and make Mr. Graham comfortable. Would you like some breakfast, Al?"

Alex now realized that he was very hungry. He longed for a dish of bean curd with black sauce, or a bowl of kasha.

"Yes, please."

"Breakfast for the man", said Av, glancing at his colleagues. One of them went out of the room.

Who is this strange person? Alex thought to himself. *Why does he smile in this way and speak with such a tone? His eyes are cynical, yet he believes in something, but he despises human beings, it seems. I know him from somewhere. But who is he?*

Presently the American who had left the room returned with a tray.

"That was fast, Eddie", said Av.

"Nuked it."

Alex ate the scrambled eggs, white toast with jam, and the patty of sausage meat in record time. His body had grown unaccustomed to Western food, and his stomach began to ache. A man in shirt sleeves, with a gun strapped to a shoulder holster, entered the room carrying a tray with six styrofoam cups of coffee. He offered one to Alex.

Alex had not had coffee in over a year, not since those final cups in the Siberian prison. He gulped it and burned his mouth.

Residual memory surged up, and Aglaya the Crow was suddenly standing in front of him wagging her finger. "Don't gulp; you'll burn yourself!"

Alex laughed. The Americans observed him curiously.

"And stop that laughing", the Crow added. "People will think you're silly in the head."

Alex began to laugh uncontrollably, bending double, fighting the pain in his gut and the hilarity spilling out of his mouth.

"Mr. Graham is feeling a little disoriented", Av said dryly. "Get him a towel, someone. He's making a mess. His Excellency will not be pleased if we spoil the carpet."

Eventually Alex calmed down, as did his stomach. He laughed to himself from time to time while they waited for the person who was overdue to arrive. He realized that this was inappropriate behavior but could not stop it.

"Something funny?" Av asked.

"Everything", Alex said.

"You must have had a fun time", Av said, smiling sardonically. "The Chinese can be so comical."

"It was the Russians", Alex said. Then for no reason whatever, he saw Konstantin's shattered head and the laughter died within him.

"Where did you go after the attack?" Av asked, his face sliding into something subtle and probing.

"The attack?"

"Yeah, the one near Novosibirsk."

A strange quiet filled the room.

"What attack?"

"On the train. Just this side of Barabinsk we lost you. By that bridge the kooks burned down."

"How do you know about that?"

"I was there."

"You were there?"

"Yes, Al, I was there. You know, you really have a bad habit of repeating things."

"I'm sorry."

"You're sorry?"

"Yes, I'm sorry. I do talk too much."

The Americans laughed.

"Why don't I explain a few things, Al, and save us a lot of useless chatter?"

Alex glanced at him curiously.

"You, Al, are a prize. You are what we call in the trade a windfall. The timing was excellent, just too good to miss. Here we are in Finland getting ready for a trip into Russia—a little fact-finding mission, let's call it—and, lo and behold, a certain Mr. Graham starts showing up at the Russian embassy in Helsinki. Now, it so happens that Mr. Graham is just the right sort of fellow to draw attention to himself—not intentionally, mind you, because he's really a quiet sort of guy. But Russians keep their eyes peeled for quiet sorts of guys, you see. Add to the package the fact that he's hot on the heels of some pretty powerful figures in Europolitics, for reasons known only to himself. The son thing cinched it."

"The son thing?"

"The missing son. It looked like classic cover story to us. Played by a pretty damn good actor, I might say."

"But it was true!"

"We know that now. But it seems you were on to some big people. And the big people—some in Russia, some in Germany, some in England, and some in our own little corner of the world—were not terribly enthusiastic about you complicating their lives."

"I still don't understand."

"It was a traffic jam, Al. A traffic jam full of dented fenders and head bangs. And quiet Mr. Graham, the lowly bookseller from rural hometown up-north, just wanders into the middle of it like Dorothy in Oz. That's when we—how shall I express this?—that's when we integrated you into our mission."

"That's crazy", Alex said. "I don't believe you."

"Ah, maybe you're right. Maybe I'm just making all this up. But let me finish my story. Anyway, in Helsinki, we smelled virus hunters from the other side, and they smelled us. But this *fact*—this certain Russian fact we'd been trying to find— was too important to leave alone. We couldn't just pack our bags and go home. We were pretty sure you were working for someone else, maybe China, maybe Iran, so we dropped a few hints here and there, just enough for the sniffers to think you'd slipped up a little on your cover story. And they took the bait. The whole pack of beagles just swerved off our trail and started chasing you. It was simple."

"Simple?"

Anger began to simmer in Alex. What had they done? What gave them the right to integrate him into their mission?

His anger grew as he saw that Av was a man very much like Arbat. Like Cui too. Yes, the same look in the eyes, the cynical contempt disguised—even from its perpetrator—by the righteous cause, the patriotism, the political idealism.

"Now, the bonus," Av continued, "the gravy on the mashed potatoes, was the unexpected trip to Siberia, because that's exactly where we needed to go. So we thought, why not take it farther? Why not just quietly swim along in your wake? With all eyes on you, we would be in the best possible position. Maybe we could go very far, all the way to Irkutsk."

"Why Irkutsk?" asked Alex, his anger still masked.

"The fact we needed to know was near Irkutsk. But the attack by the ecology arsons blew things out of the water. We lost you. For this and other reasons, the whole mission was scuttled; we packed our bags and went home. But here you are, dropped into our laps after an absence of—what is it?—eighteen months. So I guess, Al, you can understand why we wanted to have a little chat with you."

"I don't have anything to tell you."

"Not even a teensy-weensy little fact or two?"

"I can tell you about some fences with lights. That's all."

"Ah, so you did make it to Irkutsk."

"Yes, I did."

"And what did you find behind the fences?"

"I never got inside them; at least I don't think I did. Maybe the prison was there, but all I saw was a cell. I could be wrong about that; the prison could have been anywhere. You know more about it than I do."

"We know about the fences and lights. And the little white helicopter. From a rather high vantage point only. And all those reindeer. It can make a guy dizzy counting reindeer. And the mine, of course. Did you see a mine?"

"No."

"That's too bad, because we really do have our hopes set on you. As far as we can tell, you're our only eyes on the ground."

"Isn't your agent in Irkutsk eyes enough?"

"How do you know about him, Al?" Av said evenly.

"When the Russians interrogated me, they mentioned him."

Now Av and every other American in the room sat up straighter and turned cool eyes upon Alex.

"Our friend in Irkutsk has disappeared. Any idea where he went?"

"They said he'd been arrested; he was in the Lubyanka prison in Moscow. That's all I know."

"You know quite a lot. Anything else you'd care to share with us?"

"I met an American in prison. Was that your man from Irkutsk?"

"No, our man in Irkutsk is Russian. Tell me about the American."

"His name was Lesley. Carl Lesley. He let on that he worked for your intelligence agency."

Av glanced at one of the others and said, "Get on the line; check it out with Ops."

They waited for ten minutes. The Americans got up and stretched, lit cigarettes, refilled their coffee cups. There were now eight in the room, all in shirt sleeves, two with shoulder holsters. Alex stood and walked to the window. Outside was a small, parklike enclosure, in which three children were playing baseball—a pitcher, a batter, and a catcher.

An agent returned to the room and said, "Nobody by the name of Lesley is working for us. Used to be a Carl Lesley with encryption in Managua, but he retired years ago."

"How old?" Av asked, blowing smoke sideways out of his mouth, keeping his eyes on Alex.

"Seventy-three. Lives in Bloomington, Illinois, raises purebred Airedales. Hasn't left the country since he left the Company."

"How old was your Mr. Lesley, Al?"

"About my age."

"Then they pulled a name out of a hat. Your Mr. Lesley was a Russian."

"I thought he might be", Alex said. "His American accent was perfect, but he kept using old slang expressions."

"Like what?"

"Like 'The jig is up.'"

"Ooh, those clever Russians! Poor Ivan's seen too many gangbuster movies."

At that point the door opened, and in walked a distinguished man in a pinstripe suit. The Americans in the room rose to their feet, and some put on their suit jackets.

"Sir, this is Alex Graham", said Av. "Al, this is Ambassador Evans."

"Glad to meet you, Mr. Graham. You're a Canadian, I hear. I haven't been briefed yet on what exactly you're doing in China or why we have an interest in you, but I leave that to these boys. However, I do want to assure you that we can take you to your own embassy whenever you wish or have them pick you up."

"Actually, sir, I need to talk with you about that", Av said. "There are complications. Can we speak privately?"

"Of course, of course. Let's step outside in the hall."

Five minutes later the ambassador and Av returned.

"I'm new on the job here in Beijing, Mr. Graham", said Evans. "Arrived three weeks ago. So I still have a lot of blanks to fill in. But I want to reassure you that you're free to go. Our staff can drive you over to the Canadian embassy whenever you like. However, in the interests of security for both my country and yours, I would urge you to give us a little of your time."

"There are problems in your embassy, Al", Av cut in. "Some fairly serious. We had to bargain very hard to get you out of the tiger cage, and we're not really sure your own people wouldn't let you just slip back into it. The Mah-Jongg policy, you know."

"Mah-Jongg?" said the ambassador with a puzzled expression.

"Yes, sir, Mah-Jongg. That's another subject we need to discuss."

"Mah-Jongg."

"May I suggest that we get Mr. Graham a diplomatic passport so we can fly him out of here as soon as possible? He's carrying rather a lot of sensitive information in his head."

"Of course. Do anything and everything that's needed." He thrust out his hand, and Alex shook it.

"Nice to have met you", said the ambassador. "Safe trip home, now." Turning to Av, he said, "Take good care of this man, Bell."

"Bell?" Alex said to Av when the ambassador had departed. "Is your name Bell? Averell James Bell?"

"How would you know that?" Av said in a low voice, staring at Alex with a poker face.

The other agents gathered around.

"Born in Kansas City, Missouri?" Alex asked. "Recruited by Langley in 1981?"

These details surfaced in his mind with uncanny clarity, but how he knew them he could not at first recall. Then he remembered Arbat.

"Uh-oh", breathed Bell, staring at him. "Does this mean what I think it means?"

"It seems the Russians knew about you."

Bell said nothing as he absorbed this.

"They thought I was you", Alex went on in a pained voice. "So did the Chinese. Why don't the Chinese know that you're...you're you?"

Bell considered a few moments before answering. "They know me by a different name. I'm a visitor, you see. Sort of a commercial traveler."

"Oh."

"Did you hear any other names when you were in Russia?"

"I think they gave me false names, though I don't know why they did, because they planned from the beginning never to let me go."

"Because you saw the reindeer park?"

"Because I might have seen something inside the fences. I didn't, but they couldn't risk believing me."

"Tell me any names you heard—intelligence and security people's names."

"Arbat was one. He was the first interrogator."

"Arbat. They were playing with you. The Arbat is the most famous shopping district in Moscow."

"That would explain it. He called me a shoplifter."

"Describe him to me."

When Alex had done so, Bell shook his head. "Any other names?"

"Someone named Tver from Saint Petersburg who was tracking drug dealers. He tried to connect me with a criminal named Serov."

"Tver we know. Serov we know too. Tver is a patriot. Serov is pure scum. Anyone else?"

"Just a name. Kochetov. Somebody I never met, but he was important enough to make even the Russians nervous."

"He's big enough and nasty enough to scare *us*, Al, even at the remove of thousands of miles."

"They were sending me to him."

"Where was he?"

"In Vladivostok. He was interrogating some people they'd caught reporting to the West about Russian shipping."

"And they told you Kochetov was doing the interrogations?"

"I overheard it."

A dark look entered Bell's eyes.

"Does that mean anything to you?" Alex asked.

"Unfortunately, it tells us a lot." Turning to another agent, he said, "Bob, get on the blower. The Nor Pac naval inflow has been unstable for over a year. It needs a complete analysis for counter-intel."

"Friends of yours, boss?"

"People I knew. Send your-eyes-only: 'Urgent. Kochetov in Vladivistok during downtime Pacific Fleet movements. Maximum caution current data. Suspect counter-intel.'"

The agent left the room.

Turning back to Alex, Bell said, "Well, this is more complicated than I thought it would be. Looks like we need to send you to some people who see the big picture."

"Where?"

"If you're willing to help us, Hawaii. If not, I guess you can always learn to play Mah-Jongg."

Alex said nothing, just continued to gaze at Bell with an impassive face.

Bell sat down on a chair facing Alex, put his elbows on his knees, and looked Alex square in the face.

"We're your friends, Al. You're on our team."

"Am I?"

"Yeah, you are. Like it or not, you are."

Seeing that this elicited no response, Bell said in beautifully enunciated Russian, "You've been through a lot. Try to understand what's happening here. What you've told us is going to save lives."

"Whose lives?"

"Americans, Russians, maybe even some Chinese."

"It was bad news, wasn't it? You've lost some people."

"Yes. But it helps considerably with damage control. You have no idea how important these bits of information are. Spending a little more time with us will delay you getting home, but we need to ask you more questions. Are you willing?"

"I'll do what I can."

Bell exhaled, nodded abruptly, and checked his wristwatch.

"Your Russian is excellent", Alex said. "The Russian Institute at Columbia? And linguistics at Princeton?"

Bell raised his eyebrows. "For a bookworm, you're a surprising man." He paused, considering, and Alex observed his face shift subtly away from the tough professional veneer he had maintained until now. With a twitch of a smile that seemed to be human, even personal, he said: "You know that copy of *Dead Souls*, signed by Gogol, the one you have for sale in the Russian section of your bookstore? When you get home, could you set it aside for me? I'd like to buy it."

"How did you know about that?" asked Alex.

"I spoke with a lady who was dusting books in your store. Told her I was your cousin."

"An Italian woman?"

"That's right. She was worried sick over you. Shed some tears."

"She believed you?"

"Of course."

"What were you doing there?"

"Looking for you. You'd been missing a while, you realize."

"Were you that concerned about me?"

"We thought your cover story needed checking out—who you were really working for."

"I wasn't working for anyone."

"Yes, well, we know that now. But at the time we thought you might be willing to trade some useful information."

"Trade? You mean if you caught me at espionage you could have blackmailed me into working for you? Or sent me to prison if I didn't tell you what you wanted?"

"That's rather harsh, Al. I'm trying to be candid here. I'm in the information business after all. And you may have noticed that we just got you *out* of prison."

"Thank you", Alex murmured. He stared at the backs of his scarred hands for a few moments, then looked up. "I would have set the Gogol aside for you, but I'm afraid the bookshop's gone now. My home too. In fact, everything."

"That's too bad", Bell murmured in a distracted way. As if he had suddenly lost interest in Alex, he stared at the floor, thinking about bigger tragedies.

His anger now coming to a boil, Alex said to him in a cold tone: "You shouldn't treat people like objects. We're not pawns."

Bell shot him a neutral glance, stood abruptly, and left the room.

Alex spent the remainder of the morning showering and shaving in a visitor's suite in the embassy. Staff provided a light summer suit, a white shirt and tie, and brown loafers. It had been more than a year since he had worn socks, and they felt too tight. At one point, he glanced into the bathroom mirror and was startled to see Bell looking back at him. The illusion passed swiftly. Throughout his life he had wasted little time looking at his own reflection, and thus Bell's face was, to a certain extent, more real than his own. He and Bell were about the same age, and they had the same body weight, height, and coloring. Bell, of course, lacked a jagged scar at the back of his skull.

Late in the afternoon another set of Americans put Alex into a sleek embassy car, along with a driver and two agents with gun holsters visible beneath their open suit jackets. They passed through the gates, followed by a silver jeep with two more agents and two marines. Taking the main thoroughfares south to the international airport, they encountered no problems on the way, though it was obvious that Chinese security vehicles were close behind.

At Nanyuan Airport, bureaucratic and police regulations caused them to pass through a certain amount of heavy crowding, but this was far less than the procedure demanded of ordinary travelers. At one point, as they walked toward the security gate, a young woman stepped out of the crowd and faced Alex. Two agents leaped forward and grabbed her arms, but Alex told them to let her go.

It was Pin.

"In the deep waters," she said, "you will find the true word."

For a moment they held each other's eyes.

"Tell the flock in the West about us", she said. "Carry us to them. We carry you in our hearts—all the way to Paradise Mountain."

She put out her hand to him, and he shook it.

"All the way to the mountain", he said.

She nodded and disappeared into the crowd.

"Girlfriend?" asked one of the agents.

"My sister", Alex whispered.

Opening his hand, he saw that a small blue stone was lying in it. He put it into his pocket.

The airline was an American Boeing 757, and the embassy had paid for four seats in first class. Alex sat in the window seat at the front, facing the bulkhead, protected by the agent beside him and two behind. As the aircraft leveled off over the green folds of China and banked toward the sea, he closed his eyes. He kept Pin's face before the eyes of his heart, and when he was able to bear it, he took the stone from his pocket and opened his palm.

It was cobalt blue, shot with tiny particles of red. It was a carving of a bird. The bird was unmistakably a kingfisher.

Night fell. Alex stayed awake throughout the journey, holding the stone in his hand, thinking about a growing number of unanswered questions, the political, the spiritual, and the personal: How had Pin learned that he had been set free? Had John-Xia told her? How had she known when he was leaving for America? Why had she risked a meeting that could compromise her and John? Had she counted on the crowds, the anonymity? Yes, it must have been that, because she had worn peasant clothing; she looked no different from dozens of other girls in the great hall at the airport.

And how had she known so much about him—about the leap from the bridge, about his love of water, about the image of the kingfisher? How had she known that Lin Jing was a priest? How had Lin Jing known she could be trusted? It was as mysterious as a Chinese puzzle, all this knowing.

The sun rose sooner than seemed possible, and not long after, the jet landed at Honolulu International Airport. The agents told Alex that he would not leave the plane until all other passengers were in the terminal. Then they took him through a special security gate and, on the other side, handed him over to some official-looking civilians who had "intelligence" stamped all over them. Military people were also in attendance, including some in naval uniforms.

His new custodians exited the terminal through a back door and hustled Alex into a waiting military car. From there they sped west on a highway and within minutes passed through a gate into a vast guarded compound. One of the people in the car explained to Alex that he was now a guest of Hickam Air Force Base.

He was provided with a suite in a building that looked like a hotel. The windows did not open, however, and the room-service staff were young men in military uniforms. His hosts asked if he wanted to rest for a while. He did. They told him that a meeting with several officials was scheduled for one o'clock in the afternoon. They left him, and he sat down on the bed.

For the first time in many weeks, he felt completely alone. He was no longer anxious in any way, and indeed, when he thought about Pin, a quiet joy filled him. Even so, as he gazed out the window at jets taking off and landing, he felt the strangeness of the environment. He was still exhausted from his ordeals, from the long flight, and from more than a year of poor diet. Thoughts surfaced and sank, emotions also, and he began to lose parts of his memory. The sense of dissociation was not distressing, only odd. He searched for his name and after a moment or two remembered it. With a similar effort he retrieved the names of his sons. He had circled the globe, or at least the circle was soon to be completed, and he had not found Andrew. Then his hands began to shake uncontrollably, and every muscle in his body tensed.

Feeling his heart palpitating and his breath ventilating too quickly, he got up and opened the door. In the hallway two men sat on chairs on either side of the door. They had side arms strapped to their waists. They looked up at him and nodded.

"Can we help you, sir?" one asked.

"Why are you guarding this room?" Alex stammered.

"For your protection, sir."

"Do I really need that on a military base?"

"It's just a safety measure. All kinds of people come in and out of the base—food delivery, mail, couriers, et cetera. The commanding officer ordered it as a precaution."

"Oh."

"Need something to eat or drink? We'll call down for it."

"No thank you. Is there a doctor I could speak with?"

"Right downstairs, sir. Want me to call him?"

"Yes, please."

Alex went back into the room, lay down, and tried to calm his breathing. A few minutes later a naval officer entered carrying a medical bag and stood beside him. He was about sixty-five years old, dressed immaculately in a dark blue uniform, silver hair combed neatly, tanned face and hands, a thoughtful look in his eyes. He introduced himself, but Alex immediately forgot his name.

"Not feeling well?" the doctor asked with a note of sympathy. "No, I guess not. You've been through a lot, I hear."

He sat down on the edge of the bed and removed a stethoscope and other instruments from the bag. After taking Alex's blood pressure readings and listening to his lungs and heartbeat, he said:

"You've got a few palpitations there. Also, your pulse is racing. You're in reaction, and that's not abnormal. It's probably long overdue. Can I give you some medication that will help you relax?"

"No thank you. I don't believe in that sort of thing."

"All right, if you think you don't need it."

"I don't need it", Alex said with rather too much intensity.

"When was the last time you had a good sleep?"

"I had a nap on the plane. Before that, not much."

"For how long?"

"Weeks, maybe months."

"You're worn out, Mr. Graham. I'd like to do some blood tests, if you don't mind. I can take a sample here."

"All right", Alex said indifferently.

The doctor took a sample and said, "I'll talk to the officers who want to meet with you after lunch. You need to rest. They can see you later in the day."

After the doctor left, Alex took the stone bird from his pocket and looked at it for a while. It seemed to calm him. He tried to pray, but his thoughts were still unstable. He couldn't remember some of the words of the Our Father. So he just kept looking at the bird and drifted off to sleep, waking several hours later to find that the sun was setting. His heartbeat had slowed, and he could no longer feel palpitations. His nerves were steadier as well and his thoughts clearer.

Not long after, the doctor returned and sat down on a chair across from the bed.

"Good news and bad", he said with a smile. "Which do you want first?"

"The bad news."

"You're anemic, with severe vitamin deficiencies. Also, your blood sugar level is lower than it should be. When you get home, go see your doctor, have some proper blood work done, a full battery of tests. That's a day-long job, and we don't have time for it right now. In the interim, I'd like to give you booster shots of iron and B complex. Pump the proteins into you as well. What do you say?"

"Do what you think is best. Is there any more bad news?"

"Let me check your vital signs first."

After doing so, the doctor folded his stethoscope and pressure gear and put it away.

"You have some peculiar readings, Mr. Graham, but basically you're a healthy specimen, healthier than many a man your age. The palpitations are gone now, and everything else is steady as she goes. Ever suffer from heart problems before?"

"Physical or metaphysical?"

"The former."

"I had rheumatic fever when I was a boy."

"Spent some time in bed, did you?"

"Two years."

"That means it was touch-and-go for a while. It looks like you pulled through with flying colors, but you've just had quite a year of stress. So when you get home, you'll have to build up your system again. Walking and swimming are the best."

"I like both."

"Good. Begin as soon as you can. But don't push yourself. Also, you'll need to eat a very healthy diet to heal the damage done by nutritional deficiencies. Are you married?"

"I'm a widower."

"No one to cook for you?"

"Not really."

"Well, sir, may I suggest that you either hire a housekeeper or find yourself a bride, unless you're the sort of guy who's savvy enough to feed himself on a regular basis."

"Uh, Doctor, you said there was good news and bad news. What's the good news?"

"The good news is, I've put the entire security of the United States of America at risk by convincing the fellows from Washington to postpone their meeting with you till tomorrow morning. Tonight you should just take it easy and relax, if you can."

The doctor put a pill case on the bedside table. "These are tranquilizers. Very mild dose, just enough to ease your system down so the sleep mechanism takes over and you drift off naturally. One or two should do it."

After the doctor left, Alex threw the pills into a wastebasket.

In the bathroom, he filled the tub with water as hot as he could stand it, turned on the jet sprays, and sank into it with a sigh. He emerged limp and relaxed, toweled himself off, and returned to the bedroom to find a set of new pajamas folded on the end of the bed, a toothbrush, a tube of toothpaste, and copies of yesterday's *New York Times* and Toronto's *National Post*. On a cart beside the armchair was a full-scale luxury meal. He looked at it somewhat disapprovingly, then sat down in the chair, towel around his waist, and ate steadily for half an hour. Alex felt guilty at first, but he told himself that he would soon return to his home a very poor man. For that matter, he no longer had a home. He might as well eat while he could. He wished for a bowl of bean curd and another of kasha but had to make do with Black Forest cake. It was too rich—so rich that he gagged and spat it out.

43. Does Simply No One Believe Me?

"Wakey-wakey, sir. Breakfast's ready."

Standing by the bed was a young soldier.

Alex struggled into the sitting position, scratched his head, and glanced with interest at the cart parked by the armchair.

"Bacon and eggs, coffee, toast, fresh papaya, orange juice", said the boy, listing off the items proudly.

"What time is it?"

"It's oh eight hundred hours, sir. Your meeting is at oh nine hundred sharp."

Alex ate every morsel of food on the tray. He drank the coffee and felt it zinging in his system, waking him still further. Then he had a hot shower, a shave, and a tooth scrub, and finally he dressed himself in the clothes that someone had hung in the closet—tan slacks and matching socks, underwear with the tags still on them, a white polo shirt, and a light summer blazer. He hoped he would be allowed to keep them when he went home. That would make two sets of new clothes.

At ten minutes to nine the doctor knocked and entered the room. He chatted with Alex as he checked his vital signs; then he injected him with vitamins. Two guards arrived and led Alex along the hallway to an elevator and took him up to the top floor. There he was received by some of the military personnel whom he had met the day before and was conducted into a conference room with floor-to-ceiling glass along one wall, offering a view of the ocean. A dozen comfortable armchairs were arranged in a semicircle. One of the civilians directed Alex to a solitary chair facing the others.

They took their seats, and one of them, someone with a lot of gold braid on his arm, asked Alex to describe his entire journey through Russia and China. And so he did, point by point, leaving out the most personal experiences. They were, of course, very interested in what he had seen of the installation near Irkutsk. There was some disappointment when he told them that he had not seen anything really, just fences, flashing red lights, and surveillance cameras.

"Tell us about the cameras", said one of the civilians.

They asked so many questions that he soon lost track of what he had told them. The civilians in the group took special interest in getting him to repeat things, then asked questions that covered the same subject matter from different angles. The military people were interested in objective facts, the civilians in the verification of facts. After three hours of this, Alex began to wonder if some in the group did not believe his account. They questioned him like trial lawyers. A pattern was emerging in the examination, and the pattern clearly indicated that they wanted to trip him up, make him contradict himself. Once or twice he said things poorly, forgetting certain details, and the civilians pounced. Under their cross-examination he tried to correct the bad impression he had made, but their cool, analytical eyes grew steadily colder. He was mentally depleted, and the effort to collect his thoughts became increasingly difficult. Finally someone said, "Mr. Graham is not in the best of health. I suggest we break for lunch."

In the afternoon he described what he could recall about the Russian interrogations. When he mentioned the torture, he felt no emotion. His listeners grew solemn, expressing neither sympathy nor outrage. Later, when the day's examination was over, he was taken back to his room and left alone with the awakened memory. His hands resumed trembling, though it was not as severe as the day before. The doctor came in again after supper and sat down in the armchair while Alex stretched out on the bed.

"You've hit the press", he said, placing fresh copies of the *National Post* and the *New York Times* onto the end of the bed.

"Oh?" Alex replied with little interest.

"The story was deliberately leaked in a form that will give you some protection."

"Some protection?"

"Two nations want your memory erased, Mr. Graham. Or your absence from the planet."

"Do you really think a newspaper article can stop them?"

"It's the best we can do for the time being. Ever consider a change of occupation?"

"What do you mean?"

"New identity, new home, new life?"

"I prefer my old life."

"Were you aware that there were Canadians in the group upstairs?"

"No. Who were they?"

"Two guys from the Canadian Security Intelligence Service. They're your sharpest critics, by the way."

"Of course, they would be."

"Feeling depressed?"

"Not really, Doctor."

"Just sad?"

"That's right."

"You're an idealist, aren't you, Alex—may I call you Alex?"

"If you wish. It's a cultural norm in America, isn't it?"

"Who told you that bit of guff?"

"A Russian."

The doctor chuckled.

"But you can call me Alex. I'm sorry; I forgot your name."

"I'm Bill."

"Bill, can you tell me why things are so crazy?"

Bill gave the question some thought before answering.

"It's human nature, I'd say. It's always been that way and always will be until the final curtain."

"You're sure about that?"

"Reasonably sure. No faith in humanity, Alex?"

"Not much."

"How about God? You have any faith in him?"

"Yes, I do. How about you, Bill? You have any faith in him?"

"Indeed I do."

Alex paused to take this in. The doctor was observing Alex as profoundly as he was being observed.

"You know," Bill said at last, "one of my favorite lines in Scripture is where David slays Goliath. Just a small shepherd boy picking up stones. Five little stones against an unstoppable army and a ferocious giant."

"What's the line?"

"The line is, and my point is, 'The battle belongs to God.'"

"What do you think it means?"

"It means we're not going to win by our own strength or resources. Not with bombs, not with propaganda, not with sterilizing half the population of the world or any other strategy. The battle will be won in a way that we can't begin to guess."

"That's an unusual thought in the mouth of a warrior."

"Is it? Certain kinds of warriors, I suppose."

He frowned, stood up, and walked to the window, where he remained for some moments staring at whatever was out there. Turning back to Alex, he said:

"I'm rethinking a lot of things these days."

"Are you?" Alex replied, not knowing what the doctor meant.

"Read history, Alex. Study it carefully, and you'll see that the impossible battles have all been won by men who understood the principle. And not just in the Bible. It's as real as this morning's news. Tyrants come and go, empires rise and fall, but it's the Davids who make the difference."

"So you really think we can do without bombs and propaganda?"

"Yup. And collateral damage—people turned into statistics from hell."

"Pawns?"

"One could call them that."

"What are you saying?" asked Alex, trying to relate the man's words to his uniform.

"It's a moral dilemma, and we're stuck with it for the time being. But there's something wrong—wrong in a big way—on all sides."

"You mean we're all prisoners of circumstance."

"Yes, we are."

"But we don't have to be prisoners—not that kind of prisoner."

Bill nodded pensively, then seemed to shake himself free of an unwelcome, or unproductive, thought. He said:

"Whatever's under the mountain outside Irkutsk may, or may not, spell doom for East or West. But one thing is certain, Alex—the battle belongs to God."

"How do you know about the mountain near Irkutsk? I thought you were just a doctor."

"Well yes, I am just a doctor. I also happen to be a rear admiral in the U.S. Navy, assigned to the Office of Naval Intelligence. Perhaps I should have told you earlier."

"That's all right."

"I try to keep my hands clean, and I do what I can to keep the system clean."

"You have your work cut out for you. There are a lot of evil people in the world."

"You've noticed that, have you?"

Now Lin Jing's words echoed in the room: *Man here, man there, man all places want to be safe.*

"Here, there, everywhere", Alex whispered.

A wave of exhaustion suddenly hit him, and he was no longer sure what he and the doctor were talking about. He rubbed his face and looked out the window.

"Feeling okay?" Bill asked.

"I'm just tired."

"I can go if you need to rest."

"You can stay. It's just that I can't quite...I forget..."

His attention wandered. He saw Konstantin in his mind's eye.

"Alyosha", Alex murmured.

"Pardon me?"

"Nothing. It was nothing."

For several minutes they sat without saying any more. Bill watched him all the while.

When Alex could focus again, he said, "Bill, do you have children?"

"Seven. And twenty-four grandchildren, twenty-five next month."

"Do you make toy boats for them?"

"Actually, yes. And toy planes. Dollhouses are also a big item in our clan. That's what people were made for, don't you think?"

"Yes, I do."

"How about you? Do you make toy boats?"

"When I was a boy, I did."

"Make any for your children?"

"No, I didn't. I was too busy."

"Ah, the melancholic regret of the middle-age father is in your eyes. I know the feeling well. I too failed there. But you know, you should see how my sons light up when I make something for their children. Better still, when I make it *with* the grandkids. My sons can't keep their hands off it. Have to barge in, interfere with the grandfather dynamic, grab my hammers and take over my workbench. But what can an old fellow do against that kind of thing?"

"You're saying there's a fresh start, even if a father has made a mess of things?"

"Absolutely. It heals the past. The world begins all over again, every time. As long as you don't get sucked in by the theorists. Life wins, every time."

"Every time? What about the heap of victims in our times?"

Bill dropped his eyes.

"You haven't answered my question."

"Old demons replaced by new demons, Alex. Old enemies by new enemies. There'll always be an enemy, won't there?"

"You still haven't answered my question."

"There's only one answer to your question. No human answer can ever be enough. The battle belongs to God."

Bill stood up and stretched. "In the interests of honesty, I should tell you I now have to go upstairs and have a little talk with a panel of experts who are, even as we speak, trying to decide whether or not you're a counterintelligence plant."

"Does simply no one believe me?" said Alex, shaking his head.

"Wanna know what I'm gonna tell those boys?"

"I don't need to know."

"I'm gonna tell 'em you're a dangerous man."

"A dangerous man?"

"That's right. You're a shepherd with a sling. Only you don't know it yet."

Alex looked up and met his eyes.

"One piece of advice", Bill added.

"Yes?"

Bill came over and shook Alex's hand. "Don't ever stop being a dangerous man."

After the doctor left, Alex opened the newspapers and came upon a small item inside the *Times* regarding a Canadian who had been missing in Russia for more than a year and was soon to be repatriated through the good offices of the U.S. State Department. The *National Post* had an article on the front page. The *Post*'s facts were scanty, but its coverage was more extensive. Both articles said that a tourist by the name of Alexander Graham of Halcyon, Ontario, had been beaten and robbed while traveling in Siberia and had subsequently suffered from related health problems and amnesia. Lacking proper documents, the victim had languished in a remote medical clinic for more than a year, his identity unknown or uncertain. Recently recovered, Mr. Graham would be returned to his native land within days. There was no mention of China.

It was too abstract, as if it had happened to someone else. So he threw the papers onto the floor and turned on the television set and tried to learn how to operate a remote control. This challenged his mind for a while and led him to a channel that offered films. There were three hundred titles to choose from, and he could select whatever he wanted to watch. He switched it off. He fell asleep holding Pin's kingfisher in his hand.

Bill was present during next morning's meeting, though he remained in the background, asked no questions, made no comments. Someone informed Alex that the debriefing was now complete and that if he wished, he could board the next flight for Canada. There was one leaving in the early evening. Alex said that was fine with him; he'd like to go home now.

No one had any objections.

As the intelligence people stood to take their leave, Alex asked if they had discovered anything more about the mountain near Irkutsk.

"I guess we can tell you, Mr. Graham", said one of the civilians. "We owe you that much. You're going to be signing some documents under the Official Secrets Act in a few minutes from now, and anything you hear in this room falls under the scope of the act. Failure to comply with the terms of the act means a long prison sentence. Is that understood?"

"Yes."

"Well, it seems that whatever is under that mountain has been dismantled posthaste by the Russians. I leave the rest to your imagination."

"So it's over?"

"Until the next time."

"Can I go home and live a normal life?"

"If the doctor says so."

Bill came forward and said, "There's no longer a reason for any nation to erase your memory, Alex. The site's gone, and only the Russians know what it really was. Hopefully the Chinese don't have a similar institution. As far as they're concerned, the problem's resolved. Resolved for us as well. Nobody's got an interest in you anymore—except your family and friends."

"My family and friends", Alex asked. "Do they know where I am?"

"We notified your son in Toronto about an hour ago. He'll be there at the airport to meet you."

This left Alex speechless. Bill took him by the arm and said, "So, what are you going to do for the rest of the day?"

"I'd like to see the ocean."

"Mind a little company? I know a beach where the tourists never go. I can drive you there and drop you, or hang on as your bodyguard. Take your pick."

"I wouldn't mind the company."

"Great. Meet you in your room in twenty minutes."

They walked back and forth along a stretch of white sand in a cove surrounded by palm trees.

"What was it?" Alex asked. "What did they have under the mountain?"

"I can't say for certain", Bill replied after a bit of a pause. "But here's an official secret to keep under your hat. Until now, satellite intel showed only a mine inside a game preserve. The Russians knew all about our satellite schedules and made sure their technical shipments and activities occurred during our blind spots. They'd staged plenty of mining equipment as props, moved machines around like toys in a sandbox, all for the benefit of the eye in the sky. My guess is that it was a major scientific research establishment dealing with very bad stuff. Since we retrieved you, trucks have been coming out of the mineshafts twenty and thirty a day, scattering throughout the country, mostly to science cities. Seems there was an underground explosion of some magnitude this morning. The Russians blew it up themselves. There were invited Chinese observers there."

Alex stared out at the sea.

"See something?" Bill asked.

"It's more like hearing."

"Care to share it with me?"

"I don't like to bore people."

"I won't be bored."

"I hear singing in the waves, a language that crosses the abyss. I thought at first that it was my mind singing. Then I felt a prisoner close to me, and in his heart the sea of mercy sang."

"Do you know who the prisoner was?"

"Yes. Not a prisoner like us. He's different. He's locked in a cell, but he's a free man in his soul."

"Does he have a name?"

"He has a name. The indestructible name. Sometimes I feel him close. When he's near, I remember what I could have been and might yet become. Do you hear his song? Do you also hear the singing of children who will never be?"

"One of my granddaughters—age four—tells me that the world is a seashell and God has it pressed to his ear. He's listening to the waves. We're the waves, she said, the singing waves. Almost what you said."

"Do you hear the singing, Bill?"

"No, but I believe in the singing."

"Do you think I'm having delusions?"

"No."

Alex listened to the sea a while longer. Bill stood beside him, watching the surf.

"When I was a boy, I used to throw myself into it", he said. "I liked the way it tossed me around. I liked the way I survived."

"When I was a boy," Alex said, "I had a place by a river. It was just an ordinary rock where I sat for hours watching the water pass by."

"Maybe you were listening to the singing."

"I didn't hear anything."

"Maybe the music was soundless."

Alex suddenly realized how strange their conversation was, and yet not strange at all.

"You're an odd sort of sailor, Bill."

"You're kind of an odd guy yourself, Alex."

He told the doctor that his mind seemed to be acting like a radio that kept losing its frequency. He kept forgetting things and finding them again. Sometimes he had problems making sentences. Nouns and verbs disappeared and reappeared. Pictures floated to the surface and sank again. Music swelled and faded in his ears. Was he, maybe, just a little bit crazy?

Bill told him that he didn't think so. The head problems were probably due to low blood sugar, which could fog the mind of healthy people. That, combined with what he had been through, made for a potent mix. He reminded Alex to get some proper tests done as soon as possible. Alex said he would.

Bill let that hang in the air for a while as they continued to watch the surf.

"You were tortured, weren't you?" he said at last.

Alex nodded.

"Having nightmares?"

"Once in a while."

"Torture leaves its marks on the mind. You might want to talk it over with someone when you get home."

"I have a friend. A priest."

"Oh, good."

"And the Muchenik."

"The Muchenik?"

"*Muchenik* in Russian means the tormented one. He was tortured too."

"The prisoner you mentioned—the indestructible name?"

"That's right."

"I'm glad you've got that as a symbol, Alex. It'll help. But torture strikes deeply into the self. It depersonalizes. It might take years for you to recover completely."

"Maybe. But I don't think so. You see, he's more than a symbol. He was with me there in the prison. By the edge, at the drain hole. I put my fingers into the wound in his side. He put his hand into my wounds. And he's still with me."

Bill looked long and soberly at Alex, then returned to watching the sea.

Eventually he asked if Alex had any good memories from his journey. Alex began to tell him a few things, starting in Oxford and Helsinki. Then, crossing the frontiers of memory, he spoke about the important things, the people he had loved and the times when he had felt God very close. Bill listened without interruption.

When Alex could tell no more, Bill asked if there was any good fishing up where he lived. Alex said there was.

Bill said he might like to wet a line next summer. Could he check out the northern rivers? Bring a son or two along? Maybe some grandkids? Alex thought that was a fine idea. They promised to keep in contact. Bill wrote out his home address, and Alex, because his home was now gone, did not know what to give him in return. In the end, he jotted down, "Alex Graham, General Delivery, Post Office, Halcyon, Ontario". Then his mind, like a child's, drifted on a muse, and without speaking any of it, he added the sequential list: Canada, North America, western hemisphere, planet Earth, the solar system, the Milky Way galaxy, our galaxy cluster, the supercluster, the universe, existence.

After supper, Bill and two civilians drove him to the international airport. The civilians, close-mouthed individuals, boarded the Air Canada flight to Toronto and sat beside him in the first-class section. The two civilians were from the Canadian Security Intelligence Service. But Alex didn't mind. They were somebody's sons.

He slept through most of the flight. Whenever he woke a little, he saw many beloved faces: Aglaya shaking her finger at him, saying, "Now we're making progress!" Children ringing a snowhouse, teaching him to sing from the *glubina dushy*. Alyosha's weeping face, *nyet, nyet, nyet*, his eyes fixed on Alex as he pulled him out of the drain hole of the universe. The prostitute standing beside him on the bridge over the Moskva River, making a covert sign of the cross on her breast. Sergius and Serafim, Kolya the Water Skimmer, Pin and John and Lin Jing. Irina's eyes as she tried to tell him that you cannot give your heart away only to take it back again, that you cannot play at love, because love is the source of life. Irina kissing his cheek, lighting fires, burning down the kremlins of the soul. Ilya punching him in the face, apologizing, hating, loving. Kiril bouncing as he won his chess games, flinging his father's boat onto the rock by the shores of Baikal, and pulling a miraculous draft of fishes from the waters of the Sacred Sea. Crying his *exultet* on the height of the Bell Tower, kolokol, kolokol!

I greet! I greet!
I greet you, life!
I bless! I bless!
I bless you, life, for you have blessed me beyond all imagining!

Kisses and poems, blows to the skull and blows to the heart. It was all life, all immersed in the ocean of mercy. The old world was dying, the new world being born. The winter-born were gazing at the green buds pushing through the snow, trying to believe in spring. Leaping stags. Girls on galloping horses. The river of gold pouring through the holy gateways. The Mother of the burning tree and the face of the suffering Christ in the icon that had been pulled from the fire.

44. One May Circle the World

As the jet descended into the approach to Toronto's international airport, Alex recalled the words he had spoken on the train to Paradise Mountain:

"I see that the world is a splendid sphere. A man might walk around it."

"A very long journey that would be", Mr. Zhang had replied.

When the aircraft landed and came to a halt, the agents made Alex wait until all other passengers had deplaned before taking him into the terminal. They were met by another federal agent, and from there he was led through the usual barriers without stopping. Pointing to the exit door, they said he was on his own now, and then they left in another direction. Alex walked slowly through the last passage into the main reception area, wondering what he would find on the other side.

Cameras flashed, video cameras from the networks winked red lights at him, and a rabble of interviewers pressed forward, jostling for his attention, shouting questions, their microphones stabbing at his mouth. Then someone in a Roman collar elbowed his way into the herd, pushed away a few media men, and grabbed Alex by the arm. It was Father Toby. Without a word of greeting, the priest dragged him through a throng of applauding, grinning, crying, exclaiming people.

"Alex! Hi, Alex! Welcome home, Alex! Alex, Alex!"

It happened too fast for him to recognize many faces—they all seemed to know him, but he had to struggle to remember who they were. Easiest to recognize was Darla Conniker bouncing up and down, and Maria and Bruno Sabbatino looking grim. Then came two adult Russian faces with a little girl—the family of Oleg, the poet-miner-exile from Vyborg. It was impossible to reach him, but Oleg shot Alex a smile as the crowd surged past, bearing him onward.

Stunned by the noise and commotion, unable to speak, he was spilled out through the revolving exit onto the sidewalk, where a young couple stood waiting for him beside an idling car. The doors were open. The young man was familiar, but what was his name? It was—he thought it was—yes, it was his elder son Jacob.

Jacob threw his arms around him and held on. "Dad, Dad!" he said quietly.

It was so unreal, so surreal, that it was happening to someone else. But Jacob would not let him go, locked him so tightly in the embrace that he was unable to free himself. Then he did not want to free himself, and he hugged his son with a ferocity that shocked them both.

Still, he could not speak.

When it was over, Jacob led him to a pregnant young woman who was smiling shyly at him.

"Dad, this is my wife."

She stepped forward and kissed Alex on the cheek.

"Hello, Mr. Graham—Dad—I'm Meg."

"And your grandchild", Jacob said, grinning, blinking back tears. He put his arm around his wife. They both wore wedding rings.

"When?" Alex stammered.

"Three more weeks to go. If it's a boy, we're calling him Alexander."

"I mean..."

"Oh, the wedding." Jacob looked embarrassed. "We were married a year ago, Dad. Father Toby said..."

His daughter-in-law stepped forward and took his hands in both of hers. "You see, we didn't know if…"

"If I would come back?"

"Yes", she said, and burst into tears.

"I'm so glad", said Alex. "I'm so glad you married. Yes, it's the only way. Making new life—you mustn't regret it—life overturning death-in-life and the kind of death that would make death-in-death—"

They stared at him dumbly.

"Well, Alex, it's time to go home", Father Toby said cheerily, taking his arm and conducting him to the car.

Jacob bent down, talking through the open window.

"We're driving up to Halcyon on Friday, Dad. You're in good hands now. I have a case before the Court of Appeal tomorrow morning—a real cliff-hanger, but we'll see you about seven o'clock Friday evening. Then we'll have days and days to talk about what happened."

Alex said he understood. He was about to ask the most painful question of all. Had anyone heard from Andrew? Was he alive? But at that moment, more reporters and well-wishers rushed in, and in the confusion there was time only to wave good-bye.

Father Toby maintained a judicious silence as he maneuvered through evening traffic toward the highway that would take them home. Alex laid his head back on the seat and closed his eyes.

Too many details and faces, too fast. Andrew, Andrew, Andrew. The absence of Andrew. Time flowing. Rivers coursing, fragments swirling, the lake burning, the mountains slowly crumbling under the force of millennia, and the atmospheric pressure of angels warring above: the Warrior of the Spirit with his holy sword, and the Millennium Angel with his foul dart.

The news must be very bad, Alex thought. *That's why he isn't telling me. He wants to tell me when I get home.*

Home? He did not have a home.

"Where will I be staying?" he asked.

"You can stay with me if you like, Alex. As long as you want. We have lots of space at the rectory."

"Will the monsignor mind?"

"The monsignor is gone. He retired last year and is busy with his mission in Florida. He enjoys amazing success on the golf links, I hear. There have been conversions." Father Toby smiled. "I'm the pastor now."

"It will be good to be with him."

"Who?" Father Toby asked with a puzzled look.

"The Lord. I haven't been able to be with him, at least not in the Blessed Sacrament, not for a long time. I feel starved. But he came to me when I was in the poustinia on the Little-Little Ob, the night of the wolf and the stag. Iisus! The other time was when the gardener brought Jesus to me by the fish pool, under the cherry tree. Ye-su! I wish I could tell you what it was like to be that hungry, then to feel the sweet fire feed you. Then to be hungry again. Do you know what I mean?"

Father Toby did not answer.

"Am I making any sense?"

"It's okay, Alex."

"Wait, I'm forgetting about Communion in Moscow, once in Helsinki too. But it was too long a time; there was too much hunger in between."

"I'm sure you prayed."

"Yes, I prayed. Jesus came to me in his Spirit and in the words of Scripture, the parts I could remember. But it's the flesh and blood, you see; it's the love—it's the good fire."

"You don't have to talk, Alex. I think I understand."

"If you ever have doubts about your life, Toby, don't believe it."

Father Toby glanced sideways at him. "Okay, I promise."

Alex continued to ramble, and the priest listened intently as his friend described a prisoner in a cell without light, lying naked on an ice-floor, how he had put his fingers into the living wound in the stranger's side. And then how the stranger had put his own hand into Alex's wounds, though the wounds were all inside, all inside the *serdtse* and the *glubina dushy*.

"What are those?" Father Toby asked, his face worried.

Alex told him. It wasn't just a dream, he said; it was a man. Like Alyosha in the tomb of degradation and the nameless girl from Smolensk. He told him about his brother priests, Sergius and Serafim, Porfiry and Lin Jing, and what they had shown him. About the ruined hands of Aglaya's mother, about people who reach into fire to pull icons from it. About Pin and the underground Christians—maybe there were more true Christians in the darkness of the East than in all of brightly lit North America. When he could tell no more, he began to weep, a low, dull weeping that was not inconsolable but contained both grief and peace. Sensing this, Father Toby extended his arm, put his hand on Alex's shoulder, and kept it there, praying silently all the while.

Later, Alex wiped his face and opened his eyes.

"I'm sorry. I'm not quite myself. This sort of thing comes and goes."

"You'll be glad to see the Kingfisher again, won't you?" Father Toby said gently.

"The Kingfisher? You mean the bookshop? No, we don't need to go there."

"We can see it tomorrow. I'll take you."

"Thank you, but it's not necessary."

"I suppose you'll want to get it up and running at some point."

Alex looked at him. "But it's gone."

"Gone?"

"I mean the bank took it."

"No, it's still yours. Didn't anyone tell you?"

"They haven't told me much since I left China."

"China? The papers said you were in Russia."

"It was both. But it got all messed up. They were only interested in what I saw over there. Military things mostly. As for me—well, I thought everything I had was gone."

Father Toby shook his head. "So you haven't heard."

"Heard what?"

"Last year a secretary at the credit union got wind that Charles was going to foreclose on your property because of the loan default. The gears were grinding away in his back office without anyone knowing about it. It was going to be a done deal, you see. No one had heard from you for months, and it looked like you wouldn't be coming back."

"They thought I was dead."

"Well, not everyone thought so, but people were making all kinds of wild guesses."

"But didn't you get my phone messages?"

"Messages? No, nothing. The last time I heard from you was when you called me from Moscow."

"My letters from Siberia?"

Toby shook his head and then continued:

"Anyway, one day this secretary called me and a few other people, made us promise not to mention her name. She said ownership would be transferred in a week if we didn't do something about it. Word got around town that Charles was hell-bent on doing it. He had every legal right because the loan was in default. People were upset, though most of us felt pretty helpless. The law is the law, after all. Then Mr. Phillips got up in arms."

"Who is Mr. Phillips?"

"Don't you remember? Ed Phillips. Theresa Colley's father. People think he's crazy, and maybe he is, but he just wouldn't stand for it. Said we were all moping around with our fingers in our mouths, doing nothing while the kingfisher nest was handed over to cuckoos and starlings. Night and day he went door to door, begging money to pay off the loan. It was nickels and dimes at first, then the spirit of the thing caught hold, and it became fivers and tens—then hundreds started flowing in. Ed wrote a letter to the editor of the *Halcyon Leader*, and it got published. It wasn't very coherent—full of poetry and jeremiads—but it spread the news even farther. Then he rented the town hall and called a public meeting. Of course, I went. I thought maybe a dozen people would show up. Do you know how many showed up?"

"How many?"

"Over two hundred. It was a three-ring circus, Alex, the craziest meeting that ever took place in these old hills, but at the end of it people got out their checkbooks. And a lot of folks stood up to announce that if the foreclosure went through, they were withdrawing all their money from Charles and company. Ed opened an account at the Maplewoods Credit Union under the name Save the Kingfisher Fund. Within a week he got some fancy lawyer to obtain a court order delaying the foreclosure. Jacob helped with that. I'm not sure how they pulled it off—it was some technicality. Well, to make a long story short, your home and business are still there. It's in your name, the debt's paid off, and there's a little sum we've been using to pay the taxes and the furnace oil. There's only a couple of hundred dollars left, so you need to think about opening the shop soon."

Alex said nothing. It was so much to take in at once.

As the sky turned dark purple and stars appeared, the car turned north onto Highway 11.

"But Andrew", Alex said in a pained voice. "Toby, what has become of *him*? I've followed and followed. Always behind. Always too late."

Father Toby sat up straighter.

"Where is he?" Alex groaned. "Where is he?"

"What! You really don't know?"

"No matter how hard it is, you've got to tell me."

"Maybe I'll let him tell you himself."

"Who?"

"Your son, Alex. He's safe."

"Is he home?" cried Alex.

"He's in England. He's going to phone you tonight."

Beyond comprehension, Alex sank back down in the seat and stared out the window.

Father Toby drove up Oak Avenue, slowing to a crawl as they passed the bookshop. There were no lights in the windows, but under the glow of the porch lamp, Alex could see that the bushes had been trimmed and the grass neatly clipped. On the front door was a cardboard sign: "Welcome Home, Alex". Balloons were tied to the doorknob and gateposts.

Father Toby wheeled into the parking lot of Saint Mary's, braked abruptly, and turned off the ignition.

"Here we are, here we are", he said, leading Alex into the rectory kitchen. He offered to make a supper, but Alex said he wasn't hungry. He wanted to see the church. Would it be all right if he went in alone?

Father Toby replied that of course it would be all right.

Alex entered the nave and knelt down in the center aisle. It seemed strange, being there. It was old, yet there was nothing in need of repair. No menace battered at the walls.

He wanted to pray, but at first he was incapable of it. Nothing came. No flood of emotion, no upsurge of memory or nostalgia. He waited in the stillness as if he were an empty room. When he prostrated himself before the Eucharist, he felt his smallness as never before. Not the smallness he had felt when he was naked in prison, or his helplessness when he had traveled from one frustration to another across Europe and Asia. Nor was it like his disorientation when he was released from prison. This was the deepest abandonment of all, for here at last he was in the place where he had known his only fullness. And now he saw that what he had once been, in this place, was now gone.

Slowly, the words formed in the depths of his soul:

"I drowned and you held me.

I rose and you held me.

I was broken and you held me.

I was lost and you found me.

I died and you brought me to birth.

I was a stranger and an exile and you carried me home.

I am at home in the hands that formed me.

I am home."

Then the river of worship came, pouring slowly from the fountains of God into his small vessel and fountaining up again to its source.

"I love you", he said to the Presence in the language that is beyond all speaking.

I love you, came the reply.

"I love you."

Three times it was spoken, and three times the reply was given.

Father Toby entered the church an hour later and found Alex lying asleep on the floor of the center aisle. He woke him and told him that someone had just telephoned for him. The caller would ring again in a few minutes.

In the rectory parlor he settled Alex into an armchair and brought him the phone.

"I'll leave you alone now. See you later."

Alex waited. His mind was empty as he listened to the silence. His glance settled on a model sailing schooner on the mantle over the fireplace. It was the boat he had given to Toby when they were boys.

When the phone rang, Alex lifted the receiver with trepidation.

"Hello", he said.

"Dad?"

He knew the voice, knew, knew it.

"Dad, are you there?" the voice said anxiously. "It's me. It's Andrew."

Andrew.

How strange it felt to speak the word. Or had he only thought it?

"Dad, are you there?"

"Andrew?" Alex whispered.

At first there was nothing more to say, because there was everything to say, and neither knew where to begin.

"You're home", his son said.

"Yes, I'm home."

"Are you okay?"

"Andrew", he said again. How very odd to speak that name—to Andrew himself. After all this time—almost two years.

Then the terrible silence became still more terrible.

"Oh, God, I'm sorry!" cried the voice on the other end of the line. "I'm so sorry, Pa!"

Alex heard him sob for a little; then he said something that he did not know he believed until the moment it came from his mouth.

"You mustn't regret it, my son. You mustn't."

"How can you say that after what I've done to you, after I sent you through hell!"

"It wasn't hell."

"I ruined your life!"

"You didn't ruin my life, Andrew. You *are* my life."

Once again silence loomed between them. As the voice on the other end of the line continued to sob, Alex felt his mind whirl. He put the receiver to his forehead, closed his eyes tightly, and tried to cross the sea. But it was no good; the wire was too thin.

"Andrew?" he said at last.

"Yes, Pa?"

"This is too hard. It's too hard on the telephone."

"How can we ever talk normally again?"

Steadying his thoughts, Alex slowly replied, "There's so much to tell you. So many wonderful things. When will we see each other?"

"I'm coming home on Friday. I need to see you're really safe. I need to talk with you. I—"

"I'll be waiting."

A few more clumsy exchanges brought their conversation to an end. Alex sat for a time, dizzy with fatigue. He remained there staring at the carpet until Father Toby came into the room and shook his shoulder.

"How was it, Alex?"

"He's coming home."

"I know. Jacob and Meg are picking him up at the airport and bringing him straight here."

"Oh, good", Alex said abstractly.

"That'll give you a couple of days to rest."

They fell into silence again until Alex stood up and said he wanted to go home. Father Toby drove him to the King-fisher, parked by the curb, and gave him the keys to the house.

"Home sweet home, Alex. Let's go in."

"Thank you, Father, but I'd like to go in by myself."

"By yourself?"

"Yes."

"You're sure you're okay?"

"Yes, I'm fine."

Father Toby looked uncertain.

"Don't worry. I just need to rest. I'll see you tomorrow."

After Father Toby drove away, Alex waded through the balloons to the front door and let himself into the dark building. Without turning on the lights, he stood in the hallway, inhaling the smell of old books and varnish as a flood of memories rushed out to greet him. The grandfather clock quietly ticked and tocked. He supposed that someone had wound it in preparation for his arrival. It all felt so odd, as if the house had a life of its own that had continued uneventfully during his absence.

He made his way up to the second floor in the dark, holding onto the banister, feeling weak in the knees. At the top he fumbled along the hallway to his bedroom, pushed the creaking door wide open, and went in. He bent and turned on the bedside lamp.

It was a room both familiar and strange, the home of a man who had been himself, who had lived there before. A bookish and insular man. A man waiting to die. Now he was exposed, without insulation, and he no longer needed it.

He opened the window to let in fresh air. Removing his shoes and coat, he lay down on the bed and pulled a blanket over himself, then fell into a sleep so deep that it was unmediated by dreams.

On the morning after his return to the New World, Alex awoke to sunshine and a cool autumn breeze streaming through the billowing curtains. The feeling of strangeness, as if he were in a place belonging to someone else, was gradually replaced by the promptings of familiar objects and sounds, particularly the photo of Carol on the night table, and the grandfather clock ticking faintly below in the empty house. The stillness was comfortable, and this, added to the knowledge that his journey had not been in vain, convinced him that he was home.

Shortly after ten o'clock Father Toby phoned to see if Alex wanted him to come over; did he need help getting reoriented? Alex replied that he would love to have his company, but for today at least he wanted to be alone with the Kingfisher, and with his memories.

Throughout the morning he puttered around, upstairs and down, opening doors and cupboards, closing them again. In each room he stopped and looked, staring as a stranger might, waiting for the dormant portions of his mind to awake again. He walked through the aisles of shelves in the bookshop, dragging his fingers along the spines of the books, lightly touching them, as one would touch the arm or shoulder of an old friend with whom there is comfortable trust, with whom there is no need for words to retie bonds stretched by long separation.

After that, he sat down at his desk and noticed a cardboard box filled with letters. Beside it was a stuffed mailbag from the post office. Someone had taped notes to each. On the box was written "Personal and Business", and on the bag was written "Fan Mail".

Fan mail? he thought with a puzzled look.

In the box were several items demanding immediate response, but these were months old, hopelessly beyond recall.

There was also a letter from Russia, dated seven months earlier. It contained a handwritten note and a photograph of a pretty young woman and a homely young man in front of an Orthodox church. The man had his arm around the woman's shoulder. The woman had one arm about his waist, and the other rested lightly on the shoulder of a little girl who stood in front of them. Beside her a three- or four-year-old boy looked up into the sky with both arms raised, as if in greeting.

Smolensk, 2 February

Hello, Mr. Aleksandr Graham,

I think you might not remember me. Do you recall a day when we stood on the bridge over the Moskva and talked together? You gave me a gift from Saint Mary of Egypt. With the help of your money and her prayers, I have returned to Smolensk, where I have made a new life. I am now making dresses as a seamstress, and they have become popular with the local girls. The man in the picture is my husband. We were married three months ago. He is my first and only husband. And this, God willing, will be so until death parts us.

Saint Mary taught me about the mercy of the Most High. She too was an *interdevushka* who repented. I do not have her courage, but if I did, I would go out into the desert like her and live in a cave and make reparation. But I am a weak person. Also, I have my two children who need me, and this is God's will. I have told my husband about my mistake, about the time I went to Moscow, and he loves me nonetheless. We are praying that God will grant us a child. This is the kind of man he is. See his eyes, Mr. Graham, which are very gentle. He is strong also, a welder. In his spare time he makes toys from scraps of wood and metal. He gives them to the children of the neighborhood without payment. That I should find such a man is a miracle to me. Now we begin again, together. It is better not to make mistakes like I made, but God can bring good even from the badness. I do not know if this is true, but I think it is. I hope for it.

The photograph was taken on the day of my children's Baptism. My husband's name is Boris Osipovich. The children are Katerina and Nikolai. Katya is learning to sew and to play the flute. Kolya is a dreamer, and what he is to become none can say.

I am Lizaveta. I should have told you my name on the bridge, but I was ashamed.

I do not forget you, Mr. Graham. I pray for you each day. Are you a believer? I think, surely, you are. If you are, remember me before our Savior.

With cordial respect and best wishes,

Lizaveta Nikolaevna

Alex remained long with this letter, rereading it several times before placing it aside. Farther down in the pile he came upon another letter from Russia, this one postmarked Irkutsk, dated ten months before. It contained four pages neatly type-written in Cyrillic font.

Alik,

I am writing in the hope that your government has been able to extricate you from whatever trap you have fallen into. I try to envision you safely in your book-shop, selling Russian novels like exotic candy to terribly bright, terribly ignorant North American students. I try not to resent it. Most of all, I try to see you safe.

When you did not return from your hike into the mountains, I was desperate with worry. I called the *mil-itsiya*, but they knew nothing. Then the FSB came and questioned me. One of them, an officer, said you were an agent of the CIA operating under a false Canadian passport. He said your real name is Bell and that you are an American. I told them this was ridiculous, that I knew you very well and that you were an honest person. The other agent was a weasel, a dreadful man, the sort who is familiar to us from the KGB days. He said he had tracked you all the way from Saint Petersburg, where they have proof of your involvement with the narco-mafia. I told him they had made an absurd mistake, but he said there was no mistake, that they had a big criminal boss in custody who put the blame on you.

Really, I cannot believe this. It is too much like the things they used to do in the old days. But—please reassure me, Alik—is it a lie? Yes, I am certain it is a lie. I believe they were probing blindly, trying to discover who was involved with you and who was not, and for what reason. They came to see me several times, and then they gave up. I think they were finally convinced that our relationship was entirely personal. They smirked at me. Personal! That—and that alone—these *oprichniki* can understand.

Of course, it is true I fell in love with you. But I am not so naïve as to think this was anything more than feelings, the longing to find someone. Though you are lovable, that does not mean we have any right to love each other without realism. I think you also loved me. But love is a raw passion, like a rampant river that destroys if it is not contained within its shores. What sort of love do you think would have been possible between us? We are too different. Our eyes look at the same things and come up with opposing answers. You were lonely. I was lonely. That we managed to avoid capitulation was, I believe, the result of the brevity of our time together. Did you know me? Did I know you? Well, a little, perhaps. What am I to you? A person who gave you refuge at a stage on your long journey. And what are you to me? You will always be a man on a train, moving through the world as through an alien land. A man who sets fire to himself and trips over his own boots. A man who falls in love at a stroke—with pretty ballerinas and aging doctors. What is it, Aleksandr Graham, that you are really looking for? Is it your missing wife? Is it the vitality of youth? The sensations of love? Or is it, perhaps, love itself you seek?

Do not be offended by these questions, for I ask them of myself. Honesty—above all, honesty—is the necessary precondition for genuine love. For me it is too late for all that. I have my sons; I have my work. I have my memories. Were you to come here to be with me, you would not survive. "Measure seven times before you cut the cloth", we say. Although it is true that you and I are the basic material, both made of human cloth, our patterns are too dissimilar. Were I to go to your world, I would not survive. It is very hard to live in Russia, but it is harder to live anywhere else. Try to understand this.

In my thoughts, I speak to you often. I say to you, I am sorry we did not get to know you better. I am sorry you did not see our family at its best. And that you did not see me at my best. Will you be embarrassed if I tell you that late at night when the boys are asleep, I sit in the parlor and remember you? I remember our conversations. I try to change the things I said, for I regret some of it. Not much, you understand, just a little. I do not forget my strange visitor, the man who fell from the sky. We have conversations again, you and I. You explain your people to me. I explain Russians to you. Neither of us understand too well but are content.

Yevgeny's letters to his sons are a thousand times payment for the tea and medicine we gave to you. You gave a father back to his sons. If they do not yet understand what Yevgeny says to them, I think they are, nevertheless, now closer to him in the depths of their hearts. Kiril reads and rereads his letter. Ilya will not let me see his letter, though I have no doubt it is as beautiful as Kiril's.

I am in great anxiety over Ilya. He declares that he will join the army when he is old enough. Sonia has run off and married a foreign ecologist. Ilya has found no suitable obsession to replace her. He says that the only thing he wants from life is the opportunity to kill the Chinese, as many Chinese boys as he can, or Chechens, or Kosovars. The enemy changes day by day. Oh, what has caused this terrible thing in my elder son? Of course, it is because he is without direction. He is angry at life for taking his father away. He does not know who he is or what he is. If I believed in God, I would try to pray for him. But I do not have faith. Aglaya the Crow scolds me for this. If there is a God, it may be that he listens to her prayers and Ilya will be rescued. You told me that you too are a believer. Do you pray for my poor steppe wolf? Oh, do not cease to do so, please.

My only consolation is Kiril. This shining boy! This golden child who is ever a joy. A great change has come upon him. Kiril—yes, our Kiril—has become a serious young man. I will now tell you about the surprising event that has brought it about. A month after your disappearance, a visitor came to Ozero Baikal. He walked through the village one day carrying a sack on his back, and those who looked from their windows said later that he struck them at first as a beggar or a tramp. But his face was clean, his demeanor respectful. Kiril was walking home from school at that time and passed him in the lane. He stopped in his tracks, ran back to the stranger, and took his arm. The man ceased walking and looked at my son. They talked for a few minutes, and then Kiril led him in the direction of our house. I watched it all from the kitchen window.

I thought, "Oh no, not another beggar! Not another visitor!" (Forgive me, Alik.)

Kiril burst into the kitchen, dragging the poor man behind him.

"Mama, Mama, look what I have found! Can we keep him?"

The stranger bowed to me and said, "Peace to this home and to all who dwell here."

Really, the strangest peace did seem to surround the man and came into the room with him. Kiril was jumping up and down. As you know, this is a habit of his. However, the extent of his demonstration was so extraordinary, I was speechless.

"Don't you see the light all around him, Mama?" he cried.

I saw no light. I resolved to give the man a bowl of soup and send him on his way as quickly as possible.

"Why are you all covered with light?" Kiril demanded of the stranger.

"You see a light about me?" he said, smiling, and rather surprised himself. "I did not know the light could be seen with the eyes."

"I see it!" Kiril exclaimed, as if this were the most natural thing in the world.

"Who are you?" I asked.

"My name is Sergius", he said. "I am a priest."

A priest! Can you believe it? Well, as it turns out, he is a *Latin* priest. A Roman! He has lived in the village for many months now, and he believes that God has told him he must stay here for a time. He believes, moreover, that God has spoken through my Kiril. Sergius lives in the abandoned shack beside the fish shed. He works as a hired hand on Volodya's boat. Sometimes Ilya goes with them to Olkhon Island to net the omul catch. They talk together, though what they discuss, I do not know.

People have taken to the priest with surprising speed, for he does not seek to impose his religion on anyone. Aglaya Pavlovna says he is a saint, though she is not happy about his Romanism and prophesies that someone as holy as he cannot fail to see the light one day. "You will be Orthodox", she tells him with absolute conviction. He smiles at her and says little. He replies in metaphors such as the following: "The Body has two lungs and needs them both. There is but one heart beating within, and that is Jesus Christ!" Despite their differences, she is his greatest supporter. She has told everyone that he cured her cow of milk fever, and a friend in Peschanaya of an abscess. It's all in her imagination, of course. He rebukes her for spreading such tales, but who has ever been able to silence the Crow!

Has this letter reached you? Reply quickly and free me from my worry over your fate.

I am your friend,
Irina Filippovna

Alex placed the letter on the desk, pondering what it revealed. He would write to her soon. He would tell her how much she meant to him, and how much her children meant to him, and what they had taught him. He would try to explain that his journey had shattered forever his longing for a safe refuge from the radical insecurity of human existence. He would say that to love was to be exposed, to love was to bear his pain and incompleteness with dignity as he walked on the pilgrimage into eternity. To love was to bear in his heart the hearts of all the other broken ones whom God had placed there.

He would tell her also that he loved her, though no longer with the impulse of desire for mutual possession. It was true that their patterns were different and that neither of them would have been happy in the other's native land. They belonged to another country, the *terra incognita*, toward which they were journeying on different paths. They had not been given to each other for earthly consummation but for mercy and hope. They would meet in the place where Carol and Yevgeny had gone—there, where life exulted and danced and sang in the eternal wedding feast.

Around noon the ship's bell rang, and Alex opened the front door to find Father Toby grinning and waving a paper bag.

"Lunchtime, buddy. Hope you like salami sandwiches. Figured you didn't want to go down to the café on Main. There's mobs of well-wishers roaming the streets looking for you. I fended off the media too. But you won't be safe outdoors until things settle down."

"Come on in, Father. It's good to see you."

"Sleep okay?"

"I slept very well."

"Feel like your old self?"

Alex smiled but said nothing.

Upstairs in the kitchen he made a pot of tea while Father Toby set the table and unpacked the sandwiches. As they ate together, he looked at Alex uneasily and said, "I have some bad news for you. I hope you can take it."

Alex considered, then said, "You might as well tell me."

"There's a big bonanza party planned for next Sunday at the town hall. A welcome-home party. The mayor's giving you the keys to the city. And there's worse to come. Charles Findley has nominated you for citizen of the year. He's been politicking for it ever since the news broke about you coming home. Charles himself is going to award it to you the night of the party."

"That's very generous of him."

"Yeah, right."

"Any other news?"

"Uh, no, not that I can think of. What's the matter with you?"

"The matter with me?"

"You should be writhing in agony. This is the kind of thing you detest. All the attention would have killed you in the old days."

"I guess it would have. But it's my chance to thank people. I really want to thank them, Father. They saved my home and work, and a lot of them must have prayed for me too. Maybe their prayers saved my life."

"Boy, you have changed."

"You've changed too. You're looking—"

"Say it! I'm looking chubby? Pillsburyish? Michelinish?"

"That's not what I was thinking."

"Well, it's true."

"I was thinking that now you're the pastor, there's a happiness in you I never saw before."

"I *am* happy. I have my flock."

"There's a light all around you."

Father Toby regarded him dubiously. "A light?"

"It's there. I can see it."

Father Toby laughed. "Worm! Good old Worm!"

Realizing Alex's need for solitude, Father Toby left after lunch. Throughout the afternoon the doorbell and phone rang frequently, but Alex refrained from answering. He sat in the Russian room for a time, reading a little. He whispered his way through some Hopkins, savoring the feeling of familiarity as it slowly returned.

Later, he found the copy of Gogol and considered setting it aside for Av Bell. Then he realized he had no way of contacting the man. He added the book to a little stack of volumes he would send to the Pimonenko family.

Just before suppertime someone rapped steadily on the front door and would not desist. When the raps changed to loud bangs, Alex heaved a sigh and got up to see who it was. Opening the door, he found Maria and Bruno Sabbatino. Hat in hand, Bruno stepped back a pace and looked embarrassed.

Maria, carrying a glass dish covered with foil, burst into tears. She rushed forward, crying something in Italian. Bruno rescued the dish, and Maria wrapped her arms around Alex. He kissed the top of her head.

When they had all more or less regained their composure, Maria scowled and gestured with her right hand, by which Alex understood she was very happy that he had returned.

"Father Toby say it's okay we bringa you the supper, Alex", she declared in a tone of offended pride. "But he say we no come in. No *bother* you, justa droppa lasagna and *go away*! What he know anyway?" She thumped her chest. "What he know about the heart, eh?"

"He knows a lot, Maria. But he doesn't know everything. You and Bruno prayed for me, didn't you?"

"All a time, Alex", Bruno mumbled, wringing his hat. "This woman drive me nearly crazy with the praying. She do it for you. Me too, I pray."

Alex took their hands in his. "Thank you", he said. "Thank you."

"Okay, okay, enough!" Maria commanded, pulling her hands back, simultaneously wiping a tear from one of her eyes and making the sign of the cross. "Enougha dis. You home. You no die."

"No *matto-pazzo*", Alex suggested.

"Whata you talk about, *matto-pazzo*? You no crazy!"

"I am, Maria. I am a little bit crazy, but not as much as I used to be."

"No make a joke about dat, Alex. Not funny, not funny."

"But it is funny, Maria", he laughed. "It's very funny."

Her husband took her by the arm. "Maria, we go now, let Alex have a supper in peace. Alex, you come our place soon, have a *cicchetto di vino*?"

"Yes, I would like to very much, Bruno. As soon as possible."

After they had gone, Alex took the lasagna upstairs to the kitchen and ate half of it. Fatigue hit him again as he was washing the dishes. He took the phone off the hook and went to bed early.

Thursday morning dawned bright and blue. The second deep sleep helped restore his sense of well-being, and his mental abilities were recuperating as well, but he kept the phone disconnected and did not answer the door.

Slowly, slowly, the shape of the past continued to sharpen, confusion dissipating like mist burning off under summer sun. He prayed often—continuously, it seemed—wordless prayer from the *glubina dushy*, turning his attention to the presence of the Muchenik. He remembered everything that had happened and wondered at much of it.

There was a Mass at Saint Mary's in the evening. The bell in the steeple was an old friend, and Alex could not resist its call.

"Kolokol, kolokol", he answered.

He was now feeling more able to meet townsfolk and fellow parishioners and thought that any further delay would make it only more difficult. Father Toby met him at the entrance and told him that an autumn fair was under way over in Maplewoods and that the church was practically deserted. A few elderly parishioners smiled and nodded at Alex, though they did not approach. He sat up close to the front, as close as he could get to the Presence. At Communion, he rested with the Muchenik in the tabernacle of the heart. Time melted, and he was once again in the cabin on the Little-Little Ob and by the pool in Beijing. Father Toby blended into Father Sergius and Father Lin Jing, and all three became Christ—Christ in them and them in Christ, and Christ within himself. It was all light. It was all good.

45. *Will He Want Me?*

His third sleep was as deep as the previous two, and he awoke refreshed. He said his morning prayers, then showered, ate a hearty breakfast, and lingered over a pot of tea. His thoughts were often unfocused, but they cleared whenever he needed them to. After washing the dishes, he went down to the ground floor with the intention of reading more personal mail and assessing what was needed for reopening the bookstore. But his mind soon wandered again, and he went into the Russian room, where he sat down in the easy chair under the portrait of Soloviev.

There he spent most of the day waiting for Andrew's arrival, which Father Toby had said would be around seven o'clock that evening. He watched the sunlight move across the hardwood floors, strike the samovar, then illuminate this or that title on the shelves. Unable to concentrate on any task, he wandered and puttered aimlessly but always ended back in the armchair. At last he focused himself by pondering a question he had not yet had time or energy to consider: the huge question of God's role in the recent events of his life.

The presence of God was undeniable. The intentions of God were another matter altogether, specifically the mystery of what he had been doing in this one small life, this Alexander Graham. He wondered if God had foreseen everything about the journey, then corrected himself as he remembered that God was indeed omniscient.

That did not mean, however, that he had made it happen. The freedom of human will had been involved—a great many human wills. How, then, had God acted in the affair? Obviously, he had supplied the graces necessary for meeting the trials and temptations. He had answered prayers, moved people to help Alex, taught him much in the refiner's fire of experience.

Step by step, Alex retraced the journey, pondering everything that had happened. When he came to Helsinki, he paused over the memory of a dream he had had the night after he had seen Valkyries in the sauna. In a garden of herbs there was a flowering cherry tree, a pool of water, birds crossing the field of his vision as streaks of vermilion and magenta, their songs the chords of zithers and dulcimers. There a small woman helped him to open his hand and placed into it a carved piece of blue stone. That was Pin.

Now he understood that he had been given an extraordinary gift—not so much the carving but the message it conveyed. He was not alone. His small life was seen by heaven, his labor and identity were within the plans of divine providence, and every good effort, no matter how obscure, had its effect in the world. Nothing was wasted.

Only one detail was unfulfilled. At the end of the dream, following the gift the small woman had placed into his hand, there had come a second woman whose face remained hidden from him. She had taken his hand and did not let it go.

Here is the heart that is on your path. You are free to choose or not choose. But understand that not choosing is a choice.

What this meant he could not say. He supposed that in a sense it had been fulfilled on the shores of Lake Baikal, the night Irina held his hand beside the snowhouse. Then he recalled that she had let it go, and in her letter she had reaffirmed this letting go, telling him what he already knew, that they had drawn close to each other from the sheer hunger for human warmth, and that despite their feelings at the time, the attraction did not have, and could not attain, the depth of love they had known with their spouses. He did not fully understand why this should be so, but he knew it was true.

He felt some regret that it had come to this, for he cared greatly for the Pimonenko family. Yet he reminded himself that friendship was still possible, and he resolved to do whatever he could to help them during the coming years. He saw that God had answered the prayer he had made in Beijing the night before he was to enter into torment, when he had offered his coming sufferings for her, when he had finally let go of her. He had asked that a good husband be sent to her and a good father to her sons. Father Sergius' appearance in Ozero Baikal was, he felt sure, a generous response from heaven, for the priest would be a spiritual father to the boys. As for a husband, perhaps such a man was already on Irina's path.

As the afternoon wore on and the room darkened, Alex turned his thoughts to the coming reunion with Andrew. At certain moments he felt close to tears. Once, when fingering the jagged scar at the back of his skull, he experienced an outbreak of pain over his son's follies. But this was quickly swept away by the upwelling of love for him.

He could not eat anything and took only a single cup of tea around suppertime. From six o'clock onward, he paced the hall and the rooms of the bookshop, up and down the staircase, stopping only to peer out the windows from time to time. The rumble of passing cars drew him to the front door more than once.

Just after seven a shiny minivan drew up to the curb and stopped. Alex, peeping through the venetian blinds, saw Jacob get out of the driver's side. Jacob stretched, then opened the rear door and helped his wife out. On the far side of the vehicle, a tall, young man emerged and stared at the Kingfisher uneasily.

For a few seconds Alex hesitated, unable to recognize him. Then he knew him—knew, knew, knew him fully. He rushed to the front door, threw it open, and raced down the steps. For an instant, fear crossed Andrew's face as he stared at the man running toward him. Then his face crumpled, and he threw himself into his father's arms.

Alex's hands were firm on Andrew's back, Andrew's head was on his father's chest, eyes closed, holding him. Enfolding the prodigal rags, Alex heard:

"Have you lost him?"

"I have run from him."

"You must return to him."

"Will he want me?"

"Yes, he will want you."

"How is it so, this speaking between you and me? Do you know me, sir?"

"I know you. And you know me."

"Do I know you, sir?"

"More than any other."

"But how do I know you? Tell me who you are."

"I am you. As you will be, in time."

Four people connected by blood and marriage now faced the challenge of how to communicate after a long separation and radical transformation. Meg took charge with casual sureness. Leading the way into the Kingfisher, she conducted them all upstairs to the apartment. She and Jacob seemed adept at easing situations of the uncomfortable kind. They bantered, put on the coffee, opened the paper cartons of Chinese food they had brought, and told Alex and Andrew to go into the parlor to visit while they got supper ready.

Alone with his father at last, Andrew spoke for the first time.

"Dad", he whispered.

Seated side by side on the sofa, the silence between them was not strained. They both knew there would be time enough for conversation, for filling in the blanks, for all the things that needed to be remembered. They listened to the cheery clamor of dishes and silverware and the repartee of the married couple in the kitchen. Then Alex smiled at Andrew, and his son returned the smile.

Suddenly Andrew thrust his hand into his trouser pocket, withdrew something, and put it into his father's hand. Five little white stones, rounded and smooth.

"What are these?" Alex asked.

"They're for you. They're from the ocean shore at Kronshtadt, near Saint Petersburg."

Alex reached into his own pocket and withdrew Pin's kingfisher. He put it into Andrew's hand.

"What's this, Dad?"

"It's for you."

"It's a kingfisher, isn't it?" Andrew said, rubbing the stone between his thumb and forefinger, gazing at it with sober concentration. Looking into his father's eyes, he said, "Where did you get it?"

"In China."

"China? The papers said you were found in Russia."

No more could be said because Meg bustled into the parlor and called them to the kitchen for supper. They all sat down at table and joined hands, Alex between his two sons, Meg between her husband and brother-in law.

"Could you say grace, Dad?" she asked.

Alex bowed his head, made the sign of the cross, and prayed aloud in a voice shaking with emotion:

"We thank you, God our Father, for you have brought us together again. What was lost is found; what was dead has come to life. Please bless this food and all the years that are ahead of us. And bless the children who will come to us from your generous hand. In Jesus' name we pray. Amen."

"Amen!" echoed the others, Jacob and Meg in choked voices, Andrew in a whisper.

Throughout the evening Alex gave an account of his journey. He found it next to impossible to convey the immediacy of the places where he had been or the people with whom he had shared his life during the time of exile. He was no less a quiet man than he had been before the journey, and description did not come easily to him, but he made the effort and seemed to capture the full attention of his three listeners. The grandfather clock below in the hallway was striking eleven by the time he began to tell about the final stages of his imprisonment in China. The chronology and politics were confusing to everyone but him, and they began to ask so many questions, not understanding the answers, that in the end they decided to wait until morning to continue.

"Let's call it a day", Jacob said, getting to his feet, stretching and yawning. "We're going to be here the whole weekend. I even took the battery out of my cell phone."

"This", said Meg with a significant look at her father-in-law, "is a breakthrough for Jake. All through our first date he talked into one of those contraptions. And I expect he'll be talking into one as he stands at the foot of the delivery table."

"Maybe even on his deathbed", Andrew quipped, poking his brother's shoulder.

"Nah", Jacob drawled. "Births, deaths, funerals, and weddings, I leave the thing at home."

Over their protests, Alex settled the married couple in his own room because it had the only double bed in the house.

"Little Alexander, or Alexandra, needs rest", Alex said, kissing Meg on the cheek. They all laughed, exchanged hugs, and bid each other good-night.

Alone now, Alex and Andrew returned to the parlor. Alex sat down on the sofa. Andrew's face grew troubled as he sat down on an easy chair opposite his father.

"Dad", he began, leaning forward, his hands clasped together. "Tell me you're okay."

"I'm fine, Andrew. I'm very happy now."

"You're sure you're all right?" his son pleaded. "Father Toby says..."

"That I'm a little bit crazy? Maybe I am still. But I think it's a passing thing. And maybe it's the kind of madness that leaves something very good in its wake. I'm tired, and it'll take some time before I'm fully recuperated. But it was worth it—every bit of it."

"Please tell me the truth and don't worry about making me feel guilty. I need to feel guilty. I *am* guilty!"

"The truth is you made a mistake. You were tricked and misled for a time. It could have happened to anyone."

"Anyone? I don't think so. I was incredibly blind and stupid."

"You were young and trusting."

Andrew shook his head, staring at the floor. "Please forgive me", he said in a small voice.

"I forgive you, my son. And I love you."

"I know that, Pa. I know you love me. How could I not know it?"

"Do you forgive *me*?"

"Forgive you? What on earth do I have to forgive you for?"

"For failing to be the father you needed."

"Don't talk like that!"

"You went in search of something you hadn't been given by me."

"That's not true. I chose to believe those people. I let myself be convinced."

"Why did you?"

Andrew hesitated before answering. "I don't know. I'm not sure."

"There are no perfect parents in this world, Andrew. None. We all make our mistakes, and we leave marks and gaps in our children's lives. But we do love them—imperfect love, as all human love is. Then, when children become adults and have their own families, they begin to understand. They in their turn learn the need for forgiveness. In prison I learned to forgive my own father, and I saw that he needed to forgive his father. No one is exempt from this. It goes all the way back to Adam and Eve."

"You're saying that you want *me* to forgive *you*?"

"Yes, whenever you're ready, whenever you think the time is right."

"You're saying you want me to forgive the best father in the world for some imaginary crime he's committed against me?"

"Even the best father in the world passes down the ancient sin. As I did to you, you will do to your children. But there's grace now, more grace than we'll ever need. Rivers of it, torrents of it, abundant and overflowing. All we have to do is ask."

For a long time, silence stretched between them, then finally contracted.

"Okay, Pa. If you're asking me for it, I give you my forgiveness—I can't believe I'm saying this! Anyway, okay, I forgive you from the bottom of my heart for failing to be what you think you were supposed to be."

"That's close."

"Okay, I forgive you for failing to be God."

"I failed to be an image of God for you. Forgiveness, Andrew. No one is exempt."

Once again the silence resumed.

At last Alex cleared his throat and said, "We'll have lots of time to talk. I have so much to tell you. So many beautiful things."

"About your journey?"

"Yes. And I want to hear about yours. You're back in England now, I hear."

The vagueness of Alex's statement disturbed Andrew.

"I'm in Oxford", he said in a low voice. "Didn't anyone tell you?"

"Not yet. Where in Oxford?"

"At Magdalen. They let me back in. Professor Whitfield pleaded for me, and he won. I lost a year, of course, but things are going well now—very well."

"So you're a student again?"

"Yes."

The room reeled, and Alex's mind began to swim.

"But when—how?" he murmured.

Seeing his father's confusion, Andrew began to recount what had happened to him step by step. Alex listened without interruption. It took some time to reconstruct the events, and the clock struck two in the morning as they arrived at Andrew's sojourn in Russia.

In Saint Petersburg the hotel clerk had handed him the envelope containing the book of Hopkins poetry. Shaw Cunningham had also seen it and had accompanied Andrew back to his room, where she asked what the message was. Andrew had blithely opened the envelope in front of Bloch and Cunningham and expressed his surprise: who had sent it? And why Hopkins? Bloch suggested that the clerk had probably mistaken Andrew for someone else and that the book must have been intended for another English-speaking guest in the hotel.

"Shaw took the book from my hands, flipped through it, and said there was no note inside. She said she loved Hopkins' poems and asked if she could browse through it before returning it to the clerk. I felt a bit uneasy about the way it happened so fast, she not letting me have a look through it myself. But I chalked it up to her enthusiasm for Hopkins. I was in a submissive state anyway. I thought they were really advanced spiritual leaders."

"So you never did read my message. But how and when did you leave them?"

"The following morning."

"The following morning! But—"

"What happened next helped me to see what was really going on under all the beautiful philosophizing. Shaw excused herself and walked into the washroom. She closed the door, and Bloch started talking to me. But he paused for a breath and that's when I heard the toilet flush. A few seconds later she walked out and handed me the book. She said it wasn't a good edition, that it was missing her favorite poems, which I thought was kind of odd because it was the collected poems."

"And then what?"

"Then they just went on with their business. Phone calls to Moscow, to some doctor down there who was arranging meetings with important Russians. After that there were calls to Siberia, where we were all planning to go for a big superconference. While they were buzzing back and forth on the phone, I went into the bathroom and flipped through the book. There was no name on it, no message, nothing. I kind of shrugged to myself and said, Well, I guess somebody made a mistake after all; I'll take it back to the lobby myself. I sat down on the edge of the tub and read a few poems, taking my time. Then I noticed a wad of paper floating in the toilet bowl. I realized she had torn something out of the book and flushed it. But she hadn't watched carefully enough, because it didn't go down. There was writing on it. I fished it out and just had time to read 'king of Halcyon' when somebody rapped on the door, asking me if I was all right. That was so weird, to see those words. I didn't know what to think. I dried off the paper and stuck it into my pocket. Later that night I got up and went into the bathroom as quietly as I could—I was sharing a room with this guru guy from Kashmir. I see now that he was also a kind of baby-sitter for me."

"Krishnamurti?"

"Yes, that's right. How did you know that?"

"I have lots to tell you too, but it can wait."

"Anyway, he sleeps like a cat, and I heard him padding after me. I locked the bathroom door and made like it was just a routine visit. He asked if I was all right. I said, 'I'm fine, be out in a minute.' I opened the crumpled paper and found your message staring me in the eye."

"And what did you think?"

"I couldn't think. I was just stunned. It didn't add up. It didn't make any sense at all. Of course, I knew it had to be you. 'The child is father of the man...a boy who slept in the arms of a giant...a king of Halcyon.' Who else could it be? My dad? In Russia? Pretty farfetched, I thought. But if it was true, why were you there, and why were you trying to contact me this way?"

"Didn't you think you should call me at my hotel?"

"I would have, except that the paper was torn, and most of the address was gone. She must have crumpled it into two wads, and one went down the drain. All that was left of the address was 'Room 611'. Do you know how many room 611s there are in Saint Petersburg?"

"How many?"

"A lot. I tried them all."

"When?"

"During the next few days. After I left the group."

"You left the group in Saint Petersburg?"

"Yes, I did. I lay awake in the dark all night long trying to figure out what was going on. What was really happening? A light was slowly dawning inside my head. I realized they'd been keeping things from me, stuff I had every right to know. And if you had been forced to send in a coded message, then in all likelihood you had tried to reach me before, and your other messages had also been intercepted. If that was so, why had they done it? It could mean only one thing—they were isolating me. It meant they knew you were in the city, and they had set up a blockade around me so subtly that I didn't even see it. What else were they hiding from me? It hit me like a hammer blow. They had been deceiving me, and sometime before dawn I knew with absolute certainty that if they could play with the truth and manipulate people to this degree, then they weren't what they said they were.

"In the morning, when Krishnamurti was taking a shower, I just jumped into my clothes and bolted for the door. I ran like hell and went down the emergency stairs and got out of the hotel and as far away from it as I could. I had no money—that's another thing about them: they like to relieve you of burdens, and personal money's a spiritual burden, you see. They'd paid for everything, and pretty high-class living it was. I'd trusted them so completely I hardly even noticed my empty pockets. Now I noticed. I had my passport and other ID, but that's all, so I walked as quickly as I could to the Canadian consulate and told them what had happened. It took some paperwork, but they were great, really bent over backward to help me. They put me up incognito in a private apartment for a week, so the New Advent people couldn't find me. That was a hard few days, wondering what to do and trying to get my brains unfried. It was scary, because I'd sucked in a lot of poison.

"I'm ashamed to admit it, Dad, but I'd accepted their version of reality. Looking back on it now, I can't believe I fell for it. But they were so brilliant, and their absurd metaphysics was so convincing…so beautiful, it seemed at the time. As I said, it was scary getting that out of my head. Luckily, I found a Catholic church on Nevsky Prospekt, and a priest there heard my confession and prayed with me. By that time, somebody at the consulate finally found out where you'd been staying in Saint Pete's. The Hotel Moskva, not far from the Peterhof, but they told me you had checked out. I raced down there in case you were still in the lobby or at the bus stop outside, but you'd gone. At that point I figured you were heading back home. It never crossed my mind that you would follow them to Moscow. Let alone—"

"After that, what did you do?"

"I called Father Turner at Tyburne and told him what had happened. I begged his forgiveness and asked him to help me. He told me to return to Oxford immediately and said we would discuss what to do when I arrived. He said he didn't know where you were, but he thought you might still be traveling, trying to track me down. He said that the most reasonable thing to do would be to get back to solid ground and stay put until you could be contacted. He wired the plane fare, and I was back in my room at Tyburne sometime around the middle of February. I won't go into all the details now, but I'd really made a mess of things, and it took some time to piece my life back together. I learned a lot during that time. I learned a lot about who the real spiritual people are. A friend of mine, Father Xavier, was an especially healing influence on me. Father Turner was also tremendous. He's a saint, no doubt about it. John Groves—I hear you met him too—gave me a bawling out I'll never forget, and we're still not on great terms. But I learned about what freedom is, and about love. I'm still learning."

"And then?"

"And then the embassy in Moscow called to say they'd finally tracked you to a hotel in Moscow. The bad news was you'd disappeared. After that we could only wait to hear from you. We never did."

Startled by this information, Alex said, "You mean the embassy knew about me being in Russia, and about you?"

"Yes, they gave me a lot of help."

Alex shook his head, puzzling over the times he had been told that the embassy had no knowledge of his presence in Russia. Perhaps there was a simple explanation. Had the consulate in Saint Petersburg failed to communicate properly with the embassy in Moscow? Or had the state agency Intourist failed to inform the embassy of Alex's and Andrew's presence in Russia? If so, was this a case of bureaucratic error, or was it deliberate? If deliberate, why had they done it? And who had he been talking with when he phoned the embassy from Listvyanka? Who had Irina talked with? Had some secret government agency rerouted the calls from the village?

Probably he would never know the answers to these questions. The dark underworld of espionage, cults, and crime was ruled by lies—they were intertwining realms of illusion.

"Dad, are you okay? Can you hear me?"

Alex looked up and realized that he had been staring into space.

"Sorry, Andrew. What were you saying?"

"I was saying that the embassy gave me a lot of help."

"Oh, yes."

Andrew continued:

"I went back to Magdalen with my tail between my legs, but they weren't having any of it. I'd blown it. Thankfully, Professor Whitfield took me on, and after another lecture that I'll never forget—about the state of my character—he softened and offered me a job in his village. I stayed with the Whitfields at Wootton for a month, digging up their garden and pruning trees. It was the best medicine. He's one tough customer, Dad, and he was just what I needed. After a month of physical labor outdoors, he got me a job at a home for the handicapped near Beaconsfield, the place where his daughter lives."

"Philly?"

"That's right—Philly! You met her, didn't you?"

"Feedabird", said Alex.

"Flied away. Yup, that's our Philly. She was so good for me. Kind of like Darla Conniker, without the dreams and prophecy. Just lots of heart."

Andrew paused, looking into the distance for a moment. "From then on, things got steadily better. My job was to bathe the severely disabled men, push them around the grounds in their wheelchairs, tuck them in at night, clean up their messes, sing songs to them. That's where I learned the most. I saw that I was the handicapped one."

"And after that?"

"I finished at Saint Alban's this past August. Owen said that the best thing I could do would be to get on with my life, pick up where I'd left off. I applied to Magdalen for the master's program in English, and they accepted me. I think he did a lot of bargaining to get me back in."

"So you're a student again."

"Yes. That's why I can't stay long this time, Dad. I have to get back by Tuesday. But I'll be home for the Christmas holidays. A whole month. Will you be here?"

Alex smiled. "I'm not going anywhere for a long time."

"Good", said Andrew, nodding emphatically. Then he returned to his story:

"A few days ago our embassy in London contacted me and let me know they thought you'd been found—they said that a man the Russians had in custody fitted your description. I guess the Americans blew the whole thing wide open and got you out. Then some guy from their embassy came by and questioned me, asked a whole lot of questions about you. It didn't take a genius to figure out that they wanted to know if you'd ever been involved with intelligence work. He told me you'd been captured in a military zone. You had no name or papers, and you were... well, they said you couldn't tell them anything that confirmed your identity. So—"

"That's not quite what happened, but we don't need to think about that now. Tell me about the New Advent people. Are they still active in Oxford?"

"They folded their tents and disappeared into the night. The police say an account of the whole affair has been sent by Interpol to law enforcement agencies throughout Europe. It was sent to Russia too, but so far there's been no acknowledgment. I doubt it'll put a stop to their organization because they're untouchables. They haven't broken any laws, and they've got friends in high places, so high and powerful they can wiggle their way out of just about anything. Despite that, they definitely don't want any shadow on their reputations; controversy would be unpleasant for them. I wrote an article about my experience and sent it to several British newspapers, but none of them would print it. The Oxford town paper and the college rags gave it exposure, though. In the meantime, the gurus have to go more carefully, and maybe that means fewer souls will get caught in their net."

"Then it was worth it."

"I guess you're right", Andrew sighed. "I only wish I hadn't—"

"It was a gift, Andrew, a great gift."

"I don't understand that. No, not at all. I'm finding it hard to live with myself at the moment. I've been a mess ever since I heard you'd disappeared—I thought you were dead. I thought...I thought I'd killed my own father."

"That's a great suffering for you, but in the end it wasn't so. It's true that I died a little, maybe more than I know, but my life was given back to me again, and God has brought a great good out of it—out of everything."

"A good?" Andrew said in a broken voice. "I can't imagine what good. If only I'd stayed at Oxford and got my degree!"

"You learned a hard lesson."

"Who paid for it! You did!"

"We paid for it, the both of us. And that's the way it was meant to be."

"Not like this. It shouldn't have happened."

"It wasn't God's first choice for our lives, that's true. But when it happened, and the darkness fell, he brought another kind of good out of it. The pain is gone now, Andrew, and I'm home. I'm a different person, and I hope a better person."

On an impulse Andrew knelt on the floor and put his arms around his father.

46. *Kingfishers Catch Fire*

Dawn was near when Alex woke up in the semidark of Jacob's old bedroom. He lay on his back for a while, watching the pale light play with model airplanes suspended from the ceiling. He mused on the drawings of bridge engineering pinned to the walls, the ingenious Meccano invention, the neatness, the order. When the sun rose over the ridge of the Clementine hills, he got up, prayed, showered, and dressed.

The household was quiet. Jacob and Meg were still asleep behind the closed door of the master bedroom. He thought of his grandchild waiting inside. Would it be a boy? Would it be a girl who looked like Meg, or Carol perhaps? The next generation.

Through the open door of Andrew's room, he saw his son sprawled in deep sleep on the bed. His face was relaxed, his mouth half-open, the small wedge of the knife scar visible on the temple of his forehead. The room was as he had left it years before, somewhat disarrayed, shelves cluttered with pebbles, bird nests, unusual configurations of wood and stone, and his many drawings taped to the walls. The paper whale and its Jonah floated in the air above the bed.

"'All night across the dark we steer'," Alex whispered. "'But when the day returns at last, safe in my room, beside the pier, I find my vessel fast.'"

He closed the door without a sound and went back to the kitchen. He made tea and sat at the table for a while, sipping a cup, savoring the happiness of a house full of beloved people. After that he checked his watch and saw that it was nearly eight o'clock. His children would probably sleep for a few more hours. He thought that he would like to go down to the river and sit for a while beside the Clementine. It would be a pleasant and simple way to reacquaint himself with his town. He would gaze into the water as he used to do when he was a child.

Into his pocket he placed a rosary and the five smooth stones. He packed a small knapsack with some bread, a bottle of water, and a book of Hopkins' poetry. Putting on his old walking shoes and his windbreaker, he went outside to breathe the perfumed air. The weather was glorious with the kind of autumn light that turned the unwary into pantheists and believers into mystics. The hills of the Clementine were bright with maple reds, birch yellows, and the brindle-bronze of the more sedate oaks. Breezes were warming in the sun, and the air was filled with spinning seed keys and tumbling acorns. It was a Saturday morning, and in backyards a few early risers were raking leaves into piles. The smell of wood smoke was abroad, and children's melodious voices seemed to come from everywhere.

He took the route that was most meaningful to him: up Oak Avenue in the direction of the crown of Halcyon. He bowed and made a sign of the cross as he passed Saint Mary's, and proceeded on toward the crest. There he turned right and went down the steep incline of Tamarack, going slowly, digging in his heels with each step to avoid slipping on the damp leaves that had piled up in the shadows of hedges and stone walls. Arriving at the riverside road, he walked the half block upriver toward the dam. There, at the valley's narrowest point, three old men were seated on wooden crates dangling poles over the stream, chatting contentedly, waiting for bass and carp.

At the little park by the catwalk, Alex paused and looked at the place where he had fallen through the ice during his rescue of Jamie and Hannah Colley. Then he mounted the catwalk and crossed it slowly. The roar of the water on the spillway grew to a crescendo at the midpoint of the bridge, where the current rushed over the lip of the sluice, thundering on the rocks below. Reaching the far side, he turned onto the northern river road and strolled along it to Wolfe's Run. So far, his energy had sustained him, as long as he maintained a leisurely pace. Then he decided there was no reason why he should not go a bit farther up the ravine. Finding himself at the top, he turned east and ambled along a country road without any goal or intention, passing fields where farmers loaded bags of potatoes onto carts beneath honking arrows of southbound geese.

There he recognized the view that had always meant so much to him—the high perspective where one could look out over the valley and see a beautiful recumbent woman in the contours of the land. He smiled and moved on, realizing that he had grown beyond this fixed point where his soul had sought to anchor itself in a spinning cosmos. Man, he saw, was intended for both permanence and transience. He lived in an incarnate world where each soul sprang from its appointed place, its roots in the earth. But the trunk and the branches must grow beyond the fundamental soil, must reach up into the light, if they were to flower and bear fruit. There would be many times in the days and years to come when he would return here to meditate, but now he understood that this could never be the final station of his journey.

The hills rolled slowly onward, and the fields gave way to stands of swaying trees. He stopped and surveyed the surrounding hills with pleasure, wondering what the next stage would be, wondering how God would continue to shape him into what had been intended from the beginning. He noticed with some surprise that he was facing a small farmhouse nested in a grove on top of the rise. It was the Colleys'.

He did not know what to expect as he climbed the lane. At first it seemed that no one was at home, for the place was quiet with a tranquility that was not simply autumnal but contained the vibrations of a space that had recently been vacated by the vital commotion of children. Mrs. Colley and her family were away, it seemed. However, as he neared the top, Alex saw that an old man was sleeping in a lawn chair beside the front porch, and beside him a large yellow dog lay on its side snoring.

Alex came up to them and stood for a moment, looking down fondly at Mr. Phillips and Clovis. Deciding that it would be a shame to wake them, he turned to go.

"Well!", snorted the old man, his eyes flicking open.

Alex nodded. "Hello, sir."

The old man scanned him up and down with a critical gaze. "You have changed."

Dropping his knapsack to the ground, Alex went down on one knee before him, as if before a king.

"I heard what you did, Mr. Phillips. You saved my home and my bookshop."

"We are not here to speak of *me*", said the old man, pointing his finger crossly. "We are here to speak of *you*."

"Me?"

"Yes, *you!* You, Jack, have much to account for."

"In what sense, sir?"

"I cannot abide a man who is irresponsible, who does not keep an appointment."

"An appointment?"

"You accepted an invitation to dinner. That was a promise. That was an obligation. You failed to keep your word."

"I regret it very much."

"A banquet was planned for you! But you did not attend. Do you realize the trouble and consternation this caused? Do you?"

"No, sir."

"Still—you have an explanation, do you not?"

"There are reasons—but no excuses."

"Away, away he went, eh? Now he is back—but *is* he immortal diamond? Is he?"

"He is becoming immortal diamond, though first he must know he is a poor joke and a potsherd and matchwood."

The old man nodded sagely. "In the wrong mouth, that is nothing but an excuse. In the right mouth, it is a reason. What say you?"

"I say I am a man, no more, no less, and in my mouth are both reasons and excuses."

"For excuses there is no excuse. For reasons there is a reason. Did you go far?"

"Yes, it was far."

"What did you see?"

"I saw princes degraded in sewers, and liars on the high seats of power. I saw the heart that is broken, and I saw that the only whole heart is a broken one."

"This is, of course, quite true. What else did you see?"

"I saw that we must go down into deep waters before we rise again."

"Do you believe this, Graham?"

"I do believe it."

"And will you keep it alive, lest the memory fade from the West?"

"I will, sir."

"Now, tell me of the kingfisher. Did you see him?"

"I saw him, the king of birds revered in ancient myth, bright feathered, as blue as royal robes. I saw him meditating by the rivers and the sea. In other places he was hunted through the reaches of the world, and in the darkest places his song was silenced. Yet ever does he spring up again, calming the sea, coming to rest in the heart of the soul, waiting for his day."

"Some say he is no more."

"Never will he cease to speak the word he was sent to be."

Tears came to the eyes of Mr. Phillips. "Then it is true, what I always hoped for?"

"What did you hope for?"

"That the universe sings a song. And the halcyon sings with it. His is a song no other can sing."

"If this is so, it is because he is small."

"Yes, he is small. And very brave. Tell me, Graham, does he still catch fire?"

"He does, Mr. Phillips. As dragonflies draw flame."

"Christ dwells with him?"

"Christ dwells with him, crucified and resurrected."

"And does he still play in ten thousand places?"

"Yes, he still plays in the places where he dwells, and there he sings to the Father of us all."

No further speech was possible. Alex bowed his head, and toward him in unceasing streams came the faces of the many souls who were now part of his life: their colors, their songs, their forms raising their arms in greeting, though they did not yet know the one whom they greeted. Jacob and Andrew, Meg and the baby, Kiril and Ilya, Jamie and Hannah, Lizaveta of Smolensk and Alyosha of the degradation, the peasant youth in the Hermitage, Darla, Konstantin, Irina, Pin, and all the others.

Then both men went deeper and deeper into silence. It was broken only by the warble of a bird.

"Go to her, Graham", Mr. Phillips whispered.

Alex opened his eyes and gazed into the old man's face.

"Go to her."

"Where?"

"In the garden. Go, now."

Alex got up, put a hand on the old man's shoulder, then slung his knapsack onto his back. He walked slowly around to the rear of the house.

Theresa Colley was standing among the berry bushes with a tin bucket in her hand, looking up to the height of the grove, where her children were running through the trees. Beside her was a bushel basket spilling over with dark green squash; a heap of pumpkins lay nearby. Sunflowers bowed, crickets played symphonies, and grasshoppers leaped from many bridges. The wind billowed her dress. Her right arm was lifted, shading her brow beneath a wide straw bonnet.

When she turned toward the house, she did not at first see him. Her face was summer brown. A light frown and beads of perspiration played on her brow. When her eyes registered the fact that there was a man standing perfectly still only a few feet away, she was startled but not alarmed. Then a great stillness came over her, and she looked at him without moving.

He took a step toward her.

"I'm sorry I'm late", he said.

Then she came to him and took his hand, and did not let it go.

ACKNOWLEDGMENTS

Words are hopelessly inadequate to express my gratitude for the following people who contributed invaluable assistance and insights in the writing of this book. Without their help the *terra incognita* would have remained, for me, completely *incognita*: Miriam Stulberg, Marie Javora, Alma Coffman, and Father Michael Shields in Magadan, Siberia; Nikolas and Eugenia Goryachkin, Elena Ignatieva, Igor Verbitskiy, Viktor Pravdyuk, and Sasha Eovlev in Saint Petersburg; Vladimir Erokhin, Raïssa Gershzon, Olga Yerokhina, and Mikhail Zavalov in Moscow; Michael and Frances Phillips in Oxford and Aylesbury; Paul Savage, Åsa Sjoberg, and Alexandre Havard in Helsinki.

For a variety of inspirations and suggestions I am also indebted to Father Emile Brière, Anton Časta, Christopher and LeeAnn Corkery, Catherine Doherty, Jean Fox, Father Raymond Gawronski, Olga Glagoleva, James and Karen Hanlon, David and Katherine Jeffrey, Igor and Olga Kazanov, Peter Kreeft, William Kurelek, Sandra Lynch, Robert McDonald, Roxanne Mei Lum, John Paul Meenan, Mark Miravalle, and my wonderful O'Brien crew: Sheila, John, Benjamin, and most especially my eagle-eyed, creative Elizabeth. For valuable advice, thanks are also due to Vladimir Oslon, Father Robert Pelton, Father Pio Maria, Max Picard, Edoardo Rialti, John Romanowsky, Mark Ryland, Karen Van De Loop, Petroc Willey, and Christopher Zakrzewski.

And to you whose names I never learned and whom perhaps I will never meet again: as I traveled through your lands, you gave a stranger your kindness, music, food, thoughts, prayers, and stories of sorrows and joys. Above all, I thank you for the icon of your lives.

Michael D. O'Brien
Combermere, Ontario

AUTHOR'S NOTE

The characters in this novel are not intentionally based on real persons, living or dead. Those associated with real institutions are not necessarily representative of the institutions' ideals and practices. As is usual in fiction, artistic license has been employed—sometimes liberally. It should be noted, however, that many of the events in the tale are based on firsthand accounts told to the author.

*

Lines from Mikhail Lermontov's poem "Mtsyri" are from the book *Mtsyri*, translated by Irina Zheleznova (Moscow: Izdatelstvo Khudozhestvennaya Literatura, 1993).

Brief quotations are taken from Aleksandr Solzhenitsyn's *The Gulag Archipelago*, vol. 2, pts. 3–4 (New York: Harper and Row, 1973), and from Aleksandr Solzhenitsyn's *"One Word of Truth..."*: *The Nobel Speech on Literature, 1970* (London: Bodley Head, 1972).

The excerpt from Vadim Borisov's essay "Personality and National Awareness" is from the anthology *From Under the Rubble*, edited by Aleksandr Solzhenitsyn (Boston: Little, Brown and Co., 1975), originally published as *Voix sous les décombres*, © Editions YMCA-Press, Paris; used with permission of YMCA-Press.